CW00661944

Beneath the Scarlet Frost

Book One of the Fallen Reign Series

COPYRIGHT © 2023 BY MARISSA MILLER. *All rights reserved.*

No part of this book may be reproduced in any form or by any electronic or mechanical means, including information storage and retrieval systems, without written permission from the author, except for the use of brief quotations in a book review.

ISBN (hardcover): 979-8-21-826485-7/ ISBN (paperback): 979-8-21-826486-4

Front Cover Design by Jeanine Croft. Case design by Marissa Miller

Interior Layout by Marissa Miller

Illustrations (41. 420) by @Xenychan

Map art by Marissa Miller

Marissamillerauthor.com

ACKNOWLEDGMENTS

To my husband and Mother for being my biggest supporters, and loving me in spite of all my ups and downs along this journey.

To the "Core Four" who have all held my hand through the process of completing this book. You've helped me more than I can put into words. I could have given up if not for you.

To Sam for being a constant, shining affirmation amidst both the chaos and the euphoria. Your friendship and help were two of the greatest things to come from this book. Never change, you delightful creature.

To Kyra for holding the mirror I needed to see both this work and myself in. Your encouragement and analysis has kept me going and helped me to see myself and this book authentically!

To Deonna, for being both my ever-patient friend and my D.E.. This work would not exist without your analytical mind and constant support.

To my Women Writer's Group for all of the feedback, encouragement, and safe space to explore this story.

To Tatiana Nikolaevna for being the inspiration I needed most.

A thank you to my initial readers, Sam Filice, Emily Vanderbent, Marina Marcello, Bri Eberhart, and Kyra Ann Dawkins. You each contributed invaluable feedback to make this story the best version it could be.

PRAISE FOR

BENEATH
THE
SCARLET FROST

Beneath the Scarlet Frost is a breathtaking tale of love and loss. Loosely inspired by the Romanov family, this dark high fantasy is full of twists and turns and heartbreaking moments that keep you coming back for more. Miller creates a unique magic system with complex characters you can't help but fall in love with.
-Bri Eberhart, author of *Strangers in Our Heads*

Beneath the Scarlet Frost is not only a compelling invitation into the vivid world of Alse Hanya, but also a thought-provoking story that stirs a unique caliber of literary intrigue and discourse. Readers will fall in love with Sorrel, the empathetic protagonist whose change in perspective pulses at the heart of the narrative. The prose Miller uses to render the story is unmatched in its intentionality, nuance, and richness. As a gentle warning, this book will likely break your heart, but you'll be thankful for it. Trust me.
-Kyra Ann Dawkins, author of *The We and the They,* and *First-Person Archer*

Beneath the Scarlet Frost is the history-inspired, slow burn, courtly intrigue, literary fantasy novel you didn't know you needed! This book will pull you in with cozy wintery vibes and break your heart with secret reveals and political wars— let's be honest, who doesn't love romance mixed with their tragedy and lies?
- Marina Marcello, Owner of *Valkyrie Visionaries*

Perfect for fans of Russian-inspired literature, *Beneath the Scarlet Frost* is an elegantly woven tale of hope, heartbreak, and humanity. The artful world-building and unique narrative style create a compelling reading experience that is the perfect start to what is sure to be an excellent series.
- Emily Vanderbent, author of *The Timewalker Archives*

A gentle note to readers

This book deals with the following content:

Violence
Some Sexual Content
Murder
Trapped in Fire
Blood
Death
War
Corruption

Please read with this in mind if any of these topic
are sensitive for you.

BOOK ONE OF
THE FALLEN REIGN SERIES

BENEATH
THE
SCARLET FROST

MARISSA MILLER

ALSE HANYA

DIMAER

KATAHE

SIBRU

VIDEIRIA

PACHAY

LUCIO

VA

Character Names

Genri Zdraevit - (GHEN-REE Z-DREV-IT)

Geneva Zdraevit - (JUH-NEE-VUH Z-DREV-IT)

Inessa Zdraevit - (IH-NESS-UH Z-DREV-IT)

Sorrel Zdraevit - (SOR-REL Z-DREV-IT)

Yulia Zdraevit - (YU-LEE-UH Z-DREV-IT)

Kira Zdraevit - (KEE-RUH Z-DREV-IT)

Theodorvin Zdraevit - (THEE-OH-DOR-VIHN)

Friedrich Rusev - (FREED-RICK ROO-SEH-V)

Roland Rusev - (ROH-LAND ROO-SEH-V)

Arrian Rusev - (AR-REE-AN ROO-SEH-V)

Otvel Chinye - (AH-T-VELL CHIH-N-YAY)

Rafe - (RAY-F)

Vadia - (VAW-DEE-UH)

Maggie - (MAG-EE)

Sergeant Hykner - (HIGH-K-NER)

ALSE HANYA COUNTRIES

EISA (EYE-SUH) - LAND OF ICE AND SNOW

KESGOLDOL (KES-GUHL-DUHL) - LAND OF SHADOWS

DEZIDANEYA (DEZ-IH-DAY-N-YUH) - LAND OF WISHES

SLAYAD (SLAY-AH-D) - LAND OF STARS

SONYO (SAW-N-YO) - LAND OF DREAMS

VATRA (VAH-TRUH) - LAND OF FIRE AND ASH

LUCIO (LOO-SEE-OH) - LAND OF WATERS AND MISTS

PACHAY (PAW-CH-AY) - LAND OF PEACE

LUSORYIA (LOO-SOR-REE-UH) - LAND OF LUST

VIDEIRIA (VID-EE-REE-UH) - LAND OF VINES

SIBRU (SEE-BROO) - LAND OF WHISPERS

DIMAER (DIE-MEE-AIR) - LAND OF DEATH

KATAHEYDA (KAH-TUH-HEE-DUH) - LAND OF STORMS

ᏰEFORE

ivines above. I wished there was a way to know you'd gotten on the bad side of a situation before you made whatever terrible decision that had landed you there to begin with. That was the lesson I was contemplating at eight years old as I watched the blood rolling down Mama's arm while we raced through the trees towards the safety of home.

My elder sister, Inessa's, breath puffed in large white billows against the frigid air as she struggled to keep pace in the heavy snowfall. A muffled gasp sounded behind me, and I slowed my gait, glancing over my shoulder to see my youngest sister, Kira, struggling to get to her feet from where she'd slipped.

"Kira!" I cried, fighting my forward momentum to backtrack to her. I bit my lip against my fear as I spotted the blood on the freshly disturbed snow, dark crimson spiraling through the ice and fissures.

"Sorrel, help me!" Kira wailed, reaching out for my hand. She was only four years old, and her short legs and innate clumsiness made it difficult for her to keep up with the rest of us. With Mama already carrying our new baby brother, neither Inessa nor I, nor our third sister, Yulia, were big enough to carry Kira.

"It's alright, I've got you," I breathed, grasping roughly around her wrist to yank her to her feet.

"Girls!" Mama barked frantically, realizing she'd lost two of her brood.

"We need to hurry," I urged Kira, glancing nervously over my shoulder. "Or we will be caught by—"

"Too late, little princesses," a low rumbling voice growled. The sound of footsteps in the snow crunched loudly in my ears, but when I turned around I couldn't locate anyone nearby.

"Yulia, Inessa, keep going straight to the house and get help! Find your father or Friedrich— anyone!" Mama commanded, and I shoved Kira behind me as I stumbled backwards on trembling legs.

"We came here for the heir, but anyone from the Zdraevit family line will be a victory." Looking frantically from left to right, I couldn't locate the origin of the menacing voice, until my eyes locked on a flickering shadow creeping from the base of a nearby frostbitten tree.

"Run, Kira," I whispered over my shoulder. "Run as fast as you can to Mama."

"But—"

"Hurry up!" I ordered, stooping to grab a fallen tree limb. My fingers sank into the powdery snow as they curled around the branch, the cool touch soothing against my sparking nerves. Kira heeded my instructions and scrambled away towards the fast approaching sound of Mama rushing to help us. I slowly placed one foot behind the other, brandishing the branch as I kept my gaze fixed on the shadow.

"It's just a trick," I told myself firmly. There was a hoarse sound of laughter from within the puddling darkness that made my body feel heavy and sluggish. "A horrible trick."

"Grab her." The command barely broke the silence before a rugged man exploded from within the shadow, arms outstretched as he lunged for me.

A shrill scream scratched the inside of my throat as it tore through the air. The sound palpitated in echoes through the woods that dislodged clumps of snow and sent a spray of small icicles cascading from the branches above.

"Shit," the man swore as one of the ice shards punctured his arm, piercing through the thick wool of his coat down to the skin and causing a creeping bloodstain to appear on the fabric. He kept advancing despite the injury, so I swung the branch wildly in front of me. The man laughed and waved his hands in a rhythmic motion, conjuring a blade and rope from within a shimmering white glow.

"Wielder," I bleated pitifully as the man swung his magical sword, effectively cleaving my branch in two.

"Sorrel!" Mama was almost to me, but she was still holding Theodorvin close to her chest, the target of this attack. I threw each end of my broken branch at the man, but he deflected them with ease, as he continued his depraved chuckling.

"Mama, help!" I yelped, all bravado in my performance slipping away as I ran out of options to defend myself.

"Why bother with a blade," he crowed, slapping his hands together and pulling them apart to form a pistol. "When I could just shoot all three of you? Eisa knows you lot deserve it."

My eyes stretched wide in terror, but somehow my feet were still carrying me backwards. We were near the edge of the wood now.

"Nenaya, if you can kill the heir and the Empress, so be it, but take the girl alive and give her to me. We will use her to barter," a second voice hissed from the pool of shadows, this time belonging to a woman.

"Certainly, Ahska," the man called Nenaya snorted. He aimed his pistol at Mama and Theo, and I shrieked for him to stop, watching as time seemed to slow around us while his finger roved to the trigger.

A loud bang thundered around us and I fell backwards, certain that the man had fired his weapon as my head throbbed and my ears filled with a sharp collateral ringing. It wasn't until I felt an arm around me from behind, that I dared look up and see crimson blooming across Nenaya's chest.

"Sorrel, come on!" Mama's voice pushed through the ringing as she shook my shoulder. My eyes locked onto where Nenaya crumbled to his knees in front of me, a wheezing, gurgling sound pressing through his lips as blood filled his mouth. "Take your brother for me and run straight home."

Mama tugged me to my feet and handed me Theo, who was crying and thrashing in his bloodstained swaddle where Mama's wound had bled. I held the bundle close to my chest as I had seen her do and nodded.

"Aren't you coming?"

"Yes, My Darling. I'll be right behind you. Look there, see soldiers are on their way. One of them shot the bad man down to keep us safe." Mama urged me forward, pointing at the group of armed men flooding into the woods, led by my father. "I need to tell them what happened and you need to get to safety immediately."

"I thought…" I whimpered, biting down on my tongue and trying my hardest not to cry.

"This is important, Sorrel. I need you to take care of Theodorvin and bring him home. Can you do that for me, Darling?"

"Yes, Mama," I promised and trudged as quickly as I could through the throng of men towards the house.

"Someone accompany the Grand Princess and Grand Prince Heir back to the palace!" An order barked and a couple of men broke out of formation to flank me as I hurtled through the last of the snowy stretch separating me from my home.

I stumbled through the door and was immediately rushed by all three of my sisters, each one in a fit of fearful tears. Yulia covered her ears and closed her eyes, shrinking back, while Kira gripped hysterically onto my arm, and Inessa babbled a mile a minute.

"Sorrel, you're bleeding," she gasped, pointing to the small puddle that had accumulated on the floor by my bare feet.

"Where are your shoes?" Kira squeaked, pointing to my toes. She was wrapped snugly in a small red blanket, her own toes covered in a thick pair of wool socks. "Aren't your feet cold?"

"What?" I puffed, confused. The room felt stifling after running through the brisk winter air and I felt myself rapidly overheating. "I must have lost them while running."

"Did you not put on boots before you dragged us out there?" Inessa's golden eyebrows raised in surprise, and I winced at the fault I carried for the terrifying events that had transpired. "No matter. You're hurt. Let's get that looked at."

"I don't remember getting hurt..." I trailed off when I realized that Theo's crying had stopped and his breathing had grown labored against my chest. "Theo?"

"It's probably when you *saved me!*" Kira shouted dramatically, using one hand to wipe away her tears with a large snort, the other still anchoring her tiny body off of my arm.

"Kira, stop that. You'll trip her," Yulia chided, finally releasing her hold on her head to yank Kira from underfoot.

My voice wavered and I looked frantically around at the gathered maids gathered around us in the foyer. "Someone fetch Doctor Klivech immediately!"

"Right away, your Imperial Highness," a maid dipped her head and scurried off. I raced up the stairs and down the hall to the nursery. Laying my brother down, I looked at myself in horror when I realized my entire torso was also stained red.

"Sorrel, what's happening?" Inessa asked, peering over my shoulder.

My chin trembled as my teeth chattered with a fresh rush of fear. I untied the swaddle and located the source of all the blood. It was a small lengthwise cut on Theo's arm, leaking the sticky hot crimson like a faucet.

"Divines above, what happened?" Inessa blanched beside me. I took the blanket and pressed it firmly against Theo's tiny arm, remembering seeing Klivech do the same thing to stop the bleeding from a gash on Kira's knee once.

"He must have gotten nicked when that maniac cut Mama's arm at the waterfall. The bleeding won't stop, Ina!" I whimpered.

"Yulia, get word to Mama that Theo is hurt." Inessa shoved Yulia towards the door.

"How do I do that?" Yulia bleated, her big blue eyes stretching wide as saucers.

"Roland is in the school room, send him out. Or tell a soldier, a maid, whoever is closest. But hurry!"

"Is he going to die?" Kira whispered, creeping up to my other side, her voice small and frail with worry.

"No!" I replied adamantly. "I promised Mama I'd take care of him and I will. Doctor Klivech is on his way here, and Mama will know what to do."

"Why won't it stop bleeding?" Inessa whispered to me. "Did the blade have something on it? It just materialized from thin air when it struck Mama."

"It was at least two Wielders who attacked us. One came out of a shadow and made blades with his bare hands when he tried to grab me. It has to be something to do with the magic, right?"

"Divines above," Ina swore for the second time. "You're probably right."

"It cut Mama much worse than this." I tipped my chin toward Theo, nausea cramping my stomach as my head reeled with newfound concern. "Do you think she's alright? She hasn't come back inside yet like she promised. What if the blade poisoned her too?"

"Girls?" A familiar voice sounded behind us and filled my

heart with relief. Friedrich Rusev; Minister of Internal Affairs, Papa's dearest friend. His deep brown eyes locked on the bloodied blanket I was pressing against Theo. He hurried to my side. "What's wrong with your brother?"

"Theo's arm was cut by a Wielder with magic knives, but the cut won't stop bleeding. He was moving around a bunch before but now he's grown really quiet and still. Did they poison him?"

"If it was done by the Wielder's blade, I fear the bleeding may be the result of a curse."

I looked sharply at Friedrich, the word causing the hairs on the back of my neck to lift. "A what?"

"Wielder's magic stems from curses." His voice fell away, yielding to a new train of thought. "Did anyone call for Klivech?"

"Sorrel did!" Kira reported, crowding her way between me and Friedrich. "And she is pressing on owie like the doctor did when I hurt my knee." Somehow hearing Theo's condition reduced to an *owie* by a four-year old shook the ground beneath me with a clear understanding of how much more serious this was.

"Good, applying pressure is the best we can do until he arrives."

"Will he be alright?" Tears brimmed in my eyes as guilt threatened to overwhelm me. I ran my hand over Theo's forehead and flinched at the heat. He was already growing feverish. "Ina, get a cool rag."

"Only the Divinities can say," Friedrich placed a comforting hand on my shoulder. "But we always have hope."

"Where is he?" Mama's frantic voice sounded from down the hallway. My knees wobbled with relief hearing that she'd returned safely. "Where is my son?"

Friedrich stepped to the side, lifting Kira into his arms to keep her from being run over as Mama flew into the room, tears streaming down her face. Yulia stumbled in behind her. "Geneva, try and compose yourself. You'll frighten the children.

Sorrel is keeping pressure on the wound, and already sent for the doctor."

"What's wrong? What happened?"

"It seems a Wielder's blade nicked him and the bleeding won't stop."

"Mama was cut too," I reminded them quietly, looking down at the ground to check if there was more blood.

"But my wound was much deeper and it started to clot," Mama rambled, her words choked. She angled her arm to give Friedrich a glimpse at her injury. "If it's just a small cut, I don't understand…"

"Geneva," Friedrich spoke my mother's name slowly, his tone weighted with pity.

"No. A curse? It can't be. Not now that we finally have an heir for Eisa. I can't go through another pregnancy— and certainly not at the risk of another girl." Mama swayed on her feet and Friedrich steadied her.

"Wait and see. Pray to the Divinities to see him through. That's all we can do. And be grateful for your daughter's quick and helpful instincts." I glimpsed Friedrich jerking his dark bearded chin in my direction.

"You said it was important." My brows furrowed, and my voice pitched, betraying cracking composure. "I don't want anything to happen to my brother."

"Oh, Sorrel," Mama breathed, cupping my face in her hands. "Thank you for taking care of him, my darling girl. And going back for Kira. You were such a brave big sister protecting your siblings. I'm very proud of how mature and collected you were today."

"Here's the cloth!" Inessa raced back into the room and laid the cloth over Theo's forehead. "And Doctor Klivech is here."

"Thank the Divinities!" Mama gasped, pulling away from me, distracted. I could see sweat gathering on her dark auburn brow as Klivech entered the room.

Friedrich quickly ushered everyone else out except for

Mama. "Listen here, girls," he spoke firmly, setting Kira down with the rest of us. "Your brother's condition is a matter of privileged information. Only a select few may know of this incident. Do you understand?"

"Yes," my sisters and I spoke in tandem.

"And rest assured, Little Princesses, your father and I will make sure this breech in Eisa's security won't go unpunished. Any Wielder who dares think they can live within our borders will be eradicated like the monsters they are. That's a promise."

Twelve
years later...

ONE

Something isn't right.

A burst of fire shattered the frozen sky and rained scarlet on the world below. The sudden presence of foreboding spread from the nape of my neck down my spine, like a million pricks of a stray needle. My face was pressed to the frosted glass, watching the display from the window of the room I shared with my sister. The vibrant hues bounced off the spindling fractal patterns like shimmering constellations.

What was that ominous dread I just felt?

"Hurry up, and get ready. If the festival is starting, we should already be heading downstairs." Inessa, my elder sister, called over the cracks of fireworks exploding into the night just beyond the palace grounds.

"Wait! I need you to close my dress, Ina," I gasped in dismay. Turning away from both the window and the spark of disquietude, I rushed to the privacy screen to disrobe and slip into my evening gown.

Inessa made quick work of sealing me securely in the dress, and I did a spin to check everything looked alright. The main form of the garment was a deep shade of larkspur purple— a color I had chosen from one of the flowers in Inessa's greenhouse— with a sheer glittering overlay covering the skirt in midnight blue. The beading and embroidery consisted of subtle flecks of silvers, blues, and purples. I smiled, the design reminding me of a sky that was in transition between twilight and nightfall. Receiving the nod of approval from my sister, I rushed over to my vanity and somehow managed to pin my hair in a layered updo, with three rows of glittering silver ribbon wrapped around my head. Lastly, I slipped on a pair of small teardrop earrings, and Inessa and I both placed the other's tiara on our heads with a laugh.

It wasn't until seven years ago that the realities of being royalty really sank in, and winters were never quite the same again. Back home at Svyat Gavan, where we spent a majority of the year, everything felt simple. But, every winter, since my thirteenth birthday, when we would return to the capital for the season, simplicity quickly turned into exorbitance. Our daily casual frocks were replaced by opulent gowns, our privacy was exchanged for a plethora of staff, candor for decorum— and most of all, it reminded us of the world beyond our own insular family. The parties we entertained during our time in the capital also reminded us of a world beyond Eisa, the country over which we were so proud to reign.

"Ah! Shoes," Inessa squawked and we both raced behind the screen to get our shoes. "How do we always forget those until the last minute? Can you imagine if we had both made it downstairs without anything on our feet?"

"Then we might be in more trouble than Yulia and Kira for the sledding adventure they went on this afternoon," I joked of our two younger sisters.

Inessa whipped her head up from where she was slipping into her emerald green slippers and raised her eyebrows. "Yulia and Kira did *what?*"

"Yulia came back sopping wet, and freezing, while Kira had a head full of twigs. Certainly safe to assume they crashed, and Mama was beside herself trying to make sure they were presentable for tonight."

"Those two, I swear. Hearing their antics you'd never guess that Kira was turning sixteen in a few months. They still sound like children." Inessa rolled her eyes and offered me her arm. "Shall we?"

We linked arms and lifted our skirts to rush from the room and head to the stairs. We were met along the way by our younger sisters—dry and twig-free in their own glittering gowns— and found our parents waiting at the top of the flight.

"Cutting it close, young ladies," Papa's words were stern, but his eyes looked bemused. Mama, on the other hand, looked slightly strained and shook her head.

We each mumbled our apologies and found our places in our typical family formation. Papa dawned a formal icy blue jacket, embellished with medals and pins in place of embroidery, and black dress pants. At his side, Mama wore a variation of the same golden and white gown, similar in style to her daughters', that she did every year. A step behind her, Inessa stood adjacent to Papa, while I took my place behind Mama. A step out from Ina and I, Yulia stood behind Inessa, and Kira behind me. But something was missing and I leaned forward to address my mother.

"Where is Theodorvin?"

"Sorry! I was watching the fireworks and lost track of time!" My question was answered as my brother, the youngest of us five children, raced down the hall to stand between me and Inessa, directly behind our parents. Much like Papa, Theo was in a formal cobalt uniform, though instead of medals, the jacket was adorned with striking draped aiguillettes since his weak constitution and young age of twelve had not yet allowed him to earn any accolades of his own. Like a matched set, both he and Papa stood proud in their coordinating gold epaulets, red facings studded with gold buttons, and silver ceremonial sashes across their chests.

"That's alright, Theo. So long as we are all ready now?" Mama looked over her shoulder at us, and we each nodded back.

"Why doesn't he get scolded?" Kira muttered to Yulia, who poked her in the ribs as a sign to be quiet.

"Alright," Papa exhaled slowly, his body drooping for a moment into a peaceful calm before straightening to a firm alignment of strength and power. "Into the lion's den we go!"

Each of us stood a little taller, storing away all casual airs to be replaced by the regality and elegance of the roles we were to play for the evening. Our unified stance held us at a point, and with our heads lifted proudly, we descended the stairs from the third floor together to welcome our guests.

There was a brief moment of buried stillness that palpitated around me as we paused at the doors to the ballroom. Two footmen gripped around the golden handles, turning to open the entrance in tandem. As the doors pulled apart, we were greeted with decadence and smiling faces with each slow, uniform step we took into the room.

In the echoing call of the herald, announcing our entry, there wasn't a single other sound. The sea of guests parted around the scarlet coronation carpet to welcome us, their bodies dipping into bows and curtsies in a rhythmic wave of brocade silks and glinting gems. We continued wearing the royal pride and dignity that was expected of us, until we reached the platform with the imperial throne. Once more in perfect synchronicity, we turned and faced the crowd, dipping our heads in acknowledgment. Papa stepped forward, a benevolent grin outlined by his dark, sharply groomed beard.

He folded his arms behind his back. "Welcome, all. We thank you for sharing this momentous milestone in Eisa's history, as we celebrate the three-hundredth year of reign of the Zdraevit family line." Papa paused to let his gaze sweep meaningfully around the room. "I stand here before you, an emperor humbled by the faith of his people, his country, and kinsmen. With me, stands the imperial family— my family— strong, resilient, and ever loyal to the Eisan kingdom. I am but one of many to wear this crown, and after me, it will be my son and Eisa's heir, Grand Prince Theodorvin, who will take up my mantle."

My brother lifted his head proudly, the light refracting around the room turning his dusty brown hair golden. His chest puffed beneath his uniform, though I could still see the weariness in his eyes, betraying the fact he was still recovering from the fever that had been plaguing him for the past week.

"In a country that has ushered in peace and sanctuary from the wicked and reprehensible scourge of Wielders and magic-Sympathizers," Papa continued. "I am proud to stand with you as your ruler. This is just as my father did before me, and my son will after me. I would call a toast to another three-hundred years of peace, but that wouldn't be enough. No, we will continue to strive towards an *infinite* future of peace and prosperity to keep Eisa safe, strong, and the greatest country in all of Alse Hanya!"

My own chest swelled with pride at my father's speech. He spoke with such conviction, every single person in the ballroom stared at him in awe before erupting into applause, so loud I could feel the vibrations in my feet. Next, Mama stepped forward to join Papa, ready to assume her usual role. She smiled, her posture oozing a demure and regal radiance, well rehearsed for such events, as she gestured slowly around the room with a sweep of her hand.

"Please, enjoy tonight's festivities and celebrations." Her silver eyes twinkled against her pale skin. It was hard to imagine, witnessing her perfectly executed performance, how out of alignment she had always felt with the royal court. "Let the party begin!"

The footmen made quick work of rolling up the carpet to allow for dancing, and just as smoothly as the crowd had parted, it swept back together in a rolling tide of social interactions. A small nod from my parents told us that my sisters and I were free to join in. Kira's eyes blazed with enthusiasm as she was the first to peel away from our family to meld with the crowd. Inessa and Yulia descended from the platform together and were quickly engaged in conversation with some visiting dignitaries of one of our allied countries, Videiria. Mama and Papa followed suit, though they remained close to the throne as they socialized, leaving me to trail behind and slowly enter the crowd.

The orchestra was striking the beginning notes of a waltz, so I gravitated to the edges of the room and peered around aimlessly, looking to spot one familiar face in particular. I raised on my tiptoes to get a better view, but saw no sign of him.

"Your Imperial Highness, Grand Princess Sorrel," Friedrich Rusev, our Minister of Affairs, and my father's oldest and closest friend greeted me, interrupting my search for his son. He bowed respectfully and gave me a small wink at the formality as he extended his hand. "How are you this evening?"

I accepted his hand, laughing as he gave me a playful twirl and handed me a flute of champagne. "I am doing quite well, Lord Friedrich, thank you. Sorry, I mean *Lord Minister*," I copied his ceremoniousness. "All of the preparations turned out marvelously, didn't they? Did you see the fireworks at the festivals? Ina and I were able to see a few from our room."

"I did! I also heard reports of the record attendance. We had arranged to give each attendee a special memorabilia, but I'm not sure if we estimated the count correctly." Friedrich nodded, and rubbed at his chin. "I suppose the accommodations will be handled as needed by the official posted at the event. In any case, it is out of our hands tonight while we are here."

"I didn't know that there was a gift arranged," I beamed. "Papa really thought of everything. He loves Eisa so much. I just hope that the people aren't terribly disappointed if they don't get a gift."

"Always such a thoughtful girl, sweet Sorrel. I think they were starting to hand them out around an hour ago, and people were still arriving," Friedrich mused and waved his hand. "But, that's enough about that. We should be enjoying our own festivities here and now. I noticed you were sticking to the edges, not like your sister." He gestured affectionately at Kira, who had snagged herself a dance partner— none other than her constant flirtation partner, and Friedrich's youngest son, Arrian— and was gliding around the room, her face bright with energy.

"Kira is always the first one to find a dance partner," I chuckled with a small shake of my head.

"And Arrian is almost always happy to oblige her, isn't he?" Friedrich laughed along.

Arrian was looking down at Kira's beaming face as she caught my eye and grinned at me. A bemused smirk curling the edges of his lips, his eyes narrowed with fascinated discernment. At eighteen, he stood a little over two years my sister's senior and certainly was a handsome and dignified young man— tall, with rich brunette hair and deep brown eyes. He and Kira got along well enough as children, though it seemed since entering into their teen years, something a bit more had begun sparking between them as they shifted from teasing and hair-pulling to dances and spirited debates.

"Her charisma is always rather unmatched, isn't it? Looking as stunningly beautiful as you do tonight, I am sure you will be hot on her heels any time now." Friedrich looked around knowingly, pulling my attention away from my sister. "Where is my other son anyway?"

I blushed and shrugged in defeat. "I was looking for Roland just before you found me. He is rather adept at camouflaging himself when he wants to."

"Unlike his brother who always seems to be at the center of things. Those two would make quite the match, between you and me. Though, their joint shining might just blind us all." Friedrich tilted his head at Kira and Arrain. "When you find Roland— or I'm sure he will no doubt come looking for you— tell him he owes you a dance, and step on his toes for making you wait! I must continue the obligatory mingling, though to be honest, I don't mind it so much. It's rare that we entertain such a large gathering and I think we all better make the most of it."

I raised my glass in a gesture of farewell. "Thank you for the champagne, Lord Friedrich." He bowed and turned to make his way over to my parents.

I wandered around the room, entertaining various conversations with guests off and on, for the duration of another few songs, still having no luck finding Roland. Much like it seemed Arrian and Kira were setting down a more romantic path, Roland's and my relationship had been blossoming since our childhood— though we had never openly discussed the prospect of any sort of proper courtship. Part of me thought it was likely due to his reluctance to approach my mother and father for the official request. Spending the evening with him had been something I'd highly anticipated tonight, and I puffed my cheeks in frustration that he hadn't yet revealed himself to me.

"What could he possibly be doing?" I muttered mutinously to myself.

I made my way back towards where we had entered and wondered if perhaps he was lingering somewhere outside the ballroom, but along the way I was stopped by one of the dignitaries of Vatra, another allied country to Eisa, here to celebrate my family's reign. He was a tall man with deeply tanned olive skin and silver hair. His face was round, with a wide brim nose and deep brown eyes. It was his smile though that stood apart from the rest of his features. It was broad and held an unattainable warmth to it. He was accompanied by his wife, who was dressed in a burnt orange gown, her long, rich ebony hair was plated into several braids and piled intricately atop her head.

"It is an honor to be here tonight and to meet you. Your ancestors gave the world something imperative when they successfully initialized the first Prohibition of Magic Act. It was no easy feat to accomplish either, combating the Wielders with your superior technology and weapons, and gaining control back for the mortals. Positively outstanding! Emperor Valamir was a legend amongst men," the man, now introduced to me as a duke named Kenji, praised.

His wife, Duchess Kailia, nodded emphatically. "It gave the rest of Alse Hanya hope for a better tomorrow when we no longer had to live in fear under the terrors of sorcery. The Zdraevits were revolutionary visionaries."

"Thank you," I dipped my head in acknowledgment. My heart was warmed by the appreciation for me and my family's legacy. "It is such an honor to be Emperor Valamir's descendant, and I can only hope that we continue to bring honor to his name and efforts of peace and prosperity."

Kenji and Kailia exchanged a glance. "We only wish Vatra was as peaceful as here."

I furrowed my brows and tilted my head. I knew that both Vatra and Videiria were currently engaged in a war with magic wielding countries, but since both had been able to send officials to attend our celebration, I had assumed things were faring well for their side of the fighting. The look that passed between them, though, made me suppress a small shiver of dread at the thought that the Wielder's side of the war might be gaining momentum.

We are safe here. I reminded myself firmly, sipping my champagne to wet my dry mouth.

Kailia noticed my subtle shift in demeanor and jumped in with an explanation. "It's Sonyo we are having the most trouble with. They deal in nightmare curses, as I'm sure you know. They can slip into your dreams and drive you mad by tormenting you while you're unconscious. The worst bit is that they can do it from their own homeland, it seems."

"They live under the protection of the Veil of Stars, though. Finding a way to get through that monstrous defense is something we hope to accomplish so our people can once more sleep safely." Kenji bit, the warmth in his smile falling away to be replaced by flames of rage in his eyes.

I bristled at the information. "I had no idea it was that bad," I admitted remorsefully. "I'm so sorry."

Safe. Eisa is safe.

Another look was shared. "We hope to find the remedy to our problem very soon," Kailia replied vaguely, her tone leading.

I opened my mouth to express more sympathy for their plight, but faltered as a shoulder brushed roughly passed me, causing me to stumble to the side. Another song came to an end, and there was a small pause of silence as the musicians adjusted their sheet music. I regained my footing, grabbing hold of Kenji's offered arm for stability. The silence was filled with a crescendo of applause, deafening in the ornate ballroom.

A crash cut through the room as a server lost hold of a tray and the contents clattered to the ground. The cheering fell away, replaced by the antagonized bellows of a man.

TWO

"How many of our bodies are you dancing over tonight?" The man spat, his face tinged in the violet hue of heated emotion. Then the whispers began to drift back to me from the center of the commotion.

"Who is that vile man, and how did he make it into the palace?"

"Listen to what he's saying. Anti-Imperial nonsense. He must be anti-Eisa."

"Do you think he is a Wielder?"

"In Eisa? Not a chance, look where we are!"

"He could be a Magic-Sympathizer. Still dangerous, if you ask me."

Everyone in attendance knew there was nothing in this world to be feared more than a Wielder, and the very prospect that this man might be even a Sympathizer, had stolen the vibrancy from the room. Panic was growing behind cupped hands and dipped heads, and a wide space had formed around the man as the elegant figures dispersed from the dance floor. A bated quiet stole over the room, and we all hung on the bits of fevered hysteria we could make out. I took a few distracted steps forward, trying to hear more clearly.

The man was dressed like a regular merchant from the city, but his clothing was so caked in dirt and various layers of grime, the color of the fabric was no longer distinguishable. Dark smudges of blood coated his hands and face, but whether it belonged to him or someone else was unclear. The crystals on the chandeliers rattled, threatening to spill to the floor in a demonstration of his wrath. My breath caught in my throat, and Kira appeared beside me in the shuffle, gripping onto my arm.

"Who is that, Sorrel?" She whispered, staring at the man with her piercing blue eyes. Her chin was lifted in defiance to his interruption, and I prayed she wouldn't give into any of the impetuous thoughts tumbling behind her gaze.

At last, I spotted Roland across the room, standing near my parents and his father. He approached Friedrich and whispered something into his ear, received a small nod of approval, then he backed away and disappeared amongst the guests. I mentally traced his path and stiffened when I saw it pointed in the direction of the guards coming to restrain the intruder.

"We were celebrating *your reign*. What did you do to prevent this tragedy? Were you baiting us? Are you trying to wipe out another group and call it a mass casualty like you did before? The protests you keep trying to quiet will only grow after this! You can't bury it this time, not when it's your own people you're putting in the ground." The man's voice echoed with vehemence around the ballroom as he was forcibly dragged away. Roland appeared again at the exit to direct the guards.

"I apologize for the interruption," Papa's voice boomed. He stood tall next to the throne platform, unphased, calm, and collected. "Don't let the ravings of a single man spoil the fun. Please, enjoy the celebration. Any issue with merit will be dealt with." He opened his arms in a gesture of goodwill and humble offerings. Even across the room, I could see his smile, equally reassuring and disarming in its magnanimity. But I could tell the corners of his mouth were stretched too tight, and though he might seem unphased to his audience, something was unsettling him.

Guests continued whispering to each other as the music picked back up where it had faltered to veil the lingering curses of the mystery man, and everyone slowly resumed the party. The moment was lost in the sweeping trills of the violin. I caught sight of Inessa and Yulia sharing an uneasy glance before resuming their designated hostess roles and placating our company with bright smiles and gentle voices.

I looked to Mama and Papa to see how they were reacting to the outburst before answering Kira. My mother was smiling calmly while speaking quietly to my father, who nodded and patted her hand. I was able to tell, even at this distance, that Mama's nerves had been rattled, despite her outward composure, and she'd likely make her excuses and adjourn early. Her resilience to shock had declined steadily in the twelve years following Theo's accident in the woods as an infant. Every little blunder, emergency, and crisis had left her less and less able to cope. In each overwhelming situation throughout the years, unless her presence was absolutely necessary to maintain a strong front, she would excuse herself and flee to her bed. I could tell now that it was only the thread of royal protocol and expectations for tonight's event that held this performance she was putting on together.

"Sorrel?" Kira repeated. "What was all that?"

"Don't worry, Kira. I'm sure it's nothing. Go back to the party and enjoy it while it lasts." I motioned her back towards the twirling masses, but she pivoted.

"*While it lasts?* That sounds rather cryptic." Her eyebrows toggled with curiosity. "Do you know something about that man you're not sharing?"

"Of course not. But, it will be a long time before we host a gathering this extravagant again— which I know you adore— so, best make the most of it. We will be back in Eisolde at Svyat Gavan before you know it!" I smiled warmly at my sister, trying to banish the disquieting throbbing that had lodged in my chest at the thought of the peasant man.

He must have been the one who had pushed past me. Recalling

his stature conjured a visceral memory of a writhing pool of darkness beneath a frosted tree. I curled my sweating palms into my skirts, eyes scouring the vicinity lest someone else be lurking in shadows.

"I did see another particularly delectable potential suitor somewhere by the hors d'oeuvres… I think I'll go pounce!" Kira pulled a silly face behind an impish grin, indicating that my attempt as reassurance had succeeded. She turned and disappeared in the throng of weaving and dancing bodies, her long flaxen curls bobbing along behind her. Apparently, Arrian wasn't the only prospect she had her eye on.

The mesh of glittering dresses and glinting medals twinkled in a haze like a nova of starlight trapped between gilded pillars and frosted windows. The room felt hot, and a wave of anxiety churned through my stomach. What had the man been ranting about? Was Roland safe while he handled the matter? I shuffled backwards, trying to disengage from the mass of bodies twirling too fast, laughing too loud, and smiling too bright.

"Apparently there was an incident at the festivals in the city. Citizens died because it was extremely overcrowded," Inessa whispered quietly in my ear, joining me by where I rooted myself near the floor to ceiling window, trying to steady my breath.

"What happened? How many died?" I gasped, reaching instinctively for my throat in horror when my sister shrugged.

"Something to do with a stampede over a misfired firework that went into the crowd while the citizens in the Piren District were receiving their gifts, I think. The explosion set off a panic that spread through the city and caused a stampede. Yulia only heard a small piece of the explanation."

"That sounds like an accident. Why accuse Papa of nefarious intents?"

"I guess it seemed suspicious because of the particular location being near where there were rumored Sympathizers hiding." Inessa glanced at her feet, her fingers fiddling idly at her earring.

My stomach knotted at the mention of the gifts, knowing my father's honorable intentions. I thought of smiling out at the fireworks display, how we had been boasting of the large turnout, and guilt tore at my lungs. "Why not cancel the remainder of the party?"

"Perhaps to keep morale high? It is the celebration of our family's long reign. Of our ancestor's victory in saving us from the Weilder's War all those centuries ago. To cancel *this* celebration would be the same as dishonoring them in most's eyes. It is seen as our duty to maintain the peace they liberated for us and, on this day, to celebrate them. We will expect to mourn tomorrow," Inessa answered briskly, her eyes flicking around the room. The corner of her lips puckered ever so slightly in pensive thought, and I knew she was biting the inside of her cheek as a means to stay grounded beneath her thinly veiled concern. "I'm not sure how he managed to make it this far into the palace though."

"Do you think we need to worry? Everyone seems relatively pacified now, but I still feel a bit ill at ease." I hugged my arms to my chest and looked over my shoulder, like I expected to see an ambush barreling through the door at any moment. "He walked right past me, and I can't shake this feeling that something else is terribly wrong."

If he was somehow a Wielder, I feared the proximity we'd shared, even if only for a moment. Could I have been cursed like Theo? Had he just come here to berate us, or was there something more nefarious at play by getting into the middle of a room of high ranking royalty, nobles, and dignitaries? Was that the reason for the trepidation I couldn't seem to banish?

Inessa patted my shoulder gently. "He was just upset, Sorrel. He might have lost someone he loved in the accident. We don't know the volume of tragedy just yet. My guess is that he needed someone to blame, so he chose Papa. Try not to let it get you too unsettled."

"I suppose you're probably right, Ina." I clasped a hand over hers where it rested on my shoulder and gave it a small squeeze. "I'll be fine. Don't worry. Go enjoy the party."

"Alright, if you're sure. I saw Kira making questionable advances on some poor boy on my way over, so I suppose I should probably go and do my best to intervene before she does something he will regret."

"Don't you mean *she* will regret?" I laughed.

"No. Kira rarely regrets anything she does. But, that boy might regret what Kira does."

"Right, better hurry then."

Inessa bid me farewell with a smile before her lithe form slipped into the crowd. My lungs struggled to draw in breath the longer I remained in the congested space, and after a few more rapid heartbeats, I elected to step out onto the balcony for fresh air.

I pressed myself inconspicuously next to the exit door, turning the handle and whisking myself through the opening as fast as I could manage so as to not draw attention to my departure. Pushing it closed behind me, I leaned against it, ready to receive reprieve, but what I was met with as I stepped outside was something straight from a nightmare.

I was faced with the abrasive image of blood against snow, though this time it wasn't a memory surfacing in my mind amongst flickers of a lumbering man and twisting shadows. I came to the railing and stared in horror, my hands starting to reach instinctively to cover my mouth, unable to avert my gaze. From the balcony of our palace, beneath the cool wash of a full moon, I could just see the edges of the harsh scarlet crawling over the snowy streets of the city, marking the pathways death had taken that night. I trembled at the sight, knowing it was one I would carry with me for the rest of my life.

"Tuyet is bleeding," I whispered hoarsely.

Countless innocent civilians had met their end that night. Bodies were nothing more than limp, dark forms being piled together and taken away in groups from my vantage point, and it didn't seem this was even the most affected area of the city. I wished I could have said the night was still and quiet in the aftermath following the stampede, but that would be far from the truth, as the night sang the harrowing cacophony of mass grief from our surviving citizens.

I was so far removed from it all, standing there in a gown of indigo starlight, yet I felt as if the very tethers of my humanity were being pulled towards the city, yearning to help and comfort. Tears pooled in my eyes as a storm of emotion roared to life inside me, but knowing there was nothing I could do in that moment, I swallowed it down beneath a blanket of numb stoicism.

"You'll catch your death of cold standing out here." It was Papa's voice that sounded behind me, and I could feel the heat of the party radiating from within the door he held open.

"The frost doesn't bite me," I replied my usual mantra coolly, not turning around and instead keeping my gaze fixed on the calamity before me. "I don't think I can go back inside and dance with the noblemen as if I haven't seen what happened out there, Papa."

Papa came to stand beside me, snow collecting on his rich dark hair. He gripped the icy railing firmly enough for his knuckles to turn white. "I know it isn't easy to hear it all the way up here, and it's even worse to look at—"

"I think the sound is worse than the sight, actually," I whispered, the wails of anguish tumbling over each other in a mournful serenade around it. Sound was always sharper on cold nights.

"—But there isn't anything we can do right now. As frivolous as it may seem in contrast to the world out there, we are simply doing our duty, Sorrel, My Dear."

"Our duty?"

"Yes. Tonight we are required to project prosperity and strength to our guests. Turning people away now for the tragedy beyond our walls will cause too big a stir. We must lift our chins and continue on. Eisa mustn't look weak, and as the reigning power we cannot waver in this resolve."

"And then what, Papa?" I turned to face my father, looking deep into his blue eyes, imploring an answer.

He looked so regal and powerful, standing tall, but I could tell in his gaze that his spirit was weary. It had long been known in our most intimate inner circle that though my father respected his role as emperor, he had never felt completely comfortable or particularly prepared for the position, having taken the throne suddenly after his own late father's abrupt passing.

"Qualified personnel are handling the victims of the stampede now. They will take care of things down there. I will be stepping away to handle the briefing and initial protocol with Friedrich and the rest of the applicable ministry. As for you, tonight you celebrate the holiday of our family's prosperous reign. Smile, laugh, and dance—anything to keep our guests engaged and distracted. Then, after everyone has left, we will close our gates and assess. We will mourn this tragedy tomorrow."

He echoed Inessa's earlier words, and the promise of tomorrow suddenly felt so terribly hollow.

THREE

S hadows crept along the walls, spliced by the dappling light of the chandeliers. The air was cool and stagnant as I stared out the frostbitten windows. The sky beyond the courtyard was in transition between dark and dawn— Stars receding into their nebulous beds with wisps of sunlight cresting the horizon.

I glanced away from the window and surveyed the empty room. It was hard to imagine it as it was now, that hours earlier it had been the very center of celebration in our empire. Now, instead of applause, laughter, music, and the sound of shoes gliding over marble, the palace echoed with a spectral silence. I closed my eyes and drank in both the glamorous images of the previous evening and the sea of quiet that swallowed me now. My ears only honed in on the muted clattering sounds of the staff stirring and beginning the day's work. I could no longer hear the wailing of our people, but the sound haunted me until I was certain it was hissing deep within my eardrums—Low and insidious, like sand spilling over rocks, permeating my mind to rake claws along my subconscious. I clutched at my temple and shook my head to dislodge the whispering phantom from my senses, inhaling deeply.

After so many faces, so much ambient energy, and the turbulent anxieties of my own roving mind, I'd caught a second wind and found I wasn't the least bit tired yet. I'd compartmentalized the importance of duty and successfully performed my role as princess until the last guest had cleared the doors of the ballroom. But now, in the stagnance, the mental compartments cracked open, and I was transported back to that poignant moment that had simultaneously fried my nerves and stolen all the warmth from my body.

How many of our bodies are you dancing over tonight? The words thundered in the center of the memory of wails and screams from beyond the vaulted walls of this palace. Recalled from the depths of my childhood, memories of my one and only encounter with Wielders collided with the passing present, choking my mind the more I tried to make sense of the overlaps.

I couldn't help but wonder, as I stood before the same window that led to the balcony, staring out at the quiet blanket of white, what the man had meant when he'd mentioned growing protests, and my father supposedly trying to keep them quiet. Our kingdom was safe and sturdy. Nothing had happened in the last twelve years regarding Wielders, not since that day we were attacked outside Svyat Gavan. Our country was thriving, so I couldn't understand what the protests might be over in the first place. But the unbridled anger of the intruder told me there was something to his claims, a root I couldn't yet grasp at. Perhaps there was simply more unrest in Tuyet as the capital than there was in Eisolde.

What was happening now beyond our palace grounds, out in the city? Was their snow now glistening as white as ours here in the palace, or was it still tainted and stained by the blood of the innocent? Was there a storm brewing and it just hadn't reached us yet? Or had the man succeeded in some cruel attempt to sow discord in our sanctuary? So many questions threatened to overwhelm me, until the very air itself held an unbearable pressure.

I left the window and sank into one of the many chairs pressed against the walls. Willing the image of dancing snowflakes behind my lids, I closed my eyes and inhaled deeply, allowing every one of my senses to respond to the mental stimulus. The moment was so still and fragile I could have melted and frozen over amidst the snowflakes outside. It centered me, allowing a small space for peace back into my mind.

"Didn't anyone tell you the party ended hours ago, Snowdrop?" A smooth, familiar voice broke through my wall of silence, and my eyes fluttered open as if awaking from a dream. I recognized the pet name *Snowdrop*—after the precocious little flower that would emerge in the snow before spring had melted it away—that had been given to me as a child by Roland. He had declared me a snowdrop after he had seen me wandering barefoot in our snow covered gardens the day Theo had been cursed.

I smiled despite myself, and nodded to the young man with dark chestnut hair, mussed and dangling in front of his deep blue eyes. He too was still in his evening attire from the party, but had removed his formal jacket, leaving him in his white dress shirt, slouched against the door frame to my right.

"You startled me, Roland," I chided lightly, reaching a hand to brush a rogue strand of hair from my face. It tickled my nose as it grazed the skin in passing, and I crinkled the bridge in response. "I didn't see you all evening, and now you're wandering the palace in the dead of night? Don't try and tell me you thought to look for me here at this hour."

"Apologies. I'm afraid I had to play chameleon all night. But, rest assured, I definitely saw you. And you looked positively stunning. You *still* look positively stunning, I might add." Roland clicked his tongue and glided up to me, his stature leaving him towering over me. "The question is, why did I find you here at this hour?"

The heaviness in my chest began to melt away in his presence, and was replaced by the quiet palpitations of excitement.

"I wasn't tired," I answered simply, blinking in surprise as Roland extended a hand in the offerings of a dance.

"I know you, Snowdrop. There is more to it than that. I owe you a dance, and in exchange, I think you owe me your conversation."

"How forward of you to assume I owe you anything after you left me partnerless all night," I narrowed my eyes in mock reproach, though my lips still wore a bemused smile as I accepted Roland's hand and he began leading me in the steps of the dance around the empty ballroom. Flashes of white and gilded walls blurred past the edge of my vision as we moved. "And, might I point out that you are also still awake. Should I be questioning your motivation?"

"Ah, a fair point." He nodded, feigning serious contemplation. "But— and not to sound too childish— I asked you first."

I scrunched my face, but drooped in concession to the inquiry. "That man tonight… He was so angry."

"That he was," Roland acknowledged, a flash of sympathy appearing in his eyes. "He and countless others, I'm sure. There will be lots to smooth over tomorrow to say the least."

"So many people died, Roland. I saw the blood in the streets from the balcony and it was like the city had this large gaping wound. How can we ever heal it?" I thought back to the unsettled feelings I'd had at the start of the night, and how I brushed them off beneath a guise of invincibility that was suddenly feeling more and more like a delusion of childish grandeur than a plausible reality.

"I'm not sure," Roland sighed. "But, we will. I'm sorry I don't have a better answer for you. Short of turning back time— which not a magical ability in all of Alse Hanya can do— we have no real choice but to move forward and face each day as bravely as we can."

"A very diplomatic response," I murmured.

"Well, that is my job," Roland chuckled softly, the low rasping sound chipping away at my lingering unease. "There will be damage control for sure— especially once we finally have a death toll. Not to mention that there will likely be an insurgence of unruly citizens that the royal guard will have to disperse—"

"Roland?" I tightened my grip on his shoulder, interrupting his procedural ponderings. "Maybe, let's just be in the moment now. We rarely get this kind of quality time anymore, and I think I'd just like to enjoy the remainder of it."

Roland hesitated, contemplating my shameless avoidance of the topic, then cracked a grin and nodded amicably. "As you wish! Anything for the most beautiful princess in Eisa." He dramatized his statement into an official declaration, gripping around my waist and lifting me effortlessly into the air and back down to the ground again in a single sweeping motion. "But don't tell your sisters I called you that or they'll have my head."

My breath caught in my throat for a moment before I replied, "What flattery."

I knew his teasing was his way of lulling the tension from my body, something he had always been especially adept at doing. Part of me felt like I should feel guilty for indulging in flirtatious banter, while the rest of me craved the solace I felt in his arms, pretending like everything was fine. But weariness was threatening to drag me into the bowels of despair I wasn't sure I could climb out of, so I let the chaos of the night flee my brain. There was nothing left to think about besides him and me for the next few precious stolen moments.

"You need the distraction, don't you?" He dipped me suddenly, and my body yielded to his lead, despite my surprise at the movement. His face hovered inches away from mine for a moment as he grinned mischievously down at me.

"Oh, that's how you're going to distract me, is it?"

"My dear, lovely Princess, are you accusing me of something?" Roland guffawed incredulously, returning me to an upright position.

"Let's look at the facts, Lord Minister," I drawled dramatically, using his official title for emphasis. "You approach a young woman alone at a strange hour, compliment her, and lure her into a dance with no music playing to elicit such behavior. Either you lack common social graces, which I know you've been taught, or you are trying to distract me with vain attempts at seduction!"

Roland's eyebrows jumped and he beamed at me. "Ah, you do make some interesting points, Snowdrop. However, it worries me that you can't hear the music we've been dancing to."

"What music?"

"Listen closely," Roland whispered, waving his hand over my

face, dragging lightly at my eyelashes to pull my lids closed.

I obliged, and let my senses all slip away save for my hearing. I could hear the rhythmic scuffing and tapping of our feet against the floor as we moved in tandem, and the sharp jingling of the beads of my gown rattling against gems and fabrics. Somewhere caught between the two sounds was the rustling of my skirt against my ankles and legs.

I felt a light color creep into my cheeks, and I opened my eyes. "I stand corrected, I can hear the music now," I conceded softly, and our cantering steps slowed.

"So, you rescind your accusations of me using my superior dance moves with impure intentions?" Roland murmured, pulling me just a hair closer to him than was necessary for the dance. His shirt seemed gossamer and thin in the dim room as my shadow leaned against the sharp white of it.

"I rescind them," I answered gently, my gaze dropping from Roland's brilliant blue eyes to his mouth and back up again.

He mirrored me, eyes to lips, and back again. "I am doing a good job then," He gloated, his voice rasping at the edge of a teasing purr and a whisper.

"But," I replied slowly, dragging my eyes away from his handsome face, wondering if this might be the moment he finally chose to kiss me. Twenty years, and never more than a peck on the cheek had passed between us, and I never quite understood what held him back.

"What is it?" He leaned in even closer to me, and I could feel his breath brush against my cheek.

He is teasing me. I sighed internally, something instinctual telling me this wasn't the moment he'd chosen to make his move to finally kiss me. *Well, I have to pay him back for standing me up as my dance partner earlier anyway.*

I smiled and gripped harder on his hand, curling my body in with his arm, then uncurling into a twirl. At full extension, I released his hand, and spun towards the window. I let my fingers trail against the drapes, dragging them with me for a few steps, and revealing the burgeoning morning and golden sky, before the curtains slipped from my fingers and swept in to conceal the outside world once more.

I paused at the door and looked over my shoulder at Roland, who still had his arm half outstretched from my spin. "Looks like our time is up. Goodnight, Roland."

"Isn't it 'good day?'" He laughed, amusement and disbelief tumbling over each other in his words. It looked like I had successfully taken the upper hand in our game of banter, and I couldn't help but smile at my little victory.

"Mmm," I mused. "I haven't gone to bed yet, so I say *goodnight*."

"But, the sun is up, so it should be 'good morning.'" He pressed, trying to goad me into staying longer with a battle of semantics.

I clicked my tongue and shrugged before turning back towards the door. "Sounds like we will have to pick up this debate next time. But, I must warn you, you will never win."

"'Next time,' already?"

"Consider it retribution for being too late and not dancing with me at the proper time. Be thankful. Your father told me to step on your toes," I admonished with a wink.

"Wasn't this so much better? Just the two of us, without all those people," Roland implored, his tone another offering for me to stay with him longer.

I bit my lip, fighting the desire to concede. "Sorry, Roland. You'll have to wait. An exercise in patience."

"And restraint," He murmured, mostly to himself, and ran a hand through his hair. "Until next time then, Sorrel."

"Sorrel? What happened to Snowdrop?" I paused.

"No, you're being difficult so you will get no more endearments until further notice." He folded his arms to convey his resolve on the matter and I couldn't help but laugh.

I wanted to stay, to remain lost in those dazzling eyes of his, and play our game of wits and teasing. But, alas, the staff was fully up and running with the dawn, and my family would too soon be waking. The last thing I wanted was to have to explain to my mother— or worse, my father— why I was in the arms of a man at dawn. Even one as beloved as Roland. The moment had escaped us and followed the stars to bed.

"Until next time," I echoed the farewell and let the hallway beyond the doorway swallow me up like a portal back to reality— A reality that crept back into harsher clarity with each hasty step I took up the stairway.

As my hands clasped around the handle to my room, my spine stiffened, and a thin layer of sweat gathered on my palm. A low whisper of a voice I couldn't quite discern tickled my ear, light as the brush of feather. It was there and gone, quick as a flash of lightning. A small shiver crawled down my vertebrate, releasing it from its rigidity, and the perspiration in my hand evaporated, leaving only the cool touch of the handle against my skin.

I shook my head to clear it, unsure where the sudden wave of anxiety had come from, tucking it away to the back of my mind, and slipped into the room. Tiptoeing past Inessa's bed, I disrobed as quickly as possible, shedding the elegance of the party like a snake skin until it was just me, hair loose and free, in my nightgown. When I crawled into bed, sleep claimed me almost instantly. I slipped through darkness and fell away to find myself standing on a rocky cliff overlooking a forest swirling with slow, flicking shadows.

"Sorrel, have a dance?" Roland was suddenly beside me, his voice sounding like it was traveling through water. He was dressed in his formal garb and looked the picture of regality, just as he had at the celebration. One hand was extended to me, while the other held a flute of champagne.

I reached to accept his offered hand, but when I grasped at his fingers, his figure turned to dark mist and whisked through the air to join the writhing mass of shadows in the forest below. The champagne turned to bubbling crimson, shattering on the ground in a spray of blood as the flute fell through the mist. I trembled against phantom images of blood in the snow and a large man lunging towards me surged to life in my mind, lifting the hairs on the nape of my neck.

"Are you still dancing on the bodies?" A low, gruff voice growled in my ear and I whirled around to see the strange peasant man who had interrupted our party, flickering in and out of confluence with my memories. He spread his arms wide, and the rocky mountainous terrain behind him shuttered, turning into mounds of bodies, stacked by the hundreds. "See how we celebrate your reign?"

"No…" I took a step back, fear thrashing through my body—wild energy pent up beneath a rigid shell of flesh and bones, churning chaos in my chest and tangling my every nerve. Any lingering happy jitters of my encounter with Roland vanished, and I was doused once more in tragic certainty.

The man moved his parted arms inward to reach for me, the tips of his fingers beginning to bubble into darkness that dripped and spattered on the ground in front of him. His eyes glowed red and his teeth gleamed with malice. What should have been regular facial features melted away into flickering shadows, leaving the red gaze and white snarl in a rolling mass of darkness.

"Our protests will only grow, Princess." The voice sounded like slabs of slate sliding past each other, terrible and otherworldly. "How will you change to save yourself?"

"Are you… are you a Wielder?" I stammered, taking another step back, terror threatening to overwhelm me entirely. I felt transported back to being eight years old, staring down blades and barrels.

"What power can you hope to maintain as you dance over the bodies of your people?" The voice hissed, ignoring my question, though I was fairly certain I was, in fact, facing a magic Wielder, and the picture of evil incarnate.

"I didn't know. We care for our people. We've always protected our people!" I cried, pleading for the terrifying creature in front of me to believe me.

I jumped as I felt a hand slip into mine and turned to see Inessa standing beside me in her beautiful emerald party gown, dripping in excess jewels and beauty. I felt relieved to see her and feel her touch, but my solace didn't last long as I realized her hand was as cold as ice. Vines erupted from the ground and coiled around her ankles.

"It is our duty to maintain the peace they liberated for us and, on this day, to celebrate them," Inessa repeated what she had told me earlier. The vines crawled up the length of her body and were fanning out over her rosy cheeks.

"Let her go!" I screamed, looking from my captured sister to the strange creature writhing in darkness. I started tugging at the vines, but even with all my strength, I couldn't budge a single stem.

Appearing on the peaks of body-mountains, the remaining members of my family materialized. Mama, Papa, Kira, Yulia, and Theo. Each one was now dancing with a phantom shadow atop the bodies.

"No, stop!" I called out to them in horror.

One by one they halted. When our eyes met, the Wielder in front of me grinned, and each of my family members was overtaken by a magical force. Papa's feet turned to ice, and a crawling frost claimed his body. Mama was swallowed whole by a thundering cloud, and Kira burst into flames. Yulia's rich brown hair grew sallow before a hissing wind arose and encircled her. Theo, like Papa, was claimed by a shroud of ice and water. I blanched when I saw the water was tinged with blood. As each family member was overtaken by the magical assault, the shadow they were dancing with rippled before pushing their partner from the mountain peaks.

"Mama, Yulia, Kira!" Tears began streaming from my eyes as I witnessed my family fall to their deaths. "Theo, Papa!" I was left standing with a mostly encased Inessa still holding onto my hand.

"We will mourn tomorrow." Her voice echoed over a sudden harsh silence that rang in my ears like gunfire. And with that, she tipped herself backwards, taking both of us over the cliff's edge. I screamed as wind and shadow shrieked through my hair and we plummeted towards the forest of writhing darkness.

"I once glimpsed Death, and realized I didn't know how to live without her. Then came the greater realization that I would have to."

-D

FOUR

Impact was inevitable, and every old wives tale of how dying in a dream meant death would claim you in the waking thundered in my skull as the ground neared. Just before I crashed into the forest floor, I awoke with a jolt, my heart frantic to escape from my chest and flee the terror not yet leached from my bones. Cold sweat made my nightgown cling to my back, and I struggled to catch my breath.

"It was just a terrible nightmare," I whispered to myself, though the notion did little to reassure me as I was reminded of Kenji and Kailia's plight with nightmare curses. "I didn't die there, nor here. I'm safe."

Wiping my forehead, I sat up to see bright late morning sunlight splintering through the gaps in my curtains. A glance to my right showed that Inessa was already up for the day, her bed neatly made. There was a fire roaring in the fireplace, signaling that the scullery maid had already come and gone as well. I was surprised I had been permitted to sleep for so long without interruption and wondered if my sister had known about my late night dancing and chosen to let me be. I'd have to thank her later.

Swinging my legs out from under my comforter, I slipped my feet into a pair of cozy slippers, and grabbed my thick morning wrap from the reading chair next to my bed. It wasn't terribly cold in the room, but I appreciated the soft texture against my skin.

Pulling back the curtains, outside I saw Yulia and Kira. They were running about in the freshly fallen snow, their faces ruddy from the chill, but their smiles were bright. Though Kira was almost sixteen, and Yulia eighteen, they still played in the snow with the same unbridled abandon as if they were children. Likely the same sense of wonder that had taken them sledding yesterday.

Children of varying ages were running around with my sisters, partaking in the frozen activities. All of them were guests, here for the celebration last night. Kira and Yulia must have been charged with entertaining them for the morning, but neither one seemed to begrudge the task. I sighed with a strange sense of relief at seeing them all safe, though the lingering unease and confusion still coursed through my body from my eerie dream and the stampede.

"What protests was that man talking about? I haven't heard a thing about any protests before now," I mused aloud to myself as I let my fingers trail slowly down the length of my drapes, before setting them to work finger-combing through my sleep-mussed dark waves that fell to my waist. I shook myself both physically and mentally, trying to dislodge the sinister feeling that Wielders' magic would come to harm my family here in the heart of Eisa. The imagery of bodies made sense to me, but the rest of the dream's specific content had me very perplexed. Where had such thoughts come from?

I pulled the cord by my bed to summon a maid for something warm to drink. A perky red-headed attendant knocked and poked her head in, then disappeared to retrieve me a cup of tea and a newspaper. She returned shortly after with my requested items and left me to peruse the paper in peace. I chose the reading chair next to the window, where I could still see the tumbling figures of my siblings in the yard below, and curled up with my steaming cup and paper.

I thumbed through some pages as I sipped, the warmth and energy of the tea slowly thawing the stiffness I had awoken with. I stopped on an image of open grounds of the city, where bodies were being taken away in carts, and the headline read, *Festival Death Toll Climbs to Over 1,000*. My stomach lurched at the thought. Those were our people, and they had been celebrating my family's reign when they'd met their death. I felt such immense guilt, but trusted that Papa had been right, and there was nothing immediate I could do besides wait for whatever decision was made on how we were to address the tragedy as a family.

Another headline tucked in the corner of the following page caught my attention. It read, *Protests Grow in Tuyet As Citizens Seek Reformations to Magical Prohibition Act and Subsequent Living Conditions*. Protests. This must have been what the man had been referring to. Dread crept down my arched spine as I contemplated what these protests meant. Perhaps it was connected to the strange sensation of impending doom that pervaded my dream.

"If there are citizens seeking magical reformations in our country, then that means there *are* Wielders out there in the masses wanting to use magic again," I whispered aloud to myself as I stared down at my happy family. I couldn't help but wonder why I hadn't heard more about this potential threat prior to last night. If it was truly isolated to Tuyet, then I could write it off as a lapse in information since we were only here for a chunk of time in the winter. However, something nagged at me that this sort of news should have reached us in Eisolde, especially since we'd been attacked there once already. So then, why was it being withheld? Why had it sounded like that man had been accusing my father of something nefarious?

The hairs once more rose on the back of my neck and a sudden and foreign chill enveloped my body. Inessa and Papa had both told me we would mourn the losses from the festivals today. I was sure Papa would address the tragedy and we would do what we could to console our citizens. It would quiet the discontentment and things would go back to normal just as they always did.

This was *Eisa*, a country known for taking control back from the terror of Wielders. They'd tried to disrupt our sense of ataraxia before and failed. We were still in control. We were safe here. We would *stay* safe, and even if there were crowds of unruly citizens or rogue Wielders, for every one of them we had countless loyal subjects and a royal guard the size of an army to protect us from any abnormalities.

I smiled down at my siblings throwing snowballs and giggling with one another, and rose to dress for the day.

Everything will be fine.

"How are you feeling, Mama?" I inquired as I handed my mother a glass of water. We were all collected in our private drawing room, enjoying a little family solitude away from our visiting guests while they were otherwise engaged. Due to my sleeping late, I had missed breakfast before everyone dispersed for their daily obligations, and my stomach was twisting in protest to the forsaken meal.

Mama dipped her head in appreciation, her deep gray eyes warm and affectionate as she patted the sofa beside her. "I'm doing fine, Sorrel. I already told you that it was the stress of your brother this past week, your sisters' shenanigans, mixed with the excitement of the party and being around so many guests. I simply overdid my socializing." She winced. "And maybe overdid it with my back a little too. I'll just be glad when we are done with our business in the capital here and can return to Svyat Gavan. No dancing required."

"I could have danced into the morning," Kira commented loudly from where she was lounging in front of the fireplace. She ran her hands over the tops of the flames. We all liked to tease her that she would crawl in with the kindling if she could. Her eyes flicked over to me, bright with mischief. "Like Sorrel did with Roland. Guess we aren't all so lucky."

I bristled in embarrassment, grateful that it seemed Mama had returned her focus to the letter she was in the midst of writing, so I wouldn't get another lecture on royal proprietary when it came to Roland. I'd never forget the painfully awkward day in my early teen years when Mama sat me down to inform me that I could no longer run off alone with Roland, and why our preferred seclusion was no longer appropriate. "I couldn't sleep. What were you even doing awake?" I replied stiffly.

"With Roland lurking around? I imagine you couldn't sleep!" Kira guffawed, ignoring my question. "What was that old diary entry you made when you were Theo's age? Something about his *dreamy* blue eyes I think. Or was it how his voice was changing and sounding more manly?"

"I have no idea what you're talking about." I wanted to crawl inside myself. "I don't even recall if I kept a diary at that age, and certainly not one that would have been shared with you. You would have been seven."

"He certainly is manly now, isn't he? I'd stay up with him all night too, if I were you." Kira wriggled her eyebrows up and down.

"Oh, Kira. Could you please be a little less vulgar with your insinuations?" Inessa chided without looking up from where she was pouring water into a potted plant by the window.

"Vulgar? I was referring to his stimulating conversation. What were *you* insinuating, Ina?" Kira blinked rapidly, feigning innocence, but could do little to hide her pleasure at successfully trapping Inessa in her words.

"Honestly, Kira," Inessa's tone shifted in annoyance and she set her water can down abruptly, ready to launch into the goaded argument. "Are you that bored that you have to go trying to start rumors and pick fights?"

"Girls," Mama warned, rubbing at her temples, fatigue creasing her brows.

"There is nothing improper about two friends speaking to each other, or sharing a dance. I seem to recall even you being entertained with a dance with Roland at the last ball we had, Kira." Yulia plopped down next to our youngest sister and threw her arms around her shoulders. "*Are* you bored with the party being over?" I was thankful for Yulia's patience and ability to tame Kira's more uncouth and trouble-starting nature when the rest of us failed to keep our composure under provocation.

"Yes!" Kira flopped backwards against Yulia dramatically. "How will anything ever compare to a party as fine as that one? I danced with so many young men, and only two of them stepped on my toes. If they were rude, I stepped on theirs. It was perfect."

"You looked like you were enjoying the snow again this morning," I commented as I rose from my seat next to Mama and crossed the room to search the stuffed bookcase for something to flip through. "Did you invite Theo?"

"It was entirely too cold after a while, and all I could think of was a hot bath waiting for me to boil myself in. I didn't feel the need to bore Theo with the details of something he couldn't partake in. Plus, he would have just complained that I was throwing the snowballs too hard for his highness's precious royal skin if he had been able to come along." Kira's tone dipped with mockery and impatience.

"That's not him complaining about his skin. It's him trying to be mindful of his health. Unless you want to volunteer to take care of him next time he is unable to sleep through the pain, I'd think you'd be mindful of it too." I patted Kira's head as I passed her. She sighed heavily but offered no further protest.

"Why did that Wielder curse Theo in the first place?" She asked instead, causing Mama to pause her writing, pen in mid stroke. "I barely remember it all."

"It was an attack on our Eisan empire by attempting to destroy the heir to the throne. The curse, as you are well aware, turned his skin as fragile as paper and his blood thinner than trickling water." Mama's words were clipped with bitterness.

Though she loved us all, her duty had been to provide a male heir for Eisa, and we knew that made Theo her crowning jewel. His poor health she took on as a personal failure as empress, even though it had been due to a curse and nothing she could be faulted for. I supposed perhaps she blamed herself for not managing to block the strike of the knife that day, even though she took the brunt of it. Her arm still wore the scar, whereas Theo's had disappeared years ago. I bore no physical scars from that day at all, only the guilt and fear that awoke within me every time the memories surfaced. After all, it had been my fault we'd gone for the walk in the woods in the first place.

"You know the story already. We were all there," I grumbled, not enjoying the conversation taking a turn for the sinister by speaking of our poor brother's condition. It always caused him tremendous anguish as he danced on the edge of death each time he was even suffering a minor injured. Nor did I care for the reminder that Kira and I had almost been grabbed and stolen away ourselves— and that the whole reason we were there to be grabbed was because of me

Kira had no shortage of interest in the macabre fate of Theo's daily life. Furthermore, she enjoyed the cheap thrills of discussing the evil of Wielders, often asking for tales of their offenses on mortal-kind for scary bedtime stories as a child that would result in her and Yulia climbing into bed with me and Inessa. Mama, of course, tried to keep most of the curses and magic talk away from Theo, advising us all that the cruelty of his illness was all the exposure he should ever have with Wielders in his lifetime. And of course, we did not let the public be privy to his condition, lest it be taken as weakness.

"Which country has that kind of power though? The power of curses, or is it cursed objects?" Yulia frowned as she tilted her head to the side curiously and crawled over to an open arm chair to curl up in, with a blanket tossed over her legs. "I've forgotten now where that man was from."

"Dezidaneya," Mama grunted, and my stomach twisted. Dezidaneya was a country we shared a direct border with. It was terrifying to think that hateful souls who dealt in curses were our neighbors. "Though, of course, Dezidaneya isn't special, since all magic wielding stems from curses. It bears no use discussing further."

"Do you suppose the man from last night was from there?"

"That man clearly wasn't in his right mind." Mama's tone hardened abruptly, and I wondered if she had seen the paper this morning too. The air felt a little heavier, filled with a slight static tension I could practically taste. The strange dread that had nipped at my ears the previous night returned, whipped up in gust and gone again just as soon as I noticed it.

"True. Who ruins a perfectly good party like that? Spouting nonsense about dancing over bodies and unrest in our country. Utter nonsense." Kira rolled her eyes and leaned an elbow against the mantle. Her choice of words brought forth clear images from my nightmare that I forcefully blinked away.

"Kira, mind your dress. You'll catch it on fire standing that close." Mama signed her name to the letter addressed to her sister and rose to fold the paper, sealing it in an envelope at the desk in the corner.

"Did you not read the papers today, Kira?" I asked.

"No, I had to go outside with Yulia and the younger children this morning."

"I saw a headline," I ventured slowly, hoping I wouldn't upset Mama by mentioning it. "It was tracking the death toll of people who were trampled during the festivals."

"Wait, really? People actually *died*?" Kira's eyebrows raised. "So it wasn't nonsense? I feel a little bad now for mocking it."

"Over thirteen-hundred, last I saw. Equally as many, or more, were injured in a huge stampede. It's a terrible tragedy. I wondered when Papa was going to come in and tell us how we were going to respond..." I trailed off my train of thought and bit my tongue. I didn't want to seem like I was doubting my father's priorities, but it was already one in the afternoon, and as far I knew, no statement or instructions had formally been made on behalf of the royal family for the victims of the stampede.

The room fell quiet under the hidden weight of my words. Everyone knew it was horrific what happened. A sudden acrid tang scratched at the back of my throat, causing me to swallow hard. My nose stung and my eyes watered too. I lifted my nose and sniffed the air.

"Kira! Your dress!" Yulia gasped and pointed to where the flames of the fireplace had sunk their teeth into the hem of her dress. Images of her being swallowed up by fire in my dream made my stomach flip, and before I knew I had even moved, I had somehow found Inessa's watering can in my hand and was dousing the flames.

"I told you to get away from the fireplace!" Mother chided

frantically, abandoning her envelope to flutter to the ground.

Kira's eyes were wide, but she didn't carry on or cry as we all clustered around her to inspect where her leg was surely burned. I ripped her skirt back and stared in confusion at the unharmed skin of Kira's calf that greeted me, lightly pink with heat but not burned in the slightest.

"How are you not hurt?" Yulia breathed in amazement. "Do you actually boil yourself in those baths?"

"How did you not realize you were on fire?" Inessa demanded, her golden brows knitting in confusion.

"I scarcely even felt the heat. Oh, bother. My poor dress. I rather liked this one."

"Poor dress, indeed. You're lucky it was only your dress that burned up! Next time I see you being so careless with the fire, I'll toss you out in the snow before you even know what's happened." Mama scolded, though we all knew her harsh tone came from her fear of one of her precious children being harmed.

"I always tell you all that I hate the cold," Kira laughed, dusting herself off and bursting out of the circle we had made around her.

"Knock, knock" The words were followed by the sound of knuckles tapping the doorway behind us. "It smells like smoke in here. Don't tell me the Littlest Princess set herself on fire?"

I shook my head and smiled, turning around to face Roland. Kira grinned from ear to ear and skipped over to our childhood friend, jutting her leg out when she reached him to reveal her charred hemline.

"Actually, I did!"

"Oh! Are you alr—"

"Not to worry, I am right as rain." She chirped happily. "Didn't even singe my leg hair. Have to keep that to stay warm in these eternal winters, after all."

"Dear Roland, were we expecting you this afternoon?" Mama inquired politely, ushering Kira towards the door with a small hiss to go change her dress. Kira snorted in amusement but gave a small curtsy before pushing through the opposite door to Roland that led toward her bedroom. "You've caught us shirking our social obligations, I'm afraid."

"Your Imperial Highness," Roland tucked his arms and bowed deeply to address my mother. Then, in an equal display of formality, he turned to Inessa, Yulia, and myself each in turn with a gracious dip of his head. "Grand Princesses."

"Lord Roland," My sisters and I spoke in unison and curtsied behind smirks. Roland, to his credit, always tried to go through the proper addresses, though the formality was just for show.

He clearly was swallowing his own amusement as he returned his gaze to Mama. "No, you were not. But, I was told by my father to meet with him and His Imperial Highness for a discussion with the royal family about the stampede, amongst other things. There have been meetings all day, so our paths only crossed for a moment to convey the message. Lots to be smoothed over, I'm afraid. I think there were mentions of a late luncheon."

"He sent you here instead of the dining room— er, hall?" Yulia asked softly, crinkling her nose and tucking a perpetually unruly stray strand of dark hair behind her ear as she corrected her phrasing.

We had several family palaces around our country, but we typically spent most of our time in our smallest one, located in the town of Eisolde, where we could live more privately and intimately out of the public eye. That palace was our true home, and we affectionately called it *Svyat Gavan*, meaning *our sanctuary*. In the Winter Season we were often moved to the largest palace located in our country's capital, Tuyet, for our court obligations. It also happened to be in Tuyet's Valamir Palace where we held our celebratory events. Normally in our regular home, we dined in a *room*, whereas in this enormous palace, we ate in a dining *hall* instead.

"No, again. I was looking for—" Roland chuckled awkwardly, his eyes shifting to look a little too interested in Inessa's plant, and I was fairly certain he had been looking for me but wasn't fortunate enough to catch me alone. He cleared his throat and straightened, correcting himself with ease. "I was on my way there, and I smelled the smoke. I was actually relatively concerned that Kira might have gone ablaze. Funnily enough, I don't think I actually expected to be right in my first assumption. I am glad that she wasn't harmed though."

"She is fortunate that the flames decided to eat her skirt instead of her skin. Unfortunately, she likely won't learn her lesson for next time either," I sighed and gestured to the door. "Shall we adjourn to the dining hall for this meeting then? I'm quite interested in what Papa has to say on the matter."

"A woman of the people," Roland nodded approvingly at me, stepping to the side to allow me by. A jolt of electricity shot through my fingertips as he made sure his hand grazed mine while I walked past him, prompting a surge of remnant attraction from the previous night.

"As I should be."

SORREL ZDRAEVIT

2ND GRAND PRINCESS OF EISA

SORREL ZDRAEVIT

Character artwork by Xenychan

FIVE

"Oh, good. Looks like Roland found you before the staff did." Papa rose to his feet and nodded affectionately to each of us.

I spotted my father at the head of the dining table. His dark beard looked sharp against his winter bleached skin, and even at a distance I could see the lines around his mouth and eyes that spoke years of kind expressions.

Next to him sat Roland's father. Though Friedrich shared less visual evidence of warmth and laughter etched onto his face, I knew him to also be a kindhearted and nurturing man. I had never truly seen the man get angry, but something in my gut had always told me that his gaze could swallow you up and smother you in their watchful profundity.

Arrian also already sat at the table. He had no official role of state yet, on account of his inexperienced age of eighteen. Though Roland was only four years Arrian's senior, he had been a precocious exception, obtaining a ministry position at the age of twenty. Having specifically expressed interest in foreign affairs, that seat had been the one Roland had applied for with no small amount of earnest enthusiasm. He'd maintained his position expertly for two years already.

On the other side of my father, sat my brother. His expression was serious, as it usually was when we discussed any major matters of state, and he took his position as heir with a reverence beyond his years. I couldn't help but smile fondly at my brother and appreciate that, unlike so many other young princes his age, he was stolid and respectful of his position.

With our fathers and my little brother at the table, that brought the group up to nine, and it still felt too small for the grand space. It was an immense room in the palace, rivaled only by the ballroom in size and grandeur. The hall was meant to entertain large dinner parties for groups reaching over one hundred in headcounts. It felt large and conspicuous with only the few of us to fill it.

"Oh, let's not bother with formalities!" Papa blustered when Roland stooped to bow and greet his Imperial Highness.

Roland's face cracked a bemused grin and he interrupted his dignified hello. "As you wish. I was on my way here, actually, when I smelled smoke."

"Where is Princess Kira?" Friedrich asked, looking over our small assembly.

"That would be the source of the smoke Roland came across," I clicked my tongue and lifted my brows. "Don't worry, she is fine, and she will likely join us after she's changed her dress."

Papa's expression creased with momentary concern before he sighed and shook his head in resignation. "Very well. We can get started without her, and one of her sisters can relay what she missed."

Everyone nodded their acknowledgments to the sentiment and took their seats at the table, waiting patiently as the staff trailed in and out through the doors from the kitchen to bring us our meal. The servers proceeded to fill our plates with various delicious foods, and my mouth watered in anticipation, once more reminding my stomach of my missed breakfast. I could smell the distinct and sweet hints of smoked alder wafting off Mama's plate as it passed me.

Once everything was set, Papa cleared his throat. "Right. I suppose we best get onto it then."

"Ahem." Mama made a small cough, her gray eyes shifting to take in the meal before us. Her chin was dipped demurely, her dark auburn hair pulled back into an elegant updo, making her look the picture of commanding grace.

Papa nodded to his wife. She was reminding him we needed to say our blessings first for our meal. "Thank you, Geneva. First we must lift our heads and give thanks to the grace of the Divinities for our bountiful food and prospering kingdom." We all echoed the prayer, touching our index fingers and thumbs to our chest, our forehead, and finally, our lips before curling our hands upward by the pinky in the gesture of thanks to the Divinities above. We waited for Papa to take the first bite of his meal before we tucked into our own plates.

"On the topic of our prospering kingdom, as you should all be aware of by now, it suffered a tragedy last night."

I swallowed and quickly took a small swig of wine to rinse the food from my mouth before speaking. "The last update I saw, the toll was over thirteen hundred, Papa."

Papa nodded his acknowledgment to my report, and I felt a small swell of pride at having proven my knowledge, and deflated a moment later with his next words. "That is a sizable death toll that can't go unacknowledged. We have handled things on the official channels this morning, but what we need to decide now is how we, as a family, and immediate circle, are going to respond to our people."

"Especially since it was at the festivals celebrating us," I added quietly, as I imagined the bodies of innocents being forcibly stomped into the cobblestone streets and dirty fields by the lake in the central city park. I couldn't fathom the panic the public must have felt in the overcrowded groupings and the screams that had rung among the crash of fireworks, ending in silent puffs of air as life was driven from chests. I held my head, my fingers sinking through the strands of my hair, trying to banish the onslaught of guilt and empathy tearing through me.

"Don't worry, Dear Sorrel," Friedrich said kindly, the words passing by Inessa to reach me. My sister leaned over and squeezed my hand sympathetically as Friedrich consoled me. "It wasn't any of your faults, so you shouldn't take that weight of blame onto your shoulders."

"There was no way of knowing that the turn out this year was going to have this kind of volume. The streets were overcrowded, so an accident wasn't properly accounted for," Inessa added, blinking at me encouragingly.

"We weren't prepared for the numbers, that's all." Arrian spoke up for the first time from his place between Roland and Yulia, setting his glass down with a small *thunk*.

Something in his expression felt callous and too far removed from the incident to properly feel any empathy towards the plight of our people. Arrian's brazen nature often had him shining bright with charisma, just like Kira, but his fatal flaw was his brash responses to serious topics. It had always been a trait I longed for him to hurry and outgrow, preferably adopting some of his brother's diplomacy.

"And, we will be prepared in the future," Papa spoke confidently, his resolute expression melting away some of my unease.

"We will *over prepare* next time." Roland added sincerely. "Nothing like this will happen again."

"I can't help but feel terrible when I think of how we were at a party, dancing, while people beyond our gates were in panic and dying," I admitted. "I danced with my family and friends in a beautiful dress while some poor child was lost in a crowd crying for the mother they would never see alive again."

"Sorrel, you mustn't be so grim," Mama breathed, looking away to hide her own horror at the harsh reality of my words. Mama knew better than any of us what it was to lose family, having lost two of her own siblings and her mother all to illness in her childhood. Subjects that leaned more dire always deeply unsettled her to the point where she had little to no tolerance for discussing it or her own wellness would take a sudden negative turn.

"She is right though. It is terrible, and we need to show our solidarity beyond simply changing to wearing mourning clothes for the lives lost." Roland pressed the significance and severity of the situation, and I was grateful for his support. His comment poignantly acknowledged all of the colorful fabrics in the room, being as none of us had formally changed to our darker mourning palettes yet as we awaited our instructions.

"Yes, what can we do?" I nodded emphatically. "Something active, not just symbolic."

"Could we pay for funerals, perhaps?" Yulia piped up, receiving approving nods at her suggestion.

"It would be quite an expense, but I'd think we could manage it. We can broach it with the treasury. Perhaps a thousand tsena to each family," Mama obliged, looking at Papa and Friedrich for confirmation, but Friedrich was looking thoughtfully at me.

"If I may," He started, snapping his gaze from me to my mother. "The royal children aren't seen in the public very often. Sorrel, I believe there were a decent amount of citizens injured but not killed in the incident as well. Is that correct?"

"Yes." I thought back to the article and information I had been following throughout the day. "There were thirteen hundred casualties, and an additional thirteen hundred plus who sustained injuries"

"You're like a reference book sometimes," Roland chuckled, so softly I was almost certain I was the only one who heard the comment. I kicked him lightly in the shin beneath the table in retaliation to his teasing, and he startled in his seat before swallowing his laughter at my secret assault. He spoke around his glass to clarify, "I didn't say it wasn't impressive!"

"Thank you, Sorrel." Friedrich smiled and extended his hand to begin motioning to me and my siblings. "The children are rarely seen interacting with the public, especially here in the heart and capital of Eisa. I think it would be an excellent time to make a public appearance in Tuyet. Perhaps we could send them in pairs to the hospitals to visit the injured. Really connect on a personal level with the people here in the heart of Eisa."

"Do you think that is safe?" Mama queried, her eyes darting

around to her children nervously.

"Why wouldn't it be safe?" Yulia asked, eyes wide.

"I think your mother is worried about the possible threat of retaliation against the royal family… Considering the unexpected guest last night." Roland replied, popping a tomato into his mouth.

At the mention of the man, the same wave of fear from my nightmare seeped through me again. Roland caught my eye and quirked an eyebrow, obviously picking up on some new shift in my demeanor at the mention of the mysterious stranger from last night, and I mouthed the word *later*.

"Can we… talk about that man?" I mumbled.

"Speak up, Sorrel. What is it?" Papa commanded, and I flinched but raised my voice.

"The man at the party. He was raving about us dancing over bodies. I understand he was using a metaphor to implicate our party and being unaware here in the palace about the stampede. However, what concerned me was the mention he made about protests. What protests is he talking about and should we be worried about them? We never hear anything about this sort of thing in Eisolde."

"Oh, that is all just nonsense." Mama waved her hand dismissively and rolled her eyes. Papa gave a noncommittal grunt of relative agreement, while Friedrich averted his eyes.

"But, I saw something in the paper this morning about mounting protests of citizens asking for magical reparations in our kingdom for Wielders. I thought our kingdom was safe from Wielders? Rather, that our whole country was safe. What—"

"As I said," Mama's tone was clipped with impatience. "It's all just nonsense. Pay no more mind to any of that. Our country does not deal with Wielders. It's what our ancestors and your father have fought so hard to protect us from."

There was an awkward silence following her words that came off as more of a reprimand to me than a reassurance. I folded my hands together and looked down at my lap while the staff removed our dishes and cleared the remaining spread from the table.

"Of course."

"I don't believe we will have any reason to fear retaliation, but we can send some men with the Princesses. Shall we plan perhaps for the Big Pair and the Little Pair for the outing? We could even have a parent with each if that would make you feel more at ease." Friedrich glossed over the previous conversation with years of dignitary skills, and stayed focused on the pertinent details that needed our attention— showing solidarity with our citizens. Ina and I, as the eldests, were often grouped off affectionately as the *Big Pair*, while Yulia and Kira comprised the *Little Pair*, and I wasn't surprised that this was how we'd been split up for our assignment.

"Do you really think it will help?" Papa asked, bringing his hands beneath his chin to contemplate the suggestion. As long as I could remember, both my parents had been as close to royal recluses as duty would permit, avoiding the public in preference for personal time. They had no ill-will towards our people, but it was clear they felt uncomfortable on their pedestals amongst them.

Mama, in particular, struggled with the social aspects of her role as Empress, and the court knew and rebuked her for it, making the awkwardness worse. I'd heard whispers of their opinions of our family, and how we had insular tendencies, my whole life. While Papa, my siblings, and I were generally forgiven, it seemed Mama could do nothing right by them, every attempt falling flat— even before Inessa and I were born— so by the time Kira was born, Mama had more or less given up all pretenses and resolved herself to duty, faith, and family.

"Approachability is everything in today's day and age," Friedrich replied to my father's question, leaning forward with fervor. He had always been one to bridge the gap between my parents' shyness and the public and I couldn't help but admire his natural inclination for it. "Just look at your uncle in Videiria. Had his wife not gone against the grain and gone amongst the people, they would have had revolution on their hands and been overthrown by now. It would have been the end of the Videirian empire. That's certainly the last thing we want for Eisa. Our country does not boast strength in magic or the supernatural. Our strength is in our people and is measured only by what we put into those people."

"So, that would be a 'yes' then?" Papa cracked a smile at his old friend.

"Yes, it would be a 'yes.'" Friedrich chuckled and shook his head.

"Alright, then that is what we will do." Papa folded his hands. "In addition to the financial contribution, Inessa and Sorrel will visit the Piren Districts Hospitals and clinics, and Yulia and Kira will visit the Skovyet districts. They can go tomorrow."

"Where will Theo go?" Yulia looked at our father with twinkling, imploring eyes, kindly trying to be a voice for our brother, but Mama stepped in with her usual protective instincts flaring.

"Theodorvin will remain here at the palace. If there is any chance, however small, that there is danger out there, we cannot afford to put him in that situation. His place is here. I would, however, like for us to send a member of the church with the girls for added Divine protection and prayer over the patients to show solidarity from the Priests. I'll ask Otvel and one other."

Otvel Chinye, a healer gifted by the Divinities themselves who saw to my brother's ailments, had found his way to us not long after Theo had been born and cursed. Our dependence on his assistance along with our family doctor, Klivech, had prompted a rather rapid promotion from regular citizen to a head priest in the church. His connection to the Divinities was infallible, and as such, he was a favorite of Mama's. Plus, like her, he didn't share in any sort of public favor, being rather disliked by most who accused him of manipulating us. I'd always found the notion quite offensive given how much we owed him for Theo's wellness over the years, but they weren't privy to that contribution so it did little to dwell on.

Theo looked noticeably crestfallen at the decision for him to remain behind, though I highly doubted he had expected any less. Of all of us, Theo was the only one who lived like a bird in a cage. But, he carried the burden well.

"He will be with me, shadowing my meetings. It's never too early to become well acquainted with the job he'll be filling one day," Papa added to Yulia.

"Then who will be going with the girls, Genri?" Mama asked, folding her arms.

I could tell from her behavior today, along with her bout of nerves last night, that she was more frightened of the prospect of Wielders in our kingdom than she was willing to let on. As if somehow voicing her fears aloud would bring our peaceful world crashing down. That was why she dismissed any inclination towards the subject as nonsense instead, willing her words to be true. Sending her out into the public would only escalate her nervousness as it always did, though however uncomfortable she felt, she would comply since duty demanded.

"If they are split up, I can't be with both."

"Quite right. You go with Yulia and Kira. Something tells me they will need a closer eye kept on them than Ina and Sorrel." Papa winked at Yulia, the gesture absolving her of any guilt in the implication.

He was of course referring to our lovely and wild Kira. She was a force of nature and an absolute wild card and always had been since the day she was born. Papa had welcomed her birth with a grand party and parade just to show that a fourth daughter was no misfortune as some who were waiting for the male heir might say. Since Kira was the only one with a parade on her birthday, we like to joke that she came into the world with the same energy.

"Arrian, would you care to accompany them as well?"

Arrian dipped his head and smiled confidently. "I'd be honored."

"And Ina and Sorrel?" Mama prompted, raising her brows and narrowing her eyes.

"Roland can accompany them. I have no doubt he will make sure they are safe." It was my turn to be given a knowing look, to which I stared blankly back. Something in my father's subtle acknowledgment made my stomach squirm with embarrassment.

"It would be my pleasure. Will an accompanying guard post of four be sufficient as well?" Roland dipped his head obligingly.

"That would suffice, yes. Thank you, Roland." Mama was at last satisfied with the arrangement and I could see her stiff stature visibly relax in her chair.

"Then it's settled. I believe our guests will be looking for us,

Geneva. Back to the tedium of entertaining, much to your chagrin, my dear." Papa teased his wife.

Mama pulled a sour face of agreement, breaking the regal projection of empress for a moment, before once more sobering. "I'm just feeling a little run down. It will be fine. Kira can give the guests more than enough energy for both of us."

"Sorrel?" Papa prompted, rising to his feet. "Would you like to supervise the address to the public, my little secretary?"

"When would she ever refuse the offer to post a notice?" Arrian smirked under his breath, receiving an elbow to the rib from both Roland and Yulia on either side of him.

I resisted the urge to scowl at Arrian and instead beamed back at my father, appreciating the windows of involvement he would often allow me and my sisters to participate in based on our various interests, despite us not being heads of state or heirs in our own right.

Rising to my feet and clasping my hands together, I lifted my chin. "Shall we go now then?"

The sooner we dealt with this issue, perhaps the sooner that eerie nightmare and smothering grief would melt away.

SONYO

Sonyo is a southern country of Alse Hanya, sharing an island with its sister country, Slayad. Both countries are obscured from the rest of the world beneath the Veil of Stars, an impenetrable night sky that both shields the countries, as well as boosts the affinities of the Sonyotes and Slayds beneath it. The country is exceptionally insular, and has been involved in a long-standing war with its neighboring southern country, Vatra. Sonyo's most famous regional wonder is their *Dream Pools*.

Their magic type deals with dreams and nightmares.

SIX

$\mathcal{A}$fter successfully dispatching the approved press release on behalf of the family, I sank into the armchair of the sitting room adjacent to my father's study, and danced through my own mentalscape of internal monologues. There were easily a thousand things I wish I could say to the families of those injured and killed. I shivered, imagining visceral images of faces being crushed against pavement, thrashing with the discordant sounds of turmoil. From one thought to the next, the scene tumbled to the shadowy wraith of my dream, enveloping my family in darkness.

"What's on your mind, Snowdrop?" Roland cleared the fatiguing mental mist by sauntering into the room. "I was promised *something* to come *later.*"

He leaned against the desk and folded his arms across his broad chest. Though not in his formal uniform or party attire, he still looked dapper in a black jacket embroidered with frost-like designs in steel gray and wintery silver threads. His blue eyes were twinkling with curiosity, but behind the light, I could sense concern and dark foreboding.

"I can't shake this feeling like something terrible is coming," I answered quietly, not bothering to straighten from my slumped position in my chair. "It started before the party and hasn't gone away since."

"Are you worried about visiting the injured tomorrow?"

"No, I am glad we are doing that," I waved my hand to dismiss the notion. "We rarely get such an opportunity to be around the people here, and I am grateful to your father for suggesting it. He's right about our strength coming from our people. If we don't have our people, then who are we ruling? We'd be obsolete without them."

"Well, obsolete sounds awfully grim and depressing," Roland clicked his tongue and reached for my hand, which was braced against the desk. "If not that, then would you forgo the suspense, and tell me what has you concerned? You're starting to make me feel anxious right along with you, which is extremely unfair if I don't even get to know what I'm being anxious about."

"That is the very essence of anxiety: fear of ambiguous or unknown future possibilities beyond our control." My voice trailed away as I dipped back into my sea of dread.

"You're giving me a vocabulary lesson, Sorrel?" Roland rolled his eyes and started to retract his hand from mine, but I gripped onto his fingers, the small touch of our skin bringing me comfort.

"Sorry, I'm feeling very strange and dazed. I can't seem to get out of my own head. Everything feels murky like I am still lost in my own nightmare."

"Well, if you're done being a dictionary, this is all very cryptic. Did you say *still* in a nightmare?" He slid his hand fully into mine once more and gripped it tightly.

"I had this dream last night—"

"I think you mean nightmare," Roland interjected with a smirk.

"Hush." I explained the nature of my dream, careful to vocalize any imperative details in case Roland might have any insight. He was charming and socially adept, but what most people didn't see was that he had a quiet intelligence that, in my opinion, was unrivaled by anyone I knew. His ability to process information with discerning observation was extremely impressive. If anyone was going to make sense of the nightmare, I was certain he could.

Roland listened quietly, nodding periodically, until I had finished. "You have a very active imagination, my dear." He said finally after a moment of contemplation.

"So, you think it is nothing?"

"I didn't say that. But, your dreamscape sounds very exciting. Tell me, do I appear there often?" A mischievous twinkle sparkled in his eyes and I swatted his arm with my free hand.

"That isn't supposed to be the take away, you egomaniac."

"I think there are two options here." Roland's tone sobered into pragmatism, though the corners of his mouth were still curled upward. "The first being that your fears about the man last night have run away with you and manifested in some strange and aggressive— and a bit disturbing, if I'm honest— way. Remind me not to get on your bad side."

"A dream is a dream." I shrugged with a bit of relief. If Roland thought it was nothing then that would be enough to quell my misgivings on the matter.

"Right," He nodded slowly. "Except for when it isn't."

The misgivings returned with a jolt. "When it isn't?"

"I do find one thing a bit odd. You know very little about the magical abilities of other countries outside of Eisa, correct?"

"Correct. We aren't taught much of that in our lessons because magic is a banned and evil practice. We don't study crime and murder either as a matter of fact." I scowled at the notion that such dark and terrible practices would be taught in our schooling.

"I find it very odd that you would see some more elaborate demonstrations of magic you don't know of or understand— aspects you couldn't possibly arbitrarily know. Namely I am thinking of the shadow you mentioned. I know you saw a display of that as a child, but not to its full capabilities. Do you know what country that affinity comes from?"

"Not a clue. I didn't even know there was a Shadow affinity specifically." I'd never asked questions of what I had witnessed that day in the woods, too afraid to bring it up.

"Shadow is the common meaning of the name *Kesgoldol*. You also mentioned some geographical points that I am fairly certain you wouldn't be aware of. The dark forest you saw sounds like the woods at the base of the Kesgoldol territory, where magic is still prominently used, as apposed to anywhere in northern Kesgoldol that has an anti-magic stance, where you might have been at some point in your life."

"How could I dream of a magical forest I have never seen or heard of? Furthermore, what does the shadow-meaning of Kesgoldol, or Shadow affinity, have to do with it?"

Kesgoldol, like Dezidaneya, shared a border with us. While Dezidaneya was a land of curses with whom we were not allied with, Kesgoldol's northern territories were in alignment with our country's rhetoric. I only knew that the country was in the midst of a civil war between those who clung to magic and those who had walked away from its evils. I vaguely recalled Inessa mentioning the terrible beasts we'd been warned of living in Southern Kesgoldol, but other than that, I really knew nothing more about it.

"That's what I am wondering. I don't think you will care much for my theory."

"That's rather ominous."

"Sonyo is an island country south of Kesgoldol."

"I've seen a map, Roland. I know the names of the countries and where they are." I tried to fight the sensation of a snake coiling around my throat and sinking its teeth into the nape of my neck at the mention of the nightmare country. I had willed away the correlation between my conversation with the Vatrese delegates and my dream.

"Sorry, Miss Intellectual Scholar. Riddle me this; what affinity does Sonyo have as a prominent Wielding country?" Roland quizzed me, leaning forward expectantly.

I opened my mouth for a biting reply but snapped it closed again when I realized I had no answer to his question based on my own knowledge. I only knew what I had learned the night before from the Vatrese couple. I scowled and decided to take a chance on replying, "Nightmares."

"Dreams," Roland corrected, tapping his temple.

"Dreams?" I echoed, confused.

"And, by nature of the beast, nightmares as well," He elaborated. "Both sides of the coin include dreams and nightmares."

"You're right. I don't think I like where this is going."

"I think someone with a Dream affinity came in contact with you last night and messed with your dreams." Roland's expression was serious and I could see his eyes searching for a reason behind such an attack.

"That's ridiculous." I spluttered. "We don't have Wielders in Eisa."

Roland shook his head with a light scoff. "Don't be naive, Sorrel. Of course there are Wielders here. They are just hiding."

My throat went dry and my stomach churned. "But, I haven't been around anyone to have come into contact with anything. I was at the palace all day yesterday."

"You were just at a party with two hundred people last night." Roland reminded me pointedly, and I felt my face pucker at the condescending nature of his tone. "It doesn't take much for Sonyotes to get access to the dreamscapes of others. They do it with a small sample from their native dream pools that has to come in contact with your skin, or be ingested. Though it would take someone particularly powerful to alter your dreams that much."

"No, those were all formally invited guests, except for that man. They are all dignitaries and members of court," I insisted.

"Sorrel," Roland sighed and lifted his brows, his tone leading.

"You mean someone in our court is a *Wielder*?" I whispered the last word like the offender would somehow materialize with the spoken realization. For all I knew, someone with magical capabilities could very well do just that. I pulled my hand from Roland's and hugged my arms to myself for reassurance. "What does that mean? Who can it be? Am I going to be okay?"

I wanted to banish the suggestion away and choose to believe that Roland's first option was the correct one, but he had made some good points that I couldn't find a counter to. Someone had been able to curse Theo while he was a baby, and there was no denying that's what it was. None of us had ever been targeted to my knowledge since then, but it was entirely conceivable that, with the growing unrest of the warring world, attacks could be made.

I tried to remember every face I had seen at the party the night before and determine if there were any I didn't recognize. I sagged immediately when I reminded myself that we lived a relatively reclusive life in Svyat Gavan. Of course, I didn't know most of the guests by face. It would be the perfect place to blend in while in plain sight.

The world felt like it was spinning all around me, and I lurched to my feet abruptly. "Roland, am I going to be okay?" I repeated. "Do you think anyone else has been cursed?"

"Cursed?" Roland pushed off the desk and furrowed his brows in confusion.

"Yes, cursed."

"Sorrel, the Dream affinity isn't a cursing power. Something isn't automatically a curse just because it's magical in nature," Roland spoke slowly, following my every movement to discern my reaction to his words.

"That is an awfully big leap towards sympathetic speech if I didn't know any better of you. Someone *entered my mind* while I was asleep, without my consent, and threatened my family. You want to tell me that was well-intentioned?" I countered, patience slipping from my grasp. This was no time for unsolicited ideals.

"Maybe not, but it's just ignorant to call something a curse because you're too afraid to understand it for what it really is." He shoved his hands in his pockets and looked away, his mouth forming a terse line of minor annoyance.

I was taken aback and the sting of offense made the skin on my face tighten as I set my jaw. Looking around the room lined with shelves of aged books and studded with mahogany furniture, I realized we had lingered beyond our welcome in this room. "We aren't even supposed to be in here like this. We need to go, or Papa will be upset that I abused the trust he placed in me with the press release. I promised I'd be adjourning shortly after he and his secretary left."

"Fine, you're right. I'd rather not get on your father's bad side either. How mad would he be if he found us alone in here, anyway?" Roland's tone shifted, and I could tell he was trying to create some levity.

"Considering there is all kinds of sensitive information and matters of state on his desk in the adjoining room currently, I'd say he wouldn't be pleased." I pushed past Roland and made for the exit, our shoulders grazing. "You probably have another meeting to get to anyway."

My words were clipped with a curtness at our mutual irritation over the conversation, and Roland reached out to stop me, giving my shoulder another reassuring squeeze. I looked back begrudgingly, and faltered when I saw the apologetic look on his face.

"I'm sorry," He said quietly. "I wasn't meaning to sound short. I hope you understand that it is part of my job here as head of the Foreign Affairs Ministry to understand the ways of other countries and their Wielders a little differently than most others do. I didn't mean to call you ignorant. We know so little and that lack of knowledge can be dangerous and misleading. It's better to understand the root objectively. Certain aspects of religious ideals can make studying other cultures difficult."

"Ideals?" I echoed, swallowing my offense at the dismissive sound of the phrase. I gave him a long stare and mulled over his words. "Knowledge does have power," I conceded before lifting my chin and narrowing my eyes. "But, make no mistake, it is the Wielders who are the dangerous ones."

"Very well, Snowdrop." Roland's expression shifted into

something unfamiliar to me, then back to his typical friendly demeanor so quickly I almost missed it.

We exited my father's study and walked down the hall in silence for a ways, until we reached the stairs, indicating our paths would diverge. I didn't like the tension between us, and I could see a million thoughts tumbling behind Roland's eyes, like he was on the verge of saying something but kept talking himself out of it.

"Well, I wish you luck in the rest of your meetings. I suppose I will probably see you at dinner tonight." I dipped my head and made to ascend the stairs but paused when Roland spoke my name.

"Sorrel?"

"Yes?"

"I will look into what we talked about and see if there is any merit to the idea that you were targeted last night."

Having answers would help me feel better, and Roland knew that. As a Minister of Foreign Affairs, he would be a perfect person to quietly look into the matter for me. It was comforting that he would offer the assistance on his own, even if it seemed he might not share the same sort of intense foreboding I felt when Wielders were mentioned. Appreciation swelled in my chest.

"Thank you," I breathed a sigh of relief and smiled sincerely at him.

"Just," He continued, looking over his shoulder as he went the opposite direction to descend the stairs. "Don't mention it to your parents or sisters— anyone, for that matter— until I figure out what's what. No use spreading fear when there has already been so much stress and tragedy in the last twenty-four hours."

I nodded. "I'll keep it to myself until you have more information to give me."

"And be sure to let me know if anything odd like that happens again."

"Of course."

"See you tonight. May your mother have mercy on us and seat us together and not with someone insufferably dull." Roland waved his hand in farewell, continuing down the steps at a brisk cantor until he disappeared from view.

"See you tonight," I echoed his farewell with a smirk.

There was a part of me that wanted to rush to my parents with the information for reassurance and comfort, like I was a child again. But, Roland was right. The stampede aftermath was more than enough stress on the family without the idea of curses floating around without due evidence. Knowing Roland was looking into it gave me enough reprieve that I took the idea and packed it away in my mind, compartmentalizing to focus on the moment with a clear head.

If there was anything to share down the line, I would. But for the time being, I lifted my eyes and headed to join the rest of my family and our guests.

SEVEN

"Do you really think having Chinye go with the girls is a wise idea?" Papa asked Mama quietly. "He isn't always in the best favor with the public, given his rapid ascension to High Priest and his past... indiscretions."

"Don't worry so much about Otvel, Genri. He is our personal friend and, as you pointed out, a high priest. He has been blessed by the Divinities. That's all the concern we need to have on the matter. The people don't need to know his role in Theodorvin's health and recovery to appreciate his blessings, and should feel just as honored to receive a visit from him as from the girls." Mama waved her hand and adjusted the skirt of her dress. "Alright, girls, let me take a good look at you before we head out."

"That's my cue to take my leave. Have a nice day, my dears, and please be on your best behavior. Your kingdom needs to see your strength as well as your grief. Make Eisa proud." Papa lifted his chin and waved farewell, walking briskly up the steps towards Theo's room.

"Make sure Theo is up for the shadowing today! He was complaining of nightmares keeping him awake last night," Mama called after Papa who gave a nod of acknowledgment without breaking his stride and disappeared from view.

I tried not to bristle at the mention of another nightmare after my conversation with Roland as the four of us lined up in our typical birth order for Mama's inspection, and pushed the concern away for the time being. We were all wearing simple black dresses, none of the same decadence of the party remaining in our appearance. Inessa, Yulia, and I had our hair styled in smart, sensible updos, same as Mama, while Kira was still young enough to leave her winter gold hair down. Sometimes, when pins pricked at my scalp, it made me miss the relief and freedom of wearing my hair loose with a delicate air of reckless abandon in the wild locks.

"Reporting for duty," Arrian announced himself with a small bow.

"Ari!" Kira perked up, reached out to grab his forearm. "Tuyet is truly *scandalous*. You'll never believe what I heard last night about Kath—"

"Kira, don't gossip. It's in poor taste. Hello, Arrian. We should be ready to depart in just a moment. Let's fix those flyaway hairs, girls. Where is your hairpin, child? Ina and Sorrel, you're free to go." Mama fixed us with a hard look while Kira scowled and leaned in to whisper her news more discreetly, eliciting a sharp laugh from Arrian. "Don't forget your coats! The drive there will be chilly. If there is anything that feels unsafe in any way, you are to come straight home. Do you understand me?"

Ina and I dipped our heads. "We understand, Mama."

Mama gave us an approving nod and gestured for the door. "Roland and Otvel should already be waiting at the cars with your guards. Two were selected from each of your regiments."

Unlike many other kingdoms, here we princesses were given our own regiments on our fourteenth birthdays by Papa, and we were each expected to run them through their military exercises regularly. Our involvement was for our own knowledge and benefit, according to Papa, as well as keeping a well established relationship with our soldiers to bolster loyalty. Should we ever find ourselves in need, we could command our own army.

I gave my mother and little sisters a quick hug, bid Arrian a polite farewell, grabbed my coat, and followed Ina to the cars. One was completely open around the seats, the frame and doors being the only thing to really define it as a vehicle and not a wagon bed with an engine. The second, and the one we would be riding in, had an open compartment for the driver, while the back cab was enclosed and more akin to a motorized carriage.

Roland was leaning against the hood of the second vehicle, jotting something down on a scrap of paper as he chatted with one of my soldiers, Sergeant Hykner. Otvel was already waiting in the car, looking lost in thought with his hands folded neatly in his lap. He had once been condemned as a charlatan of false mysticism back in his home city of Zdenayk, but Mama and Papa had taken him on when he had shown a particular aptitude for helping Theo through his rougher episodes.

He had boasted of an audience with a member of the Divine in a moment of personal peril, in which the ethereal figure had saved him and led him to the path of the church. After proving his merit and loyalty, Mama had made sure that Otvel was promoted to the top of the church, proudly declaring how the Divinities themselves had touched him with a healer's hand. I wondered, as I watched him in the car, if he was praying for our safety and good fortune on our outing, or what else might be taking his focus a million miles away.

"Imperial Highnesses!" All four soldiers straightened and saluted Inessa and me as we approached. Roland looked at the formal reception and dipped his head in greeting, opening the door for us before the chauffeur had a chance to round the hood.

We returned the greetings with appreciative smiles and nods, climbing inside to settle in while the soldiers hopped into the other vehicle. Roland gave the chauffeur the address for the first hospital, small and more akin to a clinic, we'd be visiting, and we sat in silence while the engine roared to life, vibrating the seats with its loud mechanical purr.

I looked out the window and allowed my mind to submerge into thoughts and images of what we might find at the hospital. I tried to plan what words of comfort I could share, and how I could best help the victims smile again, but the answers to those questions escaped me. Yesterday I'd had a million words to share, and now I could hardly string a sentence together.

"You are looking particularly pensive," Otvel observed, breaking into my thoughts. Any subsequent idea fragmented and slipped like sand through my fingers. "Something on your mind, Sorrel?"

"Always," Roland and Inessa both chuckled knowingly, and I crinkled my nose at their laughter.

"I was just trying to think of what we are going to say to the patients."

"We will express our sincere condolences." Inessa tilted her head to the side. "That is what we talked about this morning. We will go in, stop by each bed, and say how sorry we are."

"Doesn't that seem…" I pursed my lips, trying to find the words to articulate. "Flimsy?"

"What do you mean?" Roland leaned forward, resting his elbows on his knees.

"Well, it's not like any of us have really gone through anything as traumatic as a stampede. I've just started to wonder if we don't have a very strong leg to stand on with this endeavor." I cast my eyes downward.

"Empathy does not require experience and qualifications. It merely asks for a kind and helpful heart with good intentions," Otvel tapped my knee to catch my eye. "And that, my dear, you have in spades. Just be human. Not royal, not mortal, or anything else. Be human, and there you will always find connection with others."

"Through humanity?" Inessa clarified.

"And humility." Otvel grinned.

"I suppose you're right." I conceded with a small smile of my own, relief and clarity tickling the inside of my chest, and soothing my tumbling stomach. "We are all just people."

"Well said, Priest." Roland nodded his approval, a sort of knowing glint in his eyes. Curiosity made my pulse quicken, and I longed to know those deeper contemplations swirling in his head.

Otvel quirked an eyebrow at the praise. Silence fell back around us like a fog, and Inessa and Roland shared a quizzical look, something unspoken passing between them. I felt a small prickle in my finger tips, a strange discomfort of not being in on the secret exchange creeping up my arms.

Inessa caught my eye and smiled sweetly, entirely unassuming in her demeanor. I gave myself a mental shrug, dispelling the odd haze of misplaced jealousy. I laced my fingers together, tethering my emotions back into place as my knuckles glided over each other, and jumped when I felt a small zap.

"Ouch!"

"Everything alright?" Roland's bemused expression beamed at me.

"Yes, I just shocked myself." All my fidgeting created too much friction. I lifted my hand and waved it front to back in front of his face before pointing my finger at his nose. My eyes narrowed playfully. "Keep laughing at me though, and I'll give you a good zap too!"

"I think we are approaching the hospital, so before you goad each other further in whatever exchange this is," Inessa pulled me back by my shoulder, brows knitting together sternly, "You'll want to settle down and prepare for our arrival so we don't appear—"

The car shook violently, its steady cruising disrupted by sudden undulations. A loud bang followed by muffled screams, snapping wood, and rocks sliding past each other caused us to stiffen, eyes wild and searching. Only Otvel remained completely composed, though he too craned his neck to try and locate the source of the commotion.

Inessa and I clasped each other's hands and squeezed. My spine straightened, pushing itself into the plush leather of the seat until it could rest against the firm boarding underneath. The car came to an abrupt halt, the brakes squealing in resistance to the jarring stagnance.

Both of us lurched forward, tumbling into Otvel and Roland. My elbow collided painfully against Roland's knee and my forehead thumped into his stomach, causing him to give a winded splutter. I fumbled to return to a dignified position, losing hold of Inessa somewhere in the awkward shuffle.

"What was that?" Inessa blustered. The chauffeur coughed in his open compartment as the car was covered by a sweeping cloud of dust. Dirt coated the snowy street side, and several indiscernible forms raced past our vehicle in the opposite direction, crying out as they went.

"A Wielder! A monstrous girl attacked the hospital."

"Did you see the power she was using? It was a tendril of pure darkness and evil."

"Stop gawking and run!"

The comments were fleeting as we were quickly the only ones remaining on the street. Roland's eyes narrowed, and he mouthed the word *Wielder* to himself in confusion. My jaw trembled, but concern split my chest like a burst of lightning.

"The patients!" I croaked, reaching shakily for the door handle. "Someone said there was a Wielder attack on the *hospital*. We have to make sure they are alright." This time I wasn't so hindered by distance on a balcony, condemned to watch but not help the plight of my citizens. This time I was here and I could help.

Roland waved his arm in front of me, warning me to let him take a look first before venturing further. The sound of shoes crunching against gritty snow alerted us to the arrival of the soldiers, marching past our windows as an armed unit. Roland waited for them to pass and opened the door, pulling his revolver free from his jacket, before slowly slipping out onto the street.

"Sorrel, be careful—" Inessa tried to grab onto my shoulder, but I leaned out of reach and thrust my trembling body out of the car before I could overthink it. I didn't have time to be a coward. Not when the already injured and ill could be suffering or in peril.

I wasn't certain I could even do much to help, but I *was* certain I had to at least try. I sucked in a deep breath and held myself tall, crowding past Roland against his protests to take in the scene before me.

Smoke coiled into the sky, and my heart thundered in my chest as I stood frozen in fear. Bricks and chunks of the building were still dropping to the ground like raindrops, the *tinking* sound mixing with the *cracks* and *thumps* of crumbling debris. A form was shifting in the plume of dust, and I recognized her as the source of the civilian's panicked comments.

The Wielder-girl looked at me from where she stood in the center of the wreckage, eyes round and unblinking. Her chest was heaving beneath her hospital gown, and her hands were shaking. There was blood running down her forearm.

She was a patient? A victim in the stampede?

A group of guards rushed towards her, weapons raised. She broke away from our stare to reach her hands to either side of her body and motioned like she was cracking invisible whips at the guards.

Maybe it is a misunderstanding, and she is just a patient that needs help.

Long, wispy black tendrils appeared from her hands and mirrored her movements, the darkness spreading from whips into large sweeping wings of shadows that collided with the soldiers, knocking them down. It was the same type of viscous shadows that the man had used in my dream.

The darkness of evil.

My blood turned icy in my veins, and every muscle in my body threatened to either collapse beneath me, or force me to run away. There was no denying what she was, even if she was young and injured. She was a Wielder and practitioner of iniquitous magic against Mortalkind.

The girl took a step forward, her big brown eyes once more fixed on me, and I matched her with a step backwards, feeling like prey caught in the sights of a predator. Her gaze roved quickly over Inessa—who had also reluctantly left the car— and Roland rooted beside me, hands poised on his gun, and the edge of her mouth twitched into an equally unnerving smile.

She lifted her chin forward and tilted her head, the movements awkward, intentional, and unnatural, like a feral beast. My mouth fell open and horror surged through me from head to toe as her cast shadow darkened and she stepped forward, falling into it out of view, while the form of her shadow remained behind.

"Where did she go?" I balked, my body trembling fiercely. The form on the ground shifted from human into an unidentifiable blob, then it shot across the icy cobblestone street, straight for me.

My eyes widened, and I took another step back, completely spellbound and at a loss of how to get away from the black mass. It was the same as the pool of darkness in the woods outside Svyat Gavan. Was she going to pull me down into it with her? Was this some strange foresight from my nightmare? Perhaps she recognized me and Inessa as Grand Princesses and wanted to try and assassinate us or finish what that other Shadow Wielder started in our childhood.

Mama's warnings and instructions to go home at the first sight of danger screamed through my mind in the wake of that very danger. Looking at the destruction the girl had unleashed on the infirmary behind her, and how easily she had bested our guards, I didn't like my chances of survival if she succeeded in reaching me. But, where could I run? Once more I was faced with a Wielder, just like twelve years ago, and once more I was out of defenses. A relentless shroud of helplessness consumed me in its grasp, uncertainty scratching my skin like ravenous claws feeding on doubt.

Otvel knelt and scratched a line on the ground in front of me. He poured the contents of a mysterious vial onto the white line and struck a match. The sparks ignited on the powdered substance, producing a display of bright and colorful, short, leaping flames. The sudden appearance of light caused the surging shadow to halt in its tracks, veering and melding into the shadow of a stack of crates. The girl reemerged from within it and narrowed her eyes at me, her neck craning in the unsettling way once more. She stooped to the street abruptly, placing her hand to the ground. A flickering pool of darkness appeared beneath her and she hopped inside it once more. Both she and the manipulated shadow vanished entirely, not a trace left behind.

"Th-thank you, Otvel," my chattering teeth struggled to allow the words through my lips.

"Are you alright, Sorrel?" Roland whipped himself in front of me, Inessa hot on his heels. It took me a moment to realize I had slowly wilted to a crouched position.

"She's just had a scare. The fear will leave her body shortly," Otvel replied for me, giving my shoulder a gentle pat. "Divine above may you reach down and resolve this child's fears with your Divine touch, reminding her of your strength and perfection. There is no fear where a Divine heart dwells, but that evil may not exist there."

There is no fear where a Divine heart dwells, but that evil may not exist there. I repeated his prayer over and over in my head.

"What did you use to make those flames?" Inessa asked, staring at where the multicolored fire had already vanished. "And how did you know to do that to block the shadow?"

"Chemical reactions," Otvel replied matter-of-factly. "Different mixtures result in different reactions. All shadows fear the light—especially the light of fire. Their evil cannot live in those flames."

"The infirmary," I rasped after a few deep, steadying breaths. There was only one reason I'd left the car in the first place. "What's happening with the patients inside? Why was that Wielder in a hospital gown?"

In front of me, beyond Roland and Inessa, I could see the soldiers had managed to get back to their feet, confused, and rattled at witnessing Wielder magic up close. One had already regained his footing, while another was clutching at his chest, hunched over, gasping for breath. The second pair were grabbing their heads and padded their bodies like they were checking they were still in one piece. I didn't blame them, and I didn't envy whatever sensation being struck by a shadow had caused for them.

"Maybe we should head to our next destination. Let the guards deal with things here," Inessa suggested gently. She leaned forward and squeezed one hand, while Roland held the other tightly. "Or head home. Mama did tell us to go home if we had any issues."

I furrowed my brows at the avoidance of my question and rose shakily to my feet, making my way towards the infirmary to see for myself just what damage had occurred. My knees were still unsteady beneath the weight of my body and threatened to buckle with each step. But, I kept moving forward, pushing down my own fears, replacing them with a resolve to help anyone who was possibly injured or frightened in the explosion.

"You're being stubborn, Sorrel!" Inessa called after me.

We came here to help, not simply pacify disgruntled citizens.

"Thank you," I addressed the guards with a grateful dip of my head as I passed. I made sure to look into each one's eyes directly, repeating my gratitude to each individual soldier until I reached the front of the infirmary.

The entrance to the building was in pieces, the damage spreading across the front facing wall and the lobby. The remainder of the structure seemed intact, so I slipped through the broken bricks and framing. Trepidation was wheezing through my lungs with each deep breath I took.

Were there going to be casualties through the next set of doors? Was there another Wielder laying in wait to attack, or would that girl reappear to finish what she had started? The questions tumbled in free fall from my mind to my pitted stomach and back again.

Behind me, I could hear shoes crunching against rubble and knew that Roland, Inessa, and Otvel had entered the building with me. Roland and the recovered soldiers began clearing the space, weapons raised. I lifted my head to harness my resolve and braced myself, pushing against the door that would take me into the first patient hallway. The creaking of the hinges rang harshly against my ears in the tingling silence. Goosebumps spread across my body the moment my first step carried my foot over the threshold into the empty room.

White gossamer curtains rippled against the draft from the open doors. Cots and bedside stands were the only forms I could see, but something pricked at the back of my mind that said this image before me might not be as it seemed.

"Where are the patients?" I whispered, stepping fully into the dim room and looked over my shoulder to my sister. "Wasn't there supposed to be displaced children and families in this hospital?"

"It's a small hospital. The smallest of the ones we were going to visit. Maybe they ran away in the chaos." Inessa offered, her arms wrapped around her body where she stood surveying the room from the entrance. "I'm going to see if there are any other rooms besides this patient hall to check. I doubt everyone just vanished into thin air."

The thought punctured my resoluteness with cold seeping dread as I realized it was entirely possible that the Wielder had swallowed them up in her abyss of liquid black. Surely there wasn't really someone so powerful that they could steal away an entire room of people? I willed away the thought and continued into the room.

A whimper, so small I questioned if I had imagined it, snapped my attention to where a pile of linens had spilled on the floor. Beside it was a tipped cabinet that had landed at an angle against a table in the corner of the room. A closer look, and I noticed some of the linens had been pulled towards the little makeshift cave. Someone was hiding inside.

I knelt and held out a hand to a cowering woman, whom I now realized was curled around a child. "Don't worry, you're safe now. We won't hurt you," I coaxed, beckoning for them to come out of their hiding place. "I have some soldiers here who will relocate you to another hospital for your remaining recovery."

"Who are you?" The woman's words were brittle and frail. Though she was healthy and whole on the outside, I could see she was little more than a husk huddling over the little boy with the last of her strength.

I blinked warmly. "My name is Sorrel. What's your name, if you don't mind me asking?"

The woman's eyes stretched wide and she lowered her head. "Your Imperial Highness." She startled when my hand rested gently atop hers, and I shook my head.

"Just Sorrel. And your names?" I repeated my question, thankful to see some of the tension dissipate from the pair in front of me.

"Yeneve, and this is Palto."

"Nice to meet you both, though I wish it had been under better circumstances. Are either of you injured? Do you know if there is anyone else hiding?"

Yeneve shook her head. "Some ran out. But there wasn't a huge group here. Almost everyone had been discharged. We were both cleared to go but we needed another day to make travel arrangements."

"You're not from here?"

"No, I came with my brother and his family from Videiria."

"That is a long trip." I tried not to wince under the weight of my next question. "And your brother?"

"We got separated in the chaos last night. Palto is my nephew. We don't know where his sister or parents are. Everything happened so fast." Yeneve's face started to crumble, and a band squeezed around my heart.

"Please, if you will go to the soldiers— ask for Sergeant Hykner— he will help you find your missing family members, and I will personally make sure your safe travels home are arranged." I pointed to my soldier, a young man with sandy blonde hair and deep brown eyes standing at attention next to Inessa. "Please accept my deepest apologies for what you have endured on Eisan soil."

Palto looked up at his aunt, and Yeneve seemed to be weighing my words. She was likely gauging them for sincerity, and I hoped she knew I couldn't truly put the depths of my sympathy into words.

"Thank you," She whispered finally, a tear rolling down her cheek. "Thank you."

"Here, let me help you up. Are you sure you're not hurt?"

"Just a few bruises and scrapes," Yeneve tentatively accepted my offered arm and guided Palto by the hand to follow me towards the door. "More than anything, we are just shaken. Everything last night was so terrible, and then to see the remaining patients here just vanish like that... It was something straight from a nightmare. I thought Eisa would be the last place we would see acts of war like that."

"Pardon?" I whipped my head around. "You said patients vanished?"

Yeneve shrank back, and I kicked myself for reacting so strongly. "Yes, when the doctor was treating a young man, he got all riled up, and the doctor's instruments started freezing. He was about to report the man when that girl got up and started throwing shadows at him. She chased him into the lobby and then—"

"Hey! There is a wounded man out here by the front desk!" Roland's alert sent a shock wave down my spine.

I thanked Yeneve for her recount, trying not to tremble beneath that knowledge that there had been not one, but two Wielders in this hospital— and both had gotten away. I waved Hykner over and introduced him to Yeneve with brisk instructions, my eyes darting over to where Roland and one of Inessa's men were pulling a bloodied man out from a pile of debris behind the desk out into the open. Otvel stooped down and checked for signs of life, pressing his ear to his chest, while he held his fingers to the man's wrist.

"He's not dead!" He called out. "Just stunned. He has had a good knock to the head."

With Yeneve and Palto taken care of, I was at the man's side in an instant, cradling his head in my lap to support his neck as he came to consciousness. "Grab some gauze for his head," I instructed Roland, who complied, plopping a roll of bandaging in my hand in a couple of heartbeats. Otvel shifted to the side and looked on as I took over.

"What are you doing? Do you *know* what you are doing with a head injury?" Roland whispered as he kneeled beside me.

I nodded. "Yes. Mostly, anyway. Remember when Yulia was

ten? She took a tumble in the garden and knocked her head against a rock. Ina, can you find a rag and some clean water?"

"Of course," Inessa dipped her head.

"Naturally, Dr. Klivech was called for immediately. Mama was an absolute wreck because head wounds bleed a lot, and she was certain that Yulia—" I swallowed, accepting the small pail and rag from Inessa. Dipping the cloth, I started dabbing gingerly at the ailing man's head. "Klivech cleaned the wound, to make sure it wouldn't get infected, but also to see the true source of the bleeding."

The white cloth quickly turned russet under the dirt and blood being soaked into its fibers. I scrunched my face, wringing the rag out, tinged water spilling through my hands, and handed the pail back to Inessa. She glanced down at it, her lips twitching, and her fingers barely holding onto the bowl. But she turned and dumped the soiled slop, replacing it with fresh water.

"There, see? The cut itself isn't so bad. I doubt it will even need stitches. Sir?" I called quietly. Otvel stepped in to wave some smelling salts beneath the man's nose and his ice blue eyes fluttered open. "Sir, can you tell me your name?"

"Uh," The doctor squinched in pain. "Um, Val. My name is Val."

"Alright, Val. You've taken a hit to the head, but we've got you all cleaned up. We have more help coming soon." I looked sharply at Inessa and raised my eyebrows. She had a sharp intake of realization and immediately whispered something to her soldier, sending him rushing away.

"Th-thank you." Val murmured.

"No trouble at all. I'll be right here with you until a doctor can look at you. Can you tell me where you are, Val?" I patted his arm reassuringly. "I always get so turned around in the city."

"We are, um, in the Piren District, Vicht Hospital, three-hundred Vicht Street."

"Ah, that's right." I nodded and tried to think of a way to keep the man talking. I vaguely remembered Klivech doing the same for

Yulia, saying it could be dangerous to let someone concussed go to sleep too soon. I didn't know if this man was in fact concussed, but I wasn't about to take any chances. "You must have been busy today. Thank you so much for all of your hard work in taking care of our people."

"Your people?" Val blinked rapidly and strained to look at me. I could see two small indents on the bridge of his nose and realized he must normally wear glasses. "Forgive me, Madam, but just who are you?"

"She's the princess!" Palto chirped from across the room, the first audible words he'd spoken, and they caused me to duck my head in embarrassment.

"Uh, Sorrel. My name is Sorrel."

"Princess? Oh my," Val blanched and tried to bolt away from me. "Your Imperial Highness! Forgive me, I lost my glasses. Please, you shouldn't be here on the ground in the dirt and—"

I pushed gently on the man's chest to keep him in place and smiled. "I'm exactly where I need to be, and where I want to be."

"Can you tell us what happened to you?" Roland asked, settling down in a seated position on the ground beside me. "We had just pulled up when that girl came out of the building."

"Ah, ah that girl? That *thing* you mean! She was a horrible monster pretending to be hurt to hide amongst the injured to launch her attack. She and that harbinger of sinful ice."

I thought back to the Wielder-girl and the blood running down her arm. It looked to me that she had been legitimately injured, but perhaps I had misjudged someone else's blood for her own.

"She looked injured when she was bleeding outside, so something must have done some damage," Roland commented, his expression neutral, but the corners of his eyes and mouth gave his underlying curtness away.

The Doctor ignored his comment and kept going, speaking only to me. "They started attacking me when I caught onto them, and next thing I knew, patients, along with the nurses and other doctors, were running out the doors. Those who stayed were swallowed up by that monster's shadows. They just vanished, and I was thrown out here. The shadows themselves turned feral and took out the wall. That's the last I remember."

Val's voice was starting to rise and I could see hysteria and shock taking root in his eyes. If he kept on as he was, he'd overexcite himself before the soldier could return with qualified help. I cursed under my breath that the other doctors had run and seemingly managed to get away so fast, not thinking of protecting their charges.

A storm was brewing in my chest just as it had the night before, and I once more swallowed it down. My own fear was not what Val, Yeneve, or Palto needed to see. They needed to know that everything was going to be taken care of.

I beckoned to Otvel and kept my voice soft and sweet as honey. "Otvel is our most devoted high priest with a special connection to the Divinities. Please, allow him to pray over you to banish any lingering evil from this attack."

"Really? Your own High Priest? You're too kind, your Imperial Highness."

"I only wish I could do more. But, rest assured, everything is going to be alright and you are safe now." I mouthed to Otvel to make sure the man didn't fall asleep during the prayers and leaned back on my hands, disengaging from the interaction as he started speaking over the rattled man. My back pushed into something hard, and I tried not to jerk in surprise, lest I risk disturbing the ritual taking place in front of me, when I realized Roland had shifted to allow me to rest against his side.

"You are remarkable, you know that?" Roland's breath tickled my ear, and I turned to see his eyes glowing behind a look of subtle awe. "The way you throw yourself into these situations and take charge. I've seen you do it countless times with your siblings too, always leaning on Klivech's every prognosis. It's really amazing"

Beyond him I could see Yeneve and Palto staring at me with twinkling expressions, hands clutched to their mouths and chests. Inessa gave me a knowing look, her eyes dragging over the intimate position Roland and I were in. Then, she looked at Val and gave me a small nod of approval.

"I just want people to know that I care. That *we* care. And that we will do whatever it takes to keep our people safe," I mumbled, biting the inside of my cheek and looking at the ground. "Without them we are nothing."

"All your people?" Roland asked, and I was confused by the question.

"Of course all of our people." I tilted my head. Inessa turned away and Roland looked at me knowingly, a darkness falling over his face.

"Even the Wielders?" The question was pointed, and I wondered if he was reminding me to be careful how I phrased my statements given the situation we were in. I recalled his words from the previous day proclaiming that Wielders lived within Eisa's borders, and had to assume he was referring to something similar.

I opened my mouth to correct him by saying there weren't Wielders in our country, but faltered. I saw with my own eyes that that proclamation was no longer true. "We need to send word to Papa immediately." I frowned and blinked rapidly, reaching for the commanding pragmatism I needed to demonstrate in this situation. "Can you see to that, please, Roland? I'm going to pray with Otvel."

Roland dipped his head and shuffled to his feet with a sigh, formality overtaking him. "As you wish."

I nodded my thanks and closed my eyes. My ears were honing in on Otvel's divine words, but my mind was once more replaying the images of those whips of darkness, the girl's odd posture, and the blood on her arm.

What was that girl? She was a Wielder. A real, powerful, terrifying Wielder, wielding actual dangerous magic. I can't explain it away.

Wielders were in Eisa, and it seemed they weren't too keen on hiding anymore.

EIGHT

"There was another Wielder attack in Pyry," Yulia sighed heavily, finishing the last of her echinacea tea and setting to the side. "I just can't believe they are in Eisa at all. We went so long without them causing any issues." She was sitting in a chair by the fireplace in the room she shared with Kira. Our younger sister was sitting on the hearth, while Inessa and I sat on her bed.

"What are you drawing, Yulia?" I tried to shift the conversation but frowned when Yulia turned her sketchbook around. The crisp white of the paper was scored with long curling wisps of black, coiling around our palace.

"I can't get these images out of my mind since you told us what happened," she admitted and went back to drawing. "The shadows are always surrounding some new place, including one I'm not even familiar with. I saw them turn white and foggy around a sort of farm house, somewhere snowy, next to a forest. It was the strangest dream. The whole thing has completely unnerved me."

Her charcoal scratches sounded like the sharpening of a knife in my ears, and set my teeth on edge.

I wondered if Yulia had also been cursed by whoever slipped into my dreams the other night and shown me such threatening images. It had been three days since the party, and two since the attack on the hospital. Nearly everyone who had shown up for the event had left, and now only a handful of guests remained. I personally couldn't wait for everyone unfamiliar to leave so I could be certain we weren't sharing our home with a hidden Wielder. All that remained now were a couple of delegates directly from the courts of our trusted allies, and they only lingered to handle some remaining business with Papa.

Since the news of the attack had broken, Mama, Papa, and the Council of Ministers had been in almost constant meetings. Even the head general had been called upon to assess if the attack was something related to the war at large. The palace was submerged into a strange bilaterally split atmosphere, with half of it existing in quiet, whispering dread, waiting for a hammer to drop, and the other side continuing on life as usual.

All of the round-the-clock meetings had left Roland virtually unavailable to see if he had found out any information on the nightmare, or if it was somehow connected to either the mystery man from the party, or the girl who had tried to attack me. I only saw him at dinner, and even then we weren't seated next to each other where a more private conversation could be carried out.

"Was it scary?" Kira's eyes were round and bright, the reflection of the flames flickering orange against blue. "It's insane to me that you went *inside* that building after being attacked. Weren't you scared?"

"*We* weren't attacked," Inessa rolled her eyes. "We were just standing there."

"Otvel said the girl melted into the ground and went straight for Sorrel!"

"Well…" Inessa blustered, her face puckering. "Otvel shouldn't be feeding your morbid curiosities. Besides, Sorrel did the honorable thing. She was worried about the people who might be hurt inside."

"I heard that Mama and Papa were really cross with you for not heading straight home," Kira grinned at me, eyes narrowing. "Who knew you were such a rebel?"

"I wasn't being rebellious. I just wanted to help." My fingers picked at a loose thread on Kira's bedspread.

"Reckless is the word you're looking for, Kira," Yulia mumbled, squinting at her drawing. "Sorrel is all logic until she isn't and it's going to bite her someday."

"It takes a Wielder attack to get her to break a rule!" Kira snorted. "Was that your first one?"

"Hey—" I started to defend myself, but was cut short.

"Not that this isn't fascinating to mull over— over and over again— but I think I am going to go check on my plants in the greenhouse before dinner." Inessa hopped to her feet, her shoulders tense. The conversation was clearly making her uncomfortable, though it didn't seem based in the obvious kind of fear, like what I felt. Her worries felt stifled beneath the surface of her skin, ready to burst out at any moment.

"You don't have a greenhouse here, Ina!" Kira called after Inessa as she headed for the exit. "That's back at Svyat Gavan."

Inessa's cheeks puffed. "Well, I am going to go check on the plants that *are* here. Someone probably has a potting shed or greenhouse somewhere. This wretched palace is certainly big enough."

"Don't forget your mittens," Yulia cautioned, her eyes flicking to the window and then back at her drawing. "And maybe an umbrella. I think it might rain."

"It's been snowing, not raining."

Yulia shrugged. "Better safe than sorry."

Inessa frowned at the window. "I guess so." She took her leave, and the three of us remaining sat in silence for a while before Kira popped to her feet.

"Today has been rather dull. I think I'll go fetch some cards or a chess board. Sorrel, care for a game?" She laced her fingers together and raised her arms over her head, arching her back in a long stretch.

"Against you?" I laughed. "You'll completely destroy me."

"That's half the fun! Come on, rebel girl. Live a little, dig down deep, and try to take me down. You never know. This might be the day!"

"You're entirely too cunning for your own good. Fine." I waved Kira towards the door. "I'll play a game or two, but if I win, then I get to pick the next game."

Kira weighed my challenge and marched up to me with her hand out. "Deal! I'll be back in two hops of a frosted frog."

I shook her hand, warmth spreading through me at her touch. She was just as adept at lifting moods as she was at getting into trouble. She shrugged her wrap up over her shoulders and zipped out of the room, her feet losing a bit of traction with her thick wool stockings against the marbled flooring.

I looked at Yulia as she swapped her charcoal pencil between her ambidextrous hands to get a better angle on her drawing. The fire crackled and popped in silence. I rubbed my thumb against my finger, and the longer I watched my sister, the more my heart quickened in pace.

"Yulia?"

"Yes, Sorrel?" She looked up and blinked at me.

"Are you alright?"

Yulia shifted her weight in the chair, tucking her legs in further under her. "Why wouldn't I be?"

"I don't know. You have seemed really out of sorts since we got back from the hospitals. You know everything will be alright, don't you? Your outing went off without a hitch, and what happened on mine wasn't a normal occurrence. We have so many people here to keep us safe, and whatever this Wielder nonsense is, it's merely an anomaly. They won't hurt us this time. They won't get the chance."

"Are you saying that to convince yourself, or do you really believe that?"

"I do. Even out there, being rushed by that young Wielder,

Otvel deterred the shadows in an instant."

"And if Otvel isn't around to protect us?" Yulia's brows lifted, her round, saucer eyes growing even bigger.

"Why wouldn't he be?"

"I don't think he always can be, Sorrel."

"Yulia, come on. You're making that face. Talk to me," I pressed, coming to stand by the fire next to her chair. "What's on your mind?"

"Nothing is on my mind." Yulia insisted. "I just keep having these stupid dreams and trains of thought." She paused, parsing her next statement in her mind before speaking it. "Sometimes, I feel like I catch these odd moments where I know how others are feeling so strongly, it's almost like I can... Well, anyway, it's very strange."

"You're very empathic. And insightful. You always have been." I nodded along.

Yulia shook her head, her loose hair swishing around her shoulders. "No, I'm frightened. No one is saying it, because it isn't the strong Eisan way, but I know everyone else is frightened too. You're scared just like I am, but the difference is that you're always so worried about soothing the rest of us, you hardly give yourself time to process what's happened between distractions. Kira is the only one who says what's really on her mind in this whole palace."

"It helps that you two are bonded at the hip." I tried to bite down the sting at my sister's uncanny assessment of me.

"Well, who else would keep an eye on her?" Yulia's mouth twitched into a half smile, and I caught her hand as she reached a charcoal coated palm to rub at her eye.

"You'll look like you have a black eye if you aren't careful." I handed her the rag resting on the arm of the chair that she used to wipe her hands.

"Thanks," She accepted the cloth and cleaned her hand before pawing at her fatigued eyes.

"You really haven't been getting any sleep, have you? You said you've been having strange dreams?" I pressed as nonchalantly as I could, my growing reservations bursting at the seams.

"Yes," She yawned and leaned her head against my side. "Sometimes, it's the shadowy stuff in weird locations. Sometimes, it's fire in a small space, other times, it's icy water from a dark hole, or a really big storm. The people with me in the dream change too. But, whatever disaster it is, it always wipes out whatever building we are in with a really loud bang. Then, I wake up."

I ran my fingers gently through her hair, and she closed her eyes with a sigh. "Those sound like some serious nightmares. I had a pretty frightening one the other night too."

"I heard."

"You did? When? I thought I only told Roland about that." I looked down at her in surprise.

"I must have passed by when you mentioned it or something. I don't really remember." She shrugged and straightened back into her seat. "I'm always overhearing the most random things. People must fail to notice I'm around."

"You are rather quiet." I nodded slowly and untethered my fingers from her hair. "I think Inessa mentioned you were the one who first overheard about the stampede at the Celebration of Reign. Did anything seem at all odd to you at the party the other night?"

"Just that man who interrupted it. Though, I suppose he was sort of rightfully upset given what happened. I just wish he hadn't chosen such a poor way to display his anger. That sort of thing could get him killed in the wrong company. I just think he didn't know how to express it any other way."

"At least he wasn't near you," I sighed. If Yulia had been touched by a Sonyote Wielder, just as Roland suspected I had been, I could rule out that man from the mix. Perhaps he truly was a disgruntled citizen and nothing more. The answer did little to console me as I realized it meant that more than likely, one of our staff or invited guests was responsible for the cursed assault. At least all those guests were gone now, and those who remained hadn't been by both me and Yulia that night to the best of my knowledge.

"Roland was acting a little strange too."

"He was?" I laughed, trying to imagine what sort of thing might be considered strange for him that Yulia had caught wind of. Having not seen him at all the night until the wee hours of the morning, I had no gauge for his behaviors, other than that he had been *playing chameleon all night.* "How so?"

"It was when he was escorting the man off with the guards. I don't know, there was something that seemed not quite right about him." She paused and scrunched her face at the memory, then shrugged and returned to her drawing. I looked down and winced at the crumpling building she was in the middle of depicting. "I guess now that I think about it, he just seemed a bit cross and concerned. Which, given the situation, was entirely reasonable. He probably would have rather been with you."

"Interesting," I mused, drumming my fingers on the back of her chair. "Well, if you have any more of those frightening nightmares, or can't get them out of your head, you can always come and tell me about it. In fact, the next time it happens, you *should* tell me, and I'll help you forget it."

"Same to you," Yulia smiled meaningfully, but didn't look up from her sketchpad. "Sometimes, I miss when Kira would beg Mama for those frightful bedtime stories about Wielders, and she and I would end up crawling into bed with you and Ina, because we'd get so scared."

"Inessa always hated it so much when Kira would choose her bed. She complained that she was an absolute bed hog. Can't say she was wrong either," I couldn't help but chuckle at the childhood memories. "You were always a much nicer bedmate."

"Sorrel, did you have plans you forgot about?" Kira asked, looking over her shoulder as she sauntered back into the room with a chessboard tucked in her arm, and a deck of cards in her hand.

"Not that I'm aware of. I have the afternoon free until dinner."

"Huh," Kira's face crinkled in confusion. "I just saw Ina in the hall with Roland and they were whispering about some plan they had tonight."

"Inessa and Roland have plans together?" I furrowed my

brows. "Odd. I haven't even seen Roland since last night's dinner."

"I assumed you'd be part of the adventure?" Kira left her statement as more of a question, prompting whether or not this was something I should be upset about being excluded from.

In truth, I felt a small tightening in my throat at the idea of being left out. Roland and Inessa had always gotten on well enough, certainly, but they had never been ones to lurk around, surreptitiously planning nightly rendezvous. Whatever it was, I was fairly positive it wasn't romantic in nature. Roland and Inessa had never looked at each other as anything other than friends, even with the three year age gap putting him closer to Ina's age than mine.

No, this had to be something else, though what that might be I hadn't the faintest idea. Moreover, I hadn't a clue what kind of secret they might be hiding. My thoughts jumped involuntarily to Yulia's comment about Roland's demeanor the night of the party. The two couldn't possibly be connected, but then why did I have such a nagging sensation like I was missing something nipping at the back of my neck?

Not thinking up anything satisfying to my internal queries, I smiled again amicably. "Not this time, I guess."

"Alright. Cards or chess? I think chess would be more fun, personally," Kira plopped down on the bed and laid out her items, all interest in Roland and Inessa forgotten in an instant.

A low deep rumble sounded from beyond the window, followed by a streak of lightning that tore the sky in two with a blinding white light. The sight sent an ominous chill down my spine, and I found myself drawn to the window, peering out at the tumultuous sky, somehow feeling at home in its rolling tide of purple and black clouds.

"A storm is coming," Yulia commented absently, flipping to another new page in her sketchbook. Her fixed stare glinted. "I think I'll draw it. Best to put those nightmares behind me anyway. There is no use dwelling on them now. Lightning makes more interesting shapes in any case."

"Since when did you become a meteorologist?" Kira snorted.

"You seem awfully concerned by the weather today. It's ghastly, like it always is at this time of year."

Yulia bit her lip. "I don't know. It just seems to be a bit restless today. Emotional, almost."

Water ricocheted off the pane and beaded down the glass. I pulled the latch and pushed the window open, a strong gust of cold, early evening air crashing over me, frigid and comforting against the growing heat in my body.

"Ah! Sorrel, for crying out loud, close that window. It took me the better part of today to finally get warm, and you're going to freeze me to death all over again," Kira squawked, flinging herself back in front of the fireplace.

Below me, an umbrella opened, and Inessa bolted from the steps, through the courtyard towards the gardens, clearly still intent on the search for the potting shed. Unless she was headed somewhere else…

I stretched out my hand, the mix of sleet and rain melting in my palm and dripping through my fingers. Sure enough, Yulia's weather prediction had come true.

"I'm sure it's nothing. Set up the board, or we won't have time to play before dinner."

"Princess Sorrel was always running outside in the most dreadful of weather." Lord Friedrich lifted his glass of wine to his lips with a jaunty laugh. "A downpour, there she was twirling between the raindrops. A blizzard? Why, I'm fairly positive Her Imperial Highness had to physically restrain her from playing in the snow."

I was staring so hard at the table I was certain my gaze was going to bore right through it to the ground. Glasses swished their contents around, forks scraped against the plates, and if there were various nonverbal reactions to the Minister's stories, I saw none of them.

"Meanwhile, little Princess Kira always tried to crawl inside the fireplace just to keep warm," Friedrich continued his reminiscing to the dinner table, recounting happily to the last of our guests left in our capital.

"Tried? I still *try*," Kira laughed along, slouching slightly in her seat. A swift poke in the arm from Yulia had her straightening back up a moment later with a small disgruntled puff.

"Tell me, Princess Sorrel, it's another cold and stormy night. Would you rather be in the eye of the storm?" Friedrich grinned at me, and I wanted nothing more than to melt into the floor when every head at the table swiveled in my direction.

"Oh, come now, Father. Stop teasing the princesses. I, for one, find all of their quirks nothing short of delightful and entertaining!" Roland jumped in on my behalf and I looked at him gratefully.

"I enjoy the cooler weather too, to be honest. Though I've quite fancied our holidays at the coast as well," the attention moved to Theo as he piped up cheerfully.

"A man meant to reign over Eisa through and through!" Papa beamed and patted Theo's shoulder affectionately. My brother's chest puffed at the praise, and he sat a little taller.

"It sounds like Princess Kira would much prefer our climate in Vatra," Kenji, who was one of the remaining guests along with Kailia, nodded approvingly to Kira. "When things have settled down, you'll have to come visit our country and see how you like the heat."

Arrian squinted playfully at Kira from his seat across from her. "I should like to see the Great Forge of Vatra myself. Perhaps we could make a grand adventure of it."

"That sounds divine!" Kira perked up, plunked her elbows on the table, and rested her chin in her hands. "Tell me more about Vatra, please. And while you're at it, lend me your secrets for how you're tolerating this insufferable cold here!"

"Kira," Mama's voice was low, and she dipped her chin to her daughter's improperly placed elbows. "I'm sure there will be plenty of time for that when we adjourn to the drawing room after the meal."

"Perhaps I could hear more about Videiria too," Inessa piped up to the Videirian ambassadors. "I'm afraid I was a bit too young to remember our last trip there very clearly."

Izadora and Warner were the other couple remaining in our charge, along with their son, who looked to be around Inessa's and my age, Bellon.

"I have read a few books on the flora there and it's very fascinating." Ina's eyes twinkled.

"It would be our pleasure, Your Imperial Highness." Izadora blinked warmly at my sister. "I'm sure Bellon could tell you anything you wish to ever know about the herbs issued in the healing poultices we use and export here, in fact."

"All in accordance with Prohibition of Magic Act's guidelines for magical content, of course." Bellon's dusky brown eyes locked with Inessa's. "And it would be my pleasure, Your Imperial Highness."

"Inessa, please. I must insist you call me Inessa." Ina chuckled, her cheeks flushing pink.

"Dowles?" Papa called to the butler, with a small lift of his chin. "I think dinner is just about finished."

"Yes, Your Imperial Majesty," Dowles bowed deeply, and he and the footmen set to their work while the rest of us disengaged from the table to stand.

Roland found his way to my side and offered me his arm. "May I have the honor of escorting you to the drawing room?"

I dipped in a subtle curtsy and accepted his arm. "You may." I contemplated asking him what he and Inessa had been talking about so secretively earlier, but was having trouble thinking of a way to articulate the question without sounding accusatory.

"The rest of you go on ahead." Papa waved us forward, and I noticed Friedrich, Kenji, and Izadora lingering by the table. "We won't be but a moment."

Warner, Theo, Bellon, and Arrian all offered their arms to the available women to escort them into the next room— A formality we only trotted out when company was present. Mama gave Papa a sidelong glance, which he returned with the smallest of nods.

"Do you need to stay too?" I asked Roland, trying to keep the curiosity that was burning in my chest out of my voice.

"I'm not sure." He looked to his father who gave a slight shake of his head.

"Go on ahead. Enjoy the evening. There will be plenty to keep you busy tomorrow, My Boy."

One of Roland's dimples appeared where his jaw ever so slightly clenched, but it melted away with the ever diplomatic smile that followed a moment later. "Very well."

"Everything alright?" I whispered as we headed for the door.

"I can't say I love being left out of the loop with the foreign dignitaries, being as it's sort of my department of ministries and that is the point of my entire job, but there must be a reason for it. Father is the head of council, and Prime Minister after all, so there is little point fighting it. No need to be consumed by pride either, especially not when the alternative is spending time with you, Snowdrop."

"I can feed you lies of how wonderful you are to boost your ego?" I offered, bumping his arm with my shoulder as we walked.

"Would you?" His smile stretched from forced to sincere. He pressed his hand to his chest in mock pomp. "Do go on then!"

"Well, where to start in your long list of accomplishments?" I sighed heavily. "You haven't read any of the marvelous books I have recommended, your horse riding can be a little lackluster, and your artistic skills leave little to be desired."

"You know, I don't think you have this inflated ego thing quite mastered. I'll have you know I can ride quite well, thank you very much, and I thought my self portrait was quite uncanny!" Roland shook his head as he extended his arm and guided me by the hand to a free seat.

"Certainly not!" I insisted with firm scowl. "You're far more handsome than that stick figure."

His eyes lit with amusement and he nodded, inching slowly

to his own seat a couple feet away. "There it is. You were burying the lead. You meant all along to inflate my vanity, and you know, I don't mind it. A little bird once told me you fancied my eyes in particular."

Embarrassment scorched my face, and I was almost certain I was blushing scarlet. "I'm going to kill Kira."

Roland laughed and settled into his seat. Both of our gazes traveled to where my little sister was hanging on every word of Kailia's description of Vatra, the rest of the world shut from her mind.

"That same little menace of a bird— who can't be trusted, mind you. Remember that, please— mentioned she spotted you conspiring with Inessa earlier today." I spoke casually, trying to keep my tone light and playful as I finally got the nerve to broach the topic of my curiosity. "Do I get to be in on the secret?"

I expected some clever dancing wordplay around the topic, teasing and pulling me along, but eventually giving in and sharing the secret. But, to my surprise, Roland quieted and laced his fingers together over his knee. I didn't miss the slight shift of his eyes from Kira to Inessa and back, and the smallest of discerning squints in their general direction.

Finally, after a few endless heartbeats, he replied, "Well, as you said, the bird can't be trusted."

"That's an awfully cagey response, even for you," I blurted, a bit sharper than I meant to.

"It's nothing to worry about. We were discussing her affinity for gardening, if you must know. And, I was trying to dissuade her from rushing out in the rain. Jealous?" He adjusted his posture.

"Your ego needs no help," I said flatly.

"I'm only teasing. I will regale you with every detail of potting soil that was discussed right now! Anything to regain your good favor."

I rolled my eyes but couldn't help but smile. I knew nothing nefarious would be transpiring between them, and Inessa had been on her way to the gardens, so more than likely, she really had been talking about potting soil, and Kira had simply embellished the hushedness of the conversation. I had no good reason to not believe him.

"Oh, alright. I won't punish you by asking for those details."

"And you're a saint for it!"

"However…" I raised my hand dramatically for pause.

"Oh no. So close." Roland winced.

I opened my mouth for a feigned condemnation of his senseless teasing, but snapped it closed when I caught Mama's eye. She mouthed the words *mingle with the guests,* and guilt evaporated the flirtation in my chest.

I cleared my throat and dipped my head to Roland. "Forgive me, Lord Roland, I have monopolized your attention. Please excuse me."

Roland looked puzzled by my sudden shift in demeanor, until he spotted the silent connection passing between me and my mother. "Ah. The mask of duty claims another pretty face. I must say you wear it well, Snowdrop." He turned his head away from the guests and spoke so quietly I was certain only I could hear him.

"No one wears it quite so well as you," I pointed out, and pushed gracefully to my feet.

As I passed Yulia on my way to get a refreshment on my after dinner drink, she smiled sympathetically at me. Of course, she would have been the only one to witness our private exchange from where Kira had abandoned her for the Vatrese woman.

I received a fresh glass of wine from the footman and was on my way to strike up a conversation with the Videirian ambassador's son when Papa entered the room, followed by the remainder of the party. Everyone froze and observed a quiet heaviness that had entered with him.

"Genri?" Mama rose hesitantly to her feet.

Papa looked at the ground for a moment, his shoulders squared, feet turned out, and hands clasped behind his back. Something official was about to be announced. I knew that stance well.

In trained synchronicity, Inessa, Yulia, Theo, and Kira

simultaneously rose to stand with our parents, equal parts hesitation and trepidation worn on their faces. Yulia and I were standing closest to my father, and with the subtlest intakes of breath, she had clearly guessed what he was about to announce a moment before he did.

Sweat mixed with the beading moisture of the chilled glass in my hand, and pooled between my fingers. The seconds that followed felt like hours of pent up anticipation banging on the inside of my forehead, and it took everything in me to swallow my swelling impatience and not speak out of turn.

"It is with a heavy heart and no small amount of deliberation that I share this news with you," Papa finally lifted his head and his gaze swept over the room, resolute and commanding.

His opening statement was enough to transfer the palpitations behind my eyes to an unsteady wobble in my hand.

"The recent events on Eisan soil are in no short supply of horror and tragedy that bespeaks a lurking evil trying to push its way into our country. That much can't go ignored." Papa continued slowly. Each word was weighted in careful calculation.

"Papa?" Kira took a tiny step forward, being the only one brazen enough to prompt Papa for the point. Her forehead creased with uncharacteristic apprehension, and Theo placed a hand on her shoulder in silent solidarity.

Papa puffed a sigh and stood a little taller. Firmer, with more reverence. We weren't going to like what he was about to say next and he was braced for it.

"Our allies, Videiria and Vatra, have formally requested Eisa's assistance in the war against Wielders."

No! I wanted to wail aloud.

"And I have accepted the request for aid to rid the world of its plague of Wielders once and for all."

No, no, no. Please tell me this is another nightmare. Wake up, Sorrel. Wake up! My brain swirled, desperately searching for a way out of the situation before Papa could complete the last piece of the announcement we were all dreading. All the stars could be falling from the heavens for how the world shook beneath me.

"Eisa will be joining the war, effective immediately. We will be remaining here in Tuyet, rather than returning to Eisolde, for the immediate future. Each of us in the Imperial family will have a role to play in this effort, also effective immediately…"

And just like that, our entire safe and sheltered world had shifted beyond recognition.

NINE

The sounds of boots marching against stone in perfect synchronicity rang through the still, early morning air. I sat atop my horse, Ortipo, dressed in my full regimental regalia, and watched my men moving through their drills with expert precision. The bright yellow accents of our uniforms caught the light, drawing attention to each crisp movement framed in navy.

I adjusted my hat, shifting the ornamental plume to the side as I gripped onto the reins in my lap. Across the courtyard, Inessa mirrored me in her light blue uniform, while Yulia stood beside her horse, watching her regiment in emerald green and gold.

The soldiers returned to starting places at the heed of our barked commands before running through their drills again. Their steps shuffled the regiments like a deck of playing cards, slipping between each other with rifles hoisted proudly at their sides.

As the men marked their march and the drill drew to end, Inessa and I slipped off our horses to join Yulia on the ground.

"It's looking well, I think," Yulia commented, leaning to peer around Inessa. "The form is good, and everyone appears to be in sync."

I nodded and tugged at the fingers of my gloves. "Yes, I think they should be ready for the send off. A few stood out as exemplary in their motions too. We should note those to relay back to Papa."

"Hykner in your regiment was hitting his mark well," Inessa offered.

"Yes, I did notice him. He made a very good impression that day at the hospital, so I've already given his recommendation for one of my accompanying bodyguards."

"Really?" Inessa perked, then tugged at the strap of her own hat, removing it from her head with a sigh. "That's better. I think Hykner would be good for that job. It will likely spare him from any drafting that might take place in the future too."

"Wouldn't we want exemplary soldiers fighting for us?" Yulia queried.

"It's also nice to know there are some left here just in case," I threw in, shooting Hykner an appreciative look. "Darion was also hitting his marks well, though I'm not sure if he would be my first choice for a personal guard. Who was that man over there?" I pointed to one of Yulia's men, standing proudly with his rifle.

"Corporal Zdrute. He is very keen." Yulia replied, lifting her chin with approval.

"Vaun also stood out to me," Inessa added then frowned. "Someone should be writing this down." She waved over one of her men and asked for a pen and paper. The soldier was still half bowed as he scurried off and returned a few moments later.

"I can't believe the first wave of soldiers are really headed to the front tomorrow," I breathed, my breath billowing in front of my face and twisting with the morning fog still hanging in the air. I rung my loose gloves in my hands and stared at my feet. "It feels so surreal."

"I don't know if that's the word I would choose," Inessa muttered, folding her arms as she finished scribbling the soldiers' names.

Yulia blinked at her and tilted her head. "You're upset by the war. Eisa's involvement specifically, aren't you, Ina?"

Inessa's lips formed a tight line, and her brows furrowed. "I think we have matters to work out in our own country before we go challenging others." She gave a signal for the assembled men to adjourn from practice for the day, and Yulia and I followed suit.

I bit my tongue, stopping myself from echoing similar sentiments. I wasn't sure what she meant by matters to work out in Eisa, but I did know that I was also very reluctant to involve our country in such dangerous affairs, knowing it would surely only invite more tragedy and duress to our empire, especially so soon after the stampede.

"If our allies are putting up a fight to maintain balance and prosperity, surely it isn't fair to reap those rewards without our own contributions?" Yulia countered.

"Videiria and Vatra have received plenty of contributions over the years from Eisa."

"I think it's noble to help in the battle against the Forsaken hold over Wielders," Yulia pressed, fidgeting at the sleeve of her uniform. "If we turn a blind eye to such evils, we are complicit, and how can we look to the Divinities for aid and guidance when we aren't first willing to help ourselves?"

"The Forsaken?" Inessa repeated, and I could see she was trying not to roll her eyes. "The Forsaken are true entities of evil— the opposite of the Divinities in every regard. You think that's who we are going to war against?"

"If we are the footmen of the Divine, then Wielder's are the other side of the coin." Yulia's brow creased in confusion. "You know all of this, Ina. I'm not sure what you're getting so worked up about."

I too felt puzzled by Inessa's adamance in arguing the basis of our entire religious upbringing, but then again, her moods could often turn sour for something unrelated before being projected on a fruitless argument. Though, usually, it wasn't Yulia who locked horns with her surliness, but rather Kira or Mama.

Inessa's blue gaze roved over both of us in turn before she closed her eyes and sighed heavily. "I don't want to argue with you Yulia, so please, let's just leave it be. I just don't want to lose lives needlessly."

"I'm sure the soldiers are proud to fight for their country," Yulia replied, with a small smile, in what was clearly an attempt at reassurance, but Inessa's eyes flashed with fresh annoyance.

I shared a look with Yulia, and tried to stifle my own brewing frustration with both sisters for their stubbornness. I knew Yulia meant well by holding her ground, and her own pertinacious behavior was delicately forceful, but sometimes her choice in timing left little to be desired. Inessa, on the other hand, often swung like a pendulum between philosophical pontifications and impetuous obstinance. Meanwhile Kira, though thankfully not present to add fuel to this particular fire as she was working separately with her own regiment on flag carrying, was brazen, willful and mischievous. Mediating between my sisters always fell to my shoulders, and usually ended with my nursing a headache and some bruised egos.

Tensions had been running particularly high since Papa's announcement to join the war, and everyone was handling it in their own way. Yulia chose to rationalize the involvement by applying Divine Tenants to our moral obligations. Inessa seemingly felt put upon and was masking her fear for our disrupted era of peacefulness with bouts of distemperment. Kira applied her mind to the strategy of it all, choosing a more removed stance, and Theo walked the faithful line of obedience and duty in Papa's shadow. Mama and Papa remained a united front, though I could see an added layer of weariness lingering behind their confidence that gave away their own internal worries for what this war ultimately would mean for Eisa.

Meanwhile, I was still struggling to discern my own feelings. I saw bright faces of young soldiers, eager to protect their country, and couldn't help but wonder how the realities of war would dull their spirits— if they returned back at all. There was a painful ignorance hanging over my head, leaving me with a gap of knowledge too great to even begin to quantify what those men would face when they joined the Vatrese on the fronts of Sonyo. How could they know anything but honor and an urge to prove themselves for their kingdom when they were heading to face an unknown? They'd be briefed, certainly, but even I knew words on a page couldn't hold a candle to the terror standing in the presence of a Wielder would elicit, especially under threat.

I felt a sting in my shoulders where my muscles tensed inside my jacket, and I released the breath I'd subconsciously been holding. Slowly uncurling my tightly balled fists, my fingers yielded stiffly to the moment as I tried to force a more relaxed posture.

"Grand Princesses?" Darion approached us with Hykner and the man Yulia had denoted as Zdrute.

"Yes, Darion?" I dropped my shoulders and turned to face the man with a smile.

"You'd mentioned you were interested in seeing the disassembly process of our rifles, and we were about to take them apart for a final cleaning before tomorrow… if you'd care to watch."

"Oh!" I straightened and clasped my hands together, grateful for the invitation of levity and distraction to dispel the gathering tension around my sisters. "That would be lovely, Darion. Yes, please."

"We'd thought about having a race to see who could disassemble their weapon first," Hykner threw in, a mischievous glint in his eye.

Inessa smirked. "Now, *that* sounds like an entertaining suggestion. I for one am up for a little friendly competition. How about you two?" She looked to me and Yulia and raised her hands in a shrug.

"You mean have one man from each regiment champion for us?" Yulia's prickled demeanor softened in an instant and she beamed with interest.

Taking the cue from the eagerness of the group, I lifted a finger. "Or, we could make it a little more interesting, seeing as it's our last meeting before the parade."

"And how would we do that?"

"We have the soldiers teach us and *we* compete with them as our judges for speed and accuracy."

"Is that safe?" Yulia asked.

"With supervision from these professionals, I think we would be in safe enough hands. What do you say, Ina?"

Inessa paused to mull over my challenge, then reached out and took Hykner's rifle from him. "A Zdraevit doesn't back down from a challenge! But, no one tells Mama." She looked at me pointedly before shifting her gaze to Yulia. "Or Kira. We don't need any lectures or tattling."

"Deal." Yulia and I nodded in tandem.

"Hykner can teach Inessa since she's already got his gun. I'll tutor under Zdrute, and Darion with you, Sorrel. Does that work?"

"One for each of us, sounds fair." I tapped my finger to my chin. "A half hour to learn should be sufficient. Shall we?"

"Go!" Inessa cheered, and we each bolted with our respective soldiers from the parade field into the barracks. We were led to individual tables and each given our soldier's rifle to practice on.

Waiting no time, Darion grasped around the bolt, lifting and pulling to the rear of the gun. "You first start by racking the bolt open, and check to make sure there are no munitions in the chamber. Then, depress the trigger and remove the bolt. Like this."

I leaned down, carefully noting the exact positioning of his fingers over the trigger mechanism and the rhythm in which he moved through the disassembly. Biting my lip in focus, I tried not to brace myself for a fire of the rifle with the trigger fully depressed.

Darion caught my eye and smiled reassuringly. "Don't worry, we've already cleared the rifle so there is nothing to fire. You always make sure the weapon is clear before performing a field strip, and never skip that step. The firing pin, that is what will ignite the bullet, is on this bolt piece here, so the rifle cannot fire without it now that we've removed it."

"Right," I nodded along and studied as Darion walked me through removing the cleaning rod, locking clips, and upper handguard.

"These guns only shoot five bullets between reloads."

"Why five?"

Darion chuckled and shrugged. "Because whoever designed the magazine decided five was all it needed."

"Wouldn't that make it hard to fight with, only having such few bullets to fire?"

"With the right training you make each shot count. Technology is constantly improving, so what we have here," Darion placed his hand over the stock, "is leaps and bounds over what he had previously. I even hear they are working on producing a rifle with ten rounds instead of five."

"Constantly evolving." I picked up the cleaning rod and rolled it between my fingers, the cold of the steel abrasive but not uncomfortable against my skin. "So what comes next?"

"Next we will be removing the magazine well. You'll need a screwdriver and a punch for this…"

I picked up the magazine release after Darion set it down and squeezed the odd clamp-like piece. "This reminds me a little of a set of tiny pliers. Kira once took a pair from a handyman and used them to crack walnuts when she was little. They looked so big in her hands. The exact opposite of this." I laughed, and Darion joined in.

Though I knew there was a competition on the line, I could tell I was feeling less urgency than my sisters stationed elsewhere in the barracks. Instead, I watched Darion's adept hands move through the motions of deconstructing the remainder of the rifle then putting it back together again for me to try.

"Darion," I started as he slid the gun across to me. I curled my fingers around the bolt, and yanked it back to open the chamber.

"Remember to check the weapon is clear before proceeding. Even though we haven't added any bullets, it should be second nature to clear the chamber."

"Right," I murmured, angling the rifle to peer into the chamber. "I was wondering something."

"Ask away," Darion folded his arms and grinned at me.

"Forgive my candor, but as a soldier, how is the war sitting with you?"

The smile melted from Darion's face and his expression grew guarded. "I'm not sure what you mean. It is an honor to serve my country should I be called to do so."

I gritted my teeth as I depressed the trigger, giving a small puff of relief that the rifle didn't go off unintentionally, and lifted the bolt mechanism clear. "Honor aside, I'm curious what would drive you to fight in a war. On a personal level, how do you quantify it? Eisa has been peaceful for a long time, and we're stepping into this fight after a considerable period of relative neutrality beyond our own borders. Do you feel satisfied fighting a foreign country on behalf of another foreign country?"

Darion was quiet for several heartbeats, carefully considering his answer. Finally he replied, "I fight to protect peace for my wife."

"And you feel that peace is threatened?"

"Peace is under constant threat. Utopia's are merely an ideal. We each perceive what ideal peace means to us differently. Ideals are fragile, easily bowled over by the tangible and the terrible. Tragedy is much easier to define than euphoria. So, as a soldier, I would like to fight against any threat against the peace my wife and I currently share together."

I paused where my fingers were coaxing the bands off the barrel and contemplated Darion's response, pleasantly surprised by both his directness as well as his thoughtful answer. What was my peace I'd fight to protect? My family, my people, my country… all obvious answers. It made sense that soldiers by the thousands would place the same merit in their roles on the front.

"I won't be doing any fighting, but I hope there will be an opportunity to do my part. I'd like to help protect peace for my family and the citizens of Eisa if I could."

"You'd be surprised at all the ways we fight calamity. Soldiers aren't just those who carry a rifle and wear medals on their chest." Darion tapped his chest. "Soldiers are those who keep marching forward despite the challenges in front of them to make the way easier for those behind them."

"I like your answers, Darion," I grinned at the young man. "Your wife is lucky to have someone like you on her side."

"Nothing could tear us apart. I'd take on the world to keep her smiling." Darion beamed fondly. Then he sobered and handed me a screwdriver. "Remove the screws. We better pick up the pace if we want to beat the others."

I ducked my head and rolled my shoulders back, going through the steps over and over until our countdown ran out. My sisters and I stood side by side with the rifles laid out in front of us, the mixed regiments clustering all around to watch the competition. Yulia and Inessa smiled brightly, eyes narrowing playfully as they readied for the race. I panned from them to the excited faces of the soldiers cheering us on, each regiment rooting for its respective colonel. At the front stood Hykner and Darion, eagerly awaiting their impromptu apprentices' possible success, along with the soldier who had guided Yulia.

The command to begin was given and we dutifully fumbled our way through the disassembly, laughing and blustering beneath the weight of a rowdy audience. Yulia was the first to finish and raise her hand, with Ina and I tying for second just a step behind her.

The men cheered for us all regardless of the results and I grinned from ear to ear, laughing as Inessa batted my plume out of her face as we were pushed together by the crowd, and soaked up the communal elation.

I thought of Darion's words, and my heart hammered in my chest till I felt lightheaded.

This. This is worth fighting for. However, I can be, I will be a soldier to protect the peace for these men and their loved ones.

"L loved me enough to rend reality in two so I could live, but not enough for her stay in that reality beside me."

-D

TEN

The cupboard opened with a loud creak that made me flinch in the quiet room. I only pulled it open enough to snake my hand through and paw for a roll of bandages. My fingers prodded multiple items before finally landing on the fibrous cotton roll. I closed the door quickly, so as not to prolong the squeak of the hinges but sighed when the door slammed against the frame with a bang.

"Sometimes it seems that trying to be quiet makes everything ten times louder, doesn't it?" I jumped at the groggy voice sounding from the cot directly behind me.

"I'm so sorry! I was trying not to wake you." I dipped my head apologetically to the young man and showed the gauze in my hand. "I was out of this in the other room."

"I was just dozing." He pushed himself up and smiled kindly at me. With a sweep of his arm he gestured to the empty bed beside him. "And I don't think you were disturbing my invisible roommate. I haven't seen you in here before, are you a new nurse?

Or a bandage thief?"

Time had surged forward in the blink of an eye since the decision to join in the war efforts. While Papa, his Council of Ministers, and the upper generals focused on the battle front, he had tasked all of us children with different responsibilities and left Mama and Lord Friedrich to maintain Eisa's internal functions. Friedrich had strongly advocated for a more hands-on approach, and I hadn't been able to agree fast enough at the opportunity to help in any capacity.

"Yes, and no," I laughed. "I have been volunteering here for about two months now, but I've just graduated from morale booster to gauze fetcher."

"I see," The man nodded along then reached out a hand to introduce himself. "Well, lucky me that both a current gauze fetcher and a former morale booster wandered into my room. My name is Rafe."

I took the offered hand without pause and gave it a firm shake, feeling a small trill of rebellion at the colloquial exchange, as apposed to all the formal royal greetings. "Lovely to meet you, Mr. Rafe. May I?" I pointed to his patient chart. I'd been studying how to read them as I graduated into some more formal nurse training.

Rafe nodded, stray strands of straw colored hair falling into his face, then held up a finger. "Of course. You're the medical professional here, or at least you're wearing the uniform. But, before I allow you to peruse my blood pressure ratings and meal plans, I must first ask that you tell me your name."

I hesitated, knowing the man clearly didn't know who I was, and that all the pleasantries of being a simple nurse would go out the window the moment I said my name. Rafe noticed my pause and looked at me seriously.

"Is it a terrible secret?" He whispered. "Your name?"

I gave a bemused snort and shook my head. "Quite the opposite I'm afraid. My name," I looked down at the shoes peeking out from my plain nurse's frock. "My name is Sorrel."

Recognition glinted in Rafe's eyes, gold like two orbs of pooling sunlight, but he merely nodded along. "Like the princess then."

"Yeah, just like the princess," I mumbled, and busied myself reading what I could off his chart. It seemed that he had been in one of our southern towns, near the border of Dezidaneya, and had gotten injured in an ambush. He'd suffered mostly minor injuries, more from physical strikes than any magical wounds, the worst of which was a bayonet wound to the left abdomen that was being monitored.

"You're much prettier than her." Rafe grinned around a stifled cough. The motion dislodged the blanket from his chest, revealing his bare torso covered in bandages and bruising around his ribs.

I spluttered at the compliment, unsure of how to take it. "Pardon?"

"The poised royal woman in the photographs. The dutiful, earnest nurse is a much better look for you." He leaned over for his cup of water, wincing, and I stepped forward and handed him the glass.

"I'm not sure whether I should be flattered or offended," I replied evenly, and motioned him to tilt forward so I could take the pillow from behind him and fluff it.

"Whichever you prefer, I guess. Clearly you're not trying to flaunt your heroism, but I have to ask, what is one of the Grand Eisan Princesses doing fluffing my pillow and…" He trailed off as I sat on the edge of the bed and guided him to lift his arm so I could look at his side. "Looking at my injuries? I'm sorry, are you qualified for wound inspections, Madam Gauze Fetcher?"

"My sister, Inessa, volunteers here too. As does my mother, when she is able to," I replied, narrowing my eyes in concentration. "I fluffed your pillow because it looked in need of it, and I'm looking at your wound because it is spotting through with some yellow. It would be very unfortunate if your scabbing bonded to the bandage and got ripped off the next time it's changed. Or worse, was infected."

"I see… and about your qualifications?"

"Oh, I have plenty of experience helping my brother with bandages and wounds," I explained, then snapped my mouth closed with an inward groan as I realized my error. I cleared my throat. "Boys can still be rough and tumble, even when they are princes."

"*You* take care of your brother?" He sounded genuinely taken aback by the idea.

"Yes, however I am able to. What I'm not, I try to learn for the next time. It's been that way since he was a baby."

Rafe glanced up at me, dubious. "You're a very odd princess."

"Why do you say that?" I finally pulled the last layer of bandages free, easing them from his stomach. Sure enough, the fibers were beginning to stick and solidify into the wound's scabbing.

"You're not what I expected."

"Have you met many princesses to have formed a proper expectation?"

"Not exactly, but don't you have a whole slew of staff to do this sort of stuff? To fluff pillows and inspect scabs? Doesn't exactly sound very regal."

"Yes, but there is something to be said of one's own self sufficiency, and I like to learn."

"Why?" The question was puffed and mystified.

"So I can help, of course." I figured the answer was obvious, but the man seemed truly stupefied by my presence. *Perhaps I ought to check for a fever as a sign of infection, in case he was wondering if he's hallucinating or something.*

"Help yourself and your family?"

"Not just them. I learn so I can help whoever I come across who might need it." I frowned, reaching around to rest the back of my hand against his forehead. "You don't feel like you have a fever."

"You are also a lot more touchy then I'd expect someone royal to be," The corners of his eyes squinched as he laughed beneath my hand.

"Sorry, I don't mean to be—" I yanked my hand away and hopped to my feet, my cheeks burning. "I'll let your regular nurse know about your dressings, straight away."

"You don't need to be sorry. I just mean, you're normal."

"I thought I was odd?"

"Yes, that too. No, I mean you're a normal person. You have a family and a little brother you look after. You aren't too high on your pedestal to help others, even lowly field workers like myself. You're a nurse and not just wearing the outfit for show. Forgive me, you're just a very far cry from what I expected. But, it's not a bad thing."

I tugged at the sleeve of my dress. "I should be on my way. It was lovely to meet you, Mr. Rafe."

"Hey, wait!"

I turned around to face him, tensing.

"You forgot this," Rafe lifted the roll of gauze I'd abandoned next to him.

"Thank you," I mumbled awkwardly, shuffling forward to snatch the gauze and flee for the door. "I can't be a gauze fetcher without this. Take care!"

Once I was safely in the hallway, I paused and leaned against the wall to collect myself. My face scrunched under the weight of embarrassment at my forwardness. I primarily assisted in the wards where there were easily thirty men in a single room and wasn't often in a one on one situation these days anymore, other than at home. Half the soldiers who returned from fighting in Sonyo were delirious from sleep confusion anyway, and didn't do much communicating during my shifts. Yulia and Kira entertained the more lively patients who were either moved to convalescence homes or to alternate clinics and hospitals.

Rafe, being a citizen casualty, was in a different, more intimate part of the hospital, where there were only two to three patients for final observations to a room. It seemed that a new roommate had not yet been assigned to him. I wanted to crawl inside myself when I thought of my behavior. I was never alone with young men other than Roland and my brother, so I hadn't given it much thought.

"Sorrel?" I jumped at Inessa's voice. "Are you alright? You look a little flushed." She was heading down the hall towards me. I immediately blanched and rushed to meet her. I hoped that her voice hadn't carried through the door into Rafe's room, alerting him that I was still loitering outside.

"I'm fine. Just collecting myself. I have the bandages, but I need to send a nurse to examine and reapply the bandages for that man."

"Why? Is there something wrong?"

"They were bonding to his scab. The... Serous drainage, I think it's officially called. Anyway, that was mixing with the platelets and was starting to dry into the bandage. It would have ripped it off... "

Inessa wrinkled her nose, her mouth pulling down into a frown. "You've been taking notes from the doctors again."

"I read some journals too." I looked away.

"You unwrapped it, didn't you?" The tone of her voice was all I needed to know the face she was making at me right then, even without looking at her. She would have her arms folded, eyes narrowed with a goading, and somewhat patronizing smile smeared across her lips as she fished for what was making me uncomfortable. I knew better than to look, since that expression had always been one of the few I found someone could make at me that instantly sent my blood boiling.

"I did." I gritted my teeth, and finally raised my head.

"And you didn't re-wrap it? You know how." Her eyebrows lifted, and her chin tilted downward. "What stopped you?"

"Well," I spluttered, almost losing track of why I had even been flustered in the first place, under Ina's pressing. I knew I'd never hear the end of it if she found some way to tease me about my forwardness with the man. I wasn't even a real nurse at this point, and I had no business acting like I was. "It didn't seem appropriate. And, I needed to get back with the gauze."

Inessa smirked and pointed to the room. "Is he in there? Should I take a peek and see if he's someone Roland should be worried about taking his place?"

"Inessa!" I gasped, completely mortified. This was going beyond forwardness and escalating to something else entirely. "That's not at all what I meant! What if someone hears you?"

"Just answer the question, Sorrel. Is he handsome?"

"Kira has been rubbing off on you." I took a step sideways, my back brushing the wall as a chasm yawned open in the pit of my stomach. "We need to get back to work."

"Avoiding the question?" Inessa matched me step for step, her eyes twinkling with amusement.

"I was looking at his *wound.*"

"So, that's a yes then? To both questions."

I hung my head, my shoulders sagging. "By all means, go harass the man and see for yourself. I have to get this back to my ward, and then I have a meeting I'm supposed to attend for Mama. I don't have time for your incessant teasing."

Inessa beamed, her smugness radiating off her like a glow. "You just rarely get so flustered, I had to take advantage of it. Don't worry, I won't tell on you to Roland!"

"There is nothing to tell, Inessa!"

"Oh, calm down. It's a joke, Sorrel. What's his name?" She chuckled and carried on down the hall past me.

"Rafe," I grumbled at my sister. "He's healing from a bayonet wound to the side, so you shouldn't pester him."

Inessa's steps slowed, and a strange jolt rippled over her body, then returned to normal so fast I wondered if I'd imagined the reaction at all. "I'll get him squared away with who he needs to take care of him. You can go ahead and head out."

Walking down the street for the final leg of the journey back to the hospital, I paused to take in the world around me— not the one I had often seen from the palace, or from the quiet safety of a royal car, but there in the center of the discord and consequence of my family's choice to bring us into the war. Though, I supposed it was more of my father's decision, than the family as a whole. We merely executed his wishes.

It was something I could only see when I managed to slip out unnoticed without guards to walk freely through streets. This occurrence had only happened twice since Eisa was brought into the war; once on our first day volunteering, and today. I knew full well that it was reckless of me to wander alone, but I felt driven to know what was happening to our people with my own eyes without them identifying me as a royal. I did my best to take in as many details as I could, wanting to make an honest appraisal of the city.

There were men and women walking around without direction, holes in their clothing, and fatigue in their collective countenance. The movement of their bodies was sluggish and abrupt. If I squinted my eyes I could envision them as some sort of undead monsters. I had heard old wives tales about such people living in Dimaer, a country that was known to house the reigning essence of death herself, though no one interacted with the terrifying country enough to ever confirm such far fetched legends. Beneath the lumbering forms, I could also see children darting in and out of the clusters of adults, flickering like hungry minnows in a dark stream of desperation.

A small sniffle caught my ear and I turned to see a little boy curled in a ball against an empty brick building. He had his head in his hands, and his clothes were tinged with days of grit and grime. I blanched, realizing that the boy looked to be only five years old or possibly even younger. A quick scan told me he didn't belong to any of the nearby adults.

I approached slowly and squatted down in front of him. "Hello, there."

The boy glanced up at me through his tumbleweed of raven hair and sniffed loudly again, but didn't respond, squirming harder against the wall of brick at his back. Empathy pierced my heart at his obvious fear. Was he displaced or abandoned due to the war?

"My name is Sorrel."

"Like the princess?" The words were meek, but beneath their frailty I could hear the tiniest bit of intrigue ignite.

"Yes, just like the princess. Will you tell me your name?" I smiled at the familiar nature of the conversation I'd had with Rafe not two hours prior, and tilted my head to the side to catch the boy's eye. I wondered why he was sitting all alone, and figured I'd have to gain his trust to find out how I could help him.

"Harvier, Miss."

"That is a very solid sounding name, Harvier. Do you suppose we could be friends?" I spoke gently, but with a sense of wonder, like becoming this boy's friend was the most important thing in the world I could possibly be doing— and in truth, I honestly felt it was. At best, he was a victim of neglect, and at worst, a displaced orphan. Either way, someone needed to treat him like a person and not just another lump of snow to pass by.

"You want to be my friend? But you're a grownup." Harvier perked up. The earnest surprise in his voice chipped at my heart.

"You say that as if you think children and adults can't be friends."

"They can't," Harvier whispered, but he had stopped shrinking away and was looking at me directly. "Adults don't care about children like me."

"Well, I am an adult and care very much, Harvier." I nodded my head firmly. I remembered that when my siblings had been small, they had a certain type of excitement over being asked their age, and figured it was an olive branch. "Can you tell me how old you are?"

The boy blinked thoughtfully then stiffly raised a hand with all five dirt coated fingers spread wide before immediately stuffing it back into his lap, no doubt hiding them from the biting air. "I am that many."

I was right, and the poor abandoned child was only five years old. I swallowed back the ambient anger that was building in my chest at the cruel reality this child was being forced to live based on decisions that were made for him.

Holding out my own hands, I opened and closed my fists twice. "I'm that many."

"Whoa. That's a lot." Harvier's eyes widened as the seemingly massive number of twenty clicked in his mind.

"Since you and I are friends now, can you tell me why you're sitting out here all by yourself?" I scooted to the side and leaned against the brick beside the boy. The ground was covered in a thin layer of frost, the edges of the spindles soiled and dark from being trod on by passers by. I knew it would soak my coat, but that was of little consequence.

"I have to stay here. My Papa told me to stay here and wait for him to come back." His face puckered with a faint pink hue and tears pricked his eyes.

I felt relieved to know that he at least had a parent returning to him, though it still unsettled me at the look of how long he appeared to have been waiting out in the cold. The anger returned, this time directed at the parent who had left his child behind. Had he been abandoned? Was that why a five year old boy, who should only know love and care, believed that adults didn't care about children like him? I could feel the agitation sparking against my nerves as the questions tumbled over each other in my mind.

"When is your Papa coming back?"

"I don't know. He was taken away by some soldiers who accused him of being a *summarizer*... He went to get us some food and I saw them take him. But he told me he'd be back, so I can't— I can't leave." Harvier's words stumbled on his lips, and his sentences began to trail off and slur together.

My stomach dropped to my feet as the pieces clicked into place. The boy's father wasn't coming back, not because he was selfish, but because he had been taken into custody as a magic-*Sympathizer*. Harvier probably didn't understand the meaning of the correct word, or that his father was being accused of a serious crime.

"How long have you been waiting here?" I pressed gently, trying to mentally brace myself for his answer, but it did little to steel my heart against his reply.

"Two days and one night. There have been two s-suns and one moon. Someone gave me a blanket, but it got wet so I p-put it over there." He pointed a shaking hand to a small sodden mound of wool. "I was given a piece of bread and some t-tea too."

Horror encased me as I realized it was far worse than being outside for several hours, or even half a day, in the cold. I reached out to touch the boy's wrist. It was cold as ice. Gingerly shifting his hand that had been balled into the fold of his shirt, I realized the tips of his fingers weren't dark from dirt, but were purple. I wished with all my heart I could suck the cold from his body and bear it myself instead. That blanket had probably been the only thing to keep him alive through the night. I needed to get him to the hospital immediately.

"You're warm, Miss-ss S-Sorrel." Harvier cracked a weak smile.

"What's your father's name, Harvier?" It took everything in me to not leap to my feet. I didn't want to frighten the boy, but he was in serious danger and I knew I was speaking too fast. It would be of little help, and would hinder us if he resisted and made a scene. I just needed to keep him calm and convince him to come with me. If it didn't work, I'd have no choice but to take him by force, and I hoped I'd be strong enough to handle him if he fought back.

"V-Vin. Vin Holok-k." The name chattered on his teeth with another seize of chill.

I rolled my shoulders back and feigned amazement. "I can't believe it! It must have been fate that brought us together to be friends today." I prayed this boy would be as impressionable as most five year olds were.

"Why?"

"It just so happens that I was sent by your father to bring you some place warm and to get some food and dry clothes."

"You were? So, I can go with you?"

"That's right. I'll bet you're very hungry too." I rose to my feet and dusted myself off, beckoning the boy to follow.

"Miss?"

"Yes, Harvier?"

"I can't walk."

My stomach lurched again in concern, but I stuffed it down. "Are your feet asleep? I know mine will go to sleep and get all tingly when I sit on them for too long."

Harvier shook his head. "No, last night when I got so cold, my toes started hurting really bad where the tips of my shoes were wet. I couldn't sleep so I watched the ice gather on them. I haven't been able to feel my feet since the pain stopped."

"I'm sorry to hear that. I think that's all the more reason we should get you dry and warm." I tried to keep my voice level and not show the fear that was mounting over the little boy's fate. "Would it be alright if I carried you?"

He thought for a moment, staring down at his feet, then reached his arms out to me in answer. I stooped and plucked him from the ground. I felt the cold emanating from his body, and at this point, I knew without a doubt, even with my limited medical knowledge, that he was in a dangerous hypothermic window.

He leaned his head into the crook of my neck and sighed. "You're so warm. And I'm so sleepy. The lady who gave me the blanket told me not to go to sleep in the cold. Can I sleep now, since you're taking me somewhere warm?"

"You can soon, I promise. But, let's stay awake long enough to get you changed and fed first alright?" I swallowed and turned around to race back towards the hospital. I kept my pace brisk, thankful that we had been so close to the building, and felt a small prickle of relief when I was met by Inessa and Sergeant Hykner— now in the regular post as one of my personal guards— at the steps.

"Your Imperial Highness?" Hykner's eyes widened when he

saw the boy in my arms.

"What's wrong with him?" Inessa breathed, coming to stand beside me. I gave my sister a stern look, not wanting to alarm Harvier. Her bedside manner was little to be desired.

"Oh, he's just gotten a bit chilled. I let him know that his father, who he was waiting for, sent me to get him for some warm food and fresh clothes," I spoke pointedly, animating my face to match the truth of the situation.

"Right, right." Hykner nodded along, playing into my white lie.

"But, it is pretty cold out here, so I think we should get Harvier inside where its warm as soon as possible." I looked down at Harvier's face, wincing when I saw his eyes were looking glazed. His skin was pale, and beneath the small tremoring breaths he was taking, his lips were tinting blue. Or maybe they had always been blue? How had I failed to notice sooner? I was too blinded by my own frustration that I failed to see what was right in front of me, making me no better than who I was condemning. "Would it be alright with you if Sergeant Hykner took you in the rest of the way, so I can get your clothes?"

"Sergeant? Like a real soldier?"

"That's right. You will be perfectly safe with him." I worried the boy wouldn't trust him since soldiers were who had arrested his father. Though at this point his cooperation was the least of my concerns, I lied anyway. "He's who your Papa sent to tell me to fetch you."

"Are you going to take me to my father?" He asked Hykner after nodding weakly, and I'd successfully handed him over. I slipped my coat off and placed it over the boy's body before Hykner rushed up the steps into the hospital.

"Maybe a bit later, Buddy. For now, let's focus on getting you settled, alright?"

"Was that the Princess? Did the princess save me?" His voice was growing weaker and weaker.

Hykner kept moving without pause, but in the doorway he

glanced over his shoulder at me with a sad smile. "It sure was."

"Tell her thank you, please." I barely caught the whisper before Hykner and Harvier disappeared into the hospital.

"What happened to him?" Inessa asked quietly, hugging me into her side. She ran her hand up and down my arm for warmth, but I could feel neither the heat of friction nor the cold of the frosted morning air. Snowflakes had begun to drift from the tumbling silver clouds above, and normally I would have enjoyed them cascading around me, but I felt entirely numb and dazed.

"His father told him to wait for him while he went to go get some food, then he was accused of being a Sympathizer and was taken away. That was yesterday, and he was still waiting for his father when I found him." My voice cracked, and I cleared my throat to quell the wobble.

"What a good little boy." Inessa's tone was soft and approving. "How terrible for him to be left out all alone in the cold."

"How could so many people be passing by and not doing anything to help him? He's just a child for crying out loud." My frustration returned in a thundering wave, my fingertips prickling under every rapid pulse.

"There are lots of people suffering, Sorrel." Inessa's brows furrowed and a tiny crease appeared next to her right eye just as it always did when she was being serious. "They probably didn't see him."

"*I* saw him. It was just luck that I was walking by and was able to stop because I snuck off to walk on my own. Do you know how many other people were standing in that street? Someone gave him a blanket last night at least, but they should have brought him inside. We were a block away from this hospital— *a block*."

"They might have tried. You don't know if he refused to go. Sounds like you had to spin a tale about his father to bring him here yourself," Inessa pressed and folded her arms across the rich velvety green of her coat. Her chin dipped to incline her head. The mood was different than earlier, when she'd given me a similar look, but her stance felt annoyingly condescending and dismissive of my anger.

I looked away sharply. "That wasn't just to bring him here. It was to spare his feelings about his father."

"What feelings would those be?" My sister released her hold around my shoulder and beckoned me up the steps into the lobby of the hospital. "Come on, it's cold out here and you gave away your coat."

"Besides abandonment, grief, and resentment?" I sighed, once more directing my resentment at Harvier's father's parenting choices. "What if his father really was a Magic-Sympathizer? That would be dangerous and he could have been corrupted."

"Interesting."

"What is?"

"I didn't realize it was part of our Divine right to deal hands of fate in the realm of morality and corruption. It'd be a terrible shame if we handed out all of this judgment in righteous anger and it turns out we were wrong in the end."

"Ina," I stopped and looked at my sister in surprise, but she merely slowed her pace and kept walking. She was heading for the changing rooms, and I was left with no choice but to follow her. "What are you saying? That sounds like blasphemy against Eisa's entire stance on magic and Wielders and—"

"No, no. Settle down." Inessa cut my befuddled exclamations short with a raise of her hand. "It's all purely philosophical. Things are never crisp, clear cut shades of black and white, Sorrel. No matter how one tries to erase the other, dark can't exist without light, and light without the dark. And, in the aftermath of their eternal quarrel, we are left with a myriad of shades of gray to try and understand. In the end, those shades become more muddled and complex when individuals set them in front of the rose colored glasses of their own preconceived notions of right and wrong. It almost makes it hard to believe there was ever such a thing as absolute truth in the first place when you think about it. I think most everyone, with exceptions of course, are just trying to do their best to survive their own existence. Everyone thinks they know what's 'best' but, in doing so, the likelihood of it being absolute is diminished and replaced with a callus blindness and intolerance to what is different and unknown."

She prattled her philosophies, her expression turning wistful and pensive as she plucked our daily charts from the rack, prepped for the afternoon shift, and handed me mine. I stared at her in contemplation, wondering where such abstract thoughts had stemmed from inside her, though I had to admit, her words had struck a chord within me— a chord I did not yet understand.

My eyes flicked down to my clipboard, quickly reviewing my tasks for the afternoon, then up to the clock on the wall that removed time from the day one tick at a time. My stop with Harvier had put me behind schedule for arrival and if I didn't hurry and change back into my nurse uniform, I'd be late to my first appointment. I was finally supposed to begin observing medical operations.

"I'll have to pontificate with you more later," I smiled and briskly patted her shoulder. "I never realized you were quite this philosophical. I'd love to hear more."

"Oh, I haven't much else to say on it really. Call it a wild hair of sympathetic nature or something." Inessa averted her gaze and scanned absently over her own clipboard. Something told me that she wasn't being entirely truthful, but I opted not to press further. "I just suppose I'd rather believe that the boy's father was innocent and that they will be reunited in the end."

"You're right. That's what I wish for too. Thank you, Ina, for guiding me away from negative assumptions. I'm sure everything will work out in the end." I gave myself a mental shake and started compartmentalizing my priorities for the immediate future. I'd check in on Harvier later. He was with the doctor and in safe hands now. After my shift, I could slip away and grab him some new clothes like I had promised.

"No problem. Come on. We had better hurry and get changed or we will be late and mother will really let us have it for shirking our responsibilities. I'm a little intimidated by looking in on today's procedures to be honest." She linked her hand in mine and we pushed through the doorway into the changing rooms.

"You saw the surgery listed?"

"It will be our first time. I hope it isn't anything gruesome."

"Would there be any terribly gruesome injuries to deal with in the first place? I haven't seen any worse than Rafe's stab wound." We slipped into our simple black frocks, and crested our heads with the headdresses required of all nurses. The source of the direct war being fought with Wielders was quite some distance for us, and mostly we hadn't seen too many typical physical injuries of conflict. We had seen some psychological cases, illness, exhaustion, but most refugees and soldiers weren't injured. "Did you get his nurse after I left, by the way?"

"Yes, I got him taken care of. Nice man. He asked if you'd stop by again, and I told him I would send you his way. Honestly, his wound was gruesome enough. I don't know how you stomach it," Inessa replied, but all the earlier teasing was gone. We both retrieved our boards and exited our changing room back into the sterile white hallway. I pushed through the door first, Inessa hot on my heels.

"Oh, alright. I suppose if he specifically asked, I can look in on him later today." Curiosity sparked in my mind of what the man could possibly want of me. "I've heard some horror stories about those coming in at the shore too, to the West, now that I think of it. Of physical wounds. I hope whoever it is we are seeing today is alright, all things considered. Oof," I gave a muffled puff of surprise as my face slammed directly into Hykner's chest on the other side of the door.

"Apologies," He took a step back and Inessa smirked behind me. I rubbed my nose and made to jokingly brush off the collision, but the smile and laughter fell away immediately when we took in the somber expression on his face.

"What's wrong?" Inessa was brave enough to ask, but searching Hykner's turbulent gaze, I had a good guess.

"It's the little boy— Harvier Holok." His hand was balled into the fabric of my coat. He swallowed and offered me the garment with a small polite dip of his head.

"Has he taken a turn?" Inessa's words tumbled out in a stilling breath that blanketed the hall in a quiet tension.

I saw it in Hykner's deep green eyes. I knew what he was about to say, but even knowing and bracing myself against it, it did little to stop the feeling of being simultaneously kicked in the throat and gut. My mouth went dry, and I sucked in a ragged breath.

"I'm afraid he didn't make it. He passed shortly after we brought him into the room. The doctor couldn't do anything. I guess his body temperature had dipped too low before we could try heating him up."

"Hypothermic exposure," I whispered. "I didn't realize it was so bad until we'd been talking for a little bit. I finally convinced him to come with me, but he couldn't walk. That's why I carried him. He had frostbite, didn't he?"

Hykner nodded, his countenance growing pallid. "The skin on his feet and ankles were black and blue. His toes, which had apparently gotten wet in the night, were the worst, and probably would have had to be amputated had he... recovered."

"I thought he had only been out there for the better part of a day, and just needed to warm up, until he told me he'd been there overnight. I feel like such an idiot." I hung my head, biting my lip against the shame blazing behind my eyes.

I found him too late. I had failed him, taking too long to notice his symptoms or take action. Why hadn't I known to whisk him in my arms and run straight here instead of trying to appease his feelings? I'd rather him be alive and hate me. Perhaps, if I had been just a few moments quicker, it might have been enough time to get his body temperature out of danger.

"I'm not sure there was much that could have been done for him, by the sound of it... Even if you had taken him here the very moment you spotted him," Inessa tried to soothe, but her words sliced the wound of guilt deeper, leaving it fester with helplessness.

His light was snuffed out at five years old. Only five years old. What have we let happen to our country?

"He told me to thank you, Grand Princess Sorrel," Hykner started quietly and Inessa slipped out of the doorway to stand beside me.

"Hykner, please. I've told you I hate those formalities since I was fourteen. Just call me Sorrel, for the love of Eisa. I'm just a person, nothing grand in the least," I interrupted bitterly.

"For saving him," He finished, then paused before looking from Inessa to me and adding, "I know you probably don't feel like it right now, but you did save him from dying on the street. He got to pass peacefully in a warm bed with the hope of seeing his father again, and the comfort of believing his father had someone send a princess of Eisa to retrieve him. I know it's not the happy ending you'd hoped for…"

"I hadn't hoped for an *ending* at all." I curled my hand into a fist, letting my nails embed deeply into the flesh of my palm to anchor the intrusive heartache brewing in my chest. "Someone should notify his father. In custody or not, that seems only decent. We don't know if he was guilty or not. Vin Holok is his name."

Hykner shifted uncomfortably.

"What else do you know?" I dared to ask, digging my nails in harder.

"While the doctor was getting Harvier settled in the bed, I asked a guard in the hall what they knew of what became of his father. Honestly, I wanted to go and try to clear the whole thing up, if I could. Turns out, there was some sort of *altercation*, and Vin Holok was pronounced dead as of last night." He leaned on the word altercation with some thinly veiled insinuation as he caught Inessa's eye. I put a mental pin in it to ask about later as I steadied myself against the weight of what he had just shared.

"Oh, no. Both of them?" Inessa bleated.

A single nod of Hykner's head gave the confirmation of the sad fate of father and son. "I'm sorry, Your—Sorrel. I know you wanted a happier outcome and you did your best to bring it about."

Inessa echoed his sentiment.

I turned away from them, slipping the coat over my arm to hang up somewhere along the way, and walked briskly down the hallway towards my first patient. Tears brimmed in my eyes, but I blinked them back into the eye of the ever growing storm within me. Another drop of emotion, bouncing with electric current, into the constantly churning chasm of forgotten hurts and stifled wrath. And that was a chasm I knew was better left locked away than ever unleashed. Least of all at a poor soldier, trying his best to help, and my sister.

I had wished for Harvier and his father to reunite, and they had— in death. Perhaps I had been foolish to look for light in a shadow. That was the downside to wishes. They dared you to hope for the impossible, but hurt you deeply if not fulfilled in the desired way. It was in that way I could see how wishes could quickly turn into curses.

ELEVEN

I pressed through the next few hours, determined to put my full attention into my work. Inessa had already headed home about an hour prior, but I had opted to stay for one more procedure, one more nugget of knowledge I could have for next time. My limbs felt heavy like lead, trying to drag me to the ground in defeat. A sharp throbbing had started in my right temple a few hours earlier and was still sending a cascading pang through my face every time I roved my eyes too quickly.

The hallway was dim in the early evening light as I made way towards the changing rooms. A shadow flickered on the wall as a bird flew past the window and my spine went rigid, images of the Shadow Wielder girl playing behind my eyes. I observed my own shadow stretched out tall on the wall from the faltering sunlight at my back.

My eyes stared so long at the place where the cast darkness met with the ambient light, the hues and shades blurred into a deep, unfocused gray. Tentatively, I reached out a hand and brushed my fingers along the line, dragging them into the shadow's core. A complex thread of relief twisted together with mystification at the idea that some shadows could sit flat and solid while others you could sink right into.

The texture beneath my fingers was faintly gritted with fine granules of dust from years of negligence, witnessing countless staff and patients passing by, all the while it stood there, structural and sound. An overlooked pivotal piece in holding this hospital up so it could be there for all the passing people.

"Am I interrupting a special moment between you and the building?" I jumped at the amused voice beside me and leapt away, hands raised.

"What?" I puffed and lowered my arms when I saw Rafe smiling down at me. I hadn't been able to tell his height in the hospital bed, but now he looked even taller than Roland. "What are you doing here?"

"Watching you stare at a wall." His head tilted, the grin widened, one eyebrow arching.

"No, I mean what are you doing out of bed? You're injured."

"I am? So that's why I'm in the hospital. It all makes sense now." Rafe's eyes were bright, and though his posture was a little stiff and slouched, he didn't seem to be in too much pain.

I narrowed my eyes at his sarcasm. "I see you were bandaged back up, so best not overdo it."

His lips pressed together and both brows lifted this time. "Since my legs are fine, I was told to take a stroll because of something with my lungs. My side is rebelling against the whole healing process a little so I gave it a stern talking to and it looks like I will be here another day or two before they send me on my way. Your turn."

"Pneumonia."

"Sounds flowery. Must be Lusoryian. Not that I've been to such a scandalous country, of course. I would never. But they do have the strangest names for things."

I finally cracked a small smile. "No, it's what they are watching for with your lungs. Too much stagnation can cause your lungs to fill with fluid. It's called pneumonia and can be fatal."

"I'm starting to believe those qualifications you mentioned, Madam Gauze Fetcher. I hope they give you a promotion. Maybe let you manage thermometers or something. Record everyone's temperatures."

I wanted to chuckle at the joke, but the laughter died in my throat. Instead, I turned to lean against the wall. Weariness had returned to snake its way through my bones, and I loosed a long sigh.

"I'm going to need an answer on the nature of your relationship with this wall before I head back. Then, I promise I will leave the two of you to your privacy." Rafe leaned his uninjured side against the wall to give a friendly pat, rubbing his fingers together afterwards. "Dusty."

"No one takes care of it," I sighed again, a bit too defensively.

"Of the wall?"

My indignation swelled. "It just sits here and dozens of people pass by it, but no one stops to give it any care."

"The wall?" Rafe echoed his question with deeper confusion.

I shook my head, a current of stifled frustration surged through my chest. "No one appreciates it. It doesn't deserve to just be forgotten here while everyone goes on about their lives. I can't be the only person to notice it. Is everyone else so self absorbed that they couldn't take a measly five minutes to stop and see if it was alright?"

Rafe nodded slowly. "This definitely isn't about the wall."

"Well, the wall does need a good dusting," I admitted and hung my head, the ambient weight of my thoughts pulling towards my chest.

"Rough day?"

"Very."

"Want to talk about it?"

"No." If I talked about how Harvier's death had made my heart ache so deeply, I was likely to lose my composure altogether, and that was something I couldn't do. I couldn't release the floodgates or it might never stop. At least, that's how it felt as the growing lump in my throat tightened its hold around my clipped responses.

"Okay." Rafe shrugged amicably. "Let's go then."

"What?"

"Follow me."

"Where are you going?" I whipped around to face him.

"To get a rag," He replied, as if the answer were obvious.

"What for?"

"To wipe down the wall. Haven't you been paying attention?"

"But—"

"Actually, you stay here and I'll be right back with one. I'm faster at item searches on my own. Plus, the wall might get lonely if we both leave. "

"Do you even know where to go?" I furrowed my brows, knowing there weren't going to be any clean rags to use in the immediate area.

"Nope. Be right back!" He waved his hand and disappeared around the corner, leaving me no choice but to either race after him or wait for him to return.

My momentary confusion was enough to take the edge off, and it didn't take long before Rafe returned, carrying a couple of freshly cleaned rags in his hand.

"That was fast," I commented, and accepted the cloth from him. "Where did you even find these? I didn't think there would be any that close to here."

"Just got lucky, I guess. Shall we?" Rafe didn't wait for my answer before he set to work dusting the wall.

I stared blankly at him, lost somewhere between being perplexed and moved by the off kilter display of solidarity. He didn't even understand why he was doing it. He didn't need to. He just knew he was doing something to help sooth the words I had chosen to share with him— the wall was dirty because no one paid attention, or stopped to clean it.

"A boy died today," I said quietly, and joined in wiping down the wall.

"Someone you knew?" Rafe didn't look at me, but a quick glance at him and I could see that a somberness had settled over him.

"We only just met."

"Family?"

"Dead, or unaccounted for," I bit, remorsefully.

"Ah. Was he quite young?"

"Five." I winced at the number all over again.

"Too young to burn," Rafe muttered, and my heart thundered. He was referencing the cremation that happened with unclaimed bodies in the hospital.

"Much too young," I whispered, and bit the side of my tongue to anchor myself.

"How'd it happen?" Rafe continued his questioning, but both his tone and posture remained casual, an unspoken agreement that I could stop answering any time I wished.

"Hypothermia."

It was Rafe's turn to wince. "No one stopped to help him, I take it?"

"That's right."

"But you did?"

"Yes, but not fast enough." I clenched my fist around the rag as hard as I could.

"Can you really measure vision with increments of time?" Rafe mused.

"What?"

"It sounds to me like you saw him."

"Well, yes. I happened upon him and stopped as soon as I saw him—"

"No. I mean you *saw* him. Took notice. Cared. That's something that isn't measured by how fast it happened. The significance is that it *happened*. Even if he died before you ever said two words to him, you still saw him, and that's important."

I paused my cleaning to take in his words. "It doesn't feel that way."

"Doesn't stop it from being true." Rafe stepped next to me and snagged the soiled rag and handed me a clean one. "You missed a spot."

"Where did this come from?" I smiled despite myself. "Stashed in your bandages?"

"Sure," Rafe shrugged, doing his best to stretch on his tip-toes to reach the molding where it connected the wall to the ceiling.

"Don't overdo it, or you'll never heal," I chided lightly, and stooped to clean the baseboard. With his tall form arching upward, I scurried along the floor, dragging the rag along with me.

"You're quite the cleaner. Another unexpected skill set."

"My mother always insisted we live very modestly despite our station. She explained to us our whole lives that we have Divine sanction as royalty from the Divinities, but none of that meant we had to be lavish and wasteful in our day to day lives."

"An interesting perspective for an Empress." Rafe's words were flat, and I snuck a curious look at him from where I still crouched on the ground.

"Your Imperial Highness?" Both our heads whipped to the side at the voice of a newcomer, and I bolted to my feet. It was one of the doctors. He gave Rafe a scrutinous stare, and his nostrils flared slightly with indignance. "Is everything alright here?"

"Oh, yes. Everything is fine. We just noticed the wall was dirty and…" I faltered in my explanation as I realized just how absurd I sounded. Of course, the wall wouldn't matter in the grand scheme of things if every person who passed by it was already suffering or helping someone.

There are lots of people suffering, Sorrel. They probably didn't see him. Inessa's earlier words drummed through my skull with greater clarity that caused a wave of numb calm to envelop me. The numbness was cold, and though my exterior was wearing the mask of duty and resolution, there still was the tiniest voice in the back of my mind telling me that if I could, I needed to be the eyes that noticed and cared for those overlooked. But, how could I do that?

How could I make sure no one else like Harvier suffered a similar fate?

"The Minister of Foreign Affairs is here to take you home to the palace, Your Imperial Highness." The doctor glossed over my words, and dipped his head. "If you'll please follow me, I will take you to him. Sir, should you be out of bed?"

I looked at the rag in my hand and offered it back to Rafe. "I'm sorry, I have to go."

"Don't worry, I'll get rid of these."

"Thank you." I smiled sincerely, and Rafe's golden eyes glinted.

"Give my best to the minister, Madam Gauze Fetcher."

"I will," I smiled then feigned seriousness. "But I think I received a promotion to Wall Inspector."

"My apologies, Inspector." Rafe tipped an imaginary hat and turned to traipse down the hall.

"I apologize that the state of the hospital was not up to your standards, Your Imperial Highness. I will speak with the staff at once about maintenance," The doctor blustered with a small bow, and a thin bead of sweat appeared on his brow.

I walked past him to start the trek to the front for the hospital. "Oh, that's—"

"It looks good, doesn't it?" Rafe called and I turned back around to see him walking backwards as he looked at me.

"What?"

"The wall, of course! Good thing you noticed!" Rafe's voice echoed down the hallway before he pivoted and disappeared around the corner.

I smiled and kept on my way with the doctor in tow. "Don't worry about it. I understand that the staff has their hands full. I just thought I'd lend a hand. Lord Roland is at the front you said?"

"Yes, Your Imperial Highness. He and Sergeant Hykner are waiting for you in the lobby."

"Most would say life is a gift and death is a curse.
But, when you live long enough, you realize that
it is life that is the curse, and death the gift."
-D

TWELVE

"Why did you come to get me?" I asked Roland as I slipped my arm into my coat and followed him and Hykner out the door to the car.

"I was on my way back from the Building of Ministries, and saw Hykner coming in. I figured if he was here, you and your sister were somewhere nearby and we could share a car home," Roland explained, opening the door for me as I slid inside the car. Hykner went around and hopped up front with the chauffeur, while Roland jumped in to take his seat across from me.

"Perfect timing," I tried to sound chipper, but even I could hear my voice betray my weariness.

"What's happened, Snowdrop?"

I looked at my hands in my lap, spotting where my fingers were stained from cleaning, and sighed heavily. "Nothing, just a long day."

"I'm sorry," Roland blinked at me, his eyes round with sympathy. "If you want to talk about it, you've got a sympathetic ear."

The sunset was reflecting off the pearly snow and ice that stubbornly clung to the landscape, bathing it in hues of orange and crimson. The image was beautiful, but the tinged snow made my mouth go dry. "Roland?"

"Yes?"

"How are things really going for our people?"

"In general, I think we are managing from an official standpoint. There are facets that could be better, of course. But, given that look on your face, you'll have to be a little more specific."

My fingers curled around the fabric of my dress. "Are children freezing in the street?"

Roland's dark eyebrows lifted and a shadow fell across his face. I half expected it to swallow his head. He folded his hands and rested them on his knee. "With recent events, current orphanages and refugee shelters are at capacity."

"Roland, the diplomat," I rolled my eyes impatiently. "So, that's a yes?"

"That's a complicated subject, Sorrel," Roland sighed, running a hand through his hair and resting it on the back of his neck.

"It's a simple question though." I narrowed my eyes. "If they are at capacity, then people are turned away and where do they go? Do we transport them somewhere new?"

"Not currently. There is no transportation plan in place," Roland admitted, keeping his voice level, though I could see a stiffness had claimed his posture. "The Ministries are all under greater strain now that the war has to be factored in."

I leaned my head against the window and closed my eyes as the car paused at the gates to the palace, waiting for them to open and allow us entrance. "So, they *are* turned out to the streets."

"There has just been a greater focus on the war front lately. Some things have slipped through the cracks but it has been—"

"Slipped through the cracks?" My eyes popped open, and Roland visibly shrunk back. Heat flushed my cheeks, and my blood was boiling. "I saw a child freeze to death today, Roland! He was five years old. Five! I carried him to the hospital myself. Did he slip through the cracks?"

"Statistically, in a cold climate like ours, hypothermia does kill—" Roland tried to quell the brewing argument with passive logic, floundering to find sense in the bits and pieces I was giving him, but an irate snarl of disgust sounded from my lips, interrupting Roland and surprising us both.

"Unacceptable," I murmured, and threw the car door open the moment we came to a stop, not waiting for anyone to formally release me. "That boy wasn't some flat statistic on a page."

I was breathing heavily, marching through the various corridors and upstairs.

"Sorrel?" I passed Kira in the hallway and her eyes widened as I ignored her and kept on walking. Behind me I heard her say to someone who'd joined after me, "She looks furious! Do you remember the last time Sorrel was that worked up about anything?"

"Not now, Littlest Princess," Roland's puffed breath sounded in response to Kira. "She's on a mission."

"Uh oh. You stoked the fire and said something stupid, didn't you?"

"Afraid so." Roland's words were full of remorse.

"Just bat your pretty eyes at her and she will forget it in an instant. Sorrel never holds grudges."

"I'd never count on that."

I wanted to turn around and scream at them. To tell them to be quiet and stop talking about me like I was overreacting or couldn't hear them. But, I didn't break my stride until my knuckles were rapping firmly on Papa's office door.

The posted guard dipped his head to me, clearly trying to not make eye contact.

"Who is it?" Papa's muffled voice carried through the doors.

"Sorrel," I called back, both the anger and exertion making my voice breathy and sharp.

"Come in." At Papa's command, the guard shifted and opened the door for me.

I stepped through the threshold into the room and realized I was trembling, but I kept my chin lifted.

"Sorrel, my dear, what's wrong?" Papa's eyes widened when he saw me and he rose to his feet and approached, then looked to his right. "Will you please excuse us for a moment, Friedrich?"

A jolt pierced my frazzled nerves as I realized that Papa and I weren't the only ones in the study. I caught sight of my disheveled appearance reflected in the ornate mirror over the fireplace. Loose hair falling out of my braided bun, my face flushed and blotchy, and a thin layer of perspiration on my brows. My chest was still heaving from rushing the whole way here.

"Of course," Friedrich acknowledged with a small dip of his head and exited the room.

Papa gripped onto my hands and gave them a squeeze before welcoming me into a full, comforting embrace. I accepted the hug and leaned gratefully against him.

"What's this about? What has you trembling like a leaf? You looked ready to burn down the place when you came in." We separated and Papa guided me to a chair, tugging one around for himself to face me.

"It was awful, Papa." I told him everything about Harvier, even my rant about the dirty wall in the hospital. The words tumbled out of me in a flurry. "I asked Roland if we had people being turned out into the streets and he—rather coldly might I add— said they were."

Papa nodded along patiently.

"I have a request," I started, suddenly feeling small and insignificant. Having a moment to calm my storming emotions, my usual pragmatism started to leak back into view and explain away my frustrations.

"You want to find a solution to help the displaced and the orphans?" Papa concluded with a soft smile, his kind eyes creasing.

I nodded, trying not to be meek. I felt strongly about this and there was no reason I should hide away from my desires for a proper solution.

My father leaned back in his chair, and rubbed his chin thoughtfully, his ringed fingers gliding over his beard with a faint *swishing* sound. "Refugee accommodations have been on the ministries' list for a while now, but it seems one of those items that's been left to sit too long. I will push it up the priority line, and will apply my mind to a solution."

"Thank you, Papa," I breathed.

He gave my hand another squeeze. "I'm sorry you had to experience that, my dear. If the hospital work is becoming too much—"

"It isn't!" I interrupted and bit my tongue. "That is, I think I actually love my work at the hospital, and would like to continue. I assure you, I can handle it."

"Sturdy, and reliable." Papa smiled broadly at me. "But so kind and caring. You make your kingdom proud. And I am proud of you too."

I wanted to melt into my seat, but a small part of me relished the praise. I was grateful that I was fortunate enough to have a father I could approach and be heard by. Not all royal families could boast the same family dynamics.

"Alright, best go and get ready for supper. I'll figure out your request on my end." Papa held out a hand to help me to my feet and walked me to the door. "Oh, and Sorrel?"

"Yes?" We paused and Papa gave me a knowing look.

"Do go ahead and make up with Roland. Men, though I hate to admit it, can sometimes put our feet in our mouths when we are trying to be helpful. Whatever he said, I'm sure it was his last intention to upset you."

My eyes widened in dismay. "How did you—?"

Papa smirked. "The look on your face, the comment you made, and the look on his face as he watched you storm in here. I've been in hot water with your mother, I know the signs. I'll bet he's waiting for you now."

I felt two inches tall. "Thank you for your time, Papa. I'll see you at dinner!" I mumbled and fled the study to, indeed, find an anxious and bewildered Roland awaiting me outside. I brushed past him, not quite ready to take a second attempt at conveying my distress.

"The crisp morning air and a little exercise I think will do us all a world of good," Mama tilted her face towards the white sunlight that was dappling the garden through the bare trees.

"And we have to plan for birthday festivities!" Kira chirped. She was bundled up in a thick sweater, two coats, and a scarf that obscured most of her face. The pink tip of her nose and ruddy cheeks peeked out between the burgundy knit and her blue eyes.

"You're *old* now, Kira Cat!" Theo jeered, poking Kira in the back with a grin.

"Am not!" She insisted. "I shall never be old. Mark my words Theodorvin, you pest."

"Everyone gets old, Kira," I threw in, pausing where Inessa had stopped our little family walk to lightly dust the frost from some roses.

"No, I will die forever young!" Kira crowed, whipping around in front of us to challenge us all.

"Kira, you shouldn't say stuff like that. What if the Divinities hear you and take you seriously?" Yulia wagged a finger.

"Well, I only mean my spirit. I don't think spirits can grow old."

"Are you doing alright, Mama?" I switched my attention from Kira's odd philosophizing to my mother. Her gait was slow and uneven, and I could tell from how she was holding herself that she was feeling stiff in the cold air.

"It's my back, I'm afraid. I think I might find somewhere to sit and read my Divinity scriptures."

"I thought you said the exercise was doing us all a world of good?" Inessa asked, a veil of irritability falling over her face.

"My heart is hammering away." Mama clutched at her chest,

and I moved to her side to offer support.

"I thought it was your back?" Ina pressed, and her expression puckered into a full scowl.

"Ina, relax. She's allowed to have more than one ailment at a time you know." I glared at my sister and helped walk Mama over to a bench in the garden.

"There is always something with her, isn't there? Nothing happens anymore without her giving up to some affliction," Inessa snorted and rolled her eyes. "I'm going inside. This was a pointless outing anyway. I knew we wouldn't make it very far."

"Ina, don't be so wretched to Mama!" I scolded but she had already succumbed to her poor mood and spun around to march back to the palace.

Though kind at her core, Inessa had always had a quick temper when it came to certain things— and people. Mama and Kira were both usually rather high on the list of irritants. It was true that as the years went on, Mama was under the weather more often than not, but there was never enough reason to assume she was exaggerating. I knew the constant issues grated Ina's nerves, Mama leaving early or not partaking in many things outside of church services and official parties, but sometimes it was just outright intolerant. It made me wonder how she had such an awful bedside manner at home but played her proper role at the hospital with relative ease.

Kira dithered back and forth, hopping from foot to foot before jogging off after Inessa. She waved a farewell. "Sorry, but if Ina spoiled the outing, I'm going inside to get warm! I'll see you all later and we can decide what we are doing for my birthday then. Feel better, Mama!"

Theo, Yulia, and I were left to stare after them.

"Don't glower, children," Mama soothed. "Ina will learn empathy someday. Life always has a way of forcing us to confront our shortcomings in order to grow them into strengths."

"The Virtues of the Divinities," Yulia and Theo replied in tandem, receiving an approving nod from our mother at the recognition of her reference to scripture.

"And can you two recite the Virtues?" Mama asked, fixing them with an expectant gaze. We had all been thoroughly brought up in the Church of the Divine, and could easily name all of the preached virtues of the Divinities in our sleep. But, something about being quizzed under Mama's scrutiny always made each of us second guess our answers.

"Patience, humility, justice," Yulia started, and Theo finished. "Compassion, charity, and diligence."

"Very good," Mama smiled.

I sat on the bench beside her, folding my senses into the silence that followed. Closing my eyes, my mind roved over each of the virtues and if I'd been exhibiting them properly. Perhaps, I had failed in some way and that was why the Divinities hadn't seen fit to let Harvier and his father survive. On the other hand, if they were magic Sympathizers, that might have also sealed their fate. Could someone as young and sweet as Harvier be condemned for evil?

My skin prickled with unease. He had merely been an obedient boy, listening to his father and staying put. Did corrupted children still obey their parents so earnestly? I'd seen the Shadow Wielder use her terrifying powers, but before that, she had been docile and, according to Yeneve, only acted out when one of her own was threatened. She had been bleeding and injured, seeking out medical help. Would the doctor have even known she was a Wielder if she hadn't lashed out?

Even so, endangering the patients in the tiny hospital seemed careless at best and wicked at worst. Where had everyone gone when they were swallowed by the shadow? Perhaps she killed them, smothering them in her darkness. Wounded or not, I couldn't forgive that. Wielders were terrifying and dangerous. Connection to the roots of evil was what gave them their abilities.

I couldn't refute that, as much as I wanted to empathize with everyone. There were those who didn't deserve understanding. Not when their sole purpose was destruction. Surely, in their case, the virtue of compassion was a weakness.

"You look stressed, Darling." I felt Mama's hand rest on mine. She inhaled sharply. "Goodness, your hand is cold as ice. Where are your gloves? Perhaps you should have gone inside with your sisters."

I opened my eyes and rested my head on her shoulder, reaching for the comfort of both my mother and the reassurance of faith in the Divine. "I'm alright. Just thinking about virtues."

"Anything you care to share?" She let go of my hand and wrapped her arm around me, holding me close. In front of us, Yulia and Theo had started dusting the frost off more flowers, just as they'd seen Inessa doing.

"How far do the Virtues of the Divine extend? Am I supposed to show compassion and patience even to those who justice is called upon?"

"Mmm." Mama ran her hand up and down my arm, and I found the gesture calming. "I don't think I have an answer that would satisfy a mind like yours. All I know is that each of the Divine Virtues has its place, and it is our duty to execute them all to the best of our abilities. Perhaps you should go visit Otvel and see what he has to say."

I lifted my head and smiled at my mother. "I think I will."

"I'm going back inside to rest. Sorry to say, I think even this was a little too much for my energy today. Take your brother and sister with you. It will do them good to hear further about the Divinities and more abstract thought. They both enjoy lectures on such topics." Mama released her hold on me and I helped her to her feet.

"Will you be able to make it on your own?" I couldn't help but fret. Mama's posture was hunched despite the fact I could see she was trying to hold herself tall.

"I'll be fine, Darling."

"Maybe you should call Klivech to look you over. I can go visit Otvel later. I'd rather make sure you are situated first."

"Alright, but promise me you'll still take those two with you.

Kira too, if you can wrangle her, though something tells me she's either firmly ensconced by a fireplace, or somewhere harassing Arrian and Roland." She waved Yulia and Theo to us, and as they raced over, eyes bright, I couldn't help but wonder what lengths I would go to in order to make sure they were safe and cared for. Would I turn to evil acts if it meant protecting them? Could the Divine forgive such selfish acts made with the best intentions?

"I promise, Mama." I nodded and continued to brace her as we headed back to the palace. Yulia quietly slipped into place on Mama's other side, and Theo fell in at the rear, ready to steady her if need be.

We walked slowly, careful to mind our steps on the frosty ground. Around us, I could see that the trees weren't fully bare anymore, and instead were showing signs of spring with tiny buds studding the branches.

Even though snow still lingered around, bits of green were finally starting to permeate the white blanket of winter. I spotted a cluster of blooming snowdrops and smiled to myself, feeling a small sense of pride and ownership over them for my nickname's sake.

When we finally entered the palace, I flagged a maid to find Doctor Klivech and send him to Mama's room. Larkin, Ina's and my lady's maid, appeared and took our coats and scarves from us and vanished in silence as quickly as she'd appeared.

"I wish this place had a lift sometimes," Theo commented absently as he trotted up the stairs.

"The stairs are good exercise for us," Yulia replied, still mirroring me on Mama's opposite side as we followed Theo.

"Spoilsport," He snorted. "We are active enough since Papa insists on a consistent exercise regime to keep our constitutions strong. Maybe that will be my first act as Imperial Ruler," He chuckled to himself.

"Your first act would be to install a lift in the palace we don't usually live in?" Yulia crinkled her nose.

"Maybe I'll want to live here in Tuyet. There is lots to do and it is the center of our country. It makes sense to live here, really."

"You'd miss the intimacies of Eisolde. I know I do." Yulia glanced down, her gaze wistful. I couldn't blame her. I missed Svyat Gavan too and longed to return to Eisolde. It was so cozy in comparison, while Tuyet's palace felt vast and cold.

"Theo, can you go on ahead and make sure the door to the room is open?" I piped up as we crested the flight of stairs that would take us to the bed chambers.

"Sure thing," He smiled resolutely and darted ahead of us. He took designated duties very seriously, using even simple ones like opening a door as practice for imperial reign. His childlike tendencies were beginning to fade, even at thirteen since his recent birthday, day by day, as he drew closer to adulthood.

"Sorrel?" I looked over my shoulder as I heard Papa's voice behind me. "May I have a word?" He looked from me to Mama and Yulia.

"Of course. Mama was a little tired after our walk, but I've already sent for the doctor to look her over," I assured as I turned to face my father fully.

"Geneva?" He took a step forward and Mama turned to wave him away.

"I'm fine, Genri. It's my back. The nerve is pinching again."

"Yulia, can you please take Mama the rest of the way?" I looked at my sister, and she nodded.

"What sweet, caring daughters I've been blessed with," Mama chuckled. "I appreciate the help, but you all needn't fuss so."

"We fuss because we care," I quipped back, giving Mama a small kiss on the cheek before briskly clearing the distance between me and Papa.

"Thank you, Sorrel, for always looking after the family's welfare so diligently."

I ducked my head in embarrassment. "Oh, it's nothing really."

"I've been thinking about your proposal last night." Papa clasped his hands behind his back and looked down at me.

"Oh!" I straightened, alert and intent on what solution he had come to. "Yes?"

"I've come to the conclusion that we are in need of a committee dedicated to seeing that more orphanages are available here in the capital, but also throughout the country," He started and my heart began to skip. "Additionally, that committee will be charged with providing the necessary transports and with working to reunite war-torn families and refugees. Does this satisfy your concern for our people's welfare?"

I clasped my hands together in delight and couldn't stop the wide smile from spreading across my face. "Oh, yes, Papa! Thank you. That will be marvelous. I can't tell you how pleased I am."

"Good." Papa grinned down at me and rested his hand on my shoulder. I could feel the warmth of happiness radiating from his touch, spreading through my body. "I'm glad you're so enthused, because I have also decided that you will be chairing the committee directly. You will need to coordinate with some members of the Ministries of Internal and Foreign Affairs— both of which being under the Rusevs, I'm sure you should have no trouble arranging. Foreign Affairs need only be involved with transport out of the country though. Roland has enough on his plate with his contributions to the war, so I'd like him to delegate and leave focus on managing our lines of communication with our allies and neutral countries. I wouldn't expect him at any meetings to help."

"I see," I blustered, my heels digging into the floor beneath me, searching for grounding.

"The Ministry of Commerce for necessary expenditures will contribute members as well. That should supply you with adequate means. I know you will do great things."

His words were meant as praise, but I stared up into his expectant gaze, the weight of responsibility and desire to prove my worth to him suddenly felt paralyzing.

THE DIVINE

The faith, practice, and church order of the Alse Hanya Church of the Divinities.

The Divinities are spiritual entities, or deities, worshiped broadly across the world of Alse Hanya by Mortalkind. This religion is one of three most commonly practiced, and is in most direct contrast with its counterpart, The Faith of the Founders.

The Doctrine of the Divine states that magical affinities belonged solely to the Divinities, and not to be wielded by mortal-kind, as magic corrupts humans and turns them to monstrous, evil beings.

In early centuries, a mortal managed to trick the Divinity of Compassion, and coveted magic for them self, stealing it from the heavens and spreading it around mortal kind. Unable to defer the corruption of pure power in impure hands, those labeled as Wielders, along with the power they then wielded were cursed to cause pain and ruin.

Ever since, followers of the Divine reject magic and its Wielders, denouncing them as evil entities with the singular purpose of spreading chaos and corruption.

THIRTEEN

The ground felt unsteady beneath my shaking legs as I walked towards the church with my brother and sister in tow. Mama had went ahead and had Dowels send word to the church of our expected arrival and my audience with Otvel while Papa had spoken with me.

His delegation to me weighed heavily on my shoulders under both honor and doubt, and I prayed to the Divinities I wouldn't buckle under it. He had called me into his office and given me paperwork on the finer details of the job, and I tucked them away in my room to review more thoroughly later.

It was a tremendous amount of trust my father was placing in me, and I was basking in the pride it filled me with. But, with that trust, came an even greater pressure to excel at my task. Not just for the sake of keeping Papa's good opinion of me as resourceful, responsible, and diligent in my pursuits, but also for the sake of those I'd been charged with helping.

My skin tingled with sympathy at the thought of families all over our country who had been torn apart. I couldn't fathom the depth of fear and pain they must be feeling. I didn't know how I would handle it if I were in their shoes. A nightmare alone was enough to rattle me to my very core at the mere subconscious implication that I might lose my family to Wielders. Would I be able to relate to these refugees and help them through the aftermath of such a harrowing experience? Was I qualified to care for the orphans I'd have to find shelter for, when there was no possible way I could reunite them with their dead parents? How could I hope to ease their suffering?

"You doubt yourself too much," Yulia assessed as she fell in step beside me. "You will do well caring for others. You always do."

My gaze shifted sideways to the soft features of her kind, earnest face staring up at me, firm in the resolve of her words. I sighed and fidgeted with the hem of my sleeve, the cool fabric against my fingers soothing to the touch.

"How did you know I was doubting myself? I haven't even told you what I'm worrying about." I smiled weakly. As my own words set in, my brows furrowed.

"Your face told me." Yulia shrugged and looked in front of her. "I heard what Papa said to you at the stairs. You're worried about the new job he gave you because you want to make sure no more families are in pain like that little boy you found the other day."

I stopped, mystification momentarily overpowering my ability to walk, and Theo slammed into my back.

"What is it?" He jumped away, startled by the abrupt pause, and I whirled around to give him a quick once over to make sure the impact, though minor, hadn't hurt him.

"Sorrel is silently pontificating her insecurities again," Yulia chuckled, never breaking her leisurely stride. The sun was in front of her, outlining her body in a golden glow, and turning her brown hair to a warm sienna. She looked beyond this world, like she could meld with the light and join the Divinities at any moment. It reminded me of when Papa used to make jokes about Yulia being not of the mortal world as a child because she was so perfect— a kind of perfect that seemed both effortless and sincere in a way that wasn't entirely comprehensible.

"And Yulia is being spooky again," I replied wryly, causing Theo to snort.

"She does that often, doesn't she?" He spread his arms out dramatically and did a quick spin to demonstrate he was, in fact, unharmed, and then tapped his finger to his skull. "I think she's deep in psychological warfare at this point. She always knows everything about everyone. She would make a fantastic spy."

"What do you know about psychological warfare?" I snickered and patted my little brother's head, though, in the last few months, and since having his thirteenth birthday, he wasn't terribly much shorter than me anymore.

"Plenty! I've been learning all I can about our country, military, and protocol systems. It's my *job* to know these sorts of things for when I take over the kingdom," Theo huffed, sticking out his chest proudly and pointing a thumb at himself.

"You do realize," Yulia finally paused, and when she tipped her chin over her shoulder at us, the sun reflected off her left eye, giving it the illusion of a milky white, while the other remained a discerning crystal blue. "In order for you to be ruler, it means Papa has to die?"

"Yulia," I breathed, ready to chide her for being so surprisingly blunt, but faltered when I saw the pain on her face. She wasn't bringing it up to be cruel to Theo, but rather it seemed that Theo's constant talking about taking over for Papa brought difficult thoughts and feelings to her when she thought of the realities of a change in leadership.

"That's not what I'm talking about, and you know it," Theo pouted, folding his arms and glowering at Yulia. He looked down at his feet and scuffed one on the frosty stone. "I just like to think about the future sometimes. I want to do right by everyone."

"Come on, you two. Otvel is expecting us." I ushered Theo

forward and Yulia turned back around. While she didn't like to think of a world without our father, and I knew Theo didn't want that either, I realized that the reason Theo talked so much about when he would someday be ruler was because he needed to believe he would survive his illness long enough to make it to that point in his life.

"Papa could live long enough that he becomes so old he can't do the job anymore, and just passes it on to me," Theo commented almost to himself.

"Like the immortal Dimaerians?" Yulia laughed, then shrugged when Theo and I gave her dubious looks in return. "What? I thought you said I was being *spooky*. What's spookier than the Wielders of death? Besides, you know that's not how succession has ever been carried out. The previous ruler either abdicates, which is the same as disgracing them self, or they die. Since Eisans are so proud, I'm not certain a father has ever seen his son take the throne here. It's sad, really."

"There is a first for everything, Yulia." Theo whisked himself in front of her, still cantering backward, and tapped his finger to her nose, eliciting a smile.

"True. And you know what, Theodorvin? I hope that you will be the one to bring that change about. You and Papa."

"Watch where you're going, please," I sighed, shaking my head as I gestured for Theo to walk normally, lest he fall and injure himself again. "I'm going to be discussing something specific with Otvel today. Do you two have any specific questions for him?" I shifted the topic to a better focal point as we approached the entrance of the church.

"I'm going to pray over Mama. And the war of course," Yulia tapped her chin rhythmically.

"I'll pray that all the Wielders in Eisa are wiped out!" Theo declared, swinging his arm out to the side. "And that the Sympathizers are dealt with."

"Just in Eisa? Wouldn't that be prayer for the world?" Yulia tipped her head to the side.

"Good point. The whole world then, but I feel no shame in having it start with Eisa." Theo nodded along, and he and Yulia kept up their discussion as we stepped into the church.

I flinched at my siblings then wondered why their words elicited such a response from me. They were good prayers in essence and would aid in the quest for restoring peace to the world. Then I thought of Harvier.

"Go on and have a seat." I pointed to the pews, and Yulia waved me off, shaking her head. They knew where to go without me mothering them. "I will be back to join you for prayer shortly."

I separated from my siblings as they took their places to pray, and wandered to the back of the church where Otvel would be waiting for my arrival. I slipped around a partition and spotted him sitting on the steps that would lead to the bell tower and other miscellaneous nooks and crannies for managing the church. I knew the passages well from when Roland, Inessa, and I would explore them as children, back before Yulia, Arrian, and Kira joined in any of our small adventures in the capital.

Otvel's hands were folded in front of his face, and his gaze was fixed on the ground in front of him, so I was certain he hadn't noticed my presence. There was something in his demeanor that felt cold and hard, unlike his typical more jovial display.

"Good afternoon, Priest Chinye!" I hailed, the address feeling foreign on my tongue, though I still found it good form to use proper titles in such a sacred space. It was expected to show such respect in the building where the priests were sovereign and everyone else, royal or common born, were equal subjects under the watch of our Divinities— even if this particular church was still on the palace grounds.

Otvel snapped from his trance and blinked at me before a smile spread across his face. The pensive tension in his brow melted away as the familiar warmth crept back into his skin.

"Good afternoon, Princess Sorrel." He inclined his head to me and gestured to the seat in front of him. "Your mother informed me that you had questions you wished to ask regarding our Divine Virtues. She also warned you'd get me thinking, so I've fortified myself. Ask at your leisure."

I always appreciated that Otvel didn't care too terribly much for formalities. Even though *I* felt it necessary to follow protocol, I never felt comfortable when it was directed at me. There were few people in this world I truly felt I could exist on the same plain with; my family, Roland, Lord Friedrich, and Otvel. I swallowed a smile as the wall cleaning man from yesterday also came to my mind as someone to add to the list of those who left the pomp and circumstance at the door.

I took my seat and twisted my fingers together until my knuckles yielded against the contortions with a loud sequence of pops. Since the conversation with my mother, I had contemplated countless ways of articulating my question and feelings, but now, facing Otvel directly, all those well-thought out theses fell away from grasp. I was well aware that once I started work on the new committee I would be met with countless children in Harvier's position, or even like the Shadow Wielder hiding as a patient in the hospital, and the responsibility wasn't lost on me.

"Speak your mind, there is nothing to fear here," Otvel urged me, leaning forward intently.

Finding my voice, I finally managed to get the words out, "I don't understand why the Virtues work for some and not for others."

"Go on, I can tell you have more tumbling in that clever mind of yours. There is no judgment here."

"I understand that the Divinities reject the unnatural abilities and condemn Wielders for stealing power from the Divinities and twisting it into terrible curses," I prattled on.

Otvel nodded along and let me continue without interruption.

"But, what of the Sympathizers? If Wielders are monsters in human form, then aren't the Sympathizers just lost, misguided souls that could be saved if we applied our Divine Virtues to them?" I implored and baited my breath for his reply, anxious for the clarity I hoped his words would provide me. Answers always made me feel better.

"I think you mistake the Virtues as gifts we bestow on others, easily and freely." Otvel shook his head slowly from side to side, his long beard mirroring the motion. "We do not show compassion to a beast when it charges against us in the way that we spare its life. Not when doing so allows our own light to be extinguished by its darkness, or to allow it to extinguish the lights of countless others. If you mistake waver in resolve for compassion, then you are doomed to a life of destruction. You become complicit in their destruction, enabling it to spread. No, your compassion is best served protecting the flock rather than allowing the wolf into the pasture to dawn sheep's clothing and kill freely."

"So, then justice becomes the primary Virtue when facing an adversary?" I tried to quantify the order of the virtues' importance in my mind, but couldn't find a sensible sequence to the effort.

"Patience, humility, justice, compassion, charity, and diligence." Otvel ticked off the virtues on his fingers. He looked in the direction of the front of the church towards Yulia and Theo, and half of his face was engulfed by the shadow of the partition. "It is *charitable* and *compassionate* to enact *justice* upon those who have broken the laws of nature for their own selfish gain—and all those who support the progression of this evil to occur in our world. You must have *patience* with the process in order to perform due *diligence* and *humbly* serve the Divinities, and the people, despite any faltering selfish desires."

"What if…" I dug my nails into the palms of my hand. "A person is good at heart? Is it not possible for them to be set straight? A child following in their father's footsteps. Surely the children are young enough to spare such a cruel form of justice? It can't be that black and white. There is more than one way to display the Virtues, right?"

Otvel's face swiveled back to look at mine, the shadow that obscured half of his features now washed away by light pouring in from the window above us as the sun started its descent towards sunset. He was emanating the glow, like one of the Divine had touched him and given him his next words them self.

"You mustn't let your resolve waver. Diligence means removing the blight of darkness in this world, and once someone has been exposed to that corruption there is no saving them. The darkness will consume them given time. They are no longer human, and it is a mercy to relieve them of that suffering."

"Even a ch—"

"—Yes. Even a child. Corruption doesn't discriminate."

My heart turned heavy as stone, and for a very rare moment, I actually felt a chill overtake my body. Had Harvier's death then been a mercy from the Divinities? Would he have grown into a man who would fight for his country, or a monster seeking destruction?

"I hear you've been given a new responsibility of bringing families together and homing orphans. I believe our discussion couldn't have come at a better time for you to begin your new role. You will have a greater purpose and power to protect your people from evil." Otvel rose to his feet and placed a hand on my shoulder and gave it a squeeze. As he did, the crack of uncertainty in my gut yawned open to a chasm of doubt. "Do you understand now, how delivering justice is compassion?"

Harvier's kind eyes and words of gratitude as Hykner carried him away lingered behind my gaze. I didn't even know if his father was guilty of being a Sympathizer for certain. Perhaps justice had been enacted prematurely. Was that a sin? Inessa's philosophical words to me on the steps of the hospital permeated my thoughts, and the true root of the question I sought an answer to crystallized in my mind.

Who were we to assume it was our divine right to deliver judgment to humanity, through the steep toll of life and death, when we didn't have the full truth ourselves?

I slowed my breathing to quell my thundering heart threatening to storm from my chest as the world spun around me. Then, finding my gravity once more, I smiled and placed my hand on top of Otvel's, nodding. The skin beneath mine felt cold and callous, but not in the physical sense—it was the conviction of his words racing through his veins beneath his skin.

I wanted to share them, but something in that touch was telling me they wouldn't sustain me. I still didn't understand well enough to share his devout conviction. Perhaps my faith was shaken and I needed to pray in solitude to tend to my own personal connection with the divinities and find clarity in the war of wicked instinct versus reverence. I'd had my dreams disturbed by a curse. Was I corrupted through contact? Would justice come to claim my head someday?

I can't answer yet. Something isn't making sense.

"Yes, I understand. Thank you," I lied.

FOURTEEN

Something heavy pressed against me, pulling me out of a pleasant dream I was having about the Singing Ice Caves to the east. I'd always begged Mama and Papa to take me there as a child, but our holidays away from Eisolde never took us to that part of Eisa, so I could only ever dream of what I'd read of them.

"Mmm," I grumbled as two fingers brushed my face and gently pulled my right eyelid open. My vision was blurred with the stupor of waking, but I didn't need much to go off for the blob of fair skin ornamented with icy gold to be recognizable as Kira.

"Sorrel?" She whispered, her face close enough for me to smell coffee on her breath. "Wake up!"

I tugged my arm free of the covers and spread my hand over her face to push her off me. "What?"

"It's first light!" Her words were muffled under my hand but it did little to dampen the enthusiasm.

"Not yet," I mumbled, and pushed my face into my pillow. Much preferring long nights, early mornings were never my favorite and I resisted them at every opportunity.

"Yes, it is. The sun doesn't rise on your schedule. We are going to miss it!" Kira ducked away from my reach and slid off my bed. Her next tactic was to rip the covers off me and tug at my arm.

I sighed and rended myself from the comfort of my pillow, sitting up to rub at my eyes and blink the sleep away. Inessa was sound asleep in her adjacent bed, and I knew she would remain there, undisturbed. A chill bit the air, and even the scullery maid had yet to tend to our morning fire, but Kira was shifting eagerly from foot to foot, an energetic heat beaming from her face.

"It took me such a long time to fall asleep, I should have just stayed awake," I muttered and yielded to Kira's impatient tugging, exiting my bed fully. My feet found slippers instead of ground and I realized she had placed them ahead of time to speed me up.

"Grab your wrap and let's go. Yulia is waiting for us and she already has your tea, so no more delays." She slipped behind my back and ushered me out of the room. I barely snagged my wrap in time before we departed. As soon as she pulled the door closed behind us, she swiveled around to my front again and tugged me along behind her, giggling along the way.

Her laughter was always so infectious, I would hear myself joining in before I even realized I had. Our cadence of steps changed to more of a skip as we laughed through the palace to where Yulia was waiting for us at the stairs, two cups of tea and one cup of steaming cocoa precariously in hand.

She handed us our respective cups and the three of us grinned at each other, clinking them together and quickly consuming them as fast as we could. Kira finished first, able to down the scolding water with greater tolerance than Yulia or I. The warmth spread like fire through me, stoking my alertness and excitement.

Every year since Kira could walk, she had been completely captivated by the rising sun first thing in the morning— so much so that she had tried to wake the whole family to share in her enthusiasm. But, only Yulia and I had agreed to sneak through the dark at the cusp of dawn to take in the first rays of scarlet streaking through the indigo of night and put the stars to bed.

Part of the splendor, we knew, correlated to the specific sunrise on her birthday, because she had come into the world at sunrise sixteen years earlier. It was early spring and our territory liked to linger in the clutches of winter, but it seemed that Kira's birthday always marked the beginning of the true thaw without fail.

So, from that first adventure, it had become our tradition that us three would rise before daybreak, and sneak out to watch the sunrise, and witness the moment when the countryside welcomed the warmth and peeled away the frost. Since Kira was always chilled, we had started incorporating a warm beverage into the ritual around her sixth birthday. We were late to the sunrise, not scheduling our timing properly, that year, but it seemed that the Divinities held off on the thaw until Kira appeared on the balcony to see it. After that, we made sure to get up a little earlier to allow for the necessary preparation.

"It's time!" Kira gasped, abandoning the cup on the stairs for some poor maid to come across later, and bolted into the sitting room that would take us to the small balcony. It was seldom used since the palace was so big, and the windows all faced directly east, making the morning stuffy on warmer days.

Yulia and I set our cups down too and linked arms to trail after Kira. She threw the balcony door open and took a deep breath before flinging herself straight to the railing. Yulia shivered and tugged at her wrap as we joined Kira, the morning air still cold enough to promote frostbitten dewdrops. A wave of wistfulness crashed over me and I thought of how different the view from this balcony was from the one I stepped onto the night of the stampede. It had been bitterly cold that night too.

I wished that the mornings had been warmer sooner this year. Then maybe Harvier would have survived, along with countless other children. As I was preparing for the first official meeting of my new committee I had been flooded with so many tragic situations, I'd felt hollow and grief stricken for days, and my talk with Otvel had done little to satisfy my confusion. So much chaos and heartache had descended upon our country in the last few months, and it was hard to not be swept away into the pits of despair and the frightful unknown.

I shook the thoughts away, and pushed my focus back into the moment. This was a happy occasion. There were no stampedes, and the mark of the new warmer season meant less children and families struggling in the harsh winter elements. This moment was *good*, not sad. I wouldn't allow my tumultuous thoughts to disturb the fragility of our blissful morning.

None of us spoke for a while, instead watching the sky intently while it transitioned from its deep infinite midnight blue, and the stars went to sleep one by one. On the horizon, a golden hue budded around the far off mountain peaks, followed closely by a ruddy pink and crisp periwinkle so sharp in contrast with each other that the rich pastel pigments collectively sliced through the dark.

As the pink rippled to scarlet with the climbing sun, I changed my view to take in Kira. Her expression was bright with wonder and so deeply affected by the experience. I could see the rays of sunshine reflecting in her eyes, and for that moment, Kira might as well have been the sun for how much joy was glowing in her face. When she made eye contact with the sunlight, that was always my favorite part to see, and every year, it seemed her connection grew stronger. Like the sun rose just for her.

"I don't think I ever noticed the first warm sunrise before Kira," Yulia sighed, mirroring our little sister's marvel. The simplicity of an everyday occurrence turned spectacular.

"We were pretty young. I wouldn't expect little girls to notice such things." I tilted my head and inhaled deeply.

"Kira noticed though."

"Yes, she did." I smiled as I looked at Kira in front of me. She was standing on her tiptoes, her chin tilted to the sun. As the light inclined over her, she closed her eyes and let her wrap slip from her shoulders to spread her arms out to either side. She was basking in the sudden glow like a sunflower. "Kira is special like that."

While Kira welcomed the warmth, I silently bid farewell to the ice and frost that had started to melt to make room for the new season. The fractals and dewdrops reflected the light like stars on a glade, and the moment felt so still and peaceful. It was a tiny spec of time that was warm inside and out. It held an energy to it of anticipation of life to come filled with endless love and laughter and hope— something that couldn't be planned or captured. But, the excitement wasn't boisterous or assuming. It existed in the folds of silent fleeting seconds, hidden until you looked over your shoulder at moments passed. This was one of those rare instances though, where each of us standing on the balcony knew we were in that folded piece of precious time, and were drinking in every last drop of it.

We felt that significance every year, just for a matter of minutes. None of us could explain it to anyone who might ask us, but we felt it all the same. It was short, beautiful, calm, and it was all ours. It was a feeling I wished I could bottle up and share with the world— anyone suffering or celebrating could have a sip and take pause to have that sixty seconds of reprieve from everything else in the world. No war, no committees to run, no loved ones lost or estranged, no wounds, no poverty, no curses or doubt or hate. Only peace and quiet euphoria. The vibrance of the moment bled through my entire body, dispelling all negativity lurking beneath my skin, replacing it only with pure uninhibited contentment.

"You look pensive," Yulia poked me in the side. "What's on your mind?"

"I thought you always knew," I chuckled.

Yulia smirked. "Not always. Just when people forget themselves and their expression shifts, or they forget I'm there and disclose private things."

"I'm just happy."

"I am too."

"So am I! It's not quite the same as Svyat Gavan, but so long as the ice melts, I'm happy wherever I am," Kira cheered, flouncing over to throw her arms around our shoulders and rejoin the conversation. Her skin was warm to the touch, and I laughed at how much of the sun she'd managed to soak up. "Sixteen! Can you scarcely believe it?"

"Not at all," Yulia and I chorused behind stifled grins.

"I hope that no matter where we go when we are all old and married, we find a way to always make sure to still watch the sunrise on my birthday together like this." Kira exhaled slowly, and the love and contentment she was feeling was almost palpable and equally as contagious as her laughter. Yulia and I leaned our heads in against hers, our own long dark locks framing the gold between us.

"Us middle children should stick together after all," I turned and extended my hand to my sisters, pinky lifted. "Let's promise, no matter where we are or what's happening in our lives, we will always watch the sun come up on Kira's birthday."

Kira grinned so broadly, I thought the smile might split her face in two. She linked pinkies with me, and somehow she felt even warmer than before from the enthusiasm radiating from her. Yulia slipped her pinky into the mix and we shook on it.

"What's on the agenda for the rest of the day?" Yulia inquired and I rested my elbows on the railing of the balcony to lean against it.

Kira perked up and poked her head through the door to check the time. "Next, I told Roland and Arrian— I'm not sure he will get up extra early for this though— to meet us down here promptly after dawn so we could play cards or have a chess tournament. Probably chess. Then breakfast, family fun for the day, and Papa is taking us all to a special show tonight."

"But you always beat everyone at chess," Yulia whined, drooping her head.

"Everyone always says that so no one ever plays with me anymore, and it's *my* birthday so we get to do things *I* enjoy for today. I enjoy chess. Besides, Roland keeps up pretty well. Arrian is the only one who ever beats me. And Sorrel isn't half bad either when she focuses. You see, Yulia, it's all about planning ahead several turns…"

As Kira launched into a small impromptu lecture on the strategies of chess playing, which Yulia took in amicably, I allowed my mind to wander while it was still steeped in serenity. I closed my eyes and enjoyed the sunshine and company of my sisters. Inessa would be waking soon, though she never acknowledged her absence from our yearly tradition, and Theo was no doubt beginning his daily routine as well. Papa was likely heading to his study, while Mama would take her coffee in bed, and wait for her whirlwind of a daughter to command her attention.

Roland was likely an early riser on account of his job with the ministries, but since all of our birthdays were basically considered unofficial holidays, he'd have been free to rise a bit earlier than usual to be dressed and ready to meet us down here right after daybreak. Arrian would either match his brother, or take advantage of the day free of duty and sleep extra late.

My eyes popped open and threatened to bulge out of my head. I replayed the last thought over. They would be dressed to meet us down here after our special sisterly moment. Our special moment was over, which meant he was due to arrive any moment.

"Kira!" I gasped, and retrieved her wrap from the damp ground, thrusting it into her arms.

"What?" She crinkled her nose in confusion, and Yulia's eyes darted between us.

"You said Roland was coming down to meet us?"

"Yeah?"

"He is here now, in fact." Roland's voice, low with an early morning huskiness, sounded through the doorway as he made his entrance.

I stiffened and, a second later, the same realization hit Yulia and she pulled her wrap around her body self consciously. Kira, however, was blissfully unaware and threw herself at Roland for a hug.

"Good morning and happy birthday, Littlest Princess!" He laughed, hugging her as best he could with the two chess sets and pack of cards he was carrying. "I couldn't get Arrian to haul himself down here for the tournament, but I brought the games as requested. He said he'd meet us for breakfast though, and I think he even has a special gift for you."

"Color me intrigued!" Kira stifled a squeal and released Roland.

He looked up and his eyes locked on me, then slowly took in my appearance from head to toe. We were all in our nightgowns, hair down and disheveled, and were in no way presentable to be in anyone's presence, let alone a lord— even if it was Roland.

"Kira, I think you might have thought this through a little better," Yulia hissed through a tight smile.

"What do you mean?" Kira took one of the chess sets from Roland and tilted her head to the side.

"We are in our sleeping attire.," I sighed.

"So? We don't get up early enough to bother getting dressed. That's why we bring our wraps. Hmm, we need a table. I forgot about that."

"It's immodest," Yulia mumbled bashfully, and scuffed her foot. "Don't pretend you weren't taught these things."

"Eh, you and I are fine." Kira shrugged, and paused her excuses to point Roland to a small table in the sitting room. "The only one he will be looking at indecently is Sorrel anyway. Who cares? It's not like we are naked. No one will be down here to scold us for a while. Come on, let's play!"

I was certain I was going to liquefy from embarrassment, and Roland quickly averted his gaze from me, his cheeks flushing red. I was torn between mortification and a small sense of satisfaction that Kira's assessment of Roland's attention had been accurate.

"Look! He's blushing. I don't think I've ever seen him blush," Kira heckled, and Yulia chided her softly as Roland set up our game table and retrieved four chairs for us before stepping back and folding his arms over his chest.

"Sorry," I muttered and he shrugged.

"The truth can hurt sometimes, can't it?" He laughed and shifted next to me while my sisters went to work setting up the chess board.

"You're being awfully forward today," I bit my lip and looked at my feet.

Roland stole a look at Yulia and Kira to make sure their attention was elsewhere, then reached forward to grasp at a lock of my hair. He let his hand slide slowly down the length of it from my chin to my waist. His fingers lightly grazed my neck as they passed, and my whole body tensed. I looked up at his face to see him looking at me adoringly, and was once more lost in the space between embarrassment and vanity.

"I haven't seen you with your hair down since you were Kira's age." His words were gruff and breathy, quiet so as to not be overheard above the clattering of chess pieces. "It's nice."

"It needs a good brush," I babbled, pawing at my hair self-consciously. "I didn't know you'd be here or I would have looked... better."

"There are plenty of terrible and ugly things to wake up to in the morning, but I can't ever see you being one of them, Snowdrop." He leaned a hair closer and his voice dropped to a rumble, and I was suddenly aware of how thin my nightgown felt around me in his presence. "I think it would make me much slower to leave bed in the morning."

My jaw dropped and I gave a hoarse laugh of disbelief. I could count on one hand the times when Roland had been so direct in his attraction to me. Each time it happened I could hardly believe it, and was more inclined to think I had imagined the whole thing. More often than not, we danced on the edge of banter and flirtation. Being direct wasn't our typical strong suit.

"Ahem," Kira's pointed cough behind Roland made me wince. "Can you drool over my sister later, please? You're here for part of *my* birthday celebration, so look sharp!"

"So much for our solidarity as sisters," I wilted at her unsolicited commentary and slunk to my seat.

Kira pumped a fist in the air. "Middle siblings forever! Just speaking the obvious. Alright, I'm going to play against Sorrel, and Yulia against Roland. Winners play the final round together."

"To be honest, I didn't really think anything of the invitation being so early and that you might not be properly attired. If you want to change into something more proper, that's fine. I don't want to make anyone uncomfortable," Roland replied briskly.

"No, we are playing," Kira commanded. " I promise we will change after our tournament, you bunch of prudes. This is the only point in the day where it will be just us four, so we don't have time to go inside. It'll just draw attention and Ina will ask Sorrel questions, Mama will hear me and Yulia go to our room. Roland will wander off while waiting for us and get roped into some job. Then all will be lost! Please? I love them, but it's just different. I want this to be just us."

I hiked my shoulders up and ran my tongue along my teeth, weighing her proposition. Being as the damage had already been done, there didn't seem much point in drawing things out by arguing. Sometimes with Kira, the quickest way out was through.

"You win, let's play," I conceded and squared up to the chess board opposite her. "But if we get caught out here, we are all blaming you, and Roland will have to get shoved off the balcony."

Everyone burst out laughing and agreed, then we respectively began our matches. It was silent except for the clicking of our pieces. Roland apologetically beat Yulia relatively quickly, and though I held my own for a respectable length of time, I too was outmatched by Kira.

The final round came down to Roland and Kira, and lasted the longest stretch of time. The pace of movement ebbed and flowed with rapid execution and thoughtful pauses. There was a rare pensive scowl on Kira's brow that told us Roland was giving her a good fight and keeping her sharp. Eventually, he brought about his own demise by losing his queen for failing to think enough steps ahead, leaving Kira the reigning champion of the tournament.

"She should win on her birthday anyway," Roland huffed, feigning poor sportsmanship for a moment before tousling Kira's hair and pointing her to the door. "Go scout ahead, and make sure we won't be spotted, little ball of mayhem."

She gave him an impish grin and yanked Yulia away from the table with her. "Your consolation prize for a worthy match, I give you my sister! Put away the games please!" And both she and Yulia vanished into the palace.

"If I had known this would be the consolation prize, I would have lost much sooner." Roland ran a hand through his hair before it dropped to cover a yawn. "She certainly does have a lot of energy and orders first thing in the morning, doesn't she? I'd even say it borders on bossy at times," He chuckled.

I stooped and collected the pieces, returning them to their case. Static pulsed between us with an electric current that made the hairs raise on my arms. "We should probably wait for her to say it's all clear, right? Or do you think she abandoned us?"

"We could dance. That went well before. Or just stand here together. Anything to be close to you, Snowdrop, even a second longer."

"You shameless flirt," I teased. Maybe it was the warmth of the morning, or I was feeling the effects of Kira's brazen influence. Or, perhaps, I was simply equally as tempted as Roland. Whatever it was, I seized the rare shift of confidence and decided to push the envelope a hair further. "All this bravado, yet you've never even bothered to even try to kiss me. You've wanted to, haven't you?"

Roland leaned across the table, placing his cheek so close to mine, my skin tingled with the anticipation of inevitable contact. "I've wanted to. But everyday since I first realized that, I've been more and more certain that if I broke down and kissed you, I wouldn't be able to stop there."

His breath tickled my ear, rough and seductive. It was almost enough for me to abandon all sense of rules and propriety and tell him to kiss me then and there anyway. But then he leaned back and cleared his throat.

"Tempt me not, Snowdrop."

"I said nothing," I laughed, though I knew even I was fighting my own urges at this point.

"When will you realize that you don't have to say a word?" Roland sighed heavily and pivoted towards the door, sweeping the chess sets and cards into his hand as he went. "Let's make our grand escape while we still can."

I stood and took several deep breaths, taken aback by both the candor and the sensual tension that had whipped up out of nowhere like a cyclone and vanished with Roland through the door. Clarity rattled me, and I suddenly felt small and embarrassed by the exchange, the impropriety we'd exhibited, and haughty words spoken.

Where did that all come from? Had I really been so bold as to asked him for a kiss? No wonder he'd fled. I hadn't the faintest idea what could have possessed me to behave in such a lewd manner.

Rolling my shoulders back, I counted to ten and followed after the others. Perhaps with the rest of the excitement, the whole thing would soon be forgotten. Or, so I hoped.

FIFTEEN

We were all thoroughly worn out from the high paced energy and early start of Kira's birthday by the time we left the palace for the final event. I tried not to think of the long day awaiting me tomorrow, full of appointments and obligations. I would be glad to get back to the hospital and was even hopeful that if we weren't out too late, I could bother Klivech for some quick lessons before my shift in the morning.

The show we were attending was a concert and ballet. Papa had spared no expense in hiring the best performers for Kira and she was bubbling over with excitement, twirling and swaying all the way into the theater. There were people in the streets still, though mostly merchants closing shop for the night, and various customers bustling to and fro to finish their errands in time. I caught a glimpse of a group of huddled figures lurking in the alleyway, their faces obscured by the shadows. Their forms were lean and hard, and when the lights of a passing car illuminated the street, I could see the eyes of both men and women were trained on me and my family until we were swallowed by the vestibule.

"What is the story? You can't tell a thing from the posters." Theo paused in the lobby to scrunch his face at a poster.

"I believe it is a romance," Arrian commented, stopping beside Theo. "A strange one at that."

Kira linked arms with Theo, too swept up in her enthusiasm to remember her usual impatience with our fragile little brother. He looked mildly surprised at the friendly display, but smiled down at her. Now that he had officially grown taller than her, Kira was the smallest in the family, and Theo was thrilled.

"It's a wonderful story," She flashed Arrian a look before continuing. "About a princess who ran away from home and was lost in the Eisan mountains for so long she fell under a curse and started to turn to ice. Do you remember that lullaby Mama used to sing to us?"

"The one about the maiden seduced by the beauty of winter?" Arrian raised his brows.

"Yes, that's the one!"

"I have a hazy memory of my mother singing that to me and Roland too." Arrian's gaze clouded for a moment, conjuring wistful memories of a mother he had never known.

"The ending was always so unclear. Does she die?" Theo furrowed his brows.

"No, silly. What is the story in that?"

"A tragedy," Yulia commented matter-of-factly, a step behind the other two.

"No one wants to hear a story about needless tragedy, Yulia. We want happy endings! Triumphs of good versus evil and hardship. Overcoming all odds!" Kira declared then turned her focus back to a captivated Theo. "This version of the story is about her rescue from the cruel winter by a dashing explorer. He reverses the snow curse placed on her and when she returns to her kingdom, they get married and live happily ever after, reigning together."

"What happened to her kingdom while she was away? Why did she get to resume her reign?" Arrian asked, grinning at his successful provocation when Kira scowled.

"Because that's the story."

"It sounds interesting, Kira," Theo offered kindly, and Kira leaned her head against his arm.

"It doesn't make much sense," Yulia grumbled.

"Oh, just wait till you see the dancing. It's Sorrel's favorite too!"

I nodded. "It's very beautiful to watch the scenes in the mountains with all the ice and snow. The Princess' costume is usually made up of a thousand crystals to look like ice. It's breathtaking."

"Exactly. And the music they use is supposed to be an homage to the Singing Ice Caves. The Ballad of Moroz is originally a warning about venturing too far into the frozen wastelands."

"I was just dreaming of those caves this morning. I always wished to visit there," I sighed and closed my eyes, trying to envision the images from my interrupted dream.

"Otvel told me the caves seem like magic, but it's some sort of natural phenomenon, so it's alright that they exist," Yulia asserted to no one in particular. The comment felt a little stilted, and not entirely connected to our discussion, causing me to cast a sidelong glance at her. Yulia herself appeared to be taking on a more prickly mood from the moment we stepped into the theater. She'd seemed fine on the ride over.

"I want to go see the caves too. I never get to go anywhere," Theo grumbled then lifted his chin to smile at me. "We will have to go together someday, Sorrel."

"You know why you can't go, Theo. You're the heir, I'm not sure why you whine about it so much," Yulia narrowed her eyes, the surly words tumbling through her lips in a muted murmur, and I almost wondered if she'd meant to say them out loud in the first place.

"I'd love that, Theo!" I grinned back and slipped my arm

into his, opposite Kira, moving past Yulia's dig. "But, Papa always talked so fondly of it, we will have to have him take us."

"I've never actually been there myself. It would be a first for all of us." Papa's voice sounded up ahead where he'd turned to join our discussion. He pressed his hand to his chin thoughtfully. "I've been procrastinating on that long enough. I think we should plan a trip there in the next year. I'll make room for it in our schedules."

"We can't do that with the war, surely," Yulia frowned, then tipped her head slightly to the side. "Does anyone else hear that peculiar hissing sound?"

I crinkled my nose at Yulia's question, straining to listen for any trace of hissing. Inessa, who was walking ahead with Mama, Friedrich, and Roland, whipped her head around. Roland paused his conversation with his father to look sharply from Yulia to my father, and then Inessa. The two shared a concerned expression, before both glanced around the lobby. He had been particularly distant following our nearly romantic moment on the balcony, only adding to my growing mortification, and I noticed that his attention had been pulled several different directions for the rest of the day.

Idiotic girl! You were ridiculous and embarrassed both of you bringing up a kiss like that.

It wasn't uncommon for his aloof side to surface in the presence of the whole family, but it still felt strange to me that he swung so drastically from deliberately voicing his desires to barely acknowledging me. However, looking at his reaction to Yulia, Papa and Inessa, I could see his focus was elsewhere, and somewhere far more important than his flirtations with me. I kicked myself mentally for my self importance, and the indecent nature of my thoughts.

"Yulia is right," Inessa assessed briskly, glossing over Yulia's second observation since none of the rest of us were able to verify it. "A trip to the caves in the east during the height of war will send the wrong message to the public."

"I'm sure there will be things in Princess Sorrel's new capacity as head of the orphanages and refugee restoration committee that will take her all over the country once it has gotten established. That will be an excuse enough to go to Kyrith and explore some caves for the day," Friedrich offered a solution for us, patting Papa on the back. "Who's going to tattle on the Imperial Emperor for 'playing hooky' for the day? Besides, it's always best in times like these to look to a brighter future. It helps it come about instead of promising a bleak one."

"But— " Yulia started to protest but was cut short by Mama.

"Yulia, please. I'm not sure what has gotten into you tonight, and I'm surprised I even have to remind you of this at your age. This is a celebration for your sister. Please don't spoil the mood."

Yulia ducked her head, and Inessa glared at Mama. She held her soured expression at our mother as she doubled back to link arms with Yulia and began talking quietly with her. It was too low to hear, but I was sure she was comforting and commiserating with her.

Mama did have a point though in that Yulia was being particularly negative. Given what a good mood she'd been in earlier, her more dry commentary felt oddly abrasive. I wondered if she was simply overtired. Being the closest to Kira, she was run ragged the most by her antics and was likely more worn out than the rest of us.

"That's alright, Yulia!" Kira spoke loudly, her voice carrying around the group. "You're always thinking ahead and that's why I am convinced you would be an excellent chess player if you would just apply that foresight into the game."

The mood shifted back to pleasantries as smiles slowly melted through the tension. Theo asked Kira more questions about the show we were seeing and she answered each one eagerly. I detached from my hold on my brother and fell behind the rest of the group, happy to observe their interactions in place of my own as we made our way to our box. I took my seat between Inessa and Yulia, and stared at my program. Trailing my fingers over the ornately designed snowflakes, I attuned my ears to the conversations of those around me.

Mama was asking for a glass of water, Papa was discussing the ice caves with Theo, and Inessa had turned around to make small talk with Roland and Friedrich sitting behind us. Arrian was tapping his foot and rolling the program between his hands. I looked up and glanced at Kira, surprised when I didn't hear her voice in the mix around me.

She sat completely erect, her eyes fixed on the stage below. We'd helped her style her hair in her first official formal updo, twisted and rolled against the length of her head with sparkling pins peaking out between the strands of gold. I noticed her matching necklace from Arrian dangling from around her neck, and recalled how Arrian had almost bashfully presented it earlier. In a more understated blush colored dress and tiara she looked so elegant and refined. Nostalgia tugged at my heart to see her so grown up.

Though it was her captivation with the approaching show that kept her calm and quiet, and I knew that she could just as easily leap to her feet and cause a commotion at any moment, I could see how she was maturing in her own way. Kira would likely always be a bit boisterous and frivolous, no matter how old she got, and there was likely no one who could tame her fully. I caught a glimpse of Arrian watching her, brown eyes flicking from her to back down at his program.

Kira, oblivious to Arrian's attention behind her, reached over and gripped Yulia's hand with a sharp intake of breath as the lights dimmed to indicate the show would be commencing shortly. The conductor stepped out on stage, pausing for the applause to die down before he tapped his stand rhythmically with his baton, and the curtain rose to the swell of strings, brass, and wind.

The ballet told the story just as Kira had described it, beginning with the princess in her kingdom and venturing into the mountains where she was lost. The prima ballerina piqued, sashayed, and arabesqued effortlessly around the stage amongst the ensemble of snowflakes, like she was little more than a breath of air in the wind.

After a series of battements, the orchestra began building behind her, signaling my favorite part of the ballet. She lifted on her toes, arms poised in front of her, then swept out to the side as she began her series of fouettés, her long leg flicking from her knee, dipping to her calve then sweeping out to the side over and over again. Faster and faster she spun, hypnotizing us all. In one fluid movement, as she brought her arms in to turn, she discreetly unhooked the pinned bodice of her dress so that the gravitational pull of her spins would tug the fabric down, revealing a shimmering white and blue costume beneath.

It was moments like these that made me wonder if magic Sympathizers were lured in by the sheer beauty of elemental magic. The prima's costume transformation from mortal princess to a relic of ice crystals was so mesmerizing, I was transfixed. If ice curses looked like that, then that deceptive beauty had to be part of the temptation.

I felt a tap on my shoulder and turned to see Roland leaning in to whisper in my ear, "enjoying the show, Snowdrop?"

"It's beautiful," I whispered back.

"You certainly are," He teased, and ran his fingers over the nape of my neck before handing me one of my own shimmering hair pins. A small shiver engulfed me at the slight touch, causing Roland to grin and me to blush. "Forgive me, this was slipping out of your hair."

"Yeah, right," Arrian snorted from beside Roland. "Who are you fooling with that line?"

"There's nothing to forgive," I lifted my pamphlet to fan at my face, a heat overtaking me.

"Look at Kira," Roland chuckled, ignoring his brother, his head still hovering just behind my shoulder. He lowered his voice to a whisper that tickled the back of my ear.

My heart increased as I tried to push away imagining what it would be like if he pressed his lips to my skin. The notion embarrassed me, and I had no idea where these sudden carnal desires were springing up from all day. I'd been attracted to

Roland for ages, certainly, but I knew nothing would ever come of anything so improper. We'd have to be married, and that was that. So, until that bridge was crossed, I had done my best to keep my more intimate fantasies buried, and it seemed they were resurfacing in waves today. It didn't help that he was being more forward in his interactions, fanning my vanity, and finding reasons to touch me, whereas normally we only ever made contact through hand holding.

I bit the inside of my lip to center myself, and took a deep breath. "What?"

"Look at your sister," Roland repeated, leaning in a little closer to point past my face at Kira. "She's quite literally on the edge of her seat."

I followed the length of his finger in front of my eyes and shifted to look past Yulia at Kira. She was leaning forward as far as she could without tipping her seat, gripping onto the back of Mama and Papa's seats directly in front of her. Her eyes were wide and her lips parted to make way for a breath of awe.

"She is definitely getting Papa's money's worth," I chuckled softly, and reached up to gently push Roland's hand out of my way. "You're blocking my view, Sir."

"Maybe I want to be the only thing you can see."

"You're a vain man."

"No, just an exceedingly desperate one. I think you and I should find a moment alone to talk. Like we did the night of the Celebration of Reign."

"To talk?" I turned further around, finding my face ready to bump into his. "Sorry."

"Yes, to talk." Roland cleared his throat, swallowing hard. His brows creased in concentration. "I'd like to... talk to you about something important."

"Oh, good grief," Arrian sighed, turning his body away from us as best he could.

My heart skipped a beat, and I was suddenly very poignantly aware of the sweat forming in my palms around my playbill.

Was he finally going to move forward on his intentions with me? Perhaps all those forward displays had been on his way to a more direct confession.

"Ahem," Inessa cleared her throat, and looked sharply from Roland to me. Then her eyes darted to Kira, and back to Roland.

Roland stiffened, as a sense of clarity washed over him and he immediately pulled away back into his chair. His attention returned to the stage, and didn't waver once for the rest of the number. I shifted uncomfortably in my seat, put off by the strange hot and cold interactions Roland was displaying with me. Despite the obvious conspicuous setting, I tried not to feel cross with Inessa for spoiling the moment before I could make plans to see Roland later, but was finding it difficult to smother my annoyance. More than anything, what most made my chest tighten and my nerves buzz with ambient energy was that there seemed to be some unspoken exchange between my sister and him that I wasn't privy to.

And I didn't like it.

Roland always shared things with me. So did Ina for that matter. I didn't understand what they could possibly both be keeping from me, and the more I tried to think my way to an answer, the more dark clouds gathered in my head.

"Ouch," Yulia grumbled as my arm brushed hers on the armrest. The light friction caused a small static shock, which she took the brunt of.

"Sorry," I muttered half heartedly, and continued to fan myself, trying to enjoy the remainder of the performance until the curtain finally fell for intermission.

"That was amazing!" Kira cheered, still clapping intermittently to herself well after the applause of the audience had died down. "Sorrel, did you see her dress?"

"I did," I mustered up a smile for Kira's benefit, but still felt my skin crawling with irritable curiosity over Ina and Roland. If there was a shared secret, it would have to date back to at least the time when Kira had spotted them talking quietly to each other in the hall. That had been months ago.

"It's quite warm in here, isn't it?" Papa stood and tugged at the collar of his shirt.

"You do look flushed," Mama acknowledged and her silver gaze honed in on me. "Sorrel does too, for that matter."

"Would you care to join me in getting out of this stuffy box for some tea, my dear?" Papa offered me his hand and I took it gladly. I needed to give myself a little breathing room to quell my rising annoyance.

"Absolutely. Thank you, Papa."

"I'll come too!" Kira chirped, bouncing after us as we headed to the door. "I'm so excited I can hardly sit still. I need to stretch my legs."

The three of us filtered out of the room, and I didn't miss Inessa following my every movement before she turned to hiss something at Roland. Was she angry with him for interrupting the show? For talking to me? Or was it something else, something deeper? Beyond them, I could see Yulia glowering at her nails, her gaze flickering intermittently towards Inessa and Roland. She caught my eye and crinkled her nose, denoting some distaste with the conversation, and I made a mental note to ask Yulia what she overheard in my absence later.

We went to our private concession stand off the main lobby, and Papa requested green tea for each of us. Kira changed hers to raspberry and began pacing up and down the small space. The movement heightened my agitation, and I could feel a headache knocking on my temples.

"Well, are you enjoying your birthday show, my darling girl?" Papa approached Kira and lifted his hand over her head, offering a single finger for her to grab onto. She giggled and complied, letting him spin her like a top, just as we used to as children.

"Oh, definitely. I love this ballet so much. In another life, I wonder if I would have been a dancer," She sighed contentedly.

"It takes a lot of discipline to be a dancer," I cautioned. "It's exceedingly strenuous on the body, and it's a difficult, unstable life."

"I know that, spoilsport!" Kira clipped back, stopping her twirling to stick her tongue out at me. "I heard that all the best dancers come from Lusoryia."

"Isn't that the country of hedonistic curses?" I quirked an eyebrow.

"Sorrel…" Papa warned, his voice dipping with disapproval.

I didn't know why I was being a killjoy to her, but I couldn't seem to stop myself. I sounded like Ina when she was in one of her moods and butted heads with Mama or Kira. "Sorry, my head is pounding. It feels like something is trying to burrow through my temple on either side just to bicker with each other in the middle. All this excitement is catching up to me."

"Don't worry about it." Kira shrugged and wrangled Papa into a dance with her. "Sorry your head is hurting. As the birthday girl, I banish it! But if that doesn't work, maybe have some more tea. Remind me to bring Yulia back hers."

"Tea does have a way of fixing all things, doesn't it?" I brought my cup to my lips and sipped slowly. The scalding beverage stung my throat as it trickled down to my empty stomach, the warm pooling distinctively. My nerves did feel a little more settled, and I took another long drink. Kira's bright smile also did its usual job of lifting my spirit. "Did Yulia ask you for tea?"

"Didn't she? Echinacea I thought was what she…" She paused her twirling around with Papa and shook her head back and forth. "Did you hear that? It's like someone is whispering somewhere overhead."

I nearly dropped my cup in my lap as a loud bang crackled through the theater, overtaking and quieting the din in an instant. The silence was immediately followed by a series of shrieking.

"What was that sound? Did something fall?" Kira's voice wavered with unease, and Papa dropped his hold on her to rush from the room towards our box.

"Stay here, girls."

"Papa, wait!" I called to him, setting my cup down so rapidly, it tipped and spilled the remaining contents all over the little table.

"Someone get help!" I heard Mama's voice shout frantically, and I was on my feet and rushing toward the door.

SIXTEEN

"**G**et the Imperial Family out of here immediately!" One of the soldiers was barking. "Clear the theater. Prioritize the Prince and the Emperor. Send medical personnel immediately— hey, what do you think you're doing?"

The door to the box slammed into my face, cutting me off from the rest of my family, and I ricocheted off of it with a thud. But wasn't before I caught sight of a spray of scarlet on the doorframe. I reached for the handle and jiggled it frantically to no avail. Someone had locked it from the inside. I pounded on the door and more banging and muffled screams sounded from inside the box.

"Roland? Yulia! Ina!" I shouted. "Mama?"

"You need to hide, Sorrel. Take Kira and go." I heard Roland shout at me, his words strained.

"Sorrel!" Kira yelped, gripping onto my arm, her fingers pushing hard into the skin. "What happened?"

"I don't know, I can't get in," I all but wailed.

"Go!" Another command sounded from Roland, and I could hear Inessa's frightened sobbing.

"I can't get the bleeding to stop, I don't know what to do." Her voice was pitching into hysteria. "I need Sorrel. Yulia, what did you do? Where is Sorrel?"

"Is Yulia hurt? Ina! Who's bleeding?" I pleaded through the door, but I was fairly positive my sister couldn't hear me.

"It'll be fine. Go!"

My heart was pounding and I felt something building in my chest beside it, beginning to unleash. It was the wrath of helplessness while I could hear the suffering of my loved ones inside. I wanted to break down the door with my bare hands, but instead I was stranded on the outside.

"Hey, who are you? Stay back!" Kira screamed behind me, and I whipped around, pushing her behind me. A moment later I relaxed as I recognized Rafe. What was he doing here at the theater?

"Rafe, what are you doing here?" I demanded.

"You know him? Is he safe?" Kira poked her head around from behind me.

"Yes, he's safe," I answered without thinking. I was relatively positive from my interactions with him up until his release that he was a kind and caring man. "He was a patient at the hospital recently."

"We have to go, now." Rafe didn't answer my question, and instead strode up to me and peeled me away from the door, leaving Kira to cling to my side like a burr and follow us. He ushered us back into our private concessions room and closed the door before turning back around to face us. "We need to find somewhere to hide you."

"Rafe, what is going on? My family is still up there!" I dropped my voice, doing my best to spare Kira any additional concern. "Was that a *gunshot*?"

"Your parents, the Prime Minister, his youngest son, and your brother made it out already."

"And what about Roland and my sisters?"

"They are still up there. I don't know what's happening."

"Was it gunfire?" I repeated my question, my voice quieting as I braced myself for the answer.

"Yes."

The world spun around me and I felt like the ground was going to open up and swallow me whole. "Why?"

"I can answer that later."

"I need to know what I'm hiding from, and if hiding means my loved ones are going to die." I did my best to keep my voice steady, and firm, swallowing hard.

Rafe sighed, his golden eyes swirling with adrenaline. "It's an anarchist group. They are targeting the royal family, and apparently knew you'd all be here tonight with less guards. It was an ambush."

"What do you mean by an anarchist group? Is it about those protests? Magic Sympathizers and Wielders are revolting?"

"It would seem so." He ran a hand through his disheveled hair, then suddenly lunged for me and Kira, knocking us both to the ground to duck behind the counter.

"Ack!" Kira squawked, and I felt Rafe's hands find mine and guide them to my ears.

"Cover your ears," He whispered to Kira, who complied, wild eyed and speechless. We held our breath as the door opened and a couple heavy footsteps sounded, scuffing against the carpet. Rafe pressed his finger to his lips, motioning for us to keep quiet. He reached behind his back, and returned his arm to the front of his body, a knife in hand. I blinked, not remembering him having a knife on his person a moment ago.

He rolled quietly from his crouched position to the balls of his feet before springing up from behind the counter, flinging the knife at our attacker. There was a sickening crunch followed by a series of splutters and gurgles, then finally a thud. Kira scrunched her eyes tightly closed against the sounds, and I knew that Rafe had struck the invader in the throat, penetrating the cartilage down to the front of his spinal column.

"You killed him." My eyes stretched wide as I raised my body to peer over the counter and confirm my suspicions. Sure enough, there was a man lying on his back in a dark pool of crimson still beading from his neck, the bloodied silver of the knife glinting in his throat.

"I did. He was going to kill us."

"How did you know he was a villain?"

"He was the one using the Whisper affinity to affect everyone's minds and judgment. We are just lucky he didn't have a pen, since he was powerful enough to wield his suggestions at that length of distance."

"What are you talking about?" I spluttered, overwhelm crushing me beneath its increasing weight. "What does a pen have to do with anything right now?"

"Damn, he's blocking the door from closing. His men will come looking for him now that the whispers have stopped, see him lying there in the doorway, and know we are in here. We need to find another way out of here."

"I don't think there is another exit," Kira peered around the immediate area.

"Worry not, Princess," Rafe mused, looking around the room. "There are always hidden exits somewhere. You just have to look a little harder for them."

"Why are you here?" I demanded, while Rafe started feeling around the ground and wall for some sort of hatch that might lead to our escape. "The last I saw you, you were being discharged from the hospital and were headed somewhere for the remainder of your recovery. You said you were going to write to me to let me know you'd settled in. Not show up to help the moment everything falls apart."

"Letter was in the mail, probably will reach you at the hospital tomorrow, thank you very much. I am a man of my word. And, Roland sent for me when he thought something might be amiss here tonight," He replied briskly, his eyes still trained on the door.

"Roland?" I echoed, confused.

"Yeah, uh. We've met. He thought I could come in as incognito backup if something turned out wrong, and looks like he had sound judgment. I'm just glad it was you I found first."

My head was spinning with questions. "When did you two possibly meet long enough for him to be comfortable asking such a thing from you?"

"Look, I'm trying to save your ass right now, and your sister's. And, hopefully I won't get myself killed along the way either. Can we save the inquisition for when we are out of danger, for the love of Alse Hanya," Rafe huffed impatiently and I bit my tongue. He had a point.

"What can I do to help?"

"Look for a way out of this room."

I nodded and started feeling around the wall and looking behind the hanging tapestries and artwork for any sign of a hidden exit. Kira sniffled and followed my lead.

"I heard you out there at the door. You were asking if Yulia was alright. Is she?" She asked quietly.

"Roland said everything would be fine," I avoided answering directly so I wouldn't have to outright lie to her, or be forced to admit I had no idea as to the state of Yulia's safety and wellbeing, nor Roland's, nor Inessa's. "And you heard Rafe. Almost everyone is out and safe."

"If they got out, then they probably had another exit on the far side that we never use. So then, the others will get out too," Kira rationalized, and I mulled over her theory of reassurance, willing it to be true with all my might. It was all I could do to push my panic to the back of my mind and focus on getting at least Kira to safety while she was in my charge.

My heart twisted as Inessa's crying and pleading for my help reverberated with phantom echoes in my ears. What use was I down here when she needed me with her and whoever she was struggling to stop the bleeding for. For all I knew, she had been injured herself and couldn't get her own bleeding to stop. At least Roland was up there with them. He'd take charge and know what to do.

"Someone is coming," Kira whispered, her whole body going rigid. "Sorrel?"

"I have a hatch here! Come on."

"Was that always there? How did we miss it?" Kira gasped.

"Hurry up," Rafe hissed, and reached for my wrist to rush me into the small crawl space. I didn't even have the chance to stoop before someone came barreling through the doorway and tripped over the body of the man. "Get down!"

To our surprise, however, it wasn't some brute coming to finish what was started. It was a young girl, likely no more than ten years old, no doubt attending the ballet with her family and had gotten separated in evacuations.

"We need to get her out of here too," I whispered to Rafe, and for the first time, I could see the strain of fear and effort to help us crease his face. He still wouldn't be in the best shape from his wound. He squeezed his calloused hand where it held my wrist.

"Sorrel, you have to stay down. You don't understand, these people are dangerous. Trust me when I say they mean to succeed in killing you. I'll go and get her as soon as a window opens, but I need you and your sister to get in the hatch right now. We are running out of time." His breathing was growing labored, and I believed he meant his last statement.

The girl looked over her shoulder at what she had tripped over, and her ruddy face twisted in horror as her body convulsed with shrieks.

"Oh schnites, that's just what we need," Rafe swore.

"Who are you?" The girl paused her screaming when she noticed us lurking behind the counter, but before we could answer, another man stormed into the room, and I balked in terror as I saw his hand was coated in a layer of free burning fire.

"Found a civilian!" He growled down the hall to someone, and then lumbered over to the little girl, raising his hand to strike her down. She screamed bloody murder and threw her hands over her head, cowering in absolute terror. I could feel my own body trembling like a leaf, and I fought my instinct to flee, trying desperately to think of a way to help her without getting us all killed since the man hadn't noticed us yet.

Rafe had stilled completely. We were both holding our breath, silently praying we wouldn't be seen, and that some miracle would spare the girl so she wouldn't be slain right before our eyes.

"Hey!" Kira shouted, ripping her tiara off her head to hurl it with all her might at the man, striking him right in the middle of his head. The metal clinked and hissed against his skin, leaving a branded mark emblazoned on his flesh. A painful shock wave of new fear surged through me, and made my bones throb. My sister had not been the miracle I'd been asking the Divinities to send.

Kira sprang from her hiding place across the room, keeping low to the floor. She was lithe and precise in her path until she reached the young girl, tugging her to her feet behind her while the assaulted man reeled and clutched at his face in pain. "Come with us, we have a way out."

The girl complied, and I breathed a sigh of relief as I shoved her into the crawl space followed by Kira. Rafe had another knife in his hand ready to throw at the second man, and as I whirled to follow Kira through the hatch, I noticed the knife was missing from the first fallen man's throat. Had Rafe gotten it back somehow? But the one he flicked from his hand before forcibly pushing me through the passageway was completely devoid of blood.

Thankfully, our exit was close to the exterior wall and we tumbled out of the theater into an alley in a matter of moments, gasping to catch our breath, as soldiers swarmed us.

"Roland sent for this man, and he's still inside," I explained briskly as I recognized Sergeant Hykner at my side.

"Understood," He nodded to Rafe and looked beyond me like he was expecting Inessa and Yulia to emerge at any moment.

"They are still inside with Roland," I breathed, and a fresh wave of desperate panic seized me as I rose shakily to my feet.

"I'm going back in to get them," Rafe squared his shoulders and I found myself grabbing onto his arm, torn between desperately wanting someone to save the others, and being concerned that if Rafe went back in, he might never come back out. I hadn't known him long, but I couldn't forget the kindness he had shown me after Harvier's passing. I didn't want to stomach the thought of our friendship being cut short so soon.

"There is a team already inside sweeping the theater," Hykner offered, noticing my concern. His eyes were darting back and forth from me to the hatch, like he was seriously contemplating rushing through it himself to find the others.

"It's clear on the lower levels." The call echoed around the crowd and more guards approached our little group. To my dismay, while Hykner successfully guided me and Rafe out of the line of focus, the guards surrounded Kira and the girl, weapons pointed at the stranger. "Step away from the Princess, now!"

The girl stared at the guns and her face crumbled as she latched onto Kira's leg from where she had collapsed on the ground. Kira's face was contorting into a scowl of defiance and disappointment. Her eyes were blazing as she rose to her full height and shifted pointedly in front of the girl, who was shaking uncontrollably.

"No."

"Your Imperial Highness, Princess Kira. We have to assume anyone unknown on the premises could be in league with the assassins." The word *assassins* made bile rise in my throat. I needed Ina, Roland, and Yulia to make it out alive.

"No. She was just hiding here," Kira insisted, unflinching.

"We must—"

"Look at her!" She snapped. "Does she look threatening to you? She is terrified that you're going to shoot her! Lower your weapons this instant."

"She's just a commoner," one of the bystanding noblemen snorted. "Who cares what becomes of her so long as it could mean our safety. If it's her time, so be it. There's a throng of countless others out roaming the streets just like her."

I stepped forward, releasing my hold on Rafe, ready to rebuke the man's impertinence, but Kira's jaw set, her hands balling into fists. I could practically feel the waves of heated anger rolling off of her. She crouched down to the sniveling girl and held out a hand.

The girl stared woefully at Kira's offered hand, but my sister didn't budge. Instead, she reached down to clasp gently onto the girl's hand, and the moment their skin made contact, she visibly relaxed. Her hunched shoulders sagged, and her puckered tear stained face slacked with a sniffle. Finally responsive, she accepted Kira's help, and rose to her feet.

I stared proudly at my sister as she squared up and brushed her hands lightly over the girl's cheeks to wipe away her tears. She looked over her shoulder at the nobleman who had spoken, and her lip curled into a snarl of disgust, causing him to take a step back.

"*I* care. No one here will harm her, is that understood?" Her face sobered to commanding disdain. "We do not treat civilians this way."

The soldiers shifted uncomfortably, and Hykner piped up. "That was an imperial order, men. Stand down."

Slowly, the soldiers compiled and instead focused on escorting us towards the front of the building where we could be shuffled into cars and taken home to safety, likely as the rest of my family had been. I could only imagine the worry they must have felt in the chaos once they realized some of us were missing. Then I spotted Papa surrounded by his guards. He locked eyes on me and Kira.

"Oh, thank the Divinities!"

"Papa!" Kira and I cried, and ran to our father's outstretched arms, as his guards were given the order to part for us. Papa held us close, and kissed our heads repeatedly.

"You girls need to get home immediately. Your mother is beside herself," He said after a moment.

"What happened when you got back in the box, Papa?" I asked, pulled back to look my father in the eye, finding I didn't like the odd flicker of sympathy swimming in the depths of his blue gaze. He opened his mouth but another voice sounded behind me before he could answer.

"Sorrel! Where is my sister?" Ina's voice called through the crowd.

"Inessa!" I sagged with relief and whipped around, my glee immediately stifled with dread as I saw her blood covered hands and dress. "What is it?"

She was still crying, and she grabbed my hand and pulled me back towards the theater.

"Inessa, I just worked very hard to get out of that building. Please tell me what's wrong. You're scaring me."

"It's Roland," Ina rasped. "He was the one who got shot. I did my best but I didn't remember the steps. I didn't know what to do to stop the bleeding. I know there are doctors on the way to take him to the hospital, but you know what to do. You always know what to do in these situations." Her shock stricken babbling faded behind me after the first sentence.

My feet had never moved so fast or with such focused intent in all my life, as I raced to Roland's side.

SEVENTEEN

It became clear to us what had happened after Roland was transported to the hospital. He had been shot in the shoulder, thankfully a nonlethal location, though he had lost a fair bit of blood despite Inessa's best, albeit frantic, efforts.

Hykner had gotten the full account from Inessa and came with me as protection to the hospital with Roland, while the rest of my family headed home. The rest I was able to piece together from my own experience. The Whisper Wielder that Rafe had managed to take out had apparently been casting his verbal curses over us since we got to the theater, planting suggestions, and even going so far as to manipulate some perception of reality.

It had been a fluke that Papa, Kira, and I had left the room when the shot was fired, otherwise we could have all suffered a much worse fate. Our leaving rattled the plans enough that things weren't executed properly. The assassination attempt was botched, resulting in Roland taking the shot to the shoulder.

There I sat, in a blood stained dress, my hair had come

unraveled, and I held my head in my hands next to Roland's bed. I felt electrically charged and viscerally angry at all the world for the events of the evening. My emotions had tangled and contorted so severely, all that was left was a white hot rage in the pit of my stomach.

"Snowdrop?" Roland croaked and I bolted upright, snatching a small basin and cloth into my hands.

"I'm here," I replied hoarsely, and dabbed gently at his head. "I'm here, Roland."

He blinked a few times, and clarity slowly pooled back into his gaze. "Don't be angry with her, Snowdrop. Please promise me."

"I'm not angry with her," I gritted my teeth.

"Yes, you are," He chuckled weakly, reaching his free arm to grab onto my rapidly dabbing hand until I relinquished the basin and rag. He ran his thumb rhythmically over my knuckles, and though the gesture was soothing, the well of frustration within me only deepened.

"I could have lost you, Roland. I could have—" My voice caught in my throat, and I paused to clear it, blinking back the tears pricking at my eyes. "I was on the other side of the door and you were hurt, Inessa was calling for help and you told me to go. I was right there. You could have bled out. And Yulia..." I faltered and swallowed hard.

"She didn't pull the trigger. She came to her senses and dropped the gun."

"She was being controlled." I bit my lip. "I can't be mad at her for that."

"That's right. In fact, given the force of power that was being used on her, it is a miracle she was able to snap herself out of it at all. Did they catch the bastard?"

"He's dead."

"Just as well," Roland snorted, and winced.

"Rafe killed him."

"Did he?"

"Apparently you know each other."

"We have met, yes."

"Where did you—"

"Is Yulia alright?" Roland squeezed my hand, and I stared at him for a couple of heartbeats, my previous questions evaporating into the intangible mists of muddled thoughts.

"You took a bullet for her," I whispered, my hands falling limply to my sides as I slumped back into my chair, utterly exhausted.

"A sister of yours is a sister of mine. That's how we always thought it would turn out, isn't it?"

I smiled wistfully. "That's what the rumors seem to say."

Roland grinned back and turned his head to look at me, his eyes growing heavy. "Tell me Nurse Zdraevit, what will become of me? Will I ever walk again?"

"Considering you were shot in the shoulder, I'd say your chances of walking are looking well," I couldn't help but chuckle at the lame attempt at joking. "The bullet is out, and the wound is clean, no fragmented bones. Tomorrow, you'll be taken home and monitored by Klivech. You will recover just fine, Darling Stupid Man."

"I'd like that title on my tombstone, please."

"I'll keep that in mind in another eighty years when you die of natural causes."

"I'll hold you to that."

"Roland?"

"Yes, Snow… drop?" His eyes drifted closed, and his chest started to rise and fall rhythmically.

"Thank you, for making sure she was okay." I balled my hands into fists and pressed them against my eyes as I leaned my elbows onto the edge of Roland's bed, fighting back the tears I knew were threatening to come out. "Everything will be alright. It will be fine."

I felt a gentle touch on my back and jumped. A fresh wave of adrenaline pulsed through my veins at the prospect of another ambush. I reached for the pen resting on the bedside table, and whipped around, poised to strike any attacker.

"Mama," I breathed when I recognized my mother, standing behind me with my father. My lip trembled. "Papa."

"Come here." Mama pulled me into a tight embrace between her and Papa, and they both held me close, rubbing my back and stroking my hair. "Poor, darling girl. Everything will be alright. Ina and Kira are curled up in bed together, getting along for once. Yulia is with Otvel, cleansing the Wielder's touch from her mind and spirit. Theo is safe as well. Everyone is under guard, and even this hospital is surrounded with armed men. You're safe now, your family is safe, and so is Roland."

"This was a terrible night," I whimpered, and it took everything in me to maintain my composure. Even though I knew my parents would not judge me for breaking down, and would likely even expect it, I couldn't bring myself to give in. Something in the thought of shedding tears over the night's events felt like I was conceding to the assault, accepting it, and allowing it to continue to wreak havoc on my life and psyche.

It was easier to mask the fear and sadness beneath a blanket of righteous wrath. If I remained stoic, my face could hide the pain my mind would replay over and over, but then at least only I would know it. Everyone else could heal. I could weather the storm and hold it back from hurting anyone else. I had to.

"That it was," Papa sighed, detaching from our unit of commiseration to the free cot next to Roland's, and his shoulders sagged with the weight of the world as he shook his head back and forth. "Friedrich said you helped with the operation and haven't left his side."

"I just helped get the instruments and tools ready, assisted with minor things. They wouldn't let me do more than that." I nodded.

Roland's father had come to the hospital and waited until he saw that his son was out of danger and was sleeping. He'd offered to escort me home, but I'd declined, wanting to make sure that when Roland opened his eyes, I was there. If he woke up in pain or confused, I would be there.

"You're a brave, diligent girl, Sorrel," Papa breathed, his eyes fixed on straight ahead, like he was staring at a separate expanse of time and space altogether. "The hospital, Roland, us, your country— Thank the Divinities we have you."

"Papa," I mumbled self consciously from where Mama still had her arms wrapped around me at her side.

"Your sisters are a wreck—Inessa and Yulia, I understand why. Theo was shaken, but he held himself tall. Meanwhile Kira apparently was barking orders at the soldiers to protect an innocent little girl, who needed her protection. No fear in Kira, nothing but fire."

"Genri, you're getting worked up. The girls and Theo are in bed, or with Otvel. They are past the ordeal now," Mama corrected lightly, but her words were firm.

"And you. You didn't hesitate once, Sorrel," Papa continued on like he hadn't heard Mama speak at all, each word growing in fervor and distress. "You help save lives everyday with your own two hands, and what's more, you're a natural at it. If you see someone suffering, you don't think. You act. You run into smoking hospitals, or dangerous theaters, act recklessly and impulsively, like nothing else matters besides helping just one more person. You march into my office and demand that changes be made to spare the anguish of children in the streets and families ripped apart by a Divinity-forsaken war."

"Mind what you say, Genri. Perhaps we ought to take a lap around the building to clear your head. Emotions are running high tonight—" Mama tried again, but once more, Papa prattled on.

"Anguish you've gone out and seen with your own eyes. Suffering you should have never had to witness if I were a better ruler."

"Oh, Papa. Please don't talk like that." The white hot anger that had lodged in my stomach melted away, and turned wriggly, like a million worms were burrowing through me. The room felt sterile and chilly, and for a moment I thought I caught a glimpse of my breath fogging in front of my mouth, but I must have imagined it. "Everyone knows you care very deeply about our country."

"If everyone knew that, my dear girl," He gave a lifeless laugh. "Then the actions of tonight would not have transpired. Yulia wouldn't have ever had her mind overtaken and pointed a gun at her brother. That soldier never would have picked it up for the same reason and pulled the trigger at her, and Roland would not be lying in this hospital for having jumped in front of the bullet."

"But..." I fished lamely for words to comfort my father, but part of me realized there was nothing I could say in this moment to ease the kind of pain he was feeling. It wasn't something I could stitch up, or bandage, or spread a poultice on. The only medicine was speaking what was in his heart.

"I passed through the hospital to get here and I saw all the wounded troops." Papa folded his fingers together and leaned forward, resting his elbows on his knees. He stared out the door into the hallway, then his gaze slowly roved back to me and Mama. "They were fighting to protect our people with their own two hands. With their lives. When they return, you protect them. A whole legion of men out there on the front, like stars flickering out in the night sky, and where am I that I have fallen so low beneath that sky? I surely know I am not above it. We are all momentary in this life, our lives going by quicker and quicker and I want mine to mean more."

"Papa, you're the Emperor. I don't think you can be promoted." I furrowed my brows deeply. "Just because they can't see your actions doesn't mean they aren't happening."

"I want to help this country to stop hurting. I want to close its wounds with my own hands. These people aren't each one single light in a sky of a million to cast aside when they dim or go out. I have been hiding behind the safety of protocol and autocracy for far too long. This chaos has hit too close to home. It's real. More real than it's ever been before. Given the Whisper Wielder's presence tonight and his potent power level, I must figure out if this is a greater act of war from Sibru— wretched timing with my

Minister of Foreign Affairs now out of commission. They did this to Roland. To Yulia, and almost to Theo. I need to do more. I *must* do more."

"Genri, what are you saying?" Mama's face crinkled with concern, but I could see in her stance that she already knew just as well as I what Papa was getting at.

"I will be going to the front, Geneva. I am," He rose from his seat and looked down at Roland, "going to start healing this country."

I stayed up all night at the hospital, until they were ready to transfer Roland back home to the palace. It was still early. Early enough that dawn had not yet crested the horizon. It had been long enough that the doctors felt comfortable sending him to Klivech, but part of me wondered if it had been pushed along on my account to get me home as well.

With Roland settled, Mama insisted I get some rest. There was a strange sensation that filled me with both fortification and stamina, as well as unparalleled exhaustion. More than anything, though I knew my body was indeed tired, it was my spirit that felt the most weary.

I bid farewell to Klivech, asking for him to please fetch me immediately if Roland needed anything. I felt so reluctant to leave him, in case he was shaken or disoriented and needed a familiar face to immediately remind him that he was safe, but I lost the battle with Mama and trudged off to bed all the same.

As I approached my room, I noticed that a guard had been posted outside the door. It was an understandable precaution after everything. I nodded to the man and asked if a maid could please bring a bowl of water and a wash rag, then ducked silently into the dark room. It took a few seconds for my eyes to adjust, and I could make out the two forms of Inessa and Kira fast asleep, curled up together just as they had many times before as children.

I made quick work of slipping behind the changing screen to peel off my stained dress, and waited silently in my shift. A light tapping on the door announced the maid's arrival, and I accepted the bowl and rag from her through the cracked opening, careful to close it quietly. I'd washed my hands and face at the hospital already, but now that my dress was off, I ran the cloth quickly over my body to clean off any excess blood that had soaked through to my skin before changing into new clothes. A proper bath would have to wait until later.

My nightgown felt cool and comforting as I pulled it over my head, and it was indescribably refreshing to be in clean clothing. My ears were ringing from the blood that had been pounding in my ears since Papa had told me and Mama his big plans. I didn't want him to leave us. I didn't know if I could take it, not having him close-by for so long. How would we know if he was staying safe and healthy when we'd rely heavily on letters, delayed by days or weeks, for communication?

Maybe he would change his mind after a good night's sleep. If we showed him we were all alright, and that our family was standing strong, then perhaps he could find some other way to help our country. I dragged my hands down my face with a muffled groan, and climbed into bed.

I was still sitting upright when a small streak of light cut through the dark and a meek head poked through the doorway.

"Sorrel?" Yulia's enormous eyes were red from crying, and tears spilled continuously down her cheeks. I fully believed she hadn't stopped crying all night long. Pity made my battered heart swell at the sight of my distraught, grieving sister.

She was such a gentle and kind spirit, we should have known something was wrong when she first started acting out of character. She'd even mentioned hearing that strange noise, and we had brushed her off for spoiling the mood. And now she was broken hearted and guilt ridden for actions outside of her control. How utterly terrified she must be.

I knew how frightened I was at the possibility that a Dream

Wielder had altered my dreams, and I didn't even have confirmation of the theory's accuracy. Poor Yulia knew full well that a Wielder had entered her mind, and that it had caused her to almost shoot her brother. She knew that same curse caused Roland's injury in her place. Inessa's hysteria probably had made it all the worse. I didn't know it was possible, but my heart found another new ache to heal.

I worked up the best smile I could, and shrugged. "Come on," I beckoned Yulia over to my bed and flicked the covers back for her to jump in with me. She looked ready to collapse with relief as she staggered over to me, and I pulled her close.

"I'm so sorry," She sobbed, her whole body shaking. "I'm so sorry. Don't hate me. Please don't hate me."

"Shhh," I whispered as I held her and gently stroked the back of her head. My eyes drifted to the window where I saw the first rays of sunrise inching into the sky, and thought back to the bliss of yesterday's morning. "It's alright. Everything will be alright."

I wanted to believe those words. Maybe, someday, I would again.

✳ Beneath the Scarlet Frost

"From nothing can come something, but from something can also come nothing. Those who claim they are unable are simply unwilling."
-D

EIGHTEEN

Long gone were the days of blissful solitude back in Eisolde at Svyat Gavan. Papa had been gone for five days, off to fulfill his duty to our country. I didn't know if he had even reached his first destination yet. All I knew for certain was that I missed him terribly and wanted him back. He was due to be gone for months, and I wondered how we would bear his absence for so long. He'd never been gone more than two weeks on his own since we'd been born, and even then those trips were few and far between.

I'd often remarked how much I adored the close knit nature of our family compared to some of the other royal and noble families in Alse Hanya. But, now it seemed that while I'd been blessed with a loving family, the drawback was that the absence of any one member created a void of loneliness only they could fill. It didn't help that in Papa's stead, Mama had taken over running our country's affairs, so she felt a million miles away herself.

Yulia was only just starting to recover from her shock and

guilt. She'd reclused herself away from everyone as much as possible, not even joining us for meals. Theo, being the kind soul he was, had gone to reassure her that he understood what had happened and harbored no ill will, but Yulia hadn't been able to even look him in the eye. The only two people she sought out were Otvel, and Kira, though I knew some of the reasoning for the latter was due to the nature of sharing a room.

Yesterday was the first day I'd seen Yulia in over a week since the incident, and she'd spent the night cuddled close after crying herself to sleep in my arms. She joined us for breakfast, but hadn't said a word. I noticed dark circles under her eyes and wondered if her sleep was plagued by nightmares. I certainly knew mine had been— no suspicions of magical foul play this time either. These were dreams I knew were entirely of my own creation, reliving the crunch of the Whisper Wielder's trachea, and finding Roland's unconscious bloody body on the box floor, over and over.

The sun shone weakly through the window, its warm light smothered by a thick gray cloud. It seemed that the weather had taken a turn for the tumultuous and stormy since Papa had left. It felt like the Divinities were displaying the same displeasure with his absence as the rest of us were.

My siblings, Arrian, and I sat at the enormous dining table in silence, each independently distracted from the act of eating our breakfast. The morning was steeped in melancholy. Mama was in a meeting with Otvel and Friedrich, so it was just the five of us, with no one to monitor us or hurry us along.

"They are going to start drafting soldiers from the royal guard," Theo commented, his voice loud against the silence yet muted as it struggled to fill the grand room. "Splitting efforts now to Vatra and Videiria against Sonyo and now Sibru.

"Mmm," Kira grunted from where she'd pushed her half eaten meal out of the way and folded her arms to rest her head to stare out the window. Her fingers drummed against the table, and the repetitive noise started to grate my nerves.

"I thought they already were drafting soldiers?" I replied to

Theo, filling the quiet to stifle Kira's ambient tapping.

"They took some volunteers at first, paired with the mobilized units of men. Now they are going to start enlisting able civilians and even some of the Imperial soldiers from our groups," Arrian explained, poking his fork at Kira's fingers to cease her drumming.

"Why are they pulling our men?" Inessa's blue eyes flicked up from where she'd been scooting her potatoes around on her plate. "Don't we need them here for our protection? Who's ordering this draft? Is it Mama?"

"The Marshal of the Eisan Federation will be the one responsible for that order, of course." I squinted at my sister, unsure of why she looked like a cornered animal, with equal parts fear and hostility radiating from her. "You know that, Ina."

"With Papa heading the front, I'm sure he sanctioned the order and Mama likely has been implementing it in her capacity here," Theo added, lacing his fingers to twiddle his thumbs. "It makes sense when you think about it."

"Does it?" Inessa quirked an eyebrow.

"Well, yes. The greater volume of power we can display, the faster our enemies will be wiped out or retreat. Then, the faster this war business is done and everyone comes home." Arrian tipped his head as he spoke, clearly surprised by Ina's response.

"Those who don't die anyway," She muttered and went back to pushing her food around, but I could see her knuckles turning white around her fork.

"I don't want any of our regiments to die!" Kira finally yielded to Arrian's jabs, swatting him in the arm, and lifted her head.

"Maybe you should join the war protests then," Inessa mumbled, mostly to herself.

"I can't do that! Those people are in league with the lunatics who attacked us. Was that dashing man who saved us from one of our regiments? He knew Roland."

"Dashing?" Arrian scoffed. "Hardly."

"You weren't even there," Kira reminded him. "I'm not siding with anyone who is out to kill us, thank you very much."

"Not everyone who doesn't agree with the war is in league with the revolutionists and terrorists, Kira."

"Careful, Inessa…" Arrian drawled, dipping his chin. "You're starting to sound a little anti-imperial yourself."

"Oh, shut up, Arrian," Inessa scowled at him, but he didn't flinch away. "Nobody asked you."

"I don't wait to be asked, Inessa," He bit back, eyes flicking to Kira. "Isn't that right, Kira? Life's too short to wait around."

"I guess so," Kira drooped. "I hate waiting."

I turned my attention to Yulia where she sat quietly observing. Her eyes looked more alert than they'd been yesterday, and I was relieved to see her coming out of her shell shock. Kira's mention of the attack had made her wince and her gaze dropped to her lap.

"Yulia, have you had enough to eat?" I asked her gently, seeing she'd only managed to nibble on half her toast and a few bites of fruit.

"I'm fine, thank you." She worked up a smile but her words were struggling to not sound flat in their delivery.

I sighed and swiveled back to Inessa.

"Are you coming to the hospital today, Ina?"

Inessa's jaw tightened and her mouth pursed slightly as she bit the inside of her cheek. "No."

I waited for a further explanation but when the silence stretched on for several more heartbeats, I shook my head and rose from my seat. Everyone was behaving just as gloomy and unforthcoming as the weather outside, and I'd had about all I could take.

"Alright, I guess I'll be heading out on my own then. Don't forget you have that new committee Mama assigned you to, Ina. And Yulia and Kira, you have an agenda starting today too if I recall," I reminded everyone curtly. I knew Theo would be shadowing Mama and needed no reminding of his duties, as apposed to my sisters who seemed thoroughly uninterested in their tasks. "Arrian, I'm sure you know your own schedule for the day. I'll see you all tonight."

"Imperial Highness, Princess Sorrel?" I turned as Dowels stepped into the room and bowed. "The Imperial Majesty and the Prime Minister have requested your presence in the study before you leave for the hospital."

"Oh," I blinked in surprise. "Alright, I will head straight there."

"Think she's in trouble?" I heard Kira crack as the door closed behind me, and I made my way to the study.

As I walked, I passed by various servants tending to the palace. This in itself wasn't unusual, except for the fact that each time one saw me, maids and footmen alike, they shifted their gaze and shied away. Some changed directions to avoid me altogether. I paused in the hallway outside the study and pursed my lips. The staff downstairs hadn't seemed out of the ordinary, so something must have shifted the mood up here and was spreading through the staff like wildfire.

I nodded to the guards, and knocked, before opening the door and stepping inside. It was odd to be met with Mama's auburn hair and silver eyes instead of Papa's gentle smile and dark beard waiting at the desk. While I expected Friedrich to be there with her, I was surprised to see that Otvel was also in the requested audience.

"Mama," I dipped my head in greeting to her first, then to Friedrich and Otvel in turn. "Dowels said you requested to see me?"

"That's right, Darling." Mama gestured for me to take a seat. "We wanted to ask a few follow-up questions regarding the assault on our family the other night."

"Oh." My stomach seized instantly. "Of course, Mama. What can I do to help?"

"There were a few details of the evening that stood out to us when we spoke to your sister and listened to her account," Otvel jumped in, and I noticed a sharpness to his gaze. "Namely regarding that young gentleman who assisted in your escape. She couldn't recall his name, and we wanted to make sure he got the recognition he deserved for his actions."

"Kira seemed inclined to believe you were acquainted," Friedrich threw in from his seat, and smiled at me. His company felt soft and reassuring against the shrewd demeanor of Otvel and Mama's removed presence. Though she had asked me here, it was clear that the meeting was being led by Otvel and Friedrich and she was more of a spectator.

"Yes," I nodded. "Rafe. I don't know him particularly well, so I'm afraid I don't recall his last name."

"How did you two have the opportunity to meet? He's not a soldier or nobleman," Otvel leaned forward.

I'd always liked Otvel and felt comfortable in his company. He'd laughed, and played, and guided us in right and wrong for most of my life. But something about him was putting me ill at ease, and I couldn't place why. He wasn't asking anything particularly odd, nor was he behaving aggressively. He wanted to recognize a friend of mine for his heroic acts, yet somehow I still felt uneasy.

Why do I want to lie to him?

"He was a patient in the hospital."

"How unfortunate. I take it he recovered from whatever had ailed him prior to the ballet?" Friedrich's expression was sympathetic. He made me feel safe in a similar way to Papa, like he would protect against any misfortune or distress that might come up.

"He was in the Piren Hospital recovering from a bayonet wound in the east. Some scuffle off the border of Dezidaneya, if I recall," I replied to Friedrich, keeping my eyes trained on him.

"A bayonet?" Otvel repeated, and Friedrich's eyebrows jumped.

"That's right. He was impaled in the side. Accidental friendly fire, I think, and he was brought with the other injured men back here to Tuyet," I recounted. "I'm especially glad that I knew him the other night when he saved me and Kira."

"Yes, yes." Otvel nodded along and looked at Mama.

"I know it's a difficult and frightening matter to relive, so we won't take up much more of your time." Friedrich cleared his throat. "We are very grateful that he was able to extract you and your sister safely, but we were curious as to how he managed it. Was he armed?"

Images of the knife in Rafe's hand flashed in my mind and I nodded. "Yes, he had a knife that he threw. Er, sorry, two knives."

"And those knives dispatched the attackers?"

"They did."

"Then you two girls were found stumbling into an alley?"

"Correct, we had to find an escape path, so we looked for a hidden exit in the private concession room where we'd had tea with Papa before the gunshot."

"Who found the exit?"

"Rafe did, but Kira and I were looking around the room too."

"Together?"

"Individually."

"Did he have the knives on him already?"

"I didn't notice them when we ran back into the room, but I'd assume so. There weren't any knives like that behind the counter, so I don't know where he would have picked them up otherwise. I suppose he had them hidden. He said he was asked to come to the theater in case something was amiss. Actually, it was Ro— "

"He sounds like a very skilled fighter. Someone who might have made a good soldier in another life," Friedrich commented, his words tumbling over mine. "Forgive me."

"Where were the knives?" Otvel pressed.

"Pardon?"

"On his person. Where did you see him pull them from, since they were apparently hidden so well."

"He reached behind his back," I answered, trying my best not to shrink away from the priest's intense gaze.

"Did he retrieve the knives?"

"No, we left through the exit after that."

"Through the hidden door that he located?"

"Yes, that's right."

"Well," Friedrich leaned forward and rested his arms on his knees. "I'm just glad there was such a resourceful man there able to help you escape and that neither of you girls were hurt in the process."

"Before I forget," Mama chimed in and reached into a drawer to retrieve the small tiara Kira had thrown at the Fire Wielder. "This was retrieved at the theater. I had it thoroughly cleaned, of course. Can you please return it to Kira?"

"Of course." I rose to my feet to take the tiara from Mama and took it as my cue that the meeting was finished. "Is there anything else I can help with?"

"Not right now, Darling." Mama cupped my face affectionately and rubbed my cheek with her thumb. "You've been very helpful. Your attention to detail is always greatly appreciated."

"Thank you, Princess Sorrel. You've told us everything we need to know, and we will find out the rest of his information to make sure he is recognized." Otvel dipped his head and Friedrich echoed the sentiment.

"We will take care of everything from here."

"I would have you return the knives to your friend," Mama said slowly as I headed for the door. "But, they weren't recovered at the site."

I paused, and furrowed my brows, looking over my shoulder. "They weren't?"

"It's possible that someone pocketed them when cleaning the area," Friedrich rose to his feet, straightening to his full stature. Otvel stood a little taller too, his gaze darkening with theories he seemed to choose not to vocalize. "Or, that someone else came along and retrieved them after you left, before the building was cleared."

"I see," I nodded and opened the door. "I'll let him know if I see him again. I don't think he was overly concerned about getting them back as much as getting me and Kira out safely."

I stepped through the door and heard it click behind me. My skin prickled with a sense of unease whose root I couldn't properly place. The words had all been correct, but the tone of the encounter felt stilted, almost rehearsed. It gave me the distinct impression that those right words spoken had been decided on prior to my arrival and that something very wrong was lurking beneath them.

Should I have lied? What do I have to hide?

Shaking myself and politely bidding farewell to the two guards, I wandered through the palace looking for Kira to return her tiara. When I couldn't find her, I looked at the clock and realized how late I was going to be for my shift at the hospital. I scribbled a note and left the tiara on Kira's bed before racing through the halls to locate Dowels and confirm that my chauffeur and escort were waiting to take me.

It had taken a lot of convincing to be permitted to even continue on my nursing duties after the assault. Neither of my parents had been too keen on the idea, but Friedrich, thank the Divinities, had managed to convince them that the image would be in our favor. That, despite the incident, at least one of the Grand Princesses was continuing on serving the people. He had warned against the perception of showing undue suspicion and prejudice towards our people. Mama wasn't easily persuaded, but Papa had sanctioned the endeavor before his departure. After our conversation the night Roland was shot, I knew he understood all too well my want and *need* to do something with myself.

The lobby had been for both me and Inessa to return to our duties, but my sister found every poorly articulated excuse in the book to avoid returning to her position at the hospital. Instead, she was claiming that she wanted to spend more time with her regiment. Outside of possibly suppressing her own fear since Kira's birthday, I found this sudden over interest in military practice odd, since it had never been a cardinal focus of hers before. I tried my best to swallow down the irritation it sparked beneath my skin.

As I whisked myself through the palace and down the stairs like a flurry, I noticed everywhere I went the staff, both upstairs and down were avoiding my eye now. I couldn't even get one to stay in my presence long enough to call to them and ask where Dowels was. Everything about the morning had felt very intrinsically *wrong*, and it unsettled me to my core.

I caught sight of Larkin, Inessa's and my lady's maid, and puffed a sigh. Though Mama had insisted we all be brought up in a more modest manner, making us self sufficient and not in particular need of a lady's maid, Larkin was still a good natured young woman who always seemed to try her best at her job when called upon. Sure enough, she paused and waited for me to approach at the sound of her name.

"Larkin," I stopped beside her and lowered my voice. "Do you know what everyone is so on edge about amongst the staff? They all seem terribly uncomfortable with my presence. Has something happened?"

Larkin's golden brows furrowed and she shifted the clothing she was transferring in her arms. "Your Imperial Highness, I'm afraid it might be impertinent to speak on this matter."

"Oh, Larkin," I sighed and rested my hand on her shoulder gently. "You know I don't care about all that formality. If there is a problem or a discomfort, I'd like to know. Maybe I can help."

"Well," She paused and looked at her shoes. When she looked up, her gaze roved around the immediate area, and she looked quickly over her shoulder. "Someone heard a rumor. The maids for the Prime Minister and the Head Priest, they sometimes talk out of turn. They said that Priest Chinye has been advising the Imperial Empress to start an active hunt and extermination of Wielder civilians hiding in the city."

"A hunt?" I echoed. "Isn't ridding the country of Wielders a good thing? Why would taking an active approach make the staff uncomfortable? Furthermore, what does that have to do with me?"

"It's the *way* they are going about it. I apologize, Highness. I'm afraid I don't know the details myself yet, but it is my understanding that the process is going to be rather intrusive to the public, and you, Highness, are part of those soon to enforce a violation to their privacy."

I stiffened. "What are they planning on doing?"

"I'm not sure I have the specifics, Highness."

"Anything at all would be helpful," My feet itched with impatience. If I was going to find out more from anyone, I needed to know enough information to ask the right questions to force honest answers.

"They want to make a public list of those suspected of Wielder abilities and magic Sympathizers. The Priest has been working on something to help get the truth from citizens. Some sort of test, but I'm afraid I don't know what kind, Highness."

"A test," I mused. "What happens if someone fails the test?"

"I don't know, Highness." Larkin sagged under my barrage of questions, and I felt a prickle of guilt.

"That's alright, Larkin. Thank you for telling me." I stepped past her to make a mad dash for the door. "Please try and ease the staff. I'm sure there is a reasonable explanation once we have the full picture and not bits and pieces of hearsay. I'll do my best to find out."

"Yes, Highness." Larkin's voice faded behind me, and I set my curiosities and uncertainties aside for the time being as I spotted the car waiting out front. I needed to focus on what was readily before me for the moment, and that was getting to the hospital to help patients through another day of healing.

It was all I could do. Everyone was trying to make sense of the new, broken world we found ourselves living in the best they knew how, and what I knew was healing suffering. One person at a time.

NINETEEN

"Sorry to pop in on you unannounced." I looked up from my papers to see Rafe standing in front of me, hands stuffed into his pockets. His hair was pulled back and secured at the nape of his neck, and his golden eyes were a warm contrast to the harshness of the hospital.

"Rafe," I stood abruptly, running my hands over the sides of my head to smooth down any fly away hairs. "Sorry, I wasn't expecting you."

"That was the *unannounced* bit I mentioned," he laughed. "I just wanted to check in and make sure that you and your sister were doing alright. Your whole family too. I got out of the way once it was said that Roland and the others were out. I heard it was Roland who took the shot?"

Nurses were whispering to each other and looking at Rafe. It had been three days since my meeting with Mama, answering questions about Rafe's involvement in our rescue. I hadn't heard anything more about it, and in truth, the matter had more or less slipped my mind. I'd been buried in tasks between working in the hospital, social obligations, looking in on Roland, and my committee work. By the time I had a chance to sit still, Mama had started insisting on an evening sermon from Otvel.

The sudden interest from the staff in Rafe's presence at the hospital confused me. He'd been a patient here once, so surely some of the workers were familiar with him. If it weren't for their creased brows and frowns, I would have likely assumed the women were finding him handsome.

With his striking eyes, well toned physique, sharp cheeks, and cut jaw lightly stubbled with the beginnings of a browning gold beard, it wouldn't be such a leap to reach the conclusion that he was a good looking man.

"Yes? Is there something on my face?" Rafe chuckled, reaching a hand to rub at his jaw. "You're glaring at me."

"What?" I gasped, and realized a moment too late that I had been squinting at him the whole time I was making my assessment. "Sorry, no. I just got lost chasing a train of thought."

"Right, I hate when that happens. Did you find it?"

"Find what?"

"The train of thought?" He raised his brows and his eyes flicked from side to side. "Are you messing with me?"

"Everything is fine!" I blurted, mortified by my distracted behavior. "Roland was the one injured in the attack, but he is recovering well."

"Did you tend to him yourself, Madam Gauze Fetcher?" Rafe leaned his arms on the table I was using to sort my paperwork, and grinned.

I couldn't help but smile back. "Now, now. Show some respect. Not only was I previously promoted to Wall Inspector, I have climbed the ranks here since your stay, I'll have you know. I assist with procedures more regularly now, and yes, I did help with Roland's. Well, I laid out the instruments and handed things to the doctor. It's not really protocol to tend to someone you know so personally, but I insisted on helping in some capacity. They couldn't have stopped me if they tried."

"I see. You seem to be enjoying your work here. Climbing the ranks and all."

"I am. I think I would have enjoyed this as a career had my life been a little different." I walked past Rafe to the filing cabinet, to return my documents, pushing the drawer closed slowly as I thought about what my life might have been if I hadn't been born a princess. Normally I was proud of my station and lineage, and there were certain things I wouldn't have changed for the world— like my family, and Roland.

"Bothersome royalty?" Rafe cracked, lifting his nose into the air in mock disdain. I wouldn't admit it, but I had seen many a nobleman make that exact expression unironically at countless formal occasions. His mocking held some undeniable truth.

"Terribly bothersome." I feigned seriousness and nodded. Silence stretched between us for a couple of heartbeats and piqued my curiosity as to why Rafe had decided to stop by rather than simply send a note.

"Your sister is quite the spitfire isn't she?" Rafe folded his arms across his chest. "I wouldn't have expected that from royalty. Then again, you surprised me too, so clearly I shouldn't keep making assumptions about your family. She must be a handful to contain in your fancy world."

"Kira? Oh, absolutely. She's a dangerous combination of wild and terribly clever."

"Fearless too. Standing up to a Fire Wielder and to a hoard of soldiers. I was impressed by her speaking up for that little girl."

"Well, she should have. That poor girl was innocent."

"The innocent aren't always sheltered." Rafe's tone dropped, and he scuffed his foot and looked at the ground. "Sorry, I'm sure you know that."

"I do," I spoke softly, and looked out the glass panels of the door to watch the steady fall of rain increasing into a downpour. The crescendo of thunder rumbling, lightning flashes, and driving rain transfixed me. "I'm trying my best to fix it too, for what little good that is doing so far."

Rafe followed my gaze and pointed to the window. "Do storms make you happy?"

"They do." I nodded. "How could you tell?"

"Your whole face lit up with the lightning for a split second while you forgot to be sad. A man tends to take stock of what takes a lady's breath away. Habits and all. And, I'm kidding, of course. But you did light up with the lightning. That part was true."

I rolled my eyes at his joke and continued to stare out the window, wishing profoundly that I could return to simpler times as a child when the world made sense. "I used to love to stand in the rain and dance between the raindrops."

"It doesn't make you ill to stand out in the pouring rain, in the freezing cold?"

"No, I don't get sick too often. I guess with a healing hand, I am thankfully relatively resilient myself." I curled my fingers around the pages I carried and jerked my chin at the door. "I love this weather, and being in it. It's one of the most refreshing experiences and makes you feel connected to something powerful."

"Then why don't you?" Rafe wiggled his eyebrows and walked over to the window. "It's certainly coming down out there."

"Why don't I do what?" I shook my head and straightened my papers, tapping them into alignment against the table before returning them to their folder.

"Go dance in the rain?"

"Because I'm not eight anymore," I scoffed, but the notion made me smile all the same.

"Something tells me it hasn't been *that* long since the last time you indulged. You probably snuck out to stand in the rain and didn't tell a soul within the last year. I'll bet you anything," Rafe goaded, sauntering back over to my table, lines forming around his eyes where they squinted smugly at me.

I opened my mouth to retort but found myself swallowing back a guilty grin. "I can't do things like that now."

"Why not?"

"Because I'm working." I walked back over to the table and stood in front of my chair but didn't sit down. Instead, I rested a hand on the back of it, using it as a sort of tethering anchor to ward against the impulsivity rearing up within me.

"Isn't your shift ending?"

"Yes, but—"

"Come on, live a little. Are you too proud now that you're a fancy nurse assistant or whatever it is you do now? Because I think Madam Gauze Fetcher would have already been out there before the storm passed on by."

"I'll get wet."

"You'll dry off."

"I'm being watched like a hawk. Guards are posted everywhere. The only reason they aren't here right now is because I sent them to survey the outside before I leave to get a moment to myself. There is one standing out there now. You probably passed him on your way in—Sergeant Hykner. No way I can go frolic in the street."

"*Frolicking* is a wonderful descriptor. Really paints an image. And I must insist on seeing it. So, let's sneak out the back. You'll come back in, dry off and go home."

"Got another secret hatch hidden up your sleeve?" I teased and Rafe snatched my arm with a wicked grin to lead me further into the hospital. I yielded to his pulling with an unsolicited shiver of excitement.

"Maybe I do, but I was thinking we could use a regular old door, if that's okay with you."

"But—" I tried to regain control of my faculties, but Rafe cut me off again before I could formulate another excuse.

"You said the rain makes you happy, right?"

"Yes, I did."

"Well you look sad, Sorrel. Be happy just for a couple minutes," Rafe urged and shoved open a door that led to an alleyway behind the hospital. "Give yourself permission to refresh a little."

"Be happy?" I echoed, the statement so stupidly simple it

resonated with profound depth. Was I not allowing myself to be happy anymore?

"Just a couple minutes." He gestured to the pouring rain pounding against the cobblestones just beyond the door.

My eyes locked on the bouncing drops, and I felt like if I listened close enough, they were beckoning me towards them. I wiggled my feet in place, torn between wanting to throw myself into the rain and maintaining my composure. In slow tentative movements, I raised my hand and held it out to catch the rain. My heart was racing, but for the first time in a long while, it wasn't out of fear or anxiety. My eyes widened as I could have sworn the rain was increasing with each palpitation, and my excitement heightened.

"Be happy," I breathed.

"Be damn joyful! Go on, Princess. I won't tell a soul!" Rafe laughed. Leaning an arm against the wall, he waved me forward. "I'll even keep an eye out for ruffians so you can say you were under guard the entire time."

Hesitating a moment more, I took a deep breath and flung myself through the doorway with a small squeal. I thought I would flinch against the icy drops, but instead I felt like I had been enveloped by a warm comforting embrace, and I felt peaceful. I felt at home. It was as if I had somehow turned back the clock and was a child again. If I closed my eyes I could picture it—a younger me spinning in the storm, a watchful Roland undercover nearby, goading my spectacle the same as Rafe. Mama shouting at me to come inside, and sitting with Kira by the fire to dry off.

All thoughts of the world, the war, the patients— everything fell away from my mind. I tilted my face to the sky and inhaled deeply. The scent of wet stone and recently churned muddy earth mixed with the smell of sodden grass and twirled around my senses. Another crack of thunder boomed overhead and the next thing I knew I was laughing and spinning around. I could hear Rafe laughing at me from the door, but I didn't care how ridiculous I looked. The puddles sloshed around my shoes, and my frock plastered itself to my body. I felt free.

"This is in your nature, you know!" Rafe called out to me. "I can tell. And it suits you! You shouldn't shy away from your true nature. Embrace it."

With a mischievous laugh, I whirled around and lunged for him, grabbing hold of his bicep and using his surprise to tug him into the rain with me. "Join me! You convinced me to come out here like a lunatic, you have to do it too!"

"Shit, that's cold!" Rafe gasped, immediately drenched beside me. But he was smiling, and popped up an umbrella over his head. "You know, if you enjoy this and legitimately aren't cold, then I think you actually might be a little insane."

"Where'd you get an umbrella?" I asked, raising my voice to be heard over the din of the rain.

"It was by the door."

"You're a very resourceful man, you know that? Or very lucky. Either way, you always seem to have the right things on hand at the right time," I observed with a playful crinkle of my nose.

Rafe hesitated, looking at me meaningfully. "I might be out of contact for a while," He shouted back, then jerked his head back to the door.

"What do you mean?" I followed behind him, feeling energized and renewed as I tried in vain to ring my skirt out before stepping back inside the building. Water beaded from his hair down his face, and the deep burgundy shirt he was wearing clung to his arms and chest. The outline on his body made me suddenly very aware of how my frock was hugging every bump and curve of my own. I hoped my cheeks weren't flushing with embarrassment, and I could only imagine what Roland would have said if he saw me in this state.

"Well, not that you and I keep in regular contact really, but our paths have crossed off and on so I thought I'd let you know and say goodbye."

"That sounds awfully final." My smile fell. "You weren't drafted were you?"

"No, thankfully my name hasn't come up on that list. I don't think it will either. But, it's time for me to go regardless."

"I'll see you again though, I'm sure. You know Roland, right? Oh, and my mother was wanting to recognize you for your help. You'll have to be around for that."

"What?"

"Maybe you'll even get to come to the palace and laugh at me surrounded by all that needless fuss and bother. I answered a bunch of questions about you and everything. I'd really like for you and I to be friends, Rafe. I think we get on quite well and I don't have many friends outside of my family. You already know Roland and have met Kira—though it would be better to know her under more normal circumstances. Regardless, you saved us, so you'd be welcome, I'm sure. Oh, that reminds me!" I sucked in a breath, pausing my uncontrollable rambling. Something inside me was growing frantic to find a reason for him not to leave, so I kept talking. "Your knives. They couldn't find them. I think they were stolen."

Rafe laughed quietly and gave a small shrug. "Not to worry. Remember the rain." He waved and left me to stand there, dripping in the hallway, while he exited out the back door and disappeared through the rain into the dark without another word. I wasn't cold, but a chill ran down my spine at his abrupt departure. It sounded like it *was* a final goodbye, and his parting words to remember the rain, I knew was him reminding me to stay happy.

I stood for some time, forming a puddle around my feet, wondering why I felt a sense of crushing loss and loneliness for this person I hardly knew. In my gut, I felt like Rafe's and my paths were meant to cross again, but the wistful expression in his eyes made me worry what conditions those might be under. He knew something I didn't, and that much was clear. Perhaps I'd overwhelmed him and he didn't want to be friends with the Princess, only the strange nurse who'd wandered into his room by chance and nearly cried over a wall.

"Is everything alright?" I started at a voice behind me and

turned to see one of the nurses peering down the hallway at me and the open door. I recognized the woman as Rayana, a nurse from the wing Rafe had been a patient in.

I looked down at my soaked dress and shook myself. "Yes, sorry. I heard a cat in the street and was trying to get it under cover."

"Where is the cat?" Rayana asked, as I quickly tugged the door closed behind me.

"Oh," I lifted my chin and hurried past the woman towards the changing room. "He ran off."

"Your hair is wet," Roland greeted me matter-of-factly when I entered the library after returning from the hospital.

I touched my head and smiled. "It was raining."

"Did you stand in it?" He looked up from the glass he was swiveling around in his hand. "Like old times?"

"Maybe a little."

"Good. It's good to know you found a little time for yourself." He took a sip of his drink and shrugged with a smile. "I can't say I fully understand the fun involved in being soaked by the rain, but I do like to see you smile."

"I never realized I was so transparent," I mumbled, finding it amusing that Rafe had said nearly the same exact thing. "How is your shoulder?"

"My shoulder is just fine, Snowdrop." Roland wiggled the fingers of his arm in the sling. "What brings you to the library?"

"Well, I was looking for a book, though that might surprise you," I joked.

Roland smirked but the smile fell immediately from his face, and he continued to stare at the ground. When the silence lingered a heartbeat too long, concern made my skin begin to itch.

I took a step closer and narrowed my eyes. "Plus, it's one of the few private spaces left in the palace right now. You look contemplative. Has something happened?"

Roland pursed his lips, deep concentration creasing stark lines on his face. "Honestly, I'm finding myself at odds with the decisions of those I care about."

"That sounds rather cryptic." I hugged my arms close to my body and looked at my feet. "Care to elaborate?"

"They posted a list today," Roland began and I saw his knuckles whiten around his glass. I stilled immediately, overtaken by the somber air that refused to lift. Roland's shoulders were raised, and every muscle in his body was tensed despite the deflation in his posture. "Arrian brought it to my attention, all too happy with his findings."

He's upset— angry even.

"Is it the draft?"

"That was posted today as well."

"I'm afraid I'm not following." I took another small step forward, unsure how to comfort him. Roland, typically amicable in nature, rarely showed the cracks of wrath or open discontent in his own mask of duty.

"They posted the draft today, and the first round of soldiers will depart in a week's time to join the battle front. The general is continuing on in the hopes of overwhelming the Veil of Stars protecting Sonyo and Slayad's land with sheer volume of men. Then add in the new wave being directed at Sibru after the attack the other night. Most everyone will be brought to the front at this rate."

"You don't agree with this, I take it?" I prompted, inching forward a little more.

"I'm not sure I understand the point, but I can track the logic."

"But that isn't what you don't agree with?" With my next step I forced myself into his line of vision. I could see him weighing a multitude of ambiguous thoughts behind his eyes, twisting them round and round, searching for something to make sense of.

"No. It is the *other* list." Roland downed another swig of what

I could now smell as brandy, and cleared his throat. "It has the names of those suspected of Wielder abilities, and those suspected of aiding and abetting them."

"Oh," I inhaled sharply, remembering what Larkin had told me a few days earlier. It seemed as though the rumblings unsettling the staff had been proven true after all. "And this was Otvel's doing wasn't it?"

"It was." Roland's brows jumped in surprise. "You knew about it?"

"Larkin mentioned something when I asked why the staff was running away every time I came into the room. But, the rumor slipped my mind."

"Well, it's certainly no rumor." His jaw tightened, and I could see the corners of his mouth twitching into a scowl. "Being that I was on bed rest, I wasn't made privy to the decision ahead of time. It has been a complete blindside."

The list, and whatever the ominous *test* was, sounded invasive. Even I wasn't entirely sold on the validity of accusing misguided Sympathizers who could potentially be swayed, but ultimately, the intent behind arresting Wielders wasn't surprising. This left only one other conclusion I could fathom that would elicit such a strong reaction from Roland.

"Was there someone on the list you know?" I asked quietly. I wondered who could have deceived him so convincingly to leak him cracking under the weight of his discovery.

Roland leaned his neck back with a hoarse laugh, and rolled his shoulders back. "Someone we both know, actually."

"What do you mean?" My skin crawled like it was covered with a million little ants, and the warm comforting feeling of the earlier rain evaporated.

Roland pointed to the waste bin by one of the century-aged reading desks. "My brother gave me a copy *after* it was posted. Seems he's been given some new duties of late himself."

I frowned and retrieved the crumpled paper in the bin. My hands trembled lightly as I unfolded it and started scanning the list for any name that was familiar. Then, my eyes finally collided with the singular name I knew Roland was referring too. I read it over and over again.

"No," I breathed in utter disbelief. "But how can that be? I don't understand…" I stammered. "And they are arresting the people on this list for certain?"

"As of today," Roland lifted his brandy up, tipping it back and forth. "Hence, the drink."

I stared at the paper in my hand, unable to look away. "Roland, I need you to take me to the theater. Right now."

"I don't know that I'm in the mood to take in a show, Snowdrop," Roland replied wryly.

"I don't need to see a show, I just need to go inside," I insisted, and gripped onto his sleeve.

"Is that allowed? I mean, will the powers that be approve of such an outing?" He sighed, and relinquished his drink to the bar cart, before conceding with a nod to the door for me to lead the way.

"I don't know, but I need to do this."

"You seem to feel strongly about it," Roland observed, not quite a question, but the statement hung in the air as one. His eyes narrowed ever so slightly like he was sizing me up for something unspoken.

"I do. And I don't want to draw too much attention to it. We can ask Hykner to be our escort. He won't say anything." I knew that he was an officer who could be trusted and was one of the few soldiers I felt truly comfortable being a personal guard.

"Sergeant Hykner has a personal matter to tend to this evening. Come on, Snowdrop. I know a way off the grounds where we won't be noticed."

"Thank you." I shifted from the lead to stand behind him and followed him through the palace and out one of the side entrances.

I recognized it as the same direction I had seen Inessa run off to that one day she claimed she was looking for a greenhouse to stew in following the Shadow Wielder's attack on that little hospital. We ended up coming to a place where the hedges along the fence grew slightly denser, and Roland gestured to it.

"There is a gap in the fence through here, but you have to slip through the hedges— gently too, so as to not draw attention to it."

"Alright," I nodded and pushed myself through the foliage without pause. Roland picked his way gingerly through behind me. "Aren't there usually thorns in these hedges to avoid this exact thing from happening?"

"The thorns were removed."

"Should I even ask why you know this exists?"

"Not unless you want an honest answer."

"I don't think I like the sound of that. I'll hold off on that conversation for another time," I sighed and felt a sense of relief when I emerged out the other side of the suffocating hedges. "Do you think we can catch a cab, or should we walk? It isn't far."

"We might be recognized if we stop for a car, but we do need to hurry or we will be missed for dinner."

"Right. On foot it is. Are you up for it?"

"A harrowing adventure to the theater, breaking some rules with the most honest and genuine creature I know? How could I not be up for it?"

"I mean your shoulder," I quipped, pushing away the guilt rising within me at the mention of defying the rules.

"I already told you, Snowdrop. My shoulder is just fine, and as you so kindly pointed out at the hospital, I can in fact walk. Don't worry about me."

"Alright, let's hurry then." I set off briskly in the direction of the theater, keeping my head down as we entered a more densely populated area of the city where the theater was located. Though the rain had been refreshing earlier, I was thankful that the sky had cleared for our impromptu excursion.

"Are you going to tell me what we are doing here?" Roland puffed with exertion, and I questioned why I even asked him to come with me in the first place.

I knew he was injured, and if I was caught, there wasn't a good reason to get him in trouble too. I supposed there was a part of me that was afraid, and I wanted someone I knew I could trust to be with me while I confronted the truth. I was grateful that Roland, though clever and calculating, had a deep-seated loyalty that allowed him to come with me with little to no information or questions asked.

"I have to confirm it," I answered simply, turning sharply towards the entrance of the theater.

The ballet had been canceled due to the attack, but thankfully there were still workers dismantling and removing the elaborate sets. I slipped through the door behind a couple of burly men exiting with a painted flat, Roland hot on my heels. Once inside, I rushed up the stairs towards the private concessions box and threw open the door.

The room was pristine, with not so much as a single drop of blood remaining. It looked like nothing had ever happened, nor that two men had died here recently. But, that wasn't what I was looking for. I slipped behind the counter and dropped to my knees to replicate my escape with Kira. My breath caught in my throat and a hole yawned open in my chest, confusion and hurt threatening to overwhelm me.

I looked from the wall, smooth and completely devoid of there ever having existed a hatch, to the heavily wrinkled list in my hand. The reason why Mama and Friedrich and Otvel had interviewed me the other day became all too clear between the evidence in front of my own eyes and the boldly scrawled words *Dezidaneyan Wielder of Curses* beside his name.

Rafe had saved me and Kira. He had saved us, *and* he was a Wielder.

"When I sought peace in a place of trust, I
was moored with curses inked in deception."
 -D

TWENTY

I staggered to my room and closed the door firmly behind me. Mercifully, it seemed that Inessa hadn't returned from her daily activities to get ready for dinner yet, leaving me all alone. I slumped against the door and slid to the ground, pressing my shaking hands to my forehead. My mind was spinning with a torrent of emotions and questions I knew I had little to no chance of answering.

Rafe was a Wielder. He was a *Wielder*. If Otvel's warning to me about corruption was true, then I'd befriended an inhuman monster, capable of great evils. What terrified me more was that there was a piece of my brain screaming at me that Rafe had been there to provide me relief when I was grieving Harvier's death, rescued me and Kira from other Wielders, and had shown up to check in and remind me to be happy. Each of our encounters had left me more or less alone with him, and he had done me no harm. Could a monster exist beside its prey without attacking and consuming it? Could I even consider Rafe to be a monster?

If I was sympathizing with him, then I was corrupted. I would be part of the very evil my family was working so hard to eradicate. I wanted to rid our country of the blight of evils, surely that had to count for something. Harvier had been unconfirmed in his affiliations, but, if I allowed myself to sympathize with Rafe, knowing what he was, then I would be consumed and Divine justice would come for my head, just as Otvel promised.

My entire body trembled uncontrollably.

When did my downfall occur? When my dreams were attacked by an unknown Wielder? When, for a moment, I had pitied the young Shadow Wielder bleeding at the hospital? Perhaps it had been the moment I doubted my own convictions with the Divinities. They could have sensed my wavering of faith and rejected me, leaving me to fend off the darkness until I was consumed only to then destroyed by those I held dear. Was that to be the fate of a Sympathizer? When would the corruption begin to reveal itself to my family? Could I corrupt those around me simply by existing in the same space as them?

I couldn't stop the questions from trampling over each other in my mind. Thinking back to my encounters with Rafe, I thumped my head against the door with a groan. The rags he conveniently had on hand, the knives that vanished into thin air, the mysterious hidden hatch at the theater, and even the umbrella— all of it had been magic, conveniently explained away, and I had accepted it blindly as honesty.

"Why do I even care?" I puffed aloud. "He left. He isn't my friend, and he left. I'll never see him again. He's gone."

I rose to my feet and started pacing, my agitation shifting to anger. All of it had to have been a lie. He was likely trying to lure me into some false sense of security. Had those Wielders at the theater even been killed? Magic by nature was deceitful and played fast and loose with the laws of nature. I couldn't trust anything I had seen. I didn't even fully know what the capabilities of a Dezidaneyan Curse Wielder entailed. My chest tightened further, imagining Rafe conjuring the same Dezidaneyan blades that had once cursed Theo.

"Was that why the room was so clean? Did anyone even die there?" I slammed my hands down on my vanity, a cold sweat gathering on my brow.

"What?" Inessa's voice sounded from the doorway, but I didn't bother looking at her. I hadn't even heard her enter the room. "Sorrel, are you alright? You look ill."

"I'm fine," I replied sharply, taking a step back when Inessa tried to approach me.

"You don't look fine. Should I fetch Klivech?" She tried again to reach for me and I stumbled away. "What in the world is wrong with you? You're acting like I have the plague."

"Not you," I muttered to myself, and held my hands in front of my face. Pushing my sleeves up I inspected my forearm for any signs of discoloration or deformity. Was I expecting to see a blight overtaking my skin like a diseased rose petal? If that happened to everyone, we would have a very clear idea of who was who. Unless the blight was under my skin, running through my very veins. I squinted harder. "Nonsense."

"Sorrel, you're acting out of your mind. I'm going to get help," Inessa opened the door and asked the guard who was the last person they saw in the hallway. "Otvel? Well, I suppose he is good at calming if nothing else. Sorrel, I'm going to get Otvel to take a look at you, alright?"

"What?" My spine went rigid. Otvel would see the corruption in me right away. He was the last person I wanted to see right now. I could be thrown in the dungeons. Was that where I belonged? "No, no. I'm fine. I swear."

Inessa closed the door, and all but charged me before I could get away. She curled her fingers around my arms and held fast. "If you won't let me get help, then you need to tell me what has made you so worked up. You're usually the most put together of all of us. If you're this upset, it has to be big. Tell me. I promise you I won't judge or tell a soul."

"I... I..." I stammered, sucking in deep breaths.

"Is it Roland? Did something happen between you two?" Inessa prompted, forcing me to look her in the eye by grabbing my cheeks and lifting my face.

"No," I spluttered under her grip, pulling away to collapse onto my bed with my head in my hands. "No, it's not Roland."

"Then *what?* You have three seconds to tell me before I march out that door and bring the whole cavalry in here to drag it out of you. Mama, Friedrich, Otvel…" She started ticking the names off on her fingers and an unexpected wave of wrath tore through me, setting my nerves ablaze.

"They tricked me," I finally managed to whisper, doing my best to keep my emotions under control.

"Who did?"

"Everyone!" I snapped, and swiped my brow with the back of my hand. I placed my hands on the back of my neck and pulled gently, trying to relieve the tension. "I'm such a fool and now I've gone and ruined myself."

"What are you talking about? How have you ruined yourself?"

"Rafe! I befriended him. He touched my arm *today.*" I waved my arm in front of her and her face scrunched in deeper confusion.

"What's wrong with befriending Rafe? Wasn't he the one who got you and Kira out of the theater?"

"He did, but why? Why did he save us? I don't understand. It must have been for some nefarious reason, right?"

"Sorrel, you need to slow down. You're not making sense right now. Walk me through what you're thinking." Inessa moved my arm away from her face, and spoke calmly.

"Rafe was listed as a Dezidaneyan Wielder to be caught and arrested today. I just saw him this afternoon. I tried to befriend him because I didn't know what he was, and I enjoyed his company." My head drooped in defeat.

Inessa listened quietly and patiently, running her fingers lightly over my head as I confessed my sin to her.

"Then I find out he's a Wielder— the same type that cursed Theo no less— and instead of condemning him on the spot like I should, I'm torn. I want to believe in the person I thought he was so badly I'm trying to rationalize the compassion and sympathy I'm feeling. But I shouldn't be sympathetic. I barely know the man! If I'm sympathetic to a Wielder, I'm corrupted. The evil touched me and I'm lost."

"Oh, Sorrel. Come here." Ina sat on the bed beside me and pulled me close. "Compassion towards others doesn't make you contaminated or evil. Anyone who would try to feed you such rubbish is wrong. Having a kind heart like yours, and an open mind to those you share this world with, is how we keep it from imploding on itself with blind hatred. It's okay to think differently, and it's okay to not agree with the way someone lives their life. But, it's always a beautiful and just thing to respect those differences and act with reverence and kindness to those who treat us well in return. If someone has done you or those you love or those who are innocent no harm, why should we condemn them for a crime they didn't commit?"

"I feel so angry," I whimpered, hugging my sister back with all my might, thankful for her comforting presence. "Mama, Otvel, Friedrich— they all tricked me into talking about him like he was my savior, praising him and all the while they were looking for confirmation to arrest him without even telling me!"

"That was wrong of them to treat you like that. If they knew what they were doing, they should have trusted you with the truth."

"It feels wrong to be angry with them, Ina. They were acting in our interest right? How could they not be?"

"You're allowed to feel what you feel." Ina cupped my face in her hands and smiled at me. "If this made you angry, so be it. You're angry. If you don't want to hate Rafe because he was born to a fate he had no choice in, then don't hate him. You're in control of your own opinions, Sorrel. Remember that."

She let go of my face, and I flopped onto my side, my head bouncing on my pillow. "I honestly don't know how I feel yet. I know what I am *supposed* to feel, but it isn't sticking. I don't want to corrupt anyone else though."

"You aren't a virus because you're forming your own conclusions. It's better to have faith in what you believe based on your own careful considerations, and not simply because someone told you to. Faith that is obligated is hollow. You need to decide what you believe sincerely. There are other faiths outside of the Divinities. Do suppose every single person who doesn't follow one specific creed is inherently evil?

"What other faiths do you even know of, Ina?" I blustered, realizing just how unaware of alternative beliefs I was.

"The Storm Witches in Kataheyda are a group that comes to mind. No one really knows what they practice, isolated up there on the stormy island, but they seem to really do no harm to the world since they keep to themselves. Even the Faith of the Founders, which is what most Wielders practice, has its rules of morality."

"Wielders attacked us. They've tried to kill us more than once. That girl attacked the hospital too. I've seen their destruction with my own eyes. But then I think of Harvier, and how I can't bring myself to believe a little boy could be corrupted like Otvel told me. Now I'm doubting Rafe, but I'm also oddly convinced I don't need to. I'm angry at him for fooling me, and I'm angry at Mama for also tricking me. I feel like a stupid pawn, more than a person. I also can't bring myself to hate him. I truly thought he was a good man," I rambled, letting my thoughts tumble off my tongue as they entered my mind.

"Maybe he is. He helped, never harmed, by the sound of it." Inessa shrugged. "I don't believe in absolutes, personally. I think there are good men written off as evil, just as much as there are evil men claiming to be good. There is an exception to everything, therefore absolutes can't exist. If your gut is telling you he is good, then maybe he is."

"I danced in the rain like an idiot right in front of him," I declared flatly, staring unblinking in front of me, positively mortified. "I frolicked in front of a Wielder, Ina."

"Well," Inessa chuckled at my monotonous deflation. "If he's anything like how he sounded, then I think he probably just enjoyed seeing you let loose a little and thought nothing of it."

I merely groaned in response.

"Have you calmed down?"

"I think so. For now."

"Good."

"Ina?" I sat up and faced her. "Promise you won't breathe a word of this to another soul while I sort this out. I'm terrified Otvel and Mama will hate me if they find out I'm even entertaining this for a single second."

"I promise. If anyone dares call you evil, they'll have to go through me." Inessa stood and held out a hand. "Come on, we better get ready for dinner. Are you going to be alright down there with everyone? I can always say you took ill."

I shook my head and drew in a long, slow, steadying breath. "No, I'll be fine now I think. I just needed to collect myself." I walked over to my vanity and looked in the mirror, blinking at the silver eyes that glinted back at me. "And as Roland says, I wear the mask of duty well."

"You've barely said a word tonight, Sorrel dear. And you barely touched your food." Mama stopped me as the group shuffled out of the dining hall. "Are you feeling well?"

I bit my tongue to keep it from lashing. "Actually, I am feeling a bit under the weather. It was a long day." It was only a half lie.

"Are you working too hard at the hospital? I swear, I'll have to have a word with Inessa about her slacking off on her shifts." Mama's brows creased as her eyes flicked to Inessa's golden hair leaving the room. "That girl has been surlier than usual and it's about time she straightened up."

"No, Mama. The work is fine. I like having something to do."

Mama smiled at me and ran her hand over my cheek tenderly. The gesture felt comforting in its intent, but I had to keep my expression from revealing how much the touch made my skin spark with rage. "You're such a good girl. There's so much of your father's spirit in you. I don't know how we got so lucky."

I shifted on my feet and glanced down, uncomfortable with the praise. I wasn't good. I was angry at my mother, I'd befriended a Wielder, snuck off the palace grounds, and now I was entertaining the idea that everything I'd been told to believe all my life was possibly misguided and fallacious.

"I think I will head to bed early tonight."

"Are you sure? Otvel was going to speak with us again. I know you enjoy his sermons."

"I'm sure. I just need some quiet and rest." I avoided looking into my mother's gaze, the same one I shared on my own face. I wasn't sure I could lie to my own eyes— but then again, I might have been doing that my entire life every time I looked in the mirror.

"Should Klivech look in on you? I can send Otvel up to pray over you as soon as he's finished with us."

"That's alright, Mama. I just really want to be by myself tonight. I think the solitude will be quite rejuvenating." A wave of goosebumps crept along my arms as my agitation at my mother's persistence grew.

Even if she'd done so with good intentions, she'd still tricked me into informing her about Rafe. She knew he had been a friend of mine, and not once the entire evening had she thought to apologize for her actions.

Does she think I am too dumb and obedient to figure it out?

I dipped my head and ducked out of the room, splitting off from the back of the group entering the drawing room for after dinner drinks, and paused to lean myself against the wall for support while I caught my breath.

That dinner had been much harder than I had thought it would be to get through. I had no appetite since my stomach was currently sustaining itself with knots of anxiety and trepidation. Inessa had been kind enough to redirect most of the conversations away from me all night, and where she failed, Roland took over.

We hadn't spoken much on our mad dash back to the palace, but both of us were processing the news of Rafe's affiliation. I knew Roland was likely struggling with wrapping his head around it too since Rafe was clearly someone he trusted in some capacity.

"Sorrel?" Friedrich's call made my hair stand on end. The last thing I wanted to endure, while I was still trying to remember how to breathe like a normal human being, was another forced conversation.

"Yes?" I ground my teeth behind a thin smile.

"Do you have a moment? I wanted to have a chance to speak with you."

"Oh, I was heading up to my room…" I wanted to run away. *Just leave me alone!*

"It will only take a moment," Friedrich pressed and there was something solemn in his gaze that piqued my curiosity despite myself.

"Alright."

"It is about your friend," Friedrich sighed heavily and glanced over his shoulder at Mama and Otvel. "I wanted to have a chance to tell you this information in private before it was released so you weren't blindsided, but Chinye jumped the gun."

"It's alright, Lord Friedrich," I ran my thumb over my nails rhythmically. "Roland showed me the list earlier."

"I see." Friedrich shifted uncomfortably before continuing. "I'm sorry, Sorrel. I know how devastating and confusing it must be to find out someone you valued and trusted was carrying such a dark and dangerous secret." There was something in his dark brown eyes that brimmed with a sincerity I couldn't question. I wondered if there had been someone on the list that Friedrich had known too.

I felt at a loss for words, but when I finally found some, they surprised me. "Was it confirmed?"

"How do you mean?"

"I want to know if it was confirmed before the list was posted, or if all of this and the warrant for his arrest is based on fact or suspicion."

"I think," He paused, choosing his words carefully. "There was enough reasonable doubt and contrasting evidence. Once he is caught, we can confirm beyond doubt. Given your recount of his aid at the theater, and the physical lack of alternative exits found in the room... It is clear one was made by other means."

"So, it *was* me who condemned him," I whispered, my shoulders sagging in defeat. I pressed my fingers against my forehead, fighting to maintain my composure as guilt consumed me.

"Are you alright?" Friedrich asked gently, placing a hand on my shoulder.

"I... I'm afraid I don't know," I replied honestly, my voice catching in my throat. I braced myself for Friedrich's passing judgment on my lack of resolve and clear distress, but it never came. Instead, he pulled me into a hug, something he hadn't done since I was a young girl, and patted my head.

"That's a very natural response. Furthermore, you should have been notified in the proper way, and between you and me, though it was done with the best of intentions, I don't approve in the slightest of how this was handled." He let go and looked me meaningfully in the eye, his brows creasing with compassion. "We did you a grave disservice and caused you undue distress, and for that, on behalf of myself, Chinye, and your mother, I hope you will accept my apology and promise to do better in the future."

"Thank you, Friedrich." His acknowledgment dampened the heat of my indignance and quelled my rising confliction. It didn't change what had happened, nor did it remove my involvement, but at least he had had the decency and respect to talk to me directly, rather than pretending nothing had happened.

"I've taken up more than a moment of your time, but I did want to clear the air. I hope you feel better with some rest. Please tell Inessa I hope she recovers swiftly too."

"Pardon?"

"Yes, she left just before you, claiming she also was feeling ill.

I hope you two haven't caught something serious."

"Hopefully not," I acknowledged the sentiment, though, if I wasn't truly sick, I knew Ina wasn't either.

She probably just wanted an excuse to bow out of Otvel's lecture, and I'd find her lounging in our room waiting for me. Friedrich gave a tiny bow in farewell and turned to join Otvel, who I realized was lingering by the door, watching Friedrich's and my exchange. He smiled at me before disappearing through the doorway with Friedrich, and I felt like my body had been finally freed from a binding of chains once I was alone again.

I wandered slowly through the palace, enjoying my solitude, and the slowness of pace to just exist without intrusive thoughts overtaking me. I knew once I joined Ina the brevity would set back in, so I wanted to enjoy the small sensation of reprieve while I could, even though I felt compelled to talk with my sister and sort out my feelings once and for all. The ambiguous nature of conflicted thought perturbed me, and I needed to land on a definitive answer before there would be peace in my bones again.

When I opened the door, to my surprise, Inessa was nowhere to be found. I waited a while, wondering if maybe she had just gone for a walk to clear her head, but as the minutes ticked on, my mounting concern started to intertwine with my curiosity. I hadn't realized how much I was relying on the prospect of verbalizing my thoughts until the option rendered itself void.

Before I knew it, I was slipping into my shoes and making excuses to the guards at the door for my departure. The men who guarded our doors were of low level military ranks, and the turnover was extremely high, as they worked in shifts. This of course made small matters of leaving our room for more secretive endeavors relatively easy to cover up with a simple and vague excuse. Likely Ina had used one and wandered off to the garden or perhaps the greenhouse.

With spring getting the upper hand on winter, more and more plants were emerging and blooming, dappling the grounds with swaths of green and various shades of reds, purples, and pinks.

I could see the beauty and understand why my sister enjoyed the season shift so much. I just wished the sweltering heat of summer didn't have to nip at its heels before the reprieve of autumn breezes returned.

Not wanting to draw attention to myself, or risk running into anyone else, I opted for a different path that would take me to the same sparsely used side entrance that Roland had taken me through earlier. It was the quickest route into the gardens anyway.

The air was crisp and smelled of roses as it greeted me in the folds of night. I poked around the various paths of the gardens for a short while before I finally found the potting shed, and my sister standing beside it. My jaw dropped when I saw she was very much so not alone in her own company, but instead was being held tenderly in the arms of none other than Sergeant Hykner.

TWENTY-ONE

I nearly dove directly into a shrubbery to avoid being seen, but managed to dodge behind it instead when Inessa looked over her shoulder in my direction.

So *this* was her secret, and the explanation for her surly mood of late. She and Sergeant Hykner were having intimate relations. I bit my lip and scowled, wondering why Inessa hadn't told me of her secret love affair. Since Hykner was in my regiment, as well as my personal guard whom I held in high esteem, I might have even been able to help her find moments to meet him.

But, where were those stolen moments going to lead? As the oldest daughter of an imperial ruler, Inessa's fate was all but sealed that she would have to marry for state and not for love. Perhaps that's why she hadn't told me. She must have assumed I couldn't relate, and maybe she was right. I had the unspoken promise of Roland, and she had a political obligation.

"I don't want you to go," Inessa whispered, pressing her forehead to Hykner's. I could see tears ready to spill down her cheeks glinting in the moonlight.

"I know," Hykner sighed. His nose brushed against hers, their lips meeting in a gentle kiss. His hands snaked around her waist and pulled her closer, deeper into the embrace.

I felt a sting of jealousy at their physical display. She might be hiding her romance in the shadows, but mine lived in the broad daylight for all to see where stolen kisses couldn't transpire. Or, *wouldn't*. Then again, one could argue mine was all but built on a flimsy foundation of possibility, and hadn't truly begun to live at all, let alone in shadows or daylight.

The two pulled apart and Hykner reached up to wipe away Inessa's tears. "It's going to be alright."

"You can't promise that. Everything is going up in flames with every passing day. It's a nightmare."

"Hey, look at me, Ina." Hykner held Inessa's face in his hands and looked her in the eye. "I *promise*." His tone was firm and I found myself relaxing, despite my initial irritation at the secrecy. I liked seeing how Hykner treated my sister so kindly.

"We will find a way to each other, always."

"But…"

"Being drafted isn't a death sentence."

"It may as well be!"

Oh, Ina. My heart broke for my sister as realization struck me. Hykner had been one of the new recruits drafted to join the front. That must have been the personal matter he was tending to that Roland mentioned earlier. She was carrying that burden all on her own, living with a new reality of sending her lover off to a war he might not return from. I wasn't sure I could bear such a thing. It was no wonder she had closed herself off more and more to the rest of us. She was in terrible pain.

We'd both seen with our eyes the spectrum of men that returned from the front. Some were maddened from sleep deprivation or terrible nightmares. Others were husks of their former selves, while more still were injured physically.

"I swear," Inessa sniffed, turning away from Hykner as she

tried to subdue her crying. "Part of me wonders if my mother somehow knows about us and put you on that list herself."

No… Mama would never be so cruel. I longed to console my sister, but that wasn't my role in the scene playing out before me.

"I think you know deep down that isn't the case. If there is one thing we know for certain, it's how much your family loves you, Ina."

We do. Well said, Hykner.

As they continued their conversation in hushed tones, I looked away and wondered if I should start backing away, to leave them to their privacy. But, I found myself ducking down as Hykner separated from my sister, cleared his throat, and walked briskly away until he was swallowed up by the blur of foliage and inky night. Inessa stared after him, her arms wrapped around herself, as she tried to swallow back her tears. She took a few shuddering breaths, sobering, and for the second time, I weighed the option of revealing myself. I could pretend like I had just arrived and hadn't seen a thing. Though I figured it might be best to retreat the way I'd come and meet her back in the sanctity of our room.

Spying on her like this felt like a breach of trust that I could ill afford if she was my only ally in my warring beliefs. It reminded me of when we were young girls and would sneak around together trying to sneak peaks of Roland in his daily lessons, though I was fairly certain he always knew we were watching him. Inessa had a short-lived crush on a visiting dignitary's son then too, but he had spurned her affections on account of her having too many freckles. We didn't sneak around after boys as much after that. I never would have thought then that one day I'd be hiding in a bush spying on her this time.

I was surprised that the longer I lingered, something compelling me to stay until she left first, she wasn't heading back to the palace. Instead she rolled her head back, and dropped her hands to her side. She glanced around every few seconds, reaching out to inspect different flowers, and under the twinkling blanket of starlight behind her, I could almost swear they were perking up at her touch.

She was still waiting for someone. Hykner perhaps? No, his departure had an air of finality to it, and I didn't expect to see him again the rest of the night. She was waiting for someone else. I waited a few moments more, and was about to give up, when her correspondent finally appeared. His tall stature, dark hair, and blazing blue eyes were illuminated as he transitioned from the shadows into the moonlight.

Roland! What is he doing out here, and why is he meeting Inessa so surreptitiously? All their strange interactions of late— Kira's observation of them in the hallway that day Papa announced we were joining the war, and their odd exchange at the ballet came flooding to my mind. I covered my mouth to keep any wandering sounds of shock at bay

"You're getting careless with covering up your tracks, Inessa," Roland sighed. "With Hykner too."

"It's fine. I told everyone I wasn't feeling well. Sorrel used the same excuse so they will think we are together." Inessa waved her hand dismissively.

"And when Sorrel mentions that you weren't in the room with her?"

"I'll just say I went for some fresh air."

"Reckless woman," Roland tutted, and Inessa folded her arms with a scowl.

"Oh, don't lecture me."

"I'm worried about Sorrel, Ina. She was really shaken up by Rafe's name on the list." Roland looked over his shoulder past my hiding place, staring at the palace in the direction of my room.

"I know. I thought she was losing her mind upstairs earlier. It's all such a wretched situation. It's hurting everyone." Inessa's irritated stance softened at the mention of me. "I hate it. I wish it were easier to just be open about everything."

"I want to tell her."

Tell me what? I suppressed the urge to jump out of the bushes and demand an explanation. I was stuck as a specter, only able to thrash and wail in the silence of my mind unless I wanted to give my position away and risk forfeiting learning valuable information that apparently was being willfully kept from me.

"I know you do." Inessa clicked her tongue and looked to the side, not giving an inch. Her stubbornness was often an impenetrable wall you didn't want to find yourself up again.

"I was *going* to tell her after the ballet."

Tell me what? Spit it out now so I can know! I bit down on my lip to keep myself from indulging my impulses, and winced as my teeth punctured the skin and drew blood. My mouth was flooded with a bitter metallic tang. Somehow I found the bitterness matching my declining disposition. More secrets. Everyone was keeping things from me it seemed.

"That was entirely premature," Inessa quipped, rolling her eyes. "And half of that I'm sure was due to Kira's unsolicited influence pumping through the box."

What did Kira have to do with this?

"Kira is beside the point. Sorrel *should* know. Once she met Rafe, I knew it was only a matter of time before things took a turn for us. Don't you trust her?"

"I don't know. Maybe. Sorrel is…" Inessa trailed off, searching for the right word to describe me, but came up short.

"She had me go with her to the theater tonight."

"When did you do that? That list was only posted this afternoon."

"Before dinner. We had to sneak out to pull it off."

"Sorrel snuck out? My my, she hasn't been that brazen since before Theo was born." Inessa's brows jumped. "You didn't show her our spot did you?"

Your spot? What do you mean your spot? What makes it yours?

It was Roland's turn to roll his eyes, his words coming out terse. "I don't have an abundance of breaches in imperial security, you know."

"Now look who's being reckless. Sorrel isn't stupid, Roland," Inessa snapped.

At least someone thinks so. I'm not so certain anymore.

"I know that! I never said she was."

"She's going to circle back around after she's calmed down enough and start asking questions about why you need a secret way out."

"She has no reason to ask right now."

Inessa narrowed her eyes with a scoff, "She'll ask."

"Come on. We've been standing here too long. She might come looking for you if she hears you said you were sick too. As you pointed out, she's not stupid."

"Fine, let's go then. I can't be gone long tonight either way at this point. We just need to make sure things are situated," Inessa sighed. "And Roland? Let's keep this a secret a bit longer. I don't know how she will react on top of everything else. Something tells me with how reserved she is all the time, if she ever snaps, whoever is on the receiving end isn't making it out alive."

"Fine. We can keep it to ourselves a while longer. But we can't keep this up forever. She's too close to the both of us. And with Kira and Yulia getting more and more untethered, something is going to come up. It's a wonder she hasn't picked up on it already."

"She's had no reason to look." Their voices faded with distance and I finally released the breath I'd been holding.

My heart trembled so fiercely, I was certain it wasn't beating in a coherent rhythm anymore. Inessa was right; I wasn't certain after everything that had thrown my life into a frenzy in the last few months, that I could handle the reality of the secret they had chosen to keep from me.

I walked partially to the palace, and back to the potting shed three times before I stalled on the path between two walls of hedges. An intricate diamond shaped planter acted as a resting space for me while I waited to see if the two would resurface.

In my pacing, I had made up my mind that I would confront them with my presence, waiting in their path. There was a sense of foreboding at what I would find out that made my skin itch from the inside out. Agitated anticipation left me wanting nothing more than to run away— from the turmoil sloshing in my stomach, from the goosebumps rippling over my arms, and from my own pitted heart hammering like a war drum.

My senses were stinging me like a million adder bites. The night felt too still, too quiet, and I forced myself to count the stars to keep from bolting. I wanted the truth. The truth ultimately was going to be far less painful than the space between blissful ignorance and the clandestine unknown.

As my pulse raced, and my nerves twisted till they were raw, I kept staring into the infinite indigo abyss above. Sometimes I liked to imagine the sky was just another unreachable sea, and that if one ever rose high enough, they could dive into the nebulae and swim with the stars. I squinted, feeling as though the longer and deeper I peered, the brighter the stars became, telling me that I wasn't alone and they would be there watching me until I found my peace. Some believed the Divinities lived above us in a parallel plane of existence, so maybe the twinkling of radiant light was meant to console me in the knowledge that they hadn't forsaken me despite my mounting doubts.

But, as I reached up a hand to the night, I felt an odd sense of confidence that if anything dwelled in that glimmering sea, it was something entirely unto itself. The thought felt eerie with a palpable longing to be part of whatever it was that explained the presence of eternal night. It was achingly familiar and beautiful, it filled me with an overwhelming sense of serene melancholy. The kind that could bring tears to your eyes, while your heart sang with bittersweet joy.

The crunching of shoes against grit and pebbles alerted me to the return of Roland and Inessa. "The stars are exceedingly bright tonight, have you noticed?" The steps stopped abruptly, one right after the other. "Sorrel."

I lowered my hand and blinked away the mystified daze I'd placed myself under until I was tethered back to reality before me, where Roland had spoken my name.

"Are you alright?" Inessa asked slowly, her eyes quickly flicking from me to the sky and back. "What are you doing out here?"

Rising slowly to my feet, I felt dizzy under the weight of suspense. "I saw you," I started flatly.

"Saw me?" Inessa laughed, but the sound was strained. Roland's eyes widened slightly. He knew instantly what I had seen and that it had been too much.

"With Hykner. I went looking for you to make sure you weren't ill." I intentionally left the second part out, gauging their reactions, and offering them a chance to tell me themselves before I brought it to light.

"Oh," Inessa croaked, her nails digging subconsciously into her arm. "I-I'm not sure what to say."

"Why didn't you tell me?"

"I don't know. It just happened and felt so precious and fragile, I was afraid if I spoke it aloud, it would all break and be gone."

I bit my lip and looked down at my feet before raising my gaze to burn a hole into Roland's. "Bliss is fragile and fleeting. Easily shattered irreparably by deceit. You're better off being honest."

"Right…" Inessa followed my line of vision with an awkward turn of her head to Roland, who was staring unblinking back at me. "I'm sorry I didn't tell you, Sorrel, I am. But now you do know, and I hope you can find it in your heart to keep this between us, as sisters."

"Seems you told Roland." My words were clipped and pointed.

"Oh, well… I didn't tell him as much as he knew on his own." Inessa looked away and scuffed her foot.

"I'll keep your secret," I spoke briskly and clenched my fists. "I've always kept your secrets. Never once have I told on you."

"I know that. I'm so sorry, Sorrel. I appreciate you keeping this a private matter. Truly, I do."

I tipped my head to the side, narrowing my eyes slightly as they continued to bore into Roland's. Finally, his gaze broke and he smirked with a side grin and shrug.

"She knows, Ina." He shook his head, speaking slowly.

"Obviously," Inessa snorted.

"No, Ina," Roland sighed and looked back at me, imploring and curious. I dug my heels in to cement my resolve to see this matter through. "If she was there for Hykner, she was here after. She *knows.*"

I felt a heat of sudden blazing indignation surge through me, propelling my feet forward until I stood toe to toe with Roland.

"Oh, I think there is a lot I *don't* know. Why don't you tell me?"

TWENTY-TWO

"You said you wanted to tell me something," My jaw set as I ground my teeth together, steadying my sparking nerves. "Now's your chance."

"Sorrel—" Inessa tried to reach out and touch my shoulder and I shrugged her off, my irritation growing.

"Alright, you caught us red handed. We were sneaking out." Roland kept his voice level and his eyes held mine. I searched them both for the presence, or therefore lack of, sincerity, but found his gaze devoid of any overtly forthcoming information or emotion. The inviting blue of his eyes I had admired many times grew sharp and hard with a guarded coldness. I had to suppress a shiver as I blinked against my own silver eyes reflecting back at me, and realized my face had also turned to icy steel.

"Why?" I demanded.

"We were checking on Rafe," Inessa jumped in, a little too quickly. Roland's eyes twitched against an instinctual squint that told me my sister had given something away. I realized a heartbeat later that though I was aware that Roland knew Rafe, Inessa had no interactions to speak of beyond her initial reaction to him the day we met. There was no reason for *her* to seek him out unless she knew him too.

"Roland?" I prompted, raising my eyebrows. "As you both so kindly pointed out, I'm not stupid."

"It's true. We were both checking in on him… and others affected by today's list."

"I hope you mean the draft," I bit, and Inessa tensed at the mention of the sore subject. Her face flushed and puckered with annoyance. I had clearly stepped on an emotional landmine with my statement.

"This is exactly why we didn't tell you," She hissed, throwing an arm out to the side. "Listen to that pious judgment in your voice! Oh, wonderful, responsible little Sorrel, always doing exactly as she's told. How we all pale in comparison to your piety!"

"Ina, calm down," Roland warned, but she forced herself between us to shove her face in front of mine.

"What could be better than a pristine little doll who doesn't speak or think for herself?"

"How dare you," I snapped, looking down my nose at Inessa. Though she was older, I still had a few inches on her, something I knew had always perturbed her, especially on the rare occasions when we quarreled.

"Don't you look down on me!" Inessa's eyes blazed, and my leering personage had struck its mark. "I am not so far up my own ass with self inflated pride that I'm just *now* noticing the shit this country has gone to. Can you say the same?"

"That's a wretched thing to say, Ina, even for one of your tantrums." I was taken aback by her foul language.

"Alright, I think this conversation is no longer serving a productive function. Why don't we all just take a breath—" Roland tried to intervene, but the argument was too far gone. Words had been spoken to ignite all of our pent up frustrations, and they wouldn't stop tumbling until a resolution was reached one way or another after the exchange of verbal blows.

"*Tantrums?*" Inessa's lip curled around the echoed word.

"Yes, you skulk around, inflicting your foul moods on the rest of us. Like you're entitled to make us suffer your mood swings over the stupidest irritants."

"You have no idea what drives my mood."

Roland hung his head and raised his hands as he backed his way over to sit on the planter, giving room for Inessa and me to finish our row.

"How could I? You don't tell me anything anymore!"

"That's a laugh," Inessa snorted. "To what end would I divulge my deepest secrets to you? So you could judge me, condemn me, or think it's your role to save me from myself?"

"How could you even think that? We are sisters, Ina. And, I thought we had always been friends too."

"I don't blindly hate Wielders who have done no wrong, Sorrel," Inessa fired back. "I think for myself on what I believe, and I believe that they are innocent until proven guilty of a crime worse than existing."

"Wielders *have* proven to be dangerous! They cursed our brother. For goodness sake, Ina, they just attacked us and nearly made Yulia pull the trigger that would have killed him. Roland was shot!"

"And what about Rafe? He is fine and wonderful until you find out he was born with abilities he had no choice in having. Those same abilities that saved not only your life, but Kira's too. How can that even be a question up for debate of what kind of person he is? Are you that far gone that you truly can't fathom thinking for yourself?"

"Corruption doesn't discriminate. Not even children." I was taken aback as the regurgitated words of Otvel flew from my lips.

A stillness fell over Inessa, and she closed her eyes. Her nostrils flared with concentration, and her brows knitted, forming deep lines between them. Then she reached an arm to the side towards the nearest hedge, and with considerable effort started roving her fingers in a rhythmical and foreign manner. The motion was akin to coiling a string around one's finger, but instead of a string, a small spindle of the hedge yielded to the invisible tug, snaking its way to her hand.

Magic.

Inessa was *wielding* magic.

My eyes opened so wide I thought they might pop from my head and I staggered backwards, all remnants of superior posturing dissolving in an instant. Roland flitted behind me, steadying me on my feet. His expression was grim, but not surprised. He already knew.

"What now, Sorrel?" Inessa's voice was frail, the words threatening to break on her lips. Her hand fell limp to her side, and the small tendril collapsed to the ground. "You've known me your entire life. Tell me, am I evil in your eyes now that you know? Are you going to go run and turn me in? That's what the church would have you do, isn't it? I'll save you the trouble and let you know now, don't waste your prayers on my soul. It's not in need of saving."

"Inessa," Roland growled. "This isn't something to spring on someone."

"What happened to wanting to tell her so badly?"

"Not like this! She's more likely to have a stroke, or a conniption than anything else!"

Their words back and forth turned to thunder grating against my ears until they burned. My blood turned to ice, and I was only vaguely aware of myself ripping my body away from Roland's hold. My vision ebbed and flowed through spinning shapes and colors as my feet carried me silently away from the others and towards the palace. I was certain they were calling after me, but there was a hollowness palpitating through my entire body, caught somewhere between nightmare and reality. When my awareness started to creep back into sensation, I was startled to find myself standing at the entrance to Kira and Yulia's room. Both of my younger sisters were sitting upright in their beds, sharing quizzical glances with one another.

"Bad dream," I managed to push the words through my lips. Kira, whose bed was the closest, flicked her covers back and patted the space beside her. She didn't ask me why I was still fully clothed despite having allegedly headed to bed hours prior, and she didn't pry into the state of my stupor. Instead, I clambered silently into her bed and she wrapped her arms around me, holding me close.

"No more bad dreams," She whispered sleepily. "Everything always looks better in the morning."

Inessa is a Wielder. The thought repeatedly crescendoed against my skull, leaving no room for sound or sense of anything else. I stared blankly at the wall, my mind growing dull. *What does this mean for the rest of us?*

Kira rubbed her hands on my back ambiently. Something in her touch felt warm and reassuring, thawing the frigid shock that had consumed my body. Kira often emanated a certain kind of potent love, her laughter was infectious, and her skin was alive with life and an inner heat.

I turned and looked at her peaceful sleeping face, her infinite smile brimming on her mouth even in slumber. Inessa had mentioned *Kira's unsolicited influence*, and under the warmth of her embrace, for the first time, I began to question where the source of that warmth stemmed from.

"Shhh, you'll wake her," My eyes remained closed, but I could hear Kira whispering from the end of the bed. "What do you think happened to shake her up so?"

"Clearly she and Inessa must have gotten into an argument," Yulia whispered back.

"You think so?"

"Why else would she choose to hop in bed with one of us when Inessa was right there?"

"Ina is grouchy and I am a very cuddly bedmate?"

Yulia sighed, and I could practically hear her shaking her head. "Didn't she say something about Inessa when she came in?"

"Did she? I thought the only thing she said was that she'd had a bad dream."

A deep, visceral dread bit the nape of my neck. *How does Yulia really always know what I'm thinking?*

"She was super cold, I felt like I needed to warm her up," Kira mumbled. "And why is she still dressed?"

Why was Kira always warm to touch, and why was I always told I was cold?

"We should check on Inessa too, I think, and just leave Sorrel to sleep. She looked completely dazed and spooked," Yulia suggested, her voice becoming muffled beneath the sound of fabric rubbing together. "Oh, look. She's out in the garden."

"What a shock."

I waited until I heard their footsteps shuffling through the door, and the latch *click* before I dared to open my eyes against the bright light of day. For a moment, I felt afraid as my initial thoughts screamed at me that Kira and Yulia were rushing to a Wielder. I threw the covers off my body and scrambled to the window, my eyes locking on the golden head of Inessa stooping over the tulips.

No wonder Inessa was so captivated by nature.

I held my breath, fear still chewing at my cognition, until I saw Kira come racing into the garden with Yulia trailing behind her. Kira pounced at Inessa, throwing her arms around her, while Inessa feigned irritation and tried to peel her off. My knees buckled, and I sagged to the floor, still peering down at my sisters.

Guilt crashed over me for my first impulse of fearing Ina's proximity. She wasn't evil, and I knew that down to my very core. She wasn't a Wielder or a mortal—she was Inessa, my sister. That hadn't changed between the moments that had passed from yesterday to now. I balled my fists and pressed them to my face as I curled into a ball, wishing once more I could flee the confines of my own body.

I couldn't believe how easily Otvel's words had leapt into the conversation last night— words I knew I didn't even entirely agree with. Yet, in that moment, when challenged, they were the words I had chosen to brandish. It gutted me to know that my own convictions were so thin and reticent, they couldn't stand on their own without the aid of someone else's authoritative backing. I was no more than a pristine doll, just as Ina had accused me of.

"Do I even have my own thoughts and beliefs?" I breathed aloud, an odd trill of panic clutching at my windpipe. "What do I really think?"

I fished for what my instincts had told me every time I had personally been confronted with the presence of a Wielder or Sympathizer, before I'd ultimately deferred to what I was taught to feel and fear. I needed to grasp at the threads of my own inclinations before they were snuffed out by forced inhibitions.

The man at the celebration had frightened me, but what had frightened me more was the devastation of the stampede, and the nightmare that had followed. I pressed my hands harder against my head as I recalled that Inessa had been encased in vines in that dream. I'd been concerned someone was threatening me with a curse, but were they warning me instead?

That's still magic, warning or threat!

When I saw the young girl wielding shadows, I was terrified, but wasn't there something before that? I had noticed she was hurt, and I had wanted to help her before talking myself into fearing her power. I couldn't believe Harvier was corrupted. In my heart of hearts, he was an innocent little boy, and I was angry that his life had been forfeit because his father had been *accused* of sympathizing. I had gone out of my way to try and find a way to redeem Harvier's innocence, and when I disagreed with Otvel's lecture, I doubted my own morality.

The one they had called a Whisper Wielder had held too much power for my comfort, but I couldn't ignore the nagging inclination that something so capable of inflicting harm could have been prevented somehow. Those men were terrifying and they meant to kill us. They were truly monsters capable of evil. But, then there was Rafe, who had stood against them. He was not the same as them. And now there was Inessa. How many people would I allow these preconceived notions to turn from human to monster before I questioned the validity in the argument?

I couldn't discern truth and sincerity anymore. Harvier, Rafe, Ina, they were all just people. Patience, humility, justice, compassion, charity, and diligence. At some point I had started determining that some people were worth the expression of the Divine Virtues and some were beneath them. I'd been poisoned by the toxic piety Inessa had slapped me across the face with.

"Schnites," I cursed. "What do you think, Sorrel? What do you really think?" I all but shouted at myself. I took a few steadying breaths, slowing the increasingly rapid rise and fall of my chest. "What do I think?"

I don't know.

The thought crystallized like a clap of thunder. I didn't know what I thought. I didn't know what I believed. But for the first time, I wanted desperately and unwaveringly to find out for myself. One thing I did know for sure as I uncurled my body and pushed to my feet; Otvel had been right about something he'd told me back at the church, something I realized I did adamantly believe, just not in the way he had relayed it to me.

Corruption didn't discriminate. It could claim any of us, and it wouldn't care if its next victim was Wielder or mortal. I needed to be through making demons out of secondhand words, and wait to see if they existed with my own eyes. Or else *I* was the one corrupting them.

TWENTY-THREE

"Sorrel!" Mama waved me over as I marched through the hallway in search of Roland to demand answers. "Good, you're here."

There were still some things I needed to clear up before I was ready to face Inessa. After her reproach of me last night, when I next looked her in the eye, I wanted to have resolve sharp and sure enough to cut glass. My determined footsteps slowed before reluctantly shifting their trajectory to join my mother. She was sitting down in one of the many unused sitting rooms with the door open.

I poked my head into the room. "Yes?"

"I was hoping you would wander by." Mama's voice was strained. "I was also hoping you could help me with a few extra tasks today?"

My feet itched to be on their way, but one look at my mother's face told me she was having a rough day physically. I stilled the urgency probing in my mind. Regardless of how it was viewed by others, I still had responsibilities to attend to as a sister, daughter, and princess of Eisa. I'd have to settle for finding Roland later. I'd gone twenty years without knowing the secrets from last night. I could wait a little while longer.

"I'll see what I can manage," I replied evenly. There was a tenseness building in my shoulders, and I tried to force myself to relax. It was true, I didn't often harbor grudges, but I was still struggling against the sting of my mother blatantly manipulating my cooperative nature to arrest someone she knew I deemed a friend. She still hadn't apologized for the insult, but was ready to call upon my dutiful nature once more. What choice did I really have but to comply?

"For starters, your father has requested some papers be sent to him along with a couple of packages— those are already prepared. Also, the household affairs need to be managed. I know you have your committee meeting today, but if you could please see if you can find the time."

"Are you feeling unwell again?" I asked gently, pushing away the nagging pinch of my resentments along with the admonishment at myself for forgetting I had my own meetings to attend today, and ran my hand over Mama's forehead. "You look a little pallid."

"I am feeling under the weather. I've been in that study night and day, it seems, since your father left, and it's certainly taking its toll on me." She slid a paper off the table into her hand and held it out for me. "But, I'm delegating. I've even made a list."

"You'll go get some rest now, won't you?"

"Yes, just as soon as I get the gumption to move."

"I can help you back to your room," I offered, but mama shook her head.

"No, no. I'll be fine and I'll rest much easier knowing you are handling today's business." She paused and tipped her head to the side. "I'm sorry to ask all this of you, Darling. Normally your sister would be helping more in this sort of situation as the eldest, but she's been so beside herself with melancholy lately, I haven't the faintest idea what to say or do to snap her out of it. Perhaps you could speak with her when you go over the schedules."

My heart twinged with a small pang now that I knew what really had been troubling Inessa so deeply. "I plan on talking to her already, so it's no trouble."

"Good girl," Mama smiled at me. "Thank the Divinities for blessing me with such a dutiful daughter."

Though her words were clearly intended as a compliment, one I'd heard time and time again, my ears burned with shame. It might have been appreciated, but perhaps I was dutiful to fault, lacking priority and conviction strong enough to form any defiance.

"I'll take care of these things today, Mama. Should I send for Klivech before I go?" I curled my fingers around the list, the paper creasing beneath my grasp with a satisfying crinkle.

"No, I'll just send for Otvel." She rubbed her face slowly.

"But if you're ill—"

"Nothing heals like prayer. If you could have Dowels send him this note, that would be much appreciated."

I hesitated a heartbeat before accepting the small letter she offered me and said my farewells. Willing my feet to fly like the wind and inwardly willing Roland to happen into my path before I'd have to relay affairs and interact with Inessa.

I paused to scan the list and formulate the most efficient order of completion. Most of the chores revolved around paperwork and communicating orders and messages. Starting in the study, it didn't take me long to finish the first set of tasks. I'd already happened upon Dowels and passed along Mama's note for Otvel on the way, so all that was left was organizing the family affairs.

I plopped down in Papa's chair to pull out the schedules to make a full compilation, but stalled as my palms ran along the length of the chair arms. I closed my eyes, imagining for a moment that I could see Papa's kind, warm eyes and have him hold my hand through all the turmoil and agitation I was biting down. I knew I couldn't truly confide in him about what was on my mind, but in a perfect world, he would understand my deliberation and help me through it.

"You look good in here. Very authoritative. It suits you."

"Roland," My eyes fluttered open, and I lost hold of the tethers to my father I'd been grasping at. Now that I was face to face with Roland, my chest felt tight. I wanted answers from him, but a growing pettiness inside me wanted to withhold myself, and show him what a breach his actions had been.

"Snowdrop?" He dipped his chin and raised his eyebrows. A question.

"You wanted to tell me?" The words came out sharp and abrasive— more so than I had intended, but I didn't apologize and adjust my tone, realizing that for once, I was speaking as I felt. I was angry with him. Even if I could understand his motives and would ultimately most likely forgive him in full, I was still angry and he deserved to know that.

"I did." His voice was firm, with no room for question.

I asked the question anyway. "Why should I believe that?"

"Because I tried to tell you that I wanted to tell you at the ballet. I was going to convince you to go for a walk with me, just us two, after hours, and I was going to broach the subject. Then everything blew up, and Rafe ended up stealing the show." The last statement was meant as a joke, but the tone in Roland's voice was hollow and devoid of humor.

"But, you sent for him. Did you know we were going to be attacked?"

"I did send for him. I'd heard some rumblings of aggravation, and then little signs started cropping up as soon as we got to the theater. I'd hoped I was wrong, but I'm glad he at least made it in time."

"How do you know him?"

"I've known him for several years now."

"That wasn't my question."

"This isn't the place for this conversation. It isn't a safe topic for these walls. Let's go somewhere and talk for real." Roland looked sharply over his shoulder, his voice imploring.

"I can't now," I glanced at the clock. "I have to get this schedule written out for tomorrow. Then I have to go to my meeting and it's in town. I have a million things to take care of, and I don't have time for any more games."

"I don't intend to play any more games."

"Give Inessa her schedule for me, and I will see you after my meeting to talk," I sighed heavily, but Roland looked eager.

"I'll pick you up."

"Fine." I didn't change my expression, keeping my words short and to the point.

"Come on, Snowdrop. I can't stand this wall between us."

"You built it, Roland. Brick by brick, every day that you kept such a colossal secret from me."

"It's complicated, Sorrel. Lives hang in the balance with this sort of thing. It's not something I can take lightly. Think of Vin Holok, that little boy's father. I assure you, his death was no accident." Roland's voice dropped to a whisper at the end and he leaned his hands on the desk in front of me.

I oscillated between my instinctual annoyance with the excuse and the logic that rang true. Vin Holok's arrest and death had never sat right with me, for more than just Harvier's loss of a father. I gritted my teeth against a scathing reply. I'd heard Roland telling Inessa he wanted to tell me with my own ears.

He had practically been begging her, and had acknowledged his trust and desire to confide in me without knowing I was present. Perhaps my anger was misdirected at him, and I was really mad at Inessa. I'd trusted her with my deepest secret, sympathizing with a Wielder, and while she had encouraged me to form my own conclusions and promised me personal amnesty, she still insisted that she couldn't trust me fully. And, it was her secret, not Roland's, to tell.

"Logically, I know exactly why you didn't tell me anything. But, it still hurts, Roland," I murmured. "My own sister is someone I've been told my whole life to fear, and you knew. It feels like you let me be afraid."

"That was never my intent. I'm still learning how to play this role myself, which moves to make and hold back on. I have to walk the line while keeping countless others, as well as myself, alive and free. I've wanted to tell you for a very long time. The whole time. That's the truth."

I took a deep breath and inched my fingers across the desk to his. "I can't bring the wall down until I know the full truth, but... I want to believe you. I want to understand. More than anything, I don't *want* to be afraid or to doubt. I'm giving you the sledgehammer. It's up to you to break down the wall or build it taller. Tonight."

"I promise you, Snowdrop," Roland's voice rumbled deep in his chest. "I will tear that wall down with my bare hands if I have to, and I won't stop until it's rubble beneath our feet. I will tell you everything."

I smiled despite myself at his blatant resolve to win my trust back. "Alright, now leave me in peace to finish my work." I scribbled down Inessa's schedule and handed the paper to Roland. "Be sure to give that to Ina. It's your ticket to an audience with me, remember."

"Are you afraid of her now?" Roland asked, taking the paper and folding it in half.

"I know Inessa isn't a monster, but I'm not ready to talk yet," I answered honestly, and went back to my papers without looking up. "What you're going to tell me tonight, it's going to change everything, isn't it?"

"Yes. It will. There will be no going back."

I swallowed hard, but kept scratching away at the schedule with my pen. "So be it."

"Just remember, Snowdrop," Roland threw over his shoulder as he exited the room. "Ignorance may be bliss, but knowledge is power."

"Yes," I mumbled to myself, sagging against the desk. "But it's a power I don't know if I'm ready to wield."

I sat, unmoving for several moments. All of the turbulent

emotions that arisen since effectively moving to Tuyet tumbled over each other until I came undone with exasperation and started tugging open drawers and rifling through files. I didn't even know what it was I was looking for. All I knew for certain was that I was tired of only having half the puzzle because others either didn't trust me enough to tell me the truth, or figured I was too dense to figure anything out. Both possible perceptions of my person made my skin boil.

Mama contorting my good intentions.

I slammed the top drawer of the desk closed and threw open the next.

Inessa's refusal to trust me. Roland keeping secrets from me.

I flicked rapidly through another file, cursing as I felt the bite of a paper cut, and abandoned the file to the desk with a disgruntled hiss. *Next drawer.*

Papa and his—

Then my eyes fell on an invoice and I stilled my clerical rampage.

"Papa?" I whispered, tugging the file free and reading it over. It showed a diverted cost to the presses of Eisa. I bit my lip and fumbled through the paperwork, pulling free more and more documents denoting random donations, costs, and surcharges to the newspapers. Most were for the presses in Eisolde, but starting from our return to the Tuyet, the charges shifted location along with us. After the date of the stampede, the donations increased substantially.

Isolated, a single document might not lead to any condemning assumptions, but laid out in front of me on the desk, it was all too clear what it was. I'd inadvertently found the paper trail of silencing the press from reporting. Substantial tsena had gone into my father making sure none of us knew about any protests or Wielder sightings. I knew without looking any further that the dates would lead back to that first attack on us in the woods. Even at such a young age, I could recall no instances of what happened showing up in the press or being discussed by the public.

I plopped back into my seat and dragged my fingers down the length of my face. Why would Papa do this? Was he trying to keep the information away from his family specifically as a kindness to spare us from worry? Or, was the raving man from the Celebration of Reign right, and Papa had simply been silencing public outcry for the sake of external image, pretending the strife didn't exist while it slowly festered?

Just how many lies had we been fed and to what end? Did Papa know what Ina was? Who was he really protecting? Furthermore, who was making sure the stories still ran despite the interference?

I swallowed hard, unsure more than ever if I was ready to accept the answer to those questions.

"We need to find more lodging options," I announced to the forum. "There needs to be more access for refugees and soldiers to convalesce after being released from the hospitals."

"They are released because we don't have enough room in the hospitals to support lengthy stays," A representative from the Ministry of Commerce, Gregor, interjected, an edge of defense in his voice.

"I understand that, but there will be more casualties to deal with if they don't make a full recovery due to being left on their own prematurely." I leaned forward. "We have seen a lot of psychological damage done as well as physical. It takes time. More time than we can give, so we need to make room for that."

"We could look in Kirsi," Alveolar, a representative from the Ministry of Foreign Affairs, suggested. "Though, I'm not sure what is affordable after the expenses being allocated to the front."

I pursed my lips and folded my hands together. "I'll look into that as well. I'm sure we can reallocate funding somewhere. This is for our people. Victims of tragedy and the brave souls fighting to keep us all safe. They deserve our focus and the best care we can offer. That brings us to our other top priority: the children. What became of that inquiry regarding the new orphanage in Zokev?"

Dansen, from the Ministry of Internal Affairs, collected a stack of papers and tapped them together. "They sent over the paperwork yesterday. I have it here."

"Perfect, I'll take it now. Thank you." I reached for the packet and added it to the folder in front of me. "Last item of business is the transportation to these new locations. That needs to be ironed out by our next meeting. If it's a matter of funding, flag it for me to inquire with the Minister of Treasury and Finance. The Minister of Internal Affairs is a long friend of his and I'm sure between the two of us, we can work it out. It just needs to be done and implemented as soon as possible."

"Have we gotten any updates on the method for separating out the Wielders and Sympathizers from the groups we are aiding?" Dansen asked.

"I…" I swallowed, more unsure than ever about the practice. "I will look into our options."

"Yes, your Imperial Highness," The room chorused. The formality made me squirm internally but I lifted my chin assertively and rose to my feet.

"We all know our tasks for the coming week. If you have anything of imperative precedence, please feel free to schedule a meeting with me sooner. Meeting adjourned." With a bang of my tiny gavel, the board dispersed, and I collected my materials from the table.

"Lord Roland," several of the departing men acknowledged, alerting me to Roland's arrival for our own little meeting.

"You are so good at this. It's a shame you don't run a country," He purred proudly over my shoulder, and I shrugged him away.

"Oh, hush," I tutted, tucking my papers into the crook of my arm before turning to face him. He was standing close. A part of me hated the fact that despite being monumentally displeased with him, there was that piece of me that wanted to lean into his chest. Inessa's intimacies with Hykner flashed in my mind and tangled with a hot wave of jealousy. "Flattery will get you nowhere,

Minister Rusev."

"Ouch. Using my surname is a surefire way to let me know I am in the doghouse." Roland's brows furrowed with feigned hurt, the inner edges creasing upward in earnest distress. "I mean it, you know. I love seeing you like this— working for the people, prioritizing their needs."

"My priority is the people. It always has been."

Roland's eyes narrowed, but the rest of his face remained neutral. "All of them?" He repeated the same question he had asked me that day the girl had attacked the hospital. Now I had a better understanding of what he'd truly been asking me.

"I'd like to think so," I replied, patting his arm as I brushed past him. "But, I guess that depends on what you have to tell me tonight."

"Fair enough."

"Come on, then." I gestured for the door. "Where are you taking me for this chat?"

"We are going for a little stroll, but first, let's drop these papers off in the car."

"Shouldn't we just take the car then?"

"I'd rather go on foot. The less bystanders and more privacy the better."

"That's ominous. The driver might get the wrong idea of this rendezvous."

"Better he thinks we are engaging in scandalous pastimes than the real topic of interest." My cheeks flushed, and it didn't escape Roland's notice. He offered an olive branch of levity, "If you don't want to make a liar out of us, I'd be willing to partake in a little scandal."

I glared at him, knowing my blush was only deepening. "I don't throw bones to dogs in the doghouse."

"Ha," Roland guffawed. "Perhaps another time then."

"Assuming I forgive you."

"I'm optimistic. Though it sounds like you aren't opposed to the idea of future scandals." He opened the door to the car and placed the file on the seat. Patting the outside of the car with two rhythmic thumps, he instructed the driver to circle around for a while, and sent him on his way. As the car pulled away, Roland turned to look at me. "Alone at last."

"Stop flirting to disarm me and start talking," I bit impatiently, hugging my arms around my torso. "This has been eating at me all day, and I'm positive I've developed at least nine stomach ulcers in the last three hours alone."

"I'm flirting because I want to." Roland ran a hand down my arm before pulling ahead with a jerk of his chin for me to follow. "No ulterior motives, I promise. Though I suppose now is not the time for sentiment. Consider it abolished, and at the risk of your stomach eating itself any further, let's go."

I followed Roland down the street, picking up my pace to walk beside him. It looked like he was taking the route towards the river that snaked through the city. It made sense since it was nearby; the path that would be considerably less populated, allowing for plenty of secluded nooks to hide away in.

"I have been attending meetings," Roland started, clear and definitive. It made me wonder if he had rehearsed what he would tell me. I didn't know if that made it earnest or calculated. "They are made up of refugees from the fallout of the war, and citizens of Eisa."

"I'm not sure I understand. *My* committee is designated to help those affected by that."

"It is, and it does. But, your aid is of a limited scope thanks to the stance of this country and its views of anyone who falls outside that mindset. It is also made up of officials. My meetings have a more modest rank of members."

"You mean Wielders?"

"I do. And Sympathizers."

My jaw clenched, and my mouth felt dry. "Are you… Are you like Inessa?" I spat the words out and braced myself for his answer.

"A Wielder? No, I have no magical affinities to speak of," Roland assured me, and I felt a wave of relief that I wasn't going to have to process another person I cared for being possibly corrupted or not, only to have it turn to ice on my shoulders. "But, I am a Sympathizer."

"I guess I should have gathered that." It wasn't surprising, but it still felt unsettling to hear the words come from his mouth so directly and without apology. It was clear he felt no shame or guilt in his affiliation.

"The meetings are where Ina and I go together. We want to help the people who are suffering under this country's prejudice. People like Harvier and his father."

"Suffering people," I echoed, the words stinging my heart. "People we treat like abominations. Monsters waiting to attack and corrupt you."

"That is Eisa's rhetoric, yes."

"You know, it almost sounds silly to say aloud."

"There are plenty of magical beasts in this world that would kill you just as soon as look at you. But, not all creatures are hostile and dangerous. Some are violent when provoked, some only fight to protect what's precious to them. And some don't fight at all, becoming prey for hunters. Wielders and people are the same. I can't promise you that there aren't those with evil in their hearts, but I can promise you there are many, many with good. Their suffering is unjust. They need someone to help them fight simply for the right to live normal lives. I know you, Sorrel, and if you could just see it for yourself, you wouldn't turn a blind eye. You'd see the truth, and help. You could do so much to help ease their suffering, it would be invaluable. You move mountains to help others. These people need some mountains moved."

I took in Roland's words and weighed them heavily. They were laden with veracity, as well as the assumption of my own character that I wasn't sure I could claim. "The girl who attacked the hospital. I saw she was injured and I didn't help her."

"Her name is Vadia."

"You know her?" I gasped. "But she destroyed part of the hospital and captured all those people. Surely at the very least she is one of the ones who—

"— Fight to protect what's precious to them," Roland finished my statement with a wistful smile. "She was protecting Lenya, an Ice Wielder who had been found out by the doctor."

"What about the people she took hostage?"

"Not hostages. *Friends*. They were other Wielders and Sympathizers who had been injured in the same area, and were trying to receive treatment. She got them out with her shadows, so they wouldn't be arrested or killed," He spoke emphatically, and with an air of awe. "She's only fourteen, you know. That's the world she lives in. One that rejects her and forces her to live in hiding, worrying about her friends and family being taken from her simply for existing."

His words struck home, and I imagined Kira and Theo in the same position. Both I knew would fight to keep any of us safe. Kira had already demonstrated this when she'd struck the flame Wielder with her tiara. I couldn't help but wonder if the shoe was on the other foot, and Wielders reigned while mortals were the abominations, we would be in the same position as Vadia and done the same. We reached the river and I paused to lean against a tree, looking out at the water.

"And when she charged me? Can you explain that one, and tell me why Otvel had to step in with his manufactured flames?"

"That was Vadia being foolish and impetuous, if I'm honest. She was trying to see your face up close so she could see what kind of person you were… If you were kind, like Inessa." Roland beckoned me forward to come sit beside him on the bank.

"How would she be able to tell my character from looking at my face?" I crinkled my nose in confusion then waved the question away at I settled into the grass of the small knoll. Vadia sounded like the eccentric type. "No matter. So, she wasn't trying to attack me? You're sure of this?"

"I'm absolutely positive."

"And Rafe?"

"I haven't seen him, but I heard he's safe. Hiding out in the city somewhere till he can leave Eisa." Roland understood the root of my question and gave an honest reply.

I took a deep breath before asking my next question. "Is he dangerous?"

"Oh, *extremely*. Thankfully though, he's on our side," Roland laughed. "He's a powerful man."

"Are you friends?"

"Yes. He's survived a lot, helped and sacrificed a lot, and I respect him immensely."

"He wields curses from Dezidaneya," I spoke the fact that was giving me pause on pardoning Rafe as a Wielder aloud. Could he Wield curses and not be corrupt with a power like that?

Roland shifted to look at me more directly. "Remember when I told you that magic hadn't been taught to you correctly, and Sonyo was a country of dreams, not just nightmare curses?"

"Yes, and I believe you called me naive. Turns out you were right," I sighed begrudgingly. I hated the idea that I had been capable of being so easily led and blind to so much. I'd been stuck in a world of black and white while Roland and Inessa had broken out, through the endless monochromatic, and were now swimming in color.

"We are rectifying that, worry not. I thought you should know that Dezidaneya deals in the *Wish* affinity, not curses. That whole angle about your brother being cursed by someone from Dezidaneya isn't true. It's not even what their affinity does. Even if some were able to contort the Wish magic to cause an illness, at best it would be temporary… And not last thirteen years. I figured that Rafe's affinity type would make you think of Theo, so you'd want to know it's not the same. But, I couldn't bring this up before in Eisa without being charged as a heretic."

"Oh," I breathed, unsure of whether I should feel relieved that Theo wasn't living under a malicious curse, or horrified that it meant he was naturally sickly and my parents had crafted some elaborate ruse to lay blame. I recalled the last time Kira had brought up the subject of the curse, Inessa had gotten annoyed with her.

She had known the truth and was frustrated by the perpetual lie. "You've given me a lot of information tonight, and I'm terrified that it's only scratching the surface. I haven't even gotten to asking about Inessa, and I think I'm reeling a bit."

"Maybe we should call it a night and pick up again another time," Roland suggested, rising to his feet and dusting himself off before extending a hand to help me up. "I think you should talk to your sister about her affinity anyway. It should really come from her."

Things were coming into clarity more and more, and even though I had more questions to ask, Roland's candor had made great strides in subduing my initial fears. If I pushed aside everything I'd been told to believe, and allowed myself for a moment to be a blank slate, I was shockingly finding myself opening up to the plights of these Wielders Roland had told me about.

I couldn't refute that Ina had done us no harm, Rafe had a perfect opportunity to kill us but saved us instead, Vin Holok's death was suspicious at best, and Harvier had been a little boy trying to obey his father. These were all truths I could validate for myself, and it was propelling me out of the black and white, further and further into the depths of gray. What surprised me most was that even as I quantified that realization of entering the gray area, I felt starved for a world of vivid color. I wanted to see what Roland and Inessa saw, and now that everything was muddied together, it would never separate back into the neat world of black and white ever again. If I couldn't go back, I wanted to move forward.

"Thank you for telling me all this. And for wanting to tell me, though I wish you had." I stretched up on my tip toes, closed my eyes, and pressed my lips gently to Roland's cheek. "A little scandal to keep our story straight."

Roland's eyes widened at my advance. "Consider me scandalized. You threw this old dog a bone after all." His hands gripped around my arms and his breathing was uneven with restraint as my cheek brushed his chin. "A dangerous move."

"I'm not afraid of *you*. That much I'm certain of," I whispered, cupping his face tenderly for a heartbeat before dropping my hand

"Scandalize me again, and you might be, Snowdrop," He teased.

"All bluster!" I rolled my eyes and folded my arms.

"Maybe or maybe not. Guess you'll just have to trust me."

"I do trust you. I trust you implicitly and honestly, it's the only thing grounding me right now. You could be feeding me a whole trove of lies to pacify me, but I believe that you're telling me the truth."

"I want you to trust me. Losing that trust would be to lose the most valuable commodity I possess. Today, waiting to see you, hoping to straighten this out, might have given me an ulcer or two myself. "

I bit my lip and slid my hand into his, giving it a squeeze. "Is there anyone else I should know about who attends these meetings?"

"Of the people you know personally, it's just Inessa, Hykner, and myself. He's not a Wielder either, by the way."

"No one attacks you or plots to attack us?"

"These are good people just trying to live normal, honest lives. No monsters."

I tilted my head, narrowing my eyes with discernment. "How can you be sure you haven't been controlled like Yulia was?"

"Tell me this; Inessa— the eldest Imperial Grand Princess of the Emperor of Eisa, and the one who the people even thought at one point might inherit the country if Theo hadn't been born— is a Wielder, and not a soul has discovered her secret. If that isn't proof of their character, what is?"

He had a point. Furthermore, it was a testament to the trust of the group as a unit protecting Inessa's secret, because I had no doubt in my mind that if the Wielders who had attacked the theater had known what she was, it wouldn't be a secret anymore. Clearly, it wasn't widely circulated in their network, and must have only been trusted to certain individuals.

"Our next meeting is in two week's time, but if you can be

patient for that long, I will show you what I've been doing so you can evaluate the situation with your own eyes. You can come with me," Roland offered when I had no refute to his reasoning. "If you change your mind in those two weeks and wish to turn us in, so be it. You want to act upon your own cultivated beliefs, well the choice is yours now."

Roland started up the bank but I hesitated. There was one more burning question I needed answered before returning home. "Roland?"

"Yes?"

"Is Inessa the only Wielder in the family?"

"No. She is not."

Tuyet/Eisa
By Imperial Order
Head of Church Otvel Chinye, Prime Minister Friedrich Rusev
Emperor Genri Zdraevit II, proxy Empress Geneva Zdraevit

ꟿWIELDER NOTICE

Whereas jurisdiction of Wielder Activity in the Seventy Second authority, begun on the 18th day of April, adopted a resolution in the words and figures following wit:

"JOINT RESOLUTION"

Proposing an amendment to the **Imperial Doctrine of Eisa** (I.D.E) ... That the following article is hereby proposed as an amendment to the **Doctrine of Magical Prohibition** which shall be valid to all intents and purposes as part of the I.D.E when ratified by conventions by the Council of Ministries, under proxy of Imperial ruling.

Article IV. of the I.D.E

Section 1. The eighteenth article of the amendment to I.D.E is hereby repealed.

Section 2. The transportation or importation into any territory in possession of "Wielder Contraband" for the delivery or use therein of magical contents, is hereby prohibited.

Now, therefore, The Imperial Eisan Empire, by authority of Emperor Genri Zdraevit II, does hereby proclaim that any person or persons found to be complicit in the act of illegal magical activity in direct defiance to the Prohibition of Magic Act (Doc 217, Article IV), whether by personal practice or abetting, shall be found a wanted criminal of Eisa. All wanted criminals will be posted, and any information regarding such parties shall be reported to the authorities immediately. Failure to report illicit activity will be classified as an act of "magical sympathizing," and be regarded as a criminal act upon Eisa.

Furthermore, it is impressed upon all citizens and residents within the jurisdiction thereof to cooperate with the Eisan government in its endeavor to restore greater respect for law and order, by continuing such involvement to agencies which have been duly licensed by the Imperial Council of Ministries for the dispersement of medicine and elixirs containing no more than 2.75% magical contents.

Observance of this request, which is made personally to every individual and every family in our empire, will result in the participation of magic, which have passed government inspection, in the break-up and eventual destruction of notoriously evil illicit magical contents and practice.

The policy of Government will be to see to it that the social and political evils that have existed in the pre-prohibition era shall not be revived nor permitted again to exist. We must remove forever from our midst the menace of magical practice and such others that would challenge at the expense of good government, law, and order.

Signed and witnessed in proxy with full authority of Emperor Genri Zdraevit II, Empress Geneva Zdraevit, Prime Minister Friedrich Rusev, Head of Church Otvel Chinye.

x. *Geneva Zdraevit*   x. *Friedrich Rusev*

x. *Otvel Chinye*

TWENTY-FOUR

My shoulders raised like hackles, and my heart reversed its pacing, jumping from rapid palpitations to a sluggish, dull pounding that echoed in my ears. "Who else?" I asked, stilled beneath an icy calm of anticipation.

Roland's eyes, downcast, squinted meaningfully, and his mouth formed a tight line before slipping into a deep frown. His reaction gave me an indication of the answer— something he no doubt felt would overwhelm me— but I needed to hear it said aloud.

"Roland, tell me who else in my family are Wielders." My head throbbed, and I struggled not to sway on my feet. I refused to topple under this information. I didn't know if I would bend or break as my world as I knew it fractured before me and fell to pieces. It had been one travesty after another, each one smothering me more and more under the mounting weight.

Something inside was screaming for me to run away and get out of this situation while I still could, before I heard the answer and everything changed. But I dug in my heels, lowered my shoulders, and lifted my head. This was a leap I had to take, and whether I would fly or fall remained to be seen. However, I still had to leap and I would do so proudly and dignified, not cowering away from an unavoidable truth. I loved my family, and they loved me. Everything I had learned so far, if I was to believe it, had shown me that monsters were made not born. The only person who could make my family into monsters was myself.

"Kira?" I pressed the first guess through my lips.

"Yes."

"Yulia?"

"Yes."

"Papa?"

"Yes."

Each confirmation struck my body like a barrage of gunfire. The drumming in my chest escalated beyond what I thought I could contain. I inhaled a sharp quivering breath, the air stinging my lungs.

"It's... all of us, isn't it?"

Roland finally looked up at me, his expression a blend of sympathy and pain. His jaw shifted to the side as he gritted and ground his teeth. He blinked slowly, contemplatively, before answering, "Yes, Snowdrop. It's *all* of you."

One foot instinctively stepped backwards, prompting me once more to run away from the conversation. My heart leapt to my throat before plummeting down to my feet, and my vision clouded. A numbness engulfed me then turned to pins and needles scoring my skin. After a moment of disorientation, I realized I was shaking my head.

"I don't understand," I wasn't sure the words had been spoken out loud, or if the voice in my mind belonged to me. It sounded distant and strangled by disbelief. My thumb twitched, finding one of my fingers, then frantically felt for the rest, my skin hot and clammy to the touch. "I don't understand."

The earlier discovery of the presses being bribed surfaced,

once more prompting the question of who was being protected. Apparently it was us. My whole family was being distanced from any mentions of Wielding, and Wielding itself was being distanced from Eisa.

"I know. It's a lot."

"How could I not know what I am?" I demanded, finding a tether of gravity to follow back into the center of my body.

"How could you know something you were institutionalized to never even consider?" Roland countered gently.

"But, my entire family's legacy is built on being mortal led, and vanquishing Wielders for the salvation of our country. There is no way a secret that big could be kept this long."

"Secrets are only as strong as the company they keep. This has been on a need to know basis for centuries. Only the heirs are made aware of it once they've entered adulthood."

"Papa knows about this?" I couldn't believe what I was hearing. "He was likely told before Inessa was born, and will tell Theo before he dies. You girls were never meant to find out about it.

"If our entire family is the same as those we are taught are evil, then why in the world are we persecuting the Wielders?"

"Like I said, each emperor is told what their duty is and what is expected of them in order to maintain structure and conformity. They are only told about it after a lifetime of being trained to think and feel a certain way."

"But that's indoctrination!"

"Yes, it is."

"Our entire kingdom and legacy is based on a lie and boosted by indoctrination," I growled, incredulous. "How long were you going to let me go without knowing this about myself? Were you ever going to tell me?"

"Actually, Inessa was."

I stilled and clenched my fists. "When?"

"When she felt it was right."

"But you knew. Why didn't *you* tell me? Did you tell Inessa?" I demanded, a fresh wave of raw wrath threatening to reignite.

"No, Inessa told me."

"What?" The brewing inner chaos fell away into static.

"She realized she had a connection to nature that transcended normalcy. Given the nature of my job in Foreign Affairs, she came to me and started asking questions about the magical affinities. I was already involved with helping the Wielders at this point, and after Inessa realized she possessed the Vine affinity, she wanted to come with me. Together we figured out the rest of the picture, piece by piece."

"I don't know what to say," I puffed.

"It actually gave me a bit of hope for the future of this country to know that this generation of royalty had the capacity for open mindedness. Given time and proper execution, there is a real chance we could change the status quo. But, we were carefully calculating each step and who we would approach next. So we kept watch and took note, trying to discern who had which affinities. We have our suspicions but now we have a new way to test for certain."

"Test... you mean the one Otvel ordered to snuff out the Wielders? Is Otvel part of this too? Does he know?"

"Ha, absolutely not, and," Roland scoffed, eyes narrowing, "he is the last person we would want to know about this."

"But are you talking about his test?"

"Yes, though our usage of it, of course, isn't sanctioned."

I had a million more questions to ask, a million answers to learn, but as my gaze caught sight of the moon lifting into the sky, I knew we were out of time. Like clockwork, I shifted the spinning gears turning in my head to reset. I needed to be pragmatic if I hoped to hold onto even a modicum of normalcy in my life. Structure and stability, that was what I needed in order to not fall with the crumbling foundation beneath me.

"We have to go home," I asserted.

"Alright... are you sure you're good to go? I know this has all been a terrible shock," Roland asked, soothing and slow.

"Yes it has, and I need to go home now."

"Okay, but do you—"

"I'm processing," I interjected, the overwhelm sharpening.

Roland stuffed his hands in his pockets and nodded. "Okay. You're processing. I'll take you home now."

"I'll have more questions. Just not right now."

"I understand. You'll find me when you're ready?"

I nodded and strode briskly back to where we were to meet the driver, just barely keeping my feet from breaking into a run. I would find him when I was ready, but the person I needed to see most right now was Inessa.

We waited no more than five minutes for the driver to appear and pick us up. My documents remained undisturbed in the back seat, almost like a sign that I had stepped out of my world for a moment and was returning to it without a second passing— like it had waited for me.

Does it know I have returned another breed of human? Or perhaps it always knew and was waiting for me to realize it.

Roland didn't say a word on the way home. Every so often he would curl his fingers into a fist, dragging them across the black of his trousers slowly, then splaying them out again as he stared out the window. His knee bounced rhythmically, lightly jostling the car.

I didn't have much to say, or maybe it was that I had too much all at once. Either way, I remained silent as well until we entered the palace grounds and I exited the car, my papers tucked under my arm. Racing up the stairs to put my parcel down, I passed Theo, nearly colliding with his shoulder.

"You were gone for a while. Did your committee meeting run late today, Sorrel? Oh, hi, Roland." He waved hello at Roland who'd entered the foyer after me. "You're back too."

"Yes, I had a late meeting," I answered, continuing past him to the second floor.

Theo turned around, looked up after me, down to Roland, and back. "Oh, I see. You and Roland *both* had an evening meeting that ran late. Is that what they are calling it these days?"

"Theodorvin!" I snapped, my face flushing.

"I'm not here to judge you, sister dearest. So long as you're happy." He smirked, spinning on his heel to continue bounding down the stairs. "See you at dinner. You'll want to hurry if you want to be on time."

"Don't you start any rumors you can't substantiate, I mean it!" I called down to my brother from the banister. "And definitely not to Kira."

Theo laughed and patted Roland's arm as he passed. "Well played, sir. It is about time you started making a move."

"Uh," Roland blustered, having missed the lead up. "Thank you?"

"Would be an awful shame if they married her off to that Videirian fellow because you played cat and mouse a bit too long." Theo wagged a finger.

"Yeah, a real shame… wait, what? What Videirian fellow?" Roland's eyes lit up and he followed after my brother. "Do you know something I don't, Theodorvin?"

"I'm heir. I should always know something you don't."

"But see, I'm the Minister of *Foreign* Affairs. That makes it my job to know if strange Videirian men are sniffing around your sisters."

"Touché, however, I don't think that title qualifies you to play matchmaker. Seems like an *internal* affair if you ask me."

"Well, I never said…" their voices faded as they left the foyer and I found myself shaking my head with a smile tugging at the corner of my lips.

The brief reprieve of levity grounded me, connecting me back to the familiar. My life was still my life, no matter what lay dormant beneath my skin. I lifted my hands in front of my face, but this time, instead of looking for blotches and deformities that might mark me with corruption, I was searching for any trace of magical affinity I might have overlooked.

What kind of affinity did I possess? Was it possible I had given myself that nightmare after the Celebration of Reign? Or was there something else cultivating in my core. Perhaps I was like Inessa. We were sisters after all. Maybe that meant we all had the same ability, though somehow I doubted that. My intuition was steering more towards my inclination to winter. Was that why I could walk in the snow?

"So, have you made up your mind to hate me?" Inessa's guarded tone confronted me, breaking me away from my tumbling thoughts. I looked up to see her jaw clenching and her hands trembling as she awaited my response.

As I locked eyes with her, silver against blue, a new wave of understanding roared to life within me. I felt a thread of new connection binding us together in a way I hadn't seen before. We were the same; creatures of many depths and many masks. Now we shared a secret so intrinsically interwoven into our being, no matter how I felt about this new truth, I couldn't deny its sort of visceral, sad unity. Laid bare before me, I couldn't rebuke it. Rather I was compelled towards it.

Maybe that made me a hypocrite, or maybe this was simply the confusing aftermath of trying to form twenty years of beliefs and opinions in a single day, but in that moment I didn't care. I realized what I valued most, and it wasn't the moral superiority I had clung to all my life.

I flung myself forward and threw my arms around my sister, hugging her tight. She staggered under me, clearly not prepared for my sudden display of affection. Tentatively, her hands clasped on my back and she returned the embrace.

"Never, Ina."

"Are you sure?" Her muffled voice trembled against my ear. "I know I am everything you hate, and I should have never sprung that on you in a moment of anger, and now—"

"Ina, shh. I'm absolutely positive." I rubbed my hand in circles on her back, and separated to hold her at arm's length. "We are in this together now, for better or worse."

"Roland told you about the meetings, didn't he? Did he tell you more about me?"

"I heard about the meetings, and he did say a little about you, but also, about me— about all of us." I looked at her meaningfully.

"He told you about…?" Inessa inhaled deeply, her brows knitting together. "I can't believe you're taking it so well."

"It's the latest in a long line of revelations, and honestly, Inessa, you're more important to me than anything else in this whole world. You and our family. I hope you know that I'd fight tooth and nail to protect all of you, whether I was a part of it or not. I'm sorry I made you ever question that and feel like you had to go through this alone. I'm here now, and we can weather this together."

"You can't truthfully have had a change of heart that fast," Inessa's eyes were wide, dubious.

"No, not fully, but I'm trying to understand. In the last twenty-four hours alone I have had a lot revealed to me, and I was already having my doubts I told you yesterday. How could I not try and understand this? It's too late to turn back, not when so many people I care about are involved." I looked around and dropped my voice to a whisper. "If believing in what I was told all this time means believing you're condemned to evil, and I'd have to suddenly reject you, Ina, then I don't want to believe that way anymore. I choose you. My faith is in you."

"That's the first time I think I have ever seen you form and stand by your own beliefs." Inessa nodded approvingly at me, her eyes brimming with tears. A lump formed in my throat as she had to pause to swallow down a failed word, her voice cracking with emotion. "Thank you, Sorrel. I know this has been a lot to wrap your mind around. Nothing would make me happier than for us to walk this road together, wherever it may lead. My faith is in you too. It should have always been to begin with." She dropped her hands to mine and held them tight. "Forever and always."

"Forever and always," I echoed, then loosed a sigh. "I feel so relieved. Free almost."

"You've been living in a glass cage of trick mirrors, and you've just thrown the door open and jumped out of it. I imagine that would feel very freeing. It sure did for me," Inessa laughed and sniffled, dabbing at her nose with the back of her hand. "Well, now what?"

"We get ready for dinner."

"And then?"

"I'm going to the next meeting with you. Roland invited me, and I've made up my mind to see this through for myself. It terrifies me, but I have to face it if I'm ever going to see both sides of the coin."

"Wow. You really are leaping into the thick of it. Very well, then I think we should meet Roland tomorrow, and get the most shocking bit over with."

"More shocking than what happened tonight?"

"Yes. We are going to find out what you can *wield*," She mouthed the last word, and my skin tightened around my whole body at the thought. I couldn't discern whether it was dread, repulsion, curiosity, or excitement. Each brimming sensation tangled with the next, making my nerves crackle like fireworks. "Has Roland told you about Otvel's test?"

TWENTY-FIVE

Inessa explained to me how Otvels's test worked. Through the Divine Alchemy research he'd done, he'd developed a sort of tincture that could be administered through injecting small amounts into the hand or arm. The result would reveal how much Wielder blood ran through your veins and which affinity was dominant. Evidently, it managed to mirror developments that a natural Wielder would experience through training. It made me wonder what sort of research Otvel had done to discover such tethers through his alchemy.

We managed to pull Roland aside after dinner and arrange to meet him in an old, unused room, which mainly served to house the overflow of books from my father's study. It was down below the main level of the palace, and with Papa away, there was no reason for anyone to be down there, allowing us a small window of privacy.

"Are you ready?" Inessa turned from her vanity to look at me, clipping in her earring.

"I feel sick to my stomach."

"You aren't having second thoughts are you?"

"No, no. Not second. More like twentieth thoughts." I laughed hoarsely. "Are you positive this can be trusted? It sounds unreliable."

"It worked on me. And they have started implementing it on the wanted citizens as of yesterday."

"Imagine people out there not having a clue what runs in their veins, just to be outed like that and taken away." I shook my head.

"That's exactly why the whole idea is abhorrent. Up until last night, that could have been you. Think about that. Only instead of the luxury of discretion, you would be hauled away into captivity without a second thought, and no chance of repeal." Inessa lifted her chin.

"Surely it isn't that absolute?" I suppressed a shudder, already knowing the answer to my own question based on the treatment of Vin Holok and his arrest. Nothing good would come of the tests, not administered as they were.

"Roland saw the paperwork on it. That's what we were sharing with the group last night. Trust me when I say that Eisa is no friend to Wielders, and they will be treated with extreme prejudice and eradicated from Eisan soil by whatever means necessary if this continues."

"That's…" I fumbled for words to articulate the sloshing in my stomach.

"Terrible?" Inessa finished for me, rising to her feet. "Yes, it is. Are you ready to head down?"

"As I'll ever—" My reluctant agreement was interrupted by the loud bang of our bedroom door being thrown open.

"Have you seen the paper?" Kira cried, bursting into the room, Yulia trailing behind her.

"No, I haven't. What happened?"

"Look!" Kira shoved the paper in my face while Inessa came to stand behind me and look over my shoulder.

"No!" She gasped.

"Yes!" Kira nodded, eyes wide. "There is an illustration on the other side."

"That's grotesque." Ina cringed, and Yulia grunted her agreement.

"'Head Priest Otvel Chinye Shares Secret Intimacies with Imperial Empress?'" I read the headline aloud, dumbfounded. "What nonsense is this?"

"The press got a hold of some letter they claim Mama sent to Otvel," Yulia explained, leaning around Kira to point to the paper. "Just there, see?"

I quickly scanned the passage and lowered the paper, confounded. The contents of the letter suggested it was the note she had given me yesterday. I had given it to Dowels and he had sent it to Otvel. At what point had it fallen off course? Otvel had come to Mama's aid as requested so clearly it had reached him.

"It's a ludicrous accusation trying to sow dissent in the public," I rationalized.

"So you don't think the speculations are true then?" Kira asked.

"Of course not! Mama would never have an affair, least of all with a priest."

"Well…" Kira's eyebrows raised and her lips pursed to the side.

"Oh, what could that possibly mean?" Inessa rolled her eyes.

"Papa went away. Suppose Mama got lonely for… how do I put this delicately? Physical contact. Haven't you heard that Otvel has a prior reputation?"

"Ugh," Yulia stuck her tongue out with a grimace at Kira's suggestion. "Don't ever suggest Mama needing 'physical contact' again please."

"Why?" Kira snorted. "It's just sex, Yulia. I don't think she would be having an affair— that part is absurd, and I'm only joking— but the notion of sex shouldn't be something to pull a face over."

Inessa, Yulia, and I stared in horror at Kira's vulgar candor. Inessa cleared her throat, while Yulia shot me a befuddled look. Kira has always been one for pushing the envelope of appropriateness, but we hadn't ever seen her be so direct.

Inessa looked sharply at Kira's fingers, which were stained a reddish purple. "Kira, have you been eating more raspberries by chance as of late?"

"I have! They are a delicious treat. I like them for my tea too."

"Maybe you should cut back. I heard if you eat too many it'll make you ill and affect your judgment."

"Well you're the plant expert." Kira shrugged, then hesitated and looked at me. "But you're the medical scholar here. Is that true?"

Ina looked at me with an unspoken plea to back her up. "Uh, yeah. Moderation in all things. I'd hate to see you get ill."

"Curious. I guess I'll switch to strawberries."

"Those aren't in season yet," Inessa commented absently, then waved her hand. "But yes, find another fruit."

"You're so weird." Kira shook her head and spun around to leave the room. "I have to get to my lessons. If any of you find out what this is about, tell me immediately! I'm dying to know. I'm going to go find Ari." She snatched the paper from my hands and exited with a little skip.

"You don't think she's done anything regrettable, do you?" Yulia folded her arms, her shoulders hiked up around her neck. "Of a physical nature? Based on that comment, I'm not sure."

"With Kira, who knows? She is impulsive, reckless, and terribly forward. It wouldn't surprise me in the slightest if I heard some private indiscretion occurred," Inessa sighed.

"With Arrian?"

"Let's save that headache for a different day. What do you think that article is about?" Inessa and Yulia turned to me.

"Yesterday, Mama had me send for Otvel with a note. I didn't read it, of course, but the one in the paper mentioned a line about where to find her. That was the same location I left her, so I think the letter is from yesterday," I replied, keeping my voice low while Ina and Yulia leaned in.

"Really? So it sounds legitimate then?" Yulia's eyes stretched wide.

"The location was at least." I nodded.

"Otvel was here yesterday wasn't he?" Inessa asked.

"Yes, so he must have gotten the note."

"Suppose someone found it while he was gone?" Yulia suggested.

"You really think someone would do that?" I gasped, though as the words slipped through my tongue, I realized how painfully ignorant I sounded.

"Otvel has enemies. Especially in the church." Yulia frowned.

"He does? I never realized he had so many problems."

"Of course he does. Even I know that," Yulia blinked. "Mama and Papa promoted him to a high station immediately after welcoming him into service. He has personal audiences with the Imperial family, a close relationship with the empress, and personally looks after the Imperial Heir. That kind of attention could make anyone jealous and spiteful. Especially when others aren't privy to Theo's dependence on Otvel's healings."

"It would be someone aiming to hurt the royal family too." Inessa nodded along.

"I suppose you're right. I feel terrible, and responsible."

"Why?"

"Mama trusted me with that note."

"You had no control over what happened to it once it left your hands. You said yourself Otvel had to have seen it himself."

I crinkled my nose and shifted from foot to foot. "What was the reputation Kira was talking about, Yulia?"

"Oh, you know… he was apparently quite a womanizer. A bit hedonistic really. That's why he turned to the church in the first place. I'm surprised you didn't know that, Sorrel."

"I guess I should pay more attention if everyone else seems to know so much. His poor wife and daughter."

Inessa glanced at the clock ticking on the wall then back at me. "Sorrel, didn't you have some paperwork to show me this morning?" She prompted.

"Right, I need to get that submitted in a timely manner. Yulia, don't you have a social engagement to attend with Aunt Maria?"

"Oh," Yulia jolted. "I didn't realize the time. But, shouldn't someone tell Mama about all of this?"

"It is front page news, I'm sure it has already been brought to her attention," I winced, feeling a wave of sympathy at my mother's inevitable mortification. "But, I'll be sure and check on her."

"Alright, thank you." Yulia waved farewell, and Inessa beckoned me forward to make our own exit.

We entered the hall and hurried through the corridor towards the staircase. My heart was pounding with amplified anticipation, though I could hardly delineate between what was apprehension and what was excitement. Whatever it was, it was twisting and writing in rolling waves of trepidation and insecurity.

"Why were you asking about the raspberries?" I broke the silence, trying to distract my tumbling mind before it convinced me to turn tail and run—or vomit.

"There is a woman who has been teaching me some of the magical qualities different herbs and plants possess," Inessa replied. "Since magical healing elixirs are still permitted under the prohibition act so long as the properties are under the limit, it isn't technically illegal information to have. She told me about raspberries the last time I saw her."

"Raspberries are magical?"

"Not exactly *magical*. But certain foods can stoke affinities if not moderated," She elaborated with a wave of her hand.

"Oh," I exhaled. "So you think Kira's... affinity is being stoked?"

"Well, it's a possibility at least."

"Do you know what hers is?"

"Not for certain, but wouldn't it explain some of the odd behaviors of late if she had Lusoryia's affinity?"

"You mean that island country that is based in manipulation curses of physical touch and emotion?"

"Oh, Sorrel," Inessa sighed and I tried not to bristle at her patronizing tone. "First things first, you have to let go of the notion that everything is a nefarious curse if you ever hope to understand any of it. Anyone can make a weapon of anything with a strong enough will. It doesn't mean that was the original intent or use. You could stab a pen into someone's neck if you wanted to. That doesn't make all pen's inherently evil."

"I suppose so. Roland said something similar to me about Sonyo's dreams and nightmares. If it isn't manipulation curse by touch, what is it?"

"Lusoryia is known for the affinity of Lust, and its power is based in love or mood, allure, and seduction."

"Goodness."

"The natives are very loose in their inhibitions, as it is part of their nature, and I think a few too many raspberries might be flaring that dormant nature in her."

"I don't think I like the sound of that."

"Me neither. But, I've been seeing a change in demeanors

lately, especially when Kira is particularly happy."

I paused and thought back to her birthday, arguably the happiest day of the year for her, and how Roland had been acting particularly forward with me. It made me squirm a little when I recalled, I also had been swept up in the moment, ready to throw myself at him at any moment.

"By the look on your face, I'm guessing you experienced her pull firsthand," Inessa smirked. "I'm sure Roland appreciated the assistance."

"Ina!"

"Oh, don't be so uptight."

"We haven't even kissed," I admitted, a bit begrudgingly.

"Sorrel… Seriously? After all this time?"

"Well, he told me he didn't know if he could hold back if he kissed me. We can't all be so brazenly experienced as you!" I sniffed and looked away, my skin prickling with indignation and embarrassment.

"Well, that's kind of romantic. It sounds very passionate. Was Kira nearby for that little exchange too?" I pursed my lips and Inessa laughed. "Ha! She was, wasn't she? I guess you can thank her too then."

"New subject, please. I can't be going into this thinking about all that, I'll be red as a tomato," I whined and covered my cheeks with my palms.

"Hot and bothered?" Inessa snickered and elbowed me affectionately.

"Honestly, you're as bad as Kira! What's gotten into you?" I all but wailed, feeling very conspicuous under her teasing.

"It's just terribly entertaining to ruffle you. You're so serious *all the time*. Take a little sisterly advice? If you love him, there is nothing bad or wrong with showing that love however you feel is best. Words, actions, or touch— Just let it come naturally. Expressing love isn't wrong, however you choose to go about it. Tell me you've at least had *that* conversation."

"No, we have not. Not directly."

"Really? Wow, I never realized how shy you two were with this stuff. Neither of you are exactly very discrete in your feelings. Neither discrete nor direct apparently. Don't be too afraid to get the ball rolling. I honestly am not even sure what his hesitation is at this point. Give him a little push! What's he going to do? Turn you down?"

"Alright, alright. Enough please."

When we reached the stairs and started to descend, we froze in our tracks at the sound of bellowing coming from the study. The source of the yelling was clearly Mama, but most of her words were muffled by the closed door.

"Well, no doubt about it. She knows," Inessa whispered to me, craning her neck. "I wonder who she is yelling at."

"So do I." Guilt roared to life in my chest, a stinging heat spreading through my lungs in a slow sweeping burn with each breath. "I hope she isn't accusing Dowels of anything."

"Dowels did his job by getting it to Otvel." Inessa shrugged and carried on down the steps. I hesitated, straining to hear what was being said.

The words *unforgivable, disgrace,* and *go back* found their way to me. I had to keep from cupping my hand to my ear, and wished I had been blessed with Yulia's incredible sense of hearing.

"Come on Sorrel!" Inessa called me from the base of the flight. "We have an appointment and Roland is waiting for us. It's now or never."

"Right," I pulled my gaze away from the study door and plodded down the steps to join my sister, taking my first steps towards identifying myself as a magic Wielder.

TWENTY-SIX

"I'm not so sure about this," I bleated as Roland hovered over my arm with a syringe. "Can't you just tell me what you think my ability is?"

"Nope," Roland chirped, flashing me a dashing grin. "You have to earn that information. Plus, we could be completely wrong."

"Can you at least have Inessa do it? I know she's been properly trained on how to use that needle." I squirmed in my seat.

"You think I'm underqualified?" Roland pouted, and I scowled at him.

"Yes!"

"Alright, not in the mood for jokes I see. Ina?" He beckoned Inessa over and she took the syringe from him.

"Calm down, Sorrel. It's going to be fine. Remember I did this once myself too."

"You also once got yourself stuck in a log. And I got stuck trying to get you out."

"I was six. My judgment has improved since then, believe it or not."

"You're certain I won't be stuck with the evidence showing?"

"It lasts no more than five minutes at the amount we are giving you. But sometimes it can go even faster," Inessa promised. She leaned in and looked me in the eye. "I know it doesn't seem like it now, Sorrel but this is an indescribable experience. I'm not sure I can explain it, but it is like it tethers you to a piece of yourself you didn't know that was there— but it's the piece that shows you who you are. It feels like *belonging*. Just for a few minutes, you're connected to something bigger and you belong with it."

I took a deep breath to steady my nerves and held out my arm, opting to look away as Inessa smiled and made to give me the shot.

"Afraid of needles?" Roland's brows raised and he leaned against one of the shelves, startling as he toppled a stack of books at his feet. "That seems surprising."

"No," I winced as the needle penetrated my skin. "But not seeing it happen makes me feel like I still have a shred of deniability."

Roland shook his head, stooping to straighten the books. "You'll be just fine, Snowdrop. We will make sure of that. Your sister might have led you into that log, but don't forget who got you out. I'll be right here if you need me."

A harsh, crystallizing sensation shot up my arm to my head.

"Here we go, Sorrel. Roland and I have wagers on your affinities, so don't let me down!" Ina quipped and I whipped my neck to face her, appalled.

"*What?*"

"Okay, this will be your first time connecting with this piece of yourself, so it's going to go to your head first, and you'll be in a sort of haze for a few seconds that's going to find your dormant ability. It might feel longer in your mental space, but it's really only seconds. Remember that. We are right here, so lean into it."

"Oh, Schnites. What have I done?" I whimpered, a fog rolling over my consciousness. I blinked and found I was standing in a void of silver, swirling specs glinting and echoing over one another. The mist twisted and rolled, looking so ethereal and soft it compelled me to reach out a hand and grasp at it. The texture was gritty between my fingers, the particles so soft it was sharp. The silver roved around my fingers, across my palm, and spindled up my forearm, cold yet comforting, until the vapors began to solidify. Gray shifted between hues of white and pale blue, beckoning me forward. I stepped into the crystallized cloud, mystified, but as I did it fell around me, like smoke pushed to the ground, billowing away.

My hand flew to my mouth when I saw that the entire voided space was coated in shimmering fractals, refracting light like a million prisms. The air was crisp, the freshest I had ever breathed. I looked down at my hands, eyes wide in amazement, as frost slowly crept across my skin where the spindles of fog had been a moment before. This was so different from the nightmare I'd seen with affinities overtaking me and my family.

My heart skipped as I caught sight of my reflection in the forming ice in front of me. I stared, looking at myself like I would into a mirror, but it was showing me an inner self I had never met before.

Her hair was down, loose and free, and her eyes twinkled like clouded diamonds and melted steel. Lips, plump and red, curled around a bemused smile set against alabaster skin. She inclined her head to me, eyebrows raising, and in that moment, though we had never met, I knew her. She was that piece of me that walked barefoot in the snow and caught snowflakes in my hand that didn't melt. She was the breath of fresh air at the onset of each winter that filled my soul with light.

I reached a trembling hand forward as she mirrored me, steady as a rock. Her fingers permeated the barrier of ice between us, freezing over as they entered the shared space with me. I closed the gap, twining my own fingers around hers as she stepped fully through the wall, a figure of pure ice and snow. A soft blue light emanated from her, and a gentle wind whipped up around us, returning her body to snowflakes spilling around me. All except for where her hand had connected to mine.

"What?" I breathed, eyes widening as I saw the same blue glow in my palm beckoning the flakes into my hand, absorbing them into the creeping frost on my arms. The wind stirred up the silver clouds until I was once more blinking through a haze, with Inessa and Roland's captivated faces staring down at me.

"So?" Inessa prompted eagerly.

"Ice," I whispered, my heart thundering in my chest. I held up my hand, bare and void of any trace of frost in my veins now.

"I knew it!" Roland cheered, folding his arms smugly. "How does it feel, Snowdrop?"

"Well—" I started, still staring at my hand, but stopped as something stirred beneath my skin, and my vision began to blur beneath wisps of purple and black. "What's happening? What's it doing?"

"Common Wielders have one affinity they can wield. Royalty, due to the nature of a long lineage of breeding with other royalty, tend to have anywhere from one to three affinities at their disposal," Roland explained, kneeling beside my chair and gripping my shoulder for reassurance.

"It will introduce you to each one," Inessa added.

"Can there be more than three?" My breathing grew rapid. Though connecting with the icy version of myself had felt pure in essence, the thought of more than one power lurking within still terrified me. I was still getting used to the thought of one.

"No. No one has ever had more than three. I only had two."

"*Two?*"

Inessa nodded and held onto my other shoulder. "Looks like you've got more than one too. Lean in. This one should go faster now that you know what you're expecting."

I had little choice but to comply as my consciousness submerged into the dark fog. This mist glittered like twisting fibers of luminescent obsidian and amethyst. The air was charged, making the hairs on my arms rise, and each breath lightly tickled my throat as it made its way to my lungs. While the ice had been cold and soothing, this somehow felt energized and revitalizing. I steeled myself, and stepped into the dark plume.

Instead of falling away like the silver mist had, it swirled and undulated around me before lifting overhead. The ground beneath me was craggy and I knew this piece of myself was not linked to the familiar icescape of Eisa, but was a remnant connection to another country altogether.

A streak of lightning split the sky and thunder cracked overhead, the flash illuminating a figure standing in front of me. I was once more met with myself, though this version varied in her appearance and persona. Her hair was also down, but tethered and twisted back to the crown of her head at the temples, and her gaze blazed with electrifying mischief, the color of lightning.

Rain poured from the tumbling cloud above drenching us both. She grinned and kicked the water, twirling and dipping through the drops in such a way I couldn't tell if she was expertly twisting between them, or intentionally targeting each one to collide against her skin. Lightning sparked off her finger tips and arched around her body like a spiraling ribbon, the sounds of the storm a serenade to her dance.

She was a maverick. The wildness, rebellion, and unpredictability that had never been fostered. She was me, untamed and entirely inhibited in herself. I laughed hoarsely, rain beading into my mouth as I thought of the moment I had shared with Rafe, when he had urged me to dance in the storm and told me it was in my nature. I now knew what he meant. Somehow he must have known.

The Storm Sorrel stopped in front of me and held my face for a heartbeat before throwing her hands out to either side of her body, summoning a strong wind that shattered her existence into charged particles that went screaming past my face and through my hair with such velocity I struggled to keep my footing. No longer able to stand my ground, I gave into the gust and was plucked from the floor in a current of wind that formed the base of what I could now see was a large cyclone.

I blinked rapidly, feeling my stomach turn from both the unstable motion, but also from unease at the lack of stability there clearly was within that affinity. When I opened my eyes, I was once more in the room with my sister and Roland.

"Oh, I think I might be sick," I groaned, lurching over.

"What was that?" Roland asked, his eyes bright with curiosity. At least someone was enjoying this ordeal, though even I couldn't deny a growing sense of fullness forming within me as I connected to these alternate pieces of myself.

"I think I was electrocuted and sucked into a tornado," I replied, smacking my lips together to wet the dryness in my mouth from the wind.

"Ah, Storm," Inessa poked Roland in the arm. "Looks like we were both right then."

"Fair enough, an even draw," Roland conceded.

"Can you two stop making bets over top of me," I groused, clutching my head. "At least it's over now."

"Two elementals isn't bad. Storm too is a less common affinity since Kataheyda is such a reclusive country." Roland squeezed my shoulder and rose from his crouched position beside me and paused, a quiet chuckle of disbelief parsing the silence. "Though, it looks like you might have one more gamut to run."

"What?" My eyes popped open and I looked at my wrists to see more light in my veins. "There's more? I thought you said this only lasted a finite amount of minutes?"

"It's only been about three minutes for us," Inessa replied apologetically. "There are never more than three though so this really will be the last one, and I'll admit I am equal parts jealous and curious about what this one will be."

"One neither of us predicted," Roland nodded along. "Should we place a new bet?"

"You're on! I say—"

"What did I say about the betting!" I raised my voice, screwing my eyes tightly closed, only to hear it echoing around me, and knew I was once more in the void. "Schnites."

The mist was indigo this time, and I was already stepping into it, hoping this experience would be less chaotic than the last. Upon entry, the haze remained, unlike the first two instances, but became dappled with a wash of a million lights. I wasn't surprised, nor did I have to go looking for the third and final Me. She was waiting, hair piled atop her head, studded with more shimmering light like a crown of stars. Her chin was lifted and proud, regality and confidence pulsing from her. To either side of her were large beasts, glowing lines encasing constellations. They bowed their heads and stooped their bodies as she took slow, deliberate steps toward me.

She was a commander, and all I could do was marvel at her resolve. She commanded stars, and a glance around me made me tremble with a shaky exhale as I realized I was in the infinite blue I had been marveling at just the other night. I reached out a hand and gasped as the surrounding indigo rippled and stars began twirling around my wrists like gauntlets.

Was this a projection of the protection the Veil of Stars provided the home country of this affinity?

The Starry Sorrel stopped in front of me and extended her hand. I looked at it for a moment before reaching my own star-cloaked hand to shake hers. She nodded with a smile, and the beasts behind her charged forward. I flinched, but stood with my heels planted firmly in the ground, and realized they were all running straight past me in a burst of light that felt endless and courageous— a heat that felt cool, like the first few moments after a dunk in a cold lake on a hot summer day.

Then it was gone and I drew in a long steadying breath, clenching my fists, as I recentered in the waking world for the third and final time.

"Is that it?" I asked quietly.

"That's it," Roland assured me.

"And you only have one minute left on the clock before the effects wear off completely," Inessa added with a puff of reprieve. "So, now you know who you are. Who you truly are with those lost pieces reassembled. How does it feel? Who did you see?"

"Don't overwhelm her, Ina," Roland cautioned. "Remember, she didn't come into this situation as thrilled and openly as you did. She might need a little time to—"

"Ice, storm, and stars. That's what I saw," I interjected. "What does that mean? Those are my affinities, or different personalities?"

"The first time someone who has never connected with their affinity identifies it in the mindscape, it manifests as something feasible for the individual's mind to process," Roland explained, gesturing elaborately, and I could see this wealth of information on the topic of magic was both intriguing to him as well as starved for a willing audience. "Most commonly, people will see a version of themselves, or a creature, they feel embodies the characteristics of the facet of them self they believe the lost affinity has bonded to. After the initial connection is reestablished though, those projections merge back into your working subconscious for intentional wielding."

"You're right," I sighed, slumping back in my seat. "I think I am overwhelmed, actually. This all sounds entirely mad, and if I hadn't seen it for myself, I wouldn't believe one shred of all that. Though, that could be some sort of mental break talking, and in reality I've truly lost my mind."

"Oh, now." Inessa rolled her eyes and swung around to throw her arms around my neck. "Don't be dramatic, little sister."

"I'm taller than you," I patted Inessa's hand, and she gave a wicked little laugh, squeezing me harder in a mock chokehold.

"Hush. You're sitting down, you're younger, you are the little one right now. Don't fight it."

"Oh, get off me. I can't breathe." I plucked my sister from my shoulders, surprised to see such light in her face. This was the most friendly and animated I'd seen her in ages, and I realized just how much this secret must have been weighing on her. "How do you know all of this information? Isn't this drug relatively new?"

Roland nodded. "To Eisa it is, but variants of it have existed in other cultures. Not to mention how other countries relate to their affinities, coming of age rituals, rights of passage, general education. I've compiled enough research on my end of that sort of thing to piece it together."

"And I," Inessa pointed to herself. "Got my hands on Otvel's research from one of his underlings. Discreetly, of course. Together, we worked with the other Wielders to understand how it worked. We were hoping to find some way to block the drug, or counteract it. Like an antidote. That's partly what Maggie— that Videirian woman I mentioned before— and I were studying the natural magical properties of herbs."

"I had no idea you were that involved in those kinds of solutions," I murmured, feeling a small twinge of inadequacy despite myself in my sister's shadow of resourcefulness.

"How could you?" Inessa laughed. "You only just learned about everything. I'm sure you'll be moving mountains for the benefit of the citizens in no time."

"So, I have this information," I glanced down at my nail beds. "This new insight into myself, and a new connection to our Wielder heritage. What happens now?"

"Well, do you want to learn how to use it? I've had someone teaching me and—"

"No," Inessa stopped mid sentence, stupefied by my response.

"But you just reconnected to these abilities. Aren't you curious?" She pressed, shoulders drooping.

I shook my head slowly. "No. It's fine and good to understand and to know, but I don't want to wield anything."

"I don't understand. I thought you were opening up to this, and that we were going to walk this path together. Were you disappointed by your affinities?"

"Inessa, last I checked, wielding is still illegal in this country. In fact, it's heresy."

"That's a stupid and prejudiced law!"

"It's still a law."

"These affinities can help people though. I would have thought that would appeal to you, of all people."

"I am willing to go to the meeting, and I am willing to try to understand and meet Wielders. I'm even willing to help others however I can who have been unfairly persecuted, but I'm not ready to openly defy our kingdom with my own hands."

"But—"

"Ina," Roland spoke quietly with a shake of his head. "Give her time. Baby steps. Her experience with this isn't the same as yours or mine and we need to respect that by not imposing our beliefs onto her. That would be no better than those we are fighting. Take the win that she is willing to go this far, and we will take it one step at a time from there."

Inessa was quiet for a long moment while I blinked at Roland gratefully. Finally Ina sighed and threw her hands up in defeat.

"I suppose you have a point. I'm not going to make you do anything you're not willing to do, Sorrel. Thank you for coming this far. I understand it's been a lot to process."

"You're welcome, Ina. If all of this is done, I have some matters I must tend to, if you'll excuse me." I backed toward the exit, feeling a pressure building in my chest.

"Do you have any questions or comments to share, before you run off?" Roland stepped forward after me, but I clasped my hands behind my back and fumbled for the door.

"No." I grasped the handle and tugged the door open but paused in the threshold. "But, I'll still go to the meeting. I still want to meet the others."

"Then, that will be what comes next. Nothing more till then, unless you give the word," Roland promised and Inessa nodded along, swallowing hard.

I knew I was disappointing her with my lack of enthusiasm, but the knowledge that I had a storm of ice and stars residing within me made my skin burn and my hair stand on end. I hadn't been expecting more than one affinity, and I didn't know how I would even begin managing three. By that count, I was more of a Wielder than Inessa.

"Thank you," I whispered and slipped into the hallway, my thumb rubbing rhythmically over the small dot on my arm from the prick of the needle— the only remaining evidence of everything I'd just experienced.

TWENTY-SEVEN

"Arrian," I looked up from the book I was reading in surprise to find myself staring into the deep brown eyes of Roland's brother. "What are you doing here?"

My voice carried amongst the quiet halls of the library and I ducked my head sheepishly as Arrian smiled and brought a finger to his lips.

"Morning, Sorrel. I was sent to find you for a mutual errand."

"A mutual errand?" I echoed. "For you and me?"

"Don't sound so surprised. Crazier things have happened."

"Sorry, I just wasn't aware that…"

"I've recently been given some new responsibilities by my father that just so happen to have an overlap with yours at this exact moment. Believe it or not, my brother isn't the only one capable of duty."

"I'm sorry, Arrian. I didn't mean to insinuate anything of the sort." I closed my book and rested it in my lap. "What is this mutual errand?"

"We are testing the patients in the hospital for Wielder traces."

"Testing them? You mean Otvel's injections?" I tried not to bristle as I recalled my own experience with the drug two days prior.

"Well, we aren't testing them on their spelling and maths." Arrian leaned against the bookshelf and smirked.

"I could do without the sarcasm, thank you," I scowled, swatting him lightly in the arm with my book as I rose to my feet.

He waved me away and ushered me out of the library, steering me from behind by arms. "Time to go."

"Arrian!" I protested. "I need to put my book away, you pest. Stop pushing me."

Arrian snagged the book from my hands and tossed it to a passing maid with a grin and wink that elicited a giggle from the girl. "Shelve that will you?"

I rolled my eyes and tried to shrug him off before he tipped me down the stairs, managing to twist away at the last moment. "What's gotten into you?"

"Do you usually change here or at the hospital?" Arrian asked, fidgeting with the cuff of his jacket.

"Either, it doesn't really matter. But—"

"Magnificent, let's just be on our way then. I already had Dowels call us a car." There was an energy in his posture, itching to complete the task at hand.

"Excuse me, but don't you think you're being a bit presumptuous?" I huffed, folding my arms. "I could have had other things to do before you dragged me away!"

"You were reading a book," Arrian replied flatly, quirking an eyebrow.

"I…"

"You're… out of excuses to drag your feet?" He countered with a smug smile. "Come on. This is important for both of us. Can't you just cooperate?"

"You've hardly given me any information to cooperate with!"

I blustered with a squeak as he returned to trying to force me down the stairs, succeeding a step. "Ari! Are you five? Stop herding me."

"Fine," Arrian conceded with a mutinous glare. "I've recently been given a position overseeing the prisoners arrested as Wielders and Sympathizers. It was brought to our parents' attention that Wielders have previously been hiding in the hospitals, which you had a firsthand account of happening. They want us to test the patients and refugees waiting for transfer at the hospital. Satisfied?"

I was far from satisfied. My stomach twisted and a small throbbing had started in the back of my head. Inessa was a Wielder. So was I. We weren't inherently evil because of it, but if we were tested, we'd be locked away without a second thought. Even Rafe had been added to the list of wanted criminals despite him saving two princesses from certain death. The Wielders in hiding who *attacked* the hospital now had names and identities that made a similar claim for innocence and provocation. What if these tests revealed more innocents?

There was a small film of sweat forming on the back of my neck, as I continued to think. The Wielders who had attacked us at the theater were dangerous though and had attempted blatant murder. Surely they were the wicked ones that deserved to be incarcerated. The same went for those who had attacked us back at Svyat Gavan.

But that wasn't the real issue at hand. No, the real conundrum before me wasn't so much the revealing of who did and didn't have magic in their veins, but rather having the time and ability to confirm which of those people were truly a threat and deserving of arrest.

I shook my head, trying to dispel the roving contradictions, unable to find my footing firmly on either side. I was operating on a bias and heavily weighed data of limited interactions with Wielders outside my family. How many patients had I possibly treated who were of Wielder decent? Surely if they hadn't attacked me, they were the threats we were making them out to be… unless they were biding their time for the perfect opportunity to strike. Would they turn on me when I revealed them?

I bit the inside of my cheek. I had thought the inside information might help me feel more ease, but in truth, it did little to quell the plethora of zaps sparking off each of my nerve endings.

"Are you trying to push Sorrel down the stairs?" Kira asked, tilting her head as she approached us from down the hall.

"It certainly seems that way," I groused, wondering if there was some way I could alert Ina or Roland to what was happening in case there was anyone they felt needed protection from the impromptu inquisition.

Kira clicked her tongue and flicked a finger under Arrian's chin. "You better be nice to my sister, Ari, or you'll have me to answer to."

"I certainly wouldn't want that," Arrian all but purred.

Kira crinkled her nose playfully and brushed past us to continue on down the stairs. "Play nice, you two!"

"Do you know where Ina or Roland are, Kira?" I called after her.

"I think Ina went with Mama to their meeting and Roland—"

"We don't need Roland for this," Arrian snapped. "This is *my* job. If you refuse to cooperate, let it be your own head. I'm going without you."

"Oh, calm down, Ari," I sighed. I'd have no choice but to navigate this situation by myself. "I'm coming."

"Good. I'll explain to you how the drug works and what we are looking for on the way."

I didn't bother telling him I already knew how it worked, and obviously did not mention I had first hand experience seeing it. Instead I let him prattle away the whole ride over. He was serious in his delivery, contemplative, and calculated. I could see no trace of emotional taxation, but rather the only emotion permeating his diligent demeanor was that of exhilaration.

"You certainly seem dedicated to your task," I smiled, trying to dispel any ambient tension I might be inadvertently emitting with my internal ambivalence.

"It's nice to finally be given my own role to play. I intend to make it a role worthy of demanding respect, so I can't afford to take it any less than completely seriously— for my sake as well as Eisa's. We have a chance to protect people *before* the injustices are permitted to happen. We are lucky to have such an honor. I'm honestly surprised you aren't more enthused yourself."

"Oh?"

"With how… how to put it lightly… *fussy* your mother can be over you lot and your involvement with the outside world, I figured you'd take it as a compliment that you were able to be involved with something this close to possible criminals."

"I suppose I owe your father a debt of gratitude then," I nodded, my mouth suddenly growing dry and scratchy. Arrian had a point. Normally Mama wouldn't allow any of us children to be in a situation that could even remotely turn dangerous. Either she didn't know and Friedrich was acting on his own, or he had somehow managed to convince her.

Was it better to be given the freedom and have the opportunity to deflect unnecessary hostility towards innocents, or would it have been easier to stay estranged from the matter? I thought for a moment, trying not to droop when I realized the answer was that neither option would be easy and I simply had to take my lumps and hope for the best. Friedrich was at least granting me a branch of trust that my mother refused to. After his apology over Rafe, part of me wondered if this was even his way of gifting me transparency in my own domain where I'd obviously know many of those being tested. Perhaps it was a kindness after all.

"Alright, I had a vehicle follow along behind us in case we have to transport any suspected or confirmed criminals. Shall we?" Arrian nodded to me and opened the door, holding out a hand to help me exit the car. "This is your realm. Where should we start?"

I took the lead and directed Arrian and his accompanying men through the hospital.

"I'm going to change into my uniform in case any assistance is needed while I'm here."

"Excellent. Maybe we can just have you give the doses then rather than pulling a scheduled nurse away from her duties. Seems more efficient that way, don't you think?"

I swallowed a groan and worked up a polite smile before whisking myself away to change. Apprehension gnawed at my stomach, and I had to resist the odd urge to bite at my nails, a habit I hadn't had since a little girl. I already felt unsteady in the position I found myself in being included in interrogating recuperating patients, but now I was not only interrogating them, I was accosting them with a drug against their will that could condemn them. They understood that as well as I did so I worried that even if every single patient turned up negative for Wielder traces, would they continue to trust me as a caregiver, or would that role be marred?

I took my time changing and reluctantly rejoined Arrian. The first three rooms went smoothly, all patients completely devoid of magical blood. I was extra careful with how I handled the solution, a part of me also growing anxious that I could somehow expose myself in the process of administration. My nerves were reaching their capacity for the abuse I was inflicting upon them as I settled in and gently roused an ailing man with pneumonia.

"Hello, sir," I started, dabbing his fevered brown with a cloth. "There has been an order to check the patients of this hospital for any possible Wielders in hiding. I'm going to give you a small injection and then we will be on our way."

"Very well," the man croaked amicably and offered his arm.

"Thank you," I replied cheerfully, and set to work. "We should be out of your hair in no time. How have you been feeling otherwise today? Is there anything I can get you before we move on to ease your discomfort?"

"What is happening with my veins? Is that normal?" The man's glassy eyes widened with forced clarity.

I stiffened and dared to glance down at his arm. Sure enough, though sparse, there were small shimmering specs of crimson glittering in his blood.

"Only for those with Wielder blood in their veins. You'll have to come with us." Arrian stepped forward, a victorious grin trying to overpower his expression of dutiful stoicism.

"I thought the ones with barely traceable amounts like this weren't considered a threat?" I pointed out, stepping between Arrian and the now cowering patient staring stupefied at his arm.

"Better safe than sorry. Right, Sorrel? I would assume you of all people would understand the importance of precaution."

"And why is that?"

"You've been under attack from those monsters directly three times now. You'd really chance a fourth?"

"I see your point, Ari." I lowered my voice. "But, the Wielders who attacked me each of those times were extremely powerful creatures. This poor man is ill and by the look of him, he had no idea anything would show up."

"That's what I intend to find out when I question him."

"Question him how?"

"However I need to in order to get the truth."

"That sounds like a thinly veiled way of saying you're willing to torture a sickly man until he says what you want him to," I challenged.

"Are you not willing to do what it takes to keep your own country safe, *Grand Princess*?" Arrian raked me over with narrowed eyes.

"I will intervene to the best of my ability with anything threatening *innocent* citizens who have not been convicted of any crime. My role here is to help those who pass through the door seeking help, not harm them," I spoke firmly, lifting my chin and setting my jaw.

"Well," Arrian shoved his face close to mine, unflinching. He jerked his head to command the guards accompanying us to restrain the patient. "I guess it's a good thing he will be exiting those doors with me."

The guards gathered the man, forcing him out of his bed and towards the exit.

"I'm sorry," I murmured to him as he was escorted past me.

"Thank you, your Imperial Highness." The man blinked warmly at me despite wincing under the tugging of the guards. "Thank you for speaking up. I won't forget."

I curled my fingers in as tight as I could then stretched them to their full extension. Frustration boiled in my stomach until I thought I might spit fire at Arrian.

"This wasn't the assignment you described to me in the car," I growled. "I didn't come here to pull healing patients from their beds without due cause."

"Word of advice, Sorrel." Arrian paused at the door. "If you can't separate out feeling from fact, you have no business claiming to aid your country. Your soft nature will only get you and others hurt— or worse, killed. Toughen up, and do the job that needs to be done until our country is safe and stable again. Then you can busy yourself nursing those who remain. Until then, don't forget your duty."

"Duty isn't the same as inhumanity," I hissed, digging my heels as hard into the ground as possible.

"Duty demands many things from us. Don't be so naive to think humanity isn't one of them. You'd better watch out, or people might get the wrong idea and think you aren't as dedicated to Eisa as you so often tout. Come on. We have more rooms to visit."

I clenched my jaw to keep it from trembling, and exhaled slowly as soon as Arrian turned his back. I spoke a silent prayer to the Divinities, asking that no one else in this hospital show any magical affinities lurking within them. Steeling myself just in case my prayer went unanswered, I slowly trailed along to the next patient's room, wishing I didn't know what I knew. Wishing I could turn it all off like a faucet and forget the uncertainty whipping at my back. The man barely had any Wielder's blood illuminated in his veins, and it was clear enough to me that he hadn't had enough to pull him into a mindscape.

Though I had my reasons to doubt Mama's approach, if this was an order coming from Friedrich, I had to trust that everything would follow proper protocol and Arrian's overcautious approach would be little more than an inconvenience.

I remembered the conversation I'd had with Larkin when she'd first told me the rumors of the test. My response to her had been cold and unconcerned. *Isn't ridding the country of Wielders a good thing? Why would taking an active approach make the staff uncomfortable?* I suppressed a small shudder as it dawned on me that had I not learned the double-edged truth about Wielders, I could have turned out just as callous as Arrian. Desperate to prove my worth to my country even if it meant harming those within it.

I watched the needle pierce the skin of the next patient and tensed. Arrian's gaze blazed with a misplaced sense of valor, while the patient held their breath, shoulders hiking with apprehension until the test came back devoid of Wielder blood.

On both sides, I realized, had I not become privy to the truth, either the enforcer and the accused could have been me.

AFFINITIES

ICE - *Origin: Eisa.* Affinity to conjure and manipulate ice and snow.

STORM - *Origin: Kataheyda.* Affinity to conjure and manipulate elements of weather and storms.

STAR - *Origin: Slayad.* Affinity to call upon star entities and employee them under their command. Additionally, light refraction.

DREAM - *Origin: Sonyo.* Affinity to enter and manipulate the dreamscape.

WISH - *Origin: Dezidaneya.* Affinity to conjure wishes, typically seen in the form of item conjuring. *Excluding wishes that go against natural means or consent (i.e. reversal of death, or wishing death).

WHISPER - *Origin: Sibru.* Affinity to hear pieces of thoughts, plant ideas, and write rules of action. *Limitations and power level relative.

LUST - *Origin: Lusoryia.* Affinity to conjure and manipulate emotions and attraction.

SHADOW - *Origin Kesgoldol.* Affinity to shapeshift into previously seen entities, and to merge with/travel between shadows.

VINE - *Origin: Videria.* Affinity to conjure and manipulate all manner of flora. Additionally, skilled healers.

FIRE - *Origin: Vatra.* Affinity to conjure and manipulate flames and ashes.

PEACE - *Origin: Pachay.* Affinity of clairvoyance.

WATER - *Origin: Lucio.* Affinity to conjure and manipulate water.

DEATH - *Origin: Dimaer.* *Not much known on this affinity as those from this country do not leave their own land.

TWENTY-EIGHT

The night to meet the Wielders had arrived, and apprehension gnawed at my stomach. Inessa had opted to stay behind and cover for any possible inquiries regarding my and Roland's whereabouts, and though I did feel safe in Roland's company, part of me wanted my sister with me for this moment as well. There was still a part of me that couldn't help but feel like Ina was different from any other Wielder I would meet— safer, gentler.

We left the palace without any trouble, and Roland led me through the city towards a mostly abandoned district. The scent of garbage and mildew hung in the air, and Roland grabbed my hand, keeping me close as we shuffled through the seedy streets with surreptitious figures tracing our movements. I was careful to keep my face obscured from any curious onlookers, but worried I'd be recognized despites the lengths we'd taken to make sure I looked as common as possible.

There was slime crawling over the stones of our pathway, and everything about this piece of the capital felt akin to a festering wound. Finally we rounded a corner that gave way to alley, aged and dry, devoid of the moist shroud we left behind us. Our path brought us to an old rundown hotel with boarded windows and cobwebs hanging like icicles from the panes. From the outside, it looked completely abandoned, and it was only the small detail of the disturbed dust on the front door hinges that tipped me off that the building was in use. Even then it was only because I knew to look for it.

"Alright, Snowdrop," Roland grinned at me, the moonlight illuminating his sharp features against the shadows of night. I could tell he was excited to welcome me into this new fold of his life, and I wished I could share the enthusiasm. "Time to go in. Say the word, and we will leave."

I nodded, but bit down firmly on my tongue, too afraid that an unnecessary sound or movement would either cause this situation to fully blow up in my face or make me get sick on Roland's shoes. He knocked rhythmically on the door, after a quick glance around to make sure no one else was in view. Counting to ten, he repeated the same knock, and this time, it was followed by a small *click* of a lock on the other side.

The room we stepped into was pitch black, and a musty smell tickled my nose. I couldn't even *see* my nose, but I could sense several pairs of eyes blinking in my direction through the darkness.

"You've brought a guest?" A gruff voice asked, and my entire body went rigid.

That voice sounds so... familiar. And it makes me want to run away even more.

"Roland," I whispered, grabbing onto his arm. "Is that who I think it is?"

"Tonight, Inessa stayed home so that I could bring Grand Princess Sorrel with me. I hope you all will receive her with as much respect and courtesy as her sister. She comes in peace, seeking understanding." Roland rested his hand on mine where I clung to his shirt.

"She looks afraid," another voice, belonging to a younger female, called out. I tried to peer through the darkness, unnerved by the fact I could be seen but not see.

"Maybe you should put the shadows down then, Vadia," Roland sighed, and I perked at the mention of the familiar name. Vadia was the Shadow Wielder from the hospital.

"And you're sure you trust her not to run back and report to the royal family?" The gruff voice grunted, and I felt myself shrink under the weight of the situation I'd put myself in.

"I trust her with my life," Roland's disembodied voice was adamant beside me.

I took a deep breath, removing my teeth from where they still were lodged in my tongue. "You have my word."

"Lower the shadow, Vadia."

At the sound of the command, the blanket of infinite black fell away around me. It took everything in me not to press myself into the exit or hide behind Roland as I was greeted by a room of weathered citizens— more than I had thought would be present based on Roland's prior prepping. My eyes locked on the two individuals I had seen before, both of whom had been the ones to speak.

"You were at the Celebration of Reign," I acknowledged the man in front of me as the raving lunatic who had interrupted our family's party, trying my best not to cower in his presence. He was still coated in grime, his dark hair that was beginning to silver was matted. I could also see a red hue peeking out from the collar line of his threadbare tunic, betraying the presence of inflammation, and possibly an infected injury.

"I was." The man folded his arms and stared me down, unblinking.

I glanced at Roland. "When you joined the guards…"

"I got Macsen off the palace grounds before he could be imprisoned or executed," Roland finished with a small nod of his head.

"So, you *are* a Wielder then?"

"No, just a regular mortal fed up with the callous and inattentive attitude towards the common folk. Bating hungry crowds and tired citizens into a cluster with a hollow gesture of gifts then turning a firework on them. All starting in the area where Wielders were rumored to have congregated. Someone needed to say something after the streets ran red with the blood of my fellow people, all while you lot danced and celebrated your own self importance— your people died beneath you," Macsen growled, his shoulders beginning to lift in agitation before he winced and relaxed.

"She feels afraid of us, but I can also tell she feels deep remorse for the tragedy. She is conflicted but feels the need to take care of others." I jumped back startled as my gaze flitted to where Vadia was standing beside Macsen only to see my own face blinking back at me. "Even us."

"What?" I gasped.

"Remember I told you that Vadia was trying to look at your face that day at the hospital? When gifted Shadow Wielders shift in form, or merge with shadows of living things, they gain an empathy link to memories and emotions," Roland explained, then frowned at Vadia. "However, it is considered poor manners to do so without one's permission."

"They shift too?" I baulked and fought the desire to shrink away.

"I believe she is sincere," Vadia's face flickered back to her own, like it had been no more than a trick of the light. I recalled the large almond eyes that had stared at me from outside the crumbling hospital before submerging in shadows.

"If you say so," Macsen sighed, fixing me once more with a menacing glare. "Just know, we fight to death for each other and don't forgive traitors here."

"I am sorry," I took a small step forward, the apology flying from my lips. "I know words don't mean much, but after everything I have learned recently, I am truly sorry, and I want to understand."

I looked down at my hands, remembering the sensations of connecting to my lost affinities, and how, for a moment, before the doubt crept in, I had felt whole in myself after revealing the third power.

"What news do you have tonight?" Macsen narrowed his eyes at me, but turned to address Roland. "Did you bring anything to show us?"

"Yes, I did. Sorrel, if you want to go ahead and talk to anyone while I go over this, go ahead," Roland gave me a brisk nod, and made to step away, but I held out my arm to stop him.

"I want to hear what you have to say too. If you have plans to reveal to them, that tells me what is causing hardship to avoid." I lifted my chin, hoping that Vadia wouldn't shift again and pick up my half truth. Part of me meant what I said, but the other half didn't feel comfortable being thrown to the wolves.

"Very well," Roland smiled kindly at me and retrieved a folded paper from his jacket, unfolding it as he stepped through the small crowd towards a central table. "I have a map and some notes."

Most of the onlookers held back, cowering towards the edges of the room. I looked at each face— young, old, plain, beautiful, scarred. While their overall appearance varied, there were several notable features that were the same. Each man, woman, and child had dark purple circles beneath their eyes. Their shoulders were either raised like hackles or slumped in defeat. Nails were caked in dirt, clothing torn and unkempt, and I could see most people in the room, if not all, had some form of injury or ailment. The air hung stagnant, smelling of dust, sweat and grime. All marks of the rejected, fearful, and downtrodden.

Beneath it all, different and alike, the one element that stood out to me most was the undeniable humanity of each person in the room. Nothing about them told me they were monsters, wicked, or Wielders. I couldn't even determine who was Wielder and who was Sympathizer. Shamefully, I realized I had half expected them to have horns, tails, and fangs. Marks of beasts I'd glimpsed in books. As my gaze passed over them I saw mothers, fathers, siblings, sons, and daughters. They were *people*. If I wasn't a Zdraevit, both myself and my family would be in the same situation. Cowed, exhausted, and fearful of every coming day.

There was hunger in their weary eyes, for more than bread and butter— for hope, justice, and safety. But, despite knowing who I was, not one person lashed out, chased, or outright condemned me. I felt my own guards fall away and the rigidity melt from my body as I realized just how narrow minded I had been.

People. My *people. And they are kind when they have every reason to harm, trusting when they could doubt, accepting when they could judge.* Something clicked in my mind as the realization collided with the advice Otvel had given me at the church. Everything he'd told me went against the very practices he was couching the hatred in.

My attention wandered further into the group of people, until despite my reservations and insistence on staying involved in Roland's conversation, my feet followed suit, carrying me into the shallow ranks. I paused beside a huddled young woman who was struggling to reach around and dab a stained cloth at a deep scrape along her shoulder. Her blonde hair was dull and matted, though I could tell under the grease and grime that it had likely been a lovely pale shade of gold, not unlike Inessa's. The ends were jaggedly shaped, recently cut by an inexperienced hand.

"May I?" I asked quietly, gesturing to the rag.

"What?" The women looked startled and shrank away.

"I can clean it for you," I offered, kneeling down to her level.

The woman raked me over with a hesitant gaze before she reached her bruised hand out to pass me the rag. "Alright, thank you. I can't reach the bottom."

"What's your name?" I asked after a few silent moments passed as I gently touched the rag to the scrape. The scabbing was still forming, crusty with dried blood and the yellow-tinted fluid fighting to repair the torn skin.

"Amary."

"Where are you from, Amary?"

"I was born and raised here in Tuyet."

Amary winced as another moment of silence passed between us, drawing her attention back to her injury and the painful contact of the cloth. I fished my mind for something to keep the conversation moving, hoping to distract her till I finished. I'd used the tactic too many times to count in the hospital, and it had spared the patient unnecessary stress and discomfort, and spared me from having to witness the excess pain collaterally by helping them.

"Have you ever traveled out of the capital?" I tried, though I had a sinking feeling that I'd asked a silly question. I caught Roland looking at me while Macsen bombarded him with questions, his gaze soft and approving to see me already moving amongst the group and helping them.

"No," Amary replied, then sighed and to my surprise continued, "I'd like to take passage to Kesgoldol. They are taking in a lot of Eisan refugees there."

"I thought northern Kesgoldol territories had rebuked Wielders and offered no sanctuary?" I furrowed my brows in confusion.

"There are some counties and cities to the north that believe that way, but the reigning family still practices the ways of the Founders. Kesgols are sharp, cunning, and could kill you in a snap, but they are also some of the kindest people in all of Alse Hanya. As long as you can make it through the northern territories to the first set of mountains and beyond, you'll be under the country's protection and not be tried without due cause," Amary explained quietly as I finished padding the wound dry. Another fact of the real world I wasn't privy to the accuracy of.

"How'd you get this wound?" I asked, handing the rag back to her.

Amary turned to look at me with large green eyes, framed by bloodshot veins. I wasn't sure she was going to answer, but once again to my surprise, she did with more open honesty than I had expected. "I was married to a man who got called to the war—Darion. He is a mortal, but he knew what I was, a Dream Wielder. When he came back on leave from fighting with the Vatrese against Sonyo, he tried to arrest me with some other soldiers. He got hold of me and started to drag me through the alley by my hair."

I blanched. "I'm sorry, what did you say your husband's name was?"

"Darion. He is a member of your regiment, actually. I don't know if you'd know him though."

I envisioned the kind eyes of the soldier who had taught me how to disassemble a rifle, and shared with me how his wife was his reason for fighting in the war. Amary was the wife he had said nothing could tear him apart from. He had known then that his wife was a Wielder, but had said he was fighting to protect peace for her. Yet, something had changed drastically for him to return home only to turn on her. How could that kind man be capable of such a betrayal?

"I remember him, yes. How did you escape?" I finally managed to respond.

"Vadia," Amary tipped her head towards the young raven-haired girl. "And Rafe— a young Dezidaneyan warrior who had to go into deeper hiding recently when his name was posted. A shadow appeared, and Vadia reached through to cut off my hair and sever his hold on me. Rafe came through too and struck Darion. Then Vadia took me into her void and brought me here. I don't even know if Darion survived."

I bit my lip, unsure of what to make of her story. I was well aware that not everyone in our military ranks were kind and just, but it was hard to imagine a soldier, someone who had never shown any inclination towards malice, could have turned so cold as to betray his wife with such brutality. I wondered if he had always been a cruel man, and I had somehow never noticed. Perhaps he had merely been wearing a mask in front of me as his superior, but somehow that theory felt hollow. No, it seemed more likely that something terrible had happened while he was away— terrible enough to rewrite his loyalty and devotion.

Hearing Darion as a threat, this was also the first time I'd heard of Rafe being referred to as a warrior. He had been so gentle and laid-back at the hospital that I never would have guessed he was some sort of skilled fighter if I hadn't seen his quick and adept actions at the theater that night. I had seen him the day the list had been posted. Had he saved this woman before or after that farewell in the rain?

It doesn't matter when, just so long as he saved her and got away. But what happened to Darion?

"I'm sorry," I replied at last. "I'm glad they were there to rescue you in time."

"I didn't get a chance to know Rafe before he left, but a lot of us are here thanks to Vadia. She is the most selfless and remarkable girl I have ever met," Amary's eyes welled with emotion, and she blinked back tears. "So many of us would be dead without her help by now. With everything she's endured in her own life, it's a blessing that she hasn't turned bitter and cruel herself. Everyday she goes out and searches for others to help. I've even heard that she saved a soldier who was being needlessly attacked by some degenerates."

"Wow," I breathed and glanced over to where Vadia stood. The girl clearly held a depth to her as deep as the voids she wielded, and I felt my curiosity to know more of her and her character ignite. I wondered how she might have gotten on in another life if she had been able to befriend Kira in a world where both girls didn't have to be persecuted for what they had been born with inside their veins. I wondered how it was fair for such diametric fates to exist in the same city at the same time, and realized it all came down to concealment and ignorance.

Kira was safe and beloved because the only magic she knew how to wield was her own energy and charisma. Something told me that her ignorance was my little sister's saving grace that spared her from the very different and darker life that Vadia knew. Though, somehow, after seeing how she handled the little girl who escaped with us in the theater, had Kira been born into this other life, she too would have done everything in her power to fight for others.

I smiled, wishing silently for a day where the two could meet for real and take on the injustices of the world together. I wished the same for every weary face cowering in this room, and that each one might soon find the peace they'd had stolen from them.

"So then, vehicle eighty-seven will be headed into this district in the morning for an orphan round up. Though I'm not entirely sure why they'd station a meeting place here." Roland's words caught my attention, and I perked up with interest.

"Excuse me." I nodded in farewell to Amary and made my way back to Roland to peer over his shoulder at his notes. "Did you say vehicle eighty-seven? That can't be right."

"What do you know about it?" A woman scoffed, folding her arms as she peered at me. "Think we can't read or something?"

"I am in charge of the committee responsible for refugee and orphan rehabilitation," I kept my voice level, but not meek. "And, I can assure you, there are no round ups happening in this district tomorrow. Furthermore, vehicle eighty-seven was flagged as unavailable for transport until two days from now."

"Could your information be out of date or there be an error?" Roland asked slowly, his body simultaneously growing both stiff and agitated.

"No, I received the updated paperwork just this morning from Krisev himself. We had to swap things around to make our delivery schedule to the new orphanage and refugee convalescence stations in Kirsi tomorrow morning. Can I see that paper?"

Roland handed me the page covered in scribbled handwriting that belonged to someone other than Roland, meaning they weren't his notes, as I had assumed, but rather notes he had managed to snag and review. There were crude drawings and locations, but a few of the words were smudged. I brought the paper closer to my face as I tried to make out the time marker for the alleged delivery, then blanched when I realized a glaring detail that turned my blood to lead in my veins.

"What is it?"

"This here," I laid the paper down and tapped it. "I don't think the time is for the morning."

"But why would anyone be doing anything in an official

capacity at nine at night? That doesn't make any sense." Macsen's forehead creased, and his burly fingers curled around the edge of the table.

"Exactly. None of this information here is accurate or normal, but everything else in the schedule is correct. It is couched."

"So they are targeting this district tonight or tomorrow morning?"

The rumbling of an engine making its way down the abandoned street answered the man's question before I could, and I flashed Roland a panicked look. The crowd of assembled vagrants and orphans scuttled backward, glancing around frantically.

"What do we do?" I whispered to Roland.

"Stay quiet." He hissed to everyone. "They are in the district, but they could drive on by."

I closed my eyes and tried to think of anything that might be helpful right now. There was nothing Roland or I could say or do to pacify the guards when we were clearly aiding what was considered a public enemy group to Eisa. It sounded like there was only one unit being delegated to the area, so if they stopped out front, we could theoretically look for a back exit to make a run for it.

"They parked across the street!" Vadia alerted, and my eyes popped back open to the dimly lit lobby. There was a small private passage with a door that led a stairway and an old lift. The stairs looked unstable, creaky, and likely unable to support the weight of a single full grown body, and I already could guess that the lift was out of order. Beyond the old dilapidated check-in counter, there was a hallway leading to a kitchen area, but the depth of that room from the vantage point didn't look like it led to the back of the structure, but maybe the side which would be too risky. Then my gaze flitted over a small hatch next to the lift that looked like it was a laundry chute for maids to have once gathered old linens more efficiently. It reminded me of the escape Rafe had made for us in the theater, and an idea popped into my head.

"Vadia, take the children out of here," a ginger-haired woman waved the children over to gather in front of Vadia. "This is your maximum capacity for your shadow, isn't it?"

Vadia nodded somberly. "I'll take them as far away as I can and come back," She promised, waving her hands to create a pool of shadows on the ground, just like the one she'd made in front of the hospital that day. "Come on kids, hop inside."

"The rest of us will have to tough it out till she gets back," the woman sighed, looking away as some of the children began crying at the separation from their family members. Vadia hesitated, waiting for the final child to be pried away, her cries of protest having to be stifled by the hand of the man carrying her to the shadows. A stab pierced my heart to see such a sight.

"Roland, we need to get everyone upstairs," I grabbed Roland's shoulder to get his attention.

"We can't—"

"Speak up!" Someone called out softly.

"If you have an idea, Princess, best share it with everyone," Macsen gestured for me to repeat what I had said, and I almost wished I could melt away into that shadow myself.

"If we can get upstairs then I think we can access the back of the building," I asserted.

"The staircases are all broken and damaged. Without a Wish Wielder to fix them, or a Shadow Wielder to transport us, we can't reach the upper level for sure."

"I can try and freeze the steps," a young man stepped forward. "It'll be slick, but it could work."

I felt my heart quicken subconsciously at the mention of the Ice affinity, and curled my fists. "That will tell them where we went, and they will be on us as soon as they get through the door," I countered evenly. "While we wait for Vadia, we can try the stairs first, and if those give out, we might be able to crawl through the laundry chute. It should be large and sturdy enough to get us up to the next level one at a time."

"There are no guarantees the upper levels are stable," an elderly woman stepped forward. Her brows were creased under the weight of urgency, but her voice was gentle.

"They are unloading and starting to look at the building next-door," someone alerted from the vantage point of a crack in the boards covering the windows.

"It's the best shot we've got." Roland gestured rapidly for us to hurry.

I swallowed hard and wondered if the Divinities would answer a prayer to spare this group of Wielders and Sympathizers. If they followed their own tenants, surely they had to. I hovered at the back of the group as everyone rushed to the staircase. If they followed their own tenants, surely they had to.

"One at a time, or no one will get out if we put too much stress on it and it breaks!" The crotchety woman who'd questioned me snapped at her peers. I saw her dull russet hair bob through the bodies as she shifted herself towards the front.

One by one, bodies filed gingerly up the escape path. Hauling themselves against the vertical incline, they shifted their weight selectively at each creak and crack of the decaying wood beneath their feet, until there were only a handful of people left hovering between the lobby and the little hallway to the stairs.

"You should have been at the front of the escape," Roland murmured beside me. "You and I absolutely cannot be caught here."

"I don't think that would win me any favors to prioritize myself over those less able," I retorted quietly. "They are injured and I am healthy."

"I applaud your selflessness, but you also need to be practical here. If we are found out, then that's it. We can't help anymore, and we run the risk of your secret getting out and the country falling into ruin. The moment danger is in the air, it's my job to get you to safety, and trust the others to know how to help themselves. They've done it thus far."

"Barely." Something burned in my stomach, a feeling I couldn't quite place. It was conspicuous and shameful, twisted with righteous indignation and something indiscernible. It flared with a sense of feeling like more of a hindrance than a help to these people— not like Inessa and what she was offering them. Meanwhile my impression would be someone who would have to think of herself before others or else risk monumental consequences no one could afford. Had Inessa ever been in such a compromising situation and had to think of her welfare before the others? My very core screamed in protest at the idea, but I knew Roland had a point. It was more complicated than I was giving it credit for, and appearances counted for nothing if we were imprisoned or killed.

A snap sounded in front of me, drawing my focus as a young man scrambled upwards from where a section of the stairs had finally given way.

"We can't use the stairs now!" Another man hissed, his hazel eyes flashing with panic. "How do we get out? Where can we hide?"

"Come on," The elderly woman waved us to the chute. "We will have to do as the Princess said and get inside. Quickly now." She turned and narrowed her eyes at me and Roland. "You two should have been long gone by now."

"Can you climb up the chute?" Macsen lifted the hatch and poked his head inside dubiously. "It looks like there is something in here…"

"I told Lenya to see if he could find something to act as a rope to help with the incline on his way out. Looks like he followed through." The woman nodded approvingly. "I'll make it. Princess, you better get to climbing."

"You two go ahead of me," I waved her and Macsen forward.

"Sorrel," Roland sighed impatiently. "What did we just get done saying?"

"He can support her if she slips." I pointed to Macsen. "If we hurry, I'll be right behind them. No time to argue."

"They are leaving the building and heading this way!" The woman who had been keeping watch on the street alerted and raced over to us. "We are out of time."

No one argued further, and instead, Macsen helped the elderly woman into the chute where she grabbed hold of a tethered sheet and used it to hoist herself upward, with Macsen right behind her. I climbed into the chute next, doing my best to shift the weight to my feet to keep from sliding backward. Thankfully, the old dented and riveted metal allowed for some resistance against the soles of my shoes, and I braced myself with my knees, elbows pressing the sides and my back arching against the roof. Above me, I could see a small light at the opposite hatch where it was left cracked open by the dangling sheet.

"Does anyone smell smoke?" Someone mumbled behind me.

"I don't think I can stand to be in such a small space," Someone else whispered at the back. "I'm going to hide in the lift."

"Me too," Another voice chorused.

"Wait," Macsen hissed, a loud banging ringing through the inn with enough force, it rattled the building. "They are breaking open the door. Stay still and don't make a sound."

But the others had already abandoned the chute in search of somewhere else to wait out the invasion. We didn't dare twitch a muscle. We didn't dare breathe or even think for fear the guards might sense our silent screams. I couldn't help but wonder, as the door thudded open with a splintering crack, what if they found us in here? The notion had felt somewhat surreal a moment ago, buried somewhere deep beneath altruistic intent, but that altruism felt hollow and flimsy in the wake of an actual threat closing in on us. Could Roland and I truly possibly be killed or thrown in jail for conspiring? Would our kingdom fall if some soldiers reported me here, or would Papa forgive me and never let it see the light of day? So much, it seemed, had been swept under the rug already. It was either that or ruin and I made a silent vow to listen to Roland next time and get out sooner. I willed away the hopeless thoughts as best as I could and tried to ignore the harsh sound of the boots on the wooden floor.

"No one's in plain sight," Someone spoke contemptuously, and I did my best to suppress a shudder threatening to claim my already straining limbs. *In plain sight* meant they must be about to search for hiding spots. I had already been holding my breath, but my stomach sucked in further as adrenaline prepared me to fight for my life.

"Right," My blood roared in my ears as I recognized Otvel's voice. "Burn it down."

Burn it down? I bit back my incredulous gasp, and almost lost my footing as all the strength left my body and was replaced with a fresh anxiety. *They are going to burn everyone in here alive!*

"You heard the Priest, boys! Light 'em up!"

We didn't know what to do; try and flee regardless of the noise it would cause, scream in terror, or beg for mercy. It was all the same. Utterly useless. But, I'd be damned if this was where I met my end. Unless Otvel was going rogue, my family was apparently sanctioning the burning of innocent civilians, and the head of our church was leading it. I was filled with repulsion, fear, and desperation. Now more than ever, witnessing the needless cruelty being shown to those who were no different than myself or my family, I owed it to these people to survive and help them all survive as well. Looking over my shoulder, I caught Roland's eye and could see my own panic stricken determination reflected there.

We continued to wait, still and silent, knowing the soldiers were setting the lobby ablaze. I wondered if those hiding on the second floor had found an exit and left, or at least realized there was a fire set. Despite being sealed inside the chute, it wasn't long before the sound of crackling flames grew to a dull roar, and a thick acerbic haze slithered around us. The smell of smoke was just starting to smother my nostrils when we heard the door slam shut, announcing the departure of Otvel and the soldiers.

TWENTY-NINE

"Do we go back down?"

"I can't believe they set the place on fire," Roland growled.

"I'll check things out!" Whoever was last behind Roland called as they slid down the chute. The hatch opened, letting in a fresh wave of smoke.

"What is Lieve doing?" Macsen glanced back at me.

Before I could reply, the hatch opened and Lieve launched himself back inside the chute. "Move it! The lobby is completely on fire. I closed the door to this hallway to buy us a little time, but our only way out now is up. Hurry!"

"What about the others? The ones who hid in the lift?" I asked.

"I'm not sure. I think they might have tried to climb down to the basement."

"They'll be trapped!"

"Keep climbing, Sorrel. Just keep climbing," Roland ordered.

The elderly woman was scrambling up the chute as fast as her trembling body would allow, aware she was controlling the pace for our escape. The metal surrounding us was quickly heating up where it shared a wall with the burning room, burning our skin where it was forced against the surface of the encased space and we fought our way to the top. Mixed with the acrid tang of smoke was the nauseating scent of burning flesh— Whether my own, someone else's, or both, I wasn't sure. I swallowed against the lump of bile rising in my throat, despite the stinging dryness that left my mouth devoid of moisture.

Feral howls of pain and terror hit my ears and reverberated off the metal walls of the chute, discordance and despair intertwined. The closed space rattled against the sound, and the sheets of metal supporting us were becoming less and less stable in the heat.

The fabric of my clothing was heating at such an alarming rate, I worried it might ignite and swallow me in flames. Smoke was clinging to the layer of sweat dripping into my eyes as I forced my blistering skin to keep propelling my body forward, and did my best to ignore the notion we were being cooked alive. Everything in me was screaming at the heat encasing me, longing for the cold. For a brief moment, I wished I had known how to activate my Ice affinity just to alleviate the pain but willed away the fruitless thought. I didn't think I could withstand the agony much longer, and my vision was growing blurry from smoke inhalation and overheating. The chute felt like it went on for eternity, and I was beginning to regret my suggestion of using it as our escape route

At last, a blast of fresh air hit my face and grazed over my shoulders as the old woman found the second hatch door and threw it open, tumbling out in a bout of coughing. Just behind her and Macsen, I pulled myself free and collapsed, curling into myself, eyes wide with agony, drawing in ragged breaths of my own. Relief flooded me as Roland erupted from the chute. I held my breath and waited for the rest of the group to follow, hoping those who had fled had somehow made it into the chute behind Roland and I had just hadn't noticed, but as the seconds dragged on and the echoing screams below suddenly fell away, I realized no one else was coming. Not even Lieve.

He'd given us a head start that he hadn't lived to see for himself. The inhuman screams and the loud thumping behind me, the burning flesh... It must have been him, and I was completely stupefied in a veil of surrealism. A man had died behind me and I had gotten out.

I looked at Roland and reeled. *Has something like this happened to you before? To Ina?* I didn't know if I could stand to know the answer to that question. Imaging a stranger felled in the flames was difficult enough, let alone to think that my own cherished loved ones could just as easily have been the ones to perish. Though even that didn't feel quite true. There was real grief in my heart, and I'd only learned the man's name as we'd fled, and didn't even know his face, nor the the identities of the others who surely hadn't survived below either.

I blinked back tears, and tried to focus on my breathing instead of the stench of burning hair and skin still permeating the air already heavy with smoke, or the searing pain covering my body. I wanted to drag myself to the comfort of Roland's side, but my body refused to comply, feeling heavy as a rock. Thankfully, though rattled and burned, he appeared to be fine.

A quick glance around told me that a fair portion of the others who went ahead of us had already escaped, and the last of the remaining people were filtering down the end of hall towards a back exit. My adrenaline was far from gone, but just escaping from the burning metal oven had taken the edge off enough to become conscious of the pain in my palms and knees. I took one brave look at the blistering skin and quickly wished I hadn't. Seeing the injury only made it hurt worse.

I knew it was psychosomatic, and had seen patients do the very same at the hospital, but I still found myself biting my lip and closing my eyes tightly. How much worse it had been for those at the back of the line— those who had chosen to flee last had been rewarded with a terrible and painful death. I had suggested the chute for salvation and it had become their tomb— if they had even managed to reach it. Guilt engulfed me, threatening to completely overtake my faculties with hysteria.

I pried one eye open to see everyone was sitting in an awkward stunned circle. The incivility of the fact that a priest had tried to burn us to death without even seeing who might be hiding in the building was utterly shocking. We were stunned, me and Roland more than the others, by the sinister inhumanity that was thrown in our faces by someone we knew and trusted. Those people who attacked us blindly weren't people. They had no morals, and when they held the fate of living beings in their hands, they didn't care simply because we believed differently than them. Our own thoughts and opinions were being used as cannon fodder against us. Otvel would have condemned me as corrupted and burned me without remorse despite our history, and that realization rattled me to my very core.

Doesn't that make them the monsters then? Not the weary friends and families taking shelter here tonight?

Seeing she was the closest to me, I half dragged myself to the elderly woman's side. She had been in the chute for the shortest amount of time of our group, but she was also the oldest. I'd check her first, then make sure no one else needed triage, not that there was much I could do without supplies. With the building burning beneath us, we couldn't afford to stay much longer. The door would only slow the spread, and our location on the second floor was one of the worst places we could find ourselves.

"Are you alright?" I asked the women gently. Her fragile blue eyes were wide and brimmed with tears. I swallowed back the lump in my throat that was forming from this helpless old woman's fear. She stared back at me without saying anything. "Are you alright?" I repeated.

This time she seemed to hear me and let out a ragged sigh. She brought her own wrinkled and blistered hands up close to her face. She was shivering from shock. "I should be asking you that. I am a healer and yet all of you suffer because I am unable to treat you." Her voice cracked with defeat.

I felt my heart immediately breaking for her. Wielder or mortal, there was nothing evil or malicious in her sorrow and regret. "It's not your fault. I'm a nurse," I replied, shifting closer to brush my arm against hers. "I feel the same way. Helpless. But we can't help that we don't have any supplies or medicine. No one will expect us to materialize a hospital."

Knowing that there were Wielders who apparently could very well materialize supplies, I suddenly felt foolish for my statement and clamped my mouth closed. But the woman nodded in agreement.

"You're right. It can't be helped right now."

"What's your name?" I asked softly. In spite of the horror we'd just survived, and the danger still lurking beneath us, I felt the need to know this woman and let her know that I cared. I'd never have that chance for the few who didn't make it out of the chute alive. She looked at me, her eyes round moons of astonishment.

"Maggie," She breathed her name in such a way that told me she hadn't expected such an interaction from me. There was something wistful in her expression, a secret thought she couldn't bring herself to voice. I recognized her name immediately as the woman Ina had mentioned as her teacher.

She placed her blistered fingers ever so gently on my hand where it was cradled in my lap, and a single tear spilled over from her eye. I felt a strange sensation of familiarity in her touch, and inhaled deeply at the compassionate contact transpiring between a Wielder and a princess of the kingdom that persecuted her. I was beginning to understand Inessa's dedication to her secret cause. This woman wore years of repression and hardship on her skin, seeming so close to breaking, and yet her kindness was shining strong and resilient.

"It's nice to meet you Maggie." I had to steady my voice as I spoke to her with the friendly formality she so desperately deserved. The next words I spoke were as much for myself as for her. "Everything is going to be okay. We will get through this."

A faint smile curled the edges of her chapped lips as I reassured her. She squeezed my hand tightly despite her burns and began to cry, unable to fight back her emotions any longer. Ignoring the knowledge that we still needed to escape a building that was burning from the ground up, ignoring the fear I normally would have felt in the presence of a fugitive Wielder, ignoring the pull to grab Roland's hand and run away back to the safety of the palace grounds— ignoring the situation all together but for Maggie, I pulled the poor fragile old woman into my arms and hugged her tightly as she sobbed against my chest.

The tender moment only lasted for a few moments before we were brought back to the reality that we still needed to escape. Smoke poured into the space from the stairway, and I could hear the flames crackling as they slowly ate away at the splintered wood. No one else was in the area, and I felt a small trickle of relief that it seemed everyone who had used the stairs had managed to make it to the fire escape. Finding a bit of my lost strength again, I gave Roland a brisk inspection while Maggie looked over Macsen. All of us were burned, with Macsen having the worst, given his size in the small chute, but we all could still manage to walk.

"Are you certain you'll be able to get around on those burns?" I asked the man as we started down the hall, and he shrugged.

"Don't have much of a choice unless I want more."

I glanced at Maggie. "When it's safe, I'm going to get some basic ointments and supplies for salves for you."

"How does your *Highness* expect to get access to what Maggie would need to treat us?" Macsen snorted.

I bit down the irritation at his biased dismissal and kept my voice level. "Actually, since the war started, I have been training as a nurse in the Piren Hospital. I have tended to many patients over the last few months, and assisted in several surgeries."

"She helped with Rafe's stab wound, and assisted the doctor when I was shot in the shoulder. Amongst many other things. Sorrel has a sharp medical mind on her shoulders," Roland added with an approving nod in my direction. Macsen merely grunted in acknowledgment, but didn't argue, accepting Roland's praise as evidence of my capabilities.

A loud bang sounded, and I recognized it immediately as gunfire. It was the same otherworldly crackling pop that had torn the silence in two when the soldiers came to rescue us from the Wielders in the woods back at Svyat Gavan. The same sound I'd heard through the door at the theater when Roland had been shot. Another resonance I would no sooner forget than the sobs of the stampede victims, or the excruciating wails of those who didn't make it out of the fire behind us.

More shots rang out, followed by the sound of broken glass. I held up my arms against the shards as a blazing object hurtled past me. Whipping my head around, I saw that they had thrown a torch through the window to spread the fire to the second level faster.

"The soldiers have caught on to the escape path!" Macsen growled as the incendiary device caught hold of the carpet and started climbing the drapes. "They are trying to trap anyone up here still in the fire."

"What do we do?" I gasped, the inferno claiming the staircase behind us. Smoke was smothering the breathable air, and I tugged my collar over my mouth to stifle a burning cough. I flinched as more flaming projectiles broke through the windows further down the path we had planned to take towards the fire exit. "Can we still get out?"

"Only one way to find out." We all jumped and turned around to see Vadia emerging from her pool of shadows.

"Thank Eisa," Maggie breathed. "Vadia can take us out."

I looked doubtfully at the twisting shadows at Vadia's feet, unable to swallow down the memory of the concealed women in the woods from my childhood. I tried to remind myself of the stories I'd heard of Vadia's rescues, and suppress the instinctual crawling of my skin.

That was a different time, with different people. Don't lock yourself away with more judgment barring the door.

"They lit the blasted place on fire!" Vadia cried in disbelief.

"I can't believe they would stoop to smoking us out or burning us alive. That's horrific, even for them!"

"It's a new low, to say the least," Roland acknowledged. "Can you take us out, Vadia?"

"I can try, but we need to get further away from this area first."

"Why?" My curiosity got the better of me and the question slipped out of my mouth before I realized it. I shrank in embarrassment, having the distinct feeling that I didn't have a place to question the girl. As she stepped out of her shadow fully and beckoned us onward, I noticed blood seeping through a wound on her leg.

"Remember our first meeting?" She raised her eyebrows at me as the five of us continued hastily down the hall. "Your priest friend stopped me from approaching you with artificial fire. Not only does the light weaken my shadows, reducing the success of a multi-bodied transportation, the shadows caused by flames are too hot to meld with. Fire acts like a living thing, but we Shadow Wielders can't shift into its cast shadows," She explained, pointing to the various clusters of fire dappling the hallway ahead of us.

Her head cocked to the side and I recalled the same gesture seeming so inhuman and unsettling the day of first seeing her. Now she was just a young, earnest girl, patiently explaining herself to me. *Did I really project all those monstrous traits onto her?* My mask of duty had left me utterly blind.

"Oh," I nodded again. I had no idea how her teleportation magic worked. I'd never seen Shadow Wielding as anything more than a curse of darkness.

Seeming to read my mind, she added, "The weaker my shadows are, the less distance I can travel, the less people I can take with me, and the greater chance we have of getting stuck in the dark space. Plus with the soldiers just outside the building here, my first jump would land us right in the middle of them."

"How did they catch on to us anyway?" Roland rasped around a cough.

"My first jump with so many children in my shadow was just outside the inn, to the side." Vadia pointed to one of the broken windows. "My second jump only took us to the end of the building. Unfortunately, by then, one of the men spotted us before I could jump again, and started chasing after us. A few of the children panicked and left the shadow. I tried to get them back, but I had to get the rest to safety."

"We can see if we can find them later," Macsen offered, shooting Vadia a sideways glance full of sympathy. "For now, save your voice and cover your mouths or the smoke will do us in before the flames do."

Vadia grimaced and stumbled under her wounded leg. We were still in a state of urgency, with the torches continuing their jobs of slowly igniting the hallway from the walls in, but there was still enough of a path towards our exit that if Vadia's injury was bothering her that much, it likely would be better to aid her now rather than when we had to flee down the ladder if she couldn't take us out in her shadow. I stepped beside her and offered my shoulder.

"May I?"

"Sure," Vadia nodded. "The darn thing is slowing me down and taking my energy away from my magic."

"You saved a lot of people today," I wheezed.

"If I were stronger, I could have saved more," she mumbled, licking her cracking lips.

I blinked at her, taking in her small frame and thin physique. Given the nature of her vagabond lifestyle, she was scrawny. The fact she could carry any other single human away was nothing short of a miracle as I saw it.

Roland doubled back, and waved me off of Vadia. "I can carry you, Vad."

"When we get to safety, we need to remove this shrapnel from your leg or it will get infected," I advised, shrinking further beneath my collar in a vain attempt to bar the smoke so I could voice my concerns of her injury. "Maybe we can try and make our way to—" my words were swallowed by another series of crashes down the hall, followed by loud pops and shouts from the others.

"Watch out!" Vadia yelped, and I felt her hand shove hard against my shoulders knocking me backwards before Roland could scoop her up. A wave of heat and light washed over me, as something shattered in the space between us. A new wave of fire raged, nearly encircling Vadia where she struggled to scramble to her feet.

THIRTY

My eyes widened as the fire momentarily flickered into hues of purple and blue before being overwhelmed by the natural pigments of red, yellow, and orange. The colorful flames were the same as the ones that Otvel had used to keep Vadia at bay that day back at the hospital. This was his doing once again, and having seen Vadia earlier, he was clearly sending a message.

"Sorrel, get down!" I barely heard Roland's warning and looked around bewildered, uncertain of which direction the threat was coming from since I was already on the ground.

"No!" Vadia gasped, reaching in my direction, her face twisted in panic. A dark form surged from behind me, and a tendril stretched in front of my face in time to block a direct hit from another flaming projectile.

I threw my arms over my face, expecting a collateral peppering of sparks and glass, but nothing ever came. Instead the crash sounded by Vadia, followed by a cry of pain.

Flames flared together to close the remaining gap in the pathway, cutting her off from the rest of us. The momentum of the explosion threw her in the opposite direction, deeper into the ring of fire. The roaring sounds around me muffled before turning to a high pitched ringing that drowned everything else out. Vadia had taken the hit that was meant for me.

When she sat up, I could see the burn wounds running up the length of both arms. Had she caught the explosive when it passed through the shadow? I recalled her explanation that her abilities were weakened in this environment, and that the shadows themselves could become too hot to handle. But surely she should have known that would happen. Why inflict so much harm on herself to save me instead of getting out of the circling fire while she had a chance?

Vadia wheezed, her face crumpling under the pain, then she threw her head back and bit down a wail of agony. She reached to her legs and cried as she tore away the smoldering fabric remaining on her trousers. Once more the air was overwhelmed with the stench of burning flesh, but this time, I could also detect a hint of tar, no doubt used in the incendiary to help the spreading fire stick. Blood was splattered and dripping down her exposed skin, beading from the plethora of nicks and cuts inflicted from the exploding glass.

I pushed to my feet and rushed over to the wall of fire, ignoring the fact that more projectiles were flying through the broken windows behind me. I was only faintly aware of the others returning to my side, as my focus fixed on the injured girl finding the last scrap of strength and endurance in her to lift her battered body from the floor.

"Vadia, come on," I begged, wishing I could do something useful to help. Again, the thought entered my mind with a longing for access to the Ice affinity. Fire likely would melt it, but I couldn't help but wonder if even that would at least dampen an escape path for the young girl.

Vadia looked around the blazing room, wild-eyed, her chest

heaving. "I can't... use my shadows here anymore. The fire is too bright, the shadows they create are too weak and too hot to go through."

"We have to find a way to get her out," Roland puffed, looking around frantically, flinching against the heat of the fire, sweat pouring down our faces. I blinked through my stinging eyes, trying to stay composed and find a solution.

"No," Vadia spoke quietly, her gaze wistful and unflinching, even as more of the floor caved in behind her. "This is it. I can't escape this time."

"Vadia," Macsen croaked, appearing beside Roland.

"But you four *can*. Hurry and go before the rest of the building comes down!" She shouted over the roar of the flames, her voice cracking with dryness. "Take Sorrel and get her to safety. She and Inessa are our biggest hopes that this sort of thing never happens again. I believe that. So, go!"

"May Dimaer receive you and the Founders be kind," Macsen whispered. Maggie and Roland echoed his prayer, and I couldn't tell if it was the sweat or tears, or both, running down their smoke stained cheeks.

"Give Rafe my condolences, Roland. Tell him that I'm sorry for his loss. Keep him alive. That menace is going to join me if he doesn't start being more careful!" Vadia's eyes creased with feigned amusement to cover her fear, but even so, the apparent affection she felt for Rafe and Roland both was evident in every line and crinkle of her visage.

"I'll get the message to him, I promise." Roland blinked against his rising emotions.

I stared dumbfounded by the helplessness. Just like Harvier, I couldn't do enough to spare another young life. I had feared this girl and thought she was evil incarnate, yet she had welcomed me, spoke up on my behalf, come back to help us escape, and put her faith in me.

"Come on, Sorrel." Roland tugged on my arm, but I shrugged him away, my eyes locked on Vadia's.

The flames were growing and the building groaned loudly, signaling a final warning that we needed to evacuate unless we wanted to be buried under the rafters. Orange and yellow flickered all around the young girl's body, and I was once more reminded of the painful fact that she was even younger than Kira, and I couldn't imagine my sister's life being cut so short. The comparison was all too glaring, bringing reality crashing down on me with a cruel vehemence. I looked at my hand and willed with all my might for it to do something—anything—that might rescue Vadia, and reached across the threshold of fire.

"What are you doing?" Macsen gasped. "There is nothing more we can do here. If you don't want to die, move it."

The heat was scorching, angering the already raw, blistered skin on my palms, but I grit my teeth against the pain and stretched myself further. Sparks licked at my forearms, singeing my skin. I knew I was leaving more evidence of my escapade, but that was of little consequence if it meant I could reach Vadia. I could make up some story to explain away a burn, but I couldn't fib away allowing Vadia to die while I survived. She had saved so many, she didn't deserve to perish like this. Someone had to stay and beat the odds to save *her* this time.

Vadia's eyes widened as she saw me leaning into the fire. A moment of hope flashed across her face and tears began pouring down her cheeks. Her brave facade was falling away, revealing the lost and frightened child staring down death underneath. She took a small step towards me, lifting her hand to reach in my direction, but as her foot made contact with the smoldering ground, it broke away causing her to lurch backwards. The rest of flooring between me and her fell, the raging fire below swallowing it whole.

"No!" I yelped, struggling against Roland trying to pull me back. He was speaking to me but I couldn't hear a word he was saying.

Tears still ran from Vadia's eyes, but when she looked at me, the hope was gone and was replaced by acceptance. She shook her head slowly and her extended hand swung to the side. Arms splayed out wide, Vadia closed her eyes and lifted her head as inky darkness erupted from her like wings. The fire bit at the edge of the shadows purging from her body, and in that moment Vadia looked the very picture of a smoldering phoenix, ready to burn and be reborn in the flames just like the legends. Another moment later, and the ground gave way beneath her. She held her form and tipped backwards into her fiery grave.

A shriek erupted from me, and everything in me wanted to somehow dive in after her, but as the scream purged from my throat, my strength evaporated, and I snatched my arm back from the fire, cradling it close to my chest. Roland threw his arm around me and gave me a squeeze.

"I know, Sorrel. Let's not make her sacrifice be in vain."

"But what if—"

"She's not coming back out," Roland's words were choked, and I saw his eyes glistening with tears of shock and rage. "Not this time. We can't stay or we will join her."

I nodded numbly, unable to blink away the image of Vadia disappearing into the smoke and embers. Following his lead, Roland and I raced through the collapsing building with Macsen and Maggie until we reached the fire exit I had hoped would be there. But when we looked down, we could see the soldiers had moved into position below.

"We can't get down without being seen," I coughed, my voice strained. "We will have to find another exit."

A loud snap sounded behind us as more of the floor fell away and flames were crawling up the brick walls of the hallway on trails of tapestries and curtains to the wooden rafters above. The inferno was building in ferocity and in pursuit, giving us little choice but to make a run for it, further into the structure. We snaked our way down a few offshoot hallways, narrowly avoiding one that led back to an already charred and smoldering portion of the inn, the flames put out by a broken water pipe. Finally, we found ourselves on the right path to salvation.

"I think we're going to have to jump," Roland sighed, poking his head back through the window. I glanced at Maggie and shook my head.

"We need to find another way out of here, then. Maggie can't make a jump like that. Your shoulder is just barely on the mend too. There has to be another way out," I insisted.

"We are out of time and out of options here. Better a broken leg than burning alive."

"She will get caught or shot if she can't run." It was my voice speaking those brave words but my head was screaming to throw myself to safety. The idea of plunging into a pit of flames and feeling every fiber of my body being charred at once was not something I intended on experiencing. Even the rest of us stood a high chance of seriously injuring ourselves if we leapt from this height.

"We will have to risk it, even if I have to drag you out the window with me," Roland croaked, and I leaned away from his vehemence. I knew he was just as scared for me as he was for himself— especially after witnessing Vadia's fall. I was scared for him too, and I wanted him to be safe, but I couldn't abandon an old woman to die, either from burning to death or from the injuries the impact of jumping would cause her.

"Maybe I can hold her and soften the fall," Macsen tried to rationalize. "Either way, we need out of this building now."

"I hate being such a burden," Maggie whimpered. "The three of you need to just leave me behind. None of this would be happening if only I hadn't—" Her words were cut short as the ground began creaking loudly beneath us. The floor was trembling and I could feel the heat through the soles of my shoes, alerting that the fire had reached beneath us. "Look out!"

Maggie grabbed hold of my wrist and yanked me backwards just in time for a portion of the floor to fall away where I'd been standing. We were both thrown down, shrinking back from the sudden burst of heat and flames surging through the new opening towards fresh air. The new blaze acted as both an uncrossable chasm as well as an impassable wall separating me and Maggie from Roland and Macsen.

"Roland!" I screamed, afraid that the two ends of the fire were going to converge on him as he yelped in pain. My eyes were streaming from the smoke, and they stung as I tried to peer through the hue of towering orange.

"We have to jump to get out. Go with Maggie and *get out*, Sorrel! I'll find you from the ground."

I could barely make out the two silhouettes of Roland and Macsen barreling through the window into the night, their figures wavering in the mirage of the blinding heat. I gritted my teeth and prayed with all my might that the two had landed safely, and we would find them again soon. Pushing from the ground, I rose to my feet, swaying for a moment as my head rushed with a dizzying darkness.

"We need to get out of this smoke and heat, or we are going to collapse before even having to worry about the flames," Maggie coughed, rising more slowly to steady me. "Stay low to the ground as you can."

I nodded and jerked my chin for us to make another dash for it. We were running out of space left in the inn, and unless we found another escape ladder, or a stable staircase down to a lower unburned level, we would have no other option than to jump as well.

Please, please let us find an exit. I can't go on much longer. I pleaded over and over in my head, willing for the Divinities to heed my calls for aid. I grimaced as I tried to swallow, but my mouth and throat had grown so dry, the motion made my throat stick together, before a sensation of pricking thorns moved down my esophagus. *Divinities, Founders— whoever might be listening. Please hear me and help me find a way out of this fire. Help me and this woman escape. She is innocent, and I pray you see her soul and know it is worth saving.* In my desperation, I felt the devout line of loyalty to the Divinities slipping away with each slowing step I took.

Then at last, it seemed someone heard and answered my prayer.

"Look! An escape ladder," Maggie cheered weakly, and tried to lift the window but it wouldn't budge.

"Watch out," I pushed past the old woman and braced myself before slamming my elbow into the glass until it yielded and broke away. Smoke rushed through my hair as the sudden fresh air acted as a vacuum, sucking the ashy plume through the hole. I slipped out the window and pulled at the ladder with all my might but it was rusted and stuck, sucking in as much fresh air as I could in a single inhale. "I can't loosen it."

"Halt! I see you up there," I stiffened as a bullet whizzed by my head and ricocheted off the ladder with a sharp *ping*. "Let the fire burn you for your wicked deeds, filthy Wielder!"

Another shot cracked through the night, and I threw my hands over my head, completely unsure of how I was supposed to get me and Maggie both to safety with a gunman below and a fire at our backs. This was our final path of escape. A few more minutes and our fates would be sealed.

Was my search for understanding worth this?

I could see flashes of light farther away, both from the defensive magic of the fleeing Wielders, as well as the illumination of the offensive gunfire from the soldiers. My spirit broke at the sight. Soldiers I might know by face and name—whom I'd treated in the hospital, who had laughed and played cards with me during their recovery, who had been put through drills by me or my siblings— were firing at frightened, starved citizens, innocent and unarmed but for their own affinities. There were parents and siblings whom the children Vadia had taken to safety were counting on reuniting with. On the other hand, the soldiers were sons, husbands, and fathers, executing orders dutifully in support of their kingdom.

The chaos was all so needless and ridiculous. None of what was happening made sense anymore.

Another bullet clattered, this time aimed next to my leg, likely hoping to make me lose my balance. I let out a cry of frustration, wondering if Roland and Macsen had made it to safety at least. With Soldiers moving into this area, the chances of him being able to help me out of this situation was slim and undesirable. He could explain his presence here just as well as I could, and of all the outcomes of this horrific night, being seen by a soldier was one of the worst outcomes I could imagine, along with dying in the ordeal— especially after Vadia had used her dying words to put her faith in my ability to help change the future for our people and country. But, I was at a loss of how to honor that faith.

"Maggie, I'm pinned in. I— I don't know what to do," I coughed, hopelessness burrowing into my skin. "We need help."

"The fire is closing in," Maggie whispered, resignation choking her voice. Horror crawled up my spine as I saw that the flames were creeping towards us. She obviously had been transfixed by the lapping tide of yellow and orange that she didn't have any more solutions to offer.

"Do you have any affinities you could use here?" I ducked back into the building to avoid another shot being fired at me.

"My affinity is Vine, and in my weakened state, I'm afraid I can't use it effectively to conjure. If I was outside and could work with connection to existing flora, I might be able to, but in here, and on the second level, I am at a great disadvantage," Maggie shook her head, her face puckering with shame.

"That's alright. I have three affinities and no clue how to use a single one because of my own shameful narrow-mindedness and fear," I croaked, feeling that my demise was nearing with each passing second, and someone might as well hear my regrets.

"Don't sound so resolved. You'll live to learn those affinities another day, if you choose to. As a royal, you should be capable of great magic if that is the path you take." Maggie joined me by the window, each of us trying to drink in what little air we still could.

"After tonight, if I do make it out of this alive, I don't think I'll look at things the same as I did before setting foot into this Divine-forsaken inn," I laughed weakly, and thought of the innocent faces I'd met, the children anxiously awaiting the safe return of the adults, the poor souls who hadn't made it, and my own family sleeping soundly at the palace, completely unaware of the danger I was in. It gave me a renewed sense of purpose, and a wave of false energy ignited within me, fueled by a final surge of adrenaline. "I'll get out of here and strive to learn my affinities. I will use them to defend others and protect real justice."

"Welcome to the cause." Maggie smiled and patted my hand, her eyes shining with pride I didn't feel I deserved. "You'll no doubt do fine things for us, Sorrel."

"I hope so, but first we have to make it out of this building without getting shot," I sighed, sweat coating me from head to toe, causing the soot to cling to my skin. I could hope to achieve a new strength in the future until I was blue in the face, but it didn't change the fact that I had reached the end of my own current abilities and limitations, and needed a rescue. As a last resort, I cupped my hands around my mouth and shouted with all my might. "Help! Someone help us! We can't get down!"

The dryness in my throat made each word feel like it was shredding the lining of my trachea, and my lips cracked as I forced them to keep forming my pleas for help. A fourth shot struck the window pane. Recalling from Darion's tutoring, I knew the soldier was down to his last bullet and no doubt was waiting for a clear shot at me or Maggie to use it.

Please. For the love of Eisa, someone please save us.

THIRTY-ONE

I blinked, feeling certain I must be falling into a delirium as I caught sight of a figure jumping from window ledges and rooftops towards us, the platforms adjusting in size to match each step and leap. A white glow shimmered around its hands and feet, revealing a Wielder coming to our aid. My eyes widened as I recognized the magic being used, and in the next instant, identified its Wielder.

In a final leap, I caught sight of a flash of blonde hair and golden eyes trained on my face peering from the window, smoke billowing around me. The soldier shouted up at us, and the white shimmering shifted into a blinding glow. The Wielder swung his muscular arms in big, arcing circles before bringing them together to materialize several daggers into his hands as he cleared the gap to land on the platform in front of me.

"Rafe? What are you doing here?"

"I was hiding a ways away so as not to draw attention to the hideout, but I saw the smoke and ran into Vadia, she brought me back here," Rafe replied, flinging his knives at the soldier, successfully forcing him to dive for cover. "I lost track of her in the chaos."

I opened my mouth to explain about Vadia, but words failed me. Instead, I shook my head and decided I'd tell him later.

"But, what are *you* doing here?" Rafe asked. He glanced over his shoulder to see the man getting back to his feet and hurled another set of daggers his way. "Last I saw you, you were dragging your feet to play in the rain and now you're in the middle of a fire? Clearly someone let you in on the big secret. Where is Roland?"

Ignoring his questions, I took the gap from the soldier diving out of range of Rafe's bladed assault to point frantically at the ladder.

"The ladder is stuck. We can't get down."

"We?" Rafe peered around me and nodded at Maggie. "If it's stuck we need to use leverage to get it loose. You push up here while I pull that way and it might loosen. If it doesn't work, I'll have to try to conjure us a ladder without getting shot," He instructed, his hands once more emitting that otherworldly ethereal glow.

This time a pry bar appeared in his hands and he made quick work of shoving it into place, while I pushed where instructed. I had to ignore the searing pain in my palms as the rough metal dug into the raw flesh.

After a few agonizing seconds, the rust binding the ladder in place finally cracked, allowing it to shift free. Rafe grabbed hold of my waist with one hand to steady me as I climbed out of the window. Another knife sailed through the air to keep the soldier pinned, and succeeded in causing the man to waste his fifth and final bullet. I scrambled down the ladder as fast as I could manage as Rafe assisted Maggie, but both my grip and my equilibrium were beginning to fail me as I neared the ground.

I dropped on shaking legs that buckled a moment later as I succumbed to a fit of coughing. The fresh air felt cool and sweet like honey. I inhaled deeply between my hacking, feeling a thirst I didn't think I could ever quench again. My relief was short lived as I heard the clicking of a gun being reloaded a few paces behind me. Five fresh bullets I didn't think I could evade.

I glanced over my shoulder, eyes locking with a young soldier. His face wasn't familiar to me, meaning he was either new or likely part of one of my young sister's regiments. My mind spun and my vision blurred in the sudden darkness as I tried to think of some explanation for my presence in this situation. It was clear by the man's expression that he recognized me immediately.

"Your Imperial—" The soldier's shocked words were cut short as he was struck down by a knife.

"Did you kill him?" I demanded, horrified. Rafe thudded beside me, and Maggie eased herself to the ground behind him.

"He saw your face. Do you want to get tried for treason and go on the run with the rest of us or keep living safely with your family?"

"Of course not, but—"

"You experienced for yourself that this is no time for idealization. Kill or be killed. That is the world we are forced to live in." The flickering of the flames reflected in the gold of Rafe's eyes, turning them to a blazing amber. I glanced upward at the window we'd just escaped from and watched as the fire consumed it and the building further buckled in on itself.

"Be kind, Rafe," Maggie chided. "This young woman got a little more of an experience than she bargained for tonight. We all did. It's been quite a shock."

"The soldiers are..." I trailed off, my eyes locking on the pool of blood spreading out from beneath the man's body. I thought of Hykner, and how my sister would feel if this had been his fate. "They are people too."

"I took out the men attacking you in the theater too, didn't I?" Rafe prompted with a shrug. "It's all good and fine to look for the good in everyone, but you can't keep everyone safe on all sides. Redemption is both a luxury and risk war can't afford. You protect your own to the best of your ability."

"I don't know who 'my own' are anymore!" I tried to raise my voice but it cracked and died in my throat. Innocent civilians were all my people, but so were the subordinate soldiers fighting against them. Duty and justice were not aligned in this situation.

"Protect who you care about the most— who needs the protection most," Maggie offered, placing a trembling hand on my back. "That's all you need to think about right now."

Rafe whipped around suddenly at the sound of advancing footsteps emerging through the jumping darkness. "Both of you stay behind me."

"Rafe, thank goodness! It's me," I sagged with relief at the sound of Roland's voice. I pushed past Rafe and threw my arms around Roland. His grip tightened around me, and I felt his chest shudder beneath a heavy sigh. He rested his face against the top of my head for a couple of heartbeats.

"You two better get out of here before anyone else spots you," Rafe's eyes flashed at me. "The less bloodshed the better."

"Rafe," Roland sighed, separating from our embrace, his brows knitting together. "Inside…"

"Vadia?" Rafe's jaw tightened.

"She couldn't get out." The words seemed almost painful for Roland to speak, and I wondered how deep everyone's connections ran. Were they like a family?

"Fuck," Rafe swore, closing his eyes tightly.

"She told me to give you her condolences. She's sorry for your loss." Roland patted Rafe on the shoulder and then gave it a rough squeeze. "I wanted to make sure you got her message."

Rafe smirked at the line, and gave Roland's hand a quick tap of acknowledgment. He hung his head and shook it slowly with a low groan. "That menace."

"We need to get moving. You'll have to circle back for any bodies, if you can. There was a band of men starting to break off and head this way." Roland scarcely finished speaking just as more gunfire erupted around us.

Roland and Rafe jumped forward to shield me and Maggie from the barrage. Roland, I realized, was brandishing a broken pipe in one hand and his revolver in the other, while Rafe had his hands splayed, the muscles tensing with effort. My breath caught in my throat as I saw the air begin to sparkle around us. Singular specs of glimmering white undulated and fused together in an orb around us, the texture reminding me of the pattern of light filtering through water.

"What is that?" I gasped, eyes wide.

The bullets suddenly stopped pelting the ground around us, and instead dull thunks sounded from in front of and above us. With each thump, the exterior of the orb rippled. I didn't need anyone to answer my question, as I realized that somehow Rafe had managed to forge a shield from thin air.

"And, looks like they caught up to us. Come on, Sorrel. That's our cue to leave," Roland huffed, lifting his shoulder to obscure his face from obvious view.

"But—" I started to protest.

"I'll give you a head start," Rafe interrupted, planting his feet firmly on the ground. As Roland turned to leave with a nod of thanks, Rafe nodded to me and added so quietly I almost missed it, "Keep her safe."

Roland nodded. "With everything in my power, always."

"You too, Mags. Get out of here." Rafe jerked his chin and fixed his blazing gaze forward as the soldiers grew frustrated and started charging forward with their bayonets brandished.

"Wait," I whirled around, desperate to not see another life cut short before my eyes. "Can't you go with us? We can all run!"

"We don't have time. Come on." Roland grabbed onto my arm and tugged me behind him. I noticed now that he was moving with a heavy limp, most likely an effect of jumping from the second story. "He's giving us our window to escape."

"I'm separating from you here," Maggie called to us, already splitting from us back into the alleys. "May the Divine and the Founders guide you to safety."

"We have to hurry," Roland urged, feeling my hesitance turning to resistance as I looked back over my shoulder towards Rafe. I could see the illumination from the gunshots growing closer with each passing moment, and if Roland and I wanted any chance of surviving the night unseen, we couldn't linger any longer.

"Don't you dare die!" I called to Rafe and picked up my pace behind Roland.

"Not on tonight's agenda," Rafe scoffed, a haughty laugher rasping in his tone. I could hear the soldiers shouting to one another but as the distance lengthened between us and them, I couldn't make out what they were saying.

With a devious grin, completely uninhibited by fear or uncertainty, Rafe threw out his arms and goaded the soldiers. "Go on then, come at me! Give it your best shot!"

He darted forward at full speed, dodging shots aimed at him. I turned away and held on to Roland as we barreled through the dark and smoky alleyways towards the palace.

I stumbled through the garden on shaking legs. My skin was coated in ash, and my lungs labored to puff breath. Roland wasn't in much better shape beside me, still limping from the aftermath of his jump. The moon was lowering, signaling an end to the night, and I pushed onward, knowing I had limited time to recover before life resumed its usual paces in the morning.

I caught sight of a figure marching back and forth at the entrance to the garden, and recognized it as Inessa. Her head whipped around at the sound of our feet dragging heavily and unevenly across the ground.

"For Eisa's sake!" She swore, rushing over to us. "Where were you two? You should have been back ages ago! I was worried sick and—"

She stopped short as she drew close enough to take in our battered appearance. I sagged under the weight of the night and threw my arms around my sister, leaning into her for comfort and familiarity. Her eyes grew wide and darkened, flicking to Roland in demand of an explanation.

"Chinye," Roland coughed. "He's burning down buildings and gunning down the survivors."

"What?" Inessa gasped, fluttering beside me as she wiped away sweat and soot from my brow and pulled my tangled hair back from my face. "Sorrel, your hands and arms are burned! Did you try to go inside?"

"We… we were inside," I huffed with a shake of my head, struggling to swallow against the dryness in my throat. "We got trapped in the fire and had to get out."

"Roland!" Inessa balked. "She was just supposed to go meet some people and hear their stories, nothing dangerous. You should have gotten her out the moment the situation turned. She could have died! On top of losing her, how would we have explained that?"

"The same would be said of you if you had gone," I waved my sister off. "Everything happened so fast and took us by surprise."

"We were lucky Sorrel was with us to catch the paperwork discrepancy or we wouldn't have had the small window we did manage to claim," Roland sighed. I could see his body slumping under exhaustion.

"In any case, we got out and made it home." I flinched at my own choice of words, knowing others hadn't been so lucky.

"Who didn't?" Ina asked, reading what I'd left unspoken.

"Vadia, Harev, Leive, and Drella didn't make it out of the fire. I'm not sure who fell to gunfire, and we lost track of a handful of children who ran away."

"And we don't know what happened to Rafe. He bought us our escape." I looked down at my feet and blinked back tears. Another rescue, another escape, another life left unaccounted for.

"Rafe is powerful, Sorrel. He's selective how he wields his magic, but he is one of our strongest. If anyone had the best chance in that situation, it was him," Roland reassured me, though I could see clouds of emotion billowing in the blue depths of his gaze, turbulent and unfocused.

How close of friends are you and Rafe? How close was Vadia? The reality that Roland knew these people personally, and for much longer than I, pulsed through my mind. I shuddered at the loss and worry Roland must be feeling.

"Come on, you two." Inessa ushered us forward gently, seeming to have subdued her fearful outburst. "You need to get cleaned up and Sorrel— we need to come up with an answer for where you got those burns overnight. Roland, you're limping. Figure that out along with your hands. Leave nothing to chance."

I nodded and followed my sister back into the palace, where Roland bid us farewell to depart to his own chambers. The halls were quiet and still, the ticking of clocks sounding sharply in the darkness. I was thankful for a change over in the posted guards, down the hall this time, so the pungent scent of smoke that clung to me was of little notice as we slipped through the door into our room. I immediately stripped free of my clothing, while Ina collected a basin of warm water to help wash away the grime of the fire.

I sat numbly as she ran the cloth over my back. "It was so terrible, Ina," I whispered, my voice hoarse. "I couldn't do anything useful to help anyone."

"I highly doubt that's true, Sorrel. It's not in your nature to stand idly by," Inessa soothed, pausing to ring out the rag and lift my hair off my shoulders. "I knew things were getting more and more dire for the Wielders in hiding, but I can't believe that such horrific measures were taken. It's hard for anyone to stand up against that kind of brutality, let alone one woman."

"We were hiding, just waiting for them to leave to get out when they set the place on fire." I looked down at my palms, gravity pulling me down towards the burns. "They were screaming so loudly behind me, Inessa, when the fire took them. I'd never felt such terrible heat."

"I can't imagine how terrifying that must have been. I've never experienced something so terrible and dangerous in all the times I've attended." Inessa's voice shook, and despite her words, I knew that she knew the fallen by face and name, and was suffering her own loss, same as Roland.

"Vadia saved me. She took an incendiary into her shadow to keep it from hitting me, despite knowing she was too weak to suppress the explosion."

"That sounds like Vadia. She is always— was," Inessa corrected herself, the word wavering on her lips. "She was always putting herself in danger to help others. Sounds like someone else I know, in fact. What do we need to do for these burns on your arm?"

I lifted my arm and squinted at the marks. "I tried to reach her, but I couldn't. The floor gave way, and she created this shadow around her as she fell. I'd never seen something so beautiful... or terrible. To die in a fire like that. The heat and—"

"You did everything you could," Inessa squeezed my shoulder, and I turned to face her.

"I couldn't help but wonder— had I not been so frightened and prideful, had I somehow had access to the Ice affinity— maybe I could have saved them from the fire. If I could have used any of those abilities, maybe I could have fought back somehow or protected more people."

Inessa was quiet for a few heartbeats, staring deeply into my eyes. "It does no good to dwell on the possibilities of the past. You'd serve yourself better to focus on the possibilities of the future."

"I know." I averted my eyes.

"You can start learning now," Inessa pressed. "There was no outcome in which you could have learned to Wield with enough power to stop what happened in the brief time since you even learned of your affinities in the first place. So, don't you dare blame yourself for any of this. The blame falls on the wickedness and inhumanity in our own officials. In Otvel. But, if you want to have the power someday to make sure you never endure a night like tonight again, then you can start now."

Remnants of the horrors I'd witnessed flashed before my eyes in rapid succession, forcing me to once more meet my sister's gaze. I could feel something building within me, until I was certain I might burst apart at the seams. I lifted my chin and nodded.

"I burned my hands trying to retrieve a journal from the fire. We will cover them to conceal the heavier damage and no one else will know the difference."

"Alright," Inessa nodded along.

"And tomorrow," I added, curling my swollen fingers slowly to solidify my convictions. "I will start to learn how to Wield all of my abilities until I'm strong enough that I'll never fail to protect an innocent life again."

"Deep below in the bowels of existence there was
only ever her. Even when she left me behind to
wander the vast bounds of nothingness."
-D

THIRTY-TWO

The warmth of the water made my burns pucker with annoyance as I slipped into a freshly drawn bath, submerging up to my nose.

My head was still pounding from the lack of oxygen the previous night, and I tried in vain to blink away the sharp sting lingering in my eyes. My throat was raw, lungs burning, skin dry, and I was still finding soot in odd places of my body.

But the worst of the aftermath of the fire wasn't afflicting my flesh and bones. Rather, my senses were all consumed by reliving the terrifying ordeal over and over again.

I grabbed a cloth and ran it gingerly over my arms, the painful sensation of rough fibers dragging over burns making me wince. The rising steam twisting through the air conjured illusions of billowing smoke, and suddenly I couldn't seem to draw enough air into my lungs. The room turned sweltering and a nagging voice in the back of my mind screamed at me that I'd never cool down again. I surged forward out of the water, turning the cold faucet on as high as it would go. As the fresh water poured into the tub, bringing the temperature from hot to tepid, the steam dissipated— but the phantom smoke lingered like a shroud enveloping me.

I shifted to lean my forehead against my knees, speckled with bruises. I shivered under a shuddering breath, trying to steady myself and calm my pounding heart. Blood roared in my ears as I counted backwards from ten.

"Ten, nine, eight…" The numbers ticked off my tongue in a mechanical cadence that felt devoid of the peril I'd faced. I scrunched my face, closing my eyes as tight as I could as I thought of those who didn't make it out alive. Those that couldn't nurse their wounds in the comfort of warm bath. Those who in all likelihood deserved to keep their life's much more than I.

I swallowed, my throat screaming in irritation like I'd just eaten thistles and gorse. The guilt building in my stomach was both frigid and burning. Shriveled and expansive. Sharp and jagged. I was certain it had formed a serrated edge within my gut and was slowly sawing me in two.

What I had witnessed, and what I'd experienced, was it something I'd ever be strong enough to completely bury? This far surpassed even the horrors of the stampede by which I'd been haunted despite being safe, locked away. I'd seen Harvier in his frozen state, along with countless patients in varying states of injury, yet I had still been removed from the danger of it all. Even the attack at the theater, where I'd seen two men fall to Rafe's knives, paled against the fire. Every body that had fallen to the inferno had been moments away from their own salvations— safety I had reached while they blistered away to ashes behind me.

No. I didn't think it was something to be buried. Everything I'd seen and endured in Tuyet was a reminder of the need for change. I couldn't let myself shrink away from the call to action the memories evoked, no matter how painful they were. I looked at my hands and arms, focusing in on the marred skin and blistering wounds. I knew these would be the scars of Vadia's death I would physically carry with me. But before they turned to scars, I had to let them heal. Was healing even an option I could fathom anymore? Did healing mean I'd forget?

I sighed heavily and let the water turn completely cold before I emerged and bandaged my burns. I watched my reflection in the draining bathwater, seeing as I stepped back into my dress, how the fabric obscured the telling marks on my shoulders and legs. A secret that was mine, and mine alone to keep.

"How did you manage to burn your hands so severely?" Mama gasped, grabbing me at the elbow to inspect my bandaged arms. I was sitting in her private drawing room, having been requested for a cup of early morning tea together. Ever since the list had been posted, Mama had been trying to spend more quality time with me— further solidifying her guilt in using me to betray a friend.

"One of my journals fell into the fireplace," I lied, and held up a charred book. Inessa burned it for me to help corroborate my story, lest there be any room for doubt over the convenient timing. "I tried to get it out. I brought it with me to see if Dowels thought there was any saving it."

I ground my teeth beneath a soft smile, still uncertain of where my mother's humanity rested. How much did she know? What had she ordered? Was ignorance and giving Otvel free reign complicit in the murder of innocents? It was hard to ask myself those questions of my own mother who'd done nothing but love me, but somehow, it was easy to lie about the involvement of my burns.

"Honestly, you girls seem to have no fear of fire!" Mama sighed heavily, and I fought the urge to shrink from the irony of her words. "Are you going to be able to perform your duties today? Or do we need to send one of your sisters in your place?"

"Actually, I think I would like to take a day to myself, if that's alright. I'm still feeling rather unwell." I wriggled my bandaged fingers. "I'll be fine in a day or two."

"Alright then, I will send Kira and Yulia down to the hospital today to entertain those recovering, and I'll presume you'll be going down there as soon as you're well?"

"That's right."

"Good, I think some of the men there could use a little cheering up from you. You all do so well with all the patients." Mama smiled and returned to her cup of cinnamon tea.

"Oh? Any particular reason for extra gloom today?"

"You haven't heard," Mama turned, grimacing. "There was some sort of attack last night out in one of the outer districts that's mostly uninhabited. Or, so we thought."

"You said there was an attack?" I startled, my own tea cup trembling in my hands. I was taken aback by my mother's candid acknowledgment, and the concerns of how much she knew raged in my chest so intense a cold sweat collected like dew on my back. I exhaled slowly as I waited to see what she would say next.

"That's right! The men stationed nearby were attacked and it turned into an all out brawl against a group of Wielders in the area. The fight ended up with one of the brutes setting fire to a whole section of buildings. Thankfully they were abandoned, and though our side suffered some injury and a handful of casualties, it's nothing compared to the chunk our men took of theirs. They fought very bravely."

"Is that so?" I replied weakly, my breakfast churning in my stomach as I recalled the stench and sights I'd witnessed. I plunked my cup on the table and covered my mouth, swallowing down a lump of bile rising in my throat.

Denial.

She was denying every stolen life on both sides with the lies she was feeding both herself and me.

"Sorrel, Darling! Are you alright? You look as though you might be ill. Did that honey soothe your throat?"

"I'm... I'm fine," I wheezed, my lungs not yet recovered from the shortness of breath the memories elicited.

"Don't worry, Dear. Like I said, most of the fatalities were on their side. We are safe another day thanks to the efforts of last night." Mama reached to squeeze my hand but faltered as she remembered my burns and instead rubbed my shoulder. The gesture would normally have comforted me, but I was finding it difficult to not wince away from the blind ignorance in what she was saying— blindness I had shared my whole life.

"Right. I think I'm going to go lay down."

"I think that sounds like a good idea. Rest today and see how tomorrow feels. When you do go to the hospital, visit the men who were on patrol at the fire. Who knows how ghastly things might have turned out without their dutiful sacrifice."

Sacrifice. The word clashed against her obliviousness, like nails scoring slate. It made me think of the loss of Vadia, the uncertain fate of Rafe— and everyone else save for Roland. I wondered if they recovered any of the bodies, and what I could do to help the gaping wound left in the scattered little group I'd met.

When words failed me, I merely nodded and all but fled the room. Mama's call for me to stay vigilant echoed behind me, and it wasn't until I was back in the confines of my own room that I felt I could breathe again. I pressed my back into the door, and closed my eyes to center myself.

It had completely escaped me that the hospital would be filled with one half of the injured parties. I could feel my pulse making the veins in my wrist jump, and I forced my eyes open as incoherent echoes of the previous losses once more played behind my lids. A waking nightmare lingering every time I stilled or blinked.

What if any of the men recognized me from when I'd been running away with Roland? I'd been in different clothing, and they'd have no good reason to suspect my involvement, even if they had caught a glimpse of me. Would they? Not unless they got a good look at us cowering behind Rafe's shield.

Tomorrow. I told myself. *It can all wait till tomorrow.*

Fatigue clawed at my eyelids and no longer able to fight it, I gave in. I changed into a concealing nightgown and climbed clumsily back into bed. The weight of the blankets felt stifling, but

I couldn't even muster the strength to throw them off of me as I drifted off.

Nothing compared to heat of the burning inn anyway.

THIRTY-THREE

A knock rapped softly on the door. Outside my room, I was surprised to see Theo standing there, hands clasped behind his back, eyes bright.

"Good morning, Sorrel! I—" he chirped then paused as he caught sight of my injuries. "Are you alright?"

"I dropped something in the fire last night and forgot I was flammable for a moment," I prattled nonchalantly, realizing he hadn't seen me the previous day since I'd stayed entirely confined to my room after my visit with Mama. I had only vaguely recalled to consciousness to eat supper and say goodnight to Inessa when she checked on me before bed.

"That sounds more like something Kira would do," Theo commented thoughtfully, then shrugged it off. "I actually was hoping to catch you before you departed for the hospital. You are still going today, aren't you?" He gestured to my hands.

"Yes, yes. I'm still going." I stood a little straighter, dressed and ready to force myself into the normalcy of a new day. "A few measly burns won't slow me down too much. Is there something you need from me before I go?"

"I would like to go with you."

"Oh!" I couldn't hide my surprise. Not only had Theo never before shown a particular interest in our direct wellness efforts, but it was rare he was permitted out into the public. "Have you spoken with—"

"Yes, Mama already knows. It's all arranged for me to go, but I thought it would be the most beneficial experience to go with *you* specifically. Given your involvement and all."

"Of course, Theo." I smiled at my brother, slowly easing the tension knotting my shoulders. "I'd love your company. It's not often these days that we see much of each other is it?"

"You're glued to your work, Sorrel," Theo chuckled. "Best call it what it is. Always up to something. This time I figured it would be fun to get up to something together. I take it you are dealing with the fire victims?"

"Pardon?" His words sent a jolt through me that left my nerves retroactively buzzing.

"The fire in far districts? I assume you heard about the incident two nights ago involving Wielders and soldiers engaging in an altercation that resulted in a large fire. It burned down a whole city block."

"Oh, right. Sorry, I am a few steps behind today. I didn't get very much sleep, I'm afraid."

"Not surprising. I caught some whiffs of smoke myself late the other night. It was the strangest thing, given how far away the fire was from here."

"Did you now? That is odd." I swallowed, wondering if Theo had caught the scent off me and Roland when we'd entered the palace covered in soot.

"I thought, with Papa away at the front, and high casualty skirmishes happening here in the capital now, it would do well for the heir to make some informal appearances."

"That's a very mature response," I beamed proudly at my

brother.

"I don't like to hear about all the dealings of our citizens second hand. Between you and me, I think I've been too far removed for too long. It's important for me to get the full scope of things if I'm ever to be a suitable emperor myself one day, don't you think?" Theo sighed and didn't wait for me to respond before he continued. "I know they all mean well keeping me pent up here, but something keeps telling me I will learn more by *seeing* first hand what's happening to our country. I'm not going to get any less fragile physically, so I should go as I mean to carry on— now, when our people need it most."

I slipped through my door and embraced Theo, squeezing tight. His words, though ignorant to my own recent brush with that reality, felt warm and reassuring. Perhaps his current open mindedness would someday foster a more understanding rhetoric for Eisa. I didn't fully doubt Papa's own convictions of doing what he believed was best, but there was some piece to the puzzle that felt like it was missing. Something that might explain why someone as compassionate and duty bound to serve as my father would turn a blind eye to the innocent suffering of those with the same magic in their veins as us.

Was it truly all a masquerade to protect us from an unruly mob that would condemn us for centuries of unwarranted prejudice and hypocrisy? Or was there more to the story that no one besides Theo would ever be privy to? I wondered once Theo knew the truth of our lineage, how he would ultimately choose to carry on, and if he was fated to wait until our father's passing or, if like Inessa and myself, he'd discover the truth earlier. If all of us children could embrace this new ideology, maybe there was hope yet for a truly peaceful transition to equality and justice.

"Sorrel?" Theo piped up from where I was still holding tightly to him. "Are you sure you're alright? You seem a little rattled."

I detached myself with an awkward laugh and waved him off. "I'm fine, really. I'll change into my frock at the hospital, so we can leave now if you're ready?"

"Lead the way, sister dearest."

Theo and I made our way through the palace to the cars and chatted the entire way to the hospital. I had been so busy the past few months, and the new revelation of our ancestry had taken all of my attention; I hadn't noticed just how much my little brother was blossoming into a more mature and kind hearted young man. He spoke with both laughter and pragmatism, and our conversation kept toggling between the humorous and the profound. With our eight-year age gap, I had failed to consider how much the war had affected him. I was impressed and comforted to be interacting with this new sensible, philosophical side of him, but also couldn't help but feel relieved that he still held a touch of his childlike exuberance and playfulness. No matter how old and wise he might grow to be, it seemed he was in no danger of losing the spark that made him undeniably himself.

We entered the hospital with more guards than usual on account of Theo's presence, and I instructed the small group to wait in the lobby while I quickly went to change into my uniform and notify the staff of our spontaneous guest.

"Alright," I puffed as I hurried back to Theo and briskly smoothed down my dress. "Where would you like to start?"

"Wherever you start, we can go from there!"

Theo followed me on my morning rounds, stopping to interact with each patient and have short but meaningful conversations with them. We had spoken to two soldiers who were admitted from the fire incident and so far nothing out of the ordinary had come up.

It was nearing lunch hour, and I was handing out medications in the final room before Theo and I would take our leave. I wasn't slated to assist in any procedures in the afternoon, so it looked as though I would have an early day. The notion brightened my spirit as my head had been torn all morning between apprehension and fantasies of collapsing into my bed the moment the day was over.

"This is the final stop for me today," I told Theo. "After I finish, I'll just need to put the extra supplies away and we can be off."

"Very good." Theo nodded as he followed me into the patients' room, shared by a group of four.

I could see immediately from their charts that these men all were here for *Wielder-inflicted injuries,* and all had been admitted the previous night. I swallowed, knowing I just had to get through the next half hour.

"Morning, gentlemen!" I announced my entrance cheerfully. "I have your lunch dosages for you. Does anyone need their dressings looked at or adjusted?"

"This bandage on my arm isn't sitting right. I think it's too tight, if you wouldn't mind taking a look," a young man with dark auburn hair raised his hand. His eyes locked on Theo trailing in behind me, and his gesture quickly switched to an awkward salute. "Your Imperial Highness! It's an honor."

The other three men sat straighter and echoed the first's words and motions, until Theo bashfully acknowledged their salute and waved them off.

"Of course I'll take a look at that bandage. I just need to get these handed out and I'll be right with you." I smiled warmly and inspected the tray of medication.

"I can help with that, Sorrel," Theo offered, appearing at my side. "You're looking a bit worn out."

"Thank you," I replied and pointed out which doses went to which man, splitting the chore between the two of us at two soldiers each.

"Divine above, I never thought there would be a day when I was receiving medical aid from a Grand Princess and the Heir to Eisa," The man closest to the door breathed. "Is this even allowed?"

"Don't be silly," I glanced at the chart to see the names listed. "It is our honor and privilege to help serve our citizens and soldiers, Private Gaerner."

Gaerner looked shocked to be addressed directly by his name, and turned a pearly shade of white. Only his cheeks remained pigmented, flushing a deep rouge. I handed him his pills and quickly instructed which ones were to be taken with his lunch when it arrived.

"You men were on duty last night at the fire in the far district, is that correct?" Theo asked, handing his own patient— a Warrant Officer Vaun— his dose of medication.

All four men nodded, and my stomach did an involuntary flip. I bit my lip wishing Theo hadn't brought up the event when I was so close to leaving for the day.

"Thank you for your service to Eisa. I'm sure each of you fought honorably," Theo praised, his eyes darting to me then back at his audience. "Were there many casualties on the offending side?"

"We took a fair bit down with us before we ended up here!" The third man, Private Fyke, assured earnestly, his singed fingers curling around his bed sheets.

"I'm glad to see none of your injuries seem too serious," Theo acknowledged slowly. "Did any of you four come into direct combat with the other side?"

"I did," the final officer, and the one whose bandage I was stooping to inspect, dipped his head. *Corporal Zdrute.* I didn't recognize his face, but his name sounded familiar to me, though I couldn't place it. "I took a knife to the arm from some deranged Dezidaneyan Wielder. Pretty sure it was the same one that was on the Wanted List."

Rafe.

I stumbled in surprise, having to catch myself on the edge of Zdrute's cot. I mumbled my apology and set to work adjusting his bandage to fit more comfortably.

"I understand the fire was fairly large. Did many perish inside? The Wielder who struck you with the knife perhaps?" Theo continued his questioning, and I could feel sweat collecting on the back of my neck. I wondered what had prompted his sudden mild interrogation of last night's events, but more than anything wished he would leave the subject alone. I knew Rafe hadn't been inside the inferno, but I still held my breath in anticipation of hearing any clarification as to if he'd met his end outside.

"No, that bastard—pardon the language—" Zdrute apologized to me. "He got away shortly after he helped another group escape. It was a strange thing because one of the girls looked remarkably similar to you, Grand Princess Sorrel when I glimpsed her face. I almost had to wonder if she was a Kesgol trying to pull one over on us."

"Oh?" Theo's voice pitched with interest behind me. "Why is that?"

"They're shifters, you see, Imperial Highness. They can take on all forms dishonestly. Their own monarchy has to wear special masks just to keep from being impersonated!"

"I do recall that tradition, yes."

"The resemblance to Grand Princess Sorrel was remarkable, though it was smoky and the Dezidaneyan mutated the air so it could have been his fault. He and that girl struck down a soldier together. Can you imagine anything more ridiculous than impersonating a member of the royal family at such a—" Zdrute stopped short, and I realized his eyes had locked on my bandaged hands.

"She dropped something in the fireplace this morning," Theo explained, catching the exchange and coming to stand beside me as I finished tying off the bandage. "Burned her hands and yet she still insists on taking care of others."

"I see. How unfortunate." Zdrute's words were scratchy and hollow. I could see something glinting behind his dark hazel eyes that made my skin prickle.

"There was that Shadow Wielder girl we got in the leg," Vaun threw in, tossing back his pills in a single gulp. "Suppose it could have been her."

Vadia.

"No, I'm fairly positive it was her remains found on the lower level of the second building. Given the size and the fact we saw her go back in the building" Fyke looked at his bunted knuckle. "I was one of the first in to check for survivors and casualties. That's where that smoldering beam got me. There were only a handful of fatalities from the actual fire, the shadow girl included. Seemed like most everyone escaped the blaze."

"I think we've finished here, gentlemen," I rose to my feet and kept my voice level and calm. "Rayana should be here anytime with your lunches. Is there anything else we can do for you before we leave?"

When the men shook their heads, I bid my farewells, trying my best to ignore Zdrute's eyes trained on me as I exited the room. I walked a few paces then leaned a hand against the wall for support as I took in a few ragged breaths that ended in a small fit of coughs. My lungs still stung, and my head was swimming. I was relieved to hear that it sounded like Rafe had most likely made it out of the area alive, but a fresh wave of agonized grief roared to life at the indirect mention of Vadia. However, what had really stopped my heart cold was the fact that Zdrute had definitely seen me and Roland.

"Sorrel?" Theo gripped my arm to help steady me.

"It's fine," I tried to keep my voice steady, but I could hear the slight wobble. "I'm going to take care of the supplies, and I'll be right out."

"Alright, I suppose I'll wander to meet some other patients before we head out."

I nodded and whisked myself away before Theo could see my mask breaking even further. I knew if I was going to be of any further use to those who fled for their lives, I'd have to snuff out this newest storm leaking through the cracks.

I covered my mouth and screwed my eyes tightly closed. *Be strong. You must do your duty to your people, and that means you must walk tall.* I reminded myself firmly, before stepping into the storage wing to put away the excess medications and linens. I paused as my own injured hands lingered over a roll of bandages, antiseptics, surgical tools… all things being used to treat the soldiers who had started the fire, while the real victims suffered without.

Lost in my own thoughts, I jumped at the low creak of a hinge. The door closed with a *click* behind me, and I whirled around to see an elderly woman dressed in a black frock not unlike my own.

"Maggie! I'm so glad you made it out safely. Have you found anyone else?" I rushed to greet her with an odd sense of familiarity I wouldn't have fostered before our harrowing escape. "What are you doing *here?*"

"Rafe told me to wait around until you showed up. He told me there was a door over there," Maggie pointed in the direction of the exit Rafe had used that one rainy day. "It would be my best chance of running into you without anyone noticing."

"Is he nearby?" I asked. I wanted to thank him for his heroism in helping the rest of us escape. Twice now he'd shown up just in time to save my life.

Maggie shook her head. "No. He left the capital altogether. It's become too dangerous for him to stay, so he will do his part to help from some other location so long as he is well and able."

"You mean so long as he survives," I surmised the true meaning of her words, trying not to droop under the all too real possibility Rafe could meet his end any day.

Maggie smiled sympathetically and patted my arm. "He was raised a warrior, you know. He won't go down easily, and you should pity the poor soul who attempts it. It was likely only out of respect to you that he didn't kill the men after we left."

I remained speechless for several heartbeats, weighing her words with less idealistic naiveté after my run in with Zdrute. My eyes wandered to the supplies, and I straightened myself. "Here, take some of these. I can't give you much, but a couple of things that will get you by shouldn't be missed under a margin of inventory error." I started pulling things off shelves and out of drawers, placing them in a pillowcase.

"Thank you," she whispered. "The kingdom would truly have prospered under a reign like yours."

"A reign like mine?" I paused and looked over my shoulder to give the woman a dubious glance.

"Someone with a head like yours on your shoulders. So much of this devastation could have been avoided had someone of power simply been brave enough to— never mind. I also wanted to thank *you* for helping me last night. I wouldn't haven't made it without your good heart and stubbornness."

I smiled and continued stuffing the pillow case. "No thanks needed for doing the right thing. I just wish…" I faltered, my voice catching in my throat.

"She made her choices," Maggie spoke gently, guessing my train of thought. "The same as you, the same as Roland, and Rafe. Everyone knew the risks they were taking with each action they took."

I bit down on my tongue, knowing the woman's words held an undeniable truth, and turned around to face Maggie with the stuffed pillowcase tight in hand. "I hope this helps at least a little, and I'll have to think of a better system to get you more."

Maggie accepted the case from me with a gracious dip of her head. "I've only come across a couple of the others. It will take a little while before we've all found each other and a new safe haven, so this should do us just fine, and you have our gratitude. Let Roland know I will let him know the usual way when we have a new location."

I agreed and opened the door to look quickly up and down the hallway for any unwanted bystanders. With a clear shot to the exit, I hurried Maggie out the door to the alley, stooping to pick up a dropped bandage roll as she raced through the exit. I stopped her to hand it back but stiffened at the sound of my name being called. I turned around with Maggie to see Theo observing us from the end of the hall. He must have just turned the corner when our backs were turned.

"I…" my head was spinning too fast to think of a decent explanation. "Supplies were in a shortage at another hospital."

Theo tipped his head to the side, as I was overtaken by another small coughing fit. His eyes narrowed suspiciously as he paced down the hall, stopping in front of me. I fully expected a barrage of questions, demands, or accusations as to my involvement with the strange woman. Though I was considerably older, as Heir, Theo did by all accounts outrank me.

I winced, awaiting the confrontation, but it never came. Instead, Theo leaned in close to me, taking my hand gently into his own. He looked at me meaningfully and smiled.

"Don't worry. I know whatever you're doing is always to help someone else. If you chose to help, I have no reason to believe it wasn't the right choice to make. Come on, the car is waiting." He dipped his head politely to Maggie. "I saw nothing."

"We won't forget," Maggie murmured.

Theo released my hand, glancing down at it meaningfully before turning and beckoning me to follow. I stared dumbfounded for a moment before following him on shaking legs while Maggie whisked herself down the alley.

He *knew*.

His questions to the soldiers, gauging everyone's reactions— including my own. The comment about the smell of smoke at the palace and the uncharacteristic explanation for my burns. And now, watching me give medicinal supplies away in secret, Theo was letting me know he knew I had somehow been at the fire, and that whatever my involvement had been, he trusted that I was acting in the right.

He had to know to some degree who Maggie was given the situation, and by his chosen statement, he knew he was letting a Wielder, or at the very least a Sympathizer, walk free because she'd done no harm, and yet clearly had received some. When did my little brother become so wise and compassionate? What had led his views to shift so rapidly in such a short time? Last I recalled, he'd been praying for Wielders to be eradicated, and now he was pardoning them simply because of my newfound faith?

Did Papa tell Theo the secret already?

I felt so moved by his response I was ready to collapse to the ground and succumb to giddy tears filled with hope for a future under his reign. Even if Papa, for whatever reason, had fallen short of understanding the plights of Wielders, and went as far as to continue to condemn them, there was still hope that things would change when Theo came to power. Maybe even sooner.

THIRTY-FOUR

I was shaken roughly by the shoulder, shuddering me out of my flame-filled nightmare. Blinking open my eyes, and sucking in a labored breath, still feeling like I was choking on the acrid tang of smoke, I stared up into my mother's concerned silver gaze.

"Sorrel, come with me."

I opened my mouth to reply, but closed it again, opting to follow the instructions instead of questioning them. Flicking back my blankets, I threw my legs over the side of the bed and hurried after my mother. After a few moments, as my tangled adrenaline and grogginess lifted, I realized we were heading for Theo's bedroom.

"What's happened?" I whispered. It had been two days since I'd seen Maggie at the hospital, and so far the soldier, Zdrute, had raised no issues for me, despite the various suspicious looks he raked me over with every time I'd seen him since. For two quiet days, everything had actually felt relatively normal for the first time in ages, save for the nightmares and bouts of suffocating anxiety I was enduring after the fire. It seemed now, hastening after Mama towards my brother, that the small window of reprieve was about to slam closed.

"He's ill," Mama replied briskly. "Klivech is already with him, but he kept asking for you. Of course Otvel is back in Zdenayk. I never should have sent him away in the first palace, over a bit of ill spirited salacious gossip."

"You haven't called him back yet?" I asked, unable to hide the surprise elicited by her remark. Three days prior, I had heard Otvel give the order to burn the old inn to the ground, with my own ears.

"No," Mama huffed. "When do you think I would have had time to do that, Sorrel?"

"Sorry," I mumbled, lacking a suitable explanation for my inquiry. "Is it the bleeding?"

"No, he seems to have contracted something from his excursion to the hospital with you. No wonder, you have been coughing for days— don't think I haven't noticed— and it sounds like Roland caught the strain as well. I should have never agreed to let Theodorvin go…"

My attention drifted away from my mother's grousing. If Theo had contracted something from the hospital, it certainly wasn't the same thing as what was ailing me and Roland. It was likely, however, that Theo didn't have high immunities since he was mostly restricted to the palace.

"Don't worry, Mama," I soothed as she grabbed the handle to his room. "We will get him back on his feet. We always do."

Mama looked at me with heavy eyes, the weariness clear as day on her face, and gave me a small smile. "That's right. We always do."

"Sorrel, is that you?" I heard Theo call as we cracked the door.

"At your service, little brother!" I replied cheerfully and plopped myself on the edge of his bed. Pressing my hand to his forehead, it was clear to see he was entering into a fevered state. "You wanted to see me?"

"I just wanted your company," Theo rasped, working up a dazed smile. "There is something that has been on my mind since the other day."

A flash of concern pulsed through me, and I was afraid Theo might mention Maggie in front of Mama. But Theo's words tumbled clumsily from his lips, and his eyes fluttered closed. His chest rose and fell in deep rhythmic puffs, indicating he'd drifted off before completing his questions for me.

I loosed a sigh and gave a small wave to Klivech. He nodded to acknowledge me and, in the dim light of the room, I could see his brows knitting together as he jotted a few notes down. I knew it likely pertained to the potential threat to Theo's condition the fever would pose if it wasn't brought down quickly. The caveat was always to determine the best way to assist him, since many medications contained ingredients that only escalate the bleeding.

I glanced from Theo to Klivech and thought of Maggie. She had said she was a healer, and I knew that many medicinal elixirs and tinctures were imported from Videiria. Though they relied on ingredients from magical plants, the prohibition laws allowed that medicinal magic was legal so long as it never exceeded 2.75% in magical components. Though Videiria was our ally and everything about the elixirs in our possession were perfectly legal, I learned a long time ago that Klivech avoided using them out of respect to the royal family and our strict anti-magic rhetoric.

"Dr. Klivech?" I slipped off Theo's bed and approached Klivech directly, while Mama settled in on the other side.

"Yes?" Klivech looked up from his notes and adjusted his glasses.

"I was wondering if you could tell me what is happening to Theodorvin," I started, and listened patiently while Klivech rattled off the symptoms and concerns.

"The fever spiked in the last fifteen minutes, and we are struggling to keep it down."

"His eyes are looking dark underneath," I commented pointing to my own face.

"He has been developing a cough. It's mild right now, but I want to be sure to keep on top of it as the fits can cause vessels to burst. The blood pooling around his eyes, though from fatigue, is also something to make sure doesn't get out of hand." Klivech nodded and quickly wrote down a note to keep track of Theo's eyes. "Thank you."

"I was also wondering," I dropped my voice and leaned in closer. "If we had any elixirs on hand that might help reduce his fever?"

"Elixirs?" Though he was clearly shocked by my suggestion, I was thankful he picked up on the sensitivity of the topic and kept his voice low. "I don't practice with those here as a matter of principle. I have never once used elixirs on Theodorvin."

"I don't see how needless pride and protocol has any place in ensuring the patient's welfare." I folded my arms and shuffled in closer. "I know I'm just a temporary nurse, Doctor Klivech, but I took the oath too, and rest assured, I didn't take it lightly. I can't in good conscience allow my family's pride to prevent us from using perfectly legal medicine in the privacy of our own home if it might help my brother."

Klivech shot a glance past me at my mother. She was leaning over the bed, rubbing Theo's hand rhythmically and humming a soft tune. Klivech sighed and shrugged.

"I do have some knowledge on the matter. We were taught it in our schooling, and as you said, it is a perfectly viable and legal medicine. But, I must say, I don't wish to upset her Imperial Highness."

"Is there something that can quickly bring his fever down?" I fixed Klivech with a sharp stare, leaving no room for wiggling. He met it head on and nodded.

"There is."

"Use it," I asserted. "Theo's safety is Mama's ultimate priority."

"But if she hears the word elixir, she will reject it."

"Don't call it that. My mother knows about as much medicine as I do the innermost thoughts of a sea snail. You get it, and I'll tell her what it is— a medicine we now have access to that will speed up Theo's recovery. Have I claimed anything false?"

I could see Klivech weighing my words carefully. There was also a hint of awestruck befuddlement to this streak of assertiveness I was displaying. If I was honest, it was a bit foreign to me to hear the commanding confidence in my own voice. But, I was realizing that after everything that had happened recently, I couldn't be idle in my docility anymore.

I'd made myself a promise that I would protect those around me, and I meant to keep it. It wouldn't be as simple as deciding to learn how to harness my affinities' powers, I realized. It was going to require a unilateral resolve to do everything within all of my capabilities. I'd been raised as a mortal my whole life, and my inclination to medicine and caretaking was a gift I'd been blessed with to help others. It was time I stopped dancing around my inclinations, and took firm hold of them.

"You've spoken no falsehoods, though I would like to point out the omissions in your intentional vagueness," Klivech took off his glasses and tucked them into his breast pocket. "But, if I might express a moment of candor, I would be remiss to allow the young Prince to endure anymore needless pain and danger based simply on a technicality."

I smiled. "Thank you, Klivech."

He mumbled something to Mama and quickly left the room, leaving me alone with my mother and brother. I retook my place at Theo's side and mirrored Mama by grabbing his other hand.

"Do you know what he wanted to talk with you about?" She asked quietly. She looked small and tired, the stiffness she carried in her posture giving away the added physical discomfort she was in.

"I don't." I curled my fingers into the fabric of my nightgown. "You know, Mama, you can go back to bed if you want to. I'll stay with him until you come back."

"No," Mama insisted, rubbing her free hand over her face. "I need to stay with him. Once he is on the mend, I can rest."

"I think the medicine Klivech will bring back will help immensely," I offered my words of solace, but when the silence that followed was filled with the ambient ticking of the clock, I grew concerned. "Mama, are you doing alright?"

"I'm fine, Darling." Mama's reply wasn't the least bit convincing.

"It's alright you know, if you're not," I spoke quietly.

"Not what?"

"If you aren't fine, Mama. No one is completely impervious."

"I'm just tired," Mama started to pacify, but then her gaze clouded and she continued, to my surprise. "With your father away, I'm left feeling like I'm losing my grip. He never felt ready to reign, and I certainly never imagined it would fall to me in the slightest. I'm trying to do right by our people, our government, friends, and our family. I seek the wisdom of the Divine everyday, asking and hoping to make it through just one more day, all the while it seems like the edges of the pillar I'm clinging to are crumbling away bit by bit. I'm left with years of rejections from those courts and citizens I am trying to play my part for, to gain their favor. And ultimately I end up here, beside my child's bed, praying he will open his eyes again after each time he closes them. And it's moments like these I know I was never meant to be a leader or diplomat— I was meant to be a mother. It's the only place I've ever felt I truly fit and have done right. You girls, Theo, and your father, you are home."

Mama's voice grew thick with a vulnerability I couldn't recall ever seeing her wear before. I knew she had found her role as empress tedious amongst the courtly obligations and parties, but I hadn't realized just how much of a toll the royal responsibilities had been for her, especially as she was always the first to preach of duty and our Divine rights. It wasn't so much she wanted less of it, rather, she didn't want it at all, and it was the closest I'd ever heard her come to questioning the Divinities in their selection of our family to bless with our station. Tears had begun leaking down her cheeks, and I quickly relocated myself to her side, hugging her close and resting my head against hers. The distance I put between us since Rafe began to shrink, and I was reminded that my parents were humans too, capable of error and sorrow the same as anyone else.

"Then be at home, Mama. With me and Theo, forget everything else for a moment, and come home to us," I whispered, and I felt Mama's body quiver for a heartbeat before sagging with equal parts fatigue and reprieve. We stayed connected like that for several moments before Klivech returned.

"I'm sorry, but it seems we don't have the medicine I was hoping to use on hand," he apologized. "But I will get some more by tomorrow. We just have to walk the young Prince through the next twenty-four hours."

I laid my hand on top of Mama's which was still clasped around Theo's. "Then that's what we will do."

"I'm certain Otvel was sent away by Mama," I mused aloud to Roland. "Last night she even confirmed it. So how was he both sent away and at the inn?"

We were taking a walk through the garden, the summer sun beating down on the crowns of our heads. It was the first spare moment Roland and I had found together since the fire, and we were trying to make the most of it.

"I heard word that she sent for him to come back because she was worried that she would bring misfortune upon Theo by taking her anger and embarrassment out on Otvel as a high priest."

"Surely she doesn't truly believe that, does she?" I shook my head, though I already knew the answer. My mother was about as superstitious and devout as they came.

"She definitely does."

"Was Otvel still working on the anti-Wielder force even when he was sent back to Zdenayk?"

"To be honest, I'm not even certain that he left the capital at all. I know my father is running the other half of that force, and I can't see him being too keen on using such violent tactics against those who haven't necessarily been deemed Wielders. His view on the people has always been a fair trial for offenses to get to an honest and lawful verdict."

"So, you think Otvel must have stayed close by to be able to keep carrying out these extractions?"

"That's the only thing that makes all of this add up."

"Do you think that my parents and your father truly sanctioned such brutal means?"

Roland paused and looked to be weighing his next words carefully. "I think the public perception of your mother's authority is a bit skewed."

"What do you mean? Are you saying she is some sort of puppet?"

"Not exactly, but I do know the ministries have been the ones handing her all of the official paperwork to sign off on. All it would take is a deviation of attention, and who knows what might be pushed through. You've seen for yourself the stance the aristocracy has taken with the injections."

I wanted to defend my mother and say she wasn't that foolish or easily misled, but my mind wandered back to her confession of overwhelm at Theo's bedside, and I couldn't deny it. Mama trusted Otvel and his connection to the Divinities more than anyone else in Alse Hanya, and it wouldn't truly take much for her to be convinced by him.

I was grateful that at the very least Friedrich should be a counter balance to Otvel's radicalism. His more reserved and gentle approach would hopefully prevent such ordeals as the other night from happening again so long as he was properly involved.

I knew he was also of the anti-Wielder persuasion, and had seen first hand his vehemence regarding our protection against them, but I also knew he was a man of the people and would do little to jeopardize their loyalty. It made me wonder his true stance on the injections and if he'd simply been outvoted or if he truly stood behind their purpose. Memories of his promise to me and my sisters when we were little girls fluttered to the surface of my mind, and I realized I had been too young at the time to question what would follow them.

And rest assured, Little Princesses, your father and I will make sure this breech in Eisa's security won't go unpunished. Any Wielder who dares think they can live within our borders will be eradicated like the monsters they are. That's a promise.

"Do you know what happened after we were attacked that day with Theo?" I asked, fighting the desire to wring my fingers together for risk of upsetting my wounds. "I never saw another Wielder in Eisa again after that. Not in the open."

"I wasn't old enough to be made privy to anything behind the scenes," Roland answered.

"Oh."

"However…"

"Yes?"

"I do know one bit about that day that you may want to know."

"Well, go on then," I prompted, and sat down on one of the many benches placed throughout the garden walkways. I patted the space beside me and waited patiently.

"The woman Wielder, the one who was in the shadows… do you recall seeing her?"

"No," I answered honestly, pulling the memories to the front of my mind. I recalled her voice clear as day, but only the Wish Wielder had been visible. "She instructed the man from within her shadows."

"If you had seen her, you might have found her familiar."

"Why is that?" I tilted my head to the side.

"She was Vadia's mother." Roland reached forward and tucked a strand of hair behind my ear that the summer breeze had plucked free from her updo. The gesture was gentle and stilled me when his thumb brushed against my cheek.

"She was?" I whispered, remembering what Vadia had told me about her mother and early childhood. It brought a whole new light to the memory that had truly spurred my fear of Wielders. The man had been the aggressor, and I recalled that the woman had only instructed for me to be taken captive in the woods that day to be used as a bartering chip. She never once had suggested harming me. She hadn't even come out of her shadows, and knowing the bare minimum of Vadia's abilities, had she wanted to, that woman could have taken us all down into her shadows without breaking a sweat.

And she was hunted down by Friedrich and Papa for attacking us. No doubt, she had paid with her life for her participation that day. Vadia must have known the cause of her mother's death, and had still chosen to show me kindness and ultimately sacrifice herself on my behalf. I was torn between a strange warm sense of connection tethering me back to the caring girl, and the smothering guilt it brought with it.

Why was it that she was able to forgive and choose to show kindness when we had not? Though we had thought Theo had been cursed all this time, it turned out, we had lost nothing and still took everything from that little girl— even her own life in the end. Had she realized it was me specifically who had fallen behind and caused enough of a delay for the duo to be caught?

"I think she understood your fear," Roland let his hand linger beside my face, before cupping it tenderly, seeming to guess where my train of thought had taken me. "When she shifted into you to access your true thoughts and emotions, I'd be surprised if she hadn't gotten glimpses of those formative memories."

"She still saved me." I closed my eyes and leaned into his hand, drawing in the grounding reassurance it gave me.

"And you still tried to save her," Roland reminded me gently.

"It was the right thing to do." My eyes fluttered open.

"It was the right thing to do," Roland echoed, tilting my face to look into his eyes. "They didn't catch her mother that day either. She made it on the run for a couple more years before they finally found her."

"How do you know that?"

"She was found on foreign territory— hiding in Videiria. The records are part of the Foreign Affairs department."

"I see." I raised my brows, impressed.

"Sorrel," Roland leaned a little closer and his voice dropped. "I can't stand to see you look so sad and do nothing to fix it. Had I any inclination to what that night would bring… Tell me what I can do to make you smile again."

"I'm not sure there is anything that can be done," I laughed sadly, bringing my own hand to rest on his where it still cupped my cheek. "But this, this is nice. Just the two of us like it used to be when we were younger. Reminds me of a simpler time."

"I wish everyday for it to be just the two of us again. I want nothing more than a future where your company is all that fills my days."

"Do you mean that?" I breathed.

"More than anything, Snowdrop. Everything I've been working towards has been because of you."

"Because of me?"

"Yes. It's all for you, to keep you and all you hold dear safe and happy. That's all I truly want. A future where you are home within yourself."

"I…" I faltered, words failing me as I stared at Roland.

I could see the love in his gaze and realized how much weight he'd been carrying trying to slowly orchestrate the shift in paradigms for an entire kingdom all on his own.

"What made you pursue the seat as Minister of Foreign Affairs?" I asked instead of spluttering incoherent sentiments of affection.

"You." Roland smiled and leaned even closer. "You and R—"

"Roland!" I whipped my head to the side and Roland's hand dropped to his lap at the sound of Arrian hurrying over to us. "Sorry to interrupt whatever moves you're trying to make here, but there is a Videirian here with the doctor and they have something to discuss with you, *Minister.*"

I ducked my head in embarrassment at our intimate moment

being witnessed. Roland sighed and rose to his feet with a shake of his head. He punched his brother lightly in the arm with a strained laugh.

"You're too funny, Ari."

"I like to think so," Ari smirked. "Sorry, Sorrel. That kiss you've been waiting for will have to wait another day. Again. Frankly, I doubt he will ever get up the nerve. Best move on already."

"Oh!" I blushed as Roland threw his arm around his brother and squeezed just a little too tight.

"Don't be a pain," he said through gritted teeth. Arrian's deep brown eyes shifted from his brother to me before blazing with mischief.

"In front of your *Snowdrop?*"

"Mock me not, brother."

Arrian rolled his eyes. "I would never think of it. You're far too important to ever be mocked. Isn't that so, Minister? Or are you working on becoming a *prince* now too? Is that how it will work with you two, or will *Snowdrop* have to take a demotion?"

"Alright, that's it. We are leaving."

I hid a small chuckle behind my hand as the two brothers strode off in the direction of the palace. I didn't miss the swat to the head Ari took from Roland for his comments before they turned the corner. Arrian's remarks reminded me of all the teasing I endured from Kira, and I realized that the two likely conspired and shared notes to terrorize the both of us.

For a couple minutes, things felt just as they had always been, and I was standing in a bubble of wistful nostalgia I was loath to disturb. But, I knew that the matter Roland had been called in to deal with likely pertained to the arrangements of the Videirian elixirs to help Theo. So, I stepped out of the bubble and followed suit back to the palace to sit with my brother and see what it was he was hoping to share with me.

I plucked a single flower on my way to bring to him, hoping it would brighten his day even if only for a moment. However, when I opened the door to his room and stepped inside, the flower fell from my hands, and I was unable to suppress the gasp of surprise that leapt from my mouth.

Theo was muttering with only a few words discernible. *Sorrel, night, fire, Wielders.* And beside his bed wasn't my mother listening to his incoherent statements. It was Otvel.

"Hello, Sorrel. Lovely to see you. Your brother has been asking for you."

I hesitated in the doorway, unsure of what to do. Otvel would have no way of knowing I was at the location of the fire the other night, and I didn't need to give him any reason to suspect me. I smiled and sat at the end of the bed.

"Hello, Otvel!" I kept my tone cheerful. "What a surprise to see you here today. I thought you had business to attend to in Zdenayk?"

"I was there, but some matters brought me back to the capital sooner than originally intended. I was fortunate to not be too far out of town when word of your brother's ailment reached me."

"You weren't already in town?"

"No, I was just a couple towns over from here in Balaev. Why do you ask?" Otvel blinked at me, and I had to force my face not to crinkle in confusion.

I had been certain that it had been Otvel's voice I had heard give the burn order. Unless he had traveled back out of town after the fire, he had to be lying about his whereabouts. But why? Why hide his work with the anti-Wielder force, even if it was to maintain the narrative that the Wielder's attacked first? As an elevated priest of the Church of the Divine, it would be clear to anyone which side of the argument Otvel would be on when it came to magic. So, why hide it?

"I see. I didn't know that," I replied, my tone becoming flat as all of the energy fled from my body.

"Sorrel?" Theo coughed, and blinked blearily at me. "I need to ask you about something."

"I'm here, Theo." I glanced up at Otvel. "Would you mind

terribly giving us just a few moments alone, please?"

"Of course." Otvel pushed to his feet and headed for the door. "I see you and Klivech have opted to switch to an elixir to heal Theo. Resorting to magic, even at the legal limit, I must admit I was surprised. Then again, perhaps I shouldn't be."

I swallowed hard and sat slowly beside my brother. "Pardon?"

"Oh, no matter. However, now that I have returned, there won't be any need to stoop to such measures. I will heal the boy with the miracles of the Divinities. He paused and smiled at the ground. When he looked up, there was a knowing glint to his eyes, and a dark shadow fell over his face. "I have a good natural remedy for fire exposure too, Sorrel. If you find yourself in need, feel free to find me."

How did he know? How *could* he know?

Sharp panic like waves of broken glass flooded my chest. But, I somehow managed to tilt my head to the side, the picture of innocence and pointed to my bandaged hand.

"It was silly of me to reach into the fire to retrieve what I dropped, but I think it is healing just fine on its own."

"You definitely want to be careful playing with that fire. Sometimes it is better to cut your losses than to reach further into the flames. As you've learned, doing so just results in burns. I'd truly hate to see something worse become of you simply because you didn't get out while you still could. Before time runs out and all is lost." His cryptic words hung in the air between us for what felt like an eternity.

Was he threatening me or warning me?

"What I wanted to ask you," Theo croaked, peeling my attention away from the priest and back to my brother. When I glanced back up, Otvel was nowhere to be seen.

"Yes?" I replied gently, ignoring the sweat that was pooling at the nape of my neck.

"You were at the fire the other night, weren't you?" He wheezed. "You and Ina?"

"I…" I hesitated, weighing my options before answering. "Ina wasn't there."

"Why did you go?"

"Because I had to, Theo."

"You helped them, didn't you?"

"I did."

"Why?" Theo's brows furrowed.

"They were the ones who needed my help. There were all kinds of people there, and they were scared and hurt."

"The man the soldiers said fought them that was from the list... He was your friend?"

"Yes," I answered honestly.

"The woman at the hospital, was she there?"

"She was."

"That's why you gave them the supplies. My question is," Theo's words were broken up by a cough. He swallowed hard and turned his head to look straight at me. "Did the Wielder's start the fire?"

I stared back unwavering, choosing my next words pointedly. "No. We didn't start the fire."

"I see," Theo muttered, a light flashing across his gaze before the dullness of fever overtook it. "I see. Thank you for your honesty. I think... I think I'm going to go back to sleep now." He had barely managed to finish the sentence before his eyes fluttered closed and he succumbed to slumber.

I gave a weak laugh and pulled the comforter up around his chest. "Well, if you remember any of this conversation, you took the news better than I did. That's for sure."

I waited a few more minutes to see if he would wake back up, but when it was clear he had fallen into a deep sleep I opted to return to my duties for the day. Each step I took towards the door felt heavy with responsibility, and I wondered what Theo's full reaction would be when he had recovered all of his faculties. I supposed if he took a negative turn to the news, I could always write it off as having been delirium from his fever. But, there was a very real part of me that dared to hope Theo had understood what

I had said to him, and just like he had shown such graciousness at the hospital with Maggie, he might continue to show open mindedness and maturity towards the information. After all, he would learn of it someday when Papa shared it with him. Perhaps alluding to it now while his mind was still very young and open would give him a better scope of reality, as apposed to living a full adult life constantly inundated with skewed perceptions.

I clicked the door closed behind me and leaned against it to catch my breath and slow the beating of my heart. I reminded myself once more of the resilience I needed to have in order to help our country mend its rifts and slowly walked myself back from the precipice of hysteria. The sound of shoes scuffing against the floor at a brisk pace caught my attention and turned it down the hall.

Roland was heading towards me, and his face brightened when he saw me. I wondered if it would stay so elated when he learned both Otvel and Theo seemed to have deduced my presence at the fire. Though there was hope for Theo's full reaction, and Roland ultimately wanted to eventually have all five of us siblings in on the secret together, I knew that Otvel's awareness posed a very real threat to our safety, as well as those we were trying to protect.

"Sorrel!" Roland huffed when he caught up to me, keeping his voice low. "I got word from Maggie. She secured a new location with a few others. She also told me to let you know that once she finds Lenya but when she does, he can start teaching you how to access your ice. If you still want to. Afraid Storm and Star will have to wait."

The words thundered dangerously loud in my head. There was an excitement born of desperation for preparedness blooming beneath my skin. Otvel's interaction had been so unnerving, I felt the irrefutable need to have my defenses ready.

"I'm ready to learn. Now more than ever. There's something I need to tell you…"

THIRTY-FIVE

"**N**urse Zdraevit, I thought you were done for the day," A man called out to me as I passed in the hallway.

"I decided to take on a double shift today, Private Malvyute. Idle hands are the Forsaken's playthings!" I chirped back, and Malvyute laughed, raising his own injured hands.

"Now you tell me."

"I believe I saw your discharge paperwork float across the desk, so you will be out of here and back to causing trouble before you know it."

"Ah, music to my ears," Malvyute sighed, leaning back in his cot. "I hope you're sprung loose from here to cause some trouble yourself."

I narrowed my eyes. "Who says I wasn't starting some right now? Have a good night, Malvyute!"

"You too!"

There was nothing left to do besides bide my time, so I kept busy. Checking on Theo, and tripling my efforts at the hospital. I wasn't taken to the new hideout on account of Roland's concerns of another ambush. I couldn't blame him after the fire. Despite my eagerness to contribute, there was a small part of me that feared getting caught in another compromising situation that could endanger myself and my family again. I had been useless to help anyone in the end there, and felt I'd be of better use where I was more in my element— at least until I could learn to wield my affinities and stand a fighting chance.

As I recalled the flames biting my flesh, I rolled my wrist, feeling the tightness of the healing skin flex beneath my bandages. It wouldn't be too much longer before I could remove them. But my burns and the intrusive memories of the burning inn weren't the only things that had stuck with me from that night.

I paused outside a private room, and took a deep breath before entering. "Sergeant Darion?"

He was thinner than when I had last seen him, almost gaunt. Deep purple circles beneath his eyes betrayed his exhaustion, and his fingers drummed rhythmically on his leg as he stared blankly ahead. He was a shell of the good natured soldier he'd once been. Had I not known where to find him, I wouldn't have recognized him.

His wife had told me he returned changed, crazed, and cruel. The twisted frown on his lips and glassy red rimmed gaze alone corroborated her story. Something about Amary and Darion's conflict had lingered in my mind, and I needed to see with my own eyes how Darion could have turned on the wife he had once claimed he would fight the world for. I knew Amary had managed to escape the building, but I hadn't been able to help her, or provide her with any solace. Perhaps there was a chance I could reach Darion, and repair the damage.

"Darion?" I repeated my greeting when he made no move to acknowledge me as I stepped fully into the room and approached his bedside. "It's me, Sorrel. I came to visit you and see how your recovery was going?"

"What?" Darion snapped his attention to me, swallowing me up in his unsettling gaze.

"I wanted to check in on you."

"Oh," He huffed, lackluster.

"I see your wound is healing nicely. That's good news."

"Oh." The same deadpan response.

"I hope you're at least getting some better rest, now that you've put some distance between yourself and all the fighting." I murmured. It was clear that despite being in hospital for a few weeks, he still wasn't ready mentally to engage in a conversation just yet.

He wasn't the first soldier I'd seen return rattled by the psychological damage Sonyotes employed through lack of sleep, but he was the first I saw the bigger picture of. The fact his wife had been a Dream Wielder of all things had probably been too much to cope with after spending so long fighting her exact kind. But for Amary, how could she possibly wrap her mind around sending the man she loved off to war only to have him return to her as an enemy? Perhaps the wound was too big to ever close, but I had to hope there was still progress to be made. I didn't want to give up on Darion. He deserved someone to fight to restore who he once was— a good man. Not the drained, mindless creature of stewing malice they had sent in his place. I wanted the real Darion back.

"I'm going to leave you to rest now," I sighed, as Darion continued to stare aimlessly around the room in a delirium I had little chance of breaking for the moment. I only wished I had thought more of what words I could say to connect to him before coming. "I'll try again tomorrow. Sweet dreams."

"Sweet dreams are their tainted webs. Monsters! All of them. I hope they burn in the fires of Vatra. Only the heat of a volcano could cleanse our world of their nightmares!" Darion's eyes widened until I was certain they might pop free of their sockets. He bolted fully upright, dislodging his covers. His body began to shake in the beginnings of shock-induced shiver.

"Darion, you need to calm down," I spoke calmly, grabbing the sheet to pull it over him. Before I could react, Darion lunged for my arm, gripping it hard. I winced as his fingers dug into my healing burns.

"I can't sleep. They lurk there and burrow into the mind. I'll never be free. Never be free. I can't ever sleep again."

"Darion, let go of me," I kept my voice level despite the pain he was inflicting. His expression was alarmingly close to a wild animal, causing my spine to stiffen. "You're not on the battlefield any more. You're home in Eisa."

"Home?" Darion released his hold on my wrist and brought it safely to my chest.

"Home," I echoed.

"Home in Eisa. With my wife."

I perked at the mention of Amary. Maybe he was coming out of his stupor at last. "That's right. Your wife is here in Eisa. I remember you telling me about her before the send off."

"Kill her! Boil her in Vatra's flames. She's one of them. She's evil! Kill her, kill her. Kill them all so I can rest!" Darion had grown manic, clawing feverishly at his blankets, eyes darting around like he was waiting for an ambush.

"It's going to be alright…" I took a step back, turning to call over my shoulder for the doctor to come and administer something to settle the man down. "I think you'll start feeling better when you get some decent sleep—"

"Sleep?" He recoiled from the word, his lip curling into a snarl. "You can't make me! I won't let you take me back there!"

"Darion, I promise I'm not—" I tried again but my words evaporated into a gasp as Darion sprung from his coil like a snake, flipping me around with my head trapped within his arms.

"Stop deceiving me!"

"Help!" I called out, his grip on my neck tightening. My voice cracked on the plea, my throat still raw from the fire. "Help, please!"

"Monster, vile, treacherous monster."

"Darion, please see reason. You know me! Remember the barracks? You know me."

"No, no, no," Darion kept whispering, constricting even more.

"What is happening here?" Relief surged through me, filling my struggling lungs as Hykner rushed into the room as fast as his injured leg would allow. He'd only recently been brought back to recover from a leg injury, and even as a patient was still right there when I needed him.

His eyes widened when he saw me in Darion's crazed grasp and he craned his head to shout down the hall for assistance. Hykner charged forward to pluck Darion's arms from around my neck.

"No, no! You can't let them go, don't let any of them go!" Darion screeched, fighting Hykner with everything he had.

Hykner held him off enough for me to wriggle free of his grasp.

I scrambled away, clutching at my neck as I sucked precious air into my already laboring lungs. Around me, a doctor and a second able soldier stormed into the room.

"Restrain him!" Doctor Ravlet shouted, as Hykner and the second man moved to hold the howling Darion down. Ravlet prepared a syringe— likely a sedative and ready to plunge it into Darion's arm.

Darion caught sight of it, and grew more frantic as he too realized what it was. His eyes grew wide and misty, and his bottom lip began to tremble.

"No, don't make me sleep! Don't send me back there. Don't send me back!"

I covered my mouth and slowly backed out of the room. Fleeing down the hall, I grasped at the wall for support before pressing my back against it and sliding down.

I pressed my palms against my eyes and breathed deeply. *Darion, what happened to you? What broke you like this?*

"Are you alright, Pri— Sorrel?" Hykner's level voice sounded above me, and I shifted my hands to blink blearily up at him.

"Darion," I mumbled. "He lost his mind."

Hykner closed his eyes, the corners creasing, and took a long, deep breath. "I'm sorry for the loss. He's sleeping now."

"He was begging not to sleep, but… I don't know how to help him. I just don't know."

"Are you certain you can?"

"What?" I blinked in surprise.

"Some people are beyond saving. They pass beyond our reach and it becomes up to them whether they will survive or succumb. Darion seems to have slipped into a part of his mind only he can find his way out of."

"I don't know if I can afford to think that way."

"Why?"

"Because I'm a nurse."

"Or is it because you're Sorrel?"

"I beg your pardon?"

"If you will allow me to speak candidly…"

"Of course," I beckoned him to continue.

"I've been in your regiment for nearly seven years. I've been your personal guard for months. I've seen, to varying degrees, how much others rely on you, and how much you rely on helping others. There is room, you know, to be Sorrel, and to not have the answer or the bandage to fix all the problems of everyone you encounter. Not even a Divinity I think could manage such a feat."

"I thought I could help somehow. I can't stand to be idle like this," I clenched my fists until my knuckles turned white. "It's too much to bear the helplessness. I fear it will rend me in two."

"Then maybe you're the one who needs the help."

"Me?"

"Yes. You are so focused on making sure everyone makes it aboard a lifeboat that you fail to realize you've stopped treading water and are going down with the ship. Look at you; Burned, bags under your eyes, and I can hear that rattle in your breathing. You can't help others if you bend so far you break. If there are hands reaching out to help you, then now is the time to accept the help, lest you drown."

"I… want everyone to be okay. To be safe and whole again. What value do I have to my country if I can't at least strive for that? So many have suffered and perished. My own family has suffered while I've been powerless to help them. Harvier at the hospital, the people in the hideout, and Vadia. I could do nothing to stop it. Even here, where I'm supposed to know what I'm doing, I'm useless."

"You can't save everyone. There are going to be times when you can't save anyone at all, you'll feel helpless, angry, and consumed with devastation. Those are the moments you make a choice to carry on. Carry on so that next time you move a little faster, stand a little taller, endure a little more. That's how you take control back. Not by bearing all the problems of the world all at once, but focusing on one thing you can do— even if it's just rising to your feet and lifting your head." Hykner reached out and offered me his hand, prompting me to rise.

"I keep seeing others die because of my inability to save them. How do I keep moving forward when it keeps happening? How can I trust myself to not fail someone else? I've nothing substantial to offer." I gritted my teeth, ducking my head to stare at my feet.

"How many wounds have you stitched closed? Bandages changed? Medicine given? You saved countless lives, Sorrel. It's only you who can't see the good you've put back into Eisa, or the lives you've touched. That little boy died, due to means beyond your control, but he died at peace. You did that."

"Could I have saved him if I'd had access to my Ice affinity?" I looked up and locked eyes with Hykner. Knowing he was as much a part of the group in hiding as Roland and Inessa, I could only assume Ina had filled him in on my recent involvements and affinities. "Be honest."

He sighed and averted his gaze. "I can't say for sure if you could have staved off the hypothermia at that point, but it's possible you might have been able to take away the cold inhibiting him."

"I can't fight the war overtaking our country. I can't fight using these abilities. I have no weapons, no armor. I can't seem to do anything in this fight no matter how I try."

"You're wrong," Hykner insisted. "Your compassion has made you brave, your empathy has made you resilient, and your tenacity has made you fierce. Can you not see what you have already endured? Did you not try to cross fire to save Vadia? You refused to abandon Maggie to save yourself in that fire. You trusted your sister instead of turning on her when everything you thought you knew was uprooted in a single moment of a heated argument. Trust me. Lesser people would have done less. Your skin is thicker than you think. You've felt every bit of your role in this world, and it is powerful. So long as you keep true to yourself, your strengths are your armor in the constant battle of life, your sword and your shield. Mark my words, you are a caretaker, Sorrel. The unsung hero. One day you will heal the wounds of this world."

I was quiet for a moment, digesting the sentiment of Hykner's words. I uncurled my fists and slacked my locked jaw to allow a small smile to spread across my lips.

"I can see why my sister fancies you," I laughed softly. "Thank you, Hykner. It's good to have you back even if it is only for a short while. Though I wish you'd hadn't had to endure an ambush and injury to return home."

He returned my smile and nodded. "Any time. Us soldiers have to keep fighting together."

"Together," I echoed the call to camaraderie and moved in to support Hykner's injured side as I helped him make his way back to his bed.

"What are you doing up?" Inessa demanded, turning the corner with a fresh pillow in hand. She had of course returned to her volunteer station, just as abruptly as she had stopped, when I notified her that there was a particular soldier who had returned from the battle with injuries. "I leave you for a few minutes to find a new pillow and my sister has to hunt you down and return you to bed?"

I slipped free of Hykner's side and transferred him to Inessa as he started to explain.

Inessa flashed me a sympathetic look and reached a hand to look at my neck and gently run her fingers over my forehead. "I'm sorry, Sorrel. Some days we don't have wins on either side."

"Hykner was a real hero." I gestured to the soldier as he sank back against his new pillow.

Inessa smacked him lightly atop his head, disturbing his dusty blonde hair and eliciting in a small yelp of indignant surprise. "You had no business being a hero with your leg still mending!"

"What was I supposed to do, let the man strangle your sister?"

"Get someone else to help her?"

I smirked at their exchange and shook my head. "I'll see you later, Ina. Enjoy your evening." I waved farewell and made myself scarce.

Pushing through the door of the hospital, I stepped out into a world bustling with evening activity. I paused and took it in, wondering how it differed from other parts of the world. Did Sonyo have hospitals with bedraggled men and women, war torn and broken? Was their capital still safe enough for citizens to carry on their regular lives behind the protection of the Veil of Stars? This image differed so poignantly with the way I had seen the street I found Harvier on, like the facade had slipped for a moment, and now was back in place.

I knew the people streaming to and fro in front of me was a guise of stability. A distraction covering the underbelly of our country's true suffering. Shops still stood in tact, selling goods despite rations, men and women still strolled arm and arm with their sweethearts in the glow of the setting summer sun. Yet, beyond the picture of normalcy, I knew children were cowering in orphanages, and men were going mad in their beds as they tried to reclaim the night for themselves. Women were meeting their loved ones as new people, forever scarred both physically and mentally, linking them to a fight they never signed up for in the collateral aftermath. All to fight in a conflict we had no business involving ourselves with. Amary and Darion were just another two casualties of my family's lies.

I plodded heavily down the steps towards the waiting car. The chauffeur opened the door for me, but before I could reach it, in my distraction I didn't see the elderly man crossing in front of me. I ricocheted off his shoulder with an undignified *oomph* and stumbled backwards.

"My apologies! I wasn't paying attention," The man gasped, reaching out to steady me.

"Grand Princess Sorrel, is everything alright here?" The guard appointed with accompanying me rushed to my side, and I waved him off.

"Yes, no harm done," I wheezed, more startled out of my thoughts than anything.

The guard nodded to the man and stepped back, facing me with a watchful eye from the car.

The elderly man released his hold on me and looked me up and down, concern furrowing his aged-speckled brow. "Forgive my impertinence, but are you alright?"

"Oh, I'm just wrestling with the eternal question of where to find the strength to keep up the good fight," I muttered, then stiffened realizing I had spoken the thought aloud. "Sorry, I mean, yes. I'm fine, thank you. I'm sorry for running into you like that."

The old man squinted at me with crinkled eyes that told of years of kind smiles. "You feel powerless so you seek strength," He acknowledged, and I had to suppress a ripple of shock from overtaking me.

"Am I that transparent in my helplessness?" I laughed half-heartedly.

The man placed his hand on my shoulder and gave it a meaningful squeeze. "You need will to wield strength, but need strength to harness will. Purpose is then what is needed to break the paradox of ineffectuality. Otherwise, you fade to nothingness. I should know for I was once nothing too."

"Pardon?" I blinked in surprise at the almost prophetic words.

"Grand Princess?" The guard called wearily as the sun dipped below the horizon. "We are expected back at the palace."

"Don't let me get in your way." The man turned away with a brisk wave and carried on his way.

I climbed into the car, overhearing the guard muttering to the chauffeur that he didn't trust the look of the man, but I was too focused on mulling over the timely advice he'd told me to speak up.

Had the word *wield* been a coincidence or had he been trying to tell me something? Perhaps he had been some sort of message or sign from the Divine… or even a Founder? Was some higher power trying to tell me to keep striving towards my purpose in this world? Had I not discovered it, and was it still yet to come? I stared down the street as we pulled away from the curb, but I found no sign of the mysterious wise man.

Otherwise you fade to nothingness. I should know, for I was once nothing too.

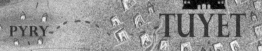

ZDE

PYRY

TUYET

KIP

GRÝKSKI

ZOKEV

SVYAT GAVAN

EISOLDE

ARANECH

DEZIDANEYA

THIRTY-SIX

"For my birthday, I was hoping we could take a day back at Svyat Gavan," Yulia announced at the dinner table a few days before her nineteenth birthday. The weather had finally started to wane from the summer heat, as August settled into full swing, transitioning into more mild Autumn weather.

"You want to go back to that tiny place?" Arrian guffawed as he pierced his potato with his fork. "There is so much more to do here in the capital though."

"I know, but it's been so long since we have been home," Yulia replied wistfully. "I miss it. I miss the calm and the peacefulness. It is nice sometimes for birthdays to be peaceful and quiet and spent with those you love."

"I think it is a great idea!" Kira cheered, leaning forward eagerly. "Do you remember the time capsule we buried out by the old well? Think it's time to unbury it?"

"I'm certainly game," Roland chimed in. "I don't even know

if I remember what I chose to put in the thing."

"Something nauseating about someone else, likely," Arrian narrowed his eyes at his brother, to which Roland grinned and wriggled his eyebrows.

"We all wrote letters to ourselves," Kira reminded us.

"The intrigue intensifies."

"Have we received any letters from Papa?" Yulia piped back up, addressing Mama.

"I did receive one this afternoon," She smiled around her sip of wine. "I figured we would save it for after dinner."

"I wonder if he will come home," Yulia fidgeted in her seat like a child.

"Don't get your hopes up too high," Inessa warned. "This hasn't been a normal year for any of us."

"Right," Yulia looked a little crestfallen, and Kira glared at Ina, ready to argue against her cynicism, but I managed to jump in first.

"He might not be able to make a trip right this moment, but I'm sure he will make every effort he can afford." I smiled encouragingly at my sister, and received a small nod of approval from Kira, who plopped a beet into her mouth instead of engaging with Inessa.

"So, what do you think, Mama? Can we all take a small trip home? I know there is a lot to do and a lot of responsibilities, but I've been missing home so much lately. I keep feeling this strong need to go back there."

"Like a Divine suggestion?" Kira made a face like she was speaking of old ghost stories, and Yulia poked her in the side.

"I think it's just a bit of homesickness, silly."

"There are a lot of things to be managed here…" Mama frowned contemplatively. "Sorrel and Inessa have duties of their own to perform as well. There have been reports on the war front that casualties are rising, and it's causing quite a stir amongst the people that we really should focus on pacifying."

"That's alright. I underst—" Yulia started but Friedrich raised his hand to interrupt.

"If I may, Geneva. I am sure with a couple days of preparations, we can afford for you and the children to take an overnight trip back to Svyat Gavan."

"Are you sure?"

"Absolutely," Friedrich smiled at a beaming Yulia. "I'd hate for Yulia to be denied her birthday wish."

"Yours should be better than mine, don't worry!" Kira snorted.

"Kira, don't be morbid," Inessa chided, and Kira glanced sideways at Yulia, remembering too late that the events of that night were still a tender subject for her.

"Sorry."

"Roland and Arrian can stay behind as well and help out around the edges as needed. Chinye is back at the palace too, so I'm sure he will be involved." Friedrich's smile wavered for a heartbeat as he mentioned Otvel, and I looked across the table at Roland to gauge his reaction. Was Friedrich discretely slighting Otvel? Roland gave me the tiniest frown to indicate he too had noticed the subtle shift in his father's demeanor.

"He had some suggestions I think I will pass on to Genri as well. We are so fortunate that Otvel has returned to us. It certainly should make your job easier again, Friedrich."

"Indeed, it should. Then, it's settled!"

"But Roland wanted to see the time capsule too!" Kira protested, her voice pitching to a whine.

"Sorry, Littlest Princess. You'll just have to bring the treasures back to me," Roland soothed, holding his pinky out to her as he'd often done with her as a child. "But no peeking or exploiting anything embarrassing that may or may not be in there from me, deal?"

Kira leaned around Yulia and hooked her pinky to his. "Deal, I will be the soul of discretion."

"I'm choosing to believe you," Roland feigned sternness but cracked a smile and returned to his food. The soft spot Kira had carved out for herself with Roland gave me no doubt that she only ever need say the word, and Roland would move mountains to grant her request.

"A terrible choice, really," Inessa murmured with a small smirk, just loud enough to be heard by the rest of us and receive an indignant squeak from Kira.

We finished our meal, and I could feel fatigue tugging at my eyelids from all of the heavy food after a long day. I'd had different committee obligations that had taken me all around the capital, making arrangements, on top of an earlier morning shift at the hospital.

Though she still made time for the other men in our charge, it was clear that Ina organized her time to spend as much time with Hykner during his recovery as possible. Out of practice with the routine, I could see that the same wave of grogginess was also catching up to her.

"Shall we read Papa's letter now?" Yulia's bright voice permeated the drowsy cloud that had settled over the room, recalling us all back to a more alert state once more.

"Oh yes, Dowels?" Mama waved the butler over. "Please bring the emperor's letter to the sitting room."

When he returned with the sealed letter on a silver tray, my siblings and I all gathered around mama in an unceremonious fashion, while Friedrich, Roland, and Arrian took their seats. I caught Arrian's gaze resting on Kira and narrowing. There was a strange darkness to his expression that made me wonder what could possibly be passing through his mind, until the edges of his lips twitched upward, and he shifted in his seat. I realized I was glad to not know what he was thinking after all and turned my attention back to the first page of Papa's letter that mama was holding up for all of us to see.

My Dearest Family,

These summer days have been long, and I count the end of each one as another moment closer to when I will be beside you all again. I hope K and Y are behaving themselves. Thank goodness for S and Ina being such dutiful role models for them. The men are likely tired of hearing me speak of how proud I am of all my wonderful children, so please allow me to express that sentiment here. I have been helping the marshal as best as I can by making strategic suggestions, but it pains me greatly that this war remains an ongoing affair. It will bring me the greatest comfort when I can be reunited with you all, my dear, loving family.

T has written to me requesting a visit, and I will be arranging a time after Y's birthday celebrations for him to see how the front is working. Worry not, Dear Wife, as I will make sure the utmost precautions are taken to ensure our safety.

By the time this letter arrives, it should be nearing dear sweet Y's nineteenth birthday. Where has the time gone that I have become an old man with such a grown, beautiful, accomplished daughter? May you have the most exceptional birthday, Sweet Yulia. I am remiss that I could not be there to wish it in person. Instead, please expect a surprise present on the actual day.

Wishing you all my love and good health,
-G

The drive to Eisolde was very long in the best possible way. As we pulled up to the modest palace, my sisters and I couldn't help but press our faces to the glass of the windows.

As soon as it came to a stop, we exploded from the car and raced inside our home. Running through the halls with the reckless abandon of our younger selves, seeing the familiar walls around us felt like we had stepped back into a moment kept in time, back to a time when we hadn't even realized how high our spirits had soared.

"It's so good to be *home!*" Kira's voice echoed from a few rooms down, and was immediately followed by a reprimand from Mama for shouting indoors. Inessa and I snickered from our own room and threw ourselves onto our beds.

"It *does* feel nice to be back," Inessa sighed heavily. "I want to make the most of it today. We should take a walk in the fields and along the stream. If we go alone, there are always some struggling plants along the banks, and I want to see if I can help them."

I stared at the ceiling, tracing the design over and over again with my eyes. Even though it had been less than a year since we'd been back home, I'd started to forget little details, and wanted to recommit every inch to memory.

Roland had stopped me before we'd gotten in the car and had asked for a full recount of the trip he was missing and to leave nothing out. A smile curled my lips as I knew I was going to give him more details than he had bargained for, but he'd likely take it all in stride as he always did.

Ina's words ebbed in and out of my awareness as she prattled off everything we could do in the day. The sun was filtering through the curtains, bathing the room in a warm white glow. The moment was so serene and peaceful, I felt all of my harbored anxieties begin to melt away. My eyes wanted to drift closed, but I didn't dare let them and miss even a second of the day.

A scream cut through the air, and Inessa and I bolted upright, instantly on alert for danger. We looked at each other, and Inessa rushed to the door while I scrambled to look outside.

"Was that Yulia?" I asked.

"Do you think she's hurt?" Inessa called back to me, craning her neck to peer down the hallway. "Where is everyone else? Wait, is that laughing?"

"What?" I abandoned the window and raced over to join Inessa. Sure enough, I could hear laughter parsing the otherwise stillness of the house. My heart leapt into my throat as I recognized one tone of voice above the others. "It couldn't be."

Inessa and I sucked in a breath and hurried to the source of the noise. Our hurried and undignified approach had us simultaneously barreling through the doorway to Yulia's room where we were both met with the most heartwarming scene we'd seen in months. Sitting with a stack of presents beside him on Yulia's bed was Papa.

"Papa!" Ina and I cheered in tandem, rushing forward to throw our arms around him where he was already balancing beneath Kira and Yulia's embrace. Mama was sitting on Kira's bed, her hands clasped to her mouth with happy tears shining in her eyes. Theo was hovering nearby, elation clear as day on his face.

"I thought you weren't going to be here for my birthday? In your letter," Yulia sniffled, pausing to wipe away some tears running down her cheeks. "In your letter you said you regretted not being here."

"Ah, but I also promised you a surprise, didn't I?" Papa grinned, and winked at Mama. "I must admit I had an accomplice in the deception. Thankfully she was able to alert me in time to travel here instead of Tuyet."

"Very sneaky," Yulia laughed.

We all disentangled ourselves as Papa presented Yulia with her parcels. He had gotten her new, specially crafted journals, sketch pads, and the highest quality drawing pencils. He also gifted her with a brand new pen and ink set, complete with several shimmering pigments to enhance her artistic lettering.

"Thank you, Papa!"

"Draw me!" Kira pounced forward, then shifted mid-motion to the door. "Wait, no. Let's go outside and you can draw me there!"

"You can go out for a half hour, then we will be having our dessert," Mama wrapped her arm around Kira and gave her an affectionate squeeze. "Have fun."

"Or, you can draw a sketch of me and Theo in a duel!" Kira gasped, grabbing hold of Yulia and dragging her with the new art materials behind her. "I have so many ideas!"

The morning turned into afternoon with all of us together as a family again. We laughed, played games, and celebrated Yulia's birthday with ample enthusiasm. Each of us sat with Papa, making sure to devour every possible moment we could with him, and talking his ear off. He told stories from the front lines of war, some amusing observations, some harrowing.

It was so good to see Papa, and to hear his voice. After

everything I had learned since he'd been away, it'd left me with so many questions. But, being with him, spending the time together, it pushed my worries and questions away, and silenced my doubts. I didn't know why Papa chose to carry out the lies of his ancestors, other than the obvious potential of putting us all at risk, but I was reminded of what a kind-hearted and remarkable man he was. He truly lived for what he believed to be the best way forward, and I knew, despite the flaws in his judgment that were showing through, my father was a good man with the best intentions.

I wondered if there would be a moment, somewhere down the line, where all of us children would know the truth and be able to speak with Papa openly about it, and maybe even sway him to change Eisa's rhetoric. I couldn't truly believe that Papa would sanction such horrific acts to befall our citizens, Wielder's or not, and it only made my suspicions of Otvel sharpen. Something seemed to be slipping through the cracks of supervision and desperately needed to be brought to light.

But, for the day, with Roland keeping watch in Tuyet, all of it could wait, and afford us a fleeting moment of family closeness that we all desperately needed to replenish our spirits. Mama looked more awake and happy than I had seen in her in ages. Kira, though always filled to the brim with exuberance, was shining even brighter in her obvious euphoria. Yulia and Inessa too looked less weary and youthful twinkles had returned to their gazes. Even as I passed my own reflection, I saw that the sadness had lifted from my shoulders. I felt light and free— both feelings I had forgotten to feel in a long while.

The late August sunshine held strong as it shifted into the evening, and the four of us sisters once more found ourselves outside, lounging beneath the shade of a tree in the open field in front of the woods. Papa and Mama had taken Theo aside to work out the details of his traveling back to the front with Papa rather than returning to the capital with us. While they were occupied, we'd stolen the moment to go and retrieve the old time capsule we'd buried years ago. Inside, just as Kira had said, each of us had written a letter to our future selves, and added in little miscellaneous trinkets. We set aside Arrian, Roland, and Theo's letters to hand off later, and sat around reading the nonsensical messages we'd each written ourselves.

With the discarded letters strewn about around us, Yulia sat with her sketchpad, drawing away, while Inessa laid on her back and plucked lazily at the grass. Kira was resting her head in my lap, as I placed flowers into her long, free flowing hair.

"Well, Yulia, was today everything you had hoped for?" I asked, my voice breaking through the humming buzz of summer.

"Yes, to have us all together and home again has made me feel so at peace. It's been everything and more. I only wish we didn't have to go back. The capital feels so ominous, don't you think?"

"It's too cold," Kira nodded. "It feels so much warmer here."

"There is a freedom too," Inessa agreed. "More privacy, less to worry about."

"It really is like a little paradise out here," I sighed. "I want to help those in the capital and the rest of Eisa, but I'd be lying if I said it wasn't tempting to want to escape all of our daily toils back here again."

"But," Yulia's smile faltered. "Is it too perfect now?"

"What do you mean?"

"A lot has happened, and we've all seen and learned so much. The war has changed our country and our way of life. I just wonder if we will ever truly come back home here after today."

"That sounds awfully morose. Why shouldn't we return here after our obligations are fulfilled in the capital? After all, we only ever went there for the social season in the winter, then we always returned back here. This is where our true home is."

"I guess it's just a feeling I've been having lately."

"That just sounds like fear to me," Kira sniffed. "You'll become a self-fulfilling prophecy with an attitude like that."

"How uncharacteristically wise a sentiment from you, Kira. I'm impressed." Ina nodded approvingly, popping a berry into her mouth.

"Thank you! I stole it from Theo."

"But, I can't shake this underlying feeling like something is missing. Is there something missing?" Yulia crinkled her nose, and ran her fingers up and down her arms, which prickled with rising goosebumps.

"The boys are missing, right Sorrel?" Kira snickered, nudging me playfully.

"Well, yes, but not all of us *had* boys to speak of, Kira," Yulia rolled her eyes.

"Didn't you once tell me you had a small infatuation with Arrian when we were around five and seven?"

"Did you now?" Inessa grinned and leaned forward. "Did Kira steal him away?"

"Don't instigate, Ina," I laughed along. It was nice to see her laughing and smiling again after having to send Hykner back off to the front when his leg had healed. The second goodbye had been harder on her than the first, and I could tell she was struggling. A trip home had done wonders for her spirit— for all our spirits it seemed.

"I neither confirm nor deny any interest in him!" Kira admonished behind an impish grin.

"I didn't really have any true infatuations towards him," Yulia blushed and tucked her hair behind her ear. "To be honest, I'm not sure I've ever felt that way about anyone before. Not like Kira, and certainly not like Sorrel."

"Speaking of which…" Kira leapt to her feet and pulled an old water stained envelope from her pocket, waving it around like a flag. "Who wants to place a wager that whatever Roland wrote in his letter to his future self pertains to a one miss Sorrel Zdraevit?" She gave a tiny bow in my direction.

"You promised Roland you wouldn't peek!" I chided, a heat creeping into my cheeks, though part of me was burning with curiosity. It made me feel like I was thirteen again.

"I told him he shouldn't trust her," Inessa sighed with a shrug.

"Now, now. I promised *I wouldn't* peek. I promised nothing of the three of you! So, who wants to open it?"

Inessa, Yulia, and I shared a look, then laughing all lunged for the letter at once. Yulia was the first to successfully wrestle it away from Kira, and ripped open the envelope while the rest of us leaned forward intently.

"Tell me your wagers before I give the grand reveal," Yulia drawled, gesturing like she was a ringmaster announcing the next greatest act.

"I'll take the bet that he wrote about something other than Sorrel," Inessa raised her hand.

"I say he most definitely did," Kira declared, turning to me. "Be our tie-breaker, Sorrel. Yay or nay?"

"Well, how am I supposed to answer that without sounding like I have an ego the size of Alse Hanya!" I threw my hands up, and my sisters shared a knowing glance, speaking in tandem.

"Yay."

"Oh, go on then, Yulia." I waved my hand. "What does it say?"

"To be honest, a lot of it is smudged— arguably our climate was a poor one for this endeavor— but what I can make out says... 'Keep focus... duty... worthiness... and—'" She paused and lowered the paper, grinning from ear to ear, her eyes gleaming with sentiment waiting to burst out of her. "'Don't mess up with Sorrel. She's worth more than you could possibly imagine and you need to hold onto that forever. If you do one thing, do this. See it through.'"

"Funny how the part about me was not smudged at all," I blustered, shrinking into my own embarrassment.

"Oh, Sorrel! He really has been pining after you most ardently all this time!" Yulia cried.

"As if there were ever any doubt. I think they've always been pretty obvious," Ina sniffed.

"Did you hear Theo tell us about his reaction when he made a joke to Roland that Sorrel might get promised off to some Videirian dignitary? I half expected him to drop to one knee then and there from how Theo told it," Kira proclaimed, my sisters nodding like I was no longer present.

"Honestly, he should any time now," Inessa agreed. "You are both of an age, and I'm in no rush to get married or leave Eisa. He needs to get off his laurels."

"Oh, I'm sure there's more on his mind than just me, and when the time is right— if he wanted to— he would ask," I quipped diplomatically, flashing Ina a look that reminded her we knew what other obligations had been taking Roland's attention. I also couldn't help but wonder if focusing on my love life was perhaps distracting Ina from the fact that Hykner had recently returned back to duty and once more left her behind in Tuyet for the war neither one of them could abide.

"But, if he asked you tomorrow, the moment we got back to the palace, what would you say?" Yulia asked, her excited words tumbling over each other and I knew she was reveling in the romantic topic.

"What, after traveling all day in a car? Where's the romance in that?" Kira shook her head. "Absolutely not. Sorrel deserves to be swept off her feet! He needs to demonstrate his love in the greatest most undeniable fashion! But then, would you say yes?"

"I…" I ducked my head feeling flustered by all the direct attention on my relationship to Roland. I pictured him leaning against the tree trunk, smiling at us and all of our sisterly antics. His tall, strong physique, handsome face, and kind eyes that had only ever seen me. I could bluster and bluff all I wanted, but I knew if I could allow myself one selfish wish in the midst of such a tumultuous era, it would be for Roland to finally declare his true feelings to me directly, and ask me to be his forever. He'd danced so close to it when Theo was last ill, but since then it had gone back to the usual teetering on the edge of actually following through. Perhaps when the war finally ended.

"Well?" Inessa quirked an eyebrow and folded her arms.

"I would say yes," I admitted begrudgingly, throwing my head back in exasperation.

My sisters squealed and all threw their arms around me. Their giddiness was infectious, and before I knew it, I had shaken off my awkwardness and joined in the commotion. We toppled over into the grass, breaking apart in a joint fit of laughter.

"How can you think anything is missing here, Yulia?" Kira sighed happily. "How long has it been since we've had an afternoon like this together?"

"Too long," I replied firmly.

"Let's just make sure we don't wait so long between these moments together, alright?" Yulia propped herself up on her elbow and fixed us all with her large blue eyes. I could see all of our faces reflected in them, and something about the image felt strangely comforting to me.

"Thanks for making sure we all came out here today, Yulia. It's been a gift to all of us."

"Yes, forget everything I said before. Today truly has been perfect. One of my best birthdays to date. It's just a terrible shame we have to go back tomorrow."

"It's time to go in to get ready for dinner," Inessa rose reluctantly to her feet and stretched. "Let's go."

"I'll race you! Last one to the door is a rotten egg!" Kira leapt up and made a mad dash, the flowers I'd placed tumbling free of her icy blonde locks behind her as she ran. Yulia, Ina, and I shrugged and pelted after her, shouting protests, all proprietary once more abandoned.

"Cheater!"

"Wait for us!"

"Out of my way, I can't be the rotten egg on my birthday!"

Artwork by Xenychan

THIRTY-SEVEN

eturning to the capital felt like we were descending into a cold, gray fog. Days felt longer, nights shorter, and the heaviness of the state of the world and Eisa pushed back into our lives. It was as though we had never left, and each of us stepped back into our daily routines without pause.

Papa's absence was possibly even more poignant than it had been before, though none of us said so for fear of seeming ungrateful for the time we had gotten to spend with him, however short it had been. Kira brought back the capsule and, snickering the whole time, handed over Arrian and Roland's letters. I had watched as Roland unfolded his letter, and a small light color crept into his cheeks. A wistful glint flickered in his gaze as his eyes rose from the paper to meet mine. I raised my eyebrows at him and turned away. Sure enough, he soon followed after me.

"I have some good news to share," He declared as he caught up to me outside the library.

"What news is that?" I asked, swallowed a yelp of surprise as he suddenly yanked me into the library and led me to the back of the room.

"They've finally found Lenya," He spoke quietly, still holding tight to my hand.

"Lenya?" I echoed, trying to recall the significance of the name.

"The Ice Wielder. One day back at Svyat Gavan and you've already forgotten everything going on here?" He teased, but his words struck a chord within me.

"Never," I admonished, then shook myself mentally. "Alright, so he can finally teach me how to use my Ice affinity."

"There is a catch."

"What's the catch?"

Roland pulled out a small notebook and offered it to me. It was worn with a plain green cover, held together by weathered and stained ribbon. I unraveled the binding and opened the book, scrambling to catch some pages that fluttered loose. Stooping to the ground to retrieve the paper I had missed, I glanced at what was written on the pages. It was all a note taker's scrawl with bits of information and diagrams sketched.

"Lenya was on his way out of the country," Roland explained. "After the last raid, and losing Vadia and Rafe, he decided to seek asylum in Kesgoldol. Maggie only just managed to locate him before he went through the Kyrith pass, heading for the evacuation tunnels. He provided everything he could think of in this notebook to give you a starting point for taming your ice."

"Was he particularly close to Rafe and Vadia?" I felt a pang in my chest that reactively set off nerves in my palms like small zaps of electricity.

"Not especially. But, those two were some of our greatest assets. I'm not sure how much you were able to see on the ground, but if you noticed, the Wielders fighting back were overpowered relatively easily and were focused on fleeing rather than fighting the soldiers head on."

I thought back to all I had witnessed that night and realized

Roland was right. I'd seen flashes of magic in the dark, but there weren't any great demonstrations of formative powers being Wielded. Not like Vadia's shadows or Rafe's wishes.

"We had four strong Wielders among us," Roland continued, raising his hand to count them off. "Rafe, Vadia, Maggie, and Lenya. Out of those four, I'd say Rafe was likely the strongest, and Lenya was the weakest by comparison. When Vadia fell, it only made sense that Rafe would wander, not to mention he's listed as a class A criminal in Eisa. It isn't safe for him here anymore, and he had nothing to stay for anymore."

"Why did it make sense?"

"Pardon?"

"You said it only made sense for Rafe to leave when Vadia fell. Why?"

"Oh, right. You probably don't know the connection there." Roland tapped his chin thoughtfully. "Remember when I told you about Vadia's mother? Well, the person who took care of Vadia after her mother was caught was Rafe. They were adoptive siblings."

"Oh," I breathed, my disposition sinking. The time I spent with my family suddenly felt all the more precious. "So, when he lost Vadia, he lost his sister. That's... I can't even imagine."

"And hopefully you never have to, Snowdrop. But, with everything that Chinye has been skulking about with lately, I find it in our best interest for you to give yourself a fighting chance." He pointed at the notebook emphatically.

"Right," I mumbled. "I'll look it over."

"Great, I'm afraid I have to run to my next engagement, but I will expect that full, detailed report from you later!"

I bid Roland farewell and held on tight to the notebook. All the accessible possibilities of learning magic were now in my hands, and I had to find somewhere to start. Maybe then the nagging sense of unpreparedness would settle, and I'd feel safe again. What was once was my greatest fear, now was my singular hope.

I woke early the following morning, and every other morning, for the next month, grabbed the little green notebook from its hiding place behind a false back on my jewelry box, and wandered out to the farthest nook of the palace ground. I did my best to go before dawn, when the air, turning crisp from autumn, was at its coldest. Lenya's notes were thorough enough to give a general comprehensive knowledge of how to establish a connection with my magic.

The affinities were split into two rough categories: conceptual and elemental. For elemental types, there was a certain degree of connection with the element required. While his notes focused on ice specifically, I imagined the same was required of fire, nature, water, and storms.

I hoped I'd be able to meet an actual Storm Wielder, since aspects of weather control appeared more complex than manipulation over temperature and movement of frozen particles. It seemed, though, that our kingdom was doing a particularly good job with keeping any well-trained and powerful entities out of the country. Something I had once been thankful for now had become more of a hindrance than an asset.

I stood alone in a small grove of trees, my breath billowing in front of my face. Glancing down at the pages in my hand, I stepped out of my shoes and allowed my bare feet to make contact with the cold ground. The sensation felt calm and soothing, as it always had, and I could now identify that as a tether to the affinity, however, I still couldn't seem to delve beyond that single thread to establish a deeper connection. Inessa had assured me that the small amount of plant manipulation she could harness had taken a long while to establish, under Maggie's guidance. Apparently it wasn't uncommon for Wielders who were late in coming into their abilities to struggle with ever establishing a strong and firm control over their magic.

But, as I curled my toes into the dew-dampened, peaty ground,

I couldn't help but feel like a failure for still having no progress to show for my efforts. Not so much as a single snowflake. I hung my head in defeat as the sun rose above the mountain studded horizon.

"What am I doing wrong?" I puffed in frustration. "Maybe Ice just isn't willing to come. Should I try focusing on Storm and Stars instead? Ugh."

I groaned loudly and grabbed my head, creasing the papers as I did so. I wondered if I had done something wrong in my mentalscape when I had initially met the pieces of my personified magic. Perhaps if I could take another injection, I could reenter the head space to form a deeper, less hesitant connection and make greater headway. As I was now, there was nothing I could do to aid in any emergency situation, and the perpetual helplessness gnawed at me.

Giving up, I trudged across the grounds, the sun now rising with the rest of the palace stirring to life. My feet were heavy, almost to the point of stomping, at my inability to execute my lessons as I made my way to my room and slammed the notebook back into its special hiding place.

"Well, that doesn't sound promising," Inessa commented as she clipped on her earrings.

"I can't get anything to work, and I'm starting to think these abilities are just a fluke that were stirred up by the injection you gave me, never to be seen or heard from again!" I groused, changing quickly into my attire to traverse around town handling committee affairs. "I need to eat something."

"I think you might just be overthinking it all. These elemental powers we have aren't something you can solve like a sum or quantify in an essay. Learning isn't the same as being studious. It's something you have to feel."

"Then why am I not feeling it?"

"Perhaps when the moment is right, your body will know and you will feel it then." Ina wagged her finger at me. "A watched kettle never boils."

"Your platitudes are of no use to me."

"My, you've gotten rather feisty since you've started on this little inner journey of yours," Inessa laughed, unscathed by my terse words.

"I'm sorry, Ina."

She leaned over and rested a hand on my shoulder, giving it a quick squeeze. "It'll come."

I sat at my vanity for a while after Inessa left the room, staring at my reflection. Focusing in on my own silver eyes, I searched for some lingering evidence that my experience in my mindscape hadn't just been a dream or regret-fueled delusion. But the irises were without splendor, cold and gray as a winter morning, just the same as they always were. It had been a few months since Otvel's warning to me, and I hadn't had any other strange interactions with him, only speaking when in the company of others or at church. Something in the quiet was almost more unsettling, and the feeling of squandering the allotted elongated time before the other shoe inevitably dropped with my ineptitude was eating me alive.

I shook my head, closed my eyes, and took a deep centering breath before rising to my feet and exiting to the hall. When I rounded the first corner, I nearly barreled straight into a footman, steadfast in reaching whatever destination he was heading towards.

"My apologies, Highness!" He bent over and, staying at a right angle, offered me an envelope.

"That's quite alright, Saarlon," I assured, accepting the letter. "What is this?"

"It arrived with the Imperial and Federation Marshal emblems just a bit ago, Grand Princess." Saarlon's eyes stretched wide as moons at my addressing him by name, and I recalled he had not been in our employ long. Likely he'd yet to have many personal encounters with us.

"Thank you, that sounds like it might be from my father. Or someone in his regiment," I mused. "I wonder why it is posted to me directly… Are you sure this was meant for me?"

"Grand Princess Sorrel?" The poor man posed it as a question, the absolute terror that he'd somehow mixed me up with one of my sisters written plainly on his face.

"Yes, that is correct then." I flipped the envelope over to see my name scrawled on the parchment, then cracked the seal and pulled out a succinct message from Papa.

My dearest, lovely Sorrel,

I hope this letter finds you well in health and mind. I wish I were writing this on better terms, but I'm afraid I have some saddening news to relay. As of Sept. 8th, it has been brought to my attention that Sergeant Hykner has been listed as missing in action. I know he was one of the top men in your regiment and often accompanied you as a personal guard. As a courtesy, I felt it important to share this disheartening news. A good soldier lost should always be mourned. With that in mind, the role of a personal guard should be permanently filled at your earliest discretion as a stand-in is no longer required.

I know you will do your due diligence to find a trustworthy replacement. Please wish your mother and sisters well. I will write a more detailed letter to all of you from me and your brother as soon as I have a spare moment.

My love to you all my darling family,
Papa.

"Missing in action?" I breathed aloud, the air being driven from my lungs. Hykner was far more important than just any other personal guard. "Saarlon?" I called, lowering the page to see he was still standing in the same place, clearly waiting for some sort of formal dismissal.

"Highness." He straightened his posture, curling his fingers earnestly.

"Please go find my sister, Inessa— Grand Princess Inessa. If she isn't on the premises, send someone to fetch her home immediately. This is important."

"Right away!"

"Wait! Roland— um, Lord Minister Roland Rusev too." I scrunched my nose, not even certain I'd relayed his title properly. "Send him as well. Tell them both I will meet them in the library."

"On my way!"

"Sorry, Saarlon?" I called him back a third time. "Please have Dowels or Larkin do the appropriate procedures to notify my appointments that I will be delayed." This time Saarlon hesitated, and I smiled apologetically. "That's all."

"Consider it done, Highness!"

I watched him hurry away to complete his task and headed straight to the library, hoping by some chance Roland wasn't in a meeting and instead was reading a book inside. Instead, as I stepped through the doorway, I found Yulia sitting at a desk, writing in one of her new journals from Papa.

"Good morning, Sorrel," she called over to me, not bothering to look up.

"Good morning," I hailed halfheartedly back, ducking through the shelves towards the back. Perhaps I should have chosen a more private location to speak with Inessa. I knew Roland and Hykner were friends, so I figured it'd be best to tell them both together, but I was doubting my decision with each passing moment. I paced up and down the back aisle, crinkling Papa's letter in my sweating palm. I had always been partial to Hykner as a soldier and a guard, but after he'd helped me with Darion, even going so far as to lift my spirits from the depths of despair, I couldn't get the twisting in my gut to ease. This loss would be felt by many, but still no one more than my sister.

I ran over countless ways to phrase the news in my head, trying to find the best option. I even tried to think of which delivery would be the least painful if I were in her shoes. Unfortunately, I knew there was no simple, painless way to relay this information.

"Did you have a break through?" Inessa's face was bright and animated as she rushed up to me. Her eager disposition made my mouth go dry, and I fumbled with the letter in my hand.

"Ina," I started shakily, then began again, this time more

composed as Inessa sobered immediately. "I received a notice from Papa."

"Is everything alright? Are him and Theo—"

"They are both fine," I interrupted and held out the creased page. "Papa notified me that Hykner was recently declared missing in action."

"What?" Inessa took a step back blinking rapidly like she was trying to wake herself up from a dream. "Why would Papa send you a personal notice about a random officer? There must be some confusion."

"Hykner wasn't just an average soldier, Ina." I offered her the page again and this time she snatched it out of my hand. I continued gently, "he was a prominent member of my regiment whom I often used as personal guard— especially after the incident with Vadia at the hospital. I... I'm sorry."

"Missing. Missing doesn't mean *dead*. It's not the same thing," She insisted, her eyes welling. "Don't speak like he's dead."

"Of course, Ina. There is no reason to give up hope for his safe return, but it also seemed prudent to notify you as soon as possible. I thought you'd want to know."

Inessa took another step backward, shaking her head. "He will return home. He... He promised he'd come back safely, so he's going to come back no matter what."

"I'm sure he's kept his word to the best of his abilities, but if something were amiss—"

"Don't patronize me with your pity, Sorrel. Just because Papa wrote you a direct letter and goes on and on about how responsible you always are, it doesn't make you my superior."

"Ina, I'm not—"

"I need some air." Inessa turned and fled the library.

After her rage at the world and all its unfairness ebbed, she would no doubt descend into an isolated despair, and I'd be able to help her then when she was ready to receive it. I retrieved the discarded letter from the ground and did my best to fold it neatly.

"You summoned me, Snowdrop?" Roland announced his

presence. He paused then rushed forward and grabbed onto where I held the folded letter, staring at it. "What's wrong?"

"Hykner is missing. I just told Ina."

"That explains her state when I passed her in the hall."

"She's angry."

"Missing, eh? How long?"

"September eighth." I looked up at Roland and saw him flinch at the date.

"It's nearly October."

"I know."

"That doesn't bode well…"

"I know."

"But that's not to say it isn't possible that he's still alive out there. He's a resilient man. For now, we can share in the hope that he will turn up."

"I do hope so. For both their sakes. Poor Inessa." I leaned against the shelves and slid to the ground, all the energy evaporating from my body, reducing me to a puddle of sympathy. "I can't imagine what she must be feeling."

"I can," Roland sighed, plunking himself down beside me. "At least a little."

"You can?"

"The moment that floor gave way between us at the inn until the moment I reached you on the ground." He shifted closer to me and grabbed my hand in his. "I had no idea if you had made it out or where you were. It was the most terrifying experience of my entire life."

"The hospital ride on Kira's last birthday might have been mine," I murmured and tentatively leaned my head on his shoulder. "I was so afraid I would lose you that night."

"You won't lose me, Snowdrop." Roland rested his head on mine and inhaled deeply. "Even if the Divinities themselves— even if Dimaer tried to take me away, I'd find some way back to you. Nothing could stop me."

"Likewise, Roland." I paused and bit my lip. "I only wish we lived in a world where we didn't have to make such promises to each other and know there was a good chance we may have to follow through on them."

"I'd make that promise anyway. I…" Roland faltered beneath a wistful tone and curled his fingers tighter around mine. "I hope you know, that this hasn't all just been some sort of infatuation to pass the time for me. It never has been."

"Roland," I started, turning to look up at his face, but he swallowed hard and continued on, his heart thundering against my shoulder.

"I know I've never made myself clear in so many words. But, if something were to ever happen to you or to me, if we found ourselves in Ina and Hykner's shoes, I suppose I'd just want to make sure you knew what you mean to me."

"And what do I mean to you?" I scarcely heard the question pass through my lips.

"You have been my greatest endeavor and the love of my life, Sorrel. As long as I can remember, it's always been you."

Roland reached into his jacket as I stared, speechless. He pulled out a small folded paper and I immediately recognized it as the letter from the time capsule. Pinching it between his fingers with a soft chuckle, he lifted it between our locked gazes.

"This was a good reminder to me. Don't pretend like you and your sisters didn't all read it, I know you did."

"Only parts of it," I laughed, warmth enveloping me from head to toe. "The rest was smudged."

"Well, I made such a fuss about not messing up, and holding on to you in this letter, it reminded me that I can't hang onto what isn't mine."

"I've always been yours, Roland. I always will be." I felt my cheeks turning numb from the shameless grin spreading wider and wider across my face.

"I am yours, Snowdrop," Roland echoed, pressing his forehead to mine, lines creasing around his eyes in the biggest smile I think I'd ever seen him wear. "And I always will be."

I reached up and traced my finger along the sharp cut of his jaw, pausing when I reached his chin. My gaze shifted to his mouth, and I brushed my thumb lightly over his bottom lip.

"Tempt me not, Snowdrop," he groaned. "We are in a library, and I can confidently say nothing scholarly will come of touching me like that."

"The temptation runs both ways you know," I admitted bashfully. "When you look at me like that, and call me the love of your life. How am I meant to react?"

"Under more private circumstances, I'd certainly be willing to explore this reaction further, however," he jerked his head towards the front of the library. "Your sister with particularly keen hearing is over there, and I'd rather not give her the wrong idea. I've already run the risk of having a very vulnerable and direct confession overheard."

"You make a fair point," I sighed and dropped my hand back into my lap. "I need to go find Inessa anyway." I stood and clasped my hands together in a demure gesture. "I guess I'll have to save mine for later."

"Save what?"

Unclasping my hands, I tapped one finger against my ear and brought the other to my mouth in the sign for a secret. "*My* confession."

Then, I spun around and whisked myself out of the library, somehow feeling heavy as lead and lighter than air by the unexpected juxtaposing turn of events of the day.

"Bye, Yulia," I called as I passed, and I caught her small smirk in a blur.

"Bye, Sorrel."

THIRTY-EIGHT

The bells of the church clanged through the air. From our seats, high in the balcony of the cathedral, the rest of the congregation appeared to filter out like grains of sand through an hourglass. I'd only half heartedly listened to the sermon, my mind wandering to other places.

My sympathy for Inessa's loss without closure warred against my own internal giddiness over Roland's declaration. I kept thinking over both the highs and the lows of yesterday, receding from the present moment.

I stiffened as my daydreams came to a grinding halt as Otvel approached our group. This wasn't an unusual proceeding for after service activities, but the dark look in his eye as it passed over me set my teeth on edge. I looked around me, trying to shrink away, but no matter where I shifted myself around the room, Otvel kept his gaze trained on my whereabouts.

Feeling like I was being caged in, I tried to hug the edge of the room and edge towards the exit, but before I made much progress,

Otvel had broken away and intercepted me from behind. He grabbed onto my arm to hold me back. His eyes were blazing with an ominous fire of reproach, making me struggle to rip myself free of his grasp and stumble a few steps backwards.

"Excuse you," I snipped. "Do not grab me in such a manner."

"You've been avoiding me." He admonished, glancing around to confirm no one had taken notice of our exchange. "Ever since your brother was ill, you've moved mountains to make sure our paths have only crossed when absolutely necessary. My patience has reached its limit. You've been keeping secrets. Ones I know you'd much rather I discuss with you in private rather than in an audience of your family."

"I have no idea what you're talking about," I bluffed.

"Is that so?" He threw the pages of my notebook at my feet, and turned away.

"How did you get these?" I gasped, scrambling to collect them and tuck them into my dress, all pretenses of denial gone.

"Something the maid came across when she knocked over a jewelry box with a false back, and thought it best to notify her priest. She did you a mercy by telling me instead of any other authority figure."

"Somehow I'm finding that difficult to believe."

"Believe what you will. If you recall, I paid you a warning months ago to get out while you still could. Before I had the chance to piece it all together without room for delusion. I'm not sure I can afford a second act of willful negligence to my station."

"You've been keeping secrets too, it seems." I narrowed my eyes. "Some unsanctioned activity, burying the truth. I know things too, Otvel."

A look of confusion passed over him, but sharpened back to a razored edge. We stood staring at one another for several heartbeats, sizing the other up for the severity of their harmful knowledge. I hoped that I was convincing in my composure, and wasn't revealing the liquefying sensation inside my body as it flooded with dread.

Otvel cracked a smile and tilted his head. "We once sat and talked of the Virtues of the Divine. I told you that corruption doesn't discriminate, and one must not waver when enacting justice as an act of mercy. Did you heed that lesson?"

"I found my own interpretation of the intentions of the Divine Virtues, one where compassion doesn't lead to death."

"If you ever take anything away from our time together, then I hope you will hear this: compassion without balance of hard resolve will only ever lead to antipathy and destruction. If compassion is the thread that ties us all together, then resolve is the needle that stitches it all down. Without both, the world as we know it unravels."

"I'm no longer bound by your ideologies, Otvel," I rolled my shoulders back and lifted my chin. "I've learned to think, see, and act for myself, and I will never go back to being dumb, blind, and paralyzed again."

"Be careful of the promises you make. The Divinities will come to test those who make idle vows."

"I do not make idle vows."

"We will see."

"What are you going to do now? Expose us?" I folded my arms.

"I have not yet prepared the next move, but for all your years of ignorant innocence and diligence to that of good, I decided to pay you the respect of knowing my findings. You can never be too certain who is waiting to pull the rug out from under you."

"Sorrel?" Roland came to stand beside me, immediately picking up on my defensive posture.

Otvel looked him up and down and smirked. "Like I said, it always pays to be careful."

"Chinye! If you have a moment," Friedrich waved to Otvel from down the pew. "There are some matters I wanted to discuss with you."

"Father was watching," Roland whispered in my ear as Otvel gave a small bow and walked away. "He saw Otvel and the notebook. How'd he get his hands on that?"

"I swear I hid it, but one of the maids found it. Things are cracking at the seams, Roland," I hissed back. "What do we do?"

"I'm not sure."

"Roland."

"I'm not. Not yet anyway."

"I was supposed to drop off more medical supplies today. I need to go, but I'm afraid Otvel will have eyes on me."

Roland looked over his shoulder towards where the two were heading out the door. "Looks like my father is heading home with him."

"That's not necessarily a comfort. He was saying all sorts of things about being thankful that the maid handed over the notebook to him and not some other authority. What do you think that was supposed to mean? What if he says something to your father?"

"Father is shrewd, but he has always been relatively collected. I can't imagine him reacting impulsively without at least having a conversation to assess the claim's legitimacy."

"Sorrel, are you walking back with us?" Kira called over to me, gesturing to where Mama, Inessa, and Yulia stood waiting expectantly.

"Didn't you have an errand to run?" Inessa offered me an out, smiling innocently. All misplaced anger gone for the good of the cause.

I nodded. "I did— I mean yes, I do. Do you want to come with me, Ina?"

"Roland can go with you, can't he? It shouldn't be a long endeavor, I imagine."

"I don't mind," Roland acknowledged.

"Alright, you two. We will see you at home. Don't be gone too long. We are having lunch at two."

"I'll go ahead and get us a car, see you out front," Roland said and peeled away. I said goodbye to my family and followed them outside into the glare of the beating sun, where Roland was already waiting by our car as promised. I hopped inside, and Roland leaned forward. "To the Piren Hospital, please."

"Can you take these?" I asked, pulling the crumpled pages of the notebook out and offering them to Roland. "I don't have any pockets."

"Hand them over. I'm not sure we will be needing a new hiding place, but on the off chance we do, then it might be better for me to hang onto this, for the time being, anyway."

I relinquished the pages with a small sting of disappointment that I'd already failed to keep my learnings a secret in such a short amount of time. Meanwhile, Roland had stayed in the clear for years. Even Inessa, as emotionally led as she was, had yet to be caught by anyone other than me.

"Don't worry," Roland said. "We will figure this all out."

We arrived at the hospital, where I was able to slip in and acquire the supplies, and dropped them off at an old clinic location for Maggie to retrieve. I picked absently at my nails as we started the course back to the palace.

"The streets seem unusually empty, don't you think?" Roland commented, peering around the city as we puttered along.

"I suppose so." I nodded and stayed focused on my fingers.

"Listen, when we get home, I'll go find my father and see—" Roland paused as the car came to a halt. "What, why have we stopped?"

"Apologies," The chauffeur called to us. "I'm afraid I can't go any further. The road is blocked."

"Blocked?" I leaned forward. "Blocked by what?"

"Looks like a group of people. I can try and back out but it looks like more are gathering behind us. We might be here a while."

"How peculiar. We aren't far from the palace, we can walk the last leg."

"Are you certain it's safe?" The man asked, and I looked to Roland. His brows were knitting together as he took in the growing assembly.

"I think it might end up being better for all of us if we aren't here," Roland replied. The chauffeur nodded with understanding. "Do what you need to, to keep yourself safe. Drive around a while, or park."

My muscles tensed as a roaring sound grazed my ears. Goosebumps rippled over my arms, and I gripped hard onto the handle of the door, bracing myself before pushing it open and stepping out into the street.

I gasped as a sea of jeering bodies stretched farther than my eyes could see. Based on their ranting, I worried they would be of the same mentality as those who had attacked us at the theater, only this time it wasn't a small band of criminals. It was the heart of the regular people banding together against the throne.

"No," Roland swallowed and rubbed his chin. "This isn't a protest or rally. This is turning into a full blown revolution. I don't know what you remember from history lessons, but those rarely turn out well for our side."

"We need to get back home as quickly as possible." I tried to slink away inconspicuously, but it seemed our attempt to slip away unnoticed was thwarted before we had a chance to even try it.

"Look there! A couple of aristocrats. Get them!" A group of men locked eyes on us and veered away from the advancing throng of protesters.

"Run, Sorrel!" Roland barked, shoving me in front of him.

I did as I was told, picking up my skirt and breaking into a full sprint away from the area. I bobbed and weaved through the empty street, looking for routes that might conceal me enough to break away. I realized after a growl of exasperation from Roland that a wedge had been driven between us, separating us into two separate escape paths. I slowed my steps to try and stay together, but he waved me on.

"Don't stop! Keep running. I'll catch up."

I nodded and continued onward, managing to keep ahead of the men charging after me for a while, but their pursuit didn't let up no matter how I seemed to flee. My lungs were burning, and I could tell that my pace was slowing, fatigue claiming my legs.

I looked wildly around the alley I'd veered into as the men were right behind me, closing in. There was only one exit, and in my mad dash for safety, I was no longer certain where the output of the route would take me. I needed to head for the grounds, but I couldn't very well lead my pursuers to the secret entrance, and heading deeper into the city was also a poor option. I'd have to hope that Roland had paid better attention to his whereabouts and would find his way back to me. Glancing over my shoulder, I let out a startled scream as a hand reached out and grabbed hold of me.

I was pushed to the ground, my face pressing into the gravel. I flailed under the weight of the attacker. The riot was growing beyond the alley, and I fought in vain to free myself. My nails dug into the cracks between the cobblestones, and the desperation felt overwhelming as my body screamed for relief.

"You little bitch," The man above me sneered and pushed harder against me. I fought to grasp at my Ice affinity, my only hope of self defense in that moment, but couldn't harness a single snowflake. "How does it feel down there on the ground?"

"You're about to find out if you don't get off of her *right now*," I jolted with relief at the sound of Roland's voice. His words held a growl that was low and dangerous, nothing like the typical diplomat I knew. "I'll put you one foot into the ground for every scratch I find on her."

"Come try it, pompous trash," The man laughed. "You might get your hands dirty."

"It's your funeral," Roland scoffed. I heard a couple of rapid footsteps followed by a series of wooden *clacks* and *thunks* before the pressure on my back released, and I pushed myself up from the ground, gasping for air.

"Sorrel, get out of here," Roland shouted at me. "Before the riot grows any more. You know the way back, I'll be right behind you."

I took a moment to get my bearings and realized Roland had

grabbed hold of a broom handle, wielding it like a sword against my attacker. The man was now lying unconscious beside me, and a few of his friends were advancing. The nearest one reached out to grab hold of me as I tried to scramble to my feet, but Roland was faster.

"Don't you dare touch her." The handle came down hard against the attacker's arm with a crack. At the same time, Roland pivoted off the momentum of the strike to take a guarded stance in front of where I was rising to my feet.

My chest heaved with labored breathing, and my head pulsed with pain as blood dripped into my eye. I reached up to dab at the wound, still a bit dazed from the impact of my skull against the ground, and wiped the blood and grit from my broken lips onto my sleeve.

I blinked through the haziness and started to run away as Roland had instructed me, but was tripped as someone tossed a spinning rope around my legs. My palms scraped against the ground, and my knees collided painfully with the stone for a second time.

I swore and rolled over onto my back to untangle my ankles. In another flurry of movement, Roland broke the handle over his knee and stabbed one of the jagged ends into the rope-thrower's bicep. I flinched against his cry of pain, but didn't hesitate in my second attempt at escape. It was clear these citizens weren't interested in peace. Instead, they were reveling in the false sense of control their violence gave them. They weren't going to show me and Roland mercy, so I couldn't afford them any in return.

"I said, *don't touch her.* Let me make it perfectly clear here," Roland spread his arms out to either side of him, giving a small bow. "Anyone else who tries to harm her, I *will* kill you. That's a promise."

I was taken aback by the ferocity of his threatening words, but what was even more surprising was the adept way in which he was fighting. I'd never seen Roland fight in all my life, so I couldn't fathom where the skill set had come from.

"We need to take him down first, then we can get a hold of her," A large man shouted at his remaining cohorts.

Roland didn't wait for them to advance for a third time, and instead chose to rush to the center of the haphazard congregation. He quickly knocked three unconscious with the dull end of the handle, a couple of quick taps to their temples did the trick. But the final man, who had called out the order to grab me again, Roland looked at like a predator finding his prey. The man sensed the danger his words had put him in. Roland had him pinned to the wall by his throat, the length of the broken handle pressing just beneath his chin.

"Did you know it only takes a minimum of thirty-three pounds of force to crush a grown man's trachea? But why bother with that? Count yourself lucky I didn't give you the chance to make good on your threat, or I'd have driven the end through your throat," Roland sneered before knocking the man out with a single punch. I stood there staring at the aftermath in awe as Roland strode back over to me, flicking the collateral blood from his knuckles with a subtle flex of his hand. "Let's go. We need to get out of here before more people notice us."

"Wait! Don't let them get away," One of the persistent goons called out, waving more from the mob who'd followed our chase over.

Roland swore and discarded the broom handle. He quickly retrieved his revolver, shoving me behind him and he aimed at the advancing men. "Stay back, or I will fire."

"He's bluffing!" Someone jeered, and Roland's jaw clenched.

"I tried to do this the easy way, but you will force my hand if you keep pressing us."

A man bolted from the growing line of taunting bystanders across from us, and Roland pulled the trigger, the loud gravely boom making me cover my ringing ears. Roland shoved me into motion again and we fled from the rapidly chaotic scene.

"Did you shoot him?" I gasped.

"No, just at the ground by his feet to cause a distraction."

"How did you learn to fight like that? With the broom. We don't train our soldiers to fight like that. You took on five men by yourself!" I didn't know whether to be impressed or slightly afraid of the beast hidden beneath that cool facade.

"They were clumsy, untrained, unarmed, and Rafe taught me some Dezidaneyan fighting techniques when we were boys. I didn't execute them as well as he would have, but I didn't forget the steps," Roland huffed with a smirk, like he was talking about remembering the steps to a dance.

"I've never seen you like that before," I murmured.

"I couldn't fight that fire with my fists, but rest assured, I would have fought it to the death had it been an option, if it meant keeping you safe."

Gunfire cracked through the air again, but this time for the direction of the initial crowd outside the palace, and I froze mid step. "Are the soldiers firing into the crowd?" I gasped in horror. "They can't do that!"

"Evidently, someone told them they could," Roland replied. "Or they heard my gun go off and got the wrong idea… Come on. Let's try and put a stop to this before things get any worse."

Taking the safest route back to the palace, we used the secret passage through the hedges and sprinted through the grounds towards the source of the commotion, entering from the back servant's entrance. We kept our brisk pace as we moved through the ground floor, racing desperately for the courtyard to call off the soldiers. However, we wouldn't make it that far. We shouldered our way through the doors to the dining hall and stopped dead in our tracks.

"Father?" Roland croaked in disbelief, and I covered my mouth as my stomach lurched.

"I'm afraid it had to be done and I will explain everything." Friedrich rose to his feet, his hands held up in a sign of no-harm. The knife he held clattered to his feet next to the blood pooling on the planks beside him.

"What have you done?" Mama screamed as she entered the

room behind us. Shouldering her way past, she rushed to the fallen body of Otvel, his eyes staring sightlessly up at the ceiling. "Friedrich, what have you done?"

"To intentionally enact tragedy upon another
is the difference between man and beast."
-D

THIRTY-NINE

"He knew, Geneva. He was ready to reveal it all."

"Mama, what does he mean?" I stepped forward.

"Watch what you say, Friedrich," Mama snapped. But Friedrich fixed me and Roland with a knowing look.

"I think these two know more than they've been letting on."

I looked at Roland, panting. We had our backs against a wall, and I was at a loss of what to do. Roland furrowed his brows and gave a short, curt bow towards our parents.

"Forgive me, I know this is an important matter, but we've just come from the city and a protest has turned riotous. Soldiers fired into the crowd, I'm on my way to take care of it."

"I'll go with him," I tried to grasp hold of the rope to leave, but my attempt was quickly thwarted.

"Sorrel, you stay behind," Mama commanded sharply, whipping around to face me.

"I'll be back, Snowdrop," Roland whispered, then made a dash for the courtyard.

"Explain yourself. What does Friedrich mean? What do you know?"

"I... I..." I stammered, shrinking away from the intensity of my mother's anger.

"Stop stuttering and someone start explaining to me what is going on!" She bellowed, and I flinched against the sound as it echoed through the empty hall. "Explain to me why you look like you've been crawling through the gutter, with cuts and bruises, and why my Head Priest is lying dead at my feet in our dining hall!"

"Roland and I got chased coming home. One of them got a hold of me but Roland fought them all off before any real damage was done," I babbled, wanting nothing more than to flee the room and my mother's wrath.

Layered emotions were warring within me, and I wasn't sure how much longer my legs would hold me. Relief at Otvel's permanent silence twisted with guilt at his demise. Confusion thundered in my already aching skull as to what would drive Friedrich, of all people, to commit such an act as murder. And fear of the peace and sanctity I had once known fragmenting away beneath my feet had sunk its claws into my entire body, overwhelming everything else.

"And this," Mama whirled around on Friedrich gesturing hysterically at Otvel, her attention diverting since it was clear I was out of immediate harm.

"You know, don't you, Sorrel?" Friedrich addressed me, his voice quiet. I held my breath trying to come up with a clever lie or diversion to the question.

"Sorrel?" Mama prompted, her initial heightened frenzy calming and falling away to an eerie stillness.

I knew Friedrich was referring to the Wielder lineage my family carried. By the way he spoke with Mama, it seemed evident enough to me that not only was Friedrich privy to the sensitive information, but so was she. It wasn't just Papa holding onto the secret for this generation.

"I know," I replied at last.

"Know *what?*" Mama pressed, her back straightening with clarity.

"I know the truth about our ancestry. I know that none of us are mortals."

Mama stared at me, her jaw trembling and her eyes slowly stretching wider and wider. She swayed on her feet, falling back into the chair. "This isn't good, Friedrich. This is very bad. With this many people knowing, it's going to be a repeat of last time with Sylvia. My own ancestral ties to Western Kataheyda aside, it's Genri's lineage that will be the most devastating."

"Aunt Sylvia?" I echoed the name of my late aunt, whom we rarely spoke of, in confusion. "Did she know before too? Did Papa tell her?"

"He told all four of us, and ultimately that knowledge led to her demise." Mama's explanation was vague and clipped, offering nothing truly informative.

"Not just hers." Friedrich's skin paled beneath a dark grimace, as phantoms of another time danced inside his head.

"No, not just hers," Mama acknowledged, sympathy flashing in her gaze. "The secret is dangerous Sorrel, and is exactly why it was only ever meant to be passed from one heir to the next— and only as a precautionary measure. So, things like this never have to happen."

I stood frozen, unsure of what to do. I didn't know whether to dismiss myself and leave Mama and Friedrich to sort through whatever veiled reference they were making, or to engage and try to comfort my mother.

She gestured to Otvel and dropped her head in her hands. "Everything is going wrong. We've killed a *priest*. How do we come back from this? From all of it! The damn protests, the tests, the war. Genri should be *here*. We were never supposed to join in this war we have no business being in. Blasted Vatra and Videiria just wouldn't let it rest. This was never supposed to happen, it was never supposed to be put on my shoulders."

"I'm sorry about Chinye, Geneva. But what other choice did I have? He was threatening Sorrel at the church and was threatening to expose us all for this. If he was successful, it would have made our losses back then all for nothing."

"You're right, Friedrich. If Otvel was truly willing to betray us in such an intentionally harmful way, then he had to go. I just hope…" Mama's face reddened with emotion, and puckered under a fresh wave of tears. She dabbed idly at her cheeks, trying to wipe them away and compose herself. "Well, what's done is done. I just have to pray the Divinities take mercy on us and provide for Theodorvin."

"We need a plan. Something to subdue the protests before they turn more violent. If we lose our people we are little more than squatters in a very expensive home in *their* city." Friedrich collapsed into his chair, his blood-tinged hand trembling.

Once more, I felt heavy in my unprecedented presence in matters far beyond my depth. I willed myself to move, but my feet stayed rooted in place, transfixed by curiosity and mortification. I nearly jumped out of my skin when Mama's steely glare of discernment roved over me.

"Do your siblings know, Sorrel?"

I hesitated, unsure how to answer the question. I'd done so much lying and secret keeping in the wings of my mother's world as of late, what was one more to spare Inessa's innocence? However, I hadn't had to outright lie to her face so directly, and despite all of the independence I had garnered, I felt compelled to tell the truth.

"I'm not sure what all they collectively know." The half truth left my lips confidently, and I pressed them together, clenching my teeth. "I've come by my own knowledge."

"And my son?" Friedrich sighed.

"I know as well," Roland announced, stepping briskly back into the room. His hair was mussed and the knuckles along his right hand were showing the bruises of his earlier altercation. "It's a secret we've held together for everyone's well being."

And Inessa. I added silently, not daring to speak the admission aloud. She was struggling enough to keep her head up, wiping tears shed for Hykner every time she thought no one was looking. It was like she had chipped under the insurmountable weight of her grief and it was only a matter of time before she broke completely.

"Well done. This wasn't your secret to share. And the discretion has put us right in the position we need to be." Friedrich nodded his approval to Roland then glanced mournfully at Otvel's body, still pooling blood on the floor. "You never know just who you can really trust until all the cards are down on the table. Nobody wants to lose their gamble in the game."

"We need to do something about…" I gestured to the fallen priest, sneaking a peek over my shoulder at the clock. "I think this would be much harder to explain to an audience."

"We will do the same as before," Mama announced, rising confidently with all the elegance of her station as empress. "Otvel was killed in an altercation surrounding the recent protests. Friedrich tried to save him but it was too late. Thankfully, he was able to dispatch his attacker. We will never speak further about what happened in this room."

I stifled a startled gasp at the ease in which my mother fabricated a new truth to cover murder so easily.

"If I may," Roland jumped in. "The gathering out there is not good. Quite frankly, with the soldiers' hasty trigger fingers, the tide is turning and simply blaming the reaction on a 'provoked assault on our priest' might just stoke the flames of revolution. The brutes who got their hands on Sorrel today could have easily killed her had I not been there. They are angry. Furious. We need to quell that storm as soon as possible or wait for them to get organized enough to storm the palace."

Mama blanched and looked at her feet. Her fingers curled into a tight fist, and she closed her eyes. "Genri, I need you home."

"The people are mostly angry about the whole testing program Chinye developed to identify Wielder blood in the people, correct?" Roland took a breath and looked around at the four of us. "What can we do to solve that?"

"Cease the tests," I replied, trying not to smile with relief. If we could turn this terrible situation in our favor and halt the hunting and persecution of the Wielders, it would help our cause greatly and settle the unrest.

Friedrich waved a finger thoughtfully. "That might seem like an empty gesture brought on by fear of the people. We want to show them we respect them." He stood and started pacing back and forth. "What if we showed them solidarity first."

"How so?" Mama asked, the desperation for guidance thick in her voice.

"If we can stage a false injection on the royal family, then it might show the people that no one is above the cost of justice, and that no one is exempt from the process we started."

"That seems like an awfully big risk!" I gasped, my hand instinctively reaching for the place where Inessa had pricked me and awakened my powers.

"Think about it. We gather an assembly, make a promise, show our cooperation, stand behind the decisions issued by our emperor, the results show no Wielder affinities in your bloodline, and the whole secret can be put to rest once and for all."

"We don't know if Chinye had followers whom he told the secret to," Roland mused, leaning a hand on one of the dining chairs. "If they try and expose it in his stead, this would serve as a sort of proof, preemptively."

"We've seen how that drug reacts. The people know how it reacts, what it looks like— everything. How are we supposed to fake that all up close?" I asked.

"Can you manage a safe replica, Friedrich?" Mama bit her thumb, eyes glazed and wild, like a caged animal.

"I believe so. I'll just need the day and we can arrange this for tomorrow."

"I don't think—" I tried to reason once more but was cut short.

"You two may go." Mama looked sharply at us. It was an order, not a suggestion. "Make yourselves scarce while we sort the rest of this out. Let the others know lunch was canceled. I have to manage the damage done out front. Friedrich, I trust you'll take care of the injection to stage a mortal reaction."

"I'll personally oversee the arrangements for tomorrow and make sure everything performs to the letter as it should."

"With all due respect to you both, are you really certain that adding more secrets is the way to go on this? I understand the timing, but it could be an opportunity to start mending rather than hiding," Roland rolled his shoulders back, and looked candidly from Mama to Friedrich.

I nodded imploringly. "If we just take a bit more time to think this through with clearer heads…"

Mama rose abruptly to her feet, slamming her hands on the table, and glared at us. Her silver eyes glittered, frustration and fear turning them to blades of steel. The aftermath of our mutual secrecy wasn't over yet, and she was through indulging me. Her trust in me had been severed and, in truth, mine in her had also been damaged despite my familial love.

"Tonight, we will let the girls know about the display tomorrow. We will hold it in the city courtyard just behind the palace, and I will get word to Genri immediately. He and Theo should come home as soon as possible while we handle this and lay Otvel to rest as our beloved friend and priest. We won't tell the children about him just yet."

"As you wish," Roland conceded under a clenched jaw. He bowed and headed for the door. I opened my mouth, feeling like I was slipping through quicksand— a million grains of misgiving dragging me down and suffocating me. Not even we could openly defy or sabotage a direct order from our empress.

"Go. Keep the others busy and send Dowels in. He's the only one we can trust to help with the body," Mama commanded and I was forced to dip my head and comply. "I'll see you at dinner."

"Yes, Mama."

FORTY

The rest of the day dragged on both painfully slow and agonizingly quick. Roland had been called away by his father, so I hadn't had a chance to confront him about my fear at this poorly thought out plan. I'd shared the news with Inessa, warning her that Mama might catch on to her own involvement. Then we all sat at the dining table, in the same hall where, hours earlier, Otvel had bled out from a neck wound. My eyes kept wandering over to the spot, looking to glean some small spec of blood that would show the foul play and end of a life, but not so much as a single drop remained. I barely touched my food, pushing it around on my plate just enough to make it look like I'd eaten a portion before the servers removed it.

I suffered through the after dinner drinks, somehow managing to smile along and make small talk. Mercifully, Mama brought the socializing to an end, reminding us we had a big day with a public appearance, and we should all get plenty of rest. Roland bid me a brisk goodnight and practically fled the room, leaving me no chance to discuss my reservations with him. His absence only tightened the knot in my stomach.

Of course, sleep was the farthest thing from my mind. Ina had openly expressed her distaste for the deceptive plan, even going so far as to challenge Mama's decision before we headed to bed. Just the same as she had dismissed me, Mama had refused Inessa's protests and questions, leaving her with little choice but to comply. Too worn out from a mixture of lingering grief and fresh worry, Ina was little company, so we both just existed in silence, watching the roaring fire burn down to smoldering embers in the fireplace. I sat by the window in our room until Inessa drifted off to sleep, then slipped out to walk the palace and hoped to clear my head.

Passing from room to room, I finally wandered down to where I'd been injected the first time, praying it might bring me some sort of lost insight or closure. Opening the door to the forsaken storage room, I was surprised to see Roland sitting on a stack of books, deep in thought.

"Roland?" I announced myself quietly, and I stepped inside, closing the door behind me.

"What brings you down here at this hour?"

"I couldn't sleep. I just can't help but feel like what we are doing is all too rushed and dangerous. Not to mention it's only adding to an unraveling web of lies. I understand the need to quell the unrest, but I wish Mama and Friedrich would see reason and simply cease the injections. They must see the damage it's causing. Even if we have to craft some ruse this one last time, if we had more time, then we wouldn't have to tamper with the existing drug and could concoct a placebo look alike with no risk attached at the very least. But tomorrow… It's so soon. I don't feel good about it. Any of it. Especially after seeing exactly how Arrian is handling his new post."

Roland ran a hand through his hair, looking weary and troubled. "The wheels are already in motion. I think today frightened everyone into action, and we have little choice but to trust in their judgment. At this point, tomorrow will be whatever it'll be. I'm headed for bed. You should too." He turned away to head for the door.

"That's it? You are just going to trust that everything will be alright?" I curled my fingers into the soft drape of Roland's shirt to spin him back around to face me. "Roland, I'm absolutely terrified. Aren't you? I heard you earlier trying to change their minds too. After everything you've been working towards all these years, you are leaving it up to chance? Everything will be fine? That's your answer?"

His body complied but his face stayed aimed away, desperately looking anywhere but at mine. "Of course it will be fine, Sorrel."

"What's going to happen to us if it isn't?" I implored, stepping forward brazenly to press myself against his chest, seeking to quell my fear. Warmth, stability— anything that would make me feel protected. He was broad and firm beneath me, an embodiment of foundation and security I was needing. "What will happen to me and my family? Papa and Theo aren't even back yet. It's Mama, my sisters, and me who have to brave going up on that scaffold to lay ourselves bare for the public, and you know Mama is already not handling things well."

"Nothing. Nothing bad is going to happen. There is a plan in place to make sure that the result is going to show that you and your family are not Wielders or of Wielder descent. That's what we have to work with. We have to trust that the plan will work. My father assured me he has it worked out and I choose to believe him."

"But…" I bleated, and at last, Roland whipped his head around to look down at me. He gripped my arms firmly between his hands, and his expression was filled with an anguish I had never seen him wear before.

"Damn it, Sorrel!" He swore before pressing his forehead to mine in defeat, a small shudder of restraint passing over him. "What do you think I can do to stop this?"

Startled by his reaction, I made to pull away, but my back slammed into the shelves behind me. The impact sent a shower of bindings and pages down between us, and I threw my arms up over my head for protection against the barrage. We were both immediately coated in a plume of dust, the freshly disturbed particles flickering in the yellow wash of light as they permeated the air. The movement shifted the sleeve of my dress, showing the place where some of my burns had turned to pink scars dappling my forearm.

I blinked through the stinging layer of flecks sticking to my lashes to see Roland's smoldering gaze locked on my marred skin, and his breathing had turned ragged with frustration. "I should have never gotten you involved with any of this. I've ruined your life." His voice was thick and hoarse, bearing the burden of a lifetime of regrets. He slipped his fingers back into his already disheveled hair and clutched at his scalp, like he was trying to contain whatever was racing around inside his skull.

Something ignited within me as the foreign sound of bitterness in his tone scraped against my ear. Before I knew what I was doing, I had my palms planted firmly against his chest, and I shoved him as hard as I could. I might as well have slapped him across his face for the look he gave me— disquieted and pained. But, I wasn't going to stand there and listen to him take the blame for tomorrow's outcome, nor yesterday's choices.

"Don't you dare!" I spat, the uncharacteristically vehement words tasted like fire as they leapt from my tongue. "I am the one who chose to follow you and Inessa. I am the one who forced you to tell me what you two were doing. *I* made those choices."

"But I didn't have to tell you the truth! I should have lied to you. It was selfish of me to share any of it with you."

"You are seriously going to look me in the eye and tell me you wish you had lied to me? What is wrong with you?" I demanded, incredulous.

"Yes! I will look you in the eye and say that. Because it would have protected you." Roland stepped forward to tower over me, and I stared defiantly back up at him. "From every burn, bruise, and agony you've endured since."

"The demands would have *still* been made. The uprising would *still* be happening! You can't shoulder that blame, Roland." I threw my arm out to the side, gesturing emphatically as I spoke.

"Yes, it would. But, you would be blissfully unaware that there was any chance they might be right! Now you must live with all of this hanging over you for the rest of your life like the curses you've been lies of. We are just two people, Sorrel. If they won't see reason, and we can't risk something going wrong and revealing a blatant attempt at lying, then what else are we left with? Lies. It would have protected you from the fear and helplessness you're feeling right now. It would have protected *me* from seeing it and being powerless to fix it for you. But, that isn't even true. I still would have *known* I was potentially leading a lamb to slaughter."

His words stilled the already stagnant air around us. It became unbearably stifling in the blink of an eye. I had no words and no more fire in me to argue back. Whatever inner flame had leapt to life within me had been snuffed out to give way to a fresh wave of frigid, inescapable despair. The truth of it was that he was just as terrified of tomorrow's outcome as I was. If a single thing went wrong, it would be the end of everything.

I hung my head and heaved a heavy sigh, then inhaled shakily, trying to dispel the raging anxiety ripping at the nerves beneath my skin. Instead, I'd treat Roland the same as any patient who needed calming before a procedure. There was rarely any certainty with those men that they'd come out of the operations alive— or, at the very least, in one piece— and somehow I could send them in, smiling, with my feigned optimism.

I didn't want to be fake with Roland. I wouldn't feign it. I would believe in the positive outcome, and I'd pour every ounce of my body into believing it until it was proven true tomorrow. For this night, I just wanted to take cover here, with him. Broken spirits and all, so long as we tried to piece the other back together until dawn came.

Quickly scanning the room we were in, I observed it was filled with mountains of Papa's ever-overflowing library. Beyond the mound I'd knocked from the shelves against the wall, the floor was studded with large towers of thick books. It made the dreary unused room feel like a fortress or sanctuary, completely separate from the rest of the palace, my family, or the kingdom as a whole. A bunker in the midst of an overwhelming reality. It was in the lower levels of the palace that were never visited by any family or staff. We would be left completely alone if we stayed here.

Raising my eyes, determination for reassurance sparking in my fingertips, I found a smile and reached up to gently cup Roland's cheek in my palm. I could feel the tiny prickles of stubble on his chin. The abrasive texture in my hand kept me tethered to the delicate moment by a thread of sensation I could focus my turbulent energy on.

When I spoke, my voice came out like wisps of cobweb in the wind. "We can hide from the world down here until morning. Ride out the storm of worries together. Just the two of us."

The vibrant azure of Roland's eyes reflected my own visage back at me as they roved over every detail of my face. I tried not to understand that he might be memorizing these details in case things did take a turn for the worse. Instead, I brought my other hand to his face and held it there, staring silently back at him.

The harsh reality was that this could be our last night together. Friedrich might not be able to fix the magic-testing instrument in time to hide our masked lineage from the world. Even if he did, the seeds of dissent had been sown, and either way, tomorrow would usher in a new way of life for me and my family— with everything in the open, for me and Roland too. Years of teasing, dancing through flirtation and banter, and the promise of an infinite forever in which we could someday possibly find our romantic footing and be together— all of that was flickering out before us with each tick of the clock that brought us one second closer to morning. In the end, if the rushed endeavor to prolong our hidden lineage failed, we would be nothing more than a tragic opportunity missed.

I didn't want that. I rejected it with every fiber of my being. I couldn't part ways with him now, tomorrow, or ever, having never so much as kissed him or told him just how deeply I loved him. He'd told me, and I'd played coy to wait for my own moment to come later. But later was never a promise. I didn't want to end up like Inessa and Hykner. Losing him, first to the stature of societal expectations and pairings, then to his military duty, had destroyed my sister's spirit.

"Stay here with me, because you have my confession. Roland, you are the love of my life." My heart racing beyond what I was sure it could physically bare, I pulled Roland's face down to meet mine, pressing my lips tentatively against his.

I felt his body tense in surprise before it gave way a heartbeat later and melted into the kiss. His muscular arms wrapped around me, enveloping me in electrifying affection. Then, when perhaps we should have separated from what would have been an innocent kiss, we didn't. Instead, the moment of repressed longing and intimacy took root and blossomed into starved desire. My mouth parted slightly, and I could feel his tongue glide softly over the threshold of my lips. Both of my hands flitted from his face, one dropping to grip his shirt at the chest, and the other snaking into his hair. The texture of the strands was silky between my fingers.

Roland leaned deeper into the kiss, like he was drinking in the moment in its entirety, until I was once more pressing my back into the shelves. I used my hold on his shirt to pull him even closer to me, our bodies pressing together at the chest. The movement dislodged our mouths, but neither of us released our hold on the other, and Roland's head dipped to my neck. I felt his breath brush against my skin and inhaled sharply. I could hardly breathe, yet standing there, panting in the heat of rising lust, gasping for air had never felt so good.

He paused in an unspoken question of whether he should proceed or not, and in answer, I inclined my exposed neck against his mouth. Something between a chuckle and a feline purr rumbled from within him, vibrating my throat where his lips were pursed, and I closed my eyes with a wicked grin.

Roland trailed from just under my chin to my collarbone before once more pausing for an indication of permission or rejection for what lay beyond that point. His cheeks were flushed and his chest was heaving. I could practically taste his hunger and was reminded of the admission he'd shared with me about not believing he'd restrain himself to a single kiss. No Lust affinity assistance needed, I placed a finger under his chin to guide his mouth back to mine, then bit gently into his bottom lip, tugging it slowly before letting it slip through my teeth.

I was hungry too. More than I'd ever realized.

The next instance was a torrent of shedding clothing, with and without assistance, barely separating from our fervor enough to peel away the garments until we were both laid bare before each other. Roland's hand traced my torso, gingerly trailing a finger around my abdomen before spreading all five to cup at my exposed chest. I would have expected myself to feel some sense of shame or embarrassment to be this vulnerable and naked in his presence, but that shroud of doubt never claimed my sensibilities or inhibition. Rather, beneath his grasp, I felt electricity pulsing through my veins, famished and begging for more— begging for him to make me his. I half wondered if Storm Sorrel, rebellious and wild, was taking the reins.

There was a strange paradox in our feverish approach as we tumbled somewhere between frantic desperation and the overwhelming desire to savor every single touch and sensation, should this be our one and only shot to do so. I lifted my arms over my head, and Roland reached up to clasp onto my wrists, holding them captive while his other hand danced from my chest down to the crest of my thigh.

The final hurdle before we crossed a line forever.

A brazen glance at Roland's naked physique from head to toe told me he was as ready as I was, and looking at him, completely unhindered by clothing, made me squirm with sudden impatience to be touched again. I shifted my hips slightly to allow his hand inward from my thigh, certain he could hear the thudding of my heart against my ribs, or feel the collateral pulsating in my wrists. I couldn't hear a sound beyond the blood rushing in my ears

His fingers roved and twirled in exploration that made me gasp and lean my neck backward in ecstasy. I locked eyes with him, and in one fluid motion, he released my arms, using one hand to grip my lower back and the other to hook my legs around him so he could hasten me to the ground. He hovered for a moment, a yearning burning in his eyes, before gently lowering himself to me. I arched to meet him and let all my fears and worries tumble away until I was blissfully lost, and mindless in the throes of passion.

This was our moment to be.

And that moment would stretch until we saw the icy pale sunlight of early morning filter through the dusty window. Until then, we were free to lose ourselves to one another, at last, obscured amongst the tomes.

FORTY-ONE

I held my breath as we marched up the steps to the scaffold, heads held high. Inessa gave my hand a quick squeeze as she took her place next to Mama with me falling in beside her. I could see her face struggling against a pucker of irritation at the spectacle we were being forced to participate in, and I couldn't help but share the sentiment. Yulia and Kira smiled at the crowd, completely unaware of the risk we were taking, nor how much we were counting on Friedrich's replacement drug to see us through to the other side of this display. Five nurses appeared beside us, one for each of us, and we presented our arms, ready to perform the same testing that countless members of our people had been forced to take.

Mama launched into a prepared speech for the occasion— she had no doubt gone over it with Friedrich, over and over again until it was just right— and while everyone else listened intently, it was all I could do to keep my nerves quelled enough to not bolt from the scene all together.

My gaze wandered through the tapestry of random faces in front of me until they finally landed on Roland. He smiled at me, and mouthed the words, *it's all going to be okay*. I took a deep breath and returned his smile, allowing myself to instead be filled with the euphoria of the night we had shared below the palace. I just needed to keep it together for a few more minutes, then I would return to his side with the whole ordeal behind us, and we could finally look towards the future together we had been chasing for so long.

I blinked affectionately at him as the nurse inserted the needle into my arm. Friedrich would make sure we got through this trial unscathed, we could return to our work helping the people of Eisa without suspicion, and Roland and I could—

"No!" A sudden scream from Yulia split the air.

The happy thoughts drifted away as a familiar sensation stirred beneath my skin, and I saw the smile melt in an instant from Roland's face. Time snapped to a still moment as I realized with sickening horror that Friedrich's plan had failed, and my veins were taking on their affinity's glowing colors.

The worst *had* happened.

"What's happening?" Kira gasped as the tendrils of orange and red climbed the veins of her forearms and shone through her skin.

The ends of her hands were smoldering black, ashes and embers fell freely from her fingertips.

Her eyes were wild, and, as she waved her arms around in an attempt to dispel the flames, the air caught fire around her. The sudden blaze lashed out at those nearest the scaffold, causing them to jump back with shrieks.

"Kira, stop fanning the flames. You need to calm down!" Inessa urged, and I could see a similar effect overtaking her own arms. Where pure fire ran through Kira's veins as her core affinity, green vines spindled from around Ina's wrists, digging into the planks of the scaffold. Water began dripping from her nails, showing her secondary affinity. The injection wasn't behaving as it had beneath the palace. I wasn't slipping into a mental space— as it wasn't my first time with the serum— and the affinities were visibly bursting in forceful pulses of wielding rather than simply showing in our veins.

I dared to look at my own trembling palms, the world dancing in and out of cadence with time as I tried to process what was happening. The tips of my fingers were covered in creeping iridescent blue frost, while my veins flickered with raging lightning and sparkled with the starlight lurking beneath my skin. All three affinities were displayed at once.

Yulia's arms were covered in an old script of winding words I knew now belonged to the Whisper affinity, and her nail beds shimmered with an otherworldly white glow. Her eyes were wide and milky, and she grasped her hands over her ears, clutching frantically at her head. Mama's arms were storming as well, rolling between flashes of white and tumbling purples of a tumultuous sky.

Citizens were starting to run away in fear, others challenging what had been done to us, and others still beginning to rally and jeer. Dizziness claimed my vision, and I flicked my eyes to Friedrich, pleading silently for him to help us. He looked horrified, and stepped forward on the scaffold. I thought he was reaching out for Mama to aid her but instead his arm extended in a sweeping command that I recognized well— it was a motion of condemnation.

He was ordering the soldiers in the square to restrain us.

"Get away!" Kira's voice pitched to a screech and she leapt backwards, her flames growing in tandem with her agitation. "I can't put the fire out. I don't want to hurt you."

"Cover that one's mouth. She will speak words into your ear that will tear apart your mind." Friedrich's voice had the air of being stupefied, but beneath it, I could hear a premeditated coldness as he pointed to a sobbing Yulia. Her eyes were glazed with shock and horror, and I had to wonder if she was hearing his thoughts thunder through her skull or if she was dipping in and out of reality and her mindscape.

He had never intended to help us, and he had always intended to betray us.

"Don't touch her!" Kira leapt in front of our dear, gentle sister, her lips curling in a snarl of unbridled defiance. The strength of her fire melted the visible air around her in a heated haze that made the advancing soldiers take pause.

"Douse that one's flames," Arrian stepped forward and asserted casually, staring unflinching into Kira's furious eyes.

"'That one?' How dare you! I am Kira Zdraevit, Grand Princess of all of Eisa, and I will not be reduced to *'that one'* by you," She spat at Arrian then turned her wrath towards Friedrich. "You planned this whole thing, you viper. Didn't you? What did those injections do to us to make this happen? What atrocity have you planted in your sovereigns' flesh?" She didn't wait for an answer, and rose to her full height, showing her station, flames blazing brightly from her arms like wings. "Whatever it was you poisoned me with, if you touch one hair on my family's heads, I will use it to incinerate you."

"Funny how you subjected your subjects to these Wielder tracers but were so pious you thought you were above it yourselves. You see, every citizen gathered here knows these mechanisms do nothing but reveal the Wielder's powers imbued in your blood. I have implanted nothing. But, I have shown the Zdraevit Family as the hypocrites they are. You condemn Wielders, ignore their pleas for reparations, all while you sit high in your castle with the very same magic in your veins. Protecting Eisa from Wielders? Laughable. Who is protecting Eisa from *you*?"

"You lied to us all, traitor." Arrain's lip curled around his cold words, and eyes that had once admired Kira now hardened with hate and disgust. "You *monster.*"

I bit my quivering lip to keep the welling tears in my eyes from spilling out. My heart was racing wildly, blindsided by the betrayal from a man I had always seen as an adoring and compassionate uncle. He had killed Otvel to protect our secret, only to reveal it here when we would be at our most exposed and vulnerable. Perhaps Otvel had never intended to reveal us after all. Or they were both traitors on different sides. I couldn't make sense of anything and dug my nails into my palms, praying to wake up from this obvious nightmare. But nothing changed, and I was trapped in this marred reality.

What did Roland think of his father's actions? What would he do after our night of love and terror spent together between those dusty stacks of books? He'd always been there when I needed him most, my rock, comfort, and voice of reason. Someone who understood me before I even understood myself. He had to have something up his sleeve to fix this. But, when I looked at him at the front of the crowd, my heart imploded. My knees buckled beneath me and slammed into the platform.

Roland's face wore the stoicism of a statue as he nodded his head along with his father's words. He didn't even look at me.

Why? How could you ignore me at a time like this? Do something! I wailed inside my head, willing him to come to our aid. But as the seconds ticked by, it was clear he wasn't waiting for an opportunity to swoop in and be our hero. He was watching everything unfold without a single trace of distress or remorse.

He knew this would happen?

Had everything been a lie? How far back into our past did this deception and betrayal run? Had everything he had shown me and Inessa been something to try to incriminate us? I thought back to him looking at my burn scars with such boiling anger. I had thought it was vehemence towards the harm that had befallen me, but could it have been frustration that I had only escaped with a few scars? All those times I had seen him play both parts; one that worked in favor of fair living for the hidden Wielders in Eisa, and the other that acted in accordance with our kingdom's rhetoric. He wore both masks without ever breaking the facade, so which one had been the real him? Who had I spent the night with? Who had I grown up with?

He used me.

He had taken my body and led the lamb to slaughter after all. Could I really believe that? I was certain he had been as wracked with anxiety as I was. Perhaps I had been nothing but an infatuated fool and he had been told to use it as an advantage. Maybe it had been his final task to keep me occupied and he'd taken it for all it was worth. Those pretty words in his letter from the time capsule took on a whole new meaning when he had instructed himself not to squander my value. It was the oldest tactic in the book, and it seemed I had fallen for it completely. When I finally caught his eye, I saw not one single hint of emotion on his face. A tear crossed the threshold, and I felt it turn to ice as it rolled down my cheeks.

"Roland, Arrian, come help restrain these traitors to Eisa," Friedrich called to his sons, and my last pin drop of hope evaporated as Roland complied. "These soldiers seem to be having trouble."

Friedrich motioned to Roland and pointed to where I had collapsed on the scaffold, the planks beginning to freeze around my body as the magic was made to not only show as it had previously, I realized, but to become unstable to paint us as dangerous. My Ice affinity was breaking through, and soon the storm and stars would unleash as well.

"Restrain that one." He knew the public statement of loyalty he was making by having it be Roland who'd collect me.

"Don't you dare!" Inessa cried out, her face twisting. "Roland, you have to help us. You can't allow this to happen this way. You were part of everything!"

The people in the crowd were leering, and the gathering was quickly turning riotous, swallowing up Inessa's pleading words. As Roland strode towards me, unwavering in his orders, I could see beyond him that Mama had already been seized, her eyes cloudy with utter disbelief. Everything she had done to try to help her country had been a manipulation to lead us to our downfall. She was still recovering from Otvel's murder, and now it would seem that her old friend had likely died in cold blood after all.

She blinked numbly at Friedrich. "Is this all because of what happened with Sylvia and Sarka?"

Friedrich loomed over Mama, leaning in so his sneering face was only a breath away from hers. "For Sarka and all of Eisa, Geneva."

I snapped my eyes back to Roland and saw his shoulders tense ever so slightly at the mention of his late mother's name. Another tear froze as it spilled down my face, my mind flickering in and out of awareness while my world fell apart bit by bit around me.

Was this all because of his mother's death? What did it have to do with us and why were we paying the price for a life lost nearly twenty years ago?

Inessa and Yulia had also been taken into custody, and Yulia had been gagged. Only Kira and myself were left to be collected. My youngest sister looked like a cornered animal, ready to lunge for the nearest jugular with her bare teeth. She was putting up the final fight. One that I knew she couldn't win. Her flames were ebbing and she was quickly doused in cold water, causing her to shiver despite it steaming from her skin. Five minutes was all it had taken.

I felt paralyzed looking up at Roland as he reached down with a gloved hand and tugged me forcefully to my feet. There was no warmth in his presence, as if he had erected a wall between us, effectively cutting away the threads of our relationship. He'd know he couldn't touch me directly. He'd planned it. There was a pressure in my chest unlike anything I had ever felt before, and I realized it must be my heart bludgeoned beyond salvation. I'd given him a lifetime of implicit trust, and he'd decimated it in seconds.

"You knew about this?" I whispered around the lump in my throat as my hands were restrained behind my back. "You knew your father was planning this?"

"You shouldn't be too surprised. Father always said the power was in the people," Roland replied, his voice was flat and the delivery was monosyllabic. He jerked his chin in his father's direction. "You said to me once to make no mistake, it is Wielders who are dangerous. That's always been the perception of this country. Eisa will no longer protect you."

The air was driven from my lungs, and my vision fell from black nothingness back to the nightmare before me. The faces of the people around us were twisting and contorting with malice, spitting and hissing in a blur of faint cognition.

"What will happen to us?" Inessa asked as we were marched back to the palace. Mother was in a stupor, while both Yulia and Kira had been gagged after Kira had in fact tried to bite a soldier I recognized as one of Inessa's company. I was certain my vocal cords had frozen over, leaving me unable to form words. Ina was the only one capable of asking that question in that moment.

"You will be taken to the palace for holding until your father and brother return with their formal abdication. Then, we will let the opinion of the people decide your fate."

"See then, what is man if not a rapid beast?
Both demand blood as monsters under
Death's reign."
-D

FORTY-TWO

We were left to wait without answers until Papa arrived by train eighteen hours later. We'd been isolated into groups in our respective rooms with guards posted at each door. Ina and I held each other and cried, purging all of our immediate fear and confusion. It was the first time I had succumbed to my tears in years. Then we spent the entirety of the day and night trying to make sense of what had taken place out on the scaffold, and what could have possibly turned Friedrich and Roland against us. We went over it again and again until we could barely speak one word after another and collapsed from emotional exhaustion. We awoke with early autumn sunlight streaming through our window, and were instructed to dress and prepare for an audience with Friedrich. Neither Dowels nor Larkin were anywhere to be found either, leaving us to fear the worst for their fates.

We did as we were told, though it was unclear if he was requesting Inessa's and my presence alone, or if it would be the whole of our family reuniting again. I wasn't sure which outcome would bring me more relief. As we entered the ballroom, it became clear that it was the latter, and everyone, including Theo and Papa, were already waiting for us to arrive. I tried not to fall back into the hollow pit of despair as I saw that both Roland and Arrian were also present.

"Now that you are all gathered," Friedrich began, his posture appearing as stiff and unfamiliar as his actions and words. "Once the assembly is all in place, we will begin."

"Begin what? What is all of this, Friedrich?" Mama demanded, incredulous. "You expect to order us around in our own palace, and not so much as deign to give us an explanation?"

"Geneva..." Papa tried to warn, but Mama was beyond rationality, and I could see from her eyes that she hadn't slept all night.

"You betrayed us out there!" She shouted. "You had this all planned out to the very last detail, and I'd like to know why! Was Otvel ever even our enemy, or was it just you? Perhaps you betrayed him too. I have my speculations of what qualms you might take with Genri and me, but the girls? How could you humiliate and frighten them like that, and then shut them away?"

"What qualms are you talking about?" Inessa jumped in, Kira joining with a similar echo.

"I want answers!" Mama's voice was pitching into hysteria and I grabbed hold of her on one side while Theo gripped her hand on the other.

"I suppose you might as well all be brought up to speed now. To start out, you are no longer royalty—"

"And what authority do you have to declare such a thing? We have a Divine—"

"Oh spare us your rants, Geneva," Friedrich growled. I had never heard such a low and ominous tone from him and it set my nerves blazing. The closest it had ever come before was his promise to me and my sisters as children that he would remove every single Wielder from Eisa...

And suddenly, the pieces of the puzzle began clicking into place. He had meant what he told us that day, but what we didn't realize was that he had included us in that lump sum. Mama hadn't revealed to me why Friedrich knew of our secret lineage, but it seemed like it was about to finally be brought out in the open. I could only imagine Kira and Yulia's confusion having no background information to work with whatsoever before being locked away for eighteen long hours. It was a wonder to me that Kira hadn't managed to force her way free in that time.

"We all know what you are and that the Divinities granted you with no Divine rights to speak of. The reign of the Zdraevit line has been nothing but a lie from the very beginning back in the days of Valamir. So, silence your infernal preaching I've been forced to listen to for the last two and a half decades!" Friedrich continued, coming to loom over Mama. His outburst served its desired intent and Mama fell silent, eyes stretched wide. "I've suffered this secret far too long, and suffered this foolish reign of yours, Genri, even longer. It's time to put it to rest."

Papa's proud stance sagged. "All this time I called you my brother."

"All this time and you chose your murderous sister," Friedrich sneered. "All the blood of the innocents on your hands from your stubbornness and pride will finally see the light of day. Your royal status built on a throne of lies won't protect you this time—any of you. Never again will Eisa walk behind a Zdraevit. You will taste the full weight of justice nearly twenty years in the making."

"Papa, what is he talking about?" Inessa demanded.

"You will go to sleep each night with the suffering of your family behind your eyes, just as I did when I had to tell my boys they no longer had a mother! So, tell me, how are you going to answer Inessa now? What will you tell her? More lies to trust in, or will you finally unbury the truth, Genri?"

Roland and Arrian stood shoulder to shoulder behind Friedrich, unmoving, their expressions fixed and menacing. I could barely register if I was breathing or not as I stared at Roland, pleading for understanding. How could he have fought so hard to save me, to have told me how much he had loved me, only to come to this? To avoid my gaze with such coldness I had never felt before.

I could only vaguely recall memories of Friedrich's wife. She had been a kind and gentle woman from what I could remember, and she had died in an incident with Wielders while traveling abroad. Papa's sister had also met her end in that same encounter. I couldn't make sense of the connections. Had all three men been carrying with them this terrible grudge against my father all this time, waiting for the perfect opportunity to betray us all?

It had all been planned so carefully. Everything had been a lie, all our lives. The contempt in their faces confirmed it, without a trace of love or kinship to be found. Roland had been using me and Inessa both the whole time. He used my affections against me, and clearly Arrian had been tasked to do the same with Kira.

"Or maybe we can have *her* tell us," Friedrich jerked his chin from Arrian to Yulia in a silent command. Arrain nodded and grabbed Yulia roughly by the back of her neck, forcing her to her knees in front of Friedrich. He leaned down to her and smirked. "Oh yes, little Whisper child. It was so cumbersome to avoid your ability when I came to realize what it was. I had to hide all my inner thoughts from leaking out where you could grab hold of them and boast of it as intuition. But I'm wide open now. Go on, Yulia, tell the rest of your family what you're hearing!"

"Stop it!" Kira screamed, her face contorted in wrathful overwhelm as more tears began spilling down Yulia's cheeks. "Can't you see you're scaring her? Stop using her to make your point and be man enough to tell us yourself, you coward!"

"Can't you see we don't care?" Arrian laughed, his fingers tightening around Yulia's neck, making her shoulders rise as she winced in pain. "You have no more power, Kira. All this time as a spitfire, and now you're little more than a dying ember."

"I don't need to be spewing fire to knock you upside the head for laying a hand on my sister! Pick on me instead, if you're brave enough."

"Kira," Mama hissed a warning, her eyes wide with fear. "Simmer down."

"Go on, read my thoughts for all to hear!" Friedrich crowed. "Your raw power was always the strongest anyway."

"You swore an oath to this family, Friedrich!" Papa bellowed, finally losing hold of his emotions.

"And you swore an oath to Eisa, Genri!" Friedrich shouted back.

Arrian rolled his eyes, and pulled a knife from his jacket, holding it to Yulia's throat. "Stop sniveling, and tell the rest of the class the answer."

"I... I..." Yulia stammered, her body shaking uncontrollably.

"It's alright, Yulia," I spoke quietly. "Just tell them what they want to hear, and it will be okay."

"I don't know!"

"You're *lying*," Arrian growled, pressing the knife against her skin until a small trickle of blood ran from the blade.

"Lady Sarka was killed in an accident caused by Papa's sister!" Yulia whimpered against the pain. "Instead of receiving justice as any other Wielder would, she was allowed to go free so long as she faked her death and agreed to never return to Eisa."

"Let her go, please," Mama begged, reaching her arms out towards her daughter. "She's done what you asked."

Arrian yanked Yulia's head back by her hair to stare menacingly down at her before throwing her backwards to scramble into Mama's arms for comfort. "Was that so hard?"

"My children had nothing to do with any of that," Papa growled.

"No, maybe not, but they would be taught to continue the same trend wouldn't they? I'll admit I waited to see what the girls would do. Whether they would remain ignorant and harmless or seek forbidden knowledge when the opportunity arose. It was only thanks to Roland that the two oldest even learned the secret in the first place. Then it was only a matter of time before they dug their own graves with their idealism and earnest hearts, sealing their fates. They even hoped to bring their siblings on board to someday openly rule as Wielders, destroying what mortals had given their lives for!" Friedrich pointed to me and Inessa, a crazed look in his eyes. "Those two committed treason with all they did. Lies and secrecy, learning about their affinities in the shadows, allowing Eisan soldiers to fall to Wielders' blades while they stood idly by. Roland witnessed all of it. Tell me, Genri, Geneva, what punishment would Inessa and Sorrel face for their crimes against the crown?"

Ina and I shared a shameful glance, cowing beneath the weight of his accusations. My legs trembled beneath me as Friedrich confirmed Roland's intentions. I wrapped my arms around my torso, wishing I could erase every vulnerable touch of his hands on my body. Every smile we'd shared. Every single stolen moment to be blinked out of existence.

"Would you not allow them to walk free and have your son, Theodorvin, take the throne under the guise of being a mortal all while carrying the secret of really being a Wielder? I knew since the day Sarka died that there was no place for another Wielder on the throne of Eisa, and the reign of terror would fall with you, Genri."

"I wouldn't have lived in secrecy!" Theo spat, his face tingeing red with anger. I'd never seen my brother so angry, and sweat began to gather on my palms at the thought of what his raised blood pressure might do to his illness.

"Oh? Tell me, young heir, how would you have been different?"

"I have lived my whole life with the secret of my cursed health. I had no such intentions to rule with another secret to shoulder to my grave. I would have fought for the equality our people deserve— the same fighting my sisters have been doing on their own because they knew that it was the people— All the people who make Eisa strong. Not the ones who betray its faith to seize power."

Amidst all of the hurt and torment, I felt a swelling of pride.

He truly would have ruled fairly just as I had predicted.

"That's just it, Theodorvin. We are not equal. Wielders have too much power. They are a menace to society, and it was the very reason they were driven into hiding to begin with. And, before you feel pity for them, remember that your father sat on their fate for twenty years, *knowing* what all of you were. He stood by through countless pain and devastation to protect the royal pride."

"It tortured me inside! You knew that, Friedrich," Papa shouted. "You heard my every remorse, and knew my hands were tied by my ancestor's choices. There was no other way to keep my family safe."

"*Your* family. Because that's all that ever mattered to you. You didn't give a damn about my family. I doubt you lost as much sleep over the orphans as your daughter did. All so long as you and yours remained safe and in your control."

"Father, the assembly is ready." Arrian pointed to the balcony.

"Assembly?" Inessa asked ruefully. "You mean the little show you put on before wasn't enough humiliation?"

"Ah, but heavy is the head that wears the crown, Ina. It's your father and brother's turn to bear their shame for all to see."

"You can't use that injection on Theo, it could cause him to bleed," I asserted, still staring at Roland, who didn't budge an inch in his stoicism. I sucked in a breath and tried one last time to reach him. "Roland?"

"He will have to endure it, the same as everyone else did." Roland's reply was monotonous. He finally looked at me with cold indifference. "You'll just have to play along. You're bound by new rules now."

His callous nature added insult to injury as I remembered how many times Roland had laughed and played alongside us. His devotion had been unshakable, how could I have been so blind as to have fallen for my enemy acting as a wolf in sheep's clothing. Just like the metaphor Otvel had once shared with me, only it seemed it wasn't Wielders it should have been applied to.

"No, I can't accept that. I can't accept that this is who you truly are," I whispered pitifully, searching for any little trace of lasting resolve in the shambles of confidence left inside me.

"You're going to have to." The unfeeling words felt like a strike to the face.

"Tell me you've been lying then! Look me in the eye and tell me it's all been a lie. That was your wish last night, wasn't it? It was all a *lie*. Not just to me, to everyone. You've betrayed us all."

"Looks like the *Snowdrop* doesn't like being crushed under your boot, Roland. You really had her wrapped around your finger all this time didn't you?" Arrian jeered.

"When did you become so cruel, Arrian?" I bit. He'd always had a darker side to him I felt lurking beneath the surface of his bright charisma, but I'd never expected this. After seeing his calloused resolve at the hospital, I should have guessed his capacity for cruelty and malice. It only ever reared its head in childish moments of defeat, and now, it seemed, in moments of stolen victory as well.

"I've always been cruel to my enemies. It's not my concern that you went and crossed the line. Idealists like to preach of all this middle area between one fixed point and another. But it's all hogwash. There is black and there is white. Gray is merely there for those stupid enough to get caught straddling the fence in their indecision to pick a side. I have no such weakness. You're on the other side of the fence now. You are my enemy. It's pretty simple."

"You're such an idiot," Kira grumbled, rolling her eyes in disgust. "All you're saying is you lack conviction to such a severe degree that you have to be told who to like and dislike. I've never heard of something so spineless."

"Say that again, Kira!" Arrian's face grew crazed, the challenge unhinging something, and he pointed his knife at her. "Do you have a death wish? I would have thought you were more clever than that to insult your captors. My mistake. Father, shall I strike her down?"

"Excuse me?" Kira blustered, clearly as equally surprised by his vehement outburst as the rest of us. I wondered how long he'd been waiting for the chance to hurt Kira instead of love her as we had all thought.

"Father, the assembly?" Roland interjected. "Honestly Ari, don't let one brat get under your skin and make you so reactive. It's your greatest weakness," Roland sighed, and both Arrian and Kira bristled at the duel insult.

"I've no intention of striking them down for good unless justice would warrant it. For now, they must serve under arrest," Friedrich mused, clasping his hands behind his back. "Starting with the emperor and heir's public admission of guilt, then begins the real atonement. If they can manage that, perhaps we can arrange something more permanent."

"If the injection isn't administered just right, you could very well be threatening Theo's life," I urged.

"Then perhaps he is meant to die. After all, the Divinities refused to grant Genri and Geneva a son for four children. Then the one they received was defective."

"I'll be fine Sorrel." Theo shifted beside me and squeezed my hand, holding his chin high. "I refuse to cower and beg beneath tyrants. I know my Divine worth."

"Friedrich, weren't the promised abdications announced spectacle enough?" Mama tried one last approach only to be ignored.

"Move," Friedrich barked, and Papa and Theo followed his instructions. Papa removed his jacket and shirt while Theo followed suit. The two fell in line between two guards, one of which I recognized with a sickening twist to my gut, as Zdrute. The soldier who had recognized me at the fire.

The rest of us were told to stand behind Papa and Theo on the balcony before a gathered crowd while Friedrich began a speech.

"I hope that Rafe has your head," Inessa growled as she passed Roland, baring her teeth. "For all you've done not just to us, but to Sorrel. He will make you pay, you can be sure of that."

"Careful the promises you make, Inessa," Roland taunted. "Now be quiet and listen."

"People of Eisa, I present to you a cowed Emperor, a Wielder like his family, masquerading as mortal while persecuting his citizens for his own sins. He has betrayed us all. We lay both him and his son, Grand Prince Theodorvin, bare in their lies with the same drug imposed upon all of you. They lived in luxury while you suffered. They lived in safety while you lived in fear. They lived as Wielders while filling you with false promises of a peaceful Wielder-free Eisa. Now let honesty bare her fruits of justice for all to see!" Friedrich recited his speech with all the right pressure points to engage a sympathetic audience, though to me, it sounded more akin to a rant than any elegant and dignified address given by a royal.

Papa and Theo were both shoved to the edge of the balcony, their arms roughly grabbed and held fast as the needles were inserted. It took only seconds for their veins to light up in tandem, revealing them both as Ice Wielders like me. Papa's veins flickered to a light pink hue and back, while Theo's undulated from icy white to deep blue, revealing his second affinity as water like Inessa. Unlike the ambush set on us, Papa and Theo's magic didn't surge out of control. This was likely a calculated precautionary measure on Friedrich's account, not wanting to risk that Papa, given advance notice unlike us, would anticipate the power and try to somehow wield it against his captors. I curled my fingers inward tightly as I wished I had acted sooner instead of being paralyzed by shock and heartbreak when the barrier between me and my affinities had been lifted.

"Emperor Genri II has abdicated on behalf of himself and his son, Grand Prince and Heir, Theodorvin. As of today, the Zdraevit line has no more claim to the throne of Eisa," Friedrich crowed victoriously.

I blinked back more tears as the crowd drank in the spectacle before them and began to boo and curse my father and brother. Condemned by the people. It was the last nail in the coffin Friedrich had been building for us. There would be no reclaiming our honor after this. Our reign over Eisa was truly at an end. Our kingdom would fall.

FORTY-THREE

"**G**et out," the command echoed, hissing against the jagged cut rocks lining the Kyrith Pass.

I peeled myself out of the vehicle, my feet crunching into the snow beside the tires. Small, drifting snowflakes coated the air like a mist, hanging around us in a heavy fog.

Kira's teeth chattered as she slipped into the icy haze, hugging her coat tightly to her body. Her arm stiff, she raised her scarf over her chin and up beneath her eyes on the bridge of her nose to protect against the wind. Inessa came next, followed lastly by Theo. Like me, Theo wasn't much affected by the cold, so with a jerk of his chin, he signaled for us to remove our own coats and hand them to our frostbitten sisters. It made me curious, looking at him less affected by the cold than our sisters but still not quite as impervious as me. He'd enjoyed the winters of Eisa and never complained, but I hadn't ever seen more than indifference from him.

Is my affinity for ice somehow naturally stronger or deeper than Theo, that

I had always been drawn to the cold?

I pushed my own scarf to cover my nose, not wanting to take any chances that my tolerance would extend to my lungs and other organs. I tapped the fabric, looking at Theo. He nodded and hiked up his covering as well.

"Move forward," The next order was given and my siblings and I complied without question.

Our spirits were breaking, little by little. None of us knew what to say to each other, and each of us quietly carried our suffering— all except for Kira, our ever bright little spirit, who never dulled her shine and optimism for more than a moment. At times, it seemed she was the strongest tether holding us all together, choosing to live life intentionally and under her own discretion despite our confinement. Slowly, as we each recovered from the shock— or in some cases bury it deep down— the rest of us started to follow Kira's lead.

We stayed locked in the palace for two months under the new Rusev reign and hardly spoke. Friedrich, Roland, and Arrian all had as good as vanished into thin air, for we didn't see them once after being relegated to the west wing, split between two rooms. In December, we received the notice that we were being moved.

That was the first time.

Every couple of weeks we were relocated, and each time, we had to travel lighter and were further and further removed from the happenings of the world. Our letters were only sent a fraction of the time, and once in a great while did we receive any communications from anyone other than the officers in charge of our captivity.

"Business?" A bearded, heavily dressed man grunted at the officer leading us.

There was a small station to our right that allowed passage into the Kyrith Plains— a perilous frozen wasteland. There was a city, but that was the only source of civilization beyond this point. The only other reason anyone ever traveled beyond the pass into Kyrith willingly was to visit the Singing Ice Caves, just as we had once dreamed of.

A little over a month ago, another notice came. Another move. Only this time, we weren't moving together. Mama, Papa, and one child were to travel ahead to this new undisclosed location without explanation. Nothing was ever clearly explained to us anymore, our rights to comprehension revoked. We sat and discussed the best option to send, each one of us reluctant to break up our unit for risk of further damage.

Theo, struggling in his health at the time, was immediately taken out of the selection process, and me along with him as his best caretaker, now that we no longer had access to Klivech. Eventually, it was decided that Yulia would be the one to make the trip. Separating her and Kira was probably one of the more difficult challenges. I could tell that, though she hid it well, Kira fretted over our fragile sister every day until, a month later, we too received our moving notice to join the others.

More than the separation of our family, more than the biting cold and long journey, there was one unspoken truth we all knew that cast the darkest shadow over us. Kyrith was where criminals that were never to be heard from again were sent, left to live in exile.

"Prisoner passage. High priority, directive order six three dash seven one eight," The soldier declared, and the gatekeeper of the pass checked his listing before waving us through.

We were flanked by dark mountains coated in thick ice, like towering walls of chipped glass. The sparse trees around the entrance were encased in frost, and the snow clumped heavily on their dipping bows. But what we all fixed our attention on wasn't the intimidating mountains or frozen flora, it was on the two facing altars on either side of the entrance to the pass.

One was etched with the scriptures of the Divinities, Tenants of the Devout, and both the Divine Virtues as well as the Forsaken's Follies. I'd tried to follow those lists, practicing everything in my power that meant the best of those words. But here I was, trudging through the snow, a prisoner condemned for being the worst of the Follies instead.

The second altar was darker, more weathered, and the etchings of a different script were hardly discernible beneath the wear. The only thing it seemed the two had in common was their shape and carving style. It was of little consequence now, but something inside me appreciated that despite the harsh treatment of Wielders in this country, neither Papa nor his ancestors had ever taken away their right to pray as they descended into their exile.

And now it is our turn. We have reaped what so many others have sewn.

As we passed the facing obelisks, standing in dark obsidian clarity against the snow, I paused as countless had done before me. Did I touch what I now understood was the Faith of the Founders pillar and seek connection to the powers that continued to remain out of reach to me? Or, did I touch the pillar for the Divinities, the faith I had been brought up under and had prayed to my whole life? Would there be anyone listening on either side of my prayers for salvation?

While Theo and Kira ran their fingers over the Divine Obelisk as they walked through, their fingers grazing across the divots left from countless touches before them, I reached out both hands. I hoped my indecision in faith didn't mark me as a religious failure in the eyes of the ethereals, but I also figured my faith was equally split between the two. I still believed in the bases for the Divinities, and felt their doctrine had been grossly misrepresented and extorted to suit the needs of those in power, but I also could no longer refute the true nature of the Wielders and where they came from. I knew little of their faith in the Founders, but something deep inside told me I respected it and wanted to form a deeper connection with my lineage's history.

As I ran my hands along both obelisks, I felt a pang in my heart to realize how much deeper the divots sank in on the Founder's obelisk. It signified just how great a difference in volume of prisoners belonging to the Founder Faith had passed through over those who belonged to the Church of the Divine. I couldn't help but wonder how many of those prisoners who wore down the stone beneath my fingers had done so under my father's reign. How many had he sent through this pass, knowing he was condemning them to never return to an Eisa they knew? Perhaps our being sent here was some sort of Divine justice after all. How many more had passed through under his father's orders, and his father's, and so on back to Emperor Valamir? How had Valamir forged such a convincing and vicious lie that would live for centuries?

"Keep moving," I felt a jab to my back, interrupting my pensive thoughts, as a soldier hurried me forward.

"Do you hear that whistling?" Kira murmured, eyes bright and searching.

"I don't hear anything," Theo replied.

"I think it's one of the caves!" Kira closed her eyes, narrowing her senses to the sound.

"Hush," Inessa commanded, and I looked over my shoulder at her, expecting to see her cross with Kira's distraction. Instead she too had her eyes closed, brows furrowed. "I'm trying to listen."

"Stop all that concentrating!" Our guard barked, his eyes narrowing suspiciously at Inessa and Kira. "One foot in front of the other, eyes *open*. That's an order."

"Come on," I grabbed Ina's hand behind me and brought her up to stand with Kira. "We don't want to make any trouble for ourselves."

"I hear it," Inessa whispered after we'd walked a few more steps.

"You do?" I looked at my sister in confusion. "I can only hear the wind."

"How did it go Kira? The Ballad of Moroz?" Inessa smiled as her eyes squinched over her vine embroidered scarf. "*There once was a young maiden…*"

"*Fair and kind and bright,*" Kira jumped in. Together they sang the wistful melody that told the tale of the ice caves and the danger of prolonged exposure to the cold. The same wistful tale the ballet we'd seen on Kira's birthday was based on.

"So loved the beauty of winter, until it took her life.
If you listen closely you can hear her song,
In the dead of winter
The Ice Caves sing along."

The guards looked at one another, but to my surprise, none of them barked for my sisters to cease singing. They likely were familiar with the old lullaby themselves, and knew there was no hidden magic with which to Wield. Though, had it been Yulia, they might have had another reaction.

Theo sighed heavily, his shoulders drooping. Then he too joined into the song, his voice low, melancholy, and rich.

Dance with me, dance with me,
Amidst the tumbling flakes.
The winters are a melody.
It called me to the mountains,
I ran far away.

When Theo nudged my arm, as if to ask if I would join in, I hesitated. I wondered if that ballad had originally been the plight of an Ice Wielder, set to wander the Eisan landscape. The melody my siblings sang was haunting, echoing tones through the frozen mountain pass, and the lyrics hit my ear differently than they ever had before. The longing for the winter, the search for connection to it eventually leading the girl far away from home in the dangerous cold— I hadn't even realized I'd placed myself in those very shoes. The notion brought tears to my eyes, but I blinked them away, worried they might freeze and alarm the soldiers. Instead I opened my mouth and joined the next verse, slipped a gloved hand into my brothers as we walked, and wondered if he felt a strange new resonance himself.

Sing with me, sing with me

In the frigid caves
The ice echoes harmonies,
Leads me to a glaciered grave.
This young girl,
Who ran away.

Hear me hear me
Whispers on the wind,
Warning me to turn,
Return to where I've been.
But the winter's hold is strong,
So I continue on,
Into the mountain, higher
I ran away.

Bite me, bite me,
With your frosted teeth.
Hungry are the winters
High in the mountains
Valleys underneath.
Devour all
In the nightfall,
So I ran away.

Freeze me, freeze me,
Over where I lay.
Cover me in ice,
So I will always stay,
This young girl—
Fair and kind and bright—
This young girl,
Who ran away.

Bury me, bury me
Beneath the fallen snow.

Under frosted waters,
Sinking deep below.
How lovely are these winters,
So that I may go?
Carry me away.
At last, I go home.

The ending of our ballad was punctuated with a clump of snow hurtling through the air and striking one of the guards in the face with a loud *oof*. Each of us whipped our heads around, the impromptu vocals still reverberating around the small space.

"Who did that?" Another guard barked while the first wiped the slush from his face. He lifted his rifle, waiting for us to give even the tiniest indication to justify using it. We each went rigid and raised our hands, lips pressed tightly closed, showing we meant no harm. Another clump whizzed down, narrowly missing the man with the gun. This time it was clear to see that it wasn't a random bit dislodging, but firmly formed snowballs.

The soldier pointed the gun to the sky, aiming wildly. "How are you doing that? When I get my sights set…" He growled.

"It's not us!" Kira gasped, also craning her neck to see where the snowballs were coming from.

"Don't fire that in here, you idiot! You want to bury us in an avalanche?" The first soldier placed his palm on the barrel of the rifle and shoved it down.

"Probably some riff raff from Kyrith intent on harassing us." Another shrugged and waved us forward. "Stop gawking. Carry on through!"

So we marched quietly, defeated, and hurried towards our next checkpoint in the frozen oblivion.

KYRITH

Kyrith is both a city and region to the east of the Kyrith Pass, in the Eisvech Mountains. Known as a wasteland lost to a perpetual winter, its populace is few, and the territory is primarily used for exiling criminals. Unlivable for most, this region was once claimed to be the home of Ice Founder, Eisa. Additionally, Kyrith is known for its *Singing Ice Caves*, a series of interconnected caves through the region with ice that shimmers so strongly, the refracted light is turned to audible musical notes, giving the appearance of a *"Symphony of Ice."* A variety of tales have been spun around these caves, but perhaps the most famous is the *The Ballad of Moroz,* and the subsequent *"Winter Maiden"* retellings.

FORTY-FOUR

"Yulia!" Kira flung herself out of the transport van and flung herself into Yulia, who had been watching for our arrival, nearly bowling her over. "Please tell me you haven't forgotten me!"

"How could I ever forget you, you goon," Yulia smiled, hugging Kira back tightly. As her lids closed, her lashes dislodged a constellation of tears falling down her cheeks. "A whole lifetime and I'd never forget you, let alone a month."

"Promise?" Kira sniffled.

"Come on, you two," I placed a hand gently on Kira's back and ushered them forward. "Let's not give them a reason to harass us. Where are Mama and Papa?"

"I would have expected them to be with you, Yulia," Inessa added.

"Mama is in bed. The stress of the separation has been particularly hard on her heart."

"I suppose I should have assumed as much…" Inessa tried

to keep the edge out of her voice at the familiar irritant of our mother's ailments. "And Papa?"

"He was with Mama, but I think he'd received a letter he was going to read before joining me to wait for you."

"You seem pretty comfortable here..." Theo murmured, trailing along behind us after Yulia paused to give each of us a proper hug of greeting.

"It's been... odd." Yulia scrunched her nose. "When we first arrived here it was with a different batch of soldiers. They were much kinder than this new lot that's been brought in with you. I think it's because they didn't have a proper supervisor on the premises to make sure they weren't being overly friendly towards us."

"That is odd." I nodded, pausing on the steps of the front porch to scan the horizon.

Everything in Kyrith was still cloaked in snow, and much of the immediate property was open and exposed. The nearest tree line wasn't for some distance, the winter ground undulating into frosted knolls before ever reaching the forest. I could see the mountains in the distance, carved of ice on one side, while the side I couldn't see from my vantage point I knew tumbled from towering glaciers to the craggy stones of Kesgoldol. I wondered briefly if Amary had ever made it safely over the border like she wished.

"I'm glad to see you've adjusted so well," I smiled at Yulia only to receive a shrug and averted gaze in return.

"We are here now, so there isn't really much to do about it. I knew Mama was worrying about Theo the whole time so I didn't want to upset her more."

"Oh come on," Kira's brows furrowed in concern before she plastered a bright smile on her lips, swiveling herself around to stand in front of Yulia. "Don't tell me you've been moping in silence all this time, dwelling on such negative thoughts when I wasn't here to cheer you up!"

"What else are we supposed to do or feel when we've been

condemned to this cursed life?"

"They aren't curses, Yulia," Inessa reminded her gently, cupping her cheek. "The affinities are as much a part of us as our ears and noses."

Yulia ducked away from Inessa's touch, her hand brushing where Ina had connected, her fingers trembling. There was a deep tempestuousness in her big blue eyes. Something warred inside her, and I had a finite number of guesses as to what it was. We were all corrupted in her mind, but while she, Mama, Papa, Kira, and Theo had been accosted with it, it seemed Inessa and I had chosen it. That fact was now in conflict with how she saw us as her sisters, and I longed to tell her I knew exactly how she was feeling. But, it seemed she wasn't in a place to receive that branch of solace yet.

"I don't think any part of what I saw was a natural part of me… or anyone." She looked at me for a moment before quickly glancing down at her feet and tugging the sleeve of her coat. "We should go inside, it's cold out here. They'll show you around the property later."

"Do you think Yulia is afraid of us?" I asked Inessa as we fell in line behind at the back of the group.

"I wish I could say she wasn't but I'm not sure. Did you ever get her to tell you what she experienced in her mind's eye on the scaffold? Before they split us up?"

"No, she refused to tell me anything about it. Then I tried to explain to her what you and I knew of the situation and she just walled herself off even more. Only Kira has any insight and even that seems to be rather sparse considering how close they are."

"How much of her did you see when we were up there?"

"Not much," I admitted bitterly. Most of my attention had been on Roland. His name, even without being spoken, left a sour tang on my tongue, and my heart seized in my chest.

"She was positively frantic and beside herself. It almost seemed like she somehow forced herself back into the mentalscape a fourth time."

"Keep moving. We aren't here to wait on all your whispering and pageantry," One of the guards reprimanded us for lingering in the doorway, dusting the snow on his fur lined hat with blatant disdain.

"What would be waiting for her that fourth time if she already met her three affinities?" I whispered, hardly even absorbing the new house we entered that we were to call home.

"I haven't a clue. Nothingness perhaps? Poor thing. I wish she would just hear us out. We could explain it all to her if she would just stop shutting us out."

"Can you really blame her?"

"What do you mean? She is making the choice to stay in the dark at this point, wouldn't you say?"

"Don't be so insensitive, Ina. She met the same affinity that possessed her and nearly killed Theo. I highly doubt any introductions would have gone smoothly."

"You have a point," Inessa sighed, her shoulders drooping with a sudden invisible weight. "I honestly always figured Yulia would be the last one to accept the Wielding anyway. It's not fair she's gotten to know what has been in our heads all this time but won't allow us even a tiny glimpse into hers. Even if it could mean helping her. Either way, I don't think she's truly *afraid* of us… maybe just unsure? Or angry for keeping it from her after what she went through."

"Girls!" Our conversation was forgotten in an instant the moment we heard Papa's voice welcoming us into the kitchen. Our feet flew across the old wood floors, a full thunderous creaking split by trills of childlike delight and we barreled into the comfort of our father's arms. The cantankerous guard's shouts of irritation at our enthusiasm echoed down the hallway, but I could barely hear it from where my ear was pressed to Papa's chest listening to his strong heartbeat.

When we pulled away I could tell there was somberness peeking through the excitement of seeing us all. Kira and Theo had already proceeded on to find Mama where she was resting, and I could hear the muffled sounds of enthusiasm lilt through the house.

"Is everything alright?" Inessa asked, clearly noticing the same malaise in Papa that I had. "I mean, outside of the obvious."

"Yulia said you received a letter," I prompted, jarred with apprehension. "Has something else happened?"

"No more," The guard barked, ripping the papers away from Papa. "We said news clippings weren't permitted on the premises."

"It came in a letter." Papa's face grew dark with reproach. "Unsolicited."

"Then perhaps there should be no more post, if you and your correspondents can't abide by the rules." The guard loomed over Papa, flecks of spit from his threat hitting my father's face. "You could be rotting in a cell. I wouldn't get too greedy."

I shrank at the disrespect, my fists clenched. I could have never imagined in my wildest dreams witnessing my father enduring such opprobrium to the point of derision from his previous subordinates. It made my skin crawl beneath an unbearable heat. But Papa stood firm, unflinching, uncowed.

The guard snorted, and threw the pages back on the table. "Get rid of this."

Once he vacated the room, Inessa and I lunged for the papers, both of our attention on the fact they had been described as *news clippings*— something we had seen little to none of since our incarceration. Splitting the fragmented pages between us, our hands began to tremble as we read the headlines. *Mass Wielder Purge in Tuyet, Citizen's Accused of Wielding Torn from Homes in Dead of Night, Streets Paved in Broken Glass Following Mass Wielder Roundup.* Friedrich had officially launched his own war on the Wielders of Eisa, and had succeeded in rallying the public to his cause.

"I thought these particular updates might be of interest to you two," Papa commented, his voice unassuming, but his posture remained stiff as he plucked the clippings from our horror-slackened grips and tossed them into the smoldering coals of the kitchen stove. "I've been receiving similar reports as these from all across Eisa.

He had not asked us to explain our involvement with the Wielders, or how we had come to garner the knowledge we had, and we had not offered an explanation. There was an invisible rift existing in the unspoken between us. A rift no one of us seemed to know how to cross without the bridge of candor we couldn't yet sustain.

It wasn't our familiar bond that had been shaken. That, I could tell, remained strong, innate, and in tact. We were and still would remain a unit. But, individually, there were questions I wish my father could both freely ask and freely answer without the strain of appearance and station barring the way. More than anything, I wanted to dispel the disappointment in me he surely must have felt when he realized his own daughter, one whom he'd held in high regard for her duty and diligence, had strayed from the path he'd carefully marked. It was a breach in trust and understanding I longed to mend, lest it tear further. Perhaps one day, I'd be strong enough to hammer the first nail into that bridge.

Papa cleared his throat when Ina and I merely managed to stare at him with large, unblinking eyes. "I'm going to join the others. I'll leave you two to yourselves for a moment. If any of the men give you trouble, it's best just to return to our room."

"Yes, Papa," Inessa and I murmured in tandem.

Papa paused in the doorway, releasing a heavy sigh. He didn't turn around, but inclined his head just enough to speak over his shoulder. "I am sorry, my dear girls, if there was a personal attachment to anyone affected." And with that, he vanished into the far hallway.

"How awful. All those people…" Inessa turned her body to face me, her face slowly crumpling. "Oh, Sorrel. I don't think I can bear it." I wrapped my arms around her and tugged her close, reaching up to run my hand gently over the back of her head.

"I know, Ina." My own voice hitched in my throat and my chest heaved with resentment so bitter it could have burned a hole like acid.

"Everyone… everything. It's all gone." Her legs started to buckled as she lost her composure to stand. I held fast and managed to spin her around to sit in the kitchen chair so she could slump onto the table.

"Steady," I murmured, pushing away the stray strands of gold sticking to her glistening forehead.

"Roland, Friedrich, Arrian, Vadia, Rafe," Ina prattled off the names of causality. "All of the innocent soldiers, and the citizens we tried to save. Eisa has shattered and it's all our faults. Now even Yulia doesn't know how to look at us the same! After everything that's happened and our blasted family still can't have a normal, candid conversation about any of it. I can't take it, Sorrel. I mean it. I just can't take it. It's going to kill me. My heart has broken too many times and it's going to kill me."

"Shhh." I knelt in front of her, cupping her face in my hands to lift her gaze to mine. "None of this is going to kill you. You're going to survive this pain, Ina."

"I can't breathe," she whispered, curling her arms around her stomach as tears poured from her haunted eyes. Her breath quickened, desperately seeking to restore the phantom air of safety and peace in her lungs. "You heard Friedrich blame us. We condemned ourselves and our sisters!"

"You're going to survive this, Ina," I repeated, my eyes pricking as I watched my sister falling apart before me.

Ever since that moment on the scaffold when we realized we'd been revealed— no, since Hykner's disappearance— I had seen her fraying at the seams, a single thread unraveling her at last. I hadn't known how to comfort her, my own spirit bludgeoned to a pulp and sifted through countless times looking for answers that weren't within me to glean.

"I'm right here with you," I spoke softly, but was resolute, the statement offered as a promise. "We will get through this trial together."

Inessa shook her head woefully and I placed my hand on her chest, tapping in a deliberate rhythm as I hummed our favored lullaby. Eventually, the rapid shuddering of her breathing slowed to match the cadence of my drumming and her heartbeat followed suit.

She sniffed and wiped the tears from her cheeks, reaching for a napkin to dab at her nose. "Sorry."

"There's no need to apologize. We've all had quite a shock. That takes time to mend."

"You can't be the only thing that keeps us from cracking apart at every turn. You're processing your own hurts and here we are, still expecting you to be this pillar for us… when you're possibly the one who needs to come undone most."

"Come on," I sidestepped Inessa's assessment, gritting my teeth under a practiced smile. Let's go see Mama and visit with everyone for a while. As a family. I think it's what we all need after so long apart."

I left out that I couldn't stand to fall apart again as I had that day in Tuyet. That I had betrayed myself to let myself fall so low when I should have done more to prevent the suffering we were experiencing now. I couldn't tell her that I needed to bide my resilience and keep my emotions stored deep within me where they couldn't lead me astray again.

That time with our family was all we really had left to claim for ourselves in this world, and I wasn't truly sure that would ever change. The sword and shield Hykner once praised in me were both battered and dull without means of repair. My days as the soldier Darion had described before joining the war, felt ever present on the horizon, so I'd have to keep marching through this haze of despair, damaged armor and all.

Whether it was hope or revenge I was clinging to, I couldn't tell anymore, and I could feel my compassionate nature threatening to curdle inside me if it meant some future promise of vindication. Whatever was brewing from the remnants of that pulp, maybe it would forge a new strength to wield. An inner strength I had yet to be acquainted with.

As I stepped into the new room we'd be called home,

overstuffed with seven cots, and my family huddled together in a clump of bittersweet reunion— as they opened their arms and beckoned me into the center to receive their unconditional love despite all we'd kept from one another— turbulence quaked within me, whipping into a cyclone of opposing emotions.

I could contain it. I could hold it and feel it all on my own where my pain couldn't be used as another means of dragging us all down.

FORTY-FIVE

"**G**o, have a look around." Papa put his arm around me and hugged me close as I stared out at the front yard from the porch.

The day after our arrival, the guards told Ina, Kira, Theo, and I that we were permitted to walk around the property, but would be shot on sight if we stepped one toe out of those established boundaries. We were to be monitored always, except for when we were sleeping or resting in the single room the seven of us now shared.

Papa's voice dropped low, laced with sympathy and regret. "A walk, I've found, gives me a sense of freedom I can't seem to muster while indoors. They might be watching you, and they might have boxed us in, but they haven't stolen the fresh air and sunshine. That's still ours to take in."

"Alright, Papa," I agreed amicably, despite the sloshing in my stomach and the weariness in my bones. I hadn't slept a wink the first night in the house, too on edge to stop mulling over thoughts and memories.

Papa pressed his lips to the top of my head and sighed heavily, and I drank in the closeness I feared I had tainted. "It's good to have you back— to have us all together. It makes hope seem possible again. Enjoy your walk."

I winced at the contrary defeat acknowledged in my father's words as he stepped back into the house. Hope only *seemed possible*. He hadn't reclaimed it yet. Everything in me wished I could restore that light for him, but once more I was powerless against an unbearable force bearing down on me. It had been too hard to make sense of my feelings, so I tried to stuff them back deep inside, but this time it seemed they refused to go back in their box. Strangled emotions and muted apathy tore my waking hours apart, unsure whether I felt everything or nothing all at once. My dreams were much the same, forcing me to relive horrifying moments, knowing there was nothing even the foresight of a dream would let me change.

"I'm going to walk around," I announced to the guard posted on the far end of the chipped wraparound porch, keeping a lazy gaze on me.

When he turned to call over his shoulder, and relay one of the prisoner daughters was walking the property, I quickly slipped my shoes off and stepped off the porch into the snow. It yielded with something between a crunch and a slosh beneath me. I paid careful mind not to stray too far.

My breath billowed in front of my face and with each step I took, I tried to connect my mind to my feet— to the ice on the ground. If I could somehow build on the little understanding of the Wielding process I'd made while studying Lenya's notes, then maybe in time I could do something to help us escape. I cursed myself for handing those pages over to Roland.

Even if we did escape, where would we go? Who would give the fallen descendants of Valamir sanctuary? Still, it was better than doing nothing. We couldn't return home to Svyat Gavan later, not with the unrest of the people, and certainly not after the brutal purging of Wielders in Eisa under Friedrich's veiled totalitarian reign, but something told me the frail promise of being sent to a farm in the middle of nowhere in eastern Eisa was something we couldn't pour too much hope into.

I bit my lip, anger and despair warring within me for dominance. My footsteps grew faster and heavier, weighed down by the gravity of the situation, until I was stomping around like a child in a tantrum. I wished I could return to the capital and freeze over the castle now homing our betrayers. All the healing I'd done, all the saving, and for what? To end up here? For those civilians to be beaten and killed in the streets and their assaults be portrayed as an act of valor?

I craved the release of destruction. My body trembled with the desire to exact revenge on The Rusevs. An icicle to the heart for every pretty lie I'd been told. A storm with wind as rough as sandpaper to tear at their skin— a grain for every tear we had shed. I'd call down the stars to rend them in two for the hope of refugees they'd taken away. I'd bury them beneath a thick layer of scarlet frost along with the dreams I'd never see come to be.

I felt a tiny crack in my chest, like a reminder that my thoughts were beginning to chip away at my own humanity, and I bit back a wail of frustration. I did my best to quell the monster I'd always feared now growing and raging with me. I'd never been good with processing my anger, and I had no idea how to begin eradicating the chaotic, steaming energy from my body every time I thought of Roland.

I felt something press against the arch of my foot through the snow. The snap pulled me from my mind and tethered me back to reality, dulling the boiling in my veins with distraction. Stepping back a pace, I stooped to see what I had stepped on.

A snowdrop.

The stem was broken and the petals crushed. I gingerly plucked the tiny trodden flower from the snow and felt the urge to hurl it against the ground with everything in me. But, as I felt the cool of the flower against my palm, I sighed, exhaling all of the violent, angry thoughts, and cradled it to my chest.

"I'm sorry," I whispered, the words catching in my throat as tears began running slowly down my face. "I'm broken too."

All the destruction inside me was merely a mask trying to stifle the spiraling anguish of betrayal. I knew I wasn't truly capable of fighting so savagely, and in truth, rather than destroy, I longed more than anything to mend and erase. But that wasn't an option now, and this time there was no last minute escape, and no one was coming to rescue us. No Rafe, no Roland, no Vadia, nor Hykner nor Maggie— all of my allies were dead, lost, or liars. It was me and my family left, and all that was left for me now was to protect them as best as I could.

Smothered beneath a blanket of hopelessness instead of wrath, I didn't try to hold myself back this time. Alone, I sank down into the snow, still clutching the flower, and squeezed my eyes tightly shut. I cried, the tears of heartbreak overflowing into the frost, and wondered if I'd ever be whole again. I hated every drop of emotion surging through me, and even more so, I hated the irrepressible need for releasing it despite my head commanding me to keep it all contained and properly managed. But, if I didn't let a little out, I feared I'd burst, just as Inessa had the day before, only there would be no one who could calm me down like I had for her.

"Sorrel?" I startled at the small, uncertain voice of Kira behind me. "Are you alright? The snow is getting your dress all wet and it's freezing out here."

I sniffed and quickly wiped the tears from my cheeks before rising to my full height. "The cold doesn't affect me," I reminded her gently, turning to face her.

"Oh, right. I forgot." Kira squinted at me, her gaze intense. "Have you been crying again?"

"I—" I faltered, failing to lie convincingly.

"I'm sorry."

"What for?"

"That you're so sad." Her eyes flicked down to the patch of

snowdrops I'd unearthed, then to the flower peeking out from where I still clutched it in my palm.

"You don't need to worry about me." I forced a smile. "I'm doing just fine."

Kira scowled at me, before the lines of annoyance began to give way into sympathy and sorrow. She rushed forward and threw her arms around me with such force I stumbled backwards.

"Don't lie to me, Sorrel," She whimpered, though her voice was firm. "No more lies. I can't take anyone else lying to my face."

I returned my sister's hug, squeezing her tight. In her embrace, I felt my spirits lift to match her earnestness until I was smiling for real. The heat of anger and devastation turned warm and soothing. Perhaps, there was still someone left who could settle me after all, and allow for a reality where I could coexist with the storms locked deep within me. Could I expect such a thing from my little sister?

"I will be fine," I answered honestly and rested my chin on her head as she held fast.

I knew her heart was morning Roland too, though as a brother rather than a lover. I wondered how that pain must differ from mine. Lovers could come and go, I knew that was a hard fact of life, but to lose a sibling— how that must hurt in a different and confusing way. I couldn't begin to fathom that kind of loss. Especially with such perceived close bonds and admiration.

Kira had loved Roland deeply as her elder brother. I'd seen her turn her wrath on Friedrich and Arrian, but for Roland, I could tell she was struggling to discern her emotions. Not to mention the toll it had surely taken on her to have been separated from Yulia for such a long stint. Kira wore her feelings on her sleeve. Having no idea what her feelings were, and having her best friend shipped away ahead of her, probably had left her feeling naked and vulnerable in a way she'd never experienced before. Had I comforted her enough these past few months, or had my suffocating emotions betrayed me again— and, by extension, betrayed my loved ones with my collateral distraction?

"Let's get you inside," I whispered gently and tried to pull away, but Kira held tight around my waist.

"No. The snow makes you feel better, doesn't it?"

"It can at times."

"Then we will stay out here."

"Kira, you're shivering."

"I want you to feel better!" Her voice rose with an edge of desperation.

"Hey," I leaned back enough to be able to cup her chin in my hands and lift her gaze to meet mine, just as I had done with Ina. Her eyes were rimmed red with emotion, but no tears had spilled. "Standing out in the cold isn't going to undo everything that's happened."

"I want you to feel better." Her voice trembled.

"I will," I promised.

"Then maybe..." Kira swallowed hard and blinked a few times. "Maybe I'll feel better. If everyone else is better too."

"Oh, Kira," I breathed, my heart breaking into a million pieces. I pulled her close again. "This hurt isn't something that's going to easily leave us. We just have to keep living, and day by day it will lessen until all that pain is just a memory."

"I don't know if I can be that patient." Her voice cracked.

"We still have each other don't we? Mama, Papa, Inessa, Yulia, and Theo— we are all going to help each other get through this moment. And then the moment after that."

"Promise?"

"I promise. So long as we draw breath, we will get through this as a family. Just like we always have. That's one thing that hasn't changed, and won't be changing anytime soon." Somehow this perspective on the same sentiment I'd stifled yesterday felt comforting. Perhaps consolidating to my family instead of the world was a blessing in disguise, rather than another act of Divine retribution.

Kira paused, her breath ragged beneath her shivering, and I could hear her teeth beginning to chatter uncontrollably. I smiled and separated from my sister— and this time she let me.

"I've had my time sulking in the snow. How about we go sit by the fire now?"

Kira smiled back and sniffled against the cold. "Deal." She slipped her hand into mine and I felt the warmth of her spirit surging within her grasp. "It's going to get better."

As I looked at her, she beamed like dawn breaking away the darkness of nightfall. It warmed my heart to realize Kira's very soul was the embodiment of the sunrise she adored so much. She held such a depth of light within her, I didn't believe there was a force in all the world that could truly rob her of it.

Together we lifted our heads and headed back to the house, our steps and hearts marching in tandem, daring to keep optimism on the horizon. Evidently there were still two soldiers trudging on.

FORTY-SIX

I woke before dawn. Our stay at the new house was finally beginning to feel normal— or as normal as it could be a few weeks in. I no longer jumped and tensed at every foreign sound, and my days had returned to a relatively standard, albeit uneventful, routine. We would wake early, make our cots, and file into the dining room for our allotted breakfast. The days were spent mostly to ourselves to read, write or other miscellaneous and unobtrusive activities. We did also help contribute to various chores such as mending, and basic housework. But this morning was a little out of the ordinary and my waking so early wasn't by chance.

"It's time," I whispered gently, shaking Yulia's shoulder to rouse her.

"What?" She bolted upright, immediately on alert for danger.

I squeezed her hand reassuringly and jerked my chin to where Kira was still sleeping in her cot. "Sunrise. We made a promise, didn't we?"

"Do you think she still wants to?" Yulia whispered, rubbing the sleep from her eyes, though I was glad to see that her unease in mine and Inessa's presence had all but dissipated since our initial arrival.

"No matter where we are or what we are doing. That was the deal." I'd watched my littlest sister carry so much on her shoulders these past few months, and in many ways it felt like she had aged several years in the span of one. I knew breaking the usual order of things came with a degree of risk, but something deep in my gut refused to let this promise be one I couldn't keep.

Yulia nodded slowly. "You're right. We should be able to see it in the next room better than in here, if we aren't caught."

I smiled and crept over with Yulia in tow to wake our little sister. "Kira?"

Her blue eyes opened in narrow slits before popping open with alarm. "What is it? Is Theo alright?"

"Theo is fine," I soothed, running my hand over her forehead.

"Oh, I had a dream one of those guards was bullying him." Kira sagged with relief. "I was just about to tackle one."

"Very noble of you. Come on," I urged.

"What for?"

"It's time to watch your sunrise." Yulia tugged on Kira's arm. "No matter where we are or what we are doing, we swore we'd always watch it on your birthday."

Kira's eyes twinkled. The sight made tears prick at my eyes. Giving so much of her own spirits to all of us, it was time someone else replenished her reserves.

"I didn't think we were doing that anymore... not after everything that happened. We don't have the freedom."

"Says who?" Yulia wrinkled her nose.

"The guards with the big guns, you goon," Kira laughed, batting at Yulia's arm.

I brought a finger to my lips and gestured to the rest of our sleeping family. "Don't wake them. If we are quiet, no one should notice us."

We had been told we had permission to wander the property so long as we notified an officer of our whereabouts and stayed within the property lines. Outside was well monitored, lest any of us get any bright ideas of escaping into the night. It had been an unspoken rule however, that these freedoms only existed in a certain time frame, daylight hours only.

"Are we leaving the room?" Kira whispered, throwing back her blanket and hopping to her feet. She hesitated, then seeing how Yulia had wrapped herself in her bedspread, she grasped the fabric and tugged it snuggly around her shoulders.

"This window doesn't face due east," Yulia explained, then pointed to the door. "But the next room over with the supplies, that one is eastward facing."

The three of us linked hands and carefully pried open the door with minimal screeches of the hinges. With hushed, careful footsteps we entered the hallway and hurried to the next room. Full of supplies, like Yulia had mentioned, there was only just enough space for us to squeeze our three faces in the frame of the window.

"They have a lot of useless stuff in here," Kira commented, shaking her foot free of a rope caught on her ankle. "I wonder if some of these shovels and ropes and things were left behind from the previous owners."

"There is a mineshaft somewhere over the hill," I nodded. "We aren't allowed over there but I heard some of the guards saying it was damaged and full of water now."

"Hey," Yulia pawed restlessly at my arm to reclaim our attention back on the window. "It's starting."

Kira and I turned back to peer through the frosted glass. On the horizon, over the tops of the nearby woods, the blazing red and golden rays of sunlight mixed with the starry indigo blue to turn the sky a rich purple. Yulia and I wrapped our arms around Kira and hugged tight, leaning our heads on top of hers.

Something in the moment felt muted. It was as if we were grasping at the echoes of previous happiness, unable to hold it firmly in our hands now. Kira's usual radiated light of euphoria, strong enough to send the frost into hiding, was a mere faint remnant of what it once was.

"The sunrise is colder than last year," Kira spoke quietly. "I don't think it's going to thaw the ice this time."

Her words drove a knife straight through my heart as they confirmed my own sentiments. Despite her best efforts, she was weakening under the constraints just the same as the rest of us. She didn't have the strength to hold herself together with her infectious smile *and* banish the winter. It was too much to ask even of her boundless optimism. Neither Yulia nor I had to think too deeply to understand that the changing of the seasons would come with or without our sister, but also the absence of warmth was still directly correlated to her disposition.

"The ice always melts," I mumbled. "Summer will return whether they like it or not."

"I know it isn't the same, Kira," Yulia added, rubbing her hand up and down her arm. "But, remember the most important part of the ritual isn't the ice melting or winter changing to spring."

"Yeah?" Kira sighed. "I always liked that part though."

"The most important part has always been this right here," she shook our little unit gently and smiled. "Even after everything they've done, this moment is still ours— just us three. They didn't manage to take that away from us, so enjoy the peace, and Sorrel and I will keep you warm until the sun gets a little stronger."

"Always," I beamed.

"Thank you. I love you both, and I hope you know how much." Kira closed her eyes and took a steadying breath. Already her touch felt a little warmer in my grip, and my own spirits lifted.

"Of course we do. We love you too, you maddening little ball of sunshine," I laughed softly. "Never change. Promise me that?"

"Why would I go and do something silly like that?" Kira snorted. "I like who I am. No one is going to steal that from me."

"Good."

"Happy birthday, Kira" Yulia sighed, and for the first time

since back in Tuyet, I could swear I heard genuine happiness on her breath.

"Happy birthday," I echoed.

The sun climbed fully into the sky, and we watched in silence. The moment wasn't grand or spectacular like it had been in previous years, but Yulia was right. It was still peaceful, and it was still ours.

"Come on, we need to hurry back to our room before the next guard passes through." Taking a quick look through the window to see the soldier still standing at attention on the porch, I tugged my sisters lightly away from the window and herded them towards the door.

"Alright, alright. No need to push," Kira grumbled, shuffling forward.

I signaled for them to wait as I peeled the door from the frame and scanned the hallway through the tiny opening. "It's clear. We need to make a run for it one at a time. Are you ready?"

"Ready," Yulia and Kira confirmed.

I yanked the door open and fled to the bedroom, slipping in unscathed. My heart pounded, but I was safe. Sticking my head back out, I waved Kira forward. She bolted to the door and poked her head out beside mine.

"Hurry—" I hissed, stiffening as I heard the door to the front of the house creak loudly, followed by the dull thuds of boots on the old wooden floors. "The guard is coming!"

Yulia's eyes stretched wide, and in a split second of deliberation she chose to make a dash for our bedroom, closing the door to the storage room tightly behind her.

She was almost in the clear, but failed to make it back to the room before the guard turned the corner. She tripped over the edge of her blanket and crashed into the floor with a hard thud. The soldier rushed over to her, and Yulia cowered on the ground waiting for the reprimand to come. But to all of our surprise, the man held out his hand to help her to her feet. He dipped his head to her, then to us in turn, spotting our heads poking through the doorway.

"Good morning," his voice was scratchy and low but his face held no trace of animosity. "You might want to have your sister apply some ice to those knees to keep them from bruising."

Yulia stared at him, eyes stretched wide. "A-alright." She stammered.

I narrowed my eyes, wondering if he was one of the men who had seen my affinities put on display in the capital. But as he turned more to the light I caught sight of a long jagged scar running from his jaw down to beneath his uniform. He had once been a patient at the hospital, I realized. I had sewn his stitches with my own hands when they had popped prematurely.

I'd used ice, I recalled, to help with many of his aches and pains. It wasn't my affinity he was alluding to, but rather a nod at the help I had given him that he hadn't forgotten. I fished my mind for the memory of his name, then stepped into the hall to take Yulia's hand and guide her back to our room.

"Corporal Unov," I acknowledged him, not missing the satisfied glint of surprise at my recognition of him. "Thank you. We wanted to see the sunrise on our youngest sister's birthday, but we will take her back to bed now." I squeezed Yulia's arm and tugged her along with me.

"Very good. Be careful Princesses. Not all guards here would look kindly on this breach of the rules."

"Of course. We appreciate your kindness and understanding."

"Happy birthday to the little one," Unov smiled and gave us a wink before continuing down the hall past us.

"Thank you," Yulia called meekly after him, a small smile curling her lips.

As we hurried back to our room, I couldn't help but feel a tiny blossom of hope blooming in my chest. Maybe all wasn't lost. Maybe enough of the soldiers knew us, or would come to know us well enough, that our time here in captivity wouldn't be so harsh. If they were capable of kindness, then we could get through this.

FORTY-SEVEN

"Zdraevit Family, report to the front lot. Immediately!" We were jarred away from our various activities by the bark of a commanding officer and herded out the front door.

"What's happening?" Papa demanded. In response, a soldier shoved him in the shoulder down the steps.

"Isn't that the man from yesterday?" Kira whispered to me before the order was given for us to line up in order. As I stepped into place between Inessa and Yulia, I saw who Kira was referring to and my stomach plummeted.

Unov was standing alone in the center of the yard, his hands bound behind his back. None of the other soldiers were interacting with him, save for the two that were posted as his guards. The longer I looked, the more the scene in front of me began to make sense. This was an execution that we were being made to witness. I could only assume the crime.

"Corporal Unov has been taken into custody for the crime

of treasonous affiliations, and those present will witness his sentence."

"No, don't! He just helped me to my feet when I tripped in the hallway. There's no need for this," Yulia pleaded. She rushed forward out of line only to be blocked by two more guards, crossing their rifles in front of her to serve as a barrier.

"Yulia," Mama hissed a warning, her body trembling with fear.

"You can't!" Yulia ignored Mama and pressed herself against the guns, trying in vain to break through. "Let him go, send him away, but don't kill him!"

"It's alright, Young Princess Yulia, the Gentle," Unov smiled sadly. "This is to be my fate."

"No! Punish me instead, I'm the prisoner, I'm the one who fell." Tears poured freely from Yulia's panic-stricken face.

I looked around, searching for any possible way to save the man. Closing my eyes, I reached for the cold, the static, the stars—I tried to grasp at any alternative option. It pained me further to know, if Yulia had been brought up with her affinities, she could save him without breaking a sweat. But then again, she would be dooming him to life on the run for desertion. If he had made peace with his fate, would it be Yulia's place to force such a life changing decision on him?

Her words had devolved into fevered, frantic wailing as the assigned guards moved into place. Seven soldiers lined up, taking guns at random so as to not know who held the bullet, and Unov was blindfolded. A tall, squirrelly looking man stepped up and placed a cigarette in Unov's mouth, muttering his condolences as he lit it. The cigarette trembled on Unov's lips, but he inhaled deeply to settle his nerves.

"Corporal Unov, you have been found to be in breach of your duties, committing treasonous affiliations with the prisoners. You have been ordered to be executed by firing squad on today, the ninth of April," Corporal Kivek read Unov his last rights. The guards lifted their guns. "Take your aim!"

"No!" Yulia sobbed, still fighting to get past the two guards barring her path. Mama and Inessa moved forward to tug her back, while Papa, Theo, and I tried to avert our eyes. Kira was shaking beside me, but her eyes were on Yulia, and I could see she was livid at her sister's pain.

"Long live the Zdraevit Family! May the Divine see them through!" Unov cried out, his words gutting all of us watching his execution.

"Fire!"

The sound of gunfire rang through the air in overwhelming claps, as the soldiers pulled their triggers. An instant later, Unov dropped to the ground, dead. Yulia's screaming ceased, and she stood horrified, shaking with shock. Her face crumpled, and her legs buckled, bringing her to her knees in a defeated slump. Mama and Inessa looked at each other, then down at Yulia between them, unsure of what to do or how to console her. The rest of us gathered around her, and I bent to help her back to her feet with Kira's help. Yulia shuddered beneath her sobs. She looked pitifully at each of the soldiers before spinning on her heel and racing back inside to our room.

Papa glared at the officers, his voice low and menacing. "You kill one of your own for a basic courtesy. What's next, you'll gun down the cook for preparing our meals?" He clenched his fists, his veins beginning to protrude from his neck and forehead as his skin took on a crimson hue. He stepped closer, his words raising into a shout. "No, you did this to make a point. To punish us— to punish my daughter!"

"Genri," Mama placed her hand on his shoulder.

Papa spat in the direction of the squad and veered away. "Rot in the pits of Dimaer." As he passed Unov's fallen body, blood pooling around it, he bowed his head and mumbled a prayer before storming off to take a walk around the house. Mama looked fretfully at the insulted soldiers before hurrying after him. Inessa and Theo turned to head back inside, their shoulders slumped and heads lowered in submission. Kira was nowhere to be seen and had likely already followed Yulia back inside. I whispered my prayer for Unov, both to the Divinities and to the Founders—to Dimaer herself— for a peaceful afterlife wherever he found himself on the other side of that bullet.

I turned away from the scene, feeling an overwhelming shroud of defeat weighing down on my shoulders. Even the most basic of kindnesses weren't permitted. Was there really any hope left for us here? We weren't in a dark, damp dungeon or jail, but it was clear more than ever that we were still prisoners, and nothing about our lives was up to us anymore. My feet carried me indoors without my awareness until I was standing inside our room.

Kira glanced over her shoulder at me, and I could see her eyes smoldering with indignation as she continued to console Yulia. Through the window, I could see Unov's body being carried off, and I shuddered, wondering just when things had gone back to such stark black and white. It seemed Friedrich was truly taking no chances that anyone spare us any small kindness or loyalty.

His hatred for us ran that deep. Merely interacting pleasantly with us was now a death sentence. But then again, wasn't that largely how our country had operated with Wielders for centuries? That's what each of us was— A Wielder. So we would be treated no differently. I thought back to Roland describing his father's rhetoric, thinking how it must have been a guise, but actually it was entirely true. He wanted offenders and criminals to have a fair and lawful verdict, governed by the laws of our country that had been enforced for generations. Wasn't that what we were receiving now? Divine retribution for the sins of our ancestors all compiled to be carried on our shoulders.

But as I saw Yulia breaking even further into herself, my sweet kind and gentle sister, the one of us who probably rejected the magic the most ardently, I felt this punishment did not fit the crime. My stomach twisted as her sobs shook against my ears, each cry sounding more and more like glass shattering against the ground, until I was so filled with rage, I stormed out of the room to pace up and down the hallway. Once more I felt the desire for destruction brimming beneath my skin. I wanted to make them all pay for hurting my family so irreprehensibly. But as that notion crystallized in my head with more clarity, my steps slowed, and I realized that was exactly the path that Friedrich must have taken to arrive here. He had taken the road to destruction and come out the other end a true and terrible monster without the ability to recognize himself. Even understanding that did little to absolve him in my eyes.

A few moments later, Kira emerged, closing the door firmly behind her. Her face was solemn but determined as she approached me.

"I need to ask you something," she kept her voice low, darting a look around inconspicuously without turning her head to see if we were alone.

"What is it?"

"You and Ina," she started. "You started learning about your abilities didn't you?"

"We did, but—"

"Do you know anything about mine?"

I was taken aback by the intensity in Kira's stance. There wasn't a trace of amusement or levity.

"I only know what they are. Fire and Lust affinities."

"How do you use them?" Her tone could have cut glass.

"I don't know. From my understanding, it's different for each affinity."

"Maybe it has a similar strategy. How did you start with yours?"

"Why?"

"Because."

"Kira."

"Because, I can't keep sitting here day after day watching everyone break around me. I don't know how to keep holding onto hope for everyone. Yulia can hardly lift her head anymore, Inessa barely speaks, Mama and Theo are declining physically. Papa won't talk about anything seriously. And you… I need to do something to end this, Sorrel!"

"There is nothing we can do about where we are now." I

shook my head, wondering what Kira's assessment of me would have been had she completed her sentence.

"I want to fight back! I don't know how this fire works, or lust, and I don't know if it is evil or a curse— but if it means protecting my family, what I need to know is if I can use it against them."

"I don't know how it all works. I was just starting to learn for myself. But, we saw for ourselves that we can't rock the boat here. We could be shot down for even speaking about it." I lowered my voice even further to barely over a whisper.

"Sorrel!"

"It's not going to help anything, Kira!"

"Fine, maybe it won't, but maybe something in the information *will*. You can at least tell me what you do know, so I can make up my own mind about it." Kira held herself tall, her posture commanding and assertive. "If we stop fighting, then we have relinquished ourselves and they win. I will not sink that low. Will you?"

"You're supposed to connect with elemental affinities," I sighed heavily and recited what Lenya had taught me through his notebook. "Find some sort of tether from your body to it. Once your connection is strong and established enough, then you can start to conjure the element, from there you take ownership and wield it to your will."

"How am I supposed to connect to fire? Stick my hand in the fireplace?" Kira demanded, taking a step past me, her mind now on a mission to set herself on fire if only it might help.

"Maybe," I reached out and caught her arm. "But, Kira, it doesn't work. At least not quickly. I've been trying to get a hold on it ever since I got here with all the snow, and nothing has worked. I was trying before all this too."

Kira shrugged me off and pointed to the door concealing Yulia. "I can't keep going night after night listening to someone crying thinking no one else hears them. That includes *you*."

"No, what you *can't* do is take on the emotions of everyone else."

Kira snorted and squared her shoulders, lifting her chin with defiance. "I can try."

She started to walk away, but I called her back. "What did you see? Up on the scaffold."

Kira pursed her lips, curiosity about my knowledge of her strange vision clear on her face. "I saw a cloud of smoke and myself clothed in flames and ash, twirling in the fire."

"Did you accept her? The other version of you, did you touch her?"

"No," Kira looked down at her feet and shrugged. "I ran away and opened my eyes to my arms spewing fire. There was another one I ran away from too. Lust, I guess? I didn't touch her either."

"Oh."

"Should I have?"

"I don't know. Inessa and R—" I choked on Roland's name, the word turning to acid on my tongue. "Inessa mentioned something about it being the first step to reconnect with your affinity. I'm not sure you can do anything else without repairing that bond."

"So there really is nothing I can do?"

"With fire? Probably not without a torch attached to one end of it."

"But Yulia can't seem to shut hers off. She's always complaining to herself about it."

"Her affinity source isn't elemental, it's conceptual. I'm not sure how that works. Though, Lust is also conceptual. It's based in allure and emotions. Maybe she touched the version of herself she saw."

"She's terrified of it, and I know she'd never use it to free us even if she knew how," Kira sighed. "Then again, maybe she's right. These abilities are the reason we are here locked up like animals. They must be evil for someone to go to such lengths against us."

For a third time she started to walk away, and this time I let her go. Words of reassurance failed me, as I was still struggling with my own bitterness and confusion over our lot in life. None of this was anything we'd chosen. We were paying the price of a sin of our ancestors, so how could I argue the virtues in our affinities? Rather than the power itself, it seemed it was the concealment of it that had been the first evil. Was it really even our price to pay so many years later, when Eisa was on the cusp of changing those poor decisions with Theo's reign— Maybe even Papa's if he could have been convinced.

Nothing felt certain or defined anymore. What once was good was now bad, and what had been condemned was some sort of possible salvation. I couldn't offer Kira any sentiments of clarity. All I could do was let her take her time processing the situation and hope that one day everything would work itself out for good.

FORTY-EIGHT

"Who is it that's coming?" Kira asked, lowering her needle and thread from where we were sewing the remainder of our precious gems and jewelry into the lining of our dresses.

Though our hope of escape was slim, we prepped our garments with potential bribery. Mama had told us a diamond broach might make the difference between safe passage or destruction, so we diligently spent a majority of our free time stitching the last of our riches.

"The guards are acting like it's someone important."

"No one important is coming," Inessa grumbled, jabbing her own needle through the bodice hard enough that it pricked her finger on the other side. "Ouch."

"But—" Kira tried to object.

"There is no one important left in that government, Kira," Inessa bit, causing Kira to fold her arms and glower.

"You know what I mean, Ina. Someone high ranking."

"It won't do any good to speculate over it," Theo tossed in from where he lay sprawled on the bed. "I can't imagine anyone high ranking now would spell good things for us."

"We could be relocated," Papa looked up from his book to join the speculation.

"What purpose would that serve?" Theo sat up, bracing himself on trembling arms. "We are already in the frozen wastelands. Where else in Eisa could they possibly want to take us?"

"It's hard to know anything since they refuse to handle any post for us," Mama sighed heavily, sagging over her needlework. "I don't understand the harm it would do to at least let us see the paper."

"Maybe it means they're hiding something," Kira offered. "Maybe they have a weakness they are worried we will figure out."

"And what weakness would that be?" I asked, tilting my head as I rubbed at my weary eyes.

"I'm not sure, but the only reason to hide things is to keep them at an advantage. It's why you don't tell others what cards you're holding, and bluff to make them think something else."

"This isn't a game, Kira," Inessa snapped, and I flinched at her burst of anger.

"I know it isn't a game, Ina," Kira snipped back, tossing her dress on the bed next to Theo. "But, you didn't exactly go showing your cards when you went to all those meetings, did you?"

Inessa's eyes blazed. "You have no idea what you're talking about."

"I know you were led to do incriminating activities, and you chose to withhold that information. And why *did* you do that? To keep your efforts at an advantage. Stop treating me like I'm too naive to understand what's happening, Inessa. I'm not stupid."

"I kept it a secret so those people wouldn't die just because those before me were too proud to acknowledge their wrongs. We went to war, joining a side we had no business being on. I've lost people important to me in this *game*."

"Ina," I hissed sharply, darting a look from her to Papa. "We have no idea what the pressures are like to actually run a country. We don't know what we would have done when faced with a similar situation."

"I do. I would have told the truth," Inessa shouted, before dropping her head in her hands in defeat. "You were in that fire, Sorrel. How can you still act like there is a reason for all this needless bloodshed?"

"You were *what?*" Mama gasped.

"That fire in the far districts, the one you were told was started by Wielders in an ambush against the guards. She was there, hiding in a laundry chute with innocent men and women who *burned alive* behind her as they tried to escape. A wonderful Wielder named Vadia used her shadows to absorb an incendiary strike that would have killed Sorrel on the spot, and she'd only just met her that night! That brave girl also burned to death in that fire, and sacrificed herself so Sorrel could live and try to help make Eisa a better place in the future!" Inessa's eyes watered, and her face had turned red with emotion. "Did you know all that?"

"Inessa, that's enough!" I barked, images of the fire and the phantom scent of burning hair and flesh stung my eyes. "What good is it telling them all this now? You're just lashing out."

"So, those burns on your hands?" Mama asked me quietly. "It wasn't your journal?"

"I was trying to save Vadia from where she had gotten trapped on the other side of the flames," I admitted reluctantly.

"Why did you—"

Papa abruptly slammed his book closed, cutting Mama short, and closed his eyes. The rest of us jumped and whipped our heads around to face him. He sighed heavily and shook his head. "Enough, girls. Enough." His voice was hoarse, and I could see the weight of every decision crushing him with each ragged breath he took.

I was reminded of the regret I had felt that day as a child when I had taken my family out to see some frozen water and wound up getting us all attacked and traumatized. I had wished then that I'd had the foresight to know I was heading for the wrong side of a situation before I had chosen it, and I could tell Papa was feeling that same heaviness ten fold. I looked from Inessa to Kira and hoped they could read the message I was conveying on my face.

Inessa hugged her arms to her chest and puffed a heavy sigh. "Sorry, I don't mean to be so cantankerous."

"I'm sorry too," Kira echoed. "All this not knowing is driving me crazy. I want things to work out again. I will fight for it if I have to."

"Someone is coming!" Theo altered with a harsh hiss. Mama whisked the gems and special bodices into the laundry in one swift motion, concealing our last grand ploy for hope beneath a pile of dingy linens.

A moment later, the door creaked as it slowly swung open to reveal the *higher up* we'd been speculating on before the argument broke out. Dark heavy boots marched deliberately across the floor and stopped right in front of Kira.

"Arrian," Mama acknowledged in disbelief. None of us expected anyone in the immediate Rusev family to show their faces here— if not for any shred of dignity in the betrayal they'd committed, at least for the fact that we had been sentenced to house arrest in the wastelands of Eisa. It was a long journey to make to an unforgiving land just for a visit.

"Oh, Kira," Arrian smiled warmly at her, and I didn't miss the mix of hope and confusion flash in her eyes as she looked up at him.

"What do you—" she started to rise to her feet only to be knocked to the ground a heartbeat later as Arrain struck her in the face with the back of his hand.

"You want to fight for freedom that will never come? I never thought of you as stupid."

"How dare you!" Papa roared, rushing forward ready to attack Arrain, only to be restrained by two large guards accompanying him. "How dare you strike her—"

Arrain waved his hand and Papa was silenced with a quick punch to the stomach, knocking both the wind and words from his lungs. Mama let out a small yelp, unsure of who to try and help, Kira or Papa, but, as another soldier hovered over her, she ultimately could do neither.

Kira crouched on the ground, stunned for a moment before she wiped away the blood that formed from the split on her lip. The previous hope was replaced in an instant by blazing fury, and I half expected her to burst into flames right then and there.

"Such hopeful talk from you, I ought to have that tongue cut straight from your mouth. We've done worse to others you know. Others far less deserving of such a fate than you. I wonder where you would be without that clever little tongue of yours," Arrain chuckled, kicking Kira in the side to knock her back on the ground as she tried to get up. "Did I say you could get up from your knees?"

"Stop!" Theo had shifted to the edge of the bed, his knuckles white and clenched. I could see he wanted nothing more than to jump to Kira's defense, but was well aware that a strike from Arrian could very well kill him.

"Oh, I suppose *you're* going to make me? Tell me, Theodorvin," Arrian picked up a needle and tapped the tip slowly. "Would this be enough to kill someone as pathetic and useless as you? If I did this to you—" He slammed the needle into Kira's shoulder, grinning when she cried out in pain. "Would that be enough?"

"Kira!" I gasped, taking an instinctual step forward to pluck the needle from her shoulder.

Theo swallowed hard, and I looked at him, shaking my head as a warning not to provoke Arrian any further. Yulia shrank away, bringing her knees up to her chest. Behind the fear in her gaze, I could tell there was a wrathful indignation, and a similar helpless desire to aid our sister, but Yulia had already been robbed of the last of her fortitude when the kind soldier had been shot down only days earlier. Her hands fluttered to her ears, and she closed her eyes. I wondered if she was being overwhelmed by the thoughts of everyone in the room.

Inessa and I, though at a definite physical disadvantage, both moved slowly to stand behind Kira in solidarity, all previous aggravations forgotten. Inessa was shaking, though from anger, I could tell, and not from fear. In truth, I knew that although Inessa was often easily provoked by Kira and bickered with her, given the chance, she would take every blow for our little sister if it meant sparing her the pain.

"Stop this, Arrian," She growled, and had she held the power to do so, I knew she would have smote the man in a heartbeat without a second thought. In truth, I would have traded an arm to have full use of my own affinities in that moment myself. I hadn't known it was possible to feel such unadulterated wrath. Seeing direct physical harm come to my family made me dizzy with the instinct to protect. I dug deep down for control of my ice but still couldn't reach anything tangible.

"Oh, yes. The two Princesses of Justice— Sorry, *former* princesses," Arrian laughed, and rolled his eyes. "That's what they are calling you two, you know. If it weren't for the impressions you made on that pitiful community of monsters and feeble minded Sympathizers, I daresay you wouldn't have a single prayer left. Yet for some reason, it seems the actions of you two girls was enough to rally a crowd behind your sad little family unit. They even have delusions of grandeur that you can be redeemed and freed."

"Your point?" I demanded through gritted teeth. Anyone sympathetic to our plight was news to all of us, and Arrian, in all his faulty pride and piety, likely didn't even realize he was feeding us the most hopeful information we'd received in ages.

Arrian knocked Kira to the ground for a third time. "They talk of the Faithful Princess who walked among them, Ina. The Healing Princess who walked through fire to save them, Sorrel. The Gentle Princess who could do no harm, Yulia. The Dutiful Prince with a pure heart, the hope of the future, Theo. And, finally," He looked at each of us and rested his gaze on Kira beneath him. "The Brilliant Princess with a smile bright enough to see them through the darkness. See, that smile they talk about, it sounds dangerous. The type of flame, if you'll forgive the pun, crowds follow behind in a band of defiance. So, naturally, I came here to make sure that light is snuffed out. The others are already broken or breaking, but shattering light is a whole other matter. I bet you two fools didn't even realize your children held so much power," He jeered at Mama and Papa.

Kira glared up at her attacker and began laughing softly to herself. "You think you can break me, Arrian? Is that it? You want to hurt me?" She sneered. "Just try it. You don't have the power."

"I have all the power in the world here," Arrian snorted, completely self-assured in his words, though he didn't knock her down again.

Kira rose back to her full height, shoving her face so close to his, Inessa and I had to intervene and yank her backwards for fear she might be struck again— or bite his nose.

"I gave you no such power over me," Kira hissed, and beneath my fingers, I could feel her skin heating at an immense rate. "My spirit is my own to do with. Try all you want, but I will *never* hand that power to *anyone*."

I flashed Inessa a curious look, only to receive a shrug in return. If Kira somehow managed to tap into her affinity and strike Arrian down, I had no idea what our next move would be. We had the gems in our dresses that could pay our way out of the country, but we didn't have any transportation. We'd never make it very far on foot, and Inessa's own powers seemed slightly stunted.

"Am I supposed to be intimidated by a pathetic speck like you?" Arrian scoffed, then lunged forward and gripped Kira by the face, squeezing forcefully. "It's a shame you had to go and be an enemy. You really were quite beautiful to me before all of this, you know. We could have had quite the life together one day. Now what are you? *Filth*."

"I'd be intimidated," Kira ripped her face away and snapped her teeth like a viper, just narrowly missing Arrian's finger tips. "You should have never gotten on my bad side, Ari because—"

"Don't call me that!" Arrian bellowed, his cool demeanor slipped away and was replaced by an unhinged animal baring his teeth. "You monsters don't get to call me that!" He struck Kira's face again, but this time she was braced and didn't topple to the ground.

She narrowed her eyes and smirked. "Oh, I meant it, what I said on the scaffold. I don't care what happens or how long it takes. You hurt my family, so I won't be playing nice. I *will* use whatever fire has been placed within me to incinerate you. Even if it takes my whole life. That's a promise, *Ari.*"

Arrian's face tinged red for a moment and he opened his mouth to shout at my brazen sister, but then something in her words seemed to click in an odd way. His mask of calm fell back over his expression and he chuckled softly to himself with a small shake of his head.

"Alright, if you say so. I'll have to hold you to that little promise of yours."

Kira glared at his patronizing words, but didn't shrink or back down. Her jaw jutted defiantly, rejecting his dismissal of her threat. I, however, could see the adamance in her face, and knew she didn't make that promise without any intention to keep it.

"I'll take my leave. Oh, Yulia? Dear, sweet, Yulia." Arrian approached Yulia's slouched body, and the closer he got, the more she appeared to recede into herself.

"Yes?" She squeaked.

"I felt it only fair to tell you," he leaned down to whisper loudly in her ear. "I've been the one who deals with the prisoners, traitors, and Sympathizers for a while. I'm the one who has been running the death sentences for them for a long while now. And, *I* gave the order to execute the soldier. If only you hadn't been so damn clumsy. His wife and three children might not be mourning him without a body. Because, you see, we don't give back the bodies of traitors here."

Yulia's eyes stretched wide and immediately filled with tears. She looked at me, guilt and horror drowning in the depths of despair. I released my hold on Kira and flew to her side, cradling her head to my chest as she started sobbing.

"Bastard!" Papa bellowed, struggling against the guards still holding him down. "Get out!"

"Get away from her," I hissed, wishing nothing more than to sink an icicle into his eye for his hateful provocations. It wasn't lost on me that Arrian was likely responsible for Vin Holok's death, and by extension, Harvier's. "You've done your damage, Arrian. Leave us alone."

"Ha, I almost forgot, lovely Sorrel. The apple of my dear brother's eye— or was it the Snowdrop?" Arrian mocked, delight sparking in his dark gaze. "I believe he should be paying a visit any day now himself! I do hope you two have a heartfelt reunion."

My throat tightened against any retorts I might have spat, had I not gone involuntarily mute at the mention of Roland's name. Kira tore herself away from Inessa and stepped between me and Arrian. She was hunched aggressively, a beast ready to lunge.

"She said to *leave*," She growled, and once more, I felt heat boiling off her in waves.

Arrian grabbed Kira roughly by the roots of her hair, paying no mind if he felt the heat too or not, and yanked her head back. His cruelty elated him, it was plain to see, but Kira smiled against the wince of pain. "You might be strong now, but as all of them crumble around you, Kira Cat, you'll break under the weight of holding them up. You're already cracking, I can tell."

"No. Power," She bit.

Arrian cupped her chin with his fingers, delicately this time, leaning in and pressing his lips forcefully to hers before pulling away with a manic laugh. He released his hold on her with enough force to send her stumbling backwards against me and Yulia behind her. She spat and wiped her mouth.

"Bewitching little creature," He murmured, licking his lips. "We'll see, Kira. We'll see. Take this one with us for a more private audience." His bemused words made my blood run cold as he waved his hands for the guards to release Papa and follow him out of the room, dragging Kira along. "Give my regards to my brother!"

No true purpose for his visit had been revealed to us, other than to sew anguish and apprehension. He was leaving us with some insidious promise of his own, and we had no choice but to sit and wait for it to play out and see what he had in store for us and for Kira to be returned to us.

FORTY-NINE

My family and I all sat in silence following Arrian's visit. Kira was returned to us within the half hour, further signs of abuse evident all over her body. She'd entered the room with her held high, though her stride was stiff with remnant discomfort. When I grabbed hold of her hand, she shook her head, a silent indication that she wasn't going to share what had been inflicted upon her, leaving me to fear the worst— especially given her underlying affinities.

The unease Arrian managed to leech into the room had stolen over us like a dense fog as we each fought our own thoughts. We continued our stitching, and one by one, Mama, my sisters, and I each finished stashing the layer of gems in our garments. Should the opportunity ever arise, we were prepared for our chance at escape. With our hands once more idle, only the ticking of the clock and the turning of pages from the book Papa was reading broke the silence.

"Something that idiot said did strike me as interesting," Kira perked up. "Did you happen to catch it?"

"Go on and tell us," Inessa waved her on impatiently.

"It's what he said about us. He told us how there are people out there rallying behind the demand for our release. Faithful, Healing, Gentle, Pure Hearted, and Brilliant," Kira beamed, tossing her hair over her shoulder in mock vanity as she spoke her own given title. "We didn't name ourselves those things. And did you hear what the soldier called Yulia yesterday? *Gentle*. The people *know* who we are! I'll bet you anything it was one of those very people who was throwing snowballs at the guards in the pass. Doesn't that just fill you to the brim?"

"No," Inessa said flatly as Kira flopped back dramatically onto her cot, hugging her arms to her chest.

"Don't you get it, Ina? Someone out there still believes in us, even after everything and all the lies. They *believe in us*. And it's thanks to you two, really." Kira pointed to me and Inessa. "You put yourselves out there amongst the people, and walked alongside them long enough to leave an impression. Smart."

"It wasn't exactly a calculated act," I murmured. "In any case, I wouldn't take much of what Arrian has to say to heart. For all we know, he is planting a false narrative to mess with our minds."

"Trust me, he isn't that clever," Kira rolled her eyes. "But, who cares! False hope is still hope to feed off of."

"Yes, except for the whole 'false' part," Theo threw in from where he'd propped himself up in bed, using the wall as a support.

"Well, I'm taking it. He wants to feed my hope for a better tomorrow, let him feed me. I'll devour every last morsel. Worst case, I have a light to hold onto while I'm living in the dark. Best case, he's an idiot and was telling the truth, which would make the hope real. Oh, can you just imagine it?"

"Freedom?" Theo asked, raising his eyebrows. "Putting all this nightmare behind us? I imagine that every waking moment. I'd go insane otherwise."

"What do you imagine?" Kira jumped up and plopped down on Theo's cot, her eyes wide and searching like a child asking for a bedtime story.

"I don't know… I imagine having my own room again, for one."

"Wow, you really dug deep for that," Kira scoffed, folding her arms.

"I imagine a quiet farm," Papa spoke up, crossing the room to place his hands on Kira's shoulders. She looked up at him and grinned from ear to ear. "We would all live there as a family, away from all of the politics and royal fuss."

"I'd tend the gardens," Inessa joined in. "Yulia would take care of all the animals, and Sorrel would boss us all around, making sure we all kept to our chore schedules."

"Hey!" I cried. "Maybe if you managed your time better, I wouldn't have to be bossy!"

"I'm fairly positive you came into this world with a to-do list," Mama chuckled. "Don't you recall, Genri? She was so particular about everything, even as a baby."

"Babies are meant to be particular. They can't communicate otherwise," I defended myself. "No matter. On this farm of ours, I think I will be in charge of administering any and all first-aid. I don't know about the rest of you, but imagining Kira with farming tools makes me think the position will be warranted!"

"Sorrel!" Kira cried and flung her pillow at me. I dodged it easily and tucked it behind me, withholding it from her, as she came to wrestle it away from me. "I'd be the best farmer there ever was!"

"Alright, alright!" I chuckled and released the pillow. "Go get in your own cot."

"Ah," Kira sighed heavily, crawling into bed. "Do you think we could ever truly have that life?"

"I don't think it's so far-fetched," Papa replied, grabbing hold of Mama's hand. "Being banished to live an ordinary life was the sentence Friedrich relayed to me before we parted ways. I think he is punishing us now for the years of suffering I inflicted upon him when I robbed him of both justice and closure. Even so, at the end of this path we've been forced onto, I think all of us will find our way to that little farm together someday."

"Or maybe we will be rescued," Kira's words slurred with sleepiness, her eyes drifting closed. "And have some marvelous adventure in a foreign country where the bastards can't legally touch us."

"Language, Kira," Mama admonished, sinking into her own bed to roll over and sleep. Yulia, Inessa, and Theo slowly followed suit.

"Papa?" I asked when the room had stilled with the muffled breathing of my slumbering mother and siblings.

"What is it, Sorrel?"

"What really happened to make him hate us so much? Why did you choose to walk the path you did, knowing the truth?"

"That's a complicated answer for this hour, My Dear," Papa sighed heavily.

"I just... I need to know. I'm sorry for going behind everyone's backs and finding things out the way I did, but now I'm asking you directly. Won't you please tell me?"

My cot was across from Papa's, and he and Mama had pushed their beds together. Mama was asleep, her back to my father, covers pulled tightly over her shoulders around her face. Papa's eyes flashed in the dark, and he patted the cot on his opposite side. I quietly slipped from my bed and sat down.

He took my hand and gave it a squeeze. "I never liked keeping the secret, and in truth I wasn't very good at it. When I found out myself, my own father had already passed away, so I didn't receive his guidance as intended. He left the sealed information in a beautiful Faberge egg for my mother to give to me if he didn't survive his convalescence at the seaside.

"The secret was to be passed down orally for obvious reasons, but my father delayed telling me because he was deliberating on whether it would be better for me to not know and hopefully lead a normal life unburdened. He decided if I could figure out the secret inside the egg, then I deserved to know. It took me a while, but eventually I unlocked the message. I shared the unbelievable news with a select few: Friedrich, your mother, and my sister, Sylvia.

"What did Mama think when she found out?"

"She was shocked, but as it turned out, she had been living with her own secret as I'm sure you've surmised." Papa's eyes roved over his slumbering wife. "But, that's a story she will have to tell you herself."

I nodded and curled my fingers together, wondering if Mama would ever give me answers to the million questions buzzing in my head. I 'd heard her mention something about Kataheyda, the country of crags and storms the north west of Eisa, and knew she must have some connection to it given both hers and my affinity for Storm. But so much of Kataheyda was lost or cloaked in mystery, I hadn't the faintest idea what history was buried there. Mama would have to explain herself, and given her obvious rejection of magic and pandering to the falsehood of curses through the Divinities, I didn't have high hopes of ever learning her true origins.

"What happened with Friedrich and Aunt Sylvia?" I asked, looking back at my father.

"Sylvia took an interest in the topic, always far more understanding and open minded than I had ever been. She looked into it and discovered her Videirian affinity."

My gaze flicked to Inessa. "Sounds like someone else I know."

"History certainly repeated itself, only this time Friedrich made sure he got the ending he wanted."

"What does that mean?" I pressed gently, seeing Papa's face turning red with emotion. "Is this what has to do with Sarka?"

"Sarka was friends with your mother and Sylvia. The three of them were thick as thieves— Sisters in their own right really. Naturally, Sylvia confided in Sarka and gained her support. Sylvia then started learning magic, and Sarka helped her. At this point, your mother had distanced herself from the pair, uncomfortable with the blatant deceptions of studying magic in private while rejecting it publicly, so she rejected it altogether. One day, while we were all traveling abroad to Videiria, something went wrong, and Sarka was killed, along some other innocents."

"What went wrong?"

"I don't know. Sylvia refused to explain herself properly. Friedrich wanted Sylvia to be tried as a Wielder who had committed murder under Eisan law. That would have meant execution, so instead, I broke the rules and sent my sister into exile, and claimed her as one of the casualties. Friedrich was beside himself at the time, but eventually he appeared to realize the impossible position I'd been put in. I was young, and didn't know what I was doing. Nothing was going to bring Sarka back. The way I saw it, Sarka had engaged in the accident willingly, so there was no harmful intent. Twenty years later, I have no idea what ever became of Sylvia, and Friedrich has finally brought justice back around."

"What he's done feels a lot more like revenge than justice," I scoffed, then stilled as Papa's grip tightened around my hand.

"It was all my fault. I dishonored my closest friends and I brought us all down— my ancestors before me and my family now. The lives of other innocents lost all just to protect a facade. A facade I was going to force upon my own son after me. I'll never forgive myself." Tears fell freely down my father's cheeks, past his trembling lips. He buried his face against his hand.

My heart broke into a million pieces to see my proud Papa reduced to this quiet crying man, grieving his mistakes. His remorse was palpable as silent sobs shook his body. I rubbed his hand softly with my thumb for a few minutes, not saying a word, until he sobered and cleared his throat.

"I'm sorry. I must be overtired. We can talk about this another time."

"Goodnight, Papa," I whispered and fled back to hide beneath my covers. I closed my eyes, drifting somewhere between consciousness and slumber for what felt like ages, still hearing the ticking of the clock, but moving through phantom wisps behind my lids.

A loud banging sounded at the door. "Wake up, get dressed,

and grab your things."

"What's going on?" Mama demanded.

"There seems to be some group calling themselves the Ivory Army, causing a commotion nearby. We are relocating you while the Scarlet Army gets in place to force them back."

"It's like what Arrian said." Kira grabbed onto my arm, her eyes shining bright. "The snowballs! That must have been them, letting us know they were there. Maybe we will be rescued after all."

"Get dressed, Kira," I whispered, not yet daring to acknowledge the same sense of hope brewing in my own chest. I wasn't sure how much time had passed since I'd fallen asleep, but a glance at the clock, reading nearly three in the morning, told me I had gotten roughly four hours of sleep. I hoped it would be enough to see me through to the next dawn.

We changed quickly, sure to wear the garments with the gems sewn in and, still groggy with interrupted sleep, we all shared a look of quiet understanding.

If the opportunity presented itself tonight, we would make a run for it.

FIFTY

We hugged our meager belongings to our chests and sides as we plodded down the stairs to the basement. We held onto them with the same grip as we did the faint hope that we were finally going to find salvation. The steps creaked loudly in the night, and the musky scent of damp wood hung thick in the air. There were rubbled chunks scattered across the floor from where they had parted ways with the concrete wall and broken. Cold clung to the stone, seeping in from the perpetual winterscape outside. It didn't bother me that much, of course, but I could see Kira's jaw chattering below her dull, sleep-filled eyes.

"It's so cold down here," She whispered, the warmth of her breath visible in a large white billow.

"Line up, in order," One of the soldiers barked at us. I recognized him as the one who replaced Unov. Yulia's eyes were downcast with lingering guilt and grief at the man's demise, and she shuffled into the center of the room without fuss or delay.

Her movements were mechanical, void of any spark of life or character. I worried that the man's death over showing kindness might have robbed my sister of the last of her will, finally breaking her spirit in a way I couldn't begin to know how to mend. Arrian's reminder to her earlier certainly hadn't helped in putting it behind her.

"How long do we have to wait down here?" Mama asked, her voice strained with pain, as she clutched at her back. "Do we know what's happening with the army approaching? Someone said an enemy group was getting too close and we were going to be relocated."

Papa was holding both Theo and Mama up on either side of him. Since he didn't have the jewelry hidden in his clothing like we did, his shirt was hanging loosely around him. He had kept up on his exercise just as he always did, but I could detect the frailty in his body that only came from heartbreak. Like Yulia, the light had faded from his eyes, the warmth had drained from his smile, and his fighting fire was extinguished, no more the Imperial ruler he once was. I wondered if our conversation a few hours ago was partly to blame, forcing him to relive his biggest regret.

"It shouldn't be too long. Someone," I stiffened, feeling the first wave of cold rolling down my spine since we'd arrived at Kyrith. My shoulders lifted against the chill like the raised hackles of a frightened animal at the sound of the voice behind me. "Please, get a chair for The Gr— the boy and his mother."

"Roland." Inessa's eyes glittered and narrowed into slits as she uttered the name I could not bring myself to say aloud.

"Ina," He acknowledged my sister, causing Inessa to practically bear her teeth at the audacity of using her pet name, and I heard him take a step further into the room just behind me. "Sorrel, it's good to see you."

I was frozen, completely unable to turn around and face the man I had always loved, but now knew I must hate. I knew I couldn't bear to look at him now that so much time had passed with so many tears shed, and have to watch him change from lover to enemy before my eyes yet again. My hands were quivering, and my breath grew ragged in panic at the onslaught of emotion his voice had stirred within me. I jumped as I felt something warm and gentle graze my fingers.

Kira had lifted her chin with defiance and slipped her hand into mine, facing Roland head on, while I kept my back to him. I turned and blinked at my little sister. There were tears in her eyes, and I could see her face trying not to crumple as she stared at him. All the hurt and betrayal we all felt she wore for him to see— So he would know what he had done to us.

The heat from her hand somehow felt like a warm summer day, full of all the remaining love and laughter we'd had stolen from us. She was holding it all: the hurt and the hope. It radiated from her body in an invisible glow of emotion, and she bathed the room in it. Blinking slowly, I realized the glow wasn't actually invisible after all. It was a subtle light, so soft a yellow it nearly looked white as it seeped into the musky air. I doubted she even realized the radiance she was emitting from the depths of her emotions.

Yulia lifted her head, and Inessa stood a little taller. Mama and Papa joined hands and leaned their heads together, and Theo shifted from leaning on Papa to stand firmly on his own two feet.

The silent solidarity Kira had ignited caught flame and breathed new strength into all of us. Her chest started to shudder as sobs slowly claimed her, tears now pouring freely from the depths of her brilliant blue eyes. But, she set her jaw and did not falter or look away.

"I said to *line up,*" The soldier shouted at us, and I curled my fingers around Kira's. "Where I can see all of you clearly, in order."

"Come on," I spoke softly to my sister and gave her hand a squeeze before releasing it. With each step, I swallowed down another storm within me, unable to let Roland see the devastation he'd brought upon me. Kira's resolve was enough for me to have the strength to walk to my place in line, between Inessa and Yulia, and finally turn around.

I kept my eyes fixed straight ahead. I wouldn't give Roland the satisfaction of drawing my gaze. I could hear him and the soldier muttering to each other, though I could make out only every few statements.

"I have it on good authority that it would be best to delay this drill till tomorrow when conditions are… better," He was saying, and the guard grunted in a non committal manner in response. "Less cold and less conspicuous."

"Look, I know you specifically requested to be on this squad, Minister, but you can't just waltz in here to fulfill some sort of blood lust fantasy and take over. I received my orders in official capacity. Papers and everything. Unless you have new papers, signed by the Prime Minister…"

"I do not have papers on me," Roland sighed, and I saw Papa flinch at the mention of his old friend being the one to sign papers that governed the treatment of our captivity. Unlike Arrian, Roland's presence had subdued my father rather than antagonized him. "I would assume being his *son* would have superseded the need for papers. I don't suppose there's time for me to get in touch with my father? I could ring him up now."

"At this hour?"

"Only if you insist on doubting me. We could continue tonight, but it has its risks of discovery that I don't think have been properly prepared for. I passed these concerns on to my father before I came here, of course."

There was an edge to his voice, though on the surface it was very well hidden— So much so I almost wondered if I simply imagined it. He was trying to buy time for something, and whatever he was up against the clock with was making him nervous.

The chimes of the upstairs clock tolled loudly, the metallic sound harsh and echoing as it filled the ambient air. It was three in the morning. A handful more soldiers filtered into the basement and closed the door behind them, effectively deadening the sound of the ringing clock with a single slam.

"The order is to wait," Roland commanded, rolling his

shoulders back to impose his looming height over the shorter soldier.

The man hesitated but finally sighed and nodded. "Yes, Lord Minister, Sir. We will wait until we receive the updated order and scheduling."

"I hadn't heard there was an update to the schedule, Roland. Surprising you'd be told and not me. When did you get the order exactly?" Arrian's voice boomed through the doorway, drawing everyone's attention to his entrance. He stood toe to toe with Roland, his broad smile never wavering.

Roland glowered at his brother. "Earlier, Ari. Not everything in the Minister's circle makes its way down the line to you I'm afraid."

"I see." Arrian's jaw clenched at the slight.

"If I recall, in fact, your specific request to be here tonight was denied by father, was it not? *I* was the one given permission to oversee this order carried out. I'm surprised to see you still here defying your own orders and not already on your way back to Tuyet. What would Father think?"

"I was detained earlier," Arrian turned his reptilian grin towards Kira, who sneered back at her attacker, lifting her chin even higher. "It would have given me such a late start home. I figured I'd stay through the night and leave in the morning. Especially since the Ivory Army has locked horns with the Scarlet Army so close to here. I'd hate to get caught in the middle of all that. Wouldn't you agree?"

Roland squinted, the finest twitch in his fingers giving away the instinct to curl them into a fist. "Fair enough. Regardless, I think it is best we head out and come back tomorrow when the proper conditions are made for the prisoner's departure. As I stated, the order is to wait. Let's go."

Finally the smile gave way on Arrian's face to a discerning frown and amicable nod. "After you."

"That was weird," Kira muttered and I had to agree.

The exchange had been strained. Arrian and Roland weren't

strangers to butting heads as brothers, but I had to wonder why odds they were clashing over now, and what it had to do with our relocating. It seemed to me that Roland had possibly caught wind of a possible rescue attempt, and acting with more discretion than Arrian, was trying to alter the schedule just enough to foil any hope of an escape— coordinated or otherwise. My skin burned with wrathful repulsion, and I grit my teeth against the seething resentment of another ray of hope being torn to shreds before our eyes.

Roland dipped his head to the soldiers. "Pack up and adjourn for tonight, men. Keep watch to the northwest for signs of attack from the Ivory Army tonight, and we will follow through with this endeavor tomorrow."

"So we aren't being relocated?" Papa asked weakly.

"No. Not yet," Roland acknowledged Papa with a brief nod in his direction before calling for Arrian to follow him out of the basement.

"I guess we will be heading to our own accommodations off the property," Arrian drawled, turning slowly to meander after his brother. He caught the eye of the head soldier and mimed a few silent gestures— a finger to the lips for discretion, a point at us, then three fingers held up with a hard stare.

My mind raced over what the secret motions might mean, but they were just vague enough for me to come up short with an explanation, but apparently concise enough for the soldier to grin with understanding and a brisk nod.

"Goodnight, Zdraevits," Arrian chuckled before disappearing through the door.

"Are we heading back to bed then?" Mama asked after a few moments had passed.

"We will wait," The soldier barked, beckoning the rest of his men close to relay classified information to.

"How long?" Papa pressed, looking down the line at his weary family.

"Until you're told to do otherwise. Be quiet!"

I flinched, and found my hands fluttering to either side, grasping at Inessa and Yulia's hands for reassurance. Ina squeezed and shuffled a little closer so her arm could brush against mine in solidarity, but Yulia's grip felt limp and vacant.

I kept mulling over the number three that Arrian had signed. What could it mean? Three of us seven? Maybe it meant three minutes before taking us back up to give them a chance to leave. But when three minutes came and went, that theory withered away. I watched the clock as it ticked by the thirteenth minute, and still the soldiers stood tense, idle, and bored.

"I don't understand why we can't go back upstairs yet," Kira complained, shifting back and forth on her feet. "It's the middle of the Forsaken night."

"*Silence*," The head soldier growled, roving a hand over his pistol. "Or I'll make you be silent."

"I'd like to see—" Kira started to challenge but Theo was quick on his feet, snaking a hand around her mouth to keep her from saying something she'd regret.

"Don't provoke them Kira Kat. We don't want any trouble," he mumbled to her, slowly releasing his hold. "The goal is to get through this. Remember that."

Kira opened her mouth to argue but instead fidgeted with the bodice of her dress and remained quiet. I wondered if perhaps she was reminding herself of the cost of escape hidden in the fabric. The chance we might be rescued was still possible, despite the guards tampering with whatever transport schedule they'd arranged. Despite her impulsiveness, Kira was shrewd enough to be working through the cost and rewards of strategic cooperation to eventually yield our escape. Even Roland had warned them to keep an eye out to Northwest. If we got free, that might be the best direction for us to flee towards in hopes of finding allies. I swallowed back a smile at the idea that Roland might have inadvertently given us our escape route.

My smugness was short lived though as the longer I thought of it, the less the situation unfolding made sense. All of Kira's carefully cultivated reassurance from earlier facing Roland evaporated in those few seconds as I finally began to piece things together.

Arrian wasn't meant to be here, meaning whatever order he'd given wasn't meant to happen. It was going against Roland's instructions to wait. For some reason the soldiers were listening to Arrian over Roland, despite ranking. I couldn't place why, but that realization chilled me to my core. Roland was cold but obedient. Arrian was mad with cruelty. Whatever he came to interfere with wasn't going to be in our favor. Maybe he was trying to sabotage his brother to stand out to his father. Either way, however he was interfering, it had to be with the sole purpose of inflicting as much pain as he could on us.

My breath hitched in my chest as that final thought sank in. This was no random drill to take shelter from nearby battles, nor did it seem we were being moved anywhere. Whatever we had been brought down here for had been specifically scheduled for this selected hour, and Roland had requested to be here for it. Whatever was happening was planned.

Twenty-eight minutes had passed since Arrian had left with Roland. Twenty-eight long minutes, when at last, the soldiers began to rouse each other. My body tensed and I couldn't make my muscles respond, or my mouth form words.

Twenty-nine minutes. What would happen when the thirty minute mark was met? Thirty was the next *three* on the clock and it was apparent that it had been the marker Arrian had meant.

"Time is up, men. Grab what gear you need and let's get to work," The head soldier grunted and my heart began racing with unshakable foreboding.

Then soldiers needed *gear* to fulfill some form of *blood lust*. We were asked to line up, one by one, completely exposed and in our birth order. My throat went dry, and I compulsively tried to swallow to keep the walls from sticking together. Sweat was gathering on my brow, and my chest tightened with an intensifying panic I could do nothing to ward against as I counted those in the room who were not my family.

Seven. They were all armed with handguns, their typical ceremonial rifles tucked behind them. The world slowed around me as they each reached for their weapons. A pinging sounded rhythmically in my ears, too sharp as it stabbed into my brain, and I realized it was my pulse jumping.

"What's going on here?" Papa's voice was muffled beneath the pinging changing to thundering drums of war and survival.

The soldiers lined up across from us. The moment was almost still, my perceptions had slowed to a near stop. The soldier across from me raised and aimed the gun, along with the rest of the assembled men, and I stared down the barrel at him with something even greater than disbelief as his lips curled into an insidious smile.

FIFTY-ONE

Shrieks and bellows of protest crescendoed around the drumming. I couldn't break my gaze away from the firing squad. The same formation that had shot Unov. Next to me, I was aware of Yulia turning to run away, the rich brown of her hair tumbling around her shoulders in a large sweeping motion. Inessa, on my other side, backed away, trembling like a leaf in the wind. The soldiers were between us and the door. There was nowhere for us to flee, yet everyone was filled with the frantic, impulsive aversion to death, and they tried to fight their fate anyway.

Kira was shouting, her voice was filled with such anguish and desperation, twisting and rising into something inhuman and feral. I heard her even call out to Roland in a final plea for him to stop what was happening and be our savior.

I wanted to scream. I wanted to unleash the myriad of storms I had stored within me my entire life, but I didn't know how, and now I was going to die with that part of me forever locked away.

I was cracking apart, and tears were starting to leak through my crudely repaired mask of stoicism that fell away from my face piece by piece. Kira stumbled towards the space between me and Zdrute, her frantic screeching and begging for him to see sense, making her body unstable and clumsy. But her pleas fell on deaf ears. Roland wasn't going to help us, likely long gone by now, and it was too late. The soldiers opened fire.

Papa was the first to go down. His body collapsed against a bullet in his chest. Mama shrieked with madness, her husband's blood sprayed over her face. She fell to her knees and threw herself over his body, shaking him. But, those infinitely kind eyes that had dreamed of nothing more than helping his countrymen and a quiet life with his family away from all the royal obligations, were now staring sightlessly at the ceiling. The warmth was gone and he had died a broken man.

Metallic *clinking* sounded all around me before the sweeping thunder of gunfire deafened me, and I felt something graze my arm at the same instance Kira pushed me to the side. A bullet nicked me and embedded in the wall behind me. I was only spared because of Kira's quick reaction and recklessness. Still, I was rooted, helpless, and exposed.

My precious little brother was the next to fall. His blood poured from his wound, his disease increasing the flow so it soaked the floor around him. Despite the obvious fact that the guns had deadened my hearing, somehow I still heard the gargles and wheezing of his final breaths, unable to move or help him. Unable to do anything.

The slant in the floor made the current of Theo's blood collide with where Yulia was huddled on the ground. Her hands were pressed into her leg, dark crimson bubbling around her fingers. When she saw our brother and realized she was trapped in a pool of his blood, she screamed manically before another shot shook the air, and her eyes rolled as she fell to the floor in a slump.

I tried to open my mouth to warn Mama that the second volley was coming but too late, and the bullet had already shot her through. I still couldn't make my body move, and I stared helplessly at my parents dead on the floor, gone in an instant, unable to breathe, let alone react. This couldn't be reality. It couldn't be.

I was trapped in a different fold of time that was filled with razor bladed emotions all slicing me open at once and a dread so deep my body was too heavy to move, my brain too sluggish to tell me what to do or how to feel. All that I was pulsed with fear that ached beyond any other pain in my life. It was like my spirit and rational thought had been pulled from my body, and I could see myself in my mind's eyes, standing there, utterly useless. My family was falling around me, just like that nightmare I had once feared so viscerally, and it wasn't until I felt a sharp tear in my throat that I realized I had been screaming all along. Still, dumb, and shrieking.

Another round of shots fired, this time coming from random soldiers, since the first two volleys hadn't killed us all, and now they were on a singular mission to get the botched job done. All formalities and order were gone. A bullet whizzed through the air and struck Inessa, still trembling next to me. The breath was driven from her lungs and she fell backwards, stunned but not dead. The jewels hidden in the lining of our dresses, I realized, were acting as armor against the barrage of bullets. Kira was panting from where one of the bullets had knocked her down too. Pain pierced my arm as it was struck directly this time.

"Stop it!" Kira wailed at the top of her lungs, her voice was hoarse and weary over the thunder as she tried to shake Mama's body awake. "Mama, get up. We have to go. We'll get Papa and Theo next. Mama! Get up!"

"They must be using their Wielder abilities to deflect the shots!" Zdrute roared feverishly, though I was only barely able to read his lips, his eyes fixed on Inessa. Some of the men had given up on the guns and retrieved their rifles, resorting to flicking out their bayonets. It was a crackling reprieve from the harsh gunfire that I was certain had made my ears bleed.

The pain in my arm restored my displaced mobility at last, setting me free from the fold of personal purgatory, and I reached out a hand to help Inessa to her feet. I turned to head for Kira, but a soldier brandished a bayonet and charged forward.

The tip of the blade impaled Inessa but stopped abruptly with a clink, and the misplaced force sent the blade slipping sideways to slice her arm. The soldier bellowed with rage, spotting the armor plate of gems through the tear in the fabric. He started jabbing Inessa repeatedly with the blade, trying to find a weakness in her protection. I flung myself forward, frantically trying to stop the man's assault. I couldn't feel the pain in my arm anymore, adrenaline blocking all my nerve receptors.

The soldier swung an arm and knocked me down with a strike to my face. Inessa hit the ground on her knees a moment later. Another soldier was on top of me in an instant, straddling over my hips, and restraining my desperate clawing hands. "They have gems in their bodices. Rip them off!"

"No!" I screamed, my words barely discernible, thrashing wildly beneath my captor. "Get off me!"

"Sorrel," Inessa gasped, her gaze cloudy. She crawled forward, numbly trying to push the man off of me. "Sorrel, we need... to help Kira. I don't know about the others. She's still... Protect her. We need to..." Her words were breaking on her bleeding lips. The soldier who had been attacking her smiled above her, he placed his pistol against the back of her head and pulled the trigger.

Blood and hair sprayed across my face, and Inessa's lifeless body thudded beside me. Her face was mostly unrecognizable beneath the aftermath of her injury, and all that remained in line of view was a scarlet cavity. I stopped fighting the man on top of me, falling limp while he set to shredding my dress. His eyes were alight with murderous glee, and he too was covered in my sister's blood. It had all moved too fast— mere seconds of irreversible carnage that to me felt like an eternity of unforgivable hesitation on my part.

Beyond Inessa, Mama and Papa's bodies were strewn on the ground, and Theo was still bleeding a river of scarlet on the stone floor adjacent to the scattered trail of my fallen family members before me. Poor Yulia was felled in the pool of the combined aftermath of her and Theo's wounds. The fresh tears on her cheeks before she'd fallen rolled into the blood.

It was only me and Kira left, and Inessa had been right. I needed to protect her as long as I could. My breath came out in a puff of icy white, and I thought hard about the cold, doing my best to try and connect with it. Then, I reached a hand weakly upward and grasped at the man's face, something sparking to life in my fingers at last, born of pure desperation. He yelped and jumped back, clutching where I had touched and made the frost bite his face.

"Yulia!" Kira's guttural screech of disbelief and grief chilled me to the bone, heightening my desperation to reach her as I pressed my fingers harder against the soldier's face.

It was enough deterrence for me to dislodge him and scramble to my knees and make my way over to the corner where Kira had crawled next to Yulia's still body, unable to wake our slain parents. She was cowering under an assault, still trying to protect Yulia's body, and was covered in blood and reddened bruises, but there was still the fire of defiance mixed with the fear and pain in her eyes.

I kept crawling forward, determined to reach her. I felt something hit my back as I neared, but kept moving. Another strike made my arms threaten to buckle as I arrived beside my sister. I threw my arms around her and put my back to the men, shielding her as best I could, ready to succumb to their attacks.

I felt more blows land against me but my body remained numb to their pain. I hoped that staying connected to the essence of the chill would keep most of the excruciating sensations at bay. Kira hugged me with all her might, her chest heaving.

"Sorrel…" She whimpered in my ear, the sound muffled like she was speaking through cloth. "I… I *can't.*"

"It's alright. I've got you. I've got you," I kept repeating the only words of solace that I could muster amidst the devastation. In truth, we were both injured and weakened. We had no weapons and had no idea of how to use our affinities to fight our way out. The likelihood of making it out alive was slipping away with each new drop of blood that spilled from our veins.

I counted at least twenty more strikes landing against me, some making contact, and others hitting one of the many remaining gems beneath my torn clothes, before I lost my hold on Kira and fell to the side. My flesh was torn, my ribs broken, my hair caked with both my and Inessa's blood.

I flinched against the sound of a sickening crack followed by repeated thudding. The soldiers had descended on Kira and were beating her with the butts of their guns, all while still thrusting bayonets at her in between strikes. She threw her arms over head trying to shrink away against the wall. Her cries of pain turned to gargles until she slumped to the floor with labored breathing. I held her gaze in solidarity as we both were bleeding out. Somehow she managed to reach her hand towards me while the soldiers were crowing their victories over us. I inched my fingers forward until they intertwined with hers.

The heat of boundless love and laughter she had given to all of us before the attack still lingered in her touch, though I could feel it ebbing with each slowing beat of her pulse, and she smiled at me. Amidst all the horror, blood and bodies around us, she managed to smile.

"I hear a voice calling me. I feel those flames in me turning to embers. They aren't evil, Sorrel. They feel like *home*," She whispered around the blood dripping from her mouth. Even now, dying on the ground, Kira's spirit would not be broken. She would not allow her existence to be evil, nor let it end in darkness. She would blaze until her final breath.

"Me too," I croaked, and squeezed her hand. "I just wish I could have had a chance to fully meet my true self as I was meant to be. I want to see what home looks like."

"Then, let's go home together. We can watch the sunrise when we get there." Her blinks were growing longer, her breathing slower, and her words fainter, but her smile never wavered. I watched as the eternal light in her eyes receded into the piece of home she found within herself.

I was the last one left breathing, though I knew with the level of blood I was losing, it wouldn't be much longer before my body shut down too. I couldn't pull my eyes away from Kira's face, frozen in death with a smile of peace on her lips. The rosy color of her skin was obscured beneath the wounds and swelling of her face, but I knew I didn't want to see the look of her when the pallor mortis set in and stole the color of life from her.

Even now, in her final moments, choosing to die with a smile— choosing to go out with that last spark of defiance, with such quiet strength, had filled me with a fresh wave of resolve.

I felt thundering vibrations of rapid footsteps sliding into the room. The voice that spoke would have surprised me if I'd had it in me to feel anything besides anguish.

"Enough!" Roland's bellow could have rivaled the gunfire in volume. "What have you done? What in Eisa have you done?"

"We were told to carry on," A soldier replied, uncertainty clear in his voice. It was followed by the sound of a fist colliding against a jaw with a snap. I lifted my bleary eyes enough to see the soldier fall at Roland's feet with a thud. Unconscious or deceased, I couldn't be certain, nor did I care.

"I said to *wait*!" Roland roared, his expression equal parts overtaken with staggering horror and unadulterated rage.

His gaze roved over the devastation and still bodies, grabbing another soldier by the throat and slamming him against the wall. His head dropped for a minute, his fingers tightening around he man's throat until he started to wheeze. Finally, he released his hold and shoved away, leaving the man to scramble to the side gasping for air.

Roland was shaking, struggling to sober from his wrath. He clawed at the back of his neck and brought a trembling hand to his mouth as he paced back and forth in front of me. "This… This dispatch on top of being unsanctioned was disgraceful. Everyone, *get out*."

Most of the soldiers didn't challenge the seething command, and fled towards the door, leaving me to drift away on the stone cold floor. All except for one.

"This one isn't dead. We were told to kill them all." I knew he was pointing to where I was writhing. I dug my nails into the ground, filled with contempt knowing that Roland was looking at me in this pitiful half dead state. The spoils of his betrayal.

"Leave, go get things ready to transport the bodies, and clean up this mess you've created so our enemies won't know what's transpired tonight should they break through our defensive line. I will finish the last one off." The edge was razor sharp in his voice, livid at the defiance to his orders. No, he'd wanted our deaths to come tomorrow at a more convenient time. Now he had to *clean up* the mess we'd made.

It was the final straw to know he was still here, towering over me and the bodies of the family he plotted to destroy. I didn't know why he was still on the property or why he felt so strongly over being defied and it didn't matter either way. All of my repressed hurt, confusion, and anger surged beneath my bludgeoned skin until I almost certain I'd rip his throat out with my bare hands if I'd had the ability.

I dug deep to grasp at the last scraps of physical strength in my body. I was soaked in dripping crimson as I plucked my feeble body off the ground and fumbled for a grip. My hands were sticky and I could feel the grit of the cement beneath that cooling red liquid with a hyper-focused sense of clarity and sensation. Streaks of blood smeared against the wall as I pulled myself up to face my final attacker. If I was to die, I would do so on my feet. I would be the last one *standing*, proud and tall. Standing strong. Like Kira, no one would rob me of this final chosen stance of dignity.

Roland walked forward, once more wearing the mask of cold indifference to our bloody fate, though his eyes were bloodshot, pupils obscuring a majority of his roses. Traits of shock? What difference did it truly make if we perished tonight or tomorrow?

The soldiers hesitated, clearly assessing the likelihood of

my survival now that I had risen. I lifted my chin and glared at Roland, though I could feel my battered legs struggling to hold my body up. Only pure spite spurred me onward. This was my choice. I'd cowered from him when he'd spoken to me last, but now I wouldn't allow him the control. He would look me in the eye before sending me to my grave.

He marched aggressively towards me in response to my defiant gesture, lingering close to my face like he had in that dusty room filled with books the night before our capture. The night before he revealed how he had deceived us all, and showed me who he really was. A cold, murderous monster.

"Go," He growled to the soldiers, not breaking his gaze from mine. He pointed his gun at my head, the tiniest shake in his hand only noticeable by me. "She was always my target in the first place. The next man to question my orders will share her fate."

As the soldiers shuffled out of the room, I was left alone with Roland for the first time since before our arrest. When the door clicked closed, I shut my eyes and readied myself for the bullet. But, it never came.

Instead the barrel moved from my head, and I vaguely felt my body be embraced. No longer able to hold myself up, I leaned into it, blinking my eyes open in confusion. I felt myself being shaken by the shuddering sobs overtaking Roland as he held me.

"Oh, Eisa," He kept muttering between gasps. "I'm so sorry. Sorrel, I'm so sorry."

"What?"

"I tried. I tried to delay it so I could get you all out but Arrian. Fucking Arrian! I thought..." He gulped in air and held on even tighter. "I thought I could find a way. I had a plan— we had a plan, but I was too late. I failed you all. I can't... I'll never be able—"

"I don't... I don't understand." I tried feebly to pull away, caught somewhere between relief and horror at his tender touch. All collection of his faculties had given way to an onslaught of sniveling regret.

"If I had known it would go this far, I never would have tried to play the long game. Father claimed after the demonstration that your family was an example, and that the goal was never to kill you," Roland continued to babble, as if he couldn't get the words out fast enough. "If I'd known, I would have fought as soon as the Whispers cleared. I'm so sorry. I'm sorry. I thought this was our best chance. I needed time to figure it all out. Your parents. Your brother and sisters. Oh, Divine Above. And Kira, how she looked at me. I couldn't expl—"

"Of course she looked at you that way," I hissed, baring my teeth at him, a fresh wave of animosity seizing control of me. These were my final moments to express the depths of malice I'd been harboring for months, so gathering every last scrap of enmity I could foster, I managed to pull away and grabbed his chin, thrusting it in the direction of Kira's body. "Look at what you did. She's dead because of *you*. I hope you live with it for the rest of your life. You, Arrian, and your father. Our blood is on *your* hands and I hope that knowledge will eat you from the inside out for the rest of your miserable life. Now, stop trying to clear your conscience and kill me already. I have no interest in satisfying your ego with pleas and promises of forgiveness if you spare me. It's bad enough all that you've taken from me, I will not fall that low." My voice faltered when I saw the expression wrought with true grief as he looked at my sisters' bodies at our feet.

"I truly thought I could stop it. I'm so sorry Littlest Princess. You shouldn't have ever had to endure any of this. Bright beautiful soul, may Dimaer receive you and be kind. I'll do whatever it takes to get her out alive," He knelt down and whispered to Kira, and I leaned against the wall for support, slowly sliding down.

Finally, confusion overtook my anger with no clear purpose present for Roland's sudden shift in demeanor. "What are you talking about? You left us on the scaffold. You tied me up and sent me here! You ordered the execution be under more favorable conditions. You knew we were all going to die when you were here earlier!" I spat.

"I didn't know what else to do in Tuyet! Everyone could see

you were Wielders, and anyone who jumped to your defense would have been arrested too. I thought my best chance at being able to get close enough to get you out and over the border was to play along, and every second of pretending that I didn't care what was happening was absolute torture. My father couldn't see any trace of doubt in me, he had to believe I was fully committed to his side, which is why he tested me by singling me out to restrain you. He used a Whisper Wielder on me that day and killed him afterwards."

"A Whisper Wielder forced you to betray us?" I sneered. "How convenient for you."

"I had to play along and make him believe it, or I never could have gotten this close to you again. I hated it. Every moment of lying to you and seeing the hurt on your face. It was killing me inside not to find some direct way to tell you, fight for you, or simply comfort you and hold you close, but it was more important to not risk your chances for freedom. If the plan was going to work everyone had to believe the act, including you." His eyes bored into mine, pleading silently for understanding, and after everything, I had no idea what to believe anymore.

My vision was blurring, and I was succumbing to my wounds and all the blood I had lost. I had wanted to be standing when death claimed me, but it seemed Roland was robbing me of that final wish too. He was letting me suffer instead, waiting until he could confirm I had stopped breathing, twisting my emotions and faculties until the last moment. It had to be another act. It didn't matter. I had nothing left to live for now anyway, and I was more than ready to fade away from the world that had crushed me and everything I once held dear.

"You're in pain," He assessed lamely, roving over my wounded and bludgeoned body. "Listen, I know you despise me, but I need you to not give up, Sorrel. I had a plan this time. It was meant for all of you, but thanks to Arrian, I wasn't enough to buy the extra time I needed, and I will regret and grieve that shortcoming for the remainder of my life. All I can do now is get *you* out. I need you to please believe me and remember me as the Roland you've always known. I'm on your side and no one else's. My only true goal of being here is to get you out and over the border."

"That must be the delirium kicking in. I could swear you just asked me to trust you," I scoffed, wincing under labored breathing.

"We are running out of time. I'll have to do the rest of the explaining later. Here," Roland reached a hand out towards my face, and I flinched away instinctively, before he revealed a tiny bottle in his palm. "It's a potion."

I curled my lip. "You're poisoning me now too? Isn't brutalizing me enough?"

"Not poison, *potion*. It's from Maggie."

"Did you kill her too?" A small part of me perked up at the mention of the kind old woman, and I remembered she had called herself a gifted healer with affinity origins in Videiria, same as Inessa's had been. My gaze fell on my sister's fallen body, and I convulsed weakly. "The horrible wicked Wielder? Did you hope she and I would both die in the fire while you got away? One less Zdraevit and two less Wielders to kill later?"

"Sorrel!" Roland snapped, though beneath his bravado he winced at my accusations. "I don't have time to argue with you. You're bleeding out and you're going to die—"

"No," I growled, blinking slowly. I couldn't tell if the sensation of liquid running down my face was from blood, tears, or both. "I don't want to listen to anything you have to say, or take anything you have to give me."

"The soldiers are going to be back to collect your bodies any minute."

"Then you'd better finish off your *target*. Go on. Put me out of my carefully orchestrated misery. Shoot me in the head, like Inessa." My words caught in my throat and the storm started to untether, my chest shaking with grief. The air in the basement thickened, pressure building in an invisible storm front. "Shoot me!" My voice pitched hysterically.

Roland hung his head, sighed, and rolled his shoulders back. "I'm not going to let it all be in vain. I won't let you die. When I get you out, I hope you'll see. I'm still on your side, Sorrel. I never stopped."

He lurched forward, taking advantage of my fragility and shoved the bottle in my mouth, effectively pouring the contents down my throat.

"What?" I spluttered in vain, my tongue too sluggish to cooperate.

"This is going to put you to *sleep*. While you are unconscious, it will do emergency triage to your vitals, mending the imperative. In essence, it is going to keep you alive while you appear dead," Roland explained in a rush. "Your body will be taken out with the rest just like you're dead. When your body has repaired enough that you're out of danger, you will wake up. At that time, I will come get you. We have some allies on standby to take you out of the country where my father's power cannot reach you. When the soldiers come back, I'm going to have to continue to play along until I can get an opportunity to grab you and run. Just know, I *will* grab you and run, and everything else is for show. We have to get through this next part before we can rest."

"Doesn't really matter," I mumbled hazily, my eyelids drifting closed. "All is lost now. There's nothing left to live for. It's all gone. You took it and killed it right in front of me." I could hear the boots of the soldiers clomping heavily down the stairs, coming to claim our bodies. My time was up either way. I didn't need to hold on any longer.

"*You* are left to live for, Sorrel," Roland spoke with such ferocity. "You are not lost. I will not lose you, no matter what you think of me. But you can't give up. That's the only way this will work. Please, don't give up." He aimed his gun at the wall and pulled the trigger, the final bang echoing around the tomb.

"I am not going to keep myself alive for you."

"Believe me, or don't believe me, but I love you, Sorrel. Not for one single second have I stopped. I was too late to save your family, and if I could trade my life for theirs, I would in a heartbeat. But I'm going to see this through, no matter what, so *you* can live."

I wasn't given a chance to respond to the rawness of Roland's promise before the door slammed open and he was on his feet in an instant, standing in front of me to obscure where my body still might show any signs of life.

"My Lord," The head soldier who had killed Inessa called out. "We heard the gun. If you've had your fun, is she finished?"

"Hurry up, we haven't got all night," Roland barked impatiently. "Where are the bodies going next?"

"The old mine shaft. It's filled with water to help obscure the bodies and it's nearly ice water so it'll keep the smell at bay till we can fill it in more solidly first thing after sunrise."

"I see. And your next set of orders are to transport the bodies?"

"Yes, sir. Transport the bodies, strip them of all clothing and throw the remains in the shaft. When it's done, we report back to the Prime Minister for confirmation." The man sounded vaguely confused as to why Roland wouldn't be briefed on the order.

"Very good. Carry on."

The group of men set to work around me. I could feel the vibrations in the ground of their heavy boots marching around, collecting the bodies of my fallen family.

I didn't care what Roland had asked or promised me. We were going to be tossed, broken and naked, into a mine shaft to be swallowed up by fresh snow melt until we could be buried or encased beneath the earth. If Roland was lying or had misjudged the potion he gave me, then in my case, I'd be buried alive if I didn't drown first. No. It wasn't worth it. Clinging to life wasn't worth it. I would give up now and be done with it all. My family was dead. Murdered before my eyes. I would never recover, and I had no reason to keep fighting.

"Sir, this one appears to still be breathing!" A nearby soldier announced.

"I'll take care of it. Collect the rest," Roland replied calmly, his boots shifting in the grit by my face.

I wanted to bolt up right but both my body and consciousness failed me as I finally tumbled into a still darkness with one last thought. One of my family members was still breathing. Whoever it was, if they were alive, I had to live to find out and make sure they were safe. I had a reason to keep fighting after all.

"Into darkness, into despair, into the greatest depths of pain, who has risen from the fathoms to emerge as the light within the shadows, the blessing amongst curses, Divine amongst man?"

-D

FIFTY-TWO

I was suspended in darkness. The world behind my eyes was pulsating between hues of black, blue, purple, and red. The colors flickered and jumped around me before breaking and flurrying into the abyss again, causing a ripple over my skin.

I opened my eyes to find myself standing in some sort of mental void, different somehow from the one I'd been in with the injection. The walls of black looked to hold infinite depth, but would occasionally shift with rolling glints of the iridescent colors, like light refracting off of solid ice, making it clear I was boxed in wherever I was.

The flicking lights were diving in and out of the dark and color, like fish jumping in a stream. Then they switched their random pathways to focus on me. I looked down at my body, now naked, covered in wounds and blood, and gasped. A metallic tang crawled over my tongue and flooded my nose. A shroud of unbearable agony pierced through my skin, and set my nerves on fire as my body remembered the brutality it had just endured. As I cried out, the shimmering lights descended upon me.

I was coated in a dress of blood and starlight. The touch of light was cool and soothing, and as I watched, I saw the crimson smears starting to lift from my skin, and float outward in the air in swirling wisps like ink in water. The beating of my heart stabilized into a steady, rhythmic hammering, and the overwhelming pounding in my head dulled.

But the images of my family broken and fallen kept permeating my mind, fighting against the starlight's best attempts at calming me. Two thoughts kept circling through my consciousness over and over again regardless of the splendor surrounding me.

Everyone is dead. I must be dead too.

The light specks dripped from my body, pouring like sand in an hourglass, then began to swirl around my body in a growing storm of radiant glow. The circulation was creating a current of wind that lifted my hair from my shoulders, and I closed my eyes against the growing illumination, letting my body be pulled and tugged by the force.

I landed gently in a crouch on my knees against the strange oscillating obsidian ground, and the dancing star flecks floated up and away, swallowed up into the empty void of space above me. The flesh on my body was torn and raw, dappled with deep bruises, but the pain had ebbed, carried away by the healing touch of the mysterious light.

Roland must have been telling me the truth about the elixir he gave me after all.

All I was left with now was the anguish left in my chest, hollowed with shock and grief. It was all I could feel. That wasn't a wound that the potion could fix. It was an agonizing nightmare that had taken root in my soul and would never leave me.

I clutched my hands to my chest and curled into myself. If I awoke from this place, I would be returning to a reality where I was all alone. One where I would have to live with images of my family's battered bodies scattered on the floor of that basement. I had been betrayed by a man I considered an uncle. I'd be going back to a world where this man, who had watched me grow up, eaten with us, laughed with us, and pretended like he loved us, had ordered our massacre.

My life now was resting on the possibility of Roland's aid. I didn't know where to begin with how I was feeling about him, and I didn't want to make room for those feelings to take root. There wasn't room within me to feel anything other than the devastating grief gripping me. Memories of my parents and siblings alive and well, happy and laughing, danced in front of my eyes before flickering away to my last moments with them, their faces twisted in fear and desperation.

For so long, I had kept everything locked up inside me. I swallowed every storm that had broiled within my chest, but this was one natural disaster I couldn't swallow. I hugged myself harder and screamed as loud as I could. I screamed until my throat was as raw as the skin on my back.

I rose to my feet and threw my hands out on either side of me, still shrieking, unleashing it all. Tears were pouring down my face and my breath kept catching in my throat, but I couldn't stop. Some part of me felt that if I kept screaming, letting the wails tear at my throat and pierce my ears, it might keep the internal pain at bay— even just a little bit.

"No!" I howled, my voice peaking in rage and guttural grief. "No!" I tried to reject everything as a nightmare someone must be inflicting upon me, but I knew that was nothing more than a foolish wish for the reprieve of denial I couldn't take hold of.

Around me, the black ice started cracking, and the air was becoming charged with electricity until lightning was bouncing against the walls. I felt the storms purging from my body, powerful, angry, and heartbroken. Billowing sweeps that cut into the ground and left deep scars in my mental scape. I kept going, ignoring the pain that started to leak through the numbness of release. Trickles of blood had started beading from my wounds, and the agitation was making my vitals unstable again. But I had to let it all go. Get it out of my body. I couldn't live with these feelings. Surely they alone had the power to kill me.

I couldn't stop to hope that whoever had still been breathing when I'd lost consciousness would be alive when I awoke. I couldn't hope that Roland would keep his word and help me escape. I couldn't stop, or I would be consumed by the fear of what would become of me if either of those things turned out to not be true while I was stuck in the world of the living, already forever dead inside.

So the storm kept raging around me, and the air got colder and colder. The lights lurking behind the ice walls were mirroring my agitation. The ground shuddered beneath me and piece by piece began to break apart. I fell through the crack, and tumbled into the canyon of darkness beneath. The storm fell away above me.

My back slammed into a cold surface and began to sink into frigid water. I wasn't as sensitive to the cold by nature, but even I found it jarring enough for my eyes to pry themselves open to the waking world in shock.

There was a curtain of foggy liquid and displaced air bubbles rushing past me as I submerged deeper. Curling spirals of red were seeping into the water in front of my eyes, coming from somewhere below me. I turned my head to see a pale hand slipping past my face.

Inessa. Her body, stripped and naked like mine, was sinking adjacent to me. The side of her face that had been blown away by the gun was facing away from me, but I saw that deep crimson was spilling from the wound and staining the water around her head. The golden gleam of her hair swaying upward in the blood.

Of all my family who might have survived, I knew Ina wasn't the one I could hope to make it out alive. The sight, even obscured, made my stomach twist, and I flinched at the memory of her being shot above me, letting out a wail and losing the breath I'd been holding in the process.

My lungs were screaming for air, but my body was sluggish in the snow water. Ice affinity or not, it seemed the power had its limits, especially with no idea how to harness it. In my efforts to propel myself to the surface, I rolled to the side, tipping my perspective downward and instantly regretting it, I screwed my eyes closed against yet another horrific image I'd be forever plagued with.

Below me, disappearing into the darker, murky depths of the hole we'd been thrown in, I could see glimpses of the other members of my family. Papa's foot, Mama's face already turning blue, Theo's back— each of them suspended in a cloud of their lingering blood that was slowly crawling through the water around me, adding to my own wisps of scarlet. The frigid temperature of the water made the spread of blood sluggish and intentional in its coagulation.

I flipped back and forced my freezing limbs to take me upward. Desperate for air and to remove myself from the waking nightmare. Thankfully, I wasn't deep, and my head broke the surface with a gasp, followed by a muffled fit of coughing. The glow of the half waxing moon gave just enough illumination for me to find the frosty mud wall of the shaft, and I leaned against it.

The unsanitary pool filled with all sorts of toxins, dirt, and human remains was one of the worst places I could find myself with my body currently covered in the plethora of open wounds. I needed to get out and get them cleaned and sanitized if I didn't want to immediately die of infection and be able to help my surviving family.

I could barely move my feet to keep myself afloat, and my body was shivering so violently I had to dig my fingers into the earthy wall to stay anchored to the surface and not sink. As my eyes adjusted, I could just barely make out an old, splintered ladder running the length of the shaft. It looked ready to break apart from who knew how long it had been exposed to such moist conditions, but it looked to be my only way out.

As I made my way over to it, I caught a glimpse of something floating beside me. Two more bodies that belonged to the two I hadn't seen below me. My two little sisters floating on the surface, naked, exposed, and undoubtedly dead. The cloudy water was now entirely tinged with blood, and bile rose in my throat while I tried to refute what I was submerged in.

Either Roland had lied about trying to save whoever the guard had announced was still breathing, or he hadn't been able to save them after all, and my heart started breaking all over again. My face was crumbling underneath the relentless chattering of my teeth as I curled my fingers around the broken base of the ladder. It was everything I had feared about clinging to life.

"Those two aren't sinking!" I covered my own mouth to conceal the scream clawing at the inside of my mouth, and pressed my back as far as I could against the wall, allowing myself to sink up to my nose in the water. I prayed with all my might to whoever might hear me. I prayed to Eisa herself that I wouldn't be spotted, just to be pulled out and tortured again. I'd rather freeze in the water than endure that a second time.

"You'd think they were full of enough holes," Another soldier joked, and I winced at his words, thinking of Inessa somewhere beneath me.

"Don't disrespect the dead." Despite myself, I felt relief course through me at the sound of Roland's voice echoing over the hole. "Whatever side you're on in regards to magic, you never want to piss off Dimaer."

"That's just a bunch of old wives tales and spun stories to scare children," The soldier scoffed.

"Well, then I guess it worked on me. Go on and pack up, and head back to the house."

"What are you going to do about the bodies floating?"

I stole another glance upward, and caught the edge of Roland's arms as he pushed his sleeves up his arm. "I'm going to take care of it. Consider it a reward for all of your hard work. I know your unit has been out here on this Forsaken piece of land for longer than any of you would care to be. With this taken care of finally, you all will be able to return home. Go, get warm and start collecting your belongings. I have a bit of energy left in me."

There was a long pause, but sure enough, Roland had

convinced them. The sound of the boots crunching through snow and scuffing over rocks faded with distance, along with the cheerful banter at the idea of returning home. *Cheerful.* Not one of them felt one shred of remorse over killing an entire family and dumping the remains out in the elements.

I held my rigid position against the wall by the ladder, and bated my breath, waiting for any signal or sign that it was in fact safe to alert Roland to my position. At this point, short of waiting him out in the freezing water, I had little choice but to accept his help and hope for the best. I hated the way my heart longed to trust him implicitly after everything he had been a part of. I couldn't allow my mind to yield to that level of trust so easily.

"Sorrel?" The whisper carried down the shaft to me. "Please, Divines Above, Founders, anyone. Sorrel, tell me you're there somewhere?" His voice was pleading and weary, the tiniest wobble giving away the desperation in his words. "Schnites. You should have woken up. You can't be dead… You can't be."

He swore when I struggled to find my voice to answer him. If he thought I was dead, then perhaps I could wait in the water a few more minutes before climbing out and making a run for it. But even then, once I was out, I had no clothing, all of the jewels had been taken, and the immediate environment was filled with snow. Not to mention having no idea where to go or how to get medical attention for my soiled wounds.

Then there was the fact that with every passing moment, my body was growing stiffer, heavier, and less responsive. I thought back to Harvier waiting for his father outside the hospital. His body temperature had gone too low and become irreversible. I could probably withstand a greater low, but I still had human limits. I didn't have extra minutes to gamble with. Not when I had no idea how long I would have to be exposed before I found shelter and warmth outside of this hole. If I could even haul myself out on the rotting ladder.

There was still the question of whether or not I even wanted to escape and survive, or die here and be forever with my family.

Despite my crippling despair, there was something ticking in my chest. Perhaps it was the innate human desire to run from the finality of death. Perhaps a part of me wanted to demand answers to unresolved questions, or maybe I wanted to avenge the deaths of my family. Maybe, there was a small kindling part of me that wanted to live on and honor them, to defy the execution of all of us by surviving. I couldn't quantify the mounting desire to escape the pit, but I did know my time to find out the reason was running out.

I did my best to catch my breath and steady my shivering body before opening my mouth to call out. I tried to say his name but I was too cold, and my voice was little more than the croak of a frog. My heart began to thunder all over again now that the option to receive potential help was being taken away by my state of weakness.

"Roland," I whispered again. The air felt sharp, like ice was forming in my lungs with each breath I took. I did my best to wave my hand, but it collapsed against the water with a dull and quiet splash. I'd have to try to climb the ladder.

"Sorrel?" I heard Roland whisper my name again, filled with a new hope that hadn't been there before. I forced my arms to grab onto the closest wring of the ladder and tried with all my might to haul myself out of the water. A moment later there was a shuffling sound above followed by a shadow and a splash beside me.

A rope ladder.

"Tug it if you are there, and I will get you." At Roland's command, I reached numbly for the new ladder and tugged with what little strength I had left. "Thank Eisa."

He was scrambling frantically down the ladder within seconds, looking down at the water every few movements until his eyes finally caught sight of me clinging to the broken wrung of the old wooden ladder, cowering and seizing with cold. Our gazes locked, and he gave a shuddering gasp. Abandoning the ladder, he jumped straight into the frigid water.

The bloody pool immediately stained the white of his shirt

as he paddled over to me. Without breaking his momentum, he plucked me from the wall and shifted me over to the new ladder. One arm was wrapped around me, strong and solid, while the other started to lift both of us out of the water. The movements were awkward and jerky, but we were moving, until my beaten body was fully out of the water and Roland paused to hug me even closer. The air nipped at the water beading from my body, stinging like a million shards of glass.

I could feel Roland's body shivering beneath me, and I knew, seeing him rush into the hole and leap into the snow melt water without hesitation or concern for his own wellbeing to get to me, there was more to validity to his explanation than I had been willing to acknowledge. The protection of his embrace, the desperation on his face when he spotted me switching to that of hope wrought with grief and regret— He was telling me the truth. This was the true Roland. The one I had known all my life and had loved more than I had ever thought possible, not the cold stranger who betrayed us on the scaffold or aimed a gun at my head. There was no one around. No one to impress, or convince by getting me out of the shaft now. As much as I wanted to keep directing all of my hopelessness at him and blame him for betraying me for no reason, as emotionally wrought as I was, logic couldn't refute what was happening at the crux of our ultimate downfall.

He was saving me.

Perhaps, there was someone still on my side. Someone who would help me, protect me, comfort me. I thought of the words Hykner had once shared with me, *If there are hands reaching out to help you, then now is the time to accept the help, lest you drown.* Perhaps Roland really had always loved me and was risking everything to show me it now by being the hand to keep me from drowning. Maybe he was safe. Maybe I could lean on him as I had many times before… Maybe I could allow myself to unbury the love I'd freely given him. And maybe, just maybe, that notion felt like a tiny glimmer of reassurance in the chasm of agony I was being carried out of.

I was so weak, I could scarcely move but I shifted my hand to brush his cheek and leaned my head into his shoulder. "Thank you," I breathed.

"Don't thank me," He replied hoarsely, his words choked with emotion.

"You've saved me."

"You saved yourself by choosing to stay alive. And, I didn't save them," He replied mutinously. One of the jarring motions of climbing the ladder one-handed, dislodged my head from his shoulder, forcing me to peer at the icy pool of death I was leaving behind.

Yulia and Kira were still bobbing on the surface of the freshly disturbed water, now dark with both the mud I had dislodged from the wall and the darkening blood still rising from the displaced current of those who had sunk to the bottom of the shaft. My kingdom had turned against me. My family was lost to me. Everything precious in my life was sinking into the past, no place in the future I would live, and was left to decay in that hole. I scrunched my eyes closed tight and wretched under the weight of it, though nothing came out.

We finally crested the top of the hole, and Roland grunted with the strain of hauling us both that final stretch onto the snowy ground. He was shaking, hunched over me. His face buckled under the emotion, and he reached a trembling hand to cup my cheek and press his forehead to mine.

"I thought I was going to lose you," He whimpered pitifully. "I still could. I know its too much to ask you to ever forgive me for failing you and your family in such an atrocious way—"

"I'm all that's left." I swallowed hard. "You aren't losing me. I know the truth now."

A shudder passed over Roland's body, and water dripped off our bodies, defiling the pearly white of the snow. He opened his mouth to say something but instead pushed to his feet and walked a few paces away to a cart before throwing a wool blanket over me. As cold as I was, it wouldn't do much to build heat, but at the very least, it was covering my naked body.

"You're not all that's left," He puffed and stalked back over to the shaft.

"Where are you going?" I whimpered, reaching out a trembling hand. The thought of him leaving me alone filled me with panic and dread I didn't feel I could bear.

"I have to go back for her. She was still breathing and I was able to give her the dregs of the potion. I just hope she's still floating and the cold didn't finish her off…" He wheezed, before descending back into the hole. He was going back into the pit of death, one filled with freezing water he couldn't withstand, to try to salvage another of our lives. Even if it was a fool's errand, his devotion to the endeavor displayed the ultimate loyalty he'd been forced to conceal. As hard as it had been to witness, his actions now spoke louder than the mechanical ones back in Tuyet. There was no reason to go into that pit a second time unless he truly meant to prove he was always on our side— even if it meant recovering the bodies of those he couldn't save.

I laid stunned and incapacitated on the ground with nothing else to do but wait. They were all dead. I saw all their bodies. I had watched each one of them meet their end, and even if they had been breathing, surely the water would have been too cold for them. I saw them in the water, still and lifeless and sinking with my own eyes.

My lip trembled as my mind tumbled over the word *floating* with a new sense of clarity, and I tried to stifle my hope. Yulia and Kira had been the only two still floating. Roland thought one of them may still be alive. My spirit plummeted and rose up and down so rapidly, I felt the sensation of vertigo as hope and reality warred inside me. Hope was screaming that one of my sisters was alive still, while reality was shouting that one being alive meant the other was dead. I couldn't choose one to hope was alive and know the other was gone. But, that was the reality I was left with.

A few agonizing minutes passed before a water logged Roland appeared over the precipice of the shaft lugging the survivor along with him. I sobbed silently in confusion when a brunette head rose over the edge of the shaft, and Yulia's body pushed to safety, before Roland descended a third time and returned with Kira. He dragged both bodies out and laid them out next to me.

"Are they both?" I croaked. Surely I couldn't have been so lucky that two more of us had survived.

Roland was breathing heavily, his body shaking uncontrollably from the cold. He dragged himself over to the cart and pulled two blankets free before stumbling back to wrap Yulia up with the first blanket, leaving only her face visible. He kept his eyes fully averted from their naked bodies, and though he had seen mine, at this point, I didn't care even if he hadn't, Yulia and Kira had been like little sisters to him. Seeing them in that state must be a different kind of unsettling that would be different from how I felt about it.

"G-give her a l-little friction, if you can. She i-isn't dead y-yet," He grunted at me and I did my best to rub my arm up and down over Yulia's core. I wept pitifully over my sister. Yulia was alive.

Yulia was alive!

Yulia was alive and Kira was…

I faltered when Roland gingerly wrapped Kira's limp body with the blanket, cradling her head, with fresh tears in his eyes, before that too was covered. I knew what it meant.

Yulia was alive.

Kira was dead.

FIFTY-THREE

I choked on another rolling wave of grief so strong I was almost certain it would kill me.

"No," I whispered. "I thought— When you brought them both back up…"

"I couldn't just leave her there when she was still floating on the surface. The others were already too deep for me to get to."

"I saw."

There was a brief pause. "I'm sorry."

I shook violently, no longer in control of my body's physical responses. I needed something to attach my weeping mind to, something with purpose. For some reason I recalled the advice given to me by the old man outside the hospital, telling me that strength was a matter of will. Strength led to will and will led to strength, purpose was needed to break the paradox of ineffectuality consuming me or I would wither to nothingness as he had warned.

"What happens now?"

"Now, I need to get us all out of here as fast as possible before they come looking for me. We need to get you warm and dressed. Both of you." Roland nodded to Yulia, and once more went back to the cart to retrieve something else. "I was able to stash these clothes for you."

"I don't think I can move to put them on."

"Then, with your permission, I will dress you," Roland offered, looking away awkwardly. So much had happened since our moment of intimacy, new lines had been drawn. "You can dress Yulia."

I nodded. "Go ahead."

"I'm hoping that the clothing will be enough to warm you so you can move on your own, given your Ice affinity, you shouldn't need that much to regain movement. But your injuries…"

"I'll make it," I replied firmly. "Hurry."

Roland set to work drying me off as best as he could with the blanket, though he was being mindful of my wounds too.

"I can hardly feel my body, just do what you need to do," I urged him, and I kept looking in the direction of the house, worried that the soldiers would reappear at any moment. I couldn't see the building from my position on the ground, but somehow it felt like the broken fragments of my heart would forever remain in its basement. A dark beacon I'd never be unaware of again.

Roland pursed his lips with a readied rebuttal but shook it away and slipped a dress over my head. The dry clothing against my skin felt revitalizing, and sure enough, just the small amount of warmth seemed to be thawing my body ever so slightly.

"What do we do…" The words caught in my throat, and all I could manage was a strangled whisper. "Kira."

"The ground is still too frozen, I don't think I can bury her," Roland exhaled and pinched the bridge of his nose. "I didn't have a plan for this. I don't know— " His voice cracked and swallowed against the emotion trembling on his lips.

"Fire," I coughed.

"What?" Roland looked at me, confusion knitting his brows.

My stomach rolled with nausea and opposition to the idea,

but I recalled Kira's dying words. *I feel those flames in me turning to embers. They aren't evil, Sorrel. They feel like home.* My lungs struggled to draw in breath as another surge of sorrow crashed over me until I wretched.

Too young to burn. The memories of Harvier's and Vadia's deaths seeped through the cracks of my battered heart as I tried to force the words through my lips.

"Can we burn her body? Return her to the fire. *Will* she burn?" I had to wonder, since my body had started to freeze over despite my affinity, if Kira's resistance to heat was something that would also waver. If nothing else, the thought of Kira being buried somewhere dark and cold felt like an insult. She deserved to rest in a blaze of warmth.

Roland looked taken aback, and he fought against his shivering body to look over his shoulder at Kira's limp, bundled form. "Her affinity won't work now that she is… gone. It leaves with the soul to the Dimaerian Gates."

"So, she will burn."

Roland opened his mouth to reply then snapped it closed again, unable to speak. I wanted to leave it alone, to not leave my family in their watery graves while I tried to find a quick solution to lay my baby sister to rest. For once, I didn't want to be thinking again, or finding a way through. I wanted to stay completely still and silent, until either the pain passed or the frost claimed me.

But, I couldn't afford to be selfish. Not when Yulia was still hanging in the balance. No amount of tears shed was going to bring Kira back, and the longer we delayed, the more certain I was that Yulia, Roland, and I would join her in Dimaer. I could see Roland's resolve breaking apart at the seams as he struggled with the realities of our next move. He'd gotten us out of the basement— out of the pit. He had an escape route for us to follow. We'd have to lean on each other to get through the final leg of the night. Neither of us were going to be strong enough without the other.

I struggled to peel my back from the ground, pushing up on

trembling arms. "Will the guards care if they see the fire?"

"Likely not…" Roland's words vibrated against his chattering teeth, his body seizing with cold. "I said, I'd take… take care of the floating bodies. They— should assume that's what I'm doing."

"The fire will warm us up too," I tossed in.

"Alright," Roland murmured, stilling for a heartbeat before forcing himself to his feet. I recognized the supplies in the cart now as the ones in the room where we'd watched our final sunrise with Kira. We'd stood amongst the tools planned for our own demise and tried to grasp at a fleeting moment of bliss. Now, Roland was building a pyre from the remnants of that stolen moment.

I kept a bleary eye in the direction of the house, trying not to flinch at every crunch of snow beneath Roland's boots, until he had the fire stoked and blazing. With Yulia between me and Kira's body, I dragged myself towards her. Untucking her hand from beneath the blanket, I placed it on Kira's wrapped torso along with my own.

I sniffled, fresh tears rolling down my cheeks. "I- I'm sorry you're not awake to say goodbye to her, Yulia. But, I hope when you wake up you will understand that we had to go." I hunched over, every muscle in my body tensing against more guttural sobs, until my head was pressed against our hands. "We have to go, Kira. I have to make sure Yulia wakes up, and I know you'll understand, but I'm— "

My words hitched, the last of my fortitude crumpling. *How do I do this? How do I say goodbye and leave her behind? I can't do this. I can't move.*

Roland sank to his knees, buried beneath his own regrets and grief a few feet away, clutching at his abdomen. His breath was ragged as he tried to sober. Tears fell freely from his eyes, and his fingers curled into trembling fists. *I have to move, anyway. For Yulia.*

"I have to go," I tried again, fighting every bone in my body that was begging me to stay. "I know you'll understand, but I'm so sorry, Kira. Please forgive me."

I ripped myself away and curled into myself, begging

incoherently for Roland to move Kira to the pyre. This time there would be no howling screams as the flames licked her skin, but I covered my mouth and nose against the inevitable stench of burning flesh I knew would come.

"Stay warm, Kira," I whispered, keeping my eyes averted from the flickering fire, and instead fixed on Yulia. I dared to feel a small trickle of relief amidst the anguish as I saw some of the color returning to Yulia's face. I bit my lip and closed my eyes. It was like Kira's endless warmth was reviving Yulia as Kira herself turned to embers, passing her light to the sister she had so adored and protected.

"We need to go, Sorrel." Roland's words were muffled in my ears as they pounded. "You might feel stronger than you are and you shouldn't move around any more than necessary until we can get you looked at. I'm going to have to carry Yulia, so I'll grab what we need from the cart and come back to help you up. We need to get into the tree line then we will have to hike to our first checkpoint. From there we will have to head to a passage in the ice caves."

"Where does the passageway go?" I asked wearily.

"Kesgoldol. They should give us sanctuary as refugees."

"Should?"

"We won't know for sure till we get there, but we can't stay in Eisa," Roland sighed and patted my shoulder awkwardly. "I'll be right back. Don't get too worked up. We have a long way to go yet."

I nodded and closed my eyes, trying to focus my energy on restoration. I had two more lives to worry about besides my own. We didn't have time to struggle any more than Yulia's and my injuries would already cause us to.

I could feel Roland's body growing weary as he scooped me up and helped me to a standing position. I reached out and touched his face. "You're getting too cold, and you're still damp. You'll get frostbite."

"I have some clothing in the bag too, but it will have to wait."

He pulled free another vile. "I have another mixture that should give you enough strength to walk, but we need to space it out so you can make the whole journey."

"And what journey would that be?" My legs threatened to give out underneath me, and a thousand needles pierced my spine at the sound of the voice behind us.

Arrian.

I didn't bother to turn around before yanking the vile out of Roland's hand and slamming back half the contents at once. "Get Yulia!" I barked, and Roland lunged for my sister.

Adrenaline pulsed with the blooming effects of the second elixir, giving me a rush of frantic energy. My legs stabilized, I grabbed a shovel from the back of the cart and swung it with all my remaining might against Arrian's rapid approach. Though weak, my blow succeeded in striking him in the stomach and driving the wind from his body enough to bring him to his knees.

"You bitch," He swore as he crumpled against the blow. "Roland, explain yourself! Why is she *still alive*?" The final words were hissed through gritted teeth, a growl of malevolence.

"Run, head for the trees!" Roland shouted at me, and checking he had Yulia safely in his arms, I leapt into motion, launching myself down the hill towards the forest.

FIFTY-FOUR

The wind buffeted against us as we fled down the hill to the tree line. Both Roland and Yulia had started shivering again, and I blanched when I saw that Yulia's lips were turning blue once more. She didn't have much longer in this state.

"What is Arrian doing here?" I demanded.

"I don't know," Roland panted, straining to keep pace while holding Yulia. "He was supposed to head back to Tuyet yesterday. I wasn't even sure why he came out here ahead of me in the first place."

"Preparing, apparently," I huffed. "What do we do now?"

"We keep hurrying, and pray we make it before he rallies the soldiers and catches up to us. Doing that gives us a little head start."

"He's seen us. You can't go back now that he's seen you helping me."

"Sorrel, I'm not going back. I never was."

I had a million responses flurry through my mind, but pushed them away to focus on the trees ahead of us. Umber trunks and snow coated evergreen bows whipped past my vision as we pelted into the forest. My lungs were already screaming, but I pushed myself forward, letting Roland take the lead. Yulia's limp form bounced against his chest, and I could tell our pace was slowing.

"We should be nearing the facility. If we can just keep our lead, and make it there, we will have a better chance of hiding." Roland glanced over at me and seemed to have come to a similar conclusion about our physical state fighting against us.

I was about to point out that Arrian and the guards would only search the building once they caught up, but decided against it. It was our only option. At this point, the meager dregs of hope left inside us were all we were running on.

"Come on," I pressed forward harder. "I'm not going to get caught again."

"That's the spirit."

Roland was right in his assessment as I peered through the flurrying snow and spotted the outline of a small barrack-like building up ahead. Our legs were shaking on the final trudge through the snow that was now packed up to our shins. By the time we reached the entrance to the ominous gray building, I was almost positive that the elixir was wearing off, and my body was going to come apart at the seams at any moment.

"Where do we go?" I asked.

"Inside, so long as Maggie is here to let us in." Roland grimaced, his footsteps clumsy. He was still in his wet shoes, and I worried what state his feet were in. He rapped his knuckles on the door rhythmically. We held our breath and waited for what felt like eternity, before there was the click of a lock and the seam of the doorway shifted, the hinges groaning loudly. The door only opened a short way before coming to an abrupt halt.

"So loud," I heard the apologetic mutter from inside, and Maggie's silver head poked out. A small sense of comfort spread through me at the sight of her. I couldn't explain it, but she immediately made me feel like I was going to be alright. "Where are the rest?"

"We are it," Roland replied somberly.

Maggie's eyes flicked from an unconscious Yulia to me, and widened as she saw what the physical state my body was in. A bullet wound in my arm, freshly coagulated blood smeared across multiple contusions, scrapes, and gashes, and deep purple and red bruises.

"Come in. Quickly." She reached out a hand and ushered us in. "Were you followed?"

"We had to handle the dead." Roland set Yulia down as he gave his briefing. "Arrian showed up just as we were leaving. Sorrel knocked him down but no doubt he and the guards are tracking us now. We don't have much time."

"We'll see if we can delay them," two figures peeled away from the walls where I hadn't even noticed them. I recognized Macsen as one and a girl I had never seen before. She had long auburn hair that was woven into long intricate braids. The color reminded me of Mama, and the world swayed beneath my feet as the reality that I'd never see my mother again with her body frozen at the bottom of the mine shaft reared to the surface of my mind.

"But— " I tried to intervene, not wanting them to put themselves in harm's way, but they were already headed for the door and gone before I could finish my sentence.

"Be careful, Eirene!" Roland called after them. "Arrian will take no mercy on a Wielder."

"Did you give her the potions I had prepared in the event of an emergency?" Maggie demanded.

"That's how she was able to make it this far. Yulia has only been stabilized and hasn't woken up yet."

"That will work in our favor. The longer she's asleep the stronger the effects of the tonic will be."

"Take care of Yulia first," I pleaded.

"The state of her... What happened?" Maggie whispered in disbelief.

"It was—" Roland's eyes shifted sideways and he swallowed

hard. "It was just Sorrel left at the end of it and I was only just able to manage to get a moment to get her the first vitality tonic."

It took me a moment of wondering why they were talking over me like I wasn't there, until I realized I had slumped to my hands and knees without even noticing, and both Roland and Maggie were laying me down on my back as they conversed. Shock was finally getting the upper hand of my awareness.

"And Inessa?"

Roland dipped his voice, no doubt trying to be discreet. "She was shot in the head, there was no saving her. They were all shot or succumbed to their wounds." He spoke candidly, only the smallest shake in his words offsetting the emotion behind the pragmatic recount. "One of the soldiers noticed Yulia was still breathing as well. It turns out she had only fainted. She has a gunshot wound to her leg and was thrown into the freezing waters of the mineshaft."

"And you?" Maggie didn't wait for Roland to brush her off. "Get those wet shoes off. There's a fresh set of clothes in the washroom."

Gunfire sounded in the distance, and a small wail pressed through my lips. Strength was failing me, but my body convulsed with the instinct to flee the sound. Red leaked into my vision as visceral blood splatters flickered in front of my gaze.

"Hold on, Sorrel," Maggie, pressed down gently against my shoulders to lay me back down. She retrieved something from a bag beside her and started rubbing a poultice all over my body. "I'll get you patched up this time."

I gasped as a blazing heat flared through my body, then ebbed, taking a majority of the aching away with it. "Thank you," I whispered. "But my sister, please."

"Your sister is much more stable than you are right now. From the sounds of it, other than the bullet wound, her fainting saved her from the same brutality you endured," Maggie commented, continuing her triage. "Shhh. No need to get worked up again."

She ran a hand over my forehead, and I realized I had started crying again at the mention of my injuries. "Sorry," I sniffled lamely.

"Don't you dare apologize." Maggie shook her head. "I can tell you all sorts of platitudes about how the pain will pass with time, but I can't heal your spirit after what those monsters put you through. I can only help your body along long enough to get you to safety. Once you're safe, you can grieve. Till then, I need you to hang on with me just a little longer."

"Is Yulia going to be alright?" My lids felt heavy and I blinked sluggishly.

"She is."

"She's going to be alright…"

"Hey," I felt a light sting on my cheek as Maggie gently slapped me. "She will be alright, but she is going to need you when she wakes up. Stay with me. Drink this."

She placed yet another vile at my lips, and I drank without question, the contents bitter on my tongue. Next, she turned and set to work on Yulia, taking care of the wound on her leg. From my vantage point beside her, I was thankful that, though inconvenient and painful, the bullet hadn't pierced any vital veins, and it seems that the cold of the water had kept it from bleeding excessively. Her skin was pink and devoid of the marks of bludgeoning that peppered my own body. I realized then that Maggie was right. Now that Yulia was out of the cold, she was going to be fine.

As the final elixir took effect, I felt a fresh wave of restoration surge through my body. Tentatively, I lifted myself off the ground, and crawled over to Yulia, who Maggie had just finished dressing in fresh winter clothing. It seemed at least the water in the shaft had rinsed away most of the blood caked on her head from sinking into the scarlet pool of her and Theo's wounds. I could see Yulia's face starting to twist with vague awareness and knew she was liable to awaken at any moment.

Roland entered the room in fresh clothing, and at the same moment Yulia's eyes fluttered open. Recognition filled her eyes and she opened her mouth, letting out a blood curdling shriek. The three of us covered our ears as the sound vibrated our skulls, and I rushed forward to hug Yulia close to me.

"Yulia, Yulia! I'm here. It's me, Sorrel. You're safe. Roland helped us escape. He's not our enemy. I'm right here," I kept repeating the phrases over and over again until the initial wave of panic passed and my sister sagged against me. Looking around and seeing none of the rest of our family with us, Yulia guessed what it meant, even as her eyes continued to search the room.

"Why?" She whimpered, turning to stare up at me. "*Why?*"

My heart broke all over again as I looked at the sorrow in her face. "I don't know."

"She needs to drink this." Maggie handed me a vile and I held it up to Yulia's mouth.

"I need you to take this medicine and then we have to go."

"Your face… your body." A frantic edge to her voice, Yulia balked at my appearance. "Where is…"

"Yulia, listen to me. Take the medicine and then we have to go. Arrian is after us. Roland is going to take us somewhere safe."

"I don't— "

"I know. I don't either," I jumped in, guessing her next sentence. "But we have to. Together."

Yulia grabbed hold of my hand and squeezed it with all her might before a faint flicker of clarity twinkled in her eyes, melting away the clouded terror. She slowly sobered, nodding. I felt a little unnerved by how quickly her disposition had shifted and wondered if she had somehow tapped into my feelings and thoughts with her own affinities that seemed much more flippant than mine.

After drinking the elixir, I helped her rise shakily to her feet. She narrowed her eyes at Roland, who had shrunken away from her screams. He kept his eyes glued to the ground, not meeting her burning stare.

"Remember he stepped in front of a gun for you once," I reminded her gently, hoping it would inspire trust.

Unblinking, she replied, "He also pointed one at you."

"We can trust him. You and I wouldn't be here if we couldn't."

More gunfire sounded, this time significantly, and Maggie

ushered Roland towards us. "I've done what I can. Get to the caves before the cavalry gets here. Roland, make sure she's seen to properly when you get to Kesgoldol." She jerked head at me, and handed Roland a small pouch to add to his bag, along with face scarves for our trek to the caves. "I'll keep them busy when they get here"

"Kesgoldol?" Yulia asked, brows furrowing. "We are leaving Eisa?"

"We don't have a choice," I said, accepting the scarf from Roland and tying it around Yulia. I nodded to Roland to lead us out. We stepped back out into the dark winter, and I suppressed a gasp of surprise as I saw that the roots of the trees had burst from the ground, creating a small tunnel for us to escape into. Maggie, in her element and at full health, was as powerful and formative as Roland had once told me.

We don't have a choice. I repeated to myself as I held Yulia's hand and trailed after Roland.

FIFTY-FIVE

"The entrance to the tunnel across the border is inside that cave," Roland called over the howling winds as we were clearing the final stretch of the frozen fjord, carefully picking our way over the icy surface. After leaving the shelter of the forest, we'd entered into a cloud of frost and flurries. Ice collected on our coats as we trudged through the elements.

"We are almost there," I hugged an arm around Yulia for reassurance. "We will be safe soon, I promise."

"Best not to make idle promises you can't keep." My whole body went rigid as the wind carried with it the sound of Arrian's mocking voice. We whipped around in tandem to see him walking casually toward us, alone. He must have kept ahead of the soldiers and separated from the main scuffle. I could make out the faint flickering glow of lights in the woods through the white haze, showing that the soldiers were back on our path.

"How did you catch up to us so fast?" I gasped.

"I thought you went home before the execution," Roland asserted, taking a protective step in front of me and Yulia.

"I was going to, but something just didn't quite add up over the past few days. Father told me he never gave the orders to go infiltrate the Wielder hideouts, you never reported a single one, and yet, the moment the Zdraevits were shown as Wielders, you had a change of heart? So much so as to want to be on the firing squad? He even had to use a Whisper Wielder's curse on you to be certain you'd comply with the initial exposure, hoping once you saw the full truth you'd follow his lead. The Wielder was killed of course afterwards— I saw to that myself. I was doubtful of my own suspicions, Roland, but I had to see for myself," Arrian laughed. "I see you couldn't help but follow your little poisoned *Snowdrop*."

"Knock it off, Ari," Roland warned.

"Feeling tough, are we? That might have worked when we were younger, but I don't live in your shadow anymore. I have my own rank and pedestal now. So, tell me. Why have you betrayed Eisa? Why have you betrayed your *family?*"

"It's not a betrayal to do the right thing, Arrian."

"The right thing is to follow the path laid out for us and to do our duty," Arrian bit back, and I winced at the same rhetoric I had also once believed. Could I have ever turned out so cruel and filled with hate had it not been for Inessa?

"At what cost? How high of a cost are you willing to pay before you admit that all of it has been wrong? That you are the corruption you've been claiming to fight!" Roland's words wiped the smile from Arrian's smug face and twisted it with rage.

"Never mind how high the cost may grow, my allegiance is to Father." Arrian rushed forward, barreling into Roland to knock him down. "I can't let you go through with this! You can't betray us."

A weakened Roland struggled to roll over onto his back. I hesitated, unsure of how to intervene or even if I should. If Roland held Arrian off, it would give me and Yulia a better chance of escaping. All Arrian could do at this point on his own was to hope to slow us down long enough for the rest of the guards to catch up.

Despite all of the tumultuous feelings towards Roland I felt, I groaned and rushed forward to try to help. After everything that had transpired, I didn't need to lose him to a frozen grave too. If we survived this night, then there would be time enough to put all the pieces back together later. I drew in a deep breath and pulled from the chilled environment around me, focusing it all into my hand.

"Sorrel, go!" Roland shouted.

"I'm not leaving you here to be shot down for treason," I retorted and clasped my fingers around Arrian's face.

He howled in pain and thrashed beneath my grip until he finally relented from his hold on his brother and struck me hard in the chest to dislodge my hold. As I fell backwards, fresh blood rolling down my ribs, I smiled seeing the frost bites scored across his cheeks.

Finally.

"Argh, Sorrel always intervening where she isn't welcome, bossing everyone around," He swore, rubbing at the blackened wounds. "I'll have the pleasure of finishing what my brother couldn't do!"

He kicked Roland in the head, causing him to collapse, dazed in the snow, before lumbering over to me and pinning me to the ground. I began shrieking manically, kicking and clawing at Arrian to try and dislodge him, images of a soldier grinning down at me flickering between blinks as thunder roared in my ears. But his weight and strength were greater than my own and he kept me down.

"Why have you become like this, Arrian? You grew up with us!"

"And I didn't know I was sharing my childhood with monsters. The very same kind of monsters that robbed that childhood of a mother and now my brother!"

Staring up at him, I could see how his warped views were the mirror opposite of my own, showing me the horrific person I could have grown to be. "Your hatred is what will cost you your brother. Your hatred is what cost him half of his own family. *My family!*"

"I wanted to do it myself, you know. I was going to be the one to cut Kira down. I wanted to save her for last and watch as she shattered before me before I drowned her in all your blood. I heard she was one of the last to fall, other than you, and my men did their job making sure she suffered at the end. I wanted her to pay for stealing the bright future from us both."

"You are a monster, Arrian. You didn't steal her light from her. She kept her power whole and she died with a *smile!*"

"She died broken. How could she not have?" Arrian's voice lilted with a deranged edge, and I was certain that all his remaining sanity had left him. "She had to suffer for going and being a Wielder despite the life we could have shared."

"She *smiled*," I spat. "You didn't take her power. Get off of me!"

"Why do you keep lying?" Arrian raved, fighting against my thrashing.

"Arrian, get off of her," Yulia whimpered, hovering between me and Roland, unsure of what to do to help us. She trembled, struggling to find her resolve until she heard my cry.

"Get off!" I shrieked, bending my wrists as far as I could beneath his hold. Ice wasn't going to help me in the situation since I couldn't make contact. I had no clue how to access my other affinities, and it had taken teetering on the brink of death to even gain access to this small amount of ice magic.

"Get off of her!" Yulia stepped forward, her voice and legs gaining more strength and stability with each step she took through the snow. Her large blue eyes narrowed into sharpened slits, and her lip curled in disgust as she looked at Arrian. Shouting sounded from the direction of the woods over the howling wind, and I turned my head to see that the soldiers had caught sight of us.

"Arrian," She hissed, and I realized I had never seen Yulia so angry. Her long brown hair whipped around her face in the growing wind, and I realized she was emitting a soft glow. "Let us go."

"Roland, wake up! We need help!" I called out, frantic.

"Let us go!" Yulia screamed over and over again over top my repeating shouts at Roland to wake up. Yulia threw her body against Arrian as he shifted his hold on my wrists to one hand and pulled free a dagger from his belt. "Let go!"

Arrian lifted the knife over my throat, and Yulia grabbed onto his arm straining to keep him from plunging it down. Tears of frustration, anguish, and hopeless desperation poured down our faces as we continued shouting against the world until eventually our words unified in one final desperate plea.

"Help us!"

A bright light flashed through the sky, cleaving the infinite indigo blue in two. Arrian released his hold on me, falling back to look overhead, and dropped the knife. Yulia tumbled backwards, losing Arrian's resistance as an anchor. I scrambled away through the powdery snow, shifting into a crouched position. The soldiers were clearing the final distance, but all slowed to a stop to stare up at the sky as the blinding light grew even brighter. Yulia lurched to her feet and yanked the dagger out of reach from Arrian, flipping it around to brandish it at him.

"What are you going to do with that?" Arrian scoffed. The soft glow encasing Yulia grew in a burst that made all of us have to shield our eyes.

"I will carry out my sister's promise to you," She promised as the light in the sky collided against the earth, knocking all of us down in a massive quake. Liquid scarlet light rolled over the landscape towards us, chasing the fissures as they ripped the ground apart. The earth buckled and began falling away to a chasm just beyond the guards who were once more running towards us, this time fleeing for their lives.

"Yulia," I yelped, leaping to my feet as I stared down the wave of advancing light and crumbling ground. "Yulia, we need to run. Now!"

I rushed to Roland and yanked him up. He was recovering from his daze, eyes widened in alarm as snow began toppling from the mountains in the beginning of an avalanche, and loud cracks started snaking across the surface of the frozen water— our bridge to the cave entrance. In moments, our escape route would be buried in snow, and possibly us along with it.

When I looked back at my sister standing with the knife still extended towards Arrian, I was startled to see that the tips of her hair had turned pitch black, and were writhing in shadowy tendrils. More waves of darkness poured from her body like a fog dripping to the snowy ground. Her eyes clouded over with an otherworldly white glow, and her shadows began to twinkle with shimmers of starlight.

I opened my mouth to call out her name over the raging discordance of the world falling to pieces around us, but words failed me as the twinkling red haze surged ahead of the quake and twirled around me in a warm embrace. It coiled around Yulia next, bleeding into the preexisting shadowy starlight leaking from her body, the night turning into a deadly nova.

"A star," Roland croaked beside me. "You called the aid of a star and it came to help you. You can trust it. Trust the light."

"Trust the light," I repeated with a breathless nod, running my fingers through the glittering scarlet. "Take us to the cave."

"*To the shadows, we flee!*" The light pulsated and a twinkling, childlike voice trilled, light and breathy. The ethereal voice took me by surprise, and I couldn't help but balk at it as it gathered its energy around us, supporting our weary and broken bodies. Yulia's affinities subdued with a look of alarm as the light swept her away with us, propelling us across the snow and ice like we were cresting the wave of destruction rather than tumbling beneath it. The guards were falling around us, unable to match the star's speed before succumbing to the tumbling snowfall.

My vision was blurring as the star pushed us onward

towards the caves. The ice began to separate beneath our feet, and dark freezing water jumped through the fractures. I shivered involuntarily, the sight too close to the horror I had endured in the shaft.

"Roland!" Arrian bellowed behind us, completely irate from where he had drifted on a jagged chunk of ice to the right of us. "Roland, you traitor! If you go through with this then you are lost to Eisa forever."

"I'm sorry, Brother," Roland spoke softly, and I could see the pain on his face as he looked across the gap of icy water between them. Even if Arrian was worthy of our pity, there was no way we could go back for him and still make it into the caves before the avalanche would catch up to us. "I've made my choice and Eisa is no longer a part of it. Father's vendetta made sure of that."

"You can't turn your back on us!"

"Goodbye, Arrian," Roland whispered as he shoved me and Yulia through the opening to the cave.

"Roland!" Arrian's shouts echoed behind us until it was completely overwhelmed by the dull thunderous roar of the avalanche burying the cave. The light trilled in farewell before shooting back into the sky, and we were left in frigid darkness. We all collapsed with a huff, exhausted and stunned.

"Sorrel," Yulia's frightened voice called through the darkness, and I crawled over to her as our eyes adjusted to the new gloom.

"You called down a star," Roland puffed, holding his head. "I can't believe it heard you and listened. No one taught you how to do that."

"I'm so tired. I don't know how much further I can make it," I croaked, tipping back into delirium.

"Come on, you can lean on me." Roland offered me an arm, and I hesitated. "I can manage," Roland insisted as I grabbed hold of his arm and pulled myself up. I felt something hot and sticky run down my arm, and I knew that Maggie's elixirs were running their course and my wounds were beginning to reopen.

"Do you know the way through this cave?" The sound of

Yulia's meek voice, so cowed and uncertain in contrast to the ferocity she'd shown Arrian, thundered in the yawning emptiness within me, reminding me I couldn't allow myself to break yet. I had to make sure Yulia made it to the other side of this before I could fall apart... Or, succumb.

"This cave will take us directly across the border to Kesgoldol," I lifted my chin and wiped my mouth with the back of my hand, leaning fully against Roland until he was more or less dragging my failing body.

"Stick close together— " Roland started to instruct us but his words were cut off by a loud cracking, followed by a dusting of ice and snow rattling loose from the ceiling. We all slowly craned our necks upward, watching as a series of fractures had started at the entrance to the cave, and were slowly making their way over us.

"The weight of the snow is too much for the ice. Move!" I instructed.

With the last dregs of energy I could muster, I raced between Yulia and Roland through the caves I had once wanted to visit with my father. As our footsteps echoed through the icy cavern, the hollowness within me grew as I realized I couldn't hear the miraculous ice melody the wonder had boasted of. I steeled myself against the memory of my perished siblings singing the tale of the Winter Maiden and wondered now if I'd share her parable fate, buried beneath the snow.

Exhausted, I looked over my shoulder and glanced down at the large streaks of blood I was leaving behind with each footstep. My head was pounding from pain, enervation, and blood loss, and I was stumbling clumsily against Roland, slumping lower and lower until I finally dropped to my knees.

"Come on, Sorrel," Roland urged shakily. "The exit is just up ahead. We are almost there. Just a little further, then we can rest."

I winced but forced myself back to my feet, hanging onto Roland's shoulder, heaving my wobbling legs every step till we stopped next to a ladder that led to some sort of overhead hatch. I realized at some point the walls had shifted from ice to rock, and it was clear when we left the tunnel we would have made it out of the Eisa at last.

Roland left me and Yulia resting on the ground to push open the cap on the tunnel and we were flooded with a stream of early morning light. It took a fair amount of effort for him to help us out of the tunnel, having given everything we could on the journey, but eventually all three of us were out. This was it. We'd made it to the dawn of a new day and left Eisa behind us for good.

The world was swimming in shadows around me as I blinked slowly to take in my new surroundings, looking for the nearest place I could safely collapse. A man stood leaning against one of the many pointed rocks in the clearing, and the sunrise lit up his golden eyes with a flash.

"Sorrel, no," He breathed in horror. "Roland, what the fuck did you let happen?"

I didn't think I could shed any more tears and crack any further, but I found myself crying and shaking once more. I pulled away from the support of Roland's shoulder and stumbled forward, losing my balance and throwing myself into the man's hesitant embrace. I pressed my face into his chest and sobbed and screamed until I couldn't anymore, free to fall apart at last, and all that I could manage was a single whisper.

"Rafe."

"Behold the God for the godless to walk behind.
Let all else be forsaken."
-D

KEEP READING FOR TWO BONUS CHAPTERS

YULIA

A heat spread up my arm as the needle pierced my skin, until my whole body was engulfed in fire. No, not fire. What was this sensation? It traveled over my shoulders before spilling down my back and chest, pooling in the arches of my feet.

I blinked, my lashes barely brushing my cheeks before the ever-present din of the surrounding crowd grew muted. I found myself in a rolling mist, no sign of the capital in view. Swaying grass tickled my toes, and I stooped to duck clear of the fog. My eyes widened and my shoulder muscles rippled as I looked out across a vast expanse of fields— fields I knew I had never seen before. Below the mist, the sound was clear and sharp, like I could hear each blade of grass whistling in the wind to make a ballad just for me.

"Hello?" I called out, hesitantly at first, my voice little more than the croak of a frosted frog. I tried again, this time louder. "Is anyone there?"

You are here.

An echo ricocheted within my ears, and my spine went rigid as I recognized my own voice but not repeating what I knew I had said. Laughter followed, and once again, I recoiled at a familiar sound my lips had not uttered.

"Kira? Are you playing some sort of trick on me?" I asked, hoping against reason that my younger sister had suddenly learned to imitate me to such an indiscernible extent. "This is another nightmare."

No, silly. You are playing tricks with yourself. Come into the field to meet me. I'm waiting for you. I've been waiting for you for such a long time now.

My chest heaved, and my ears twitched against the invasion of the voice speaking to me somewhere between my eardrums and my mind. A soft wisp of consciousness I'd never realized was there. I blinked rapidly and peered down the fields until they began to dip and undulate into knolls. Atop the nearest one, I could just make out a figure facing me, her hand cupped to her mouth in the sign of discretion.

Hurry.

The whisper cut through the air, keen as a blade. I trembled where I crouched in the grass, unsure of whether I should approach the mysterious figure in what certainly had to be a dream, or wait until I woke up. I tried pinching my skin, but all it did was somehow make the sound of ringing silence more discernible.

Your words have power, Yulia. Speak them, collect them, wield them to cleave this world in two and begin anew.

Wield?

"No!" I shouted. "Stop talking to me. Get out of my mind!" I clenched my fists, trying to make sure this time there was no gun in my hands. Though, I could tell these whispers were very different from the ones in the theater, and those had not taken me to a vision of a foreign land. "Your whispers will not control me, Forsaken."

Take my hand and trust me, Yulia. Trust the words I speak. You will need me with you or all will be lost to you someday. You must make friends with the voices and they will help you.

My eyes stung with tears and I covered my ears to try and block out the whispers coiling around my skull, noticing the figure was rushing through the grass towards me.

"I call unto the Divinities to shine their light into this desolate place and spare me from the sins of this forsaken creature," I frantically began to pray, grasping for the repetitions Otvel had told me after the Whisper Wielder had managed to possess me and nearly killed both Theo and Roland.

Yulia! Listen. You mustn't reject—

"The Forsaken have no power to cover my body and with the Divine in my heart, I reject the darkness that approaches me. I reject it!" I whimpered, as the figure I now recognized as myself, hair loose, skin pale in a black dress, written words spiraling around her wrists like a snake, lunged forward and grazed my fingers.

I snatched my hand away and looked around wildly, the foggy domain around me vanishing back to the courtyard in an instant. The air was still, palpable as my family stood beside me. But something was shifting. Something was terribly wrong. Glancing down at where the false me had touched me I balked in horror to see her curse had made contact and words were slithering around my forearms.

"No!" I screamed, and felt Sorrel tense beside me. A fresh wave of heat blazed on my other side and I snapped my head to look at Kira.

"What's happening?" She yelped, and I stood speechless to see my little sister waving her flaming arms around frantically.

"Kira, stop fanning the flames. You need to calm down!" Inessa's voice crackled into a muffled roar.

Had I somehow set her on fire while the Forsaken creature had been inside my mind? I opened my mouth to call to Kira but was suddenly enveloped in velvety, inky darkness.

"What? No, no, no." I floundered in the infinite black, searching for the light of my sister. "Kira? Are you there? Sorrel, help me! Inessa, Mama please! I didn't mean it, I swear I didn't mean to let the voice in again! I've tried so hard…" I begged, tripping over my own feet as I tried to flee.

To my surprise, I slipped through the darkness like a knife through butter until I was no longer sure if I was falling or floating. My feet somehow once more found solidity beneath them. Did these shadows feel safe? Like they were holding me, keeping me from harm?

Surely not. It had to all be more deception. Whatever was happening would vanish just like the fields. A sharp prickle of nerves raked over my body at a small tap to my shoulder. I whirled around and stumbled backward, seeing another Yulia blinking curiously at me.

Her hair was pleated in a long braid down her back, and this time, I realized I wasn't being overwhelmed by sound like I had been before. Instead, my body itself felt attuned to every sensation I'd been perceiving before arriving here— perhaps even what was happening around me while I was detained in the darkness.

I rubbed my fingers together, realizing I'd also felt the tap in my own finger the same as if it had been the one to touch my shoulder.

"Who are you?" I demanded, trying my best not to cower. "Why won't you leave me alone? Tell me who you are and what you want with me!"

"Who do you want to be?" The other Yulia asked cheerfully.

I took another step backwards on shaking legs as I watched her face flex and contort from my own visage into the features of Kira— pouty lips, large almond eyes, and long flowing icy blonde hair. Her appearance suddenly shifted and sharpened into the collected and turbulent face of Inessa. Then, from the roots down, the locks darkened until they were nearly black, and the brilliant blue eyes were replaced with a shrewd, discerning silver gaze.

"Sorrel?" I whispered her name, every nerve in my body sparking in response to what I was seeing. It had to be a Forsaken, but I prayed with all my might it was somehow truly my sturdy, nurturing sister ready to comfort and save me. "Sorrel, if that's you, please tell me what's happening here. I'm so confused. One second I was on the scaffold and the next I'm here. You have to have the answers. Please tell me how to get back home!"

I reached out a hand to Sorrel's arm and flinched as an onslaught of images and emotions surged over me, dragging me into the depths of her feelings and memories like an undertow I couldn't escape or dare even hope to survive. Gasping, I recoiled my hand to my chest as the sensation of fire scorching my skin flared in my palm followed by inexplicable guilt and pure terror. Adrenaline, desperation, and horror swirled within my chest until I could no longer bear it.

The pain ebbed and flashed between a torrent of other flickers and emotions, pride, compassion, sorrow, fear, rebellion and everything in between. Next, it blossomed into a fervor of lust pulsing in my stomach, and I saw Roland's cool blue eyes staring into mine. The moment was fleeting and was quickly replaced by a cold, relentless dread seeping into every inch of me, until I was certain I was sodden with despair and sinking into the earth beneath me. A quick withering look to the ground and a shrill scream pressed through my lips to see I was in fact being swallowed slowly by a writhing pool of liquid ebony. Twisting tendrils beckoned me down as I looked back up at Sorrel only to watch as she morphed back into my own reflection.

The magnitude of her emotions rattled me to my core, and my throat constricted against the idea that I was somehow feeling what my sister had felt, seeing bits and pieces of moments in her life. I was merely a vessel for her pain, joy, and regrets for those few seconds, and I couldn't imagine what she had been through to elicit such heightened responses. Reaching out a hand as I slipped further into the pool of black, and I implored myself to help me out of the shadowy quicksand. The other Yulia smiled and accepted my silent plea for help, but the moment her hand clasped around mine, her body broke apart into a black fog and began to coat me, seeping into my skin.

"No! What are you doing?" I yelped, flailing frantically.

I blinked and wriggled my toes against solid ground as I found myself once more on the scaffold, watching as the crowd's faces began to turn sour, in the same instant that I realized all of my family's arms had developed varying tracks of pigment rushing through their veins just like mine, revealing something sinister lurking within us all. Before I could clearly identify what was happening, I was ripped away from the world I knew and thrust somewhere else.

This time, I stood in the center of some sort of clouded prism, moments in time playing out in each crystal pane. Some blazed with fire, others filled with blood, and others still frosted over beneath murky waters. It was as if every nightmare I'd had since the Wielder attack on the hospital had been immortalized. A dull crackling thunder sounded, shaking the walls around me, and I whirled around looking for some way out of this prison of what appeared to be various snippets of calamity. Finding no escape, I flung myself against the crystal, pounding with all of my strength.

"You can't escape fate," A quiet voice murmured behind me, and I didn't bother to turn around. Once more, it was my own voice. Another me trying to invade my mind.

"I will escape! I reject your evil. Divine see me through," I wailed, continuing to beat my fists against the wall as I recited prayer after prayer for the Divinities' aid, sobbing uncontrollably as I tried to ignore the devious creature curling her arms around me to hug me from behind. Despite my pitiful attempts to shake her off, she hung on, filling me with an infinite capacity for bursting hope and insurmountable foreboding. Finally, the prism walls vanished, sending me lurching forward a step, as I lost my balance beneath the misplaced momentum, back on the scaffold.

I grit my teeth and clutched onto my ears, tears pouring down my cheeks.

"Cover that one's mouth. She will speak words into your ear that will tear apart your mind." I wilted, hearing Friedrich give the command to contain me. Was it because I was endangering everyone yet again? Did I deserve this? Confusion and desperation rattled me to my core as I tried to discern any minuscule semblance of understanding amidst the chaos.

Everyone was in danger around me because I was such a weak target. I glanced around and my stomach plummeted as I saw Kira still ablaze jump in front of me, acting as a shield with the heat of her fire growing in strength.

"Don't touch her!" She growled, and as I looked at her smoldering hands radiating light, I shuddered. She'd somehow been corrupted too. Had I cursed her? Inessa was sprouting vines, and Sorrel was spreading a frost around her body. Had I cursed them all? Before I could answer my own question or watch the scene play out in front of me, my subconscious submerged for a fourth time. How much more could I endure?

I recoiled into myself, screaming against a million voices raging in my skull for the Divinities to save my family and deliver me from this possession. I coughed and wretched with hysteria, fighting the pull into another delusion. But I still found myself in a silver twinkling mist that fell away to reveal yet another image of myself, hair braided and piled atop my head, lounging amongst beasts comprised entirely of the night sky. The impostor tilted her head at me, calculated and probing before pushing to her feet and approached me. I tried to shrink away, too weak and weary to attempt another escape if all it would do was summon me back to another false me, but she was faster, in more control of her actions, grabbing hold of my wrist.

"You will need me," She promised, before breaking apart into fragmented night and stars and forcing her evaporated form under my skin. The quickest of the four nightmares, I was out of the mist and back in the waking world. I braced myself to be stolen away again, but no other possessions followed. Instead I was finally left to stare at the aftermath unfolding in front of me.

Arrian was ordering the soldiers to douse Kira's flames and she was challenging him, somehow unaffected by the fire consuming her body. Sorrel collapsed in shock, ice spreading from her body onto the planks of wood , her face crumpling in response to an emotionless Roland approaching her. Terror gripped me even harder as I saw the tears freezing on my stoic's sister's cheeks, knowing that could only mean that this was more devastating than I had imagined. Inessa was completely surrounded by vines and soldiers were also coming to restrain her. Mama was already being taken away by the guards.

I didn't know what had happened and yet, somewhere in the chaos before my eyes and shouting in my mind, deafening my wherewithal, I knew.

We had been betrayed, my family and I had been possessed by wicked magic, and now we were certainly all corrupted, no longer worthy of salvation by the Divinities. Forsaken, as my mouth and hands were bound and I was overcome with the emotions of everyone on the scaffold. Defiance, hopelessness, confusion, and fury. I felt it all burning within me until I thought I would burst at the seams, the voice in my head growing louder and louder with more than just my own, but Kira's, Sorrel's, Arrian's, Friedrich's, Mama's, and Ina's too. Only Roland's voice remained silent. Pain of too many sensations and feelings tearing me two was too much to bear and all I could do was weep. I knew it had to have been my fault for ever letting the voice in. I was the contagion that blighted us all.

Then one voice, low, menacing, and not my own, rang like gunfire on a cold barren night. I glanced at Friedrich, seeing the smile curling his lips towards his ears with glee.

For you, Sarka. At last.

ROLAND

There was a tearing sensation in my sternum as I left the basement with Arrian hot on my heels. Kira's face staring at me, wearing all of her emotions, was burned into my brain. She had been asking me for an explanation I couldn't give her yet. She had been begging for my help, and for clarity as she'd held the hand of the sister whose heart I'd broken. The sister who it took everything in me not to run to.

Even when I offered Kira nothing, I could see the shift in her from vulnerability to quiet strength— strength she shared freely with her family to help them endure. I could see her affinity seeping into the air, but it was more than that. Had she not one drop of magic in her veins, I knew her spirit still would have held the same type of power. Something in her expression gave me hope though that in a few hours when my plan was in effect and we'd left this basement behind us, Kira would believe me. She could find it in her infinitely bright and loving heart to forgive me, and maybe, just maybe, the others could someday believe me too. Once we were in Kesgoldol. I bought us our time ticket to get there by delaying the execution, we just needed to get there. Until then, I needed to push my selfish wants aside and figure out how to address the greatest wrench in my escape plans. Arrian.

"Where are you staying?"

Where else in this forsaken pit of ice? I'm staying at the Kyrith barracks. Aren't you?"

"Of course I am."

"Good then we will just head back there together for now."

I grit my teeth, weighing the pros and cons of simply knocking him out and stashing him somewhere out of sight. A quick glance around yielded little opportunity, and I couldn't count on how long he'd stay unconscious.

I'd told Macsen, Maggie, and the others that I'd be delaying the order around this time and that we then needed to allow for time for everyone to return to bed before they were to cause a distraction under the guise of threat from the Ivory Army's advances. By then, I should have already made my way back into the house and alerted the family to run when the time was right. Theo and Geneva both looked frail, so I prayed they'd be able to make the journey. Macsen could likely carry at least one of them once we met up.

The two wild cards left in the match were whether or not I could convince the Zdraevits to listen to me, and now, my brother hovering over me. I knew Sorrel and the rest of her family would likely never believe that my father would go to such lengths to make sure I acted on his side. Nor were they likely to accept that I had been backed into a corner of a board that forced me to hold out for a long game victory, deceiving them as thoroughly as I possibly could to ensure their eventual safety. In truth, they were all likely lost to me forever, but that was of little consequence so long as I could get them successfully out of Eisa.

My biggest concern regarding the family was going to be Ina. She loved fiercely but did not forgive lightly. She would be carrying with her not just the perceived betrayal of her family, but also all those in hiding we'd sworn to help. If she truly made up her mind to ignore me, I wasn't sure I could budge her. I'd still have to try. I made up my mind that I might have to carry her out kicking and screaming, but at least she wouldn't be dead. She'd live on in her stubbornness another day. The second walls of obstinacy I'd face would be Sorrel and Yulia. I'd have to pray they'd put the chance at salvation above their hurt long enough to get out. But, I hadn't a clue how I could possibly find a reason to go back inside. Perhaps I could point out the cold and suggest we rest for the night here. At least alone in a room I had the chance of containing Arrian.

"Are you coming or what? It's freezing out here."

"Did you hear something?" I asked lamely, turning away from my brother with the only excuse I could muster to keep us on the grounds.

"Only the sound of you dragging your feet. Why is that, Roland? Is there some reason you want to stay behind?" He demanded and I balled my hands into fists.

"Did you fail to hear the warnings before coming out here, or do you only pretend to listen to Father?" I countered evenly, not bothering to conceal the small smirk of satisfaction as Arrian immediately bristled.

"Of course I listened!"

"Then you'd know we were told to treat any hint of rebellion with extreme prejudice and do our due diligence to make sure no one tried any last minute escapes. You were just worrying about their threat enough as a reason to delay your departure. Unless you want to be the one who has to explain it—"

"Fine," Arrian bit, scowling to hide the already forming crease in his brow from concern.

I patted him on the back. "Good. It's nice to have you as a team player for once. Let's take a look."

There was a piece of me that grieved even now leaving my family behind. My brother, difficult as he was, was still my little brother and I wished him no ill will. But, in every game of chess, there were only two sides and the lines had been drawn down the center of the board my father had set up for us. He knew the reprehensible wedge he'd driven between me and the Zdraevits and that there was no plausible future for me with them, so I'd have no choice but to accept my place under his reign, despite my devotion to Sorrel. He knew. And it was an act of betrayal I could never forgive. No, my father died before my very eyes that day when he chose to betray the Zdraevits. Arrian had made his choice clear as he stood with the coup, and his already prevalent callousness was being carefully fostered to a cruelty I could no longer abide or turn a blind eye to.

I'd mourn the father and brother I might have had in another life— a life where perhaps my mother had lived and kept the balance. However, stewing over faint strands of memory and sentiment wouldn't help when I crossed the line between Rusevs and Zdraevits, effectively allowing capture from the opposing side to avoid another moment spent as my father's pawn. Arrian would carry on just fine without me. In fact, he'd likely rise in greater power without me in his way.

I shuddered to think of all the harm he'd already dealt Eisa, dragging people from their homes, allowing ransacking of their belongings, leaving a trail of broken glass and tears of terror with every step he willingly took down this new path. But the board only had two sides, and just like him, I'd chosen mine. No more would I play both roles. After tonight, in a few hours, we'd all be over the border and meeting up with Rafe— the brother I chose.

Arrian and I plodded about in the snowy shadows for what had to have been a good twenty minutes before he'd reached the end of his rope with the effort. "Clearly you're an idiot with a death wish to freeze because there's nothing here!" He snapped. "Let's go. We don't even have our gloves or hats to be out this long."

"Go on without me, I think I'd be more comfortable keeping an eye out to make sure nothing unexpected happens." I folded my arms, tucking my frigid fingers between in search of any spare warmth.

"For fuck's sake, Roland! Nothing is going to happen tonight. I haven't heard a single—" He stopped short in his rant to whip around at the sound of boots crunching in the show behind us. "Who's there?"

I licked my lips against the chapping winter air to hide my surprise to see Hevyen, one of Sympathizers in league with the escape party, approaching us dressed in a soldier's uniform. This wasn't part of our plan. Were they improvising after seeing my struggle to rid myself of Arrian?

"Pardon me, but there have been some signs of movement in the area. This way…" Hevyen waved us over the way he'd come, from the direction of the old mine shaft and forest just beyond. Our escape path.

Arrian flashed his eyes at me, clearly trying to weigh the likelihood that I had somehow orchestrated this just to prove him wrong. I lifted my brows smugly, completely able to truthfully deny any such claims.

"Come on then," I sighed and waved us forward.

"I think I see some disturbed snow up ahead on that bank," Hevyen continued as we marched further from the house and up a small hill.

Quite the risk, Hevyen. I nodded to the man, thankful for his quick thinking despite the danger he was playing with. He had once been a patient of Sorrel's and when he'd learned of her fate, he pledged loyalty to her and her salvation— just as she had once saved him.

I halted a few steps behind the others at the crest of the hill and bit the inside of my cheek. We all had a role to play tonight and mine needed to happen inside the house not tromping through the snow. This was the only chance I had left to get Arrian away from me long enough to make our run for it. It wouldn't be as thorough as I had hoped but so long as we got free of the house and into the woods, at least we had Maggie and Eirene waiting as backup.

When Hevyen noticed my lagging, he too paused and raised a hand respectfully to his head. "See here," he pointed to a tree with scuffed bark and muddied snow at the base of the trunk, where he must have been hiding before coming to my aid. "There are similar marks like this all around the parameter. If they are surrounding the area in an ambush it might be worth dividing our forces and intervening before they have a chance to reach position and strike."

"I'll keep to this area, you two check the far side," I ordered.

Arrian opened his mouth to protest but I snapped before he could get any words out. "Don't forget, I still *outrank you*. I've listened to quite enough of your complaining tonight, little brother. Now, for Eisa's sake, shut up and do as you're told."

Fire flared in his gaze but faced with a direct order, he struggled to defy it. "Fine. Take some of the soldiers in the house and I'll take the others posted at the gate. We'll head them off… *If* anyone is there. And there's better be," Arrian conceded gruffly, all but stomping away to follow Hevyen to the far side of the property.

It seemed my window had arrived. It couldn't have been any more than thirty minutes we'd been delayed, so I crossed my fingers that the soldiers remaining inside would have separated off while the Zdraevits went back to bed. I placed one snow dusted boot forward when a loud bang tore the night in two with a repetition of crackles.

Gunfire.

"It couldn't be. I halted the order," I wheezed, scrambling forward, struggling to get traction in the snow. The house suddenly felt out of reach, stretching further and further away as more and more shots rang out. As I finally thrust my trembling body onto the porch the firing ceased. No one else was running to the sound. No one was surprised to hear the shots. No one but me.

No. The word palpitated with every hammering beat of my heart as I sprinted through the house and down the steps to the basement. I threw open the door to the room, blanching when my shoes slid in grit and blood.

No.

Their bodies were splayed across the floor in front of me, mutilated, bludgeoned, and irreversibly dead.

No. Too late. I can't have been too late.

My vision flickered as my pulse raced beyond where any sort of typical adrenaline would have pushed it. I was dying. Surely I had to be because I wasn't breathing anymore. I heard a crack and looked down at my hand, startled to see the knuckles bruised from impact and the soldier collapsed at my feet. When had I moved?

No. They can't all be dead. Kira would never give in so easily. Sorrel would somehow manage the impossible to protect her family. And Inessa would be far too stubborn—

It took everything in me not to vomit on the spot when I realized no amount of stubbornness could have saved Ina from the wound I could now see had blown away half of her skull. The same hand with the bruises of a punch I hadn't realized I'd thrown was around another man's throat in an instant. I was leering at him but not of my own conscious volition. Was I being controlled again? No, that wasn't it. It was my instincts leaching through the gossamer facade I was struggling to contain.

With considerable effort, I released the soldier's throat and pushed away from him, allowing my hand to paw at the back of my neck, nails grating against the nape desperately trying to refrain from completely losing control. I couldn't contain the compulsions overtaking me a moment longer. The need to rip and tear the world in two seared the inside of my skin, while the weight of loss coated me in a coldness sharper than any bite of frost. I needed to get outside of my own body and run away, flee from the anguish, but I couldn't. I had to stay here and either reap or salvage the consequences of my failure.

Settle yourself. Inessa might not have made it, and I would mourn her deeply, but maybe someone else did. *Play just a little longer.*

"This... This dispatch on top of being unsanctioned was disgraceful. Everyone, get out." I scarcely heard the growl leave my lips. The world around me had all but faded away to palpable despair. It was hazy and muddled beyond recognition, blurred in hues of scarlet. No one on the ground around me was moving or showing signs of life. I'd been too late. Everything I'd tried to plan was over before it'd begun. It was no mistake that Arrian had shown up at the house when he did. He did this. I'd failed and now there was only nothingness.

It wasn't until the muffled words of a soldier grazed my ear that everything snapped back into focus, so poignantly I almost dropped to my knees, the relief cutting like a slice to the gut.

"This one is still alive." He was pointing to Sorrel. Sorrel had done it! Sorrel was still alive, and nothing else in all of Alse Hanya mattered until I got her out of this tomb.

I looked down at where she was clinging to life on the stony floor, her back weeping from countless wounds where most of her dress had been torn away. I knew in an instant she had taken the blows in place of someone else... someone else who hadn't made it. Not if she was the only one alive. Those silver eyes I looked to in my mind to see me through every lie and falsity I had to put forth, they stared at my feet, glazed with pain and contempt. Beside her, I saw Kira's sightless gaze and broken body. The breath I inhaled felt like a million grains of glass, as I put the two together. Sorrel had thrown herself in front of her little sister only to somehow survive while Kira had perished.

I'd never have the chance to explain to her. To show her how the branch of hope and continued confidence in me hadn't been for nothing... No, because ultimately it *had* been for nothing. That brilliant young girl whom I'd loved as my own little sister was lost forever, so horrifically, and I was no longer certain I could remain on my feet.

Save Sorrel. She still needs you. I reminded myself mechanically.

"Leave, go get things ready to transport the bodies, and clean up this mess you've created so our enemies won't know what's transpired tonight should they break through our defensive line. I will finish the last one off."

I suspended myself in a bated breath, forcing my body not to lunge forward to help Sorrel, and the soldiers began to shuffle hesitantly towards the exit. I was certain the pressure building in my veins was going to burst and I needed them to leave faster. If I didn't help her she'd be dead either way. I couldn't afford to wait any longer. I'd give it thirty more seconds. If they didn't leave in thirty seconds, I'd have to drop the facade and fight to death to save her, but even then if I couldn't get her to take the emergency potion Maggie had given me in case of injury, fighting might still condemn her fate. There was no more time to waste.

These weren't chess pieces on a board as I'd tried to steel myself with during their captivity to avoid caving under the pressure. The broken bones and torn flesh littered around the room showed just how human this devastation was. What was more human than mortality? My resolve was slipping, seeping from my body and resigning itself to die here with them. I couldn't walk out of here alive without a single one of them.

Then the most single handedly remarkable thing happened. I stared, dumbfounded, as Sorrel slowly dragged herself up the wall to a standing position. Long rivers of blood scored the stone where she'd pressed against it and I bit my tongue to keep from once more swaying on my feet.

When she turned, half dead but spirit still ablaze, and finally looked me directly in the eye, my feet were flying towards her and I only just managed to catch myself from clutching her in my arms. Instead I lifted my gun in a final performance. My other hand was already snaking for a hold of the vile stowed in my jacked pocket, ready to act.

"Go," I hid the plea under a low command to the soldiers, not breaking my gaze from hers, hoping somehow deep down she would see some little spark of the real me and understand I was here for her. The gun shook in my hand and I chose my next words carefully, willing her to find it within her to understand. "She was always my target in the first place. The next man to question my orders will share the family's fate."

I meant the threat. I'd massacre them in a heartbeat just as they had done. I'd rip their ribs from their cages one by one if it meant Sorrel walked free— with or without me. But she needed the potion. At last the sound of the door clicked closed behind me and I finally yielded. I embraced Sorrel and she sagged against me but I knew it was from weakness not affection.

Oh, Eisa," I gasped, sobs finally free to rack my body in slow sweeping waves as the gravity of utter loss pulled me down into the depths of despair. "I'm so sorry. Sorrel, I'm so sorry."

"What?" She whispered, her voice cracking.

"I tried. I tried to delay it so I could get you all out but Arrian.

Fucking Arrian! I thought..." My grip tightened around her and I wasn't sure I could ever find the strength to let her go again. The explanation I thought I could swallow, the regrets of grief eating me alive, the desperation for her forgiveness was too much for me and I couldn't stop the words from tumbling out. "I thought I could find a way. I had a plan— we had a plan, but I was too late. I failed you all. I can't... I'll never be able—"

"I don't... I don't understand," Was all she could manage to murmur, attempting to pull away from me but I resisted, trying to support her anyway.

The potion. I needed to heal her but it seemed all that was left in me was a frantic energy, incapable of decisive action. I needed to pull myself together. I reminded myself of this over and over even as the words kept pouring out of me, even when she forced me to look at Kira's fallen brutalized body, even when I stopped to apologize, I struggled to regain control of myself.

We weren't out of danger yet and I could see her will to live leaving her with each labored breath. I'd have to keep going a little longer.

Fight, Roland. If you love her, you will get her through this. And after you will step aside and let her go. She will be free, even if that means eventually being free from me. She will be free.

OTHER WORKS

YA Mashup/Retelling
The When Wicked Series

Middle Grade Contemporary Fantasy
The Grim and the Fantastic

Instagram @marissamillerauthor
www.marissamillerauthor.com

ABOUT THE AUTHOR

Marissa Miller can often be found frolicking about in thunderstorms, drinking her weight in tea, playing with one of her numerous beloved pets, or with her nose shoved into a book. When she isn't found any of these places, Miller is at her desk, writing one of her fantasy novels. Her works include a gripping middle grade contemporary fantasy, *The Grim and The Fantastic,* and her young adult mashup/retelling series, *The When Wicked Series.* Taking on high fantasy with a literary spin, *Beneath the Scarlet Frost,* upon its release, will be the first installment of her adult fantasy series, *The Fallen Reign Series.*

Miller believes fundamentally in the power of imagination and creativity, and seeks to use her expression of splendor, no matter the circumstances, to overcome whatever obstacles life throws our way. Not afraid to delve into dark or heavy topics, Miller's works embody the motif that no matter the depth of darkness, and weight of topic, there is always a little light and a harrowing story to be found in the shadows. With an emphasis on character-driven narratives, her themes often touch on overcoming inner demons and trauma, the abstract of morality, and the intricacies of creative construct.

Milton Keynes UK
Ingram Content Group UK Ltd.
UKHW010652101123
432322UK00003B/135

9 798218 264864